GW01403140

Vol. 5

Vol. 5

Published by NRM Books.

ISBN: 978-1-965179-08-6

CREDITS
Cover Art by: Nathan Reese Maher

Table of Contents

Clermont

By Regina Maria Roche

CHAP. I.

Far retired
Among the windings of a woody vale,
By solitude and deep surrounding shades,
But more by bashful modesty conceal'd,
Together thus they shunn'd the cruel scorn
Which virtue sunk to poverty would meet
From giddy passion and low-minded pride.
Thomson

In a retired part of the province of Dauphiny stood the cottage of Clermont; its remote obscurity was well suited to the mental solitude of its tenant, and its neat simplicity corresponded with his refined taste. Fifteen years he had been an inhabitant of it; and from the elegance of his manners and the dignity of his mein, his rustic neighbours, were of opinion that he had once seen better days. To this impression, however, he studiously avoided giving any sanction; nay, it was evident he wished by every means in his power, to discourage the idea of opulence or greatness having ever been his portion.

His chief employment consisted in superintending a little farm, from which his principal support appeared to be derived, and his highest amusement and pleasure in studying the works of nature, and cultivating the mind of his daughter; who, with an elderly female servant whom he had hired after his arrival at the cottage, were the only human beings that shared with him the fruits of his retirement.

Madeline, but two years old at that period, could consequently recollect nothing previous to it; but, from the striking difference between her father and the surrounding rustics, she could not help adopting their opinion of him, and thinking that he had once moved in a circle very different from that in which he was then placed.

She more than once hinted this opinion, and enquired of her father the cause of their retirement, and whether they had no relatives, no friends, in that great world from which they were secluded? but she never received any satisfactory answer. The agitation he always betrayed at those enquiries, made her at last resolve to suppress a curiosity so painful to his feelings. It however confirmed her belief of his having experienced severe misfortunes; and from this conviction, she redoubled her attention, trusting that, if she could not obliterate, she might at least soften their remembrance.

But to do so in reality, was, alas! beyond her power. 'Tis true, he sometimes forced himself to wear the semblance of cheerfulness, although his heart was ever a stranger to it; oppressed by a sorrow which the boasted efficacy of time, the solicitude of filial attention, or the tenderness of sympathy could not mitigate;—a sorrow, which anticipated the work of time, had already faded his cheek and furrowed his brow, though yet in what might be termed the prime of man's life, not having attained his fortieth year; and sometimes so far overcame him, as to render him unable to bear even the society of his daughter, his only earthly comfort. At those periods he always wandered to the wildest and most sequestered spot that he could find in the neighbourhood of his residence.

'mid

.....thorns and mire;

......all forlorn,

To muse at last, amid the ghostly gloom

Of graves, and hoary vaults, and cloistered cells,

To walk with spectres thro' the midnight shade,

And to the screaming owl's accursed song,

Attune the dreadful workings of his heart.

Though one of his chief sources of pleasure (as I have already said) was derived from the culture of his daughter's mind, he was often tempted to forego this gratification by reflecting on the inutility of accomplishments to her, who, like the desert rose, seemed born to waste her sweetness in obscurity. The task, however, was too delightful to be relinquished; and he at last rejoiced that he had persevered in it; for, as he carefully guarded her against all refinements which could render her dissatisfied with her humble station, he found that the expansion of her mind, by opening new sources of amusement, increased her happiness: he cultivated to the highest perfection that taste which the

Source divine of ever-flowing love,

And his unmeasur'd goodness, not content

With every food of life to nourish man,

Implants within his heart to make,

By kind illusions of the wand'ring sense,

all

beauty to his eye,

And music to his ear;with which

well pleased he scans

The goodly prospect, and with inward smiles,

Treads the gay verdure of the painted plains,

Beholds the azure canopy of heaven,

And living lamps that over-arch his head

With more than regal splendour.

Never did a pupil render the toils of an instructor less difficult than did Madeline those of her father; and as she grew up, her perfect knowledge of the historian's record, and just conception of the poet's beauty, rendered her a companion well qualified to diversify his lonely hours.

She possessed besides an exquisite taste for drawing and music, and accompanied the soft melody of her lute with a voice which, though not strong, was inexpressibly sweet; melodious as that which the rapt poet at the visionary hour of twilight sometimes thinks he hears

> chanting from the wood-crown'd hill,
>
> the deep'ning dale, or inmost sylvan glade.

The liveliness of her fancy was equal to the strength of her understanding, and often raised a visionary paradise around her; softness and animation were happily blended in her disposition; and with equal delight she could enjoy the gaiety of innocent mirth and the lonely hour of solitude: feeling and precept had early taught her pity for the woes of others; and with cheerfulness she could tax either convenience or comfort to supply the claims of poverty. To her person Nature had not been less liberal than to her mind; by her prodigality to both, it seemed indeed as if she had been anxious to make amends for the deficiency of fortune.

She was tall and delicately made; nor was the symmetry of her features inferior to that of her bodily form: but it was not to this symmetry that they owed their most attractive charm,—it was derived from the fascinating sweetness diffused over them. Her eyes, large and of the darkest hazel, ever true to the varying emotions of her soul, languished beneath their long silken lashes with all the softness of sensibility, and sparkled with all the fire of animation; her hair, a rich auburn, added luxuriance to her beauty, and by a natural curl, gave an expression of the greatest innocence to her face; the palest blush of health just tinted her dimpled, fair, and beautifully rounded cheek; and her mouth, adorned by smiles, appeared like the half-blown rose when moistened with the dews of early morn.

Such was Madeline Clermont, who, ignorant of the great world, neither practised its follies, sighed for its pleasures, or dreaded its vices; her highest wish was gratified when she could steal from the brow of her father its usual sadness, and render him for a moment forgetful of his sorrows.

Their house stood on a little eminence, in a deep, romantic, and verdant valley, which wound to a considerable extent between cultivated hills, where the vine spread her treasures to the sun, and the husbandman often gathered a luxuriant harvest; woods of variegated verdure stretched up many of their steep ascent, and the summit of one of the highest was crowned with the ruins of a once noble castle, the residence, according to tradition, of some of the ancient Counts of Dauphiny. This shattered pile, the record of departed greatness and the power of time, was carefully shunned by the peasant after sun-set, for the village legends were swelled with an account of the horrid noises, and still more horrid sights, heard and beheld within its dreary walls: but though feared by superstition, it was the favourite haunt of taste and sensibility; and thither, as the last beams of the sun glimmered o'er the scene, Clermont and Madeline often wandered; they loved to explore its grass-grown court and winding avenues, and picture to themselves the scenes that had once passed to all appearance within them: they also frequently ascended to its broken battlements, covered with wild vegetation, where the birds of night held their unmolested reign, startling by their melancholy cries those persons whom chance or necessity conducted near the spot, from thence to feast on the delicious prospect beneath; whilst the breeze sighed amongst the surrounding trees, (whose ponderous trunks and matted branches declared them long inhabitants of the soil) as if the genius of the pile still haunted their recesses and mourned its desolation. The hills were completely surrounded by a chain of mountains, bleak, barren, and desolate, except in the summer months, when the shepherd led thither his little flock to crop the sweet herbage that then grew amongst their interstices.

A narrow river run through the valley, whose calm current was in many places interrupted by projections of rocks, which served as rude bridges for the villagers to pass from one side to the other; numerous herds enlivened its banks, along which a low brushwood crept, intermingled with a few tall trees, weeping willows, and sweet-smelling shrubs, which formed embowered seats for the solitary angler. A number of neat cottages were scattered about the vale; and it was delightful of a fine evening to behold their young inhabitants dancing to pastoral music on the little grassy lawns before them;—

Like fairy elves,

Whose midnight revels by a forest side,

Or fountain, some belated peasant sees,

Or dreams he sees; while over head the moon

Sits arbitress, and nearer to the earth

Wheels her pale course, they on their mirth and dance

Intent, with jocund music, charm his ear.

The cottage of Clermont was embosomed in a small grove, through which a broad grassy path, enclosed by a rude paling, led from the valley to the house; o'er the door honeysuckle and wild roses, during the summer, formed a kind of portico, and half shaded its latticed windows; its interior was as simple as its exterior, and it was ornamented, as Madeline grew up, by her fanciful drawings. Midway up the hill that rose at the rear of his cottage, Clermont had continued his garden, as the space which lay between it and his dwelling was too narrow to yield sufficient vegetables for his family, small as it was; a silvery stream descended from this hill that gave fertility to the flowers which Madeline cultivated; and immediately above the garden it projected into craggy points of rock, which allured thither, by the fragrant herbs that grew about them, not only the industrious bee, but the wild and adventurous goat; and though the garden, its fences being readily overleaped, sometimes suffered from having the latter in its vicinity, Clermont could not think of driving away a neighbour, whose appearance on the heights added to the romantic and picturesque scenery of the spot. On the southern side of the hill lay a small vineyard belonging to Clermont, which he diligently cultivated.

Unchequered by incident, unruffled by discontent, the days of Madeline glided away till she had attained her seventeenth year; at which period their calm current was interrupted.

CHAP. II.

Oft let me hear thy soothing voice
Low whisp'ring thro' the shade.
Barbauld

It was in a fine autumnal evening that Clermont, seized with one of his usual fits of melancholy, abruptly withdrew from the cottage, and left Madeline to amuse herself as fancy might direct. Habit had failed of its usual effect upon her mind; for, on every return of her father's dejection, she felt as much distressed as if she had never before witnessed it. To endeavour to alleviate this distress, she now walked out and pursued her course along the margin of the river till she reached the old castle, o'er which the last beams of the sun now glimmered; its gloom rather invited than deterred her from entering it: passing, therefore, through its dreary courts, she ascended a flight of half-broken stairs that led directly to a large chamber which opened to a kind of rude balcony that stretched along one wing of the building. This was a favourite seat of Madeline's. The landscape seen through the intervening trees which rose before it never satiated her eye; upon every view some new beauty, some new charm, if possible more lovely than the last, was discovered by her.

The solemn shades surrounding her, o'er which the dusky hue of twilight was now beginning to steal, and the profound stillness of the air, only interrupted by the faint warbling of retiring birds, or the yet fainter sighing of the breeze among the trees, now and then intermingled with the hum of distant voices, by degrees calmed the painful emotions of Madeline's mind, and she became again, if not cheerful, at least composed.

"How sweet, how soothing (cried she) is this tranquil hour to the afflicted heart! it seems to give a respite to its cares, as it does to those of labour. How delightful to gaze upon the glories by which it is attended! to listen to the soft breeze that seems to die away amongst the waving trees, and the low carol of the peasant hastening to his cottage to enjoy the meal sweetened by contentment, and earned by industry."

Occupied by ideas similar to those which she had expressed, Madeline was almost abstracted from the scene which had inspired them, when her attention was suddenly awakened by an oboe from the valley; nothing could be more congenial to her present feelings than its melody, and she listened with exquisite delight; her spirits alternately rising, alternately sinking, as the sounds swelled with grandeur on the air, and tremblingly died away, till only their faint echo amongst the mountains could be distinguished: at last they ceased entirely; but, as if unwilling to relinquish the pleasure they had given her, she immediately began singing the beautiful air she had been listening to, and with which she was well acquainted. She however soon ceased, imagining that she heard a low voice beneath the balcony repeating her words. Somewhat startled, she hastily arose, and looked over it; but no object was visible, and all again was silence. Her fancy, she was then convinced, had deceived her, and her composure returned in consequence of that idea; but the night being now far advanced, she delayed no longer quitting the castle.

The next evening her father again left her to herself. Slinging her lute across her arm, with which she was wont to amuse herself in her moments of solitude, she again proceeded to the castle, and sought her favourite seat; but scarcely had she gained it, ere the following lines, penciled on a smooth white stone that had once formed part of a supporting pillar to the door of the chamber through which she had passed, caught her eye, and filled her breast with inexpressible surprise.

the lines.

Midst grass-grown courts, the "ivy mantled tower,"
Where legends say afflicted spirits mourn
O'er the sad records of departed power,—
I restless watch for dewy eve's return:

For then the chantress of the woodland vale
Awakes the echoes of the dreary pile,
With sounds that o'er my tortur'd soul prevail,
And all its cares and agonies beguile.

The evening star, the pale moon's silver ray,
I raptur'd hail, that gives her to my gaze:
Her form, her smile, harmonious as her lay,—
The mild expression of her angel face.

Should this weak record of ill-fated love
E'er meet her eye,—ah, may one tender tear
Be shed for him, whom fate forbade to prove
His ardent passion or his truth sincere!

Ah! may she pity then, compassion is his claim,
'Tis all he dares to ask—'Tis all he hopes to gain.

The moment Madeline had read those lines, she recollected the voice which she fancied she had heard the preceding evening, and was convinced her ear had not then deceived her.

A stranger, she was sure, had visited the ruins, for to none of the inhabitants of the valley, all the rough and illiterate children of industry, could she ascribe them; neither could she avoid believing them addressed to herself; not from any conscious superiority of charms over the rest of the village maids, but from a conviction that they never visited the castle, on account of the superstitious dread they entertained of it.

An idea that the person who wrote the lines might be loitering about the ruins, now struck her; and she instantly determined to quit them. Scarcely had she done so, when she heard the sound of a step in the adjoining chamber; she hastily bent forward, and looking through the little arch which led to the balcony, she perceived a man gliding from the opposite door into an obscure corner of the room; there was just sufficient light within to enable her to perceive he was a stranger: her heart beat quick; she trembled, and shrinking back, regretted the thoughtless temerity which had exposed her to danger, by tempting her to visit the lonely pile at such an hour.

That it was the author of the little sonnet she beheld, she could not doubt; but the tender sentiments it expressed could not inspire her with sufficient courage to bear the idea of throwing herself entirely into his power, which, by attempting to leave the castle, she must do, her only passage being through its innermost recesses; she deemed it safer therefore to continue in her present situation, where there was a chance of not being observed, and of obtaining assistance by crying out if she should find it necessary, either till she was assured the stranger had departed, or that some hope of protection presented itself to her view.

Eagerly she listened for some sound from the valley, that might inspire this hope, but in vain; by the silence which reigned over it, interrupted only by the barking of cottage dogs, as if they bayed the moon, she was at length convinced that care and industry had already retired to repose.

he late hour to which her father prolonged his nocturnal rambles, and the timidity of their servant, gave her little reason to hope deliverance through their means: scarcely suffering herself to breathe, she continued a long time in a state of greater agony than she had ever before experienced. At last she heard a step; but her almost fainting spirits were soon recalled by a conviction that it was not approaching her; and in the next minute she caught a glimpse of a figure (the same she was sure she had seen in the chamber) descending a winding path near the balcony. Her strength and courage immediately returned, and with a quickness that scarcely permitted her to touch the ground, she left the castle, and reached the valley by a different path from that which the stranger had taken. She had scarcely quitted it, when a sudden rustling among the trees behind her induced her to look back, and she perceived him slowly emerging from the midst of them. The speed of Madeline was now if possible increased, and, faint and breathless, she gained the enclosure before her father's cottage. As she fastened the little gate, she paused and leaned over it, but almost instantly retreated from it to the house, discovering the stranger to be within a few yards of it.

Her father was not yet returned; and the maid, busied in preparing the supper table, took no notice of her agitation. The idea of security soon restored Madeline's composure; she then resolved not to acquaint her father with the incident that had alarmed her, least it should agitate, and render him uneasy, if at any future time chance prevented her returning home as soon as he expected. She also determined not to visit the castle again till she was convinced the stranger had forsaken it, nor even then at so late an hour as she had hitherto done; to know who he was, to have a perfect view of him, she could not help wishing.

The next morning, immediately after breakfast, when her father withdrew to the vineyard, Jaqueline, the servant, entered the room; she was a faithful creature, much attached to Clermont and Madeline from the number of years she had lived with them, and now appeared with a face full of importance.

"Lord, Mam'selle, (cried she) I have been wanting to speak to you this long time; I have something to tell you that will so surprise you! I dare say, if you lived to be an hundred, and were all that time guessing, you would not find it out."

"Very likely (said Madeline, taking up her work); so do you save me the useless trouble of trying to do so."

"Why this morning (began Jaqueline) before the sun was risen, I went down to the river to get a pail of water, and there I saw the most handsomest young man I ever beheld in my days."

Madeline dropped her work, and fastened her eyes eagerly upon Jaqueline's face.

"Claude Dubois and Josephe le Mure, though counted so handsome, and to be sure they are the best looking young men in the village, (resumed Jaqueline) are not to be compared to him. So, as I was saying, I found him standing by the river looking so earnestly at this cottage, as if there was something or somebody in it he wanted to discover. God bless my soul, says I to myself, if he should be looking at it with any bad intent!—for you know, Mam'selle, there are people wicked enough to go about the world trying to do mischief; so I laid the pail upon the bank, and, thinks I, I will try to discover what he wants, or what he means; but how to begin to speak to him, I did not know; for though I did not feel afraid, I felt some how or other an awe of him: he saved me the trouble however of inventing an excuse for speaking to him, by asking me whether I lived in the house he had seen me come out of. So after I had answered him, I was just going to beg in return he would tell me why he stood looking at it, for all the world as if he wanted to take its length and breadth and all its dimensions, when Margarette Duval, going to market with some kids, came up to me for the price of a new hat which I had desired her to buy me the next time she went there, and whilst I was untying my glove to take out my money, away he marched, notwithstanding he saw I was going to speak to him when she came up."

"Perhaps you said something about him to Margarette," said Madeline.

"Nothing that could offend him, I am sure, (cried Jaqueline); I only said, when she asked, as I was taking out my money, whether that handsome gentleman near me was a sweetheart of my young lady? 'heaven knows who he is; he may be a sweetheart of yours or mine as well as of hers, for ought I know.' I must confess, indeed, she stared at him with all the eyes in her head, which perhaps drove him away; for I am sure my words could not: this I took care to tell her, after he was gone, was a piece of very bad manners. Before I came home (proceeded Jaqueline), I met some neighbours, to whom I described him, in order to find out if they knew any thing about him; but they were quite ignorant of any such person; it is evident, therefore, that he does not lodge in this valley, or he would be known to its inhabitants."

'Tis strange, thought Madeline, that visiting it as he does, he should not be known to any of them.

"I was all in a flutter till I told you about him (said Jaqueline); and should be glad to know whether you would have my master also told, that in case of any bad design against the house, he may be upon his guard."

"I think I may venture to say there is no bad design formed against it (exclaimed Madeline); consequently there is no occasion to speak to him on the subject."

"Very well, Mam'selle (answered Jaqueline); I am sure you have more wisdom and discretion than I have, notwithstanding I am the oldest; I shall therefore do as you please."

Madeline resumed her work as Jaqueline quitted the room; but not with her wonted diligence did she pursue it; her eyes continually wandered from it to the valley, where, however, they met no object to which they had not been accustomed.

In the evening her father invited her to walk; this invitation she accepted with pleasure; nor was her satisfaction diminished on finding that he proceeded in the direction to the castle.

CHAP. III.

Each lonely scene shall thee restore,

For thee the tear be duly shed;

Belov'd till life can charm no more,

.......Collins

They had nearly reached the castle, when Clermont, recollecting some business he had to settle with a cottager who lived at the opposite side of the river, or rather brook, for it scarcely deserved a better appellation, desired Madeline to stop where she was, and, promising to return in a few minutes, crossed over to him.

A little above the spot on which her father left her, hid from it by intervening trees, was a low rock overshadowed by willows, upon which Madeline loved to sit, and watch the gambols of the summer flies upon the water, and those of its speckled inhabitants. Somewhat fatigued by her walk, she determined to go thither, and there wait the return of her father.

As she passed the castle, she turned her eyes towards it, but all around was awful uninterrupted solitude. The stranger she concluded had departed: but how great was her surprise when, on advancing a few steps farther, she beheld him, the same she was convinced of whom she had a transient view the preceding evening,—the same, she had no doubt, that Jaqueline had described to her in the morning,—seated on the rock, retouching a landscape laid against a book, and which, by the distant view Madeline had of it, appeared to be one of the surrounding scenes.

His attention was so much engrossed, that the light step of Madeline did not disturb him; and she paused—paused to contemplate an object who, though unknown, had strongly interested her.

He appeared of the first order of fine forms; and to all the graces of person and bloom of youth, united a countenance open, manly, and intelligent, but overcast by a shade of melancholy, which seemed to declare him acquainted with misfortune, and from nature and self experience formed to sympathize with every child of sorrow; his hat lay beside him, and the breeze had wafted aside his dark hair from his forehead, and discovered his polished brows, where, according to the words of the poet, "sate young simplicity;" in his eyes, as he sometimes raised them from the paper, was a fine expression, at once indicative of refinement and sensibility; and as Madeline gazed on them, she involuntarily said to herself, one glance from those benignant eyes last night, would at once have dissipated every terror.

As if riveted to the spot by a magic spell, she stood immovable, till roused by the voice of her father calling her at a distance. She started, and as she turned to obey the summons, she caught those eyes she had just been admiring, the consciousness of which perhaps occasioned the blush that instantly mantled her cheeks and an agitation that scarcely permitted her to walk: yet was her emotion faint to that which (though she but glanced at him) she saw the stranger betray when disturbed by the voice of her father; he looked towards her, starting from his seat; the paper he held dropped from his hand, and wildly, yet delightedly, he gazed on her.

She met her father on the spot where they had parted, and informed him, though not in a very articulate voice, of the motive which had made her quit it; her agitation was too great to escape his observation, and he enquired if any thing had frightened her? No, said she, nothing. Clermont therefore imputed it to the haste she had made to meet him. As they had walked a good way, he now proposed that they should return home, to which she did not object; but never had she been so silent, so absent before, since of an age to be his companion as she was at this time with her father.

On arriving at the cottage, they found supper already prepared, to which they immediately sat down: they had scarcely finished, however, when one of the young villagers rushed into the room, and with a trembling voice and pale face, besought Clermont, for the sake of heaven and his own soul, to come out and give his assistance to a poor gentleman whom he and his brother, returning from their daily labour to their cottage, had found lying bleeding and senseless, as they supposed, in consequence of a fall, at the foot of the hill upon which the castle stood. 'Tis surely the stranger, thought Madeline, and instantly her colour changed.

"Do you know him?" asked Clermont, rising as he spoke.

"No," replied the young peasant. Nevertheless he and his brother had carried him to their mother's cottage, who had laid him upon her best bed, and was then trying to bring him to himself. "But (added he) except his wounds are dressed, she can be of little service to him."

I have already said, that studying the works of nature was a favourite amusement of Clermont, and from that study and reading, he had learned the healing property of many simples, which he carefully gathered and administered with success to the external as well as internal complaints of his poor neighbours: to him the young peasant had therefore come without hesitation to solicit relief and assistance for the wounded stranger.

"You will go, my father?" said Madeline.

"Go, my child! (said he); yes, and happy I am to think I can in any degree mitigate the sufferings of a fellow-creature." He hastily collected what things he wanted, and went out.

Madeline left her supper unfinished, and in a state of agitation, such as she had never before experienced, watched in the little grove before the cottage for his return. The moment she saw him approaching the gate, she flew to meet him.

"Well, my dear sir, (cried she), is there any hope?"

"Hope! (repeated Clermont), heaven forbid there was not; the unfortunate young man, though severely, is not dangerously hurt; and I trust, and make no doubt, but that in a few days, with proper care and attention, he will be able to rise: his senses, which the shock of the fall alone deprived him of, were completely restored ere I went to him, and he was perfectly sensible of every thing I did for him, though too much exhausted to express his thanks, which his looks evinced him anxious to do, but which indeed a common act of humanity like mine does not merit." Clermont proceeded to say that he thought the stranger, though in such a situation, one of the finest young men he had ever seen. Madeline blushed; and, perfectly relieved from her uneasiness, felt a conscious pleasure at her father's opinion coinciding with her's.

The next morning, before breakfast, Clermont went to visit his patient; when he returned, his countenance announced pleasing intelligence.

"Well, (said he, seating himself at the breakfast table) I believe I shall soon grow vain of my skill, and declare myself a professed physician; as I prognosticated, my patient is already better, and I have had some conversation with him." Madeline looked earnestly at her father.

"He had learned (resumed Clermont), from the good dame of the cottage that I was not a surgeon, but merely attended him from good will; in consequence of which he would have loaded me with thanks, had I not stopped him by declaring, that if he persisted in talking of obligations, I would instantly bid him a final adieu.

"After I had silenced him on that subject, he proceeded to tell me his name was de Sevignie, and that a love of rambling, inspired by a wish of seeing all in nature and art worthy of observation in his native country, had led him to a little hamlet about a league from our valley, where enquiring, as was his custom whenever he halted, if there was any place in the neighbourhood worth visiting, he had been directed by his host to the old castle, as one of the finest monuments of art and antiquity in this part of the country. 'I visited it almost immediately, (said he); and from that time, which was about a fortnight ago, have never failed repairing to it every evening at sun-set, attracted thither by an irresistible impulse.'

"I am sorry (said I), your visits were at last so unfortunately terminated; your present accident is, I suppose, to be imputed to them."—His reply was 'Yes'; he had wandered unheeding whither he went, into a wrong path, extremely rugged, where, his foot slipping, he fell from the top to the bottom of the hill. His spirits seemed low, (continued Clermont); so I rallied my own to endeavour to raise them.

"There is I believe (said I) some spell, in that castle which allures, or rather draws, people thither, whether they will or no; I have a little girl who is always gadding to it, in defiance of all the ghosts, hobgoblins, and fairies, which, according to the account of the villagers, continually haunt it."

Madeline felt her cheek glow; and, withdrawing her eyes from her father, she pretended to be busy in pouring out the coffee.

"My forced gaiety was however lost upon him (said Clermont); he grew agitated, so I took my leave, promising to call upon him again in the course of the day; and, at his desire, sent one of the young men of the cottage to the hamlet for his servant, whom he wished, in preference to a stranger, to attend him. As soon as you have breakfasted, my love, I wish you would take a loaf of white bread, which cannot be procured where he is, and a bottle of last year's vintage to the cottage for the young stranger."

No commission could be more pleasing to Madeline than the present one. The moment she rose from table, she tied on her hat, and putting the bread and wine into a small osier basket, proceeded to the cottage, at the door of which its mistress sat netting.

"Ah! how kind (said she, rising and taking the basket from Madeline), is Mr. Clermont! heaven will requite him for his goodness: won't you come in, Mam'selle; 'tis a warm day, and I am sure you must be tired by your walk; all my folks, old and young, are gone to the vineyard (it was now the vintage season), and I am a little lonely or so in their absence."

"Your guest is better?" cried Madeline, entering as she spoke, and taking a chair.

"Yes, Mam'selle, heaven and your father be praised for that; he is a fine youth, and it would be a pity indeed if any thing ailed him long. I must, now that I have so good an opportunity, show you, Mam'selle, a little picture, which I think belonged to him, as my Claude found it near the spot where he fell." So saying, she opened a drawer, from whence she took the picture, and presented it to Madeline, who, the moment she cast her eyes upon it, recollected it to be the same she had seen in the hands of the stranger; and this convinced her of what indeed she had scarcely doubted before, that he and de Sevignie were the same person.

She now found it to be a highly-finished landscape of the castle and surrounding scenes, in which a small female figure was conspicuously drawn. This bore so great a resemblance to her own person, that she had no doubt of its being designed for her. Such an indication of attachment touched her young and simple heart more perhaps than the most impassioned declaration could have accomplished.

"As soon as he departs, I shall pin this picture up (proceeded his hostess); it will look so pretty against the wall; but till then I should be afraid to do so, lest he should demand it."

"I think (said Madeline, who feared the good woman or some of her family might discover the resemblance which the figure in the drawing bore to her), you had better return it."

"No, indeed (replied Janette), I shall do no such thing; he does not know I have it, so there can be no harm in keeping it."

"Well, do as you please," said Madeline, rising to depart, and taking up her empty basket. All the way back, her thoughts were engrossed by what she had seen; and she felt agitated at the idea of being introduced to Sevignie, which she supposed would now be the case as soon as he had recovered.

The attentions of her father were unremitted; and he returned from every visit more and more pleased with his new acquaintance, who, though too severely hurt to be able to rise for some days, was perfectly capable of conversing with him.

"I never (said Clermont to his daughter, on returning one evening), met with a mind more indebted to nature, or more improved by education, than that of de Sevignie; yet, with all his abilities and acquirements, he is unobtrusive, unassuming, and unaffected; he does not study for subjects calculated to display his talents, as too many possessed of such would ostentatiously do; instead of leading, he is rather led to them; and his modesty, not only from its intrinsic merit, but its novelty, greatly heightens his perfections."

Such encomiums on de Sevignie were inexpressibly pleasing to Madeline; they seemed to give a sanction to the tender interest she felt for him; and they made her, besides, feel a sensation of gratified pride at being an object of regard to so amiable a youth.

At the end of a week, her father told her that his patient was able to rise, and expressed a wish that she would take some little delicacies, which he mentioned, to the cottage for him.

Madeline never obeyed a wish of her father's more readily; tying on her straw hat, she proceeded almost directly to the cottage with her osier basket upon her arm, well filled, and covered with a napkin. The cottage door lay open, but Janette (as in general was the case) was not there; neither was she nor any other person in the little room it opened into. Madeline, not willing to depart without seeing her, proceeded to an apartment which looked into the garden, and was divided from the one she had left by a long passage, at the door of which she tapped; it was instantly opened by Janette, and Madeline was entering, when the appearance of de Sevignie, who had not, she imagined, yet left his room, seated in a wrapping gown at an open window, as if to inhale the balmy and refreshing sweetness of the air, made her suddenly start back. Janette, however, prevented her retreating entirely:—"Lord, Mam'selle, don't be frightened (cried she), 'Tis only Monsieur de Sevignie you see, who has left his chamber this morning for the first time; do pray come in, and wish him joy of his recovery; he will be very glad I am sure to see you."

"Permit me, Madam (said de Sevignie, who on her first appearance had risen, though with evident tremor and difficulty), permit me, Madam, (advancing to her) at least to have an opportunity of thanking you for your humane attention to a stranger. Oh, to the daughter suffer me to express what to the father I am forbade—my warm, my fervent sense of the obligations which both have conferred upon me."

"You rate much too highly, sir (said Madeline, raising her eyes from the ground), any little attentions we had the power of paying you."

"See, Monsieur (cried Janette, taking the basket from Madeline's arm, and uncovering it), how good Mam'selle is to you, what nice things she has brought you: do pray come in, Mam'selle, and take some refreshment; Monsieur, I dare say, will be very glad to have you sit a bit with him."

"Glad," repeated he with energy, while his eyes were fastened upon Madeline; "that were a poor expression indeed for what I should feel if I were so highly honoured."

The words of Janette, and the looks of de Sevignie, heightened the blushes which had already overspread the beautiful cheeks of Madeline.—"I cannot stop another minute," said she, confused, and turning to Janette as if solely to address her.

"Well, I am sorry that you can't (replied Janette); but before you go, won't you tell Monsieur how happy you are at his recovery."

"I am very—happy indeed (said she with some hesitation), that he is so well.—Adieu, sir (again glancing at Sevignie, whose eyes eloquently expressed his wishes that she would comply with the request of Janette, though diffidence and timidity prevented his seconding it); adieu, sir, I trust you will soon be perfectly recovered." She then, without waiting for him to speak, hurried to the outer room, followed by Janette—"I assure you, Mam'selle (said she), if you had sat a little while with Monsieur, you would have liked him vastly, he is so gentle and good-humoured; did you observe what a beautiful smile he has?"

"Yes—no," answered Madeline moving to the door.

"Do you know, Mam'selle, (cried Janette, still following) I was obliged to restore the little picture; he enquired so particularly about it, and seemed so uneasy at the idea of losing it, that I could not find in my heart to keep it from him."

As Madeline walked back, she regretted the confusion she had betrayed at the sight of de Sevignie, which she feared he might impute to a consciousness of his sentiments towards her; and his wish of concealing them was so obvious, that the idea of being suspected of knowing them, shocked her beyond measure. She therefore resolved, if ever they again met, to have a better guard over her feelings, to endeavour to remove such a suspicion if it really existed.

Her resolution was however easier to plan than to carry into effect; for when, on the second day after her interview with him, of which she informed her father, Clermont ushered him into the parlour where she sat at work; she suddenly rose from her chair with an emotion that rendered her for some minutes incapable of speaking.

"You and my daughter have already met (said Clermont to him); any introduction is therefore unnecessary. Madeline, my love (addressing her), I am sure you will feel happy at Monsieur de Sevignie's being able to come abroad again, and at his kind intention of devoting this, his first day of recovered health, to our gratification."

"I shall indeed, sir," said Madeline bowing.

The eloquent eyes of de Sevignie seemed to thank her for this assurance. Clermont made him take a seat by her; and her confusion gradually subsiding, they soon entered into conversation. The situation, simplicity, and ornaments of the cottage were pleasing themes to de Sevignie; the latter he particularly admired, perhaps from knowing they were Madeline's performances; and Clermont listened with unspeakable delight to the praises bestowed upon the taste and ingenuity of his daughter, nor could he forbear, with the pride so natural to a paternal heart, joining in them.

"Yet, 'tis not so much from the beauty of these works that I derive my pleasure (said Clermont) as from the consideration of their being specimens of a taste which will always furnish my child with agreeable employment, and prevent her from feeling that most disagreeable of all sensations, weariness of herself: but excuse me, my love (seeing a blush steal over the cheek of Madeline), for speaking as I have done; modest merit I know always shrinks from public praise. Monsieur de Sevignie will also I hope have the goodness to pardon me; to speak of what we love, is a foible we are all, particularly a parent, liable to; and some years hence, when he is himself perhaps a parent, he will be able to make allowances for its being indulged."

"You do not know my heart (said de Sevignie, with warmth), or you would not suppose I could not now make these allowances:—cold and unfeeling indeed should I consider that soul which was not proud, which did not boast of, such a treasure as you possess."

After dinner, when the heat of the sun had declined, they walked out to the garden; and from thence ascended by an easy path to the summit of the hill which overlooked it, to enjoy the lovely prospect and the fresh breeze that played around so delightful after the oppressive warmth of an autumnal day.

Immediately before them, they could only see the white chimneys of the cottages rising amidst embowering groves; but, on either side, they commanded a full view of the valley, o'er which the sober colouring of closing day was already spread, heightening the gloomy solemnity of its hanging woods, and giving a deeper tint of green to the smooth and sloping banks of the stream which, now clear and beautifully serene, reflected, as in a glass, those sloping banks, the neat cottages, the waving woods, that rose above them, and the blue firmament, yet marked by the glories of the setting sun; whilst beside it lay its ruminating herds, and all around was silence, as if nature and her works were hushed to repose by the declining hour.

"How delicious is this prospect (said de Sevignie, in a voice of rapture)! the eye could never be tired of it; yet is its tranquillity even more pleasing to the mind, than its beauties to the eye."

"'Tis delightful indeed (cried Clermont), to a mind that has been harassed by care."

"Would to heaven (exclaimed de Sevignie, with fervour), fate had destined a situation of such tranquillity for me!"

"Not now," cried Clermont.

"Yes, at this very period," replied de Sevignie.

"Suppress such a wish, my friend (said Clermont); it is unworthy of you; it would be an ill requital to the goodness of Providence, if you sought to bury such talents as it has given you (talents calculated to benefit mankind) in obscurity; besides, you could not at present enjoy such a situation."

"Not enjoy it!" repeated de Sevignie, with a degree of astonishment.

"No (replied Clermont); at your time of life you cannot have seen much of the world, or experienced many of its vicissitudes; and without doing so, we can seldom, or rather never I should say, understand the real value of rural tranquillity.

"Think you the sailor, who always glided upon smooth seas, would thoroughly enjoy his haven of security?—no; 'tis the remembrance of the perils he has experienced upon those seas, which renders it so delightful to him: he vaunts to his friends of the dangers he has encountered with an exultation, a happiness which those could never feel who always enjoyed a state of safety; and with that exultation and happiness is intermingled gratitude of the most fervent nature to that Almighty Being who lent his supporting arm through those dangers; and, should any little crosses arise, all murmurs, on their account, are instantly suppressed, by reflecting how insignificant they are, compared to what he has already suffered.

"Thus have I attempted to prove, that to render retirement truly pleasing, we should first intermix in active life, and understand what we gave up in withdrawing from it; and also, that a knowledge of its difficulties will silence that discontent which is too apt to rise at every little trial; for he who has witnessed or braved the storm, will never shrink from the biting blast."

The arguments of Clermont were too just to be controverted; at least de Sevignie had not the temerity to attempt doing so: they continued to converse till the lovely prospect they had been admiring, became all one swimming scene, uncertain if beheld. They then rose to return to the house.

De Sevignie offered his hand to Madeline: as she took it, she felt it tremble. A rising moon began to dissipate the darkness as they descended the hill, and soon o'er all her silver mantle threw,

And in her pale dominion check'd the night.

"How lovely is this scene (said de Sevignie, stopping at the foot of the hill); how soft, how pleasing the shadowy light of the moon! how beautifully does it tip the waving trees with silver; and what a solemn glory does it cast upon the mouldering battlements of yonder castle."

They entered the cottage; supper was prepared for them, and they sat down to it with no other light than what the moon afforded, and by an open window, through which a soft breeze wafted delicious odours; no sound could now be heard in the valley, but the melancholy rippling of the water.

After supper, "this is an hour (said Clermont), which my Madeline often devotes to music; the soul is never more suited for the enjoyment of harmony, than at such an hour as the present, when the busy cares of day are over, and the more painful ones of recollection are softened by the universal tranquillity of nature and her works: you, de Sevignie, are I am sure a performer, and you will not, I hope, refuse to accompany my Madeline."

De Sevignie spoke not, but his smile declared his readiness to oblige; Clermont put his oboe into his hands, and they proceeded to a rustic bench, beneath the spreading branches of a chestnut tree, near the cottage. Here they passed a considerable time in a most delightful manner; the execution of de Sevignie was in the most masterly style, but his taste if possible surpassed it, and never had his companions been more gratified than they were by listening to him: at last they rose to return to the cottage, and he then bade them farewell.

From this day de Sevignie became almost an inmate of the cottage: and as Clermont, then engrossed by the vintage, could not devote much time to him, Madeline was almost his sole, and during the mornings, his only companion; those mornings were generally spent either in reading poems to Madeline, to which the harmony of his voice imparted new charms, in watching the progress of her pencil, or in listening to the melody of her lute. The melancholy which oppressed him made Madeline exert all her powers to try and beguile it, but without effect; every day seemed to add to it; and often, affected by its soft contagion, Madeline has swept the chords of the lute with a disordered hand, and abruptly quitted the room to wipe away the tears it occasioned: – she ascribed, she wished to ascribe, her feelings for him to pity, but they proceeded from even a tenderer impulse than pity.

At length her altered looks and manner discovered to her father the secret of her heart: bitterly he then regretted the hospitality which had introduced so dangerous a guest to her knowledge; and wondered he had not timely foreseen the probable consequences of such a measure, and avoided them. His attentions immediately slackened to de Sevignie; and he scrupled not to hint in pretty plain terms, that his visits at the cottage were attended with inconvenience. Severely however was his generous nature wounded at being compelled to speak in this manner; and as the words passed his lips, he averted his looks from de Sevignie, whose faded cheeks were instantly flushed by a pale hectic. Had Clermont seen a probability of his daughter's attachment ending happily, he would not have acted as he now did; but of this he beheld not the remotest prospect; for though de Sevignie appeared by his looks to admire her, and by his delay in the valley (now that he was sufficiently recovered to leave it), to be attached to her company, not a word expressive of that admiration or attachment ever escaped him: even if he had declared a passion, there would still have been a bar to Madeline's happiness from her father's ignorance of de Sevignie's real situation and circumstances; both which it was obvious he wished to conceal, as Clermont had more than once introduced a conversation calculated to lead to the mention of them, from which, with with visible confusion, de Sevignie instantly withdrew.

The day after the alteration took place in Clermont's manner, an alteration Madeline wept in secret, de Sevignie absented himself from the cottage till the close of evening; he then entered the room where Clermont and Madeline sat dejectedly together, and informed them he was come merely for the purpose of taking leave, having fixed on the next morning for his departure: delighted to hear this, Clermont lost all coldness, and would have conversed again as usual with him, had the spirits of de Sevignie permitted him to do so; but Madeline was unable to speak; pensively she sat in a window, wishing, yet fearing, to quit the room, lest her father and de Sevignie should suspect the motive which tempted her to do so.

At length de Sevignie rose to depart; Madeline also involuntarily arose.—"Farewell! sir (cried he, addressing Clermont with a kind of solemnity in his looks); I cannot do justice to the feelings that now swell my heart; I shall not therefore attempt to express them.—Once more, sir, farewell! (taking his hand, and pressing it to his breast) may that happiness you merit be ever yours,—greater I cannot wish you: then turning to Madeline—"and you, Mam'selle, who, like a ministering angel, tried to soothe the sorrows of a stranger!"——He paused—a tear at that instant stole from beneath the half-closed eyelids of Madeline, and gave him emotions he could scarcely conceal; he tried, however, to proceed, but in vain; and, clasping her hand between his, he bowed upon it the adieu he could not articulate: then snatching up his hat, rushed from the house, followed by Clermont; not indeed, from any idea of overtaking him, but merely to give Madeline an opportunity of recovering herself.

"He is gone then (said she, sinking upon a chair); we have parted to meet no more!—Oh, de Sevignie! I now almost regret we ever met!"

Absorbed in melancholy, she forgot the necessity there was for trying to suppress her emotions before her father's return, till his step, as she imagined, in the hall roused her from her reverie, and made her precipitately fly to another room which opened immediately upon the stairs. She had scarcely gained her chamber, when Jaqueline entered.

"Come down, Mam'selle (said she), Monsieur de Sevignie is below, and wishes to speak with you."

"With me! (repeated Madeline, starting from the seat on which she had thrown herself); good heaven! (in inexpressible agitation, the agitation perhaps of hope) what can he have to say to me?"

"I am sure that's more than I can tell (said Jaqueline); but I will go and inform "I am sure that's more than I can tell (said Jaqueline); but I will go and inform him you are coming." So saying, she descended the stairs, followed by Madeline as soon as she had wiped away her tears. De Sevignie was waiting for her at the parlour door—"I came back (said he in a hesitating voice as she entered) to return the poems which you were so obliging as to lend me, and which I forgot this evening when I came to take leave."

The colour which had mantled the cheeks of Madeline died away, and she took the book in silence from him.

"Permit me now (cried he) to return those thanks for your attentions, which, when I saw you before this evening, I had not the power of doing. Oh, Madeline! (as if with irrepressible emotion) who can wonder at my being then incapable of speaking." — Madeline turned from him to conceal the feelings he inspired, and walked to the window; he followed her — "this evening (cried he) I have bade a final adieu to felicity; to-morrow, to-morrow at this hour, oh, Madeline! and I shall be far, far distant from this spot! — I shall only behold this lovely face in idea: — tell me (he continued, taking her hand, and looking at her with the most touching softness), when I am gone, may I hope sometimes to be remembered, as a friend? — to think of living in the memory of those I love, would be to me a soothing pleasure, the only pleasure I can enjoy."

Madeline promised not to forget him; 'twas a promise her heart told her she would truly perform. De Sevignie still lingered after receiving it; — "I must be gone at last (cried he); every moment I stay but increases my reluctance to depart. Oh, Madeline! no words can express my heaviness of heart at thus bidding a last adieu to — — — " He paused — but his eyes expressed what his tongue left unfinished. Madeline sat down; her tears fell in spite of her efforts to restrain them: de Sevignie grasped her hands in his; he looked at her with a countenance full of anguish. — "I must fly (said he), or I shall no longer have any command over myself." The breeze that blew in at the window had wafted aside the hair of Madeline from her forehead; de Sevignie pressed his lips against it for a moment; and, dropping on his knees, "bless, heaven (he cried) bless with the choicest of thy gifts, the loveliest of thy works!" — then rising precipitately, he once more rushed out of the house.

Madeline, more dejected than ever, returned to her chamber; nor could any effort she made for the purpose so far restore her composure as to enable her to join her father (whose walk had been purposely lengthened on her account) at supper: she excused herself by pleading a head-ache. Clermont sighed, as he thought that a heart-ache was what she should have said. The departure of de Sevignie Clermont trusted would check the passion of Madeline; and that, like an untoward blossom of the spring, it would gradually die away — the "perfume and the suppliance of a moment:" how greatly therefore was he disappointed when convinced of the falsity of this idea, by the alteration which took place in her after the departure of de Sevignie; the rose forsook her cheek; she pined in thought, and neglected all her former avocations: with an anguish which no language can express, he watched over her; he did not hint at the observations he had made; but gently and by degrees he strove to lead her back to her former pursuits, well-knowing that employment was the best antidote against melancholy: he also frequently hinted, that she should be particularly watchful of her peace, as his entirely depended on it. These insinuations at length recalled her to a sense of what was due to him and herself; and she felt guilty of ingratitude in so long giving way to feelings which, by injuring her tranquillity, had interrupted his: a conviction of error was followed by a determination of making every possible atonement for it; she therefore struggled against despondency, and applied herself more assiduously than ever to her wonted occupations: success crowned her exertions; her health returned, and with it its almost constant attendant—cheerfulness; a cheerfulness, however, which derived its principal support from the hope of again beholding de Sevignie, and which sometimes, losing that support, sunk into despondency.

The winter glided away without any event happening in the least interesting to her feelings or her father's; and without lessening the impression which de Sevignie had made upon her heart: the scenes he had particularly admired about the cottage, she still wandered to; and the old castle still continued her favourite haunt; she copied the lines, though her doing so was unnecessary, for they were already deeply impressed upon her memory; and often visited the house where he had lodged, and where every tongue was eloquent in his praise.

CHAP. IV.

Friendship, of itself a holy tie,

Is made more sacred by adversity.

-Dryden

One night in the latter part of spring, as Clermont and Madeline were preparing to retire from the parlour for the night, a loud and violent knocking at the hall-door suddenly startled them: an apprehension of danger however never entered their thoughts; some neighbour taken ill, they supposed, had sent for relief; and, under this idea, Clermont hastened to open the door; but how great was his amazement on doing so to perceive a total stranger.

"Don't be alarmed, sir (said the man, who was young and appeared agitated, on perceiving him step back); I am servant to a lady of distinction, who is travelling from Paris to her chateau about ten leagues from this, and has met with an unfortunate accident in the valley, her coach being there overturned, and so much damaged, that she cannot proceed on her journey till it has been repaired: at a loss, in the mean time, for a place to stay in, she has sent to the owner of this cottage, who I suppose, sir, (bowing) you are, to request he will have the goodness either to permit her to remain a few hours in it, or inform her where she can gain admittance."

Clermont instantly desired him to present his respects to his lady, and inform her that he was happy he could have the honour of accommodating her. The servant bowed again, and hurried away, while Clermont put the light into Jaqueline's hands, and returned to the parlour to assist Madeline in settling it. In a few minutes approaching steps were heard, and a lady, somewhat advanced in years, but of a dignified and benignant aspect, entered the room. Clermont approached to welcome and receive her, but suddenly stopped, as did the lady, and, to the inexpressible amazement of Madeline, they both gazed on each other with all the wildness of surprise.

"Good heaven! (exclaimed the stranger, first breaking silence) do I really behold a friend so valued, so long anxiously sought after—do I really behold my ever esteemed—."

Clermont started; turned his eye upon his daughter; as quickly glanced it at the lady, and laid his hand upon his mouth: she seemed to understand the sign; sighed—paused—and looked down; then again raising her eyes—"I bless the accident (cried she), which has been the means of discovering to me the retreat of a friend so valued."

"I cannot indeed regret it (said Clermont, advancing, and taking her hand to his heart); I cannot regret what has again introduced me to the notice of the Countess de Merville,—what has convinced me that a being still exists interested about the unfortunate Clermont."

"Clermont! (repeated the lady, with a mournful voice); oh, my friend! but there is no name, no title by which you would not be equally estimable to me."

"Allow me (said he, looking at his daughter), to introduce another recluse to your ladyship."

She bowed; and Clermont advancing to Madeline, who, lost in wonder, had hitherto stood contemplating them, took her trembling hand and led her forward. The Countess clasped her to her bosom; then suddenly held her to a distance from it, and exclaimed—"what a resemblance!"

"A fatal one (cried Clermont); it often embitters the pleasure I take in gazing on her; the eyes, the voice, the smile!"

"Come, my good friend (said the Countess), reflect that there is no earthly pleasure without alloy, and try to support the common lot with fortitude: I believe I need not bring any proof to confirm the truth of what I have said, that the cup of joy never comes into mortal hands unmixed with bitter ingredients."

"No (replied Clermont), I want no proof of the truth of your words."

"I hope and believe (said she), that the destiny of this dear young creature will be happier than was that of the person she resembles."

"If not (cried Clermont, raising his eyes), grant, oh thou supreme Being! that I may never live to see it fulfilled." His own energy struck him; he recollected himself: handed the Countess to a chair, and briefly informed Madeline, whom he saw almost stupefied by surprise, how she should arrange matters for the accommodation of their guests; entreating her at the same time, to hasten whatever supper could be procured. She directly left the parlour, but was greatly surprised to find two females standing in the hall, younger, but not quite so well dressed as the Countess. She expressed her regret at their having continued so long in such a situation, and her wonder at their not having accompanied the Countess into the parlour: they smiled on each other at this, and said they were only her attendants. Madeline blushed at her mistake, for she had supposed them companions of the Countess, and conducted them into a small room adjoining the parlour, used by her father as a study: here, having procured lights, she left them. She found Jaqueline stirring up the fire, and asked her how she could suffer the strangers to continue so long in the hall?

"Why, Lord a mercy, Mam'selle (said Jaqueline), how could I think of every thing? here have I been in such a fuss, ransacking my brain to know what we should do about supper. Lord, what an unlucky thing it was that Father Pierre dined here to-day; he has always such an appetite; only for him some of the fowl at least would have been left, and then I could have made some rich gravy, and tossed it into a fricassee in a moment. I am sure I am as sorry as the lady herself can be about the accident; not that I should have cared a pin about it had it happened in summer or autumn, when one would have had nothing to do but put out their hand to gather something nice; but now nothing can be got for love or money."

"I am sure (said Madeline, with a look of distress), I don't know what is to be done."

"Well, Mam'selle, there's no use in fretting any more about the matter; I'll dress a good dish of eggs, and what with them and the new cheese, and some of your sweetmeats, we'll be able to furnish the table pretty tolerably."

"We must bestir ourselves, my good Jaqueline, for the rooms are yet to be settled; my father is to have a mattress brought down to the study for himself; and you must make up a bed here for yourself, as I shall be obliged to take your's in consequence of giving my own to the Countess."

"Holy Virgin! what a hurly-burly's here, (exclaimed Jaqueline); Lord what ill luck we had that they should fix on our cottage in preference to any other in the valley."

"Hush, hush, (said Madeline); consider how ill-natured it is to regret giving shelter to those who were benighted and distressed."

"Well, Mam'selle, if you'll lay the cloth, as I am so busy; I'll be after you in a moment with supper."

"Very well (replied Madeline as she took it up); and pray do not forget the strangers in the study." She then proceeded to the parlour, where she found her father and the Countess sitting by the fire, apparently engaged in an interesting discourse, which her presence interrupted. Clermont rose to assist her in laying the cloth; and the Countess watched her every movement with looks that spoke the warmest admiration: never indeed had Madeline appeared more beautiful; surprise and agitation had heightened the faint glow of her cheek to a bright crimson, which increased the lustre of her eyes, and rendered it almost dazzling. With downcast looks and hesitating accents, she apologised to the Countess for the frugal fare she was compelled to set before her. Jaqueline soon made her appearance with it; and ere she retired, was again reminded of the servants in the study, for whom she received some of Madeline's nice sweetmeats, and Clermont's best wine.

Either from compliance to the delicate feelings of her entertainers, or from real inclination, the Countess seemed to enjoy her supper; every thing indeed, though simple, was excellent in its kind. Her conversation now turned on general subjects, and Madeline was disappointed beyond expression, for she had flattered herself it would have recurred to former days, and of course explained to her what she had so long sighed to know, namely, the real origin of her father, and those misfortunes which had occasioned his present seclusion: and her disappointment rendered her unable, as she otherwise would have done, to enjoy the conversation of her new and noble guest; which, like her eye, still retained all the fire of youth, and indicated a spirit at once penetrating and benignant.

Clermont appeared unusually animated; and Madeline, amidst her wonder and disappointment, blessed the chance which had produced an incident so pleasing to him. Soon after supper, the Countess complained of fatigue: Madeline immediately took the hint; and having seen that a chamber was ready for her, offered to conduct her to it; an offer which the Countess instantly accepted; but her attendance was not permitted; the Countess's women were summoned, and from their lady's room repaired to the one allotted for them.

Madeline returned to the parlour, hoping that her father would explain whatever appeared mysterious to her, but she was disappointed; for he instantly said that he must wish her good-night, as he was extremely fatigued. Madeline could not help believing this was a pretext to avoid entering into conversation, and with involuntary dejection she received his adieu, and retired to her little chamber. Here she sat a long time pondering over all that had passed, and wondering why such profound secrecy should be observed to her: wearied at last with conjectures, she repaired to bed, but her mind was too much disturbed to let her rest as quietly as usual. About the middle of the night she was startled by a noise from below stairs; trembling she sat up in the bed to listen more distinctly; and in the next moment heard a soft tap at the door of the room adjoining hers, in which the Countess slept; she immediately stole out of bed, and unlatching her door, opened just as much of it as would permit her to observe what was going on without being discovered. She had not stood here a minute, when the Countess's door was opened with as much caution as her own had been, and she saw her coming from it with a light; and then, to her inexpressible amazement, beheld her father standing in the passage, who, taking the hand of the Countess, led her softly down stairs. It was some time before Madeline could move, so much was she astonished; a number of uneasy sensations rushed upon her mind; but she was too innocent to harbour any ideas prejudicial to her father and his friend: she concluded they had chosen this time as the best for talking over affairs which they wished to conceal. What an opportunity, thought Madeline, is there now for discovering those affairs:—she instantly flew to the chair on which her things were thrown, and snatching up a wrapper, threw it over her with breathless impatience, and hastened to the lobby;—but here she paused and reflected,

"Good heavens! (cried she, whilst she felt her cheeks suffused with the burning blushes of shame); good heavens, what am I about doing!—going to steal meanly upon the privacy of my father and his friend!—a father, from whose uniform tenderness I might well suppose that nothing which had a tendency to promote my happiness would be concealed; —a father, who has so sedulously cautioned me against any action contrary to virtue; that any deviation in me is inexcusable.—Fie, fie, Madeline, what a wretch art thou! how unworthy of his goodness! how little benefited by his precepts!" She returned to her chamber, fastened the door, and sitting down upon the bed, burst into an agony of tears—"I shall be ashamed to meet my father's eyes in the morning (cried she), I am sure my looks will betray my guilt: well I am resolved I will punish myself for it; henceforward I'll never express the smallest curiosity to be acquainted with his affairs; and never more will I scold Jaqueline when I catch her with her ear to the key-hole listening to our discourse."

She continued lamenting her conduct and imploring heaven to forgive it, till she heard the Countess, notwithstanding the lightness of her step, returning to her chamber. Roused by this, she then first perceived that day was dawning, and cold and exhausted crept into bed, where she lay till it was time for her to rise. As soon as dressed, she went down to assist Jaqueline in preparing breakfast, and found her the only person yet up.

"Why, Mam'selle (said she, the moment she saw Madeline), I believe you slept but poorly last night, for you look very pale."

"Do I," said Madeline, with a sigh.

"Yes, indeed; and I fancy I don't look vastly blooming myself, for my rest was not over good I can assure you; I thought I heard strange noises last night; do you know, Mam'selle, I don't half like those strangers."

"We must give them their breakfast however (said Madeline); so pray, Jaqueline, let us lose no more time in talking."

"Bless you (cried Jaqueline), you'll find I have lost no time in getting it ready; the coffee is ready for making, the things are laid, and I am just going to the dairy for the butter and cream."

Madeline turned into the parlour, and walked to the window, but not now, as heretofore, to gaze upon the prospect with delight: her mind was sunk in the heaviest dejection; for, for the first time, it was conscious of error; and all that had before charmed, was now disregarded.

Oh, Innocence! first of blessings! how tasteless without thee would all the pleasures of life appear to a heart of sensibility! as no state can be happy without thee, neither can any be truly wretched with thee; thy smiles can give fortitude to the weak; thy power can blunt the arrows of adversity: he who cherishes thee shall, in the hour of misery, be rewarded by thy consolations,—and blessed, thrice blessed are they who know them.

Madeline was not long in the parlour ere her father entered. After the usual salutations, he began a conversation which seemed contrived for the purpose of knowing whether Madeline felt any curiosity about the proceedings of the last night; he at length took her hand, and leading her to a chair, seated himself by her,

"My dear Madeline (said he), you were no doubt surprised at what you saw last night; and your silence respecting that surprise, pleases me more than I can express, as it at once convinces me of the command you have over yourself, and the respect you have for me."

Praise so undeserved was more cutting to the heart of Madeline than the severest reproaches could have been; she burst into tears; declared her unworthiness, her contrition, and implored her father's forgiveness.

"An error (exclaimed Clermont, after the pause of a minute, and taking the hand which he had suddenly relinquished), so ingenuously acknowledged, so sincerely repented, I cannot deny my pardon to: but, my dear Madeline, let the conviction of your weakness, render you more fervent than ever in imploring heaven to strengthen your virtuous resolutions: let it also influence you to make allowances for the frailty of others; 'tis inexcusable in any one to triumph over the indiscretions of another, which perhaps the want of similar temptations alone prevented their falling into; but doubly inexcusable in those who are conscious of having committed them."

"From the first pang of remorse, judge of the horrors which ever attend misconduct, and strive to avoid them by ever resisting inclinations that side not with your duties: to oppose our passions, is finally to conquer them; like cowards, they are tyrannical with the weak, but timid with the brave: and no victory can be so glorious as one obtained over them; 'tis applauded by our reason, sanctioned by our conscience, and applauded by him who records the smallest effort in the cause of virtue."

"Oh, my father (said Madeline), henceforward I trust I shall convince you I have profited by your lessons."

"Be your error forgotten (resumed Clermont), or only remembered as a caution against any future one. And now, my child, to return to last night; you were no doubt astonished at the feelings manifested by the Countess de Merville and me at our unexpected meeting; but strong as is our mutual regard, friendship is the only tie between us: how that friendship commenced, or was interrupted, would not be more painful to you to hear, than to me to relate, supposing our stolen interview was for the purpose of talking over affairs which we wished to conceal; a wish dictated by regard to your tranquillity; as the Countess knew my past, so was she now acquainted with my present situation; and in consequence of being so generously noble, humanely offered to take you under her protection."

Madeline started, and would have spoken, had not a motion from Clermont enjoined her to silence.

"You know not (he continued), heaven only knows it, the load of anxiety her offer has removed from my heart; unnumbered have been the sleepless nights, the wretched days I have passed on your account; looking forward to the hour which should deprive you of my protection (a tear dropped from Madeline on his hand); which should leave you forlorn in a world too prone to take advantage of innocence and poverty: the asylum of a cloister was the only one I had means of procuring you; but to that you ever manifested a repugnance, and I could not therefore influence you to it; the free-will offering of the heart is alone acceptable to heaven: besides, I do not thoroughly approve such institutions; I think they are somewhat contrary to nature; and I can never believe that beings immured for life, can feel gratitude so ardent, piety so exalted to the Almighty, as those who, in the wide range of the world, have daily opportunities of exploring his wonders, experiencing his goodness, and contemplating the profusion of his gifts. The Countess de Merville is just the guide to whose care I can consign my beloved girl with confidence and pleasure; her virtues are as fascinating as her manners; and though her ability to do good is great, her wish is still greater.

"With her you'll move in a sphere of life very different from your present one; and against the dangers so often attending sudden exaltation I would caution you, did I not know that she will at once cherish you with the tenderness of a parent, and watch you with the sedulity of a friend: all I shall therefore say is, that I trust you may ever continue the unaffected child of nature; ever remember that modesty is the best ornament of a female, and simplicity her chief attraction: the Countess departs after breakfast, and you then accompany her."

Madeline again started; all the pleasure she might from a lively fancy have derived at the prospect of such a change of scene, was damped by the idea of leaving him;—"oh, my father! (she said, bursting into tears), how can I leave you!"

"Equally affected as herself, and bitterly lamenting the cruel necessity which could alone have caused a separation, he clasped her to his bosom, and mingled tears with hers; in pity to his feelings, he besought her to moderate hers; to consider the tranquillity he should enjoy from having her under such protection. He told her in a few months, if it pleased heaven, they would again meet, as the Countess then intended to return to Paris, and had promised in her way to it to make some stay at his cottage.

Madeline, comforted by those words, wiped away her tears, and said, she would try to compose herself. Clermont then took a small picture, plainly set, from his pocket; "I know (said he), your tenderness will be gratified by this present; accept therefore, my dear Madeline (putting it into her hand) the copy of what your father was when his cheek was unfaded by age or care, his spirit unbroken by disappointment."

Madeline had never before seen this picture, she received it with transport; though from its being done at a very early period, she could now scarcely trace any resemblance in it to her father.

The Countess now entered the parlour with a countenance open as day, and irradiated with the sunshine of good-humour: —"Well (cried she to Clermont), have you told our young friend that I mean to run away with her?"

"Yes (replied he), and she has no objection to the measure, but what proceeds from her reluctance at leaving me."

"If she did not feel that reluctance, (said the Countess), she would be lessened in my esteem; but while I admire, it will be my study to remove it."

"I am convinced it will," said Clermont.

"And I, madam, (said Madeline), am truly sensible of your goodness; I feel it at my heart; and it will be the height of my ambition to merit it: oh, what joy should I derive from it, but for quitting my father!"—A tear, in spite of her efforts to restrain it, trickled down her cheek; but she hastily wiped it away, and seated herself at the table, to which Clermont handed Madame. The emotions of Madeline prevented her eating and she lingered over the breakfast things, long after her attendance was necessary, till the Countess, looking at her watch, begged she would pack up whatever she wanted to take along with her, as she expected the carriage every moment, and was anxious to begin her journey that it might be terminated at an early hour, the roads about the chateau being very lonesome.

Madeline immediately rose and repaired to Jaqueline to obtain her assistance, and inform her she was going.—"Alack a day, it was an unlucky hour which brought those strangers to our cottage! (cried the good-natured Jaqueline); here they have come to disturb our happiness and comfort, and leave me and my poor master like two solitary hermits: we never more shall have any pleasant music! never more any midnight serenades, or dancing on the lawn—no, no! Claude and Josephe will never more come about the house with their flutes when you have left it;—poor lads! often and often have I scoffed at them for doing so, and said they might as well pipe to the kids on the mountains as to you, who was a lady born, I was sure. And then, Mam'selle, if the Chevalier de Sevignie should ever re-visit the cottage, how sadly he'll be disappointed at finding you gone; for I'll never believe but what he was deeply in love with you; what else could have kept him in the valley so long after he was recovered, or make him come loitering about the cottage as I discovered him one morning?"

Jaqueline had now touched a chord which could not bear vibration. Madeline from being pale, turned red, and then pale again; and, hastening up stairs, desired Jaqueline to follow her directly, Jaqueline obeyed; and Madeline, too much agitated to do much for herself, gave her the things to pack up which she wanted to take with her; then leaning pensively against a window which commanded a view of the castle, "I am going then, (said she to herself); going, I may say, into a new world, without really knowing the family to which I belong,—the mother from which I sprung, or one circumstance about her: but why do I indulge this restless curiosity? oh, let me try to repress it, as well from the resolution of last night, as from the conviction, that could the knowledge I desire add to my happiness, it would not be kept from me:—never, therefore, may my rashness again attempt to raise the veil which prudence as well as tenderness, I must believe, has cast over past events."

"Well, Mam'selle (cried Jaqueline), your things are now packed, but heaven knows most unwillingly. Is there no way by which you could avoid going?"

"No, (replied Madeline), for my father wishes me to go, happy to have me under the protection of a lady who is as good as she is great."

"She may be very good indeed (said Jaqueline); but that's more than her attendants are, I fancy; I don't like them at all, they did so titter at me last night when I went to the study with their supper, though I am sure I paid my compliments to them very handsomely: Lord they think, because they have been in Paris, that no body but themselves knows any thing of good-breeding."

Madeline now descended to the parlour; and in a few minutes after the coach appeared. She trembled and wept, and the fortitude of Clermont almost forsook him; he blessed, he embraced her with unutterable tenderness; he put her hand into the Countess's, and said he committed to her charge his only earthly happiness,—the only treasure he had preserved from the wreck of felicity,—his sole friend, almost his sole companion, for fifteen years.

The Countess, convinced that to delay would rather increase than diminish the emotions of both, hastened to the carriage,
The Countess, convinced that to delay would rather increase than diminish the emotions of both, hastened to the carriage, led by Clermont, and followed by Madeline, her attendants, and the weeping Jaqueline.

"I shall certainly break my heart (cried the latter as she walked by Madeline), and this great lady will have my death to answer for: Lord send she mayn't have any more sins upon her conscience; they say those Paris folks are sometimes very wicked."

Madeline cast her pensive eyes alternately on her father, his cottage, and the lovely prospect surrounding it: "oh, dear preceptor of my youth! oh, solitary scenes of early infancy! (she cried to herself) how gladly would I resign all the pleasure which, perhaps, awaits my entrance into another situation, to continue the companion of one,—the peaceful inmate of the other!"

More dejected than words can express, she entered the coach, whose swiftness soon made her lose sight of her father; but while one glimpse of his habitation could be seen, she did not turn her eyes from it; and when a winding of the valley hid it from her view, she again sighed, and implored the protection of heaven for its beloved owner.

CHAP. V.

—in those woods I deem some spirits dwell,

Who, from the chiding stream and groaning oak,

Still hear and answer to my moan. Douglas

The soothing attentions of the Countess de Merville at length abated the grief of Madeline; she gradually revived and began to converse and admire the new and beautiful scenes, through which she passed. In the course of conversation she learned that her amiable friend was a widow, and had one only child, a daughter, married about three years to a Monsieur D'Alembert, who generally resided in Paris; in which place the Countess had also lived for that period, for the purpose of enjoying her daughter's company:—"but at length, weary of the dissipation that prevails there (said she), and in which I was sometimes obliged unavoidably to join, I found myself under the necessity of giving up my daughter's society for a time, in order to recruit myself by country air and retirement."

They stopped, in the meridian of the day, at a small house on the borders of an extensive forest through which they were to pass, to procure some refreshment, and rest the horses. The room in which the Countess and Madeline dined looked into the forest; and the cool shade which the trees cast upon the windows, rendered it delightful after the intense heat they had been exposed to whilst travelling. At some distance, proudly rising above the trees, appeared the antique towers of a castle.

"What a gloomy residence must that be, madam," said Madeline pointing to it."

"Gloomy indeed," replied the Countess.

"Ah, my ladies, (cried their host, who was attending them, an old grey-headed man), I remember the time (with a melancholy shake of his head) when that castle, notwithstanding its situation in the forest, was neither sad nor gloomy, but one of the gayest mansions in France."

"And what occasioned an alteration in it?" said Madeline, after waiting a minute to try if the Countess would ask the question.

"Death, my Lady,—death, that pays no regard to rank or riches. The Count de Montmorenci, (continued the old man, advancing a few steps nearer to Madeline), the lord of that castle, had an only son, one of the finest youths perhaps that ever was seen,—the admiration of the rich, the comfort of the poor, the pride and darling of his parents; this beloved son was murdered about seventeen years ago upon the Alps, and ever since that period the Count has never held up his head. To complete his misery, the Countess, on whom he doted, died in two days after she heard the fate of her son; and poor gentleman, from that time to the present, he has led a wretched and unsettled life, wandering about from one seat to another, (for he has many in France) as if he hoped change of scene could give him comfort;—alas! nothing in this world can do so. He has now been two years absent from Montmorenci Castle; we therefore expect him soon at it. While he is away, 'tis always locked up: and from his frequent absences, and the neglect shown to every thing when in it, 'tis become, both within and without, quite an altered place. The only pleasure he has experienced since his son's death, has been in doing what he thought would show respect and honour to his memory: he has had a fine monument erected for him in the chapel of Montmorenci Castle; and on the left side of it, at a good distance, you may see, my lady, (approaching the window, and pointing out the spot to Madeline), rising above a thick clump of trees, the top of a monumental pillar, which he placed there to his memory."

"Yes, (said Madeline) I see it; there appears to me an urn upon it."

"You are right, my lady, there is an urn ornamented with a wreath of laurel, withered ere half blown. Some people say that the Count in his youth, (resumed the old man), committed actions which deserved the chastisement of heaven. For my part, I say nothing; when a man is in sorrow, his faults should be forgotten."

"Not always, my friend, (said the Countess, who had hitherto sat silently listening to the conversation); I agree with you, a man should not be reproached for them when in trouble; but they should be remembered to prove the justice of Providence in sending that trouble, and that, sooner or later, he will punish the evil doer."

"Very true, very true," cried her host, bowing to the ground.

The Countess was now informed her carriage was ready, and she lost no time in re-entering it: it passed within a few yards of Montmorenci Castle; and through the bars of the massy iron gate which opened into its spacious court, Madeline beheld that court strewed with fragments of the building, o'er which the high grass waved in rank luxuriance. "The pride, the glory of the family belonging to that castle (said the Countess, bending forward to look at it), is gone for ever; dazzling was its splendour, but rapid its decline: greatness unsupported by goodness can never be durable."

"You think then, madam, (cried Madeline), that the Count really merited his afflictions."

"'Tis an unpleasant subject, my dear, (said the Countess) we will change it"; 'twas accordingly dropped.

About sun-set they reached the chateau, which the Countess de Merville possessed in right of her father; it was built at a very distant period, and its architecture was rude in the extreme; for the pride of its possessors would not permit the smallest polish or improvement, considering its rudeness an honourable date of their own antiquity. Time, however, had been less sparing, and marked it in many places with visible decay; some of the windows were dismantled from the failure of the stone work, and many of its battlements had mouldered away: it stood upon an elevated lawn, sequestered in the bosom of an extensive wood, whose mighty shades appeared coeval with itself: on one side a narrow stream crept from a little shrubby hill with sluggish murmurs through the brushwood, expanding by degrees, till it formed a spacious lake, whose rising banks were covered with a profusion of fragrant and flowering shrubs; the myrtle, the laurestine, the flexile osier, and the weeping willow here intermingled their beauties, and fantastically fringed its margin; while on its bosom lay a few small islands of variegated verdure, the haunts of lonely and aquatic fowl, whose melancholy cries heightened the natural solemnity of the evening hour. Behind the chateau lay its old fashioned gardens, full of fountains, labyrinths, bowers, and mutilated statues; and above them, bounding the horizon, were seen the towering Alps, those gigantic sons of creation, to whom compared, the proudest monuments of art are as insignificant as the ray of the glow-worm to the solar blaze. The gardens were terminated by a narrow valley, to which there was a descent by steps cut in the sod: it lay between stupendous mountains, whose summits, at a distance, appeared tinged with blue vapour, and proudly reaching to the clouds; and in it stood the remains of a religious house, built and endowed by an ancestor of the Countess, many years prior to the erection of the castle, and at which this period had been long uninhabited in consequence of its decay; it still however continued to be the Countess's place of worship; hither, whenever she resided at the chateau, she was wont to retire at the close of day, and pass an hour in prayer and solemn meditation; and here a priest (belonging to the community that had once inhabited it, and for whom her father had procured another habitation) officiated at stated periods. The chapel was still in tolerable preservation; but all beside, except a flight of stairs that led to the dormitory above, was in irreparable decay. The numerous religious devices and heavy gothic windows of the chapel, were of themselves almost sufficient to have inspired a holy awe: relics of saints and departed warriors covered great part of the walls; and banners presented by knights crusaders on their return from the Holy Land, as grateful offerings to heaven for its protecting care, still hung from some of the pillars, waving, as if in sullen dignity, o'er the sculptured marble that covered their remains. For religious retirement, no place could have been better adapted than the valley; its towering mountains excluded every prospect that could have allured the heart to wish to stray beyond it; and the gloom of the hanging woods invited to meditation, which there was no sounds to interrupt, except the dashing of distant waterfalls, and the cawing of rooks: a thick mantle of grass covered the valley, and here the thistle shook its lonely head, and the moss that crept over the buttresses of the monastery whistled to the wind. This building communicated with the castle by means of a subterraneous passage, now never used on account of its vicinity to the burying vaults.

The vast magnitude and decaying grandeur of the chateau, impressed Madeline with surprise and melancholy; which were almost heightened to awe and veneration on entering a gloomy-vaulted hall of immense size, with small arched windows, and supported by stone arches, ornamented with rude sculpture, and hung with rusty coats of armour; while against the walls the ancient implements of war were placed in curious devices of suns, moons, and stars. At one end of the hall was the picture of the founder of the castle, and at the other the grand stair-case, whose sides were covered with historical pictures reaching to the ceiling.

The old domestics of the chateau were here assembled to welcome the return of their lady; and their delight at seeing her was a convincing proof, if such a one had been wanting, of her goodness. She addressed them all kindly and severally, nor betrayed the least impatience at their tedious enquiries. She then led Madeline into a large parlour, where she embraced and welcomed her to the chateau, which she desired her in future to consider as her home. Coffee was immediately brought in, and the house-keeper soon after followed; presuming on her superiority over the rest of the servants, she had come in to hear and relate all that had happened since her lady's departure; she was a little woman, almost double with age, and neat even to preciseness. The Countess, who esteemed her from her long residence in the family, and her fidelity, made her take a cup of coffee, and sit down.

"Well, madame (said the little creature, while her eyes twinkled with pleasure at the kindness of her lady), has my young lady yet given an heir to Monsieur D'Alembert?"

"No," replied the Countess.

"Dear heart! I am sorry for that; I had hoped by this time to have heard there was a grandson born to my beloved lady." She then proceeded to mention her pleasure at the Countess's having procured such a companion as Madeline, one who would prevent her missing her daughter as much as she had formerly done.

The Countess sighed at these words; and a shade of melancholy for a few minutes obscured her countenance. The eyes of Madeline, meanwhile, were busily employed examining the apartment; many things within it excited her surprise and curiosity; and scarcely could she keep herself from asking a number of questions about what she saw. While the Countess and Agatha were talking over family matters, she retired to a window which commanded a beautiful prospect of the lake, now glittering with the beams of a setting sun: the scene recalled to her mind the manner in which she had been situated the preceding evening; and the sigh of involuntary regret mingled with the pleasures of recollection.

With her father she had then viewed the retiring glories of the sun from the little lawn before their cottage;—glories which he had likened to those that attend the departure of the virtuous—calm, awful, and lovely: together they had enjoyed the fresh breeze which played around; and heard the soft voices of the peasant girls chanting the evening service to the Virgin, in which they joined, elevating their hearts like their eyes to that heaven whose goodness they experienced. Enraptured with the scene, they thought not of returning to the house; but continued to watch the moon gradually breaking through the fleecy clouds, mellowing the extensive landscape, and casting long tracts of radiance aslant the trembling waves; while the owl, from his ivy-mantled bower, hailed her with notes of sadness, and the young cottagers came forth to dance beneath her beams. "Oh, my father! (cried Madeline to herself) if I did not think such evenings would return, how wretched would be now the heart of your child!"

As she leaned pensively against the window, she was suddenly roused by lively music from the wood; and immediately after, saw a troop of rustics emerging from it, dressed in their holiday clothes, and adorned with large bouquets of the gayest spring flowers. Those were the Countess's tenants come to celebrate her arrival. She directly went forth to meet them, followed by Madeline, who derived unspeakable pleasure from such a sight. They all eagerly crowded round their beloved mistress, each anxious to be first noticed; some weeping for joy, and others blessing heaven for permitting them again to behold her face. Affected by those proofs of love and gratitude, the heart of the Countess swelled with sensibility, and a tear rolled down her cheek: oh, how delightful! how different her sensations from those experienced by the selfish beings who neither feel nor interest themselves about the welfare of others; but, like the haughty tyrant, seated

– – – – – – –amid the gaudy herd

Of mute, barbarians bending to his nod,

close their eyes upon the distresses of mankind, because elevated above them; and say within themselves, let not

– – – – – – –the clam'rous voice of woe

Intrude upon mine ear!

After conversing some time with the peasants, the Countess returned to the parlour; from whence she and Madeline watched them resuming the dance, and partaking of refreshments laid out for them on large tables about the lawn. The gaiety of the scene somewhat amused, but could not entirely remove the dejection of Madeline's heart; her father, sad and solitary in his cottage, was present to her view: and she sighed almost unknowing to herself. The Countess perceived her dejection, and loved her the better for it, as she knew the amiable source from which it proceeded: she tried, however, to beguile it by her conversation; and related a number of pleasant anecdotes; described the different places she had seen; and gave a particular account of Paris, its customs, and diversions.

Subjects so new to Madeline could not fail to amuse and interest her; and she expressed her pleasure in the liveliest manner.

"Yet this charming place (said the Countess, alluding to what Madeline had said on hearing Paris described), I should never visit but on my daughter's account. At my time of life, its gaieties begin to tire: besides, I love retirement, particularly the retirement of this chateau; I venerate its woods; they were planted by my forefathers; and if ever departed spirits are permitted to review this world, their spirits I think sometimes revisit them. Often, at the solemn hour of twilight, have I fancied their voices mingled in the gale which sighed among the trees: such fancies, perhaps, you'll say are weaknesses; the generality of mankind would consider them so; but they rather strengthen than enervate my mind: they are more soothing to it than language can express; they calm, they refine, they almost exalt it above mortality, and gradually prepare it for that hour which, in the course of nature, I may soon expect. But think not, my love (continued she, on seeing a gloom again stealing over the countenance of Madeline), that you are come to live with a dismal recluse; no,—I love innocent and rational society, and shall continue to do so, while I have health or spirits to enjoy it."

In this manner they continued to converse, till supper was announced in another room. Hitherto a stranger to any thing like luxury or splendour, Madeline was astonished on entering it at the elegance and grandeur exhibited to her view; for the Countess, though of the most domestic turn, still kept up that state her high rank and fortune entitled her to. She gazed alternately at the table, the attendants, and the massy plate which covered the side-board; and began to fear she should make but an awkward figure in a situation so very different from her former one.

Fatigued by her journey, the Countess soon after supper proposed retiring to rest; a proposal extremely agreeable to Madeline, whose spirits still felt agitated. The Countess conducted her to her chamber, which was near her own, and at the end of a long gallery that overlooked the hall; here they parted; but a servant remained, who offered to assist Madeline in undressing; an offer which she, never accustomed to such attendance, refused; and, feeling a restraint in her presence, dismissed her; yet scarcely had she done so, ere she felt an uneasy sensation, something like fear, stealing over her mind as she looked round her spacious and gloomy apartment; nor could she prevent herself from starting as the tapestry, which represented a number of grotesque and frightful figures, agitated by the wind that whistled through the crevices, every now and then swelled from the walls. She sat down near the door, wishing herself again in her own little chamber, and attentively listening for a passing step that she might desire the servant she had dismissed to be recalled; but all was profoundly still, and continued so; and at length she recollected herself, blushed for the weakness she had betrayed; and, recommending herself to the protection of heaven, retired to bed, where she soon forgot her cares and fears. She awoke in the morning with renovated spirits; and, impatient to gratify her curiosity by examining the contents of the chamber, instantly rose: the furniture was rich but old-fashioned; and as she looked over the great presses and curious inlaid cabinets, she thought indeed she must have not only a great fortune, but great vanity if she could ever fill them. Thus employed, she forgot the progress of time, till one of the Countess's women appeared to know if she was ready for breakfast, as her lady waited. She immediately descended to the parlour, where she was received with the utmost kindness.

Breakfast over, she wrote a long letter to her father, and was then amused by looking over the chateau. In the course of a week she received an answer from her father; and the pleasure he expressed at her situation, joined to the unremitting attentions of the Countess, entirely restored her spirits. Every day raised her benevolent friend still higher in her estimation, and love and esteem were soon united to gratitude and respect.

The Countess determined not to receive any visitors, nor if possible let her arrival at the chateau be known, till she had recovered from the fatigue occasioned by the dissipations of Paris. But the total retirement in which she at present lived, neither tired nor depressed Madeline; with the Countess, it was, indeed, impossible to experience any dullness; she had received and profited by all the advantages of a liberal education; and her almost constant intercourse with the great world, contributed, as well as her knowledge of books, to render her conversation entertaining and instructive. But not alone by her conversation did she try to enliven their solitude; she varied it by excursions about the domain and to the most romantic places in its neighbourhood.

She also diversified it, by seeing carried into execution a number of benevolent schemes for her poor tenants: she went amongst them herself to see if they had every thing requisite for comfort; and whether their children were taught to reverence the power that gave them being; she loved to watch their labours, and encourage industry by reward. Madeline, who always attended her in her rambles, beheld with the most exquisite delight the cheek of youth dimpling into smiles at her approach, and the eye of age glittering with tears; while she seemed to tread in air, and her cheek, warmed by the glow of benevolence, again displayed a colour that might have rivalled the brightest bloom of youth. Next to these, the most delightful of the hours passed by the Countess and Madeline, were those in which they rambled through the wild wood walks of the forest; at that time of day when all the

— —air is hush'd, save where the weak-ey'd bat,

With short shrill shrieks, flits by on leathern wing;

Or where the beetle winds

His small but sullen horn,

As oft' he rises 'mid the twilight path,

Against the pilgrim borne in heedless hum.

A month glided on in this manner, when the Countess, having recovered from her fatigue determined to emerge a little from her solitude on account of her young friend.

CHAP. VI.

The joys of meeting pay the pangs of absence.

The nearest neighbours the Countess had, were a Madame Chatteneuf and her daughter: they resided in a garrison town at the foot of the Alps, about three leagues from the chateau. They were people of fortune, amiable, elegant, and accomplished; and their house was the constant resort of all the gay and fashionable people in its vicinity. To them the Countess determined to introduce Madeline, not only as a means of improving, but preparing her for the yet more brilliant society of Paris.

She accordingly one morning set out with her for this purpose; and, during the ride, endeavoured to re-assure the timid Madeline, who wished, yet dreaded an introduction, lest she should not acquit herself properly: the lively conversation of her friend, and the novelty of every thing she saw, pretty well however dissipated her fears ere she reached the house; which stood at the farther end of the town, in a large court surrounded with rows of chestnut trees, and wearing an appearance of cheerfulness that justly indicated the temper of its owners. The Countess had the satisfaction of finding them at home, and was immediately ushered into a room, where they sat alone. They both flew to her with open arms; but when they heard how long she had been returned to the country, could not refrain reproaching her amidst their embraces for not letting them know of her arrival. She gave the real reason as an excuse for not doing so; and the first compliments being over, took the hand of Madeline, who, timidly standing behind, had not hitherto been noticed, and presented her to them. The reception she met with was truly flattering, and quite revived her spirits; for she was convinced that nothing satirical could lurk beneath the benevolent smile of Madame Chatteneuf, or the delightful vivacity of her daughter. The charms and simplicity of Madeline, exclusive of her being the avowed favourite of the Countess, immediately interested them in her favour; and they assured her with real sincerity, that they should be happy to cultivate her friendship.

"Though I am angry (said Madame Chatteneuf, addressing the Countess when they were seated), at your having so long concealed your return to the chateau; yet now I can scarcely wonder at it, as I am sure that Mam'selle Clermont rendered solitude so delightful, that in relinquishing it, you rather diminish than promote your own happiness; (the Countess smiled, and Madeline bowed), but now that we have discovered the treasure you possess, be assured, my good friend (continued she), we shall not suffer you to monopolize it entirely to yourself."

"Do not wrong me so much (said the Countess), as to suppose I ever harboured so selfish an idea; no, be assured I would not do society so much injustice."

"I am particularly pleased (said Madame Chatteneuf), that you have come to-day, as my daughter gives a little ball this evening, which, to her and her whole party, I am sure will be doubly agreeable from having your company and Mam'selle Clermont's."

"How unfortunate (exclaimed the Countess), that we had no presentiment of this, for then we should have put on all our airs and graces."

"Nature has already done that," replied Madame Chatteneuf.

"Well, but seriously (said the Countess), we shall not be able to appear in our morning dresses before company so brilliant as I know yours always to be."

"Every one (cried Madame Chatteneuf), will be dressed quite in a simple stile, I can assure you, for it is to be quite a rural affair; we are to dance in the garden, and have a collation in the banqueting-house; and should I now be deprived of the pleasure of your company and Mam'selle Clermont's, after the hope I entertained of enjoying it, I should derive little from the amusement."

"Enough (said the Countess), we will not mortify ourselves by refusing your invitation."

The conversation then turned on general subjects, and Madeline became if possible more pleased with her new friends. After dinner they proceeded to the garden which was large and beautiful: on a spacious and level green, at the remote end of it, surrounded with trees, stood the banqueting-house, a light and elegant structure, elevated on white marble steps, and encompassed by a balustrading of the same: it opened entirely in front in form of a pavilion, supported by fluted pillars, which were entwined with fragrant shrubs that, creeping over the roof, fell through its lattice-work and formed a canopy of "in-woven shade:" orchestres were erected in the most sequestered parts of the garden, and the walks were ornamented with arches and festoons of coloured lamps. Madeline was struck with admiration at all she saw; and her friends anticipated the yet greater pleasure and surprise she would experience when the company assembled and the garden was lighted: nor were they mistaken; she could then have almost fancied herself suddenly conveyed to the regions of fairy-land; the brilliancy of the lights, heightened by the darkness of the grove through which the walks they ornamented were cut;—the softness of the music that seemed to steal from the very bosom of retirement;—the elegance and animation of the company that were scattered about in groupes,—altogether formed such a scene as Madeline had never before seen, or even conceived; a scene, crowned by a prospect of the majestic Alps, whose awful cliffs appeared in many places to overhang the garden, and tinted as they were with the purple rays of evening, united richness and solemnity to gaiety and splendour. The ladies, engaged in receiving their guests, could no longer pay her particular attention; and the Countess, who had a numerous acquaintance, was drawn from her into a chatting party with some of her old friends, but not till she had seen her in a general manner introduced to the company, with, whom she then supposed she would intermix and amuse herself; but poor Madeline was too diffident to join any party unsolicited; and they were all too gay and thoughtless either to solicit her or deem it necessary to do so. Left to herself, she felt awkward at standing alone, and accordingly repaired to a bench placed round the trunk of an old tree near the spot destined for the dancers. Some ladies and gentlemen occupied the same seat, though at a little distance from her, and thus prevented any impropriety in her situation. Here she was sufficiently amused by attending to what was going forward; but when she saw the company preparing for the dance, an universal terror seized her least she should be asked to join them: fearful as she was that she should not be able to acquit herself like them from never having mixed in any but the simple dance of the peasant, she took care to place herself as much out of the way as possible: but while enjoying her obscurity, a party of officers suddenly emerged from a winding path near her seat, and in passing it, they could not avoid observing her; they stopped as if involuntarily, and their eyes were immediately fastened on her. Confused by their ardent gaze, she was bending hers to the ground, when a gentleman, who had hitherto stood rather behind them, suddenly starting forward, exclaimed,

"Good heaven! do my eyes really deceive me, or do I behold Mademoiselle Clermont?"

The heart of Madeline vibrated to his voice, and looking up, she beheld de Sevignie. The pleasure, the agitation of that moment cannot be expressed;—a pleasure, an agitation which, even in a greater degree he seemed to experience.

"For once (cried he, taking her hand and pressing it between his), for once has chance been my friend!—oh, how often have I wished for such a moment as this!—but hopelessly I wished—despairingly I sighed for it."

Madeline blushed and trembled; she was not more confused by his manner, than by the looks of the officers, whom she perceived smiling significantly at each other: her countenance betrayed her feelings, and made de Sevignie recollect himself; he resigned her hand, endeavoured to repress his agitation, and turning to his companions, asked them if they would join the dancers?

"That is to say (cried one of them with a significant glance) that you wish us to do so."

"Yes (replied de Sevignie, colouring, and half smiling as he interpreted the glance); and to follow your example, if Mademoiselle Clermont is inclined, and will honour me with her hand— — —"

Not more unwilling from diffidence, than unable from agitation, Madeline in a faint voice, said she could not dance, but begged she might not prevent him.

"A wish to promote my own felicity will prevent me (said he in a low voice); for oh, how much more delightfully will my minutes be spent if you permit me to devote them to you."

The officers now moved on; but their yet more expressive glances as they did so, so shocked Madeline, that, unable to bear the idea of being thought anxious for a tete-a-tete with de Sevignie, she rose abruptly and walked towards an avenue crowded with company; de Sevignie followed.—"Do you fly me then? (said he) after so long a separation, so unexpected a meeting, do you refuse me a few minutes conversation? ah, Madeline, you once permitted me to call myself your friend,—a permission which, I fear, you have now forgotten. You once promised to remember me;—a promise which, like too many in the world, was made I fear without thought, and forgotten without remorse!"

Those were reproaches poor Madeline did not merit; and the soft melancholy and confusion of her looks too plainly told him so; he caught her hand, and attempted to lead her back to the seat she had just quitted.

"I cannot go (said Madeline, struggling to disengage her hand); your companions will think it so strange if they see us there."

"They are too much engrossed by their amusement either to observe or think about us: and of this be assured (cried de Sevignie), you cannot be more tenacious about every thing which concerns your delicacy than I am, and ever shall be."

Madeline no longer opposed him; even if inclined to do so, her emotions were almost too violent to have permitted her; and he led her back to the bench, which they found deserted by the company they had left upon it. De Sevignie now enquired particularly for Clermont, for whom he expressed the warmest esteem and gratitude; and then to what fortunate circumstance he owed his present happiness.

Madeline briefly informed him a friend of her father's had taken her under her protection; and in turn enquired whether he resided at V– – –?

"No, (he replied), chance merely brought him to it, and hospitality and kindness detained him in it. By accident (said he), I got acquainted with the officers quartered here soon after my arrival, and they introduced me to the inhabitants, whose politeness and attention have from day to day induced me to put off my departure.—And for once (glancing at Madeline), I have reason to be happy at following the bent of inclination. Though I never dared to think (said he) of again intruding on the hospitality of Monsieur Clermont, yet a thousand times on the airy wings of fancy I have been transported to his cottage, to the side of his Madeline, listening in imagination to the soft pathos of that voice, which had power to thrill through every fibre of my heart; oh, happy and delightful days when I was not indebted to illusion for the sound! never has the remembrance of them been absent from my thoughts; compared to them, how insipid appear those I now pass. Tell me, (he continued, gazing on her with the most impassioned tenderness), did your father, or did you ever condescend to bestow one thought upon me after we parted?"

"Yes, sometimes (said Madeline hesitatingly and blushing), my father has talked of the unlucky accident you met with, and expressed his hopes of your having quite recovered it."

"A more unlucky accident indeed (said de Sevignie, laying his hand expressively upon his heart), than he was aware of."

"I am sorry for it," cried Madeline, who, though she understood his meaning, wished to appear ignorant of it.

"His simples, for once, were unsuccessful (resumed de Sevignie); yet, notwithstanding their failure, through his means only I could expect the wound completely cured."

Madeline could no longer disguise her confusion; and averting her eyes to avoid his, to her infinite surprise and embarrassment, beheld the Countess de Merville at a little distance attentively observing her: covered with blushes, she snatched away her hand from de Sevignie, and starting from her seat, hastened to the Countess.

"I have been seeking you every where, Madeline (said her friend in a grave accent), and was disappointed at not finding you amongst the dancers."

"I should be particularly honoured (exclaimed de Sevignie, who had followed Madeline, and conjectured this to be her protectress, bowing as he spoke), if Mademoiselle Clermont would permit me to lead her to them."

Madeline bowed, but refused; she thought to dance with him now would be to acknowledge a wish of receiving his attentions; and delicacy made her shrink from any conduct which could excite such an idea.

"We will go into a more frequented walk then," said the Countess.

There was something in her manner which made Madeline believe she was not quite pleased with her; and she bitterly regretted having staid with de Sevignie against her better judgment. He seemed in some degree to share her distress and confusion; and attempted not again to address the Countess, who had merely noticed him by a slight inclination of her head.

"I presume (cried she to Madeline, when they had got some yards from him), you are well acquainted with that young gentleman."

"Yes, madam," replied Madeline.

"And pray by what means?" asked her friend.

Madeline, as well as her confusion would permit, related the accident which had introduced him to the notice of her and her father.

"Is he agreeable?" enquired the Countess.

"Yes—very—that is, I mean rather so," answered Madeline, blushing, and bending her eyes to the ground.

They now reached a large party, amongst whom was Mademoiselle Chatteneuf. She rallied Madeline for having so long hidden herself;—"you certainly did so (said she), to tease and mortify those who wished to engage you to dance: were you not a total stranger, I should suspect that you and some sighing swain had been courting the rural shades together."

The Countess smiled significantly at Madeline, who, oppressed by consciousness, turned away her head.

Mademoiselle Chatteneuf now introduced a gentleman who wished to engage her for the ensuing dance. Madeline hesitated how to answer, not merely to avoid dancing, but on de Sevignie's account, to whom she considered herself engaged, though she feared saying so before the Countess. De Sevignie, however, had followed her; he therefore, on perceiving her situation, stepped forward, and asserted his prior right to her hand. "Is this the case, Mam'selle?" asked the other. She replied in the affirmative: and expressing his regret at his late application, he retired.

The dancing soon commenced again; and Madeline, notwithstanding her diffidence, had too much real taste not to acquit herself with elegance; the harmonious symmetry of her form, the charms of her face, heightened by the glow of modesty, and the grace and animation of every movement, excited universal admiration; and all who had not before seen, were anxious to learn who she was. When the cotillion was over, the Countess contrived to have her seated by herself, and thus precluded all further conversation of an interesting nature between her and de Sevignie: he still remained, however, near his lovely partner, and by his eyes expressed his feelings: but even the little pleasure derived from a restrained conversation, and those glances, he was soon deprived of; for as the Countess rose to repair to the banqueting-house, a party of her friends surrounded her and Madeline, and rendered all his efforts to rejoin the latter unsuccessful. The gentleman who had been prevented by him from dancing with Madeline, now led her in triumph to the supper-table, and seated her between the Countess and himself. Had the mind of Madeline been less occupied by its own immediate concerns than it now was, she would have been delighted with the scene exhibited to her view; the beautiful foliage that crept through the roof of the building was intermixed with lights which glittered like so many stars amongst it; and its drooping boughs were carelessly intermingled with festoons of coloured lamps that hung between the pillars, through which a grand perspective of illuminated arches were seen terminated in a dark grove, from whence the softest music stole, and seemed to keep time to the murmurs of a fountain which played directly before the banqueting-house.

Madeline perceived she was attentively watched by the Countess, and endeavoured to appear amused; but the scene had no charms for her. She could not prevent herself from stealing a glance at de Sevignie, who sat opposite to her; she caught his eyes at the moment, and hers were instantly withdrawn, yet not without observing a pensive expression in his face, which seemed to say his gaiety, like hers, was only assumed.

She felt pleased, as if about being relieved from a disagreeable restraint, when the company broke up; as she was quitting the banqueting-house with the Countess, de Sevignie contrived to approach and enquire, in a low voice, whether she returned to the chateau that night. She replied in the negative, having just been informed by the Countess it was her intention to continue in town till the next morning. He then begged to know whether she would permit him to wait upon her the ensuing day at Madame Chatteneuf's. The emotion those words gave Madeline, almost took from her the power of granting him the permission he requested. The moment he had obtained it, he bade her adieu.

The ladies were too much fatigued to continue long together after their return to the house. Madeline was delighted when she found herself alone; in the privacy of her chamber she could uninterrupted indulge the pleasing ideas which had taken possession of her mind; ideas which her second meeting with de

Sevignie had given rise to: never before had his language been so expressive of love, consequently her hopes relative to him had never before been so sanguine; every word, every look, now declared her ascendancy over him, and prospects of felicity opened to her view which she had scarcely ever before permitted her thoughts to dwell on;—prospects which, if realized, would elevate her to the summit of her wishes; and that they would, she now began not to doubt: the words, the looks of de Sevignie, above all the interview he had requested, flattered her hopes, and her expectations. "Ah, how little did I think (cried she), when I left the chateau of the happiness that awaited me! how little think that, ere my return to it, I might be— — —." She paused, she blushed,—yet felt that if indeed she was, ere her return to it, the affianced wife of de Sevignie, she would be one of the happiest of her sex.

CHAP. VII.

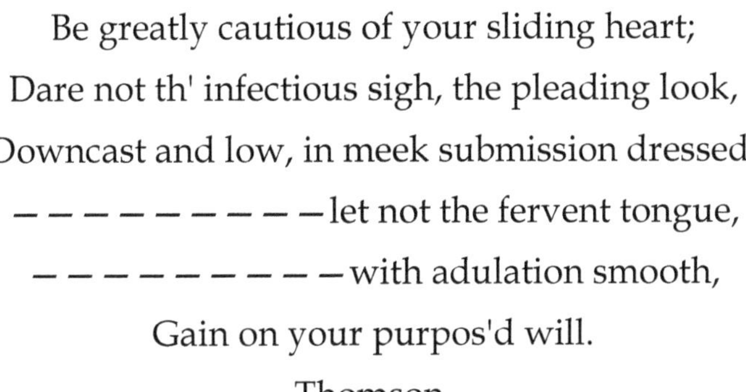

Ah, then
Be greatly cautious of your sliding heart;
Dare not th' infectious sigh, the pleading look,
Downcast and low, in meek submission dressed;
– – – – – – – – – – – let not the fervent tongue,
– – – – – – – – – – – with adulation smooth,
Gain on your purpos'd will.
Thomson.

The next morning at breakfast, Mademoiselle Chatteneuf rallied Madeline about the sudden conquest she had made of de Sevignie. Madeline said she had known him before; and then mentioned the accident which had introduced him to her acquaintance.

"Do you know where he lives in general?" asked Olivia.

"No (replied Madeline); I neither know his residence nor family."

"He has been here some weeks (resumed Olivia), and is universally noticed and liked, though no one (at least that I can learn) knows any thing of his connexions; there can be no doubt, from his manner and stile of living, that they are respectable."

The Countess saw that Madeline was confused, and changed the discourse. After conversing some time on various subjects, Olivia said they might expect an early visit that morning. "The officers are to give a concert and ball this evening, and I know some of them intend coming here to request the honour of your company, Madame (addressing the Countess), and Mademoiselle Clermont's."

"I hope they will not take that trouble (cried the Countess), for I could not accept their invitation."

"Not accept it!" repeated Mademoiselle Chatteneuf.

"No (replied the Countess); two nights of dissipation would be more than I could bear."

The sparkling eyes of Madeline, which had been turned towards her, were instantly bent to the ground; and the gloom of disappointment overspread her countenance.

"Suppose then, my good friend (said Madame Chatteneuf, who saw, by the looks of Madeline, the wishes of her heart, and knew her daughter would be mortified at losing her company), that you and I enjoy a tete-a-tete this evening, and entrust our girls to the care of some matron less soberly inclined than ourselves."

"I thank you for your obliging offer (replied the Countess); but I can neither let you relinquish an amusement you have sufficient health and spirits to enjoy, nor give up my determination of returning to the chateau this day: and I am too well convinced of Madeline's regard, to think she will feel any other regret in accompanying me, than that which proceeds from quitting you."

"Certainly, madam (said Madeline, recollecting herself at these words, and endeavouring to dissipate all appearance of chagrin), I should be ungrateful if I did."

"Do not suppose, my love (cried the Countess), from bringing you home to-day, that it is my intention to make you refuse every invitation which I do not choose to accept myself; no, such conduct would be unreasonable in the highest degree; on the contrary, I shall be happy sometimes to let you mix in the diversions of this town, with your amiable friends here, who have already requested to let you now and then pass a few days with them for that purpose."

Madeline bowed, and thanked her friends for their obliging wishes to promote her happiness.

It was now settled, that in three days Madame Chatteneuf and her daughter should call for Madeline. They had just arranged this matter, when a footman entered with a letter, which he presented to Madeline; saying, "Mam'selle, the Chevalier de Sevignie's servant waits for an answer."

Madeline started up in universal trepidation: she forgot, in the agitation of the moment, the inference that might be drawn from her manner: she forgot, in short, that there was any being to observe her. She believed that she held a letter containing a full explanation of de Sevignie's sentiments; and that belief drove every idea not connected with it from her mind. She turned to a window, and, eagerly breaking the seal, read as follows:—

"M. de Sevignie presents his most respectful compliments to Mademoiselle Clermont; he is extremely concerned he cannot have the honour of waiting on her this morning: but, though prevented by very particular business from making personal enquiries after her health, he still flatters himself he shall hear that she is well, and perfectly recovered from any fatigue that might have attended the amusements of last night."

Such a letter from de Sevignie, so cold, so formal, instead of the one she expected to receive from him, gave a shock to Madeline that almost annihilated every pleasing hope, every pleasing expectation. She sighed,—she leaned pensively against the window;—"I was mistaken then (said she to herself), in imagining de Sevignie had any thing important to say to me when he requested an interview; he only meant to have paid me what it seems is a customary compliment."

"The servant waits, my dear," said the Countess at length, rousing her from her reverie."

Madeline started, and felt ready to sink with confusion, as she thought, for the first time, of the remarks she had probably excited.

"If that letter requires an answer (cried the Countess), you had better give one directly."

Madeline again glanced at it; she thought, or rather wished to think, that the last lines expressed something like anxiety about her; and, judging of de Sevignie by herself, supposing, like her, he would be delighted to receive even a line from a beloved hand, she determined to answer the letter, and went to a table, on which was an open writing desk, for that purpose.

"What are you going to do, Madeline?" asked the Countess.

"I am going to write, madam," answered Madeline.

"Does your letter require a written answer? (again asked the Countess, in an accent of surprise) young ladies should be very careful how they write to gentlemen."

Madeline dropped the pen she had taken up. She began to think that to write to de Sevignie, without consulting the Countess, or showing her his letter, was not only a breach of respect to her, but of duty to her father, who had put her under the care of his friend, with a firm conviction, that she would never follow her own judgment without having it first sanctioned by hers. She took up the letter, and, going to the Countess, put it into her hand. "Will you have the goodness, Madame (said she) to tell me what answer I shall send?"

"It does not require a moment's consideration to determine that (cried the Countess); bless me, child, could you ever imagine this letter required more than a verbal answer? tell Monsieur de Sevignie's man (continued she turning to the servant), that Mam'selle Clermont is well, and thanks his master for his polite enquiries after her health."

Madeline sat down in a state of the most painful confusion, from which she was soon, in some degree, relieved by the entrance of the officers: they were immediately introduced to her and the Countess; and then requested the honour of their company for the evening. The Countess politely thanked them for their attention, but declined their invitation; and their mortification at her doing so, was evident. The conversation, however, soon grew lively, and was supported by all but Madeline with the utmost spirit.

"Pray (asked Mademoiselle Chatteneuf, during the pause of a minute, addressing one of the officers), what is become of de Sevignie to-day? I think he is generally your companion in your morning visits and rambles."

"I met him (replied the officer), not many minutes ago, and told him where I was coming; but I could not prevail on him to give up a solitary walk he was going to take to the mountains."

"Oh, shocking! (cried Olivia) to prefer solitude to our society; I really shall not readily forgive his want of gallantry."

A pang of wounded pride and mortified tenderness now touched the heart of Madeline. She felt equally surprised and hurt to hear, that he had in reality no business to prevent his coming to see her; and that he had even refused an invitation to do so.—How ill did such conduct agree with the delight he had evinced the preceding evening at their unexpected meeting, with the anxiety he had expressed to see her again. The hopes, the expectations which that delight, that anxiety, had given rise to, and which his letter had damped, not suppressed, now entirely vanished like the fleeting pleasures of a dream; and she began to fear he had either feigned or forgotten the sentiments he expressed for her.

She saw she was observed by the Countess and Olivia with an earnestness that seemed to say they wished to develop her feelings; and she immediately forced herself into conversation; but never before was one so painful to her; her thoughts were perpetually wandering from the subject; and she rejoiced when the officers rose to depart.

The Countess then ordered her coach; and she and Madeline were just going to it, when M. Chalons (the gentleman who had wished to dance with Madeline the preceding evening) appeared: finding the ladies on the point of departing, he regretted the lateness of his visit, and paid his compliments in a manner so pleasing to the Countess, that she invited him to accompany her friends whenever they paid their promised visit at the chateau; an invitation which he accepted with rapture, and a glance to Madeline, as if he wished her to think the exquisite pleasure he derived from it, was owing to the idea of seeing her again.

His glance, however, was lost upon Madeline, so much was her mind engrossed by its own concerns; and the moment the carriage drove off, she forgot such a being existed.

The Countess's motives for hurrying Madeline back to the chateau, is perhaps already understood. She thought, indeed, she should ill fulfill the sacred trust reposed in her by Clermont, if she did not particularly enquire about the commencement, and try to discover the strength of the attachment it was so obvious his daughter entertained for de Sevignie, that she might be timely guarded against indulging it, till assured (if that was not already the case) that she never would have reason to repent it: and as she could not (at least without interruption) make those enquiries, or give those cautions she wished at Madame Chatteneuf's, she brought her away for the purpose of doing so.

"Well, Madeline (said the Countess, first breaking silence after they had proceeded a few yards), you were agreeably amused last night."

"Yes, madam," replied Madeline.

"And agreeably surprised," cried the Countess.

Madeline blushed, faltered, and at length answered in the affirmative.

"Will you oblige me (said the Countess), by giving me now a more particular account of your first acquaintance with Monsieur de Sevignie than you did this morning?"

Madeline wished to gratify her friend; and she thought she could do so without betraying the feelings of her heart; but this was a mistaken idea. As she described her first introduction to de Sevignie, and the scenes she had passed with him, she involuntarily revealed her sentiments: but while she discovered the tenderness of her heart, she so fully proved its simplicity and integrity, that she was rather raised than lessened in the esteem of the Countess.

When she had concluded,—"Your narrative, my dear (said her friend), convinces me more than ever of the innocence and sensibility of your disposition; and woe be to the man who should ever seek to beguile one, or pain the other!—That a being exists who could be capable of hurting either, perhaps you doubt; but, alas, I am sorry to say, too many are to be found who would little scruple doing so! 'Tis unpleasant to hold up objects of a disagreeable nature to the view of youth; yet 'tis necessary to do so, in order to instruct it whom to shun. They who have made a perilous voyage, would be inexcusable if they did not caution those they saw about undertaking the same, of the dangers which lay in their way, that, by being timely apprised, they might endeavour to shun or at least acquire skill to overcome them.

"I, my dear Madeline, have made this perilous voyage, and against its dangers I wish to warn you: to none is the young, the lovely, the inexperienced female so particularly exposed as to those which proceed from a sex, ordained by heaven for her protectors, but of whom too many seem to forget, or rather disregard their original destination. Yes, my love, there are beings who make it their study, sometimes their boast, to ensnare the unsuspicious, and entail shame and sorrow upon her who would never perhaps have known either, but for a too fatal confidence in their honour. Others there are of a nature scarcely less hateful to virtue or injurious to society, who from a mere impulse of vanity, seek to gain the affections, which are no sooner won than disregarded; while they triumph aloud over the credulity and weakness that afforded them such a conquest.

"That you have never met, never may meet, with such characters I believe and trust: but liable as we all are to be mistaken, too much caution cannot be observed in receiving attentions which have a chance of touching the heart. In short, my discourse has only been (as I make no doubt you already guess) to lead to the subject of the Chevalier de Sevignie; his eyes declare love and admiration, and his language I dare say accords with their glances: but oh, my dear Madeline, fortify yourself against such seductive eloquence, except convinced his intentions are serious; if they are, believe me they will be speedily divulged; if not, if his situation prevents their being so, he will quickly cease to be particular, except destitute of honour and sensibility; for the man who possesses these, though he may, from the impetuosity of passion, be unhappily led into expressions of admiration, will never persevere in a line of conduct that may inspire tenderness which cannot properly be returned."

"Your precepts, your advice, my dear madam (said Madeline), I will treasure up as I would the means of felicity: oh, how gratefully do I feel your kind solicitude about me."

By this time they had reached the chateau, and its gloom and stillness formed a melancholy contrast to the gaiety and splendour of the preceding evening, and increased the dejection of Madeline's spirits; a dejection partly owing to her conversation with the Countess. She was shocked to hear of the depravity of mankind; and shuddered least she should find de Sevignie one of the worthless characters the Countess had described to her. "Yet, no (she cried to herself, trying to dispel the horror such an idea gave rise to), 'tis impossible; vice could never lurk beneath an appearance of such integrity and candour."

She was unable to converse as usual with the Countess; and her friend was too delicate to notice her dejection, any otherwise than by an increased attention; an attention which at last had the desired effect. Madeline no sooner perceived the efforts made to amuse her, than she felt ashamed of the weakness which had rendered such efforts necessary, and rallied her spirits; she tried to cheer, to tranquillize them, by reflecting that, in a few days, in all probability she would again behold de Sevignie; and that, as she had been taught a criterion whereby to judge of him, her suspense relative to him must soon be terminated. So soothing was this idea, that almost as soon as conceived, it dissipated her melancholy; and she was again able to converse and enjoy the conversation of the Countess. She wrote to her father an account of her meeting with de Sevignie;

but she could not bring herself to tell him the agitation that meeting occasioned. The Countess also informed him of it, and the observations she had made; but charged him not to give way to uneasy sensations in consequence of them; assuring him that she would watch over Madeline as she would have done over her own daughter if she had been in a similar situation: and also that, from Madeline's disposition, she was convinced she could easily be made to give up the object of her affections, if once assured by prudence and experience greater than her own (because more tried), that he was unworthy of them.

CHAP. VIII.

His cheeks, where love with beauty glow'd,
A deadly pale o'ercast;
So fades the fresh rose in its prime
Before the northern blast.
Mallet

At the appointed time, Madame Chatteneuf and her daughter came to the chateau; nor did M. Chalons forget his invitation; but he was a much more welcome visitant to the Countess than to Madeline, as his presence restrained her conversation with Olivia, from whom she imagined, if he was not by, she should hear something of de Sevignie. They walked about the lawn before dinner; and while he stopped to make some observations on a distant prospect of the Alps to the elder ladies, she and Olivia rambled on.

"Well, my dear (said the latter when they had got a sufficient distance not to be overheard), our ball the other evening was delightful; there was only one person that appeared dejected at it; and who that person was, and why dejected, I dare say you can guess."

"Impossible," (said Madeline, while a rosy blush at the same moment declared her consciousness of the object.)

"Poor de Sevignie (resumed Olivia), expected to have met you; and, in consequence of his disappointment, neither danced, talked, or did any thing like himself the whole evening."

It was this expectation then perhaps, thought Madeline, which prevented his coming the other morning. The idea was too pleasing to be rejected; and every shadow of uneasiness vanished from her mind. Dinner was served at an earlier hour than usual; and soon after they had taken coffee, the Countess bade them adieu, the road between the town and the chateau being extremely lonesome.

She tenderly embraced Madeline at parting; and said, as she gave up one of her highest sources of pleasure in resigning her company, she could not wonder if she soon recalled her.

"Remember (cried Madame Chatteneuf), whenever you desire her return, you must come for her yourself; for, of our own accord, we cannot relinquish her society."

Pleased with the idea of soon beholding de Sevignie, and still more pleased at being able to account in any kind of satisfactory manner for his conduct, Madeline was unusually animated, and chatted with almost as much vivacity as the little voluble Olivia, who, on reaching home, proposed a walk upon the ramparts of the town, the fashionable promenade of the place. Thither they all accordingly repaired, except Madame Chatteneuf, who felt somewhat fatigued. The sun was already set, and all was soft, serene and lovely: beneath the ramparts lay a delicious plain, scattered over with clumps of thick and spreading trees, a few neat cottages, and groups of cattle now reposing in sweet tranquillity. The river, that flowed in beautiful meanders through the plain, had already assumed the sable hue of evening, and thus heightened the brilliancy of the stars it reflected. The majestic Alps bounded the prospect, their feet hid in gloomy shadows, and their summits just beginning to be touched by the beams of a rising moon, which, as it ascended higher in the horizon, partly dissipated those shadows, and revealed in some degree, the romantic recesses they had concealed.

The company were just beginning to leave the ramparts; but the fineness of the night prevented Olivia and her companions from following their example, and they were soon the only party on them. As they proceeded, admiring the sublime and beautiful prospect they beheld, which touched their hearts with a kind of pensive pleasure, they nearly overtook a gentleman who walked before them, with downcast looks and folded arms, as if in deep and melancholy meditation: his air, his figure, had a strong resemblance to de Sevignie's; and Madeline was almost convinced it was him; but she feared saying so, lest she should betray the agitation the idea had excited. Olivia, however, free from all such emotion, instantly declared it was him; and, quickening her pace, found she was not mistaken. He started at the sound of her voice, and betrayed the greatest confusion while attempting, vainly attempting, to return her raillery: he caught a glimpse of Madeline, who had hitherto stood rather behind her friend: again he started; and, leaving unfinished what he was saying to Olivia, he took the trembling hand of Madeline with one equally tremulous, exclaiming, "This is indeed an unexpected pleasure." The soft beam which stole from her eye at that moment, convinced M. Chalons, who watched her with the most critical attention, that the fate of her heart was already decided; and he rejoiced at having made the discovery ere his own affections were more entangled, resolving from that period to pay her no other attentions than what common politeness demanded, that the world might have no reason to rank him in the list of unfortunate lovers.

De Sevignie appeared no longer dejected; his eyes sparkled with their wonted fire; and he was able to answer the raillery of Mademoiselle Chatteneuf with his accustomed spirit. He accepted her invitation to supper; and never had minutes been so delightful to Madeline as those she passed at it. In his looks, as well as words, there was a tenderness, whenever he addressed her, which convinced her of his sincerity. "The tongue (said she to herself), might be taught the language of deceit, but the eyes could never be instructed in it; they have ever been famed for telling truth."

The next morning after breakfast, she and Olivia walked out for the purpose of seeing some of the town, and purchasing some things which she wanted to wear at a large party to which she was to be taken in the evening, and which the Countess had amply given her the means of procuring. They had not proceeded far ere they met de Sevignie.

"Well you are a good creature (said Olivia), for I presume you are coming to pay your devoirs at our house, as I meet you in the high road to it." He made no reply; and she continued, "you shall not however be disappointed of the pleasure of our company; we are going to take a ramble, and will permit you to be our escort."

"Your permission honours me (said he); but I am unfortunately prevented by very particular business from availing myself of it."

"Go, go; you are a shocking creature I declare (cried Olivia); this business is the same with that which prevented your waiting on Mademoiselle Clermont the other morning according to your promise." His letter had been shown, and the reason of it explained to Olivia and her mother.

De Sevignie coloured highly, and looked confused. "You speak sometimes from supposition I fancy," said he to Olivia.

"Not now I can assure (replied she); I know very well that what you have just said to me, is a mere pretext as well as what you wrote to Mam'selle Clermont the other morning."

"Well, allowing that you are right (cried he), what can you infer from my trying to avoid her company and yours? but that I am sensible of the danger I run in being with either; and that, unlike your military heroes, I rather fly from it than brave it."

"You should always have that apprehension of danger about you then (said Olivia), and not ask a lady's permission to wait upon her, and then send a frivolous excuse."

"We are not always collected (cried he), and the reflection of the morning often destroys the resolution of the night." He then bowed and walked away.

The solemn accent in which he had delivered the last words shocked Madeline as much as the alteration in his looks and manner had already done; he was pale and languid; and his eyes, instead of anxiously seeking, assiduously avoided her; while a cool salutation was the only notice he took of her.

"De Sevignie is really one of the most altered beings within those few days I ever knew (said Olivia, as they pursued their way); his conduct is really quite incomprehensible: was he an unfortunate lover, one might be able to account for it; but of that (continued she, looking archly at Madeline), there is little danger."

The pale cheeks of Madeline were instantly crimsoned over; and the distress and confusion she betrayed, precluded all farther raillery from Olivia.

In pity to her companion, who she saw scarcely able to stand, she hastened their return home; and, hoping solitude would enable her to recruit her spirits, under the pretext of dressing, proposed retiring to their respective chambers; a proposal which, as she imagined, was eagerly embraced.

The moment Madeline was alone, the tears, which pride had suppressed in the presence of Olivia, burst forth: but while she wept the alteration in the conduct of de Sevignie, her heart secretly applauded it as a convincing proof of his honour and sensibility. "Either his reason or his situation does not sanction his attachment to me (said she), and he thus delicately, thus feelingly tries to suppress mine by remitting his attentions.

"Never does he now address me with tenderness, but when we accidentally meet, as if thrown off his guard at those moments by surprise: for whenever a meeting might be expected, he shuns it with anxiety; and if it does take place, treats me with the coldest indifference. Oh, let me (she continued), aid his efforts; let me endeavour to expel from my heart an attachment which, it is evident, can only end in unhappiness. Nor is it my own peace alone I shall consider by doing so; no, the peace of my father, dearer to me than life, is also concerned. I promised to my benevolent friend to resist the indulgence of feelings which had a tendency to embitter my tranquillity, and I will not wilfully violate that promise;—no, ye dear and revered preceptors of my youth! ye who, like benignant spirits, have watched over your Madeline, she will not make so ill a return to your care as to yield herself unresistingly a victim to sorrow—if she cannot attain, she will at least try to be deserving of the felicity you wish her!" She sighed heavily as she spoke; certain that that felicity never now could be hers; and that her efforts to conquer her attachment would be vain; when, at the very moment she wished to make them, the object of it was raised higher than ever in her estimation.

She thought not of dressing till Mademoiselle Chatteneuf tapped at her door to know if she was ready: she opened it with much confusion; and, apologizing for her tardiness, hurried on her clothes, and was soon able to attend her to dinner.

The entertainment to which they went in the evening, was pretty much in the stile of that given by Madame Chatteneuf: all the officers and most of the fashionable people in town were assembled; but de Sevignie was not to be seen; his absence did not surprise, but it pained Madeline; she was sure ere she went, that he would not be present, from a fear of meeting her; and she sighed to think a sad necessity existed for his wishing to avoid her. She would not have danced, but from a fear of appearing particular if she refused. Her partner was a stranger; for though M. Chalons was present, he did not, in conformity to his resolution, attempt to engage her; he sought, indeed, to avoid as much as possible the fascination of her looks, which had already made too deep, and, he feared, too lasting an impression on his heart.

The next morning she went with her friends in their coach to pay visits, and take a survey of the town; and the charms of their conversation, joined to the novelty of every thing she saw, insensibly beguiled her sadness. A select party assembled at dinner; de Sevignie was invited, but sent an excuse; the first, Olivia said, they had ever received from him, though they had frequently asked him, as he was not only a favourite of hers, but of her mother.

CHAP. IX.

The sprightly vigour of my youth is fled;
Lonely and sick, on death is all my thought;
Oh! spare, Persephone, this guiltless head;
Love, too much love, is all thy suppliant's fault!

The sadness which marked the brow of Madeline could not escape the notice of Madame Chatteneuf and her daughter; but they were both too delicate to mention it, yet left no effort untried to dissipate it. She had expressed a wish of visiting the Alps: and, in hopes of amusing her, Madame Chatteneuf made her and her daughter take an excursion thither the evening following the day which has already been described, to the cottage of Olivia's nurse.

They set out in a chaise drawn by mules, leaving Madame Chatteneuf engaged at cards with a select party in the banqueting house; and, after travelling about a league, reached the cottage: its situation was romantically beautiful; it stood a little above the foot of a lofty mountain, which was surmounted by others equally tremendous, and overlooked a deep hollow, scattered over with a profusion of wild flowers, darkened by majestic pines, and washed by a clear rivulet, which proceeded from a mountain torrent at some distance: on a little grassy seat before the cottage, the nurse sat working, one of her daughters was milking the goats that browsed around it, and another was seen rambling about the neighbouring heights, gathering the herbs which grew upon them.

The romantic situation of the cottage, the simple appearance of its inhabitants, and their yet more simple occupations, altogether formed a pastoral scene inexpressibly pleasing to Madeline; to whose mind it recalled the scenes she had been so long accustomed to; and she gazed on it with emotions of tenderness, such as she might have felt on seeing features in a stranger which, by some striking resemblance, suddenly brought to view those of a beloved friend.

The nurse threw aside her work, and her daughters forsook their employments, the moment Olivia descended from the chaise, round whom they gathered with the most rapturous delight. She returned their caresses with affection: and enquired most kindly after the nurse's husband and son.

"A few days ago (replied the good woman), they went higher up the Alps, as usual, to keep flocks for the rich herdsmen during the summer months. Winter (she continued), winter, my dear young lady, is my season of happiness, for then I have all my family assembled about me, and we enjoy together the earnings of industry."

Olivia now led Madeline into the house, the interior neatness of which perfectly corresponded with that of its exterior; and from thence into the garden, a wild and romantic spot, which, with a small vineyard, stretched midway up a steep ascent, broken into a variety of grotesque hollows.

– – – – – – – – – – – Moss-lin'd, and over head,

By flowering umbrage shaded, where the bee

Stray'd diligent, and with th' extracted balm

Of fragrant woodbine fill'd his little thigh.

Oh how noble, how sublime did the prospect appear which Madeline now viewed! she felt struck with astonishment and veneration as she cast her eyes towards the summits of the congregated mountains piled before her; and her heart was more exalted than ever towards the author of such glorious, such stupendous works,

– – – The Parent of Good, Almighty – – –

Her fancy pictured the exquisite pleasure which would be derived from exploring their sequestered solitudes; or, on the wings of the morning, penetrating to their innermost recesses. With mingled curiosity and enthusiasm, her mind soothed and delighted, she wandered about, till followed by the nurse, entreating her to sit down and partake with Mam'selle Olivia of the fruit and cream she had brought out for them.

She complied with the entreaties of the good woman, and seated herself by her friend in one of the little hollows already mentioned, which was impregnated with the most delicious fragrance from the herbs that grew about it.

The dun shades of twilight were now beginning to steal o'er the prospect, and touched it with a sombre colouring, which rendered its beauty more interesting, and its solemnity more awful; the gloom, however, was still a little cheered by a yellow track of radiance which the sun, as it revealed its sinking orb between two parted cliffs above, cast along the projection of the hills; but by degrees this radiance faded away, and then the damp and dreary shadows, that had been gathering below, began to ascend; and, as if warned of their approach, the distant tinkling of sheep bells was immediately heard from the heights, intermingled with the rustic melody of shepherds' pipes. Delighted with those pastoral sounds, the enthusiasm of Madeline's soul revived; and with the eye of fancy she beheld the grand, the wonderful, the luxuriant spots from whence they descended. She saw the simple herdsman penning his flock for the night; while his dog, the faithful partner of his toil, as if endued with more than common instinct, watched beside, that none should straggle from the fold. She heard with the ear of fancy the neighbouring shepherds enquiring how each had fared throughout the day; and beheld some hastening to their romantically situated cottages; while others laid them down beneath the shelter of embowering pines; the last beams of the sun glimmering o'er all, as if loath to quit such scenes of innocence and beauty. It was now indeed a time particularly adapted for such fancies as she indulged; a time when all

The fragrant hours, and Elves

Who slept in flowers the day,

And many a nymph who wreaths her brows with sedge,

And sheds the fresh'ning dew; and lovelier still,

The pensive pleasures sweet,

Prepare the shadowy car of eve.

A tender melancholy began to steal over the mind of Madeline; nor was Olivia's entirely free from it: 'twas a melancholy in union with the scene, and which taste and sensibility are so apt to feel and to indulge; as the landscape, that charmed by day, gradually fades upon the sight, and, to the moralizing mind, presents an emblem of the transitory pleasures of life. Silence had returned many minutes ere Olivia or Madeline thought of stirring; they were at length rising for the purpose of departing, when they were again riveted to their seat by the soft breathings of an oboe, which seemed to come from some cliff above them at no great distance. The air was simple, tender, and pathetic; and played in a stile which evinced exquisite taste and feeling in the performer.

"How soft, how sweet, how melodious (cried Mademoiselle Chatteneuf, during the pause of a minute, for till then she and Madeline had been wrapped in attention too profound to permit them either to speak or move), what pathos, what masterly execution: but hark! the echoes revive the strains which we imagined had utterly died away; they seem celestial strains, and almost tempt one to believe the tales of the poets, and ascribe them to the genii of these mountains."

"Lord a mercy, my dear young lady (said the nurse, who only caught the last sentence), what a conceit! from a genius indeed; no, they come from a poor young gentleman, who frequently rambles about the heights, playing such mournful ditties as often and often makes me and my girls weep; and we think, to be sure, he has been crossed in love, and that nothing else could make him so melancholy, and so fond of being alone, and sitting for hours together in the deepest solitude by himself; and a pity it is he should have met with any thing to trouble him, he is so gentle and so handsome, and looks so good."

"Do you know his name?" asked Olivia, whose curiosity was strongly excited.

"No, Mam'selle; but I know he comes from V— — —, for I asked him one day if he did not, and he said yes."

"And pray how came you to have any conversation with him?" enquired Olivia.

"Why one day, Mam'selle, about a fortnight after I had first noticed him, as he was passing the cottage, he appeared very much fatigued; so I asked him, for I was sitting before the door at work, if he would be pleased to walk in and take some whey; he thanked me courteously, and accepted my invitation, and sat a good bit with me chatting, for all the world with as much affability as if he did not think himself a bit better than me; so, from that time, he seldom comes this way without giving me a call, and frequently takes whey and fruit in the cottage; for which, indeed, in spite of all I can say, he will always pay more than they are worth."

"Is it possible to get a glimpse of him?" asked Olivia.

"Dear heart yes, if you stay a little longer; this is about the time he generally returns to town, and he almost always descends by the path near this recess."

"I will stay a few minutes longer to try if I can see him," said Olivia.

"Pray do not (exclaimed Madeline, laying her hand, which trembled violently, upon Olivia's arm); the darkness increases fast, and if we stay much longer, we shall be quite benighted."

"No, no, there's no danger of that (replied Olivia); but if you wish it I will return immediately: dismiss however, I beseech you, the terrors you have conjured up to alarm you; for if you tremble in this manner, you will scarcely be able to reach the chaise."

It was not any apprehension of danger however which agitated the soul of Madeline, it was the agony of thinking that de Sevignie was the sad and solitary mourner to whose sweet and melancholy strains she had been listening; for in the air she heard she perfectly recollected one she had taught him during his visit at her father's house; and she wished to avoid his presence, least she should betray the emotions a knowledge of his dejection had inspired. Again she pressed Olivia to depart; who, in compliance with her wishes, was moving from the spot, when the nurse hastily exclaimed, "Stop, Mam'selle, stop, he's coming now, for there's his dog. Ah, 'tis a good-natured soul (cried she, patting the head of a large spaniel which suddenly sprung into the garden, and fawned about her); he is a faithful companion to his poor master, and attends him in all his rambles: there he sits for hours at a time, upon a point of rock beside him, looking up in his face while he plays upon the oboe, like any christian, as if he knew his sorrows, and pitied them."

"I think I know that dog," said Olivia.

"Aye, like enough (cried the nurse); and see there comes his master."

Olivia raised her eyes; but the light was too imperfect to let her discern the features of the person descending: but in a few minutes, as he drew nearer, she started, and exclaimed—"Gracious heaven, de Sevignie!" Madeline withdrew her hand involuntarily from Olivia, and reseated herself.

"I thought, indeed (said Olivia), it could be no other than de Sevignie, when I heard of an eccentric being always wandering about those solitudes. Pray (continued she, while overpowered by confusion and surprise, he stood transfixed to the spot where he had first beheld her), have you yet chosen a cell for your retirement? for I suppose you will soon renounce the world and its vanities for ever. But seriously, de Sevignie, 'tis rather unfortunate that you and I should lately have only met at periods when (at least) one of us wished to avoid the other."

His confusion, if possible increased; he knew she alluded to his conduct the last time they had met. "If I ever harboured such a wish (said he), it was because, as I have already told you, I apprehended danger in your company."

As he spoke, his eyes glanced round as if in search of another object, and at last rested on the recess where Madeline sat, whose white robe rendered her conspicuous.

"Mam'selle Clermont (said he) is it not— —" advancing to her. She rose at his approach; and, withholding the hand he attempted to take, passed him to Olivia, and again entreated her to return home.

Her curiosity gratified, Olivia no longer hesitated to comply with this entreaty; and they directly left the garden, without taking any farther notice of de Sevignie. Olivia was too much offended, and Madeline too fearful of betraying her feelings, to bid him farewell. That fear, however, was soon lost in the superior one she felt at the idea of his going the solitary road that lay between the cottage and the town by himself; and she stood hesitatingly at the door of the chaise; wishing to declare her apprehensions, yet dreading to do so, least she should betray her feelings.

De Sevignie, in the mean time, heart-struck by the manner in which she had declined his notice, remained some minutes fixed on the spot where she had left him. "Oh, Madeline! (he sighed), is it thus you heighten the pangs, the anguish you have caused me. Yet, alas (he continued), why do I accuse her? unwillingly she caused that anguish; and how, without knowing, can she pity it: but am I assured her pity would follow that knowledge?—no; her averted looks give me no reason to suppose it would." Slowly he quitted the garden, and, passing through the cottage, to his infinite surprise, found she was not yet departed. Hurt, however, by her coldness, he merely bowed to her and Olivia; and was hastening away, when the latter, who saw through the motives of Madeline's delay, and determined to gratify her, though somewhat offended with de Sevignie, exclaimed, "so you are decamping, without having the gallantry to offer your protection."

"The assurance, you should say (cried de Sevignie, returning), conscious as I am that I have (though heaven knows how unintentionally), offended you."

"Well, I'll forgive you this once; so you may hand us into the chaise, and take a seat yourself."

"But will your friend, Mam'selle Clermont, be equally generous," asked he.

"Oh, I dare say she will follow a good example; what say you, my dear?" cried Olivia, turning to her.

"I cannot pardon, because I have not been offended," said Madeline in much confusion, too clearly perceiving that Olivia suspected the state of her heart.

"Nor never may you be by me (cried de Sevignie, with fervour, and taking her hand), for then I should be wretched indeed. Oh, Madeline! (he continued in a low voice though I dread your smiles, I could not bear your frowns."

He handed Olivia first into the chaise; and thus contrived to have Madeline next to himself; something he would have said to her after they were seated in a low voice; but she turned her head from him, and entered into conversation with Olivia. Her hand he took however in spite of her efforts to withstand it; nor resigned it till they stopped at Madame Chatteneuf's. After handing them into the house, he bade them adieu; but it was a most unwilling adieu; for he hesitated as he spoke, and lingered on the threshold instead of departing. He was at length turning from it, when Olivia suddenly invited him to supper; and it struck Madeline that she had only delayed doing so for the purpose of teasing him. He accepted the invitation; and they all repaired to the banqueting-house, where Madame Chatteneuf and her friends were still engaged at cards, and enjoying the fragrance and refreshing coolness of the evening air.

Olivia gave an account of their excursion; and made de Sevignie colour highly by hinting at the manner in which they had met him, and at what she had heard from the nurse concerning him.

The light gave Madeline an opportunity of observing the strong expression of grief his countenance betrayed: he seemed even more altered than when she had before seen him. Pale and languid, the fire of his eyes was fled, and the discomposure of his hair, which the mountain breeze had blown carelessly about his face, heightened its sad expression. He appeared no longer desirous to shun her; on the contrary, he betrayed the strongest anxiety to be near her: but, notwithstanding her pity, her affection for him, pride determined her to avoid attentions which she imputed to the mere impulse of unguarded tenderness: for she could not bear to be one day the object of his particular notice, and the next of his pointed neglect. She accordingly placed herself at the card-table, in such a manner as to prevent his sitting by her; and, with a look of unutterable disappointment, he turned away, and entered into conversation with Olivia, if that could be called conversation, which consisted, on one side, of laconic answers, and, on the other, of questions relative to the motives which made him so fond of solitary rambles.

Unable to bear the dejection of his looks, Madeline fixed her eyes upon the card-table, as if intently watching the game, though in reality she knew not what was played. But she could not, by this measure, save her heart from one pang; for, though her eye was averted from the melancholy of his countenance, her ear was still open to the soft melancholy of his voice; and scarcely could she conceal the emotions it gave her. The entrance of a servant with a letter to her, that instant come from the Countess de Merville, somewhat relieved her from this painful situation. She started up; and, retiring to a little distance from the table, read as follows:—

To mademoiselle Clermont.

"Will my dear Madeline return to-morrow to solitude and her friend. She may accuse me of selfishness for so soon recalling her; and perhaps with justice, considering the pleasure and benefit attending her return will be so materially on my side: but, as it is a failing so prevalent among mankind, I trust, from its being so general, it may be excused. I cannot, as I intended, call for her; but shall hope and expect to receive from the hands of Madame Chatteneuf, and her amiable daughter, the precious charge I entrusted to her care. The natural eloquence of my Madeline will, I trust, prevent any disappointment; who, in believing me her sincere friend, will only do justice to

Elvira de Merville."

Madeline guessed the purpose of this letter ere she opened it, consequently it gave her no surprise. She placed her friend's anxiety for her return to the account of de Sevignie, whom she knew she wished her to avoid; a wish she felt it necessary to comply with, if she desired the return of tranquillity.

She handed the letter to Madame Chatteneuf; who, fearful it contained some unpleasant tidings, had laid aside her cards the moment it was brought in. Her regret and Olivia's at losing her so soon, was expressed in the most flattering terms; and they promised to attend her to the chateau the next morning. A heavy sigh from de Sevignie at this moment reached her ear. She involuntarily raised her eyes, but again bent them to the ground, on perceiving his fastened on her with the most melancholy earnestness.

The Countess's servant she was told waited for an answer; and she now hastened to the house to give one. In the hall she met him, and had the satisfaction of hearing that his lady was well. Her answer finished, she would have preferred retiring to her chamber to returning to the company, so oppressed was her heart, but that she knew her doing so would excite enquiries, and perhaps unpleasant remarks.

Slowly she pursued her way back to the banqueting house, and had reached the centre of the long and darkly shaded walk which led to it; when a sudden rustling among the trees on one side, made her pause, from a sensation of fear, and an uncertainty whether by advancing or retreating she should put herself more in the way of danger, if indeed, any threatened her; the pain of suspense was however terminated in a minute by the appearance of de Sevignie. She started; and his thus seeming to watch for her, gave her emotions which agitated her whole frame; she tried however to check them, and was again proceeding when he stopped her—

"Will you not bid me farewell then (said he in a reproachful voice), ere we part?"

"Part! (repeated Madeline) don't you sup with Madame Chatteneuf?"

"No; I feel myself extremely ill, and have just apologised to her. You return then to-morrow (he continued), to the chateau; and you know not perhaps when you may revisit this town?"

"No (said Madeline), I do not."

"To me indeed, it is of little consequence to know (cried he), for I propose to leave it soon myself; would to heaven I had done so some days ago. Yet how can I tear myself from a place where I know there is a chance of beholding you:—oh,

Madeline, to do so requires a resolution I am scarcely master of."

"I dare say (exclaimed Madeline, endeavouring to rally her spirits, and disengage the hand which he had taken between his), you'll not find any great difficulty in acquiring such a resolution."

"You doubt my sincerity then (still detaining her); oh! would to heaven I could, I durst convince you of it: yet, alas, why do I utter such a wish, when I know not whether that conviction would be of any consequence to you; know not, do I say?—your altered manner too plainly assures me that it would not."

"Pray let me go (cried Madeline, inexpressibly agitated); I am impatient to return to Madame Chatteneuf, for I know she will wonder at my long absence."

"Go then, madam (said de Sevignie, instantly dropping her hand);—go, madam to the happy beings you regard, and excuse my having detained you so long from them: I see you are displeased at my having done so; I see my society is hateful to you. There was a period when---(he paused, then again proceeded)—when I imagined Madeline Clermont would rather have sought to mitigate than fly from the sorrows of a friend; would have enjoyed an exquisite pleasure in fulfilling the claim, the sacred claim, which misery has upon compassion."

"Oh, de Sevignie (thought Madeline), how little do you know my heart when you thus reproach me. Your society hateful to me!—alas 'tis infinitely too precious for my peace."

"I am sure (said she, speaking with almost as much agitation as he had done), I am sure—I wish—I should be happy was it in my power, to remove, to lessen any sorrow you may feel."

"You wish—you should be happy—(he repeated in a softened voice, as if touched by her gentleness).—Yes, Madeline (again taking her hand), I am convinced of the sincerity of that wish; and nothing, no, nothing but a degree of madness could have tempted me to reproach you as I have just done;—could have tempted me to ask your pity for feelings which I wished, from principles of honour, gratitude, generosity, to conceal from you. Oh, Madeline, I cannot ask your pardon, for I cannot myself pardon my conduct to you."

"Unasked would I give it (cried Madeline), had I been offended, but that be assured is not the case."

At this instant a distant step was heard; both started; and Madeline instantly attempted to disengage herself.

"Do not leave me yet (cried de Sevignie), it may be long ere we meet again; long do I say? alas, we may never, never meet again!—Spare a few minutes longer to me; let us turn into this walk (pointing to the one he had just emerged from), and we shall not be observed; though I said but an instant ago, I would not solicit your pity, yet my heart now tells me, that an assurance of it can only mitigate its wretchedness."

"Receive that assurance then (said Madeline, making another effort as she gave it to withdraw her hand; for, though she wished, she feared to comply with his request. Her reason opposed her inclination for doing so, by representing the folly, the impropriety of any longer listening to the dictates of a passion which she had cause to believe a hopeless one). But excuse me (she continued) from staying any longer with you; the step which alarmed us approaches, and I should be sorry we were seen together."

"Farewell! then (he exclaimed), most lovely and most beloved; I regret, but cannot murmur at your refusal: may the happiness you deserve be yours, and be not only pure as your virtues, but lasting as your life: may every change in that life, be to raise you to still higher felicity: and when you make that great that important change which will fix its destiny;—when you give the precious hand I now hold to some happy, some highly-favoured mortal, some peculiar favourite of heaven,—oh, may you then meet with a heart as tenderly, as firmly devoted to you as de Sevignie's." These last words were spoken almost in a whisper; and Madeline felt by his hands the tremor of his frame. "Farewell! (he cried, after the pause of a minute); if I have pained, if I have disturbed you, let the idea of my never more intruding into your presence banish all resentment for my having done so."

He rested his cold cheek for a moment upon her hand; then suddenly letting it drop, he instantly darted amongst the trees and disappeared.

An icy chillness crept through the frame of Madeline, at the idea of seeing de Sevignie no more. She listened with fixed attention to the sound of his steps, till they could no longer be distinguished; then, starting, she wrung her hands together, and exclaimed—"He is gone, and we shall never, never meet again!"

Every hope relative to him now become extinct; hopes which, notwithstanding the alteration in his manner, had lingered in her heart till this moment; hopes which had cheered her in the long period that separated them, by making her look forward to a second meeting, in which he should disclose sentiments he had before only revealed by his eyes. That meeting had taken place,—those sentiments had been disclosed; but, instead of promoting her happiness as she expected, had, for the present at least, destroyed it; and she wept that crisis to which but a few days before she had looked forward with the most flattering expectations.

Yet not for herself alone she wept, her tears fell also for the wretchedness of de Sevignie; and she regretted having refused to stay a little longer with him, falsely imagining their parting, if less abrupt, would have been less painful. "He prayed for my felicity (she cried); but, oh, de Sevignie, except assured of yours, how unavailing must that prayer ever be!"

The voice of Mademoiselle Chatteneuf calling on her, now roused her from her mecholy musing. She instantly conjectured it was her step which had driven off de Sevignie; and, wiping away her tears, advanced, though but slowly, to meet her.

"Why you must have written a volume instead of a letter, if you have been all this time employed in writing (said Olivia the moment she saw her); but the truth I suppose is, that de Sevignie intruded disagreeably upon you, and delayed you."

"No, he did not I assure you," said Madeline.

"You have seen him however, since you quitted the banqueting house."

"Yes; I met him as I was returning to it."

"And you stopped no doubt (cried Olivia), to wish him good-night."

"Well, supposing I had, would there have been any thing extraordinary in such a common act of civility?"

"No to be sure, nor in his detaining you almost an hour to thank you for it: though he pretended to us the moment you were gone, that he was taken so ill he could scarcely speak or stop another moment. Pray, Madeline, did he tell you the nature of his malady?"

"I never enquired," answered Madeline, blushing.

"But he might have told you without asking; and I shrewdly suspect he did. Pray did he ask you to prescribe for him?"

"Prescribe for him! (said Madeline, pretending not to understand her meaning) do you suppose he took me for an old nurse?"

"No indeed (replied Olivia), I suppose no such thing; but I am not so certain that he would be wrong in taking you for a young nurse."

"I have not spirits to answer you (cried Madeline); so be generous, and do not take advantage of my inability."

"And pray to whose account may I place your dejection," asked Olivia.

"To whose you please; I may as well have the pleasure of giving you a latitude which, whether I please or not, you will take."

"Well, I won't tease you any more (said Olivia); but let us quicken our pace, for supper waits."

They accordingly hastened to the banqueting-house, and the whole party then sat down to supper.

"I am sorry (cried Madame Chatteneuf), that de Sevignie could not stay with us to-night. Poor fellow, he looked extremely ill; but indeed I think he has done so for some days past."

"Yes, and so do I (said Olivia). I trust, however, his malady is not of an incurable nature;" and she glanced archly at Madeline.

"Heaven forbid it was (cried her mother, who took her in a serious light); I know few people whom, on so short an acquaintance, I should so much regret as de Sevignie; there is an elegance, a sweetness in his manner, which declare a soul of benevolence and refinement; he does not by slow degrees conciliate esteem, but, on the first interview, excites a pre-possession in his favour; which, upon a greater knowledge, you have the pleasure of finding no reason to regret; so that though an interesting, he is not a dangerous, acquaintance."

"Let us ask Mademoiselle Clermont's opinion as to that (cried Olivia). Why do you blush, my dear; you know you have been acquainted with the Chevalier a much longer period than my mother has, and of course can better determine whether he is or is not a dangerous creature."

"No one I am sure (said Madeline, endeavouring to suppress her confusion), can ever doubt the justness of Madame Chatteneuf's discernment."

"Ah, Madeline (cried Olivia in a low voice), I see you can some times be guarded."

"Would to heaven I had been so in matters more material than the present," thought Madeline.

When she found herself again alone in her chamber, she again regretted not having staid a little longer with de Sevignie. "It was a last request (said she), and I might on that account have complied with it; he might then have opened his whole soul to me: he might then have revealed the whole circumstances which oppose his wishes: — yet, alas! of what use could it be to know them, since separated it could give little consolation to know by what means."

But, notwithstanding those words, Madeline wished to know them; it was a wish however which, she was convinced, would never be gratified; for, though she was sure de Sevignie had no reason to blush in avowing them, she was equally sure he never would do so.

Madame Chatteneuf's coach was ordered the next morning at an early hour, as she wished to spend a long day with her friend; but an unexpected circumstance retarded her journey to the chateau till a late hour. Just as she was setting out, a letter arrived from Verona, from a sister of her deceased mother's, who had married an Italian nobleman, and had long been settled in Italy, informing her, that her lord was no more; and that, finding herself oppressed in spirits, and declining in health, she ardently longed for the society of her niece, feeling herself rather forlorn, now that she had lost her husband, in a place where she had no connexions of her own about her. Moreover, that as he had left every thing in her power, and she intended making a will in favour of her niece, it was absolutely necessary she should be with her at the time of her death.

Affection for her aunt, whom she tenderly esteemed, and consideration for her daughter's interest, to whose fortune the possessions of her aunt would make a very splendid addition, determined Madame Chatteneuf to accept this invitation without delay; and she immediately ordered preparations to be made for her journey the ensuing day; and, in overlooking those preparations, and arranging domestic concerns, was detained at her house till within a short time of the Countess de Merville's usual dinner hour.

Amidst all the bustle that was going forward, Madeline sat motionless, and in the deepest dejection. She regretted the intended departure of her friends, not only as a means of depriving her of the exquisite pleasure she enjoyed in their company, but as a means of destroying her hopes of again beholding de Sevignie; for, notwithstanding what he had said, she was convinced he would continue a little longer at V———; and she had flattered herself that the Countess would again have permitted her to visit Madame Chatteneuf, and thus have afforded her once more an opportunity of seeing him; an opportunity she could not help sighing for, though now assured their attachment was hopeless.

In their way to the chateau, Olivia made her promise to correspond with her; a promise which Madeline gave with pleasure, yet with diffidence from a fear that she might not prove as entertaining a correspondent as her friend expected.

On entering the chateau, a presage of ill struck her heart at not beholding the Countess, who generally came forward to the hall with a smiling countenance, like the genius of hospitality, to welcome her friends.

"Where is your lady?" asked Madeline, turning to one of the servants.

"Above, Mam'selle, in her dressing-room; she has been rather indisposed to-day."

Madeline heard no more. Heedless, or rather forgetful at that moment of all ceremony, she instantly flew up stairs, leaving Madame Chatteneuf busy in ordering her servants to have the coach ready at an early hour), and found her friend sitting, or rather reclining, in a great chair, with an appearance of illness and dejection, which equally surprised and alarmed Madeline.

"Oh, madam! (said she inexpressibly affected, and taking her hand, which she pressed to her lips and her bosom), why, why did you not send for me before?"

"Because I did not wish to break in upon your happiness," replied the Countess returning the pressure of her hand, while her heavy eyes brightened with a sudden ray of pleasure, and a smile broke through the gloom of her countenance.

"Alas, madam (cried Madeline mournfully), you could not have broken in upon my happiness, for I experienced none (said she, suddenly recollecting herself), which I could have put in competition with that of attending you."

"I am truly sensible of your affection, my love (cried the Countess), and am grateful for it."

"You must have been indisposed longer than to-day I am sure, madam?" said Madeline.

The Countess acknowledged she was right in thinking so.

"And why, madam (said Madeline), did you permit your servant to deceive me last night by saying you were well?"

"I did not wish to give you pain while it was possible to avoid doing so," answered the Countess.

"Ah, madam (said Madeline, with an involuntary sigh), pain is doubly great when not expected."

Madam Chatteneuf and her daughter now entered, and both, by their words and looks, expressed their regret for the illness of the Countess. The former tenderly reproached her for not having immediately acquainted them of it.

"Why you may know (said she) by the short stay which Madeline has made with you, that I have not long concealed it from you. I was only taken ill the evening after she left me; and, had I grown better, I should yet a little longer, in compliance with your wishes, have debarred myself the pleasure of her company. But do not distress me (she continued, raising herself in her chair, and looking round with her wonted benignancy), by this melancholy; I am already better; your presence, my friends, like a rich and precious cordial, has revived me."

The exertion she made cheered her friends; and the conversation soon took a more cheerful turn. Madame Chatteneuf apologised for not coming at an earlier hour, by assigning the reason of her delay; and the Countess sincerely congratulated her on an event which had given her such pleasure.

"From the prospects of my friends (cried she), I must now derive my chief satisfaction."

"If they are as bright as your own (said Madame Chatteneuf) they must be pleasing ones indeed."

The Countess sighed deeply, but spoke not.

Olivia saw dejection again stealing round, and rallied her spirits to drive it away. No very difficult task indeed for her, as she was delighted with the idea of her journey to Italy. She talked of the conquests she expected to make; declared nothing less than a Marquis would satisfy her: and said the moment she was settled in her palace, she should invite the Countess and Madeline to it.—"And we will then try (she continued), whether our fair friend will follow my example, and give her little French heart in exchange for an Italian one."

"Seriously (cried Madame Chatteneuf, addressing the Countess), if we stay any long time at Verona, I shall flatter myself with a hope of having the pleasure of your company and Mademoiselle Clermont's."

"Do not indulge such a hope (said the Countess); for, be assured, my good friend, it would end in disappointment. There is but one journey which I can now look forward to."

The solemnity of her voice and manner, gave them no room to doubt the nature of the journey she alluded to.

"My dear friend (cried Madame Chatteneuf) you will really infect me with your gloom, and I shall begin my long and fatiguing journey with quite a heavy heart. At your time of life you may well look forward to many years. And, as I know of none whose continuance in life is more anxiously desired, so neither do I know of any who should more fervently desire that continuance themselves than you should, possessed as you are of every blessing which can render it happy—affluence—universal esteem—the consciousness of deserving it—and an amiable daughter who adores you, and is settled as happily as your fond heart can wish her to be."

"I am truly sensible of the blessings I possess (cried the Countess), and truly grateful for them, impute my melancholy not to discontent, but to illness."

Dinner was now served in the dressing-room; and, soon after its removal, Madame Chatteneuf rose to depart, having many important matters yet to arrange at home. She assured the Countess, but for the material reasons she had for hastening to Verona, she would have put off her journey thither till she saw her perfectly recovered. This was a measure the Countess declared she never would have consented to, and one by no means necessary to prove the strength of her friendship.

Madeline attended her friends down stairs, and in the hall received their adieu. She wept as they gave it; for their pleasing manners and kind attentions had inspired her with the truest regard.

"Farewell! Madeline (said Olivia, tenderly embracing her); remember your promise of constantly writing; and may heaven grant us all a happy meeting to make amends for this melancholy parting."

"Amen!" said Madeline in a faint voice as she followed her to the coach, where Madame Chatteneuf was already seated, and which now drove off without any farther delay.

Perhaps no sound strikes the heart with greater melancholy than the sound of the carriage which conveys from us the friends we tenderly love, in whose society we have been happy, and whom we know not when we shall behold again. At least Madeline thought so; and her tears were augmented as she stood listening at the hall door to the heavy rumbling of Madame Chatteneuf's coach wheels. "Heaven grant we may have a happy meeting (cried she, repeating the words of Olivia): and yet, was I to give way to the present feelings of my heart, I should little expect such a meeting; but I will not (continued she, turning from the door to rejoin the Countess), I will not deserve evil by anticipating it."

CHAP. X.

Some melancholy thought that shuns the light,

Lurks underneath that sadness in thy visage.

Rowe

She found the Countess leaning against the side of the chair, as if quite overcome by the parting with her friends. Madeline hung over her, but was too much affected to speak. In a few minutes she raised her head—"I feel rather faint (said she), and I will go upon the lawn, for I think the evening air will revive me."

She accordingly rose, but was so weak, she was obliged to lean upon the arm of Madeline in descending the stairs; and was then so exhausted by this exertion, that she had only power to reach a seat beneath the spreading branches of a chestnut;—a seat to which she had often led Madeline, as to one peculiarly dedicated to love and friendship; it owed its formation to her lord, whom the noble size and situation of the tree had charmed; and this circumstance, together with a complimentary line, devoting it to her, was carved upon its rind: in a beautiful opening of the wood it stood, commanding a fine view of the lake, and all around

The violet,

Crocus, and hyacinth, with rich inlay

Broider'd the ground.

"I love the shelter of those venerable boughs (said the Countess); they recall a thousand tender recollections: at such an hour as this, when day was declining, often have I sat beneath them with my lord, watching the sports of our children, —the lovely boys, whose loss first taught me the frailty of human joys, first convinced me that it is hereafter we can only expect permanent felicity. 'Tis a conviction of this kind, which loosens the hold the world too often almost imperceptibly gains upon the heart; let us therefore never dare to murmur at events that draw us still closer to our God."

Madeline sighed; she felt indeed that nothing will so soon

detach us from life as disappointment.

"I fear, my love (cried the Countess), that I have infected you with my gloom."

"No, madam (replied Madeline) you have not."

"I fear (resumed the Countess, regarding her with earnestness), that some secret sorrow preys upon your heart; a sorrow which, perhaps if I knew, I might be able, if not to remove, at least to lessen."

"Oh, no, madam," exclaimed Madeline with involuntary quickness, terrified at the idea of revealing her hopeless passion.

"Then heaven forbid (cried the Countess), I should seek to probe a wound I could not heal."

"Forgive me, madam (said Madeline), I spoke unthinkingly. I know of none more qualified to heal the sorrows of the heart than you are; but—but my feelings (continued she, hesitating and blushing), require more the exertions of my own reason, than the sympathy of a friend; and—and be assured, madam I, to the utmost of my power, will use those exertions."

"I trust so, my love," said the Countess, who guessed the sorrow of Madeline proceeded from the disappointment of her hopes relative to de Sevignie."

"I trust so, my love; not only on your own account, but your father's, who, from your happiness, hopes to receive some consolation for the numerous, the dreadful, the unprecedented calamities of his youth."

"Ah, Heavens (cried Madeline, starting, and forgetting, in the horror and agitation of the moment, the resolution she had once formed of never attempting to discover the nature of those calamities), you shock my very soul by your words. Oh, why, why is there such a silence observed as to his former life!—a silence which makes me tremble lest some heavy misfortunes, in consequence of the events of it, should still be hanging over him."

"Madeline (said the Countess in a solemn voice), in my concern for your father, I spoke unguardedly; and I already repent having done so from the situation I see you in: but, as some atonement for doing so, I will take this opportunity of cautioning you against all imprudent curiosity; let no incentive from it ever tempt you to seek an explanation of former occurrences; be assured your happiness depends entirely on your ignorance of them: was the dark volume of your father's fate ever opened to your view, peace would for ever forsake your breast; for its characters are marked by horror, and stained with blood."

Madeline grasped the Countess's arm in convulsive agitation;—"I swear (said she, raising her other hand, and looking up to heaven), from this moment, never, by any means, direct or indirect, to try and discover ought that my father wishes to conceal."

"I rejoice to hear this resolution (cried the Countess, kissing her cheek); I rejoice at it on your own account. And now, my love, let us change this discourse. You have promised (she continued) to try and recover your spirits; and I shall attentively watch to see whether you fulfil that promise. Oh, Madeline, grief in the early season of youth, is like frost to a tender flower, unkind and blighting; and no tongue can describe, no heart, except a parental one, conceive the bitter, the excruciating anguish which a parent feels at seeing a beloved child wasting the bloom of youth in wretchedness,—pining, drooping, sinking beneath its pressure.—From such wretchedness may heaven preserve your father! Oh, never, never may the distresses of his child precipitate him to his grave!"

Madeline almost started, she looked earnestly at the Countess; and fancied that the energy with which her words had been delivered, declared a self-experience of the sorrow which she mentioned. The idea however was but transitory; and as she dismissed, she wondered she had ever conceived it. "No," she said to herself, "the Countess has felt no sorrow but what the common casualties of life have occasioned."

Both were silent for some minutes; Madeline at length spoke:—"It grows late, my dear madam, and I fear your staying longer in the night air may hurt you."

The Countess instantly rose, thanked her for her kind solicitude about her; and, leaning on her arm, returned to the house; they supped together in her dressing-room, and parted soon after for the night.

Madeline retired to her chamber deeply affected by the incidents of the day,—incidents which had increased the dejection she felt in consequence of those she had experienced at V— — — to a most painful degree. Instead of undressing, she sat down to indulge her melancholy thoughts, but was soon interrupted by a tap at the door; on desiring it to be opened, Floretta, one of the Countess's women, entered.

Whenever attendance was necessary, it was she that waited upon Madeline, who liked her much for her liveliness and good-nature; she had been in the Countess's suite at the time she stopped at Clermont's, and was daughter to an old and favourite deceased waiting-woman, whose place since her death she had filled.

"I was longing, Mademoiselle (said she with a smile and a courtesy), for an opportunity of welcoming you back to the castle. I hope you had a pleasant time at V— — —; but indeed I dare say you had, for Madame Chatteneuf sees a power of company they say; and she is in the right of it—company is the life of one; besides, it gives her daughter a chance of being married soon; I warrant she has a number of admirers; and I make no doubt but you, Mam'selle, came in for your share."

"You are mistaken indeed Floretta," said Madeline smiling.

"Not entirely, Mam'selle: Lord, didn't Jacques and Philippe tell me the first evening you went to Madame Chatteneuf's, there was no one there half so much admired as you were; and how you danced with the handsomest gentleman present who looked so tender on you, Monsieur—lord, I forget his name, but I dare say you recollect, Mam'selle."

Too well, thought Madeline. She sighed, but made no reply; and, rising, began to undress in order to conceal the agitation which the mention of de Sevignie had excited in her mind.

"You are come back to a dismal house, Mam'selle (said Floretta, echoing her sigh, which she imputed to regret for past pleasures), to a dismal house indeed, (shaking her head), now that my poor lady is ill."

"Its gloom on that account will soon be dissipated I trust (cried Madeline), by the perfect restoration of her health."

"Alas! I fear not (said Floretta with a greater seriousness than Madeline had ever before remarked in her countenance), her mind is too much disturbed to permit me to think it will."

"Disturbed! (repeated Madeline in an accent of the greatest surprise, and turning to her), why what has happened to disturb her mind?"

"Lord, don't you know?" asked Floretta with a kind of eager stare.

"No, I can't even conjecture," said Madeline.

"Well, I could never have supposed my lady would have been so secret with you (cried Floretta, after the pause of a minute); though after all it does not surprise me, for I know it shocks her to have any one suspect his wickedness."

"Whose wickedness (asked Madeline eagerly)? you astonish me beyond expression by your words."

"Aye, and I could astonish you much more, Mam'selle (said Floretta), if I was to tell you all I know; for, from my mother's being a favourite with the Countess, and from my being always in her service, I know more of her affairs than perhaps any other person except Agatha does; often and often she has made me promise to keep them all profoundly secret; and to be sure so I have, and would always, except (continued Floretta, whose passion for telling secrets was equal to her passion for hearing them), except with a little hesitation, to such a friend as you are to her."

Highly as the curiosity of Madeline was raised, she instantly recoiled from the idea of learning the Countess's private affairs through the channel of a servant.

"No, Floretta (said she), except from the Countess, I can never hearken to such secrets as you would impart; had she wished me to know them, she would have communicated them herself. Had I been surprised into listening to them, I should have blushed tomorrow when I beheld her face, from the consciousness of having acted meanly and basely towards her; and so would you I am confident, at the idea of having violated your promise, and betrayed what should be ever sacred to you, the confidence of your Protectress and friend."

"But I am sure (she continued, seeing the cheeks of Floretta covered with blushes, while she trembled so she could not stand), you spoke without thought, or perhaps from an idea that the disclosure of the secrets you hinted at would have gratified me; but be assured, Floretta, that would not have been the case, for I early learned, my good girl, that pleasure could never be attained by acting contrary to truth and virtue; and I hope you either do or will in future believe the justness of that saying as firmly as I do."

"Yes, that I shall to be sure, Mam'selle (cried Floretta, somewhat recovered from her confusion, and again raising her head). As you have said, Mam'selle, nothing indeed but an idea that I should have gratified you by revealing my lady's secrets could ever have tempted me to mention them."

Madeline did not appear to doubt her, but said she would no longer detain her. Floretta therefore courtesied, and retired with great humility.

Left to herself, Madeline reflected on all she had heard, and the more she reflected, the more she was astonished at it: to surmise how or by whom the Countess was distressed, was impossible.—"But to know the source of her grief could scarcely, I think, augment my regret for it (cried Madeline); alas! what an aggravation of my sorrow is it to know that the two beings I love best in the world, are oppressed by griefs which, by concealing, I must suppose they deem too dreadful for me to be acquainted with it."

She continued in melancholy meditation till the whole castle was wrapped in silence. She then retired to bed; but her rest was broken and disturbed by distressing dreams; and she longed for the return of morning to chase away the gloomy horrors of the night. She arose at an earlier hour than usual, before any of the family, except some of the inferior servants, were stirring, and walked out upon the lawn to try if the freshness of the air and exercise would revive her spirits. A solemn stillness reigned around, and the dewy landscape was yet but imperfectly revealed; but by degrees its grey veil was withdrawn, and the stillness interrupted by the twittering of birds and the carol of the early peasant. Madeline sighed at the contrast she drew between the cheerfulness of the scene and the sadness of her own mind.

"And oh, when (she cried as she saw the gloomy vapours of night flying before the beams of a rising sun), oh, when shall the clouds that involve my prospects be dispersed!"

After walking about some time, she sat down beneath the shelter of the chestnut, where she and her friend had rested the preceding night; and as she looked at the opposite but distant mountains, she thought of Madame Chatteneuf and Olivia, who had fixed on this morning to commence their journey; and her regret at their departure was augmented by believing that their presence would have been a comfort and relief to the Countess.

Full of the idea that they had already begun to ascend those stupendous precipices, which together they had so often viewed with mingled awe and veneration; she gazed upon them with a melancholy kind of pleasure, as if by doing so she could once more have beheld the travellers.

She remained thus engaged, till Agatha called to her from a window, and informed her the Countess was up. She directly returned to the house, and, going up to the Countess's dressing-room, met her just as she was entering it.

With the most anxious solicitude she enquired how she found herself. "Somewhat better," (the Countess replied). But whether the imagination of Madeline was affected by what Floretta had said the preceding night, or whether it really was the case, she thought there was no alteration in her countenance to support this assertion; the same look of languor and dejection prevailed; and she involuntarily repeated her enquiry with an earnestness that intimated the doubt she harboured, and hinted a wish of having a physician sent for.

"I thank you for this kind anxiety about me, my dear girl (said the Countess); but I can with truth assure you I am better; and even if I was not, I should never think of sending for a physician; medical skill (continued she in a low voice), could be of little avail in my malady."

"Ah! (thought Madeline) this is indeed a confirmation of all that Floretta told me; she gives me to understand by those words, that her malady is upon her mind;—would to heaven I could alleviate it!"

They sat down to breakfast; the table was laid near an open window, from whence they inhaled the sweetness of the morning air, and beheld the dewy landscape gradually brightening to their view,—beheld along the forest glades the wild deer trip, and often turning, gaze at early passenger: grey smoke arose in spiral columns from cottages scattered about its extremity, painting the rural scene with cheerful signs of inhabitation: and soon the industrious woodman was beheld commencing his toil, and the careful shepherd driving his bleating flock along the grassy paths to taste the verdure of the morn, while on every side

Music awoke

The native voice of undissembled joy,

And thick around the woodland hymns arose.

"Oh, how lovely is this scene! (said the Countess), this is Nature's hour for offering up her incense to the Supreme; and cold and unamiable indeed must be that heart which is not warmed to devotion by it. What real enjoyment do the children of indolence and dissipation forego by losing, in the bed of sloth, those moments when every blooming pleasure waits without: how cheering even to the soul of sadness itself, is the matin of the birds! how reviving to sickness or to languor this pure breeze, which, as it sweeps over tall trees of the forest, bends their leafy heads, as if in sign of grateful homage to the great Creator."

"It is an hour which I particularly love indeed (cried Madeline), one in which some of my most delightful rambles have been taken; with my father I have often brushed the dews away, and on the side of some steep and romantic mountain, caught the first beams of the sun, and watched the vapour of the valley retiring before them."

"Our friends (continued Madeline, after the pause of a few minutes), have ere this, I dare say, commenced their journey; by this time they have probably got a considerable way, and at this very moment perhaps may be sitting down to breakfast in the cottage of some mountaineer, attended by him and his family with assiduous hospitality; or else beneath the shadow of some cliff, o'er which the light chamois bound, and tall pines cast a solemn shade. Oh, how delightful must such a situation be!—how delightful, how elevating to the mind to be surrounded by the noblest works of nature,—by scenes which bring the heroes of other days to view!—how pleasing to listen to the soft melody of shepherds' pipes, to the bleating of his numerous flocks, intermingled perhaps with the lulling sound of waterfalls, and the humming of bees, intent on their delicious toil!"

"You speak like a poet, Madeline," said the Countess, smiling.

Madeline blushed at this observation, and wondered, when it was made, that she could have given such latitude to her imagination.

Fatigued by talking, the Countess lay down upon a sofa after breakfast. This debility, in a mind so nervous and a frame so active as hers had hitherto been, gave the most painful apprehensions to Madeline; and, under a trifling pretext, she left the room in order to communicate them to Agatha, and enquire from her whether she did not deem some advise requisite for her lady.

Agatha shook her head mournfully on hearing them; but relative to her enquiry, answered in the negative, saying that rest and quiet were all that was necessary for the Countess, "if those don't do her good (said she), nothing can."

"Alas! (cried Madeline, as she turned from her), 'tis too true! 'tis sorrow that undermines her health, and medicine could not reach her malady. Oh! what, what is this sorrow which so dreadfully affects her,—which is so carefully concealed that even her most intimate friends know it not, for such I know Madame Chatteneuf and her daughter to be, and they, I am confident, are ignorant of it?"

When she returned to the dressing-room, the Countess requested she would read to her; and thus employed, except at short intervals, when her ladyship made her pause to rest herself, she continued till dinner was served, at which the Countess was unable to preside; she grew better however in the evening, and again entered into conversation with Madeline.

The discourse turned upon the time she had passed at V———; and the Countess now requested to hear a particular account of it. This was a request which Madeline, if she could, would gladly have declined obeying; for, in almost every amusement, almost every scene she had partaken of, or mixed in while there, de Sevignie was so principal an object, that to describe them without mentioning him, she feared would be scarcely possible; to mention him without emotion, she knew she could not; and to betray such emotion would be, she was convinced, to confirm in the Countess's mind the suspicions she knew she already entertained of her attachment to de Sevignie; and now to have them confirmed, now, when not a hope remained of their being ever more to each other than friends, she felt would be humiliating and distressing in the extreme.

She attempted however to comply with the request of the Countess, but she faltered in her talk; and, by trying to omit what she wished to conceal, rendered what she would have told almost unintelligible.

The Countess saw and pitied her distress; she pitied, because she guessed the source from whence it proceeded. She was now more convinced than ever, from the dejection of Madeline, her confusion, and a few involuntary expressions that dropped from her, that all hope relative to de Sevignie was over, and, since terminated, she meant not to enquire concerning him, certain as she was that that termination was owing to no impropriety in the conduct of Madeline, or in his either, else she would not thus regret it. Time and kind attention, she trusted, would heal the wound which disappointed affection had given to the bosom of her youthful friend.

By degrees she turned the conversation to one more pleasing to her; and they both parted after supper with more cheerfulness than perhaps either had expected.

The next morning Madeline had the exquisite pleasure of meeting her beloved protectress at breakfast, with a greater appearance of health and spirits than she had witnessed the preceding day.

No attentions which could contribute to render this change a permanent one, were wanting on the part of Madeline; her assiduities were indeed unremitting, and the Countess received them with every indication of gratitude. A week saw her restored to her usual looks and serenity; and thus happily did the storm which had threatened the peace of her friends and family, appear overblown.

Occupied by attention and anxiety about her friend, Madeline, during her indisposition, had had no time to ruminate over past scenes; but now that her recovery allowed her more leisure, they arose in gloomy retrospection to her view. She saw herself deprived of all those hopes which had hitherto cheered her mind, assured, almost solemnly assured, that her destiny and de Sevignie's could never be united; and sad and solitary in the extreme she anticipated her life would be after such a disappointment, for de Sevignie she considered as her kindred spirit, and could not hope, or rather deemed it utterly impossible, she should again meet with one so truly congenial to her own.

Another week elapsed without any thing material happening, during which the Countess heard from her daughter; she gave the letter to Madeline to read, and the vivacity with which it was written, and the assurance it contained of her own health and happiness, clearly proved that Madame D'Alembert was entirely ignorant of her mother's late illness and disquietude.

The wonder of Madeline was increased at finding she concealed this disquietude even from her daughter. Surely, she thought, its source must indeed be painful when she thus hides it from those who are most interested about her.

In vain she tried to assign some cause for it in her own mind; the more she thought upon it, the more impossible she found it to conjecture from what or from whom it proceeded, and that she never would know, she was convinced; and now that she saw her friend had (apparently at least) overcome it, her curiosity was somewhat abated.

In about ten days after Madame D'Alembert's letter, she received one herself from Olivia (as did the Countess from Madame Chatteneuf), written in the most lively and affectionate manner, and containing a particular account of their journey over the Alps, their reception from her aunt, who was not quite in so declining a state as they apprehended, and the amusements they partook of at Verona.

She concluded by charging Madeline to write immediately; and said she expected to hear from her all that had happened in and out of the chateau since her departure, and particularly whether she had since seen de Sevignie. "But that you have, I cannot doubt (she added); and, jesting apart, believe me, my dear Madeline, I hope to learn from you that every little uneasiness which lurked in your mind, and his, is removed by the mutual acknowledgment of a passion which, to the penetrating eyes of friendship, it was evident you entertained for each other. Blush not, my dear; the secret which friends discover is guarded by them as sedulously as their own; and, should concealment be necessary, be assured of mine. But I will not harbour an idea that it is; no, I will not believe that de Sevignie will be contented with the mere possession of your heart:—ere this, perhaps, preparations are making; ere this, perhaps, the happy knot is tied; if so, accept my sincerest congratulations; every one who regards you, will congratulate you and themselves on such an event; for the wife of de Sevignie must, if not her own fault (which can never be your case), be completely happy."

Madeline's whole soul felt agitated as she read those lines; since hopeless, she was distressed that her attachment should be known; and she sighed with the heaviest sadness at the contrast which she drew between her present feelings, and what they would have been, had her friend's conjectures relative to de Sevignie and her been just.

She felt shocked at the idea of being asked to show this letter (which she had read in her own chamber) to the Countess; but that lady, perhaps from surmising some of the contents, gave not the smallest intimation of a wish to read it.

But though her fears respecting it were removed by this silence, her dejection continued. The surmises of Olivia hurt and embarrassed her; and she feared, when she declared their fallacy, that she should be regarded as a slighted object; and to pride, youthful pride, perhaps no idea could be more mortifying.

To complete her sadness, the Countess seemed relapsing into melancholy; and, though they both conversed, conversation in both appeared but as the faint effort of feeling to try and beguile the sadness of each other.

The efforts she made to converse during the day were painful in the extreme; and when the Countess retired in the evening, as was her usual custom, to the ruined monastery in the valley, for the purpose of prayer and meditation, Madeline hastily threw a scarf around her, and went out upon the lawn, as if she had feared a longer continuance in the house would subject her to society, which, in the present agitated state of her mind was irksome to her.

END OF VOL. I.

CHAP. I.

– – – – – – – Witness ye Pow'rs

How much I suffer'd, and how much I strove.

Dryden.

The evening was far advanced when Madeline went upon the lawn. It was now the dusky hour of twilight, when the glow worm "'gan to light his pale and ineffectual fires" amongst the tangled thickets of the forest, and the vespers of the birds and the toils of the woodman had ceased. The beetle had now commenced its droning flight, and the owlet her sad song from the ivy mantled turrets of the castle, intermingled, or rather lost at times, in the hoarse and melancholy cries of waterfowl returning to the little islands on the lake, across which came the hollow sound of a distant convent bell.

Madeline stood some minutes upon the lawn as if to enjoy sounds, which by suiting, soothed the dejection of her mind; but the kind of pleasing trance into which they lulled her, was of short continuance; all the perturbed thoughts which anxiety and attention about the Countess had, during the day, in some degree dissipated, soon returned with full power; and as she cast her eyes on the bleak and distant mountains, fancy, torturing fancy presented de Sevignie to her view, a sad and solitary wanderer about them. His head unsheltered, exposed to the unwholesome dews of night; his ideas unsettled, perhaps wandering after her, who like himself was a child of sorrow.

Wrapt in melancholy meditation, heedless almost whither or how far she went, she now wandered down a lonely and romantic path, which led along the margin of a lake to a stupendous mountain that terminated it: in this mountain were numerous cavities, some of which had been formed into agreeable summer retreats by the Count and Countess de Merville; the foremost of these was a spacious grotto, whose sides and roof were formed of rugged stone, ornamented by beautiful crystalline substances, which sparkled in the rays of the sun, that sometimes pierced through crevices in the roof like the finest brilliants; its floor consisted of smooth pebbles curiously inlaid, and its arched entrance was nearly overgrown by a thick foliage of ivy, whose dark green was enlivened by the bright tints of several wild flowers: while thick around the myrtle, the laurestine, and the arbutus, reared high their beauteous and fragrant heads, stretching their fantastic arms through its crevices: immediately above them rose a wood of solemn verdure, which reached half way up the ascent; the rest of the mountain was rocky and bare of vegetation. The beauty and sweetness of the shrubs; the lovely prospect it commanded of the lake and skirting woods, and the solemn shadows cast upon it by the trees above, rendered the grotto a delightful place for retirement.

– – – – – – – – – – – – – – In shady Bower,

More sacred or sequester'd tho' but feign'd,

Pan or Sylvanus never slept, nor Nymph,

Nor Fauns haunted.

From this cavity, through an irregular but not inelegant arch, formed by a chasm in the rock, was an entrance into another, in the centre of which a deep and spacious bath had been contrived many years back, which was constantly supplied by the cold limpid streams of the mountain; this bath, like the grotto, received its only light from apertures in the roof, from whence wild shrubs hung in fantastic wreaths; and about it were smaller caves that answered the purpose of little dressing-rooms; but those caves, the bath, and grotto, had been long neglected: for since the death of the Count, who had constantly resorted to them for health and pleasure, the Countess had never been able to bear the idea of approaching them. Her desertion confirmed the superstitious stories, which had long been in circulation amongst the servants and peasantry, of their being haunted by some of the former inhabitants of the chateau; nor would one of them venture near the mountain after sun-set, for almost any consideration.

Hither, as I have already said, Madeline now wandered, almost without knowing whither she was going; but when she found herself at the grotto, feeling a little fatigued, she sat down upon a moss covered stone at its entrance: the present scene was perfectly adapted to her feelings, and like the poet she might have said,

Those woods, those wilds, those melancholy glooms

Accord with my soul's sadness, and draw forth

The voice of sorrow from my bursting heart.

The grotto behind her was now involved in utter darkness, and the lake, which lay before her, tinctured with the gloom of closing day, appeared black and dismal; except where it reflected one of the beautifully chequered clouds of evening, or the scattered stars that alternately glittered and disappeared: as if unwilling to disturb the silence of the hour, it stole with gentle undulations to its green banks; and no sounds, but those of its soft murmurs, the melancholy rippling of the water within the grotto, and now and then a hoarse scream from a wild-fowl on the lake, could be distinguished.

The thoughts of Madeline were therefore not interrupted; and fancy again represented de Sevignie rambling about the gloomy heights, whose outlines she could just discover: She shuddered at the idea of the dangers to which such conduct exposed him.

"Oh, de Sevignie! (she cried aloud, speaking in the agitation of her soul,) would to Heaven we had never met, since by meeting, we have only become sources of wretchedness to each other; painful as is our separation, that pain to me would be mitigated, did I know you were in any degree happy; but while I imagine you miserable, peace must continue a stranger to my breast."

She paused, for at this instant a deep sigh, from the innermost recesses of the grotto, pierced her ear, and made her start with terror from her seat. Though she had early been taught to contemn the weakness which gives rise to superstition; and, though in the hour of composure she derided it, yet there were moments when her spirits were exhausted, such a moment as the present, in which it found admission to her breast.

Every fearful story, which she had heard of the grotto and other caves of the mountain, now recurred to her memory, and she almost feared the spectres they described would start to her view; for of a human creature being in the grotto at an hour of darkness, such as the present, she had not an idea, from the dread she knew entertained of it. She was hastening away as fast as her trembling limbs could carry her, when the sound of an approaching step took from her all power of motion, and she sunk to the earth in an agony of fear; almost instantly, however, she was snatched from it, while a voice to which her heart vibrated, the soft the tremulous voice of de Sevignie, assured her of her safely.

"Madeline! (he exclaimed, while he prest her to his throbbing heart) my Madeline! can you forgive the terror I involuntary caused you."

"Good heaven! (said Madeline, raising her head from his shoulder) do I really behold, (as if doubting the evidence of her ears, and eyes,) do I really behold de Sevignie,—why (she continued) why, for what purpose did you come hither."

"Ah, Madeline! (he said) cannot your own heart inform you; have you no idea of the sympathy which drew me hither, to wander round the mansion you inhabit; to indulge my feelings by treading, or fancying I trod, in the paths you frequented. Oh, Madeline! what to happiness would be trifles, are to sorrow and despair matters of importance."

While he spoke, the tremors of Madeline had somewhat subsided; but emotions different from those of fear, though not less painful, still agitated her mind; emotions which delicacy, dissatisfied with itself, had given rise to; she did not desire, nor ever had attempted to conceal her friendship for de Sevignie, but situated as they were, she did not wish him by any means to know, it was of so fervent a nature as her expressions in the grotto must have implied; and overwhelmed with confusion at the idea of them, she endeavoured, as soon as she could move, to disengage herself from his arms, in order to return home.

"Against your inclination I will not detain you, (said he) and yet (contradicting his words by still holding her to his breast) to part with you so soon, at such a moment as this, is almost more than I can bear; oh Madeline! to affect ignorance of what you said in the grotto, would be to betray insensibility; I have heard you (he continued, with a voice of rapture) I have heard you in accents which pity might acknowledge her's, pronounce my name. Think then, Madeline, and excuse my doing so, whether at a moment which has given me the sweet assurance of being sometimes thought of, sometimes pitied by you, I can without the utmost reluctance let you depart immediately."

"You have heard me, de Sevignie (cried Madeline, trying to speak in a collected voice,) but on your honour, on your delicacy I rest, to bury in oblivion what you heard."

"In my heart eternally," said de Sevignie.

"You must promise to forget it, (proceeded Madeline) that I may try to be reconciled to myself."

"Forget! (repeated de Sevignie) no Madeline, never will I give a promise which my heart protests against fulfilling; the memory of what I have heard I will cherish; I will treasure, as all that can give pleasure to my existence; in all my wanderings, amidst all my cares, I will recur to it for comfort and support; for never can I feel quite forlorn, never utterly miserable, while I imagine I am regarded, I am thought of by you."

Madeline sighed, and averted her eyes from his, in order to conceal the feelings his language excited. Reason opposed a longer continuance with him, by convincing her a lengthened conversation would only add to her subsequent anguish when they parted: but her heart recoiled from the idea of quitting him so soon, so abruptly, when perhaps they might never meet again; she wished too, to stay a few minutes longer, to caution him against the dangers which his wild and solitary rambles exposed him to.

For this purpose, after a little irresolution, she ceased to make an effort to leave him, and opened her lips but her voice faltered; and she felt that she could not express her apprehensions for his safety, without betraying the tender interest she took in it. Suddenly, therefore, she broke from him and moved on.

For a minute he stood transfixed to the spot where she had left him; then starting, he exclaimed thus, "thus, do I ever find my happiness transient! oh, how exquisite was that, which but a few moments ago pervaded my soul at the idea of your pity;—a pity, which your abrupt departure convinces me you either wish to disavow or suppress."

"Alas! (cried Madeline, involuntarily pausing, and turning to him) of what avail would be my pity."

"Oh, it would sooth my cares; it would assuage my sorrows: Repeat, then, my Madeline, repeat the sweet assurance of it, and spare a few minutes longer to wretchedness and me."

"No, (said Madeline, who ashamed of her past weakness resolved to give no farther proof of it,) it grows late, and I must quit this place; to continue much longer here, would, I am convinced, occasion a search after me, and consequently might subject me to the reproach of carrying on clandestine proceedings."

"Go, then, Madam! (exclaimed de Sevignie, in passionate accents) go, Madam! obey the rigid rules of propriety, and disregard my sufferings; sufferings, which you yourself have caused. Yes, Madeline, 'tis on your account my youth is wasted, my hopes o'erthrown, my comforts blasted: but go—no assurance of pity now would sooth me; for I am now convinced, what you feel for me is not a settled feeling, but a mere involuntary impulse, such as any son of sorrow may equally excite."

He turned abruptly from her, and with quick, yet tottering steps hastened to the grotto, against whose side he suddenly flung himself, as if for support.

At another time to be accused of insensibility might well have inspired Madeline with resentment; but now she could only feel compassion and tenderness for him, whose pale and disordered looks gave such melancholy evidence of his sufferings. Not more affected by his words, than terrified by his manner, to depart without seeing him in some degree composed, was impossible, and she walked slowly towards him, trusting, that at her approach he would rise, and that she might then be able to prevail on him to quit the Forest. He did not move however, and after standing a few minutes by him she ventured softly to pronounce his name. Still he continued silent and motionless, and her alarm increased; she stooped down, but could not hear him breathe,—his hand lay extended from him, she gently raised it, but almost immediately let it drop with horror at finding it cold and lifeless.

He was dying perhaps, and she had not power to assist him. "Oh, de Sevignie! (she exclaimed, in the agony of her soul) de Sevignie! speak to me for heaven's sake, or I shall sink with terror."

He started, as if the vehemence of her words had roused him; turned and surveyed her for a minute with a vacant eye. His recollection then returned, and with it all his gentleness.

"I have been ill, (he said) extremely ill; I never was so disordered before, but 'tis the effect of weakness; this is the first day I have been able to come out since we last parted."

"Good heavens! (cried Madeline) what imprudence to come hither; oh, de Sevignie, what can make you act in a manner so injurious to yourself, so distressing to your friends."

The energy of her voice, the paleness, the wildness of her countenance, proved to de Sevignie the alarm he had given her.

"Ah, Madeline, (said he, taking her soft trembling hand in his,) I seem fated to give you uneasiness; but be composed I beseech you, and also be assured, I never more will intrude into your presence;—to-morrow, I leave V——— for ever. Too long indeed have I persecuted you; I blush at the recollection of my impetuous conduct; to apologize for it as I wish is impossible; but never, never, shall I cease to regret it. Permit me, (he added) to leave you near the house, the way to it is solitary, I will then depart."

"No, (replied Madeline) there is no danger in my going alone; besides, if I permitted you to accompany me, I should bring you out of your way: for this path near the grotto is the shortest one to the road."

"Farewell, then (cried he, pressing her hand to his cold lips,) farewell, (he repeated as he resigned it,) but as this is the last time we shall probably ever meet, let me have the comfort of hearing from you, that you do not utterly detest me for the uneasiness I have caused you."

Madeline attempted to speak, but her voice was lost in the emotions of her soul, and she hung her head to conceal the tears which trickled down her cheeks. They did not, however, escape the penetrating eyes of de Sevignie: he again took her hand, "I cannot leave you, (said he) "in this situation; you weep, you tremble; oh, my Madeline, rest upon me."

"No! (cried she, resisting the effort he made to support her) I am now better; let us therefore part, and part for ever."

De Sevignie repeated the word, then yielding, or rather overcome by the anguish of his heart, he fell at her feet; he implored the choicest blessings of heaven for her; he besought her forgiveness for the rashness, the impetuosity of his conduct. "The remembrance of such forgiveness may at some future period (he continued) a little alleviate the pain of separation."

How unnecessary for Madeline to assure him by words, of that forgiveness which her looks exprest; with streaming eyes she hung over him; yet not their separation alone caused her tears. His broken health and spirits were subjects of yet greater regret, and scarcely,—scarcely could she prevent herself from kneeling on the earth beside him, and supplicating that heaven he had so recently addrest on her account to restore them; but though the supplication did not burst from her lips, it was breathed from the very depth of her heart.

In a moment of agitation like the present, the feelings of that heart could no longer be supprest, and de Sevignie now beheld the strong hold he had of its affections.

But the confirmation of her affection could not lessen his wretchedness, on the contrary, it seemed to increase it: He arose from her feet.

"Oh, Madeline! (he said) how inconsistent is the human heart; but a few minutes ago, and I fancied the assurance of your pity and regard would render me in some degree happy; now when you have permitted me to receive it, I feel myself more miserable than ever, and think, since the obstacles to our union cannot be conquered, I should have been less so had I still imagined you indifferent."

Madeline shuddered, "would to heaven! (cried she, emphatically) we had never met." Scarcely was she able to forbear asking what those obstacles were which he alluded to, but propriety checked the question; she regretted bitterly, regretted the divulgement of her sentiments, and the consciousness of its being an unpremeditated divulgement, could scarcely mitigate her regret for it; anxious to avoid the imputation of total weakness, either from de Sevignie or herself, she now summoned all her resolution to her aid, and after the silence of a few minutes, addrest him in a collected voice.

"Let us (said she) endeavour to reconcile ourselves to an inevitable necessity, the efforts of fortitude and virtue can never fail of being successful, and how can they be more nobly exercised, than in trying to repel useless sorrow. Let us from this moment, that no interruption may be given to such efforts, determine sedulously to avoid each other."

"Yet we shall meet again; (exclaimed de Sevignie in a passionate accent, and grasping her hand) our souls were originally paired in heaven; and though now separated by a wayward destiny, they will, my Madeline, be re-united in that heaven."

A tear, in spite of her efforts to restrain it, strayed down her pale cheek, but she wiped it hastily away. "'Ere we part for ever in this world, (she proceeded with a softness she could not repress) let me entreat you, de Sevignie, to exert that fortitude, which from reason, from education, from principle, you ought, nay you must if you please, be master of. 'Tis an injustice to yourself, to society; above all, to that divine Being who implanted such noble faculties in your mind as I know you to possess, to let them be destroyed by sorrow; besides, what grief must not the conduct which impairs your health and weakens your mind, give to all your connexions."

"My connexions! (repeated de Sevignie, looking steadily at her) my connexions;" and his eye loured on her.

"Yes, (replied Madeline) to your connexions, if their feelings are at all like mine. Oh, de Sevignie! if you really regard my tranquillity, promise, ere we part, to try and conquer your dejection, and to give up your solitary rambles; the idea of the dangers to which you expose yourself by them terrifies me."

"Ere we part, (said de Sevignie, who seemed only to have attended to those words) Oh! what a death-like chill comes over my heart at the idea of doing so. Never—never, Madeline, if honour, if gratitude permitted, would we separate."

"If they are combined against us (cried Madeline) it were not only foolish but criminal to think of acting otherwise than we are now doing."

"They are! (exclaimed de Sevignie) for would it be not dishonourable, ungrateful in the extreme, to attempt leading the daughter of Clermont—he to whose compassionate care, under heaven, I perhaps owe the preservation of my life; would it not, I say, be base, to attempt leading her from ease, security, the enjoyment of all that affluence can give, into care, danger, and obscurity. No, Madeline, I am not selfish; I am not a villain: I would not, for the mere gratification of my own passion, involve the woman I adore in trouble; nor should I gratify it by such conduct:—that storm which I could brave alone, I should sink beneath with her."

The obstacles which he had alluded to, seemed now explained: from fortune, want of fortune, Madeline was convinced they sprung. Charmed by the noble, the generous conduct of de Sevignie; ignorant of the difficulties and sorrows of life, when unpossessed of a competence; and believing, firmly believing, that her attachment for him could never be conquered, she was almost tempted to offer him her hand. To assure him ease, security, the enjoyment of all that affluence could give, would gladly be relinquished by her for the sake of sharing his cares, dangers, and obscurity; but delicacy, that celestial guardian of her sex, checked the rash impulse of romantic tenderness. She suddenly recollected herself, and recoiled, from the idea of the action she had been about committing, as if from a precipice.

"Gracious heaven! (she exclaimed within herself) how mean how despicable should I have appeared in his eyes, who can so nobly triumph over his own passion. Had I followed the impulse of mine, and offered my hand unsolicited, unsanctified, by the approbation of a parent or a friend. Ah, Madeline, you may well blush for your weakness."

Lest she should betray that weakness, she determined not to stay another minute with him, and bidding him a hasty adieu, she walked on. De Sevignie in a few minutes followed her, but he continued many by her side, ere he again spoke to her; at last he stopped, and taking her hand to detain her—"Madeline, (said he, as if hitherto absorbed in profound meditation,) do you think, if I could render my situation more prosperous than it at present is, that your friends, if you had the generosity to desire it, would permit our union."

"I do (cried Madeline, hesitating, yet not able to repress this acknowledgment of tenderness,) I think they would not oppose what would contribute to my happiness."

A sudden smile, the smile of rapture, illumined the countenance of de Sevignie; he clasped her hands in his; he raised them to heaven.—"Oh, what transport! (he said) to be able to contribute to your happiness; grant, heavenly powers, such blessedness may yet be mine! May I detain you Madeline, a few minutes longer to acquaint you with the plan, which I have just conceived, for conquering the obstacles that at present impede our wishes." Madeline could not reply in the negative, and de Sevignie began:

"To another"—said he.

At this instant an approaching step was heard, and in the next, the shrill voice of Floretta, calling upon Madeline.

Provoked by this interruption, de Sevignie attempted to lead Madeline amongst the trees which bordered the path; but though as much disappointed as he could be, she resisted the effort.

"No, (said she) I cannot go, 'tis the Countess, I am convinced, that has sent after me, and she would be terrified if I could not be found; besides if her servant discovered me trying to avoid her, what might she not say. Some other time must do for the explanation which you were about giving, and which I will confess, you could scarcely be more anxious to utter than I to hear."

"What time, (asked de Sevignie) I shall be all impatience, all suspense, till we meet again; to-morrow evening you may surely come hither."

"Perhaps," said Madeline.

"No perhaps, (cried de Sevignie) you must give me a positive answer."

"Well then, you may be confident, if in my power I will come."

"Adieu, then," cried he; again pressing her hand to his lips, then suddenly darting into the nearest path, he was out of sight in a moment.

Madeline paused on the spot where he had left her, to reflect on all that he had said, and congratulate herself on the prospect of felicity which was now opening to her view.

Her pleasing meditation was soon, however, interrupted by the appearance of Floretta. "Well, I am sure, (cried she,) I am glad I have found you. Lord bless my soul, Mam'selle, how can you venture into such lonely places by yourself. I am sure nothing but compulsion could make me do so."

"I hope none has been used to-night," said Madeline, as she proceeded with her towards the chateau.

"That there has, indeed, nothing but the absolute commands of my Lady could have made me come hither; I wonder, I am sure, what could make her fix on me to look for you. She might have known it was not proper to send any girl by herself into such wild places."

"Your Lady knew there was no danger, (said Madeline,) as none but her own peasants and servants are about them."

"Why, I don't say Mam'selle, there is any danger of meeting thieves, but there is of meeting much worse. Ah, Mam'selle, you know well enough what I mean; and you must be either very incredulous or very hardy, to venture near the grotto, after the horrid stories you have heard in the chateau about it; besides those stories, I could tell you others of it, which if you heard, would frighten you so much, that I dare say you would not be able to move."

"If you think they would have that effect upon me, pray don't tell them at present, (said Madeline,) for I want to make haste to the chateau."

"Indeed I don't intend to do so, (cried Floretta,) the very telling them would frighten me, and I am sure I am sufficiently terrified already."

"Why did you not get some one to accompany you," asked Madeline.

"A likely thing indeed, that any one would accompany me in the dark to such places; not but I tried, I can assure you. The butler was the first I asked; but no truly, he was getting his knives and spoons ready for supper. Then I entreated Mr. Jacques, the coachman, but he was just going to visit the horses; and as to the footmen, I know I might as well try to bring the pillars of the hall along with me. I tried the maids also, but one was going to settle the chambers, and another wanted to help the cook to get supper ready; and another—but in short they had all some frivolous excuse or other."

"Well, (said Madeline,) though you did come alone, you met with nothing to frighten you."

"That shall never prevail on me, however, to venture again to such a place by myself, if I can help it."

By this time they had reached the chateau, and Madeline being informed by a servant, whom she met in the hall, that the Countess was in the supper parlour, directly repaired thither.

CHAP. II.

Let my tears thank you, for I cannot speak,

– – – – – – – – – – – – – – – And if I could,

Words were not made to vent such thoughts as mine.

Dryden.

"You have taken a long walk to-night, my dear, (said the Countess, as she entered,) I really was beginning to grow a little uneasy."

"I am concerned I caused you any uneasiness, Madam, (cried Madeline,) I hope you will forgive my doing so. I shall take care in future not to stay out so late."

The Countess answered her with her usual gracious sweetness, and they both sat down to supper, which was served immediately after her return.

The revived hopes of Madeline had re-animated her countenance with all its usual vivacity. The glow upon her cheek, the lustre of her eye, the smile that played about her mouth; the ready cheerfulness with which she entered into conversation, and the unusual length of her walk; altogether contributed to convince the penetrating mind of the Countess, that in this walk, something uncommonly interesting had occurred; and what she believed that something to be, may easily be imagined. Considering Madeline as she did,—a sacred deposit, and exclusive of that consideration, deeply interested about her from her innocence and sweetness, she deemed it absolutely necessary, to enquire into what had past in the interview, which she was convinced had taken place between her and de Sevignie. Well knowing that the eager eye of youth and passion, too often overlooks those dangers, which strike the cooler and more experienced one of age.

"Your walk to-night, my dear Madeline, (said she with a smile, after the things were removed and the servants withdrawn) was as pleasant, I hope, as it was long."

Her smile, and the expressive glance which accompanied it, assured the conscious heart of Madeline, that the Countess suspected it had not been a solitary one; and her face was immediately crimsoned over: yet Madeline never had an idea of carrying on any proceedings against the knowledge of the Countess. She had determined within her own mind, the moment she was acquainted with the plan of de Sevignie, to unfold to her every circumstance, every hope, relative to him. The reason therefore of her present agitation, was a fear, that a premature discovery might make the Countess imagine she had meant to carry on a clandestine correspondence, and, consequently lessen her in her esteem.

"I see, Madam, (said she, after the pause of a minute, bashfully raising her eyes from the ground) I see that you suspect something, and I acknowledge you are right in doing so; but oh! dearest madam, do not think me ungrateful, do not deem me imprudent, do not suppose to chance alone you owe the discovery of my thoughts or situation; I only deferred acquainting you with both; I only delayed opening my heart to your view, till I had something more satisfactory than at present to inform you of."

"Unbosom it now, (said the Countess) "and trust me, my dear Madeline, I would not desire the communication, did I not mean to take as great an interest in your affairs as a parent would. Unbosom your heart to me as to a Mother; and be assured, if my advice, my assistance, my friendship, can in any degree forward your happiness, I shall derive real satisfaction myself from doing so."

Thus kindly urged, Madeline rather rejoiced than regretted being surprised into the relation; for she had long sighed, though withheld by diffidence from desiring it; for the counsel of a person more conversant, more experienced than herself in the intricacies of the human heart. To elucidate every circumstance which had happened in her interview with de Sevignie, it was requisite to mention those which had past at V– – –.

She began, but it was with the involuntary hesitation of modesty; and from the same impulse she tried to pass over, as lightly as possible, the pain she had experienced on de Sevignie's account; but though her language might be unimpassioned, her looks plainly indicated what her sufferings had been.

Her relation ended, the Countess sat many minutes without speaking, as if absorbed in profound meditation. She then broke the silence, by thanking Madeline with the most gracious benignancy for the confidence she had reposed in her.

"Your narrative, my dear Madeline, (she cried) confirms the opinion I entertained, since the evening I saw you together, of the strength of your attachment for de Sevignie;—nay, do not be confused, my dear; love, excited by merit, we have no reason to be ashamed of.

"It will please you, no doubt, to hear, that I think his attachment as tender as your own; but it is one, with which his reason is evidently at variance. Why it is so, the latter part of his conversation this evening seems to me to explain. A distressed situation has hitherto pointed out the necessity of his trying to conquer his passion; but I own it appears to me strange and mysterious that a man of his elegant appearance and enlightened education, should be in narrow circumstances and obscurity. If however, he can properly account for this obscurity and want of fortune; if the one proceeds neither from ignoble birth nor dishonourable conduct; and the other from no idle extravagance, no degrading folly, we will not wait for the realization of his plan, be it what it may, to realize his happiness. You are perhaps surprised (she continued) to hear me speak in this positive manner, as if I had an absolute power to dispose of you; but know my dear, that in me your father vested such a power. As soon as I understood your situation with regard to de Sevignie, I communicated to him all I thought concerning it, and requested his advice; he answered me immediately, and begged in future, I might never apply to him on the subject, but depend entirely on my own judgment; he entreated me to do this, he said, from a firm conviction that I would watch over you with as much solicitude and scarcely less tenderness than he would himself. His confidence was not, I trust, misplaced."

Madeline would have spoken in the fullness of her heart, but the Countess motioned her to silence.

"To contribute (she resumed) to the happiness of his child, will, as I have already said, impart the truest satisfaction to me; should we therefore, receive from de Sevignie the satisfactory explanation we desire, I shall immediately give to the adopted daughter of my care, that portion, which from the first moment I took her under my protection, I designed for her; a portion, which though not sufficient to purchase her all the luxuries, is amply so to procure her all the comforts of life; and, to a soul gentle and unassuming as is my Madeline's, those comforts will, I think, yield more real felicity than all its luxuries or dissipations could do. Should the little portion I can give her, be a means of procuring for her that felicity which she deserves and I wish her;—blessed—thrice blessed, shall I consider the wealth consecrated to such a purpose."

She stopt, overcome by her own energy; Madeline was many minutes before she could speak; but she took the hand of her benefactress, she pressed it to her quivering lip, her heaving heart, and dropped upon it tears of gratitude, affection, and esteem.

"Oh, Madam! (she at length exclaimed) well might you bid me unbosom my heart to you as to a mother; sure, had I been blessed with one, I could not have experienced more tenderness; language is poor, is inadequate to express my feelings."

"Then do not attempt expressing them, (said the Countess, with her usual benignant smile) but let us resume our, to you to be sure, very uninteresting conversation. You say, to-morrow evening you promised to meet de Sevignie."

"Yes, Madam, (replied Madeline) with some little hesitation."

"Inform him then, (continued the Countess) that you have made me your confidant, also what I said concerning him, and my intentions; if he can give the required explanation; but remember Madeline, you tell him, that it must be an explanation so clear,—so full, that not a shadow of doubt shall remain after it; that, except every thing mysterious is fully elucidated, Madeline Clermont and he, must in future be strangers to each other."

"I shall obey you in every respect, Madam, (replied Madeline) and indeed (unable to conceal the high opinion she entertained of de Sevignie's virtues) I have not a doubt but we shall receive as satisfactory an explanation as we could desire."

"Heaven grant you may, (cried the Countess) but till you do—till there is some certainty of your being united to de Sevignie, I shall not again mention him to your father, who now imagines from a late letter of mine, that every hope relative to him is over; and I will not undeceive him, except I can do so with pleasure to him and myself."

They soon after this separated for the night; but not to rest did Madeline retire to her chamber: joy is often as wakeful as sorrow; and joy of the most rapturous kind she now experienced; alternately she traversed her apartment, alternately seated herself to repeat all that had past between her and the Countess, to ruminate over her felicity; felicity which now appeared insured; for that de Sevignie could give such an explanation as would rather raise than lessen him in the estimation of her friend, she did not harbour the smallest doubt of.

So sanguine is the youthful heart—so ready to believe that what it wishes will happen. Alas, how doubly sharp does this readiness render the barb of disappointment.

Oh, how great was the raptures of Madeline, to think she should be enabled to put de Sevignie in possession of a competency; every feeling of generosity of sensibility, was gratified by the idea, and she implored the choicest blessings of heaven for the benevolent woman, who had been the means of occasioning her such happiness. "May heaven (she cried, with uplifted hands) remove from her heart all sorrow, as she removes it from the hearts of others."

How light was the step—how bright was the eye—how gay was the smile of Madeline when she descended the next morning to the breakfast parlour, where she already found the Countess seated; the appearance of every thing seemed changed, the awful gloom which had so long pervaded the apartments, was banished; and in the landscape before the windows Madeline now discovered beauties which had before escaped her notice. The weather had been remarkably fine for some weeks, yet Madeline thought the sun had not shone so bright for many days as on the present.

Such is the magic effect of joy, which, like the touch of an enchanter, can raise a thousand charms around us.

With her friend she took a delightful ride about some of the most delightful parts of the domain after breakfast; and the remainder of the day was past in social converse together.

As soon as twilight began to shroud the earth, the Countess dismissed her to her appointment. "Do you think, Madeline, (cried she with a smile, as she was retiring from the room) it would be amiss if I ordered Jerome to lay an additional plate on the supper table tonight."

"Perhaps not, Madam," replied Madeline, blushing. She thought indeed, it was probable that de Sevignie would immediately wish to express his gratitude to the Countess.

CHAP. III.

My lab'ring heart, that swells with indignation,

Heaves to discharge its burden, that once done

The busy thing shall rest within its cell.

Rowe.

Expecting every moment to behold him, she took the path to the grotto; but reached it without having that expectation fulfilled. Surprised and disappointed she stopped before it, irresolute whether to return to the chateau directly or wait a few minutes there; she at last resolved on the latter, and seated herself on the moss covered stone at its entrance. The deep gloom of the grotto made her involuntarily shudder whenever she cast a glance within it, but in spite of terror she continued on her seat, till the dark shades of night began to involve every object, and warned her to return home: as she arose for that purpose an idea darted into her mind, that illness or some dreadful accident, had alone prevented de Sevignie from keeping an appointment so eagerly desired, so tenderly solicited, and regretting the time she had wasted in expectation, she now rather flew than walked to the chateau, in order to entreat the Countess to send a servant to V– – –, to enquire about him; she had not proceeded many yards, however, when her progress was impeded by the object who had caused her apprehensions and solicitude. So little did she now expect to see him, that as he slowly emerged from amidst the trees, she started back, as if he had been the last creature in the world she had thought of seeing. Ere she could recover sufficiently from her agitation to speak, de Sevignie, rather negligently bowing, said, "he hoped he had not been the means of keeping her out to so late an hour."

"The officers (continued he, but without looking at her) to whose hospitality and politeness I have been so much indebted, since my residence at V– – –, insisted on my dining with them to-day, and though I wished and tried to leave them at an early hour, they would not suffer me to do so, nor to depart at the one I did, had I not promised to return immediately to them."

The coldness of his manner, the frivolous excuse he made for his want of punctuality, and the intention he avowed of quitting her directly, without any reference to their conversation of the preceding night, all struck Madeline with a conviction, that his sentiments were totally changed since that conversation had taken place: for a change so sudden, so unaccountable, tenderness suggested an enquiry, but pride repeled it, and she would instantly have quitted him with every indication of the disdain he seemed to merit, had her agitation permitted her to move."

"Will you allow me, Mademoiselle Clermont (cried de Sevignie, still looking rather from her) to attend you to the castle, 'ere I bid you adieu; and also to hope, that at some other time, I may have the honour of seeing you."

"Never—(said Madeline, recovering her voice, and summoning all her spirits to her aid) never—no sir.—No, de Sevignie, except in the presence or the house of the Countess de Merville, never more will I permit you to see me."

"In her house, (repeated de Sevignie with quickness, and turning his eyes upon her.) How could I attempt seeing you in the house of the Countess, unacquainted as I am with her."

"The Countess (replied Madeline) would never be displeased at my seeing any one in her house whom I considered as my friend. Besides—besides—(added she, hesitating, doubtful whether to stop or to go on) besides—(after the pause of a minute) she gave permission to have you introduced to her."

"When, on what account did she give that permission; (demanded de Sevignie, with yet greater quickness then he had before spoken) did she discover, or did you tell her that we had met."

"I told her (said Madeline, with firmness, and looking steadily at him.) The Countess is my friend;—she is more. She is the guardian to whose care my father has consigned me, and concealment to her would be criminal. I told her we had met. I told her every circumstance of that meeting; every circumstance prior to it; I communicated every thought, I revealed my whole soul."

"I admire your prudence," exclaimed de Sevignie, in an accent which denoted vexation, whilst the melancholy of his countenance gave way to a dark frown, and the paleness of his cheek to a deep crimson.

"I rejoice at it, (cried Madeline) my friend will strengthen my weakness, will confirm my resolves, will give me a clue to discover the dark and intricate mazes of the human heart."

Her language seemed to penetrate the soul of de Sevignie, he turned from her with emotion, then as abruptly turning to her again, "for what purpose (asked he) did the Countess give you permission to introduce me to her."

"For the purpose—" Madeline paused, she had been on the point of saying, for the purpose of promoting our happiness, but timely checked herself. And ah, thought she at the moment, from the altered manner of de Sevignie, I cannot believe that his happiness could be promoted by the intentions of the Countess.

"Tell me, I entreat, I conjure you," said de Sevignie, with earnestness.

Madeline hesitated.—Yet 'tis but justice (she thought) to my friend, to de Sevignie himself, to confess her intentions; if the alteration in his manner is occasioned by finding the plan he recently conceived impracticable, the divulgment of her generous intentions will again set all to rights; catching at this idea, and flattering herself it was a just one, she briefly related the conversation which had past between her and the Countess; de Sevignie listened with fixed attention, but continued silent many minutes after she had ceased to speak, as if in a profound reverie; then suddenly raising his eyes from the ground he fastened them on her with an expression of the deepest melancholy, and thus addressed her:

"Great (cried he) is my regret, greater than language can express, at being unable to avail myself of the high honour the Countess designed me; but though unable to avail myself of it; though unable to profit by her noble her generous intentions, my inability to do so, has not suppressed my gratitude for them.

"Why, why, that inability exists, I cannot explain; but let me do myself the justice of saying, that candour would not err in putting the most favourable construction on it. In this moment, when declaring the renunciation of every hope relative to you, I would apologize for the presumption, the impetuosity, the inconsistencies of my conduct to you. Could I do so as I wish, but as that is impossible, I must, without pleading for it, cast myself upon the sweetness of your disposition for forgiveness. I often, before this period, declared I would never more intrude into your presence; I now solemnly repeat that declaration, for I am now thoroughly convinced of the folly of my former conduct, and he who is sensible of his error, yet perseveres in it, is guilty of weakness in the extreme; such weakness is not mine. In future, I mean to avoid every pursuit, to fly from every thought which can enervate my mind."

His voice faltered, and a deep sigh burst from him. "farewell, Mademoiselle Clermont, (said he, after the pause of a moment) too long have I detained—too long have I persecuted you—with my last adieu receive my best wishes for your happiness, may they be more availing than those I formed for my own." He cast another lingering look upon her, then turning into a winding path, disappeared in a moment.

Every flattering hope, every pleasing expectation of Madeline's, was again crushed, without the smallest prospect of their being ever more revived; like the unsubstantial pageants of a dream they faded, nor left a wreck behind. Oh, what a vacuum did their loss occasion in the heart of Madeline: at first, she almost fancied she had dreamt the conversation of the preceding night, and that it was only now, the illusions of that dream were flying from her. But by degrees, her thoughts grew more composed, and then every wild or soothing suggestion of fancy died away, and she began to reconsider the conduct of de Sevignie. His last words had not been able to make her think favourably of it. "No, (she cried) I am convinced, without some motive for doing so, which he durst not avow, he never would have with-held the confidence he was so kindly invited to repose in the most amiable of women. And yet—(she continued, after pausing some minutes) he with-held it, perhaps, not from having any improper motives to make him wish concealment, but because his sentiments were altered respecting me.—Though no, (she proceeded, after another pause) that could not be the case; 'tis impossible in one night so great an alteration could have taken place. 'Tis evident then, too evident, that a cause exists for concealment, which he either fears or is ashamed to acknowledge; and also, that his coldness this evening, sprung from a wish of trying his power over me, for they say neglect is the test of affection;—but de Sevignie, your artifice caused you no triumph, and never—never more, shall you have an opportunity of exercising it on me; like you, I will in future avoid every pursuit, fly from every thought which can enervate my mind."

The striking of the castle clock now reached her ear, and she hastily walked to the chateau; alarmed on finding the usual supper hour over, least she should by her long stay, have again given uneasiness to the bosom of her friend.

On reaching the chateau, a servant informed her, that the Countess was in her dressing-room: slowly Madeline ascended to it; she felt ready to sink with confusion at the idea of the mortifying explanation she must make to the Countess. "She will think (cried she) that I have hitherto been the dupe of my own fancy; and that de Sevignie, but in my own imagination, has been amiable." She paused at the door for a minute, from a vain hope that by so doing, she should regain some composure.

"Well, (said her friend, smiling as she entered) I find, Madeline, by your long stay, that you could not withstand the pleasures of a tête-a-tête; but where is the Chevalier de Sevignie, (she continued, on seeing Madeline shut the door) were you afraid to bring him, least I should rival you."

"He is gone, Madam," answered Madeline, in a faint voice, as she sat down on the nearest chair, unable any longer to support herself.

"Gone! (repeated the Countess, in a tone of amazement) but bless me, my dear, you look very pale, are you ill."

"No madam," Madeline attempted to say, but her voice failed her, and she burst into tears.

"Gracious heaven! (exclaimed the Countess, rising, and going to her,) you terrify me beyond expression. Madeline, my love, what is the matter."

"Nothing, madam, (replied Madeline) only, only, (sobbing as if her heart would break) that I think, I believe—the Chevalier de Sevignie, is not quite so amiable as I once imagined."

"Try to compose yourself and speak intelligently my dear, (said the Countess) for I cannot support, much longer, the fears you excite." The tears she shed somewhat relieved the full heart of Madeline; and the Countess taking a seat by her, she was able in a few minutes, to relate the conduct of de Sevignie, and acknowledge the sentiments it had inspired her with.

"His behaviour is strange, is inexplicable, indeed (said the Countess) and I perfectly agree with you in thinking, that he is an unworthy character; too undeserving to have an effort made to solve the mystery which he has wrapped himself in; had he any sensibility, had he any nobleness, he never would have wounded your innocent, your ingenuous heart as he has done.

Had he respected, had he regarded you properly, he never would have regretted your making me your confidant; that regret confirms my belief, notwithstanding his solemn protestations of seeing you no more, that he still entertains designs concerning you; designs, I am sorry to shock your nature by saying so, of a dishonourable nature. Should he therefore, again throw himself in your way, as I apprehend, shun him, I entreat, I conjure you, my Madeline; as you value your happiness, your honour, the peace of your friends, the esteem of the world."

"Ah, madam, (cried Madeline) I hope you do not doubt my resolution;—my tenderness is wounded, my pride is roused, and thinking as I do of him, could I now permit an interview with de Sevignie, I should be lessened in my own eyes."

"I do not doubt your resolution, my love, (replied the Countess, kissing her cheek) and I beg you to excuse the caution, the unnecessary caution of age. (She now expressed her pleasure at not having written to Clermont, since things had taken so different a turn from what was expected.) I rejoice to think, (continued she) that he will not know how unworthy de Sevignie was of the kindness he showed him."

Madeline sighed deeply at those words, the violence of offended pride was abated, and in this moment of decreased resentment, an emotion of softness again stole o'er her heart, and made her regret having exposed de Sevignie, by her own animadversions, to the still severer ones of the Countess. She regretted, because from this returning softness she was tempted to doubt his deserving them, and to impute the inconsistencies of his conduct, to difficulties too dreadful perhaps to relate; and she shuddered at the idea of having, in addition to his other misfortunes, drawn upon him the unmerited imputation of baseness; but from this idea, torturing in the extreme, reflection soon relieved her, for when she re-considered his conduct, she could not help thinking he deserved that imputation.

"Yet is it possible, (she cried to herself) that de Sevignie, he who appeared possessed of the nicest delicacy, the most exalted honour, the steadiest principles of rectitude; is it possible that he can be unamiable? Alas, why cannot I doubt it still;—but no, let me rather rejoice than regret not being able to do so; rejoice, that passion no longer spreads a mist before my eyes: to endeavour to doubt his unworthiness now, would be to try and blind my reason, and weaken my resolves."

But notwithstanding what she said, she still fluctuated between resentment and tenderness, candour and distrust,—alternately acquitted, alternately condemned him.

With the utmost gentleness, the Countess tried to sooth and steal her from her sorrow; she did not, like a rigid censor, chide her for weakness in indulging it. She knew what it was to have the projects of youthful hope overthrown; the anguish which attends the shock of a first disappointment, and that time must be allowed to conquer it. That time, aided by reason, would heal the wound which had been given to the gentle bosom of her Madeline, she trusted and believed.

On retiring to her chamber, Madeline could not suppress her tears at the contrast she drew between her present feelings and those of the preceding night; and again she began to fancy de Sevignie more unfortunate than unamiable; when suddenly recollecting her resolution of expeling this idea, she hastily tried to divert her thoughts from it.

"That we are separated, I am assured, (cried she) and to ascertain whether I have reason to esteem or condemn him, (though soothing perhaps to my feelings to think the former) can now be of little consequence to me."

CHAP. IV.

Ah where is now each image gay

The hand of Fairy fancy wove,

The painted spring, elizium gay

The babbling rill, the cultur'd grove.

Her night was restless and unhappy.

"Ah, (sighed she) how differently did I imagine it would have ended." Pale, trembling, dejected, the very reverse of what she had been the preceding morning, she descended to the breakfast parlour, where her melancholy was, if possible, increased by observing the Countess's, who either from sympathy for her, or from a return of her secret uneasiness, or perhaps from a mixture of both, appeared languid and dejected. She tried, however, to appear cheerful but the efforts she made for that purpose were too faint to succeed, and unable either to beguile her own sadness, or that of her young companion, the day wore heavily away. As they sat, at its decline, by an open window in one of the parlours, and beheld the sun sinking behind the western hills, a deep and involuntary sigh heaved the bosom of Madeline, at reflecting, how very different her feelings were now, from what they had been on the same hour the preceding evening.

The Countess interpreted her sigh, and taking her hand, pressed it between her's. "My dear Madeline! (she exclaimed) my sweet girl, it grieves my heart to see you thus depressed. Your present disappointment, I allow, is great; but reflect, and let the reflection compose your mind: how much greater it would have been, how much more poignantly you must have felt it, had you married de Sevignie, and then, when too late, found him to be the worthless character you are now apprehensive he is.

"Few there are, my dear Madeline, whose situations, however bad, might not be rendered worse; we should therefore try not to deserve an augmentation of calamity, by bearing that inflicted with resignation.

"Why calamity is the prevalent lot of humanity—why our virtuous hopes are so often overthrown—why the race is not always to the swift, nor the battle to the strong; both reason and religion teaches us will be explained hereafter; in the mean time, let no disappointment, no vicissitudes, however painful and unmerited we may consider them, ever tempt us to doubt, or to arraign the goodness and wisdom of that Being, from whose hand proceeds alike the cup of good and evil.

"Think not, (she continued) as too many perhaps might do, that I preach what I do not practise; or, that my lessons are those of a woman, who herself, untried by disappointment, can exhort others to that submission which she never knew the difficulty of acquiring. This, believe me my dear Madeline, is not the case; I know what it is: when we extend our hand for the rose to gather the thorns—when we open our bosom to hope, to admit despair—when we bask in the sunshine, to be surprised by the storm, and have it burst with fury o'er our unsheltered heads."

"Oh, from every adverse storm may you be sheltered!" exclaimed Madeline, with uplifted eyes.

As she spoke, Father Bertrand, confessor to the Countess, and officiating priest to her household, stopped before the window: he belonged to the community which has been already mentioned, and frequently rambled at the close of day from his convent, to the wild solitudes of the wood surrounding the chateau. He was upwards of sixty, and one of those interesting figures which cannot be viewed by sensibility without pity and veneration; his noble height still gave an idea of what his form had been, when unbent by infirmity; and that form, like a fine ruin, excited the involuntary sigh of regret for the devastations time had made upon it. His hairs were white, and thinly scattered over a forehead, more deeply indented by care than age; and the sad, the solemn expression of his countenance, denoted his being a son of sorrow, and proved his thoughts were continually bent upon another world, where alone he could receive consolation for the miseries of this.

"How fares the good ladies of the castle this evening," cried he, leaning upon his staff, as he stopped before the window.

"Why not so well, father, (replied the Countess) but that we might be better; here we are, like two philosophers descanting upon the vanities of life; and when women talk philosophy, the world says, they must either be indisposed or out of temper."

"Well, I shan't pretend to contradict what the world says, (cried the good man, smiling) nor since so well employed shall I longer interrupt you, ladies."

The Countess asked him to come in and take some refreshment, but he refused, and after chatting a little longer, rambled away to the wildest parts of the wood.

"The story of Father Bertrand, (said the Countess, as he retired) is a striking proof to all that know it, that we should never be too eager in the pursuit of our wishes. As it is short, and rather applicable to what we have been talking about, I will relate it.—

"He was son to a gentleman of good family, but still better fortune, who lived in the vicinity of this chateau: the large patrimony he was to inherit, made his parents anxious to give him such an education as should teach him to enjoy it with moderation and elegance.

"After learning every thing he could learn in his native country, he was sent abroad to improve himself by visiting various courts, and acquiring that knowledge of men and manners, which is so requisite for those destined to mix in the great world, and which in a fixed residence it is almost impossible to obtain. In the course of his travels he paid a visit to England; and here, in a small town in that kingdom, he became acquainted with a young lady, who at an early age was left an orphan and a dependant on an old capricious aunt, whose only motive for keeping her in the family, was, that on her she could vent that spleen and ill-nature which no one else would bear from her. The fair orphan and Bertrand frequently met each other at different houses; and the beauty of her person, the soft dejection of her manner, and the patient sweetness with which she bore her situation, soon gained a complete conquest over his heart; nor did hers retain its liberty.

"The declaration of his attachment Bertrand would have accompanied by an offer of his hand, had not duty and respect to his parents prevented his taking such a step without their knowledge and approbation: he wrote to them for their consent; but instead of receiving it, he received a pressing entreaty to return home immediately; and also an acknowledgment from them at the same time, that they could not bear the idea of his marrying a foreigner and a protestant, as was the lady he paid his addresses to. Bertrand did not attempt to write again, or disregard their entreaty; his duty to them, and his consideration for his own happiness, prompted him to return home without delay, for he knew their hearts, and was convinced, when he once pleaded his cause in person, he would not be refused: calming the disquietude of Caroline by this assurance, and pledging to her vows of unalterable love and fidelity, he embarked for his native country, and as he expected, succeeded in his suit. It was then the depth of winter, and his parents dreading his undertaking a voyage in that inclement season, conjured him to defer, till the ensuing spring, going to England for Caroline, whose marriage they insisted on having celebrated in their own house, from an idea, that if their son was married according to the forms of her church, (which they knew would be the case if his nuptials took place in her country) some heavy calamity would befall him in consequence of that circumstance.

"But the wishes of Bertrand were too impetuous to comply with theirs; he rallied their fears, opposed their arguments, and returned, without delay, to England. The friends of Caroline; for her friends increased when fortune began to smile, now tried to detain her and her lover in England, as his parents had tried to detain him in France, till a more favourable season, but they tried in vain; the youthful pair dreaded no dangers, or rather overlooked the idea of any, in their impatience to quit a place which retarded the wishes of one, and brought continually to the mind of the other, a thousand cruel slights and mortifications. They accordingly embarked, elated with hope and expectation; the ship was bound to Normandy, near whose coast Bertrand had some friends settled, who promised, on his landing there, to accompany him to his father's house, in order to be present at his wedding; the weather continued favourable till they had nearly reached their destined port, when it suddenly changed, as if to mock their hopes, and teach the heart of man no certain felicity can be expected in this life. The sailors endeavoured to make for the shore, but in vain, the storm raged with violence, and after tossing about a considerable time the ship at length bulged upon a rock; the long-boat was immediately thrown out, though from the fury of the waves it afforded but little chance of deliverance: this chance, however, was eagerly seized—Bertrand calling upon every Saint in heaven to preserve her, bore the fainting Caroline into it, the sailors crowded in numbers after them, and it almost directly upset. The shock of that moment separated Bertrand and Caroline for ever in this world,—the waves cast him upon a rock, from whence, almost lifeless, he was taken up by some fisherman and conveyed to a hut; here his friends, whom the expectation of his arrival had drawn to the coast, discovered him. Their care, their assiduity, soon restored his senses—but with what horrors was that restoration accompanied,—the deepest moans, the most piercing, the most frantic cries, were all, for a long time, he had the power of uttering: he then insisted on being taken to the waterside, and here attention alone prevented his committing an act of desperation, by plunging himself amidst the waves which had entombed his love! one day and one night, he sought her on the "sea beat shore;" the second morning her body was discovered on the strand; but how altered, by the cloaths alone it was known to be that of the Caroline he had lost. Kneeling on the earth, Bertrand solemnly vowed, by the chaste spirit of her o'er whose remains he wept, never to know another earthly love, but to devote the remainder of his days to heaven. His friends conveyed him and the body to his parents, who endeavoured to prevail on him to cancel his vow, but in vain, and as soon as the necessary formalities could be gone through, he took the religious habit.

"His parents, disappointed in their hopes relative to him—their hopes of seeing a little smiling race of his prattling about them, pined away, and were soon laid beside the bones of her, who had been the innocent cause of their trouble.

"Bertrand then gave up the house of his forefathers, and the greatest part of the fortune appertaining to it, to a near and distant relation; by this time the turbulence of his grief had abated, and he soon after became, by his benevolence and strict, but unostentatious piety, one of the most respected members of the community he had entered into: his story interested me, and on the death of the old monk, who had been my confessor and chaplain, I appointed him to those offices. But though time and reason have meliorated his sorrows, there are periods when all their violence is revived.

"When the rough winds of winter howl round his habitation, and bend the tall trees of the mountains by which it is surrounded, 'tis then the remembrance of past events swells his heart with agony; 'tis then he thinks he hears the plaintive voice of Caroline mingled in the blast, and fancies he beholds her shivering spirit stalking through the gloom, and beckoning him away.

"The wedding garments, which the pride and fondness of his mother prepared for his intended bride; the picture, which, on their parting in England, she gave him, he still treasures, as the hermit would treasure the relics of a saint. I have beheld them—I have wept over them—I have exclaimed within myself, as I have gazed on these mementos of lost happiness—'Oh, children of the dust! what folly to place your hopes, your wishes, on a world whose changes are so sudden; whose happiness, even while it appears in our view, even while we stretch out our arms to enfold it, flies never to return.'

"Oh, Madeline! as Bertrand has shown me the ornaments designed for his Caroline, and told me their hapless tale, while the big tear of tender recollection and poignant regret has rolled down his cheek, I could only quiet the strong emotions of my heart, by saying, like the holy man himself:

'Father of heaven! thy decrees must surely be for the wisest purposes, else thou wouldst not thus afflict thy creatures; thy will, therefore, not our's, be done.' The sorrows of Bertrand (resumed the Countess, after pausing a minute) were heightened, by thinking himself accessary to them, in consequence of not regarding either the supplications of his parents or friends for postponing his voyage till a more settled season: so true is it, that those who yield to impetuous passions, will sooner or later have reason to repent doing so."

The mind of Madeline was insensibly calmed, and drawn from its own cares by the discourse of the Countess; for the precept of wisdom, the tale of instruction is ever pleasing to the children of virtue.

But with that quick transition of feeling, so peculiar to the youthful mind, she felt, with returning composure, a kind of distaste to a world, which daily experience convinced her teemed with calamity.

Soon after the Countess had concluded her little narrative, she requested Madeline to take her lute—a request, which Madeline attempted not to refuse. In the present state of her mind sad or solemn strains were alone congenial to her feelings, and she selected a hymn to the Supreme Being, celebrating his goodness, and the happiness prepared for those hereafter, who patiently support the trials of this life. Just depressed by a conviction of its sufferings, Madeline derived a kind of divine consolation from words, which gave so consoling an assurance of their being rewarded. At first her voice was weak, and her touch faint and tremulous; but by degrees, as if animated by the subject, her voice regained its strength, and her hand its steadiness; and high on the swelling notes her soul seemed ascending to that heaven, whose glories appeared opening to her view, when a deep sigh, or rather sob, suddenly startled her. Her hand involuntarily rested on the strings, o'er which it was lightly sweeping, and she cast an eager glance towards the Countess. How great was her surprise—her consternation, to see her fallen back, pale, and weeping in her chair. The lute instantly dropped from Madeline, and starting up, she instinctively flung her arms round her benefactress, exclaiming, "Good heavens! Madam, what is the matter." Then, without waiting for a reply, she was flying from the room for assistance, when the voice of the Countess made her stop.

"Return, my dear, (said she, raising herself on her chair) I am now better. It was only my spirits were overcome. Your solemn strains awoke in my mind recollections of the most painful nature; the hymn you were playing was a favourite of my lord's. The evening preceding the illness which terminated his life, as pale and languid he sat by me in this very room, he requested me to play it for him; his words, his looks, while he listened, as afterwards considered by me, have since convinced me that he knew his end was approaching, and that he fixed on this hymn as a kind of requiem for his departing spirit. In that light I have ever since regarded it."

Madeline shuddered; she thought there was a ghastly paleness in the countenance of the Countess. "Oh, Madam! (said she), why did you not prevent my playing it?"

"Because, my love, (replied the Countess) though it pains, it also pleases me. I am now better (she continued), and will retire to the chapel for a little time."

"Ah! Madam, (said Madeline), permit me to accompany you tonight, for perhaps you may be again taken ill." "No, my love, (cried the Countess), there is no danger of my being so. I thank you for your kind solicitude about me, but I cannot let you come with me; my composure I know will be perfectly restored by visiting the chapel. Tell Floretta, therefore, to bring me my scarf."—Madeline obeyed, but with a repugnance she could not conquer,—and the Countess wrapping it about her, departed, assuring Madeline she would hasten back to supper, and would then expect to find her cheerful.

Madeline, left to herself, strolled out upon the lawn. It was now the dusky hour of twilight, and solitude and silence reigned around. Her thoughts, no longer diverted by conversation, again reverted to past subjects, and deeply ruminating on them, she continued to walk till it grew quite dark: she then returned to the castle, and not finding the Countess in the room where they had parted, she rung for a servant, to enquire whether she was yet come back; the man replied she was not. Her long stay, after promising to return so soon, filled the mind of Madeline with terror, lest her delay should be occasioned by a return of her illness: and going directly to Agatha, she communicated her apprehensions to her, and entreated her to accompany her to the monastery—an entreaty the faithful creature readily complied with.

CHAP. V.

The wand'ring breath was on the wing to part,

Weak was the pulse, and hardly heav'd the heart.

As they proceeded thither, Agatha expressed her regret at her lady's persevering in visiting the chapel. "She is there, (said she) encompassed by the dead, and remote from human aid, if such should be required; often and often have I shuddered at the idea of the dangers to which she exposed herself by going thither alone; and often have I taken the liberty of entreating her not to do so, but without effect: she has a particular pleasure in its solitude, and in praying where not only the bones of her ancestors, but those of her husband and children rest."

"I own (cried Madeline) I am surprised she can go, at the lonely hours she does, to so dreary a place, which appears to me surrounded by every thing that can appal the imagination."

"For my part (exclaimed Agatha) nothing in the world could tempt me to do so;—Lord! I should be scared out of my very senses by apprehension, if I stopped a few minutes in it after it was dark. Holy Virgin! (cried she suddenly, as they advanced down the valley) protect us;—nothing but love for my lady could tempt me to go on, this place is so frightful."

Madeline could not wonder at the terror she betrayed; the scene was calculated to inspire it, and she felt a degree of it herself:—on either side the mountains rose in black masses to the clouds, and the wind issued from their cavities with a hollow sound, that had something particularly awful in it, whilst the ravens screamed horribly from the trees which waved about their feet. Madeline began to regret not having procured the protection of one of the men, but that regret, with the fears which excited it, she concealed from her companion; both, however, were too much disturbed to continue to converse; and in silence they reached the monastery, and were just turning into it, when the figure of a man, standing beneath a broken arch, near the entrance, caught their eyes; both started, and Agatha, who, from being foremost, had a better view of him than Madeline, instantly exclaimed, but without withdrawing her eyes from him, "The Lord defend my soul! what brings you hither?" She received no reply however—the man who had neither noticed her nor her companion till she spoke, started at the first sound of her voice, and, after surveying them for a moment with a look of affright, precipitately fled down the valley.

"Oh, my lady! my dearest lady! (exclaimed Agatha) some evil, I fear, has befallen her."

"Oh, heavens! (cried Madeline, trembling so she could scarcely stand) what evil do you apprehend? who is that stranger? why, if he knew you, as I suppose he did from your knowing him, did he fly from you?"

"Because he is a villain," (replied Agatha, as she rushed into the chapel followed by Madeline, whose terror and amazement were beyond language to express.) The moon then at its full, aided by the twilight of summer, gave a full view of the interior of the chapel; and as they entered it, they beheld another man darting out of a small door opposite to them. Madeline involuntarily caught the arm of Agatha, and both pausing, strained an eye of agony and terror after him: they paused however but for a moment; for a deep groan reaching their ears, made them hastily rush up the aisle from whence it proceeded, where, with feelings too dreadful to relate, they beheld their friend, their benefactress, lying stretched before the monument of her husband, apparently lifeless, and a small stream of blood issuing from her side. A shriek of mingled grief and horror burst from Madeline, and, unable to stand, she sunk beside her and clasped her trembling arms around her. Agatha, though equally afflicted, was not so much shocked as Madeline; for from the moment she beheld the stranger whom she had addressed outside the chapel, she had from secret reasons of her own been almost convinced, on entering it, she should behold a sight of horror. From being in some degree prepared for it, she was in some degree collected; and kneeling down, soon discovered that her lady still breathed, and trusted, that from the small quantity of blood which issued from it, her wound was not of a very dangerous nature. She now called upon Madeline to assist her in staunching it, ere she went to the castle for some of the servants to assist in carrying her thither.

The almost fainting senses of Madeline were recalled by her voice, and starting up, she wildly demanded if the Countess lived.

"Thank heaven! she does," said Agatha.

Madeline dropped upon her knees in a transport of joy.

"Gracious heaven! (she exclaimed) receive my thanks. (Then hastily rising) had I not better fly to the castle (said she) for assistance."

"First help me to bind her wound (cried Agatha). Madeline was habited in a lawn dress; she now instantly tore it from her waist, and giving it to Agatha, supported the head of the Countess upon her bosom, while a bandage was bound round her. The motion of raising her and binding her wound, served to bring the Countess to herself; as she regained her sensibility, with a deep groan, and without opening her eyes, she extended her hand, and made a feeble effort to push away Agatha, exclaiming as she did so—

"Murderous ruffian, forbear! 'tis not in mercy to me, but to your unnatural employer I ask you to spare my life; for never will peace or joy revisit his heart, if my blood rests upon his head."

"Oh! my friend, my more than mother, (exclaimed Madeline, pressing her cold cheek to the yet colder one of the Countess) no murderous ruffian is now near you."

The Countess sighed heavily, and opening her dim eyes, looked round her some minutes before she spoke, as if doubting the reality of what she saw; then in a faint voice, but one that evidently denoted pleasure, she cried, "Great and glorious Being, I thank thee—I shall not die far from those I love, beneath the cruel hand of an assassin."

"Dearly shall he, who raised that hand against you, rue his crime! (exclaimed Agatha); I know the villain—I discovered his accursed confidant near the chapel, and I will bring him to punishment, though my own life should be forfeited by doing so."

"Mistaken woman, (said the Countess in a hollow voice) how would you avenge me? is it by exposing to infamy and death those more precious to me than life—by giving to my heart a deeper wound than my body has sustained?

"This spot I will not quit!—no aid will I receive—on this cold marble will I die—except you promise to give up such an intention—except you swear, solemnly swear, within those consecrated walls, never to divulge to mortal ear the author of my injuries."

"My dearest lady, (cried Agatha, terrified by her expressions), though to see vengeance executed on the wretch who attempted to take away your life, would rejoice my very soul, I will do but what you please; I will promise what you wish."

"Swear then!" exclaimed the Countess.

"I do, (replied Agatha) by all my hopes of happiness here and hereafter, to lock within my heart, from every human ear, all I know concerning this black transaction."

"And you, Madeline (resumed the Countess), must do the same."

"She knows not (said Agatha, interrupting her lady) by whom the atrocious deed has been committed."

"Thank Heaven! (cried the Countess) even from her, though I might confide in her prudence, I would conceal him—conceal my having a relative, who, from self-interest, could be tempted to take away my life. But Madeline, my love, (continued she, looking at her) will you not quiet my troubled heart by the assurance I desire, from every being, I except not even your father; you must conceal my wound being occasioned by premeditated treachery; you must, like Agatha, to all my household, to all who shall enquire concerning it, declare it owing, as I myself shall do, to some unknown and wandering ruffian."

"Hear me swear, then, (said Madeline with energy) by every thing precious to me in heaven or on earth never to disclose what you have desired me to conceal."

"Enough," cried the Countess in a weak voice; and the next instant, as if overcome by the exertions she had used, she fainted away.

"Fly, my dear young lady, (said Agatha to Madeline) our efforts to recover her without other assistance will be vain."

"Madeline started up, and walked with hasty steps halfway down the aisle; she then paused—paused from the most horrible suggestions of fear. "Should the murderers return—(cried she, gasping for breath at the very idea)—should they return before assistance can be procured, and complete their dreadful design; or should they be still lurking about the chapel, will they not seize me as I go for that assistance, and sacrifice me to their own safety!"

In an agony of fear—an agony which took from her all emotion, she leaned against a pillar;—a deep groan from the Countess in a few minutes roused her from this situation. "Oh heavens! (she exclaimed, rushing forward) she expires through my means. (She instantly quitted the chapel)—If I die, (said she, as she did so) I die in the cause of friendship." A cold dew hung upon her temples, and she could scarcely drag her trembling limbs after her; every yard, almost, she involuntarily stopped to listen, and to cast her fearful eyes around: ready at the first intimation of danger, to retreat to the walls of the monastery. But she received no such intimation, and when she came within sight of the garden, her courage revived; her strength returned with her courage, and, like an affrighted lapwing, she then almost flew to the house, and, scarcely touching the ground, rushed into the servants' hall. A figure as terrific as the one she now exhibited, they had never, either in reality or imagination, seen; her face was pale as death, her hair dishevelled, and her clothes torn and stained with blood. She attempted to speak, but her voice died away inarticulate; in about a minute she made another effort, and, in a voice so hollow, that it seemed issuing from the very recesses of her heart, exclaimed, "Fly!—your lady—there's murder in the chapel!"

Struck with terror, the servants eagerly crowded round her to know what she meant. "Ask no explanation! (she cried, in almost breathless agitation) a moment's delay may be fatal." The men no longer hesitated to obey her, and unable to endure her suspense till they returned, she went back with them to the monastery; but by the time she had reached it, she grew sick with apprehension that the ruffians had returned and finished their bloody work; and whilst the servants entered it, she was compelled to clasp her arms round a pillar at its door for support. Whilst she leaned here, a cry of horror reached her from the chapel, and her spirits grew fainter. "She is gone for ever!" she exclaimed, sinking upon the earth, no longer able to stand from the tremor that seized her. In a few minutes she heard the servants approaching; she then raised her head, and beheld two of them bearing out their lady. "Does she live?" asked Madeline.

"Live, (repeated the weeping Agatha), yes, dear Mam'selle, she still lives, and notwithstanding this dreadful accident, will live, I trust, for many years to come."—Relieved from the horrible fears which had overwhelmed her, Madeline again recovered her strength, and was able immediately to return with the servants to the castle.

By the time they reached it the Countess had regained her senses; and as soon as she was laid on her bed, she commanded, whoever went for a surgeon not, on any account whatsoever, to inform him for what purpose he was sent for till he came to the castle; and that at the peril of being dismissed from her service if they disobeyed her. Her domestics should strictly conceal what had befallen her from every one out of her house, assigning as a reason for this command, that if known, she should be teased by enquiries about it; but to Agatha and Madeline, it was evident it proceeded from a fear of having the ruffian detected if his atrocious crime was mentioned. The servants promised obedience to their lady, and two of the men directly set out for the nearest town to procure a surgeon, whilst another went to the convent for Father Bertrand, who on every emergency was the counsellor and consoler of the family; he came without delay, and the moment he entered the Countess's chamber, who had sent for him, she dismissed every other person from it.

Nothing but the solemn promise which Madeline knew Agatha to have given, to conceal the author of the Countess's sufferings could now have prevented her from asking who he was. The more she reflected on the horrible affair, the more mysterious it appeared to her, and the more astonished and perplexed she felt. How strange that a woman of the Countess's benevolence, whose temper was gentleness itself, whose heart was the seat of charity, and whose liberal hand ever kept pace with the wishes of that heart, should have provoked the enmity of any one. Yet not enmity alone provoked the attempt at her life; her words in the chapel on first regaining her senses, declared its being also prompted by some view of self-interest. —This was another mystery to Madeline, for she knew of none but Monsieur and Madame D'Alembert, that could be materially benefited by the death of her benefactress.

Agatha left her soon after they had quitted the Countess's room, to prepare things for her lady against the surgeon came. But Floretta continued with her, in hopes of having her curiosity, which exceeded both her sorrow and surprise, gratified by hearing the particulars of the attack made upon the Countess by the robber, as she and all the rest of the servants supposed the assassin to be.

"Lord Mam'selle, (cried she, interrupting the deep reverie of Madeline) you must have been terribly frightened when you first beheld the villain. I protest it was well it was not I but Agatha who went with you, for I should certainly have dropped down dead at once upon the spot; I dare say he was a frightful looking creature."

"I do not know, (said Madeline) for I did not see his face."

"Lord, I am very sorry you did not, for then if you ever met him again, you might have sworn to him at once, and have had him taken up. Well, to be sure, I always thought my lady would come to some harm by going to that old ruin; I wish with all my soul it was all tumbled down, I don't know any thing it is fit for, but to enclose the dead or secret a robber;—many and many a time have I quaked with fear, lest my lady should have desired me to attend her to it. Certainly, 'tis a horrid thing to live in such a dismal place as we do; I dare say we shall all be murdered some night or other in our beds: we have nothing in the world to defend ourselves with, for the old guns are so rusty that I am sure it would only be wasting powder to try and do any thing with them. I think it would be a wise thing Mam'selle, if you would try and prevail on my lady, to send her jewels and plate away, for if the gang, to which no doubt the villain who attacked her in the chapel belongs, once heard a rumour of their being gone, and that they assuredly would from always having their spies about, they would never, I am sure, think it worth their while to break into the castle.

"Well, many men many minds, and many women I suppose the same. For I am certain if I was my lady, I would never live with the fine fortune she has, amongst these dismal woods and mountains. No, no, Paris would be the place for my money."

"Do you think Floretta, (asked Madeline, who sat as pale as death, and almost motionless) that the surgeon will soon arrive."

"Why that depends, Mam'selle, (replied Floretta) upon the haste Antoine and Jerome make in going for him, and the haste he makes in coming back with them. Though upon reflection indeed, I should not be surprised if none of them ever reached the castle; for 'tis extremely probable they may may all fall into the hands of the gang, who no doubt are lurking about the castle."

"I have not a fear of that nature," said Madeline.

"I am sure I hope mine may be an idle one (cried Floretta); poor fellows! they would die a melancholy death if such an accident befell them. Well, Mam'selle, I must now leave you; there is fortunately a sliding wainscot in my chamber, and I shall go directly and hide all my good clothes within it; I shall then try if I can't prevail on the men to see what can be done with the old fire arms. But after all, Mam'selle, (resumed she, after pausing a minute) if the rogues once broke into the house, what comfort could I receive from knowing my clothes were hid, for to be sure I should be killed as well as the rest of the family, and what avails fine clothes or money, if one has no life to enjoy them." She now retired, and Madeline remained alone in a state of the most dreadful disquietude, till the arrival of the surgeon. Father Bertrand then came to her, and Madeline eagerly enquired what he thought about her friend.

"With respect to her wound (replied he) I cannot give an opinion, as I left her room the moment the surgeon entered it; but with respect to her mind I think her an angel."

It instantly struck Madeline, that to this venerable man the Countess had imparted every secret of her heart, and that his warm, his energetic praise, proceeded from admiration at her mercy and forbearance, in not attempting to punish the monster who had injured her. "To a much later date (he continued) may heaven preserve the life of a woman, whose charities and example are so beneficial to mankind."—"Oh! long, long may she be spared (cried Madeline, with uplifted hands) who amongst the children of distress would have such reason to mourn her death as I should."

Father Bertrand informed her, that as soon as he had seen the surgeon, he should go and write to Madame D'Alembert to come directly to the chateau.

"Poor lady! (cried Madeline, with a sigh) how dreadfully shocked and affected she will be to hear of the injury her mother has received!"

"I do not mean to inform her of it," replied he.

"But when she comes to the chateau, she cannot be kept in ignorance of it," cried Madeline.

"Such precautions (said the Father) will be used, that even then she will not know it. The sight of her amiable and beloved child will, I trust, have a happy effect upon the estimable mother."

The surgeon now made his appearance; the faltering accents of Madeline were unequal to the enquiry her heart dictated; but Father Bertrand, more composed, soon learned, that the Countess's wound was not dangerous. "My principal fears, (said the surgeon) arise from the fever with which she is threatened, in consequence of the agitation of her mind." He then mentioned his intention of continuing at the castle till he had dressed her wound the next morning.

Madeline, no longer able to control her strong anxiety to be with her friend, and certain that Agatha would have every proper attention paid to him, now bade him and Father Bertrand good night, and repaired to the chamber of the Countess, where she resolved to continue till morning. All was quietness within it, for the Countess, exhausted by the pain she had suffered during the dressing of her wound, and her long conversation preceding it with Father Bertrand, had fallen into a slumber; and her attendants, Agatha and Floretta, fearful of disturbing her, would not move;—the latter, however, could not avoid whispering to Madeline, that she had prevailed on the men to collect some of the fire-arms, and that they had promised to double-bar all the doors.

Deep groans frequently escaped the Countess, but she continued tolerably quiet for about two hours; she then, in a weak voice, called for drink; which the ready hand of Madeline instantly presented to her.

"Why, my love (said the Countess, as Madeline, bending over her, raised her languid head), why do I see you here?"

"Ah! Madam (said Madeline), the only comfort my heart can know is in watching by you."

"I thank you for your tenderness (replied the Countess); but I must now insist on your retiring to bed: nay, do not attempt to refuse doing so (seeing Madeline about speaking); I will not go to sleep (and want of rest you may be sure will injure me), till you leave me."

Those words conquered all opposition on the part of Madeline; and, after kissing her benefactress's hand, she withdrew, though with the greatest reluctance, to her chamber. She could not bring herself to go to bed, lest she should not in a moment, if called upon, be ready to attend her friend; she took off her torn garments, and putting on a wrapper, lay down; but though fatigued to a degree, her mind was too much agitated, too full of horror, to permit her to sleep: and, after passing a few restless hours, she arose as soon as it was light.

CHAP. VI.

Let's talk of graves, and worms, and epitaphs.

Madeline rose with a heaviness of heart which left her scarcely power to move; the day was as gloomy as her mind, and added, perhaps, by its melancholy to her's:—a slow, but penetrating, rain was falling, and the cattle that grazed upon the lawn were dripping with wet, and retiring to the most sheltered parts of the wood:—the waters of the lake looked black and troubled, nor did any brightness in the sky give a promise of a finer day. To complete the dejection of Madeline, on going to the dressing-room adjoining the Countess's chamber, she was informed by Agatha, whom, with Father Bertrand, she found there, that soon after she had left the Countess, she had had a fit of the most alarming nature. "I directly called the surgeon (proceeded Agatha), and he sat with her the remainder of the night, during which she had many returns of it: he has already dressed her wound, being under a necessity of departing at an early hour, and he says it bears a much more dangerous appearance than it did at first. Her fever too is augmented; but he dreads nothing so much as a return of the fits, which, in her present exhausted state, are, he says, enough to kill her."

"Oh! why, why (cried Madeline, whose agonies, at hearing this melancholy account, were inexpressible), why was I not called when so dreadful a change took place?"

"At first we were really too much confused to think about you (said Agatha); and when my Lady recovered, and we would have gone for you, she commanded us not to disturb you."

Madeline burst into tears at this proof of her friend's consideration for her amidst her own sufferings.

"Be composed, my dear young Lady (said Father Bertrand), Providence may perhaps produce another change more favourable to our wishes."

Madeline now asked if she might not see the Countess. Agatha answered in the affirmative. She accordingly entered the chamber. The foot-curtains of the bed, and those of one of the windows, were open, and Madeline had thus sufficient light to perceive the striking alteration which had taken place in the countenance of her friend; her lips were livid, her eyes were sunk, and a ghastly paleness overspread her face. The tears of Madeline increased; and when the Countess, whose heavy eyes opened on hearing her light step, called her to her bed-side, and, extending her hand, asked her how she was? deep convulsive sobs prevented all reply.

"Pray moderate this concern (said the Countess); 'tis true it excites my gratitude, but it also gives me unutterable pain;—the soothing attention of a friend is the best cordial I can receive, but that cordial you will not be able to administer if you yield to those emotions."

"Oh! Madam (cried Madeline, sinking on her knees, and pressing the cold hand of the Countess between her's), Oh! Madam, I will try to repress them; I will try to do every thing which can give me the smallest power of serving you."

"I am convinced you will, my love (replied the Countess), and the conviction is soothing to my sick heart. Oh! Madeline, 'tis not my frame, so much as my mind, that is disordered."

Weakness precluded farther conversation for the present, and Madeline seated herself beside the bed, nor stirred till absolutely commanded by the Countess to go into the next room to breakfast. She took but little, and quickly resumed her place by her friend.

About the middle of the day, the Countess had another fit. Apprised of its danger, the distress and terror of Madeline almost reduced her to the same extremity, and some of the servants were compelled to carry her from the room till their Lady had recovered. On regaining her senses, the Countess ordered Father Bertrand to be sent for; and, on his arrival, she dismissed every one else from the room. While he was shut up with her Ladyship, dinner was served in the dressing-room for Madeline, but served in vain; the grief and anxiety of her mind would neither permit her to eat nor drink, though pressed to do so by the faithful Agatha and the voluble Floretta, both of whom, but particularly the former, had a very sincere regard for her. She was informed by the latter on Agatha's quitting the room, as a great secret, that the surgeon had been requested by the Countess to bring a notary with him the next morning from the town where he lived, in order to make her will. "We all guess, Mam'selle (said Floretta), that 'tis on your account she is going to make one."

"Heaven grant (cried Madeline with fervour), that from her own hand alone I may ever receive any mark of her regard."

"Why to be sure, Mam'selle (said Floretta), that might be as pleasant a way as the other; but 'tis a comfort at any rate to be certain of it. One way or other, I am a great advocate for people making their wills; for you must know, Mam'selle, I lost a great deal by an old uncle of mine in Burgundy dying without one. He always promised to leave me every thing he had; but he was always of a shilly-shally disposition: so death whipped him off without his putting his promise into execution, and his property was then divided amongst all his relations. Had he kept his promise, little as folks think of me now, I can assure you, Mam'selle, I should have been an heiress, for he owned two very fine vineyards and an excellent house, and several large flocks of sheep; and with all those I think I might have held up my head pretty high."

"I think you hold it up high enough already," said Agatha, who had entered before the conclusion of the speech.

"Not higher (replied Floretta pertly), than I have a right to do."

"That point might be disputed," cried Agatha.

"Oh, not at present," said Madeline, to whom every sound was irksome, that did not convey some tidings of the Countess.

Father Bertrand continued a considerable time with the Countess; and when he left her, he passed hastily through the dressing-room. Madeline then returned to the chamber, followed by Agatha, and resumed her station. The Countess did not appear worse; and desired they might be left together.

"You have heard, my love, I suppose (said she, turning her languid eyes upon Madeline as Agatha closed the door after her), that Madame D'Alembert is sent for."

"I have, Madam," replied Madeline.

"I hope (resumed the Countess) she may not arrive too late."

"Heaven forbid! (cried Madeline shuddering); I trust when she arrives, she will find your Ladyship pretty well recovered."

"Believe me, my dear (said the Countess), 'tis on her account I principally desire to recover; she still chains me to a world, to which I am in a great degree grown indifferent, from the loss of several of my dearest connexions, as well as many other heavy calamities;—but for her, I should look forward to the idea of quitting it with pleasure, as I should to a release from pain and trouble—should consider it with delight, as a means of re-uniting me to those whom, while on earth, I must for ever mourn.

"For the sake of my beloved child I wish to be spared a little longer; with increasing years, she may perhaps acquire that fortitude which I fear she would at present want to support my loss. But should my wish be disappointed—should she arrive too late to receive my last blessing, my admonition against a sorrow, not only useless, but inimical to every duty—to you, Madeline, I entrust that blessing, that admonition for her; certain that, as one will be delivered by solemnity, so the other will be enforced with sympathy. Should it be my destiny never more to open my eyes upon her in this world, to you, Madeline, I leave the task of consoling her;—a task not unacceptable, I am convinced, to your grateful nature, and one well suited to its gentleness. She is already prepared to love and to esteem you; and, from a predilection in your favour, will listen patiently to all you say. Represent, therefore, to her (if indeed it happens), that the event she regrets, could not, according to the laws of human nature, have been much longer delayed. And, Oh! Madeline, I adjure you, never let her know how it was accelerated."

"May Heaven only prosper me (cried Madeline) as I keep inviolably from her knowledge the injury you received."

"Excuse my betraying a doubt of your doing so (resumed the Countess), after the solemn promise I have already received from you to that purpose; my fears for her urge me even to unnecessary caution. Oh! Madeline, great as was the pleasure I ever derived from your society, 'tis now heightened by considering you in the light of my child's comforter;—you will console, you will strengthen her, you will reconcile her to my loss."

"Impossible! impossible!" exclaimed Madeline, in the fullness of her heart, and bursting into tears.

"Ah! Madeline (said the Countess, affected by her emotion), do not embitter moments like these by a sorrow which will destroy all the hopes I entertained of your being a consoler to my child."

"May every event (cried Madeline, sinking on her knees), may every event (with uplifted hands) which could place her in want of consolation, be far, far distant from her. But should such an event now happen, Oh! may Heaven grant me power equal to my inclination to give it to her!"

"After my death," proceeded the Countess.

"Oh! Madam (interrupted Madeline), do not talk of it—you stab me to the very soul by doing so."

"Rather rejoice than grieve to hear me do so (said the Countess); how much more dreadful, at the very moment when I stand, perhaps, upon the brink of the grave, to find me trembling, shrinking at the idea of dissolution! I have always tried to act so as to be prepared for it; I have always prayed, that I might be composed when it approached—might be able, in the last extremity of nature, to hold out my hands to my Creator, deprecate his wrath, and implore his mercy. Oh! my love, but for the precious ties I have still remaining, I should welcome it as a release from a world that teems with troubles. But I will not, by perpetually reverting to those troubles, cast a cloud over the youthful prospects of my Madeline."

"Alas! (thought Madeline) they are already clouded."

"Life (resumed the Countess) is a chequered scene, and, by a proper performance of our duties, we may enjoy many comforts in it; 'tis the use we make of those comforts, and the manner in which we support their loss, that fixes the peace or misery of our last moments. Oh! happy are they (continued the Countess, while a faint spark of animation was rekindled in her eye), Oh! happy are they, who can review their past conduct without regret! who can think, to use the language of a poet of a sister country, that when their bones have run their race, they may rest in blessings, and have a tomb of orphan's tears wept over them.

"But to resume the subject you interrupted.—After my death, Madame D'Alembert, I am sure, will seek retirement; and the retirement of this chateau I am confident she will prefer to that of any other place, should Monsieur D'Alembert permit her to remain in it. Till more happily settled, I hope, and believe, your father will allow you to be her companion whenever she visits, and while she continues in it alone; for your society, I am convinced, will ever prove a source of comfort to her. But remember, I never desire you to be her companion, except she is without the company of Monsieur D'Alembert: and believe me, my Madeline, I am not so selfish as not to hope that you may soon have tenderer claims to fulfil than any she can have upon you. Let not the disappointment of your first expectations make you suppress all others; oppose reason to despondence, and the latter will soon be conquered. 'Tis a duty you owe your father as well as yourself, to try and do every thing which can promote your happiness; endeavour, therefore, to erase from your heart those impressions, which can only give you pain, and to prepare it to esteem and be propitious to some worthy man.

"Should chance again throw de Sevignie in your way, fly from him instantly, I conjure you, except he offers a full explanation of his conduct. Excuse me, my love (on hearing a gentle sigh steal from Madeline) for mentioning a subject that is painful to you; but you are so innocent, so totally unacquainted with art, that too much caution cannot be used in guarding you against it. And even then (continued she, returning to the subject of de Sevignie) if he should offer to account for his conduct, do not listen to him; refer him to your father to give the explanation; for an unimpassioned ear he cannot deceive. If by any chance you should ever discover him to be the amiable character you once fancied, you will find by my will, which I purpose making to-morrow, that want of fortune will be no hindrance to your union."

Madeline could not speak, but tears, more eloquently than words could have done, expressed her feelings.

"But I am wrong (resumed the Countess), in having suggested the idea of such an union to you—an idea which may counteract all I have before been saying."

"No, Madam (said Madeline in a low voice), it will not."

"Please me, my Madeline (cried the Countess after a pause), by saying that you will remember what I have said to you."

"Remember! (repeated Madeline); Oh! Madam, could you think I could ever forget aught you said?—Remember!—I will do more—I will try to fulfil every injunction you have given me, if indeed (in a scarcely articulate voice) it should be necessary to do so."

"I thank you for saying so (replied the Countess); I thank you not only for this, but for the many proofs of affection and attention I have received from you. Your society has been a greater happiness, a greater comfort to me than I can express; it has frequently beguiled the cares which oppressed me—cares which the generality of people considered me a stranger to. I wished to be thought happy, and I endeavoured to appear so; but no tongue could describe the anguish which has long preyed upon my heart. Never, however, let this involuntary effusion of confidence escape you; let it be buried in your breast with all you know concerning the black transaction in the chapel—a transaction which I fervently hope may never be known to more than the few already unhappily acquainted with it;—from every eye I would conceal its author;—my forgiveness is his, and my earnest prayers are offered up to Heaven for its forgiveness also for him."

The evening was now far advanced, and the Countess appeared exhausted by speaking. Madeline besought her to take a reviving cordial; she complied with the entreaty, and then said she would settle herself to rest. She charged Madeline to retire at an early hour to bed. "You look pale and agitated, my love (said she); but cheer up—the mention of death does not make me nearer dying. farewell! may good angels for ever watch around you!" Madeline pressed her lips to her cheek; and then rising from her knees, closed the curtains of the bed, and withdrew. She sent Agatha and Floretta to the chamber; then retired to her own, where she offered up a fervent prayer to Heaven for the restoration of her valuable and beloved friend; after which, finding herself still very languid, and the rain being over, she descended to the garden, hoping the evening air might revive her.

CHAP. VII.

When the sun sets, shadows that show'd at noon
But small, appear most long and terrible;—
So when we think Fate hovers o'er our heads,
Our apprehensions shoot beyond all bounds;
Owls, ravens, crickets, seem the watch of death;
Nature's worst vermin scare her God-like sons;
Echoes, the very leavings of a voice,
Grow babbling ghosts, and call us to our graves;
Each mole-hill thought swells to a huge Olympus,
While we, fantastic dreamers! heave and puff,
And sweat with an imagination's weight.

Lee.

Madeline went upon a high and graveled terrace to avoid the wetness of the low and grassy paths beneath it. But though the rain was over, the evening was extremely unpleasant, a cold and piercing wind howled through the trees, of whose increasing violence the hoarse screams of water-fowl gave sure and melancholy intimation, the clouds seemed staggering with giddy poise, and the moon vainly endeavouring to emerge from them, if for a moment she was discovered,

Riding to her highest noon,
Like one that had been led astray,
Through the Heavens' wide pathless way.

Her watery lustre rather increased than diminished the solemn gloom. Madeline, however, pursued her way, and as she cast her eyes upon the long perspective of black and distant mountains, she thought of the friends that had so recently travelled over them, and her regret for their absence was heightened by believing their company would have been a source of pleasure and comfort to the Countess. From them her thoughts reverted to another object, one she dared not think her friend, yet could not call her enemy; the idea of his being now exposed upon the cheerless heights she viewed, to the inclement blast, wrung her heart with agony; she tried, however, to repel it, by reflecting that it would, by enervating, render her unable to pay the attentions she wished to her benefactress; and also, that to think voluntarily of him, was acting contrary to the solemn resolution she had formed, to try and forget him. She continued out till the wind grew so violent that it quite chilled and fatigued her; as she returned to the chateau she saw on every side a blackening train of clamorous rooks seeking their accustomed shelter among the tall trees surrounding it, while, assiduous in his bower, the owl plied his sad song, and the water-fowl, wheeling from their nests upon the lake, screamed along the land.

Madeline slowly ascended the stairs, and repairing to the dressing-room, found Agatha and Floretta there; she eagerly enquired about the Countess, and they informed her, that she still slept, and had done so almost from the time she had quitted her. They also said, that her Ladyship had desired them to sit up in the dressing-room, as a light in her chamber was disagreeable to her. Madeline instantly declared she would keep them company, and felt rejoiced to hear of the repose of her friend, flattering herself it was a sign of her being better.

Every thing, which could give comfort to the night, was already provided. A cheerful fire blazed in the grate, the brightness and warmth of which were truly reviving to the depressed spirits and chilled frame of Madeline; and before it lay a table, covered with bread, meat, and rich wines. Madeline took a bit of bread and some wine, and seated herself beside the fire. It was now the hour at which the servants generally went to rest, and with light steps they were soon heard retiring to their respective chambers; a profound stillness then reigned throughout the Castle—a stillness, however, which was soon interrupted by the wind, that had now increased to a tremendous degree. Sometimes it howled dismally through the long galleries; sometimes came in such sudden squalls against the doors, that it almost burst them open, whilst the forest was heard groaning beneath its fury; and ever and anon loose stones came tumbling from the battlements of the Castle.

The dejection of Madeline's heart returned—a dejection, which the account she received of her friend had a little dissipated, and with it a terror she could not suppress; she laid down the cup of wine, and casting her eyes upon her companions, perceived, by their countenances, they were equally affected.

"How mournfully the wind howls (said Agatha, in a low voice); the Lord have mercy (devoutly crossing herself) upon all who are at sea! many a stout heart will go to the bottom, I fear, to-night. 'Tis very odd, yet very true, that the night before my Lord the Count de Merville (Heaven rest his soul! again crossing herself) died, there was just such a storm as there is now; the noise it made throughout the house was just as if people had been fighting and shrieking about it. I thought at the time, the sounds were presageful ones; particularly as the birds kept such a screaming and fluttering about the windows, for their screams are always sure foretellers of death. Indeed they have not been very quiet to-night."

"No (cried Madeline, wishing to check the involuntary horror with which the words of Agatha had inspired her), because they are now, as they were then, disturbed by the storm; 'tis well known, that their screams not only foretell, but last during one. I have heard my father say, that people who live near the sea always take warning by them, and never (if possible to avoid doing so) venture upon it, while they continue."

"I shall never be made, however, to believe that they do not forebode something more than a storm (cried Agatha); no, Mam'selle, be assured they are certain prognostics of death; but such warnings as these are not confined to one family, like others that I know of: For instance, in the Castle of the Marquis de Vermandois, about two leagues from this, a great bell always tolls before the death of any one belonging to it; and there never was any change about taking place in this chateau that there was not a dreadful storm before-hand, accompanied by the fall of an old suit of armour, which hangs on the left side of the hall, nearly opposite the dining parlour, and which belonged to the founder of the mansion."

"I know the suit you mean (said Madeline); I have often examined it as a curious piece of antiquity; but the reason it falls, when there is a storm, is, because the wind then gets through the crevices of the walls, and blows it down."

"You are very incredulous, Mam'selle (cried Agatha); but you'll never be able to make me believe otherwise than I do now. Lord! I still tremble at the recollection of what I suffered, when I heard the armour fall with such a crash a few minutes before my Lord's death. I was alone with him, and that, to be sure, augmented my terror; for my lady, overcome by grief, had fainted, and was carried from the room by the other attendants."

"I have heard say, indeed (cried Floretta, who had hitherto listened to the words of Agatha with the most profound attention) that those warnings of death are very common."

"God, of his infinite mercy (said Madeline) may perhaps give such warnings to the wicked, in order to awaken them to repentance; but to the good, to those whose lives prepare them at any hour for his summons, I never can believe he does."

"I shall enter into no argument about the matter (cried Agatha); for nothing could persuade me out of my own opinion."

"Yet what Mam'selle says seems just enough (said Floretta); for why should the good, who need no preparation for death, be warned of it as well as those whose bad actions render it necessary they should, in order to have them brought to repentance."

"Well (replied Agatha), I have not a doubt but what they come to both?"

"What a dreadful thing it must be, to have a troubled conscience, when one is near dying," resumed Floretta.

"Ay, or at any other time either (exclaimed Agatha); many a foul deed has it forced people to reveal."

"There is a memorable story told about that (said Floretta), in the part of Burgundy I come from."

"Well, tell it (cried Agatha); it will help to pass away the time."

"There stood, about fifty years ago (began Floretta, drawing her chair closer to her companion's), near the village where I was born, an old mansion, which had for many years been uninhabited, for its owner, being given to travel in foreign parts, never gave himself any trouble at all about repairing it; so that, owing to his neglect, it went by degrees so much to rack and ruin, that two servants, who had been left in it, thought it unsafe to continue in it, and accordingly quitted it.

"Well, in process of time, the unthrifty master of this old chateau died; and never having been married, it fell to a distant relation, who was delighted (as you may well think) to have the fine estate surrounding it become his: he was neither given to squandering nor gadding; and knowing what the comforts of a good home were, he directly ordered the ruin to be pulled down, that he might have another house built in its place. This you may be sure was a joyful order for the tenants; for 'tis the life of the poor souls to have a rich landlord live amongst them, particularly one that is generous and good, as was the gentleman I am speaking of. They set merrily to work, and soon demolished most of the building; for 'tis a true saying, that willing minds, like many hands, make light work.

"As they were destroying the wall of a vault, which had once been used for family stores, they found, within a niche of it, against which a parcel of loose stones were piled, the skeleton of a full-grown person.—You may well conceive their consternation at such a sight; for it immediately struck them that this was the skeleton of a murdered person, else what should bring it there.

"The discovery was soon spread throughout the village, and all the folks came flocking to the place. They were all of one opinion, that some one had been murdered in the house, and that the crime had been committed after it became deserted. They strove to recollect whether any person, within their memories, had been suddenly missed from their neighbourhood, but could not remember a circumstance of the kind.

"While they were busy talking over the matter, there came riding by an elderly gentleman, well dressed, and of a grave and comely appearance; so seeing the crowd, he stopped his horse, as was natural enough, and alighting from it, entered the court-yard, and enquired what was the matter.

'A sad affair, master (replied one of the oldest of the villagers); we have just discovered that a murder was committed within the walls we have been destroying.'

'A murder! (repeated the gentleman, changing colour); a murder!—Pray, my good friend, how did you discover it?'

'Why, by finding a skeleton hid within a vault: you may be sure, if the person to whom it belonged had died fairly, it would never have been stuffed into such a place. They, to be sure, who committed the cruel act, thought they were secure enough of its never being found out by hiding it there, but you see they were mistaken. The watchful eye of God is over all; he seldom suffers murder to escape the punishment it merits: and indeed I can scarcely doubt that the discovery of the skeleton is but the forerunner of the discovery of the murderer.'

"The old man and the stranger were standing by a wall, against which the skeleton was placed; but the latter had hitherto been kept from seeing it, by some women who stood between it and him; they now drew back, supposing that, like themselves, he would be curious enough to wish to examine it.—Scarcely had they done so, when, just as the old man had finished his last sentence, a violent gust of wind arose, which blew down the skeleton, and it fell plump at the stranger's feet. He started back, as any one indeed might have done at such an accident, and attempted directly to leave the place; but some how or other, his foot was entangled by the skeleton, so that he could not move. Well, when he perceived this, he gave a deep groan, and sunk upon the ground. The people hastened to his assistance; he was lifted up—but it was many minutes ere he showed any signs of life; and when he did, it was at first only by dismal sighs. At last opening his eyes, he took the old man's hand, who helped to support him— 'Oh! my good friend (cried he) your words were but too true; the discovery of that frightful spectacle but foreruns the discovery of the murderer; in me you behold that guilty wretch.'—At this there was a general cry, and all praised the wonderful Providence of Heaven.

'You shall have (he continued) a full confession of my guilt; I no longer wish (even if it was possible to do so) to evade the punishment due to it.'

"As he spoke, he fell into such agonies, that they thought he would have died, and were forced to get him some wine to take.

"Being a little revived by it, he was seated on the grass, and thus began:—

'To the old, as well as the young, my story may be instructive; it will prove to the former, that their authority over youth should never be too much relaxed; and to the latter, that those who are disobedient to their parents or guardians, and waste the morning of their life in idleness or vice, may assuredly expect to end its evening in misery. I was born of reputable parents, in a small town in this province. The comforts they enjoyed, which were sufficient to satisfy humble dispositions, were procured by their own industry, and, with the inheritance of the little property they had acquired, they trusted I would possess a spirit temperately to enjoy, and honestly to increase it; but their over-indulgence marred their wishes. I soon discovered their easiness of temper, and, in consequence of that easiness, grew importunate in my demands—demands which they soon lost the power of refusing; and I became, from their compliance, giddy and dissipated in the extreme. Too late my parents perceived their error, in allowing me such latitude as they had done, and in not checking, at the beginning, the propensities I early showed to idleness and dissipation. Their remorse, together with the disappointment of their hopes relative to me, terminated their lives (while I was yet in the prime of my youth) and they died within a short period of each other. I felt some little compunction and regret; but the first call of pleasure drove them from my heart, and I resumed my former courses. A continuance in them soon dissipated the little property I possessed. I then resolved to abandon my native country, and seek subsistence in another part of the world. This resolution I imparted to a particular friend, a youth about my own age, and, like me, an orphan. Our attachment had commenced at the first dawning of reason, and a kind of infatuation seemed to bind him to me; he was ever ready to join me in my schemes, and often, latterly, assisted my declining purse. Through my means, his fortune had been considerably injured; but though his fortune was not wrecked like mine, he now declared he would accompany me to any part of the world I should like to go to; a declaration I rejoiced to hear, as he had the means of keeping me from hardships I otherwise, from the low state of my finances, expected to undergo. He accordingly gathered the remains of his wealth together, and we set out on foot (the better to conceal the distressed situation in which we left the place of our nativity) for Rochelle, from whence we purposed embarking for the West Indies, thinking that the best place for adventurers.

'About sun-set, the first day, we came within sight of this ruined mansion, and feeling extremely tired, we turned into it, and refreshed ourselves with the provisions we carried about us. We thought we could not find a better situation for spending the night in, and we had scarcely determined on doing so, when my companion, more fatigued than I was, fell asleep.

'Evil suggestions, which I had not grace to subdue, then rose in my mind. If the remnant of his wealth was mine (I cried), how much sooner could I realize the schemes I have formed for making my fortune. The idea was too tempting to be resisted, and, with the knife, with which but a few moments before he had helped me to bread, I pierced him to the heart; he never opened his eyes; one deep, one deadly groan, was all that escaped him; it still sounds in my ears, and ascended to Heaven to call down vengeance on my head.

'After I had committed the execrable deed, I searched for a place to hide the body in; and having discovered a vault, I dragged it thither, and covered the traces of the blood with rubbish. Oh that the mouldering walls had crushed me to atoms, while thus impiously employed! Yet wretch as I am! Oh, why do I say so? Rather let me bless the Power, which mercifully granted me leisure to repent—which perhaps spared me then in order to warn others, by my narration and punishment, from crimes similar to mine.

"To be brief, my dear auditors, I pursued my original intention, and embarked for the West Indies, where every thing succeeded even beyond my expectations. It seemed as if Heaven allowed me to prosper but to prove how mistaken I was, in supposing wealth alone could give me happiness. Alas! dreadful mistake, to think any could be enjoyed from a fortune, whose foundation was laid in blood:—with riches, wretchedness, if possible, increased, 'tis now fifteen years since I murdered my friend; and from that period to this, peace has been a stranger to my breast. Remorse pervaded my soul; horror pursued my steps, and the blood I had shed continually swam before me.

'Having at length secured an ample independence, and being disgusted with the place where I lived, or rather, as is often the case with the wretched, imagining change of scene might alleviate my misery, I resolved on returning to my native country; but the abode of my youth I was destined never more to behold; my conscience would not suffer me to remain unconcerned on beholding the skeleton, and thus did Providence, I may say, make me call for justice on myself.'

"In consequence of his confession (continued Floretta), he was committed to prison, and soon after tried, condemned, and executed on the spot where he had committed the murder. A little time before his death, he deposited a sum of money in the hands of a priest, for the purpose of having mass said for the soul of his murdered friend, and a monument erected to his memory in our village church, where his bones were buried.

"Often and often have I seen that monument, upon which, according to his desire, the priest had inscribed the particulars of his strange story, exactly opposite the churchyard; and at the side of the high-way he was interred himself:—his grave could plainly be distinguished when I was last in that part of the country, though all overgrown with grass and weeds, as was the stone placed at its head, to signify the reason he was denied Christian burial. Many and many a time, particularly after it grew dark, I have taken a long circuit to avoid passing it; for 'tis confidently said, and believed by our villagers, that his spirit, and that of the unhappy gentleman he murdered, take their nightly rounds about the place moaning, lamenting, and uttering the most piteous cries. My poor old grandmother, from whom I have repeatedly heard the story, told me she was once almost frightened to death, from fancying she had a glimpse of them near the church-yard; and the servants in the house that was rebuilt, have often been almost scared out of their senses, by the noises they have heard within it.

"Thus (continued Floretta) my story proves the truth of what we were saying, namely, that an evil conscience has often occasioned the discovery of foul crimes. It was owing to it that the stranger imagined the falling of the skeleton not an accidental circumstance, but one immediately ordered by Heaven, and from that idea did he betray himself."

"True (cried Agatha, who had listened with deep attention, and great delight), 'tis an old saying, and a just one, that a guilty conscience needs no accuser.

"Lord! if people were to allow themselves a little time to consider, half the bad actions that are committed would be left undone; for they would then reflect, that neither riches nor titles can make amends for that peace of mind which a wicked deed destroys. No person's lot can be truly miserable, who, on retiring to their beds, can lay their hands upon their hearts, and say within themselves, I may go to rest in peace, assured of the protection of Heaven, from never having wilfully injured man, woman, or child. Such a thought as this will support one through many distresses. May it support us at the hour of death!"—"and in the day of judgment!" (cried Madeline, with involuntary fervour, and raising her hands and eyes to Heaven)—"Amen," rejoined Agatha.

"As one story begets another (continued she), if you have no objection, Mam'selle, I can tell one something to the same purpose of that we have been listening to."

"Objection (repeated Floretta)! Lord! no, to be sure she can't (answering for Madeline); there is nothing, I think, can delight people more than hearing stories; many and many a winter's night I have passed in hearkening to my grandmother's, who had such a budget of them, there was not a great house for many leagues around us, that she could not tell something wonderful about, and she has frequently sent me to bed shaking with fear."

"Well, Mam'selle (asked Agatha, turning to Madeline), are you of Floretta's mind?"

"Yes," replied Madeline, who saw that Agatha would be dreadfully disappointed, if not permitted to tell one of the wonderful tales in which she abounded.

Breathing astonishment, of witching rhymes,

And evil spirits; of the death-bed call

Of him who robb'd the widow, and devour'd

The Orphan's portion; of unquiet souls

Ris'n from the grave to ease the heavy guilt

Of deeds in life conceal'd; of shapes that walk

At dead of night, and clank their chains, and wave

The torch of hell around the murderer's bed.

"In the reign of Lewis the Ninth, commonly known by the title of St. Lewis, from the holy war in which he engaged, there there stood (said Agatha), about a league from the boundaries of this chateau, a noble castle, the ruins of which are still visible upon a fine eminence, scattered over with wood; and I dare say, Mam'selle, in your way to Madame Chatteneufs, you have taken notice of them." — "I have," replied Madeline.

"This Castle, at the period I have mentioned (resumed Agatha) belonged to a nobleman of an ancient family, and very large fortune; but notwithstanding his rank, which should have made him generous, his fortune, which enabled him to do so, and his having only one child to provide for, he was of a mean and miserly disposition, grudging to himself, and all about him, the necessaries of life; and treated his son, a fine noble youth, brave, generous, and accomplished — in short, his reverse in every respect, in such a severe manner, that he determined to leave him, if an opportunity offered for permitting him to do so, without having his real motives known; for though he could not esteem his father himself, he yet wished, if possible, to keep him from the censures of the world.

"The opportunity he desired occurred upon the King's determining upon a crusade; for it was natural, you know, that a youth of his prowess should wish to embark in so glorious a cause. He accordingly repaired, without delay, to the royal standard, and bade an adieu to his native country.

"His only regret, at doing so, was occasioned by his separation from a young lady, whom he had privately made his wife, and by whom he had a son, then some months old. She was an orphan, and the descendant of a good, but reduced family. He saw her at the house of the relation's, to whose care she had been consigned, and who, not caring to be burdened with her, determined to settle her in a cloister. They did not know each other long, ere a mutual attachment grew between them; and well knowing it would be vain to solicit his father's consent, or her relations, for fear of disobliging him, he stole her away, and, after their nuptials, placed her in a small house near his own residence, which he had taken for that purpose.

"The only person entrusted with the affair was his father's butler, an old man, who had lived long in the family; had often dandled him in his infancy, and was, he knew, faithfully attached to him. To the care of this good creature, who respected the lady, and doted on the child, he left his treasures.

"He had but just reached the Holy Land, when his father died. Poor Peter, who, without authority, could not do any thing, apprised him, as soon as possible, of this event, and requested either his immediate presence, or orders how to act.

"So great was the anxiety of the noble youth, to see his wife and child, and have them publicly acknowledged as such, that without loss of time, he knelt before the King, and entreated his permission to return to his native country, in order to settle his affairs. This the King most graciously granted: but alack! he only returned to find a grave within it.

"Within a league of his castle, he was way-laid and murdered by two ruffians, masked; and the sad intelligence was conveyed to his expecting family by his faithful squire, then his only attendant, who, in attempting to save his life, received such desperate wounds, that he died in two days after.

"Peter was greatly grieved; but, alas! what was his grief to that of the poor lady's; she lost all relish for this life, and in less than a week after her husband's death, was laid beside him in the grave. In her last moments, as well as in those preceding them, she besought Peter to be a steady friend to her child, and see him, if possible, put into possession of his rights. Peter promised to do all he could, but that all, he feared, would be but little. The certificate of her marriage had been destroyed in a box, with many other valuables, by an accidental fire some months prior to her death; and Peter knew too much of the world to think the gentleman, who was heir to the estate, in case his master left no lawful issue, would take his single testimony for the legitimacy of her child, and thus give up a fortune he much wanted; being an extravagant spendthrift, addicted to every vice and folly, and who would for many years have been in the greatest distress, but for the bounty of his poor murdered relation. Well things turned out as Peter thought; the gentleman came from a distant part of France, where he lived, to take possession, and declared he did not give the smallest credit to there being any other heir than himself; he did not doubt, he said, the child being his cousin's, but his legitimate one, he was convinced it was not; and all poor Peter could prevail on him to do, was to allow a small stipend for its support. Peter, with the rest of the servants, was retained, and none of them had reason to complain of their master. For some time, he rendered the castle a scene of constant gaiety; but suddenly his spirits drooped; he shut out company, and appeared to have taken a dislike to all the pleasures he before delighted in; but though he avoided company, solitude seemed equally irksome to him, and he almost continually had one or other of the domestics in the apartment with him. The sudden alteration in his manner, the involuntary horrors he sometimes betrayed, appeared strange circumstances in the eyes of Peter, and from them he drew an inference that shocked him. Determined to know whether it was, or was not a just one, he devised a scheme, which, when you hear it, you will say was a bold one.

"He was the domestic his master generally selected to be near him, and, at the close of day, they frequently walked together up and down a great Gothic hall.—One evening, as they were thus engaged, Peter, whom his master allowed to converse familiarly with him, from his long residence in the family, and well-known attachment to it, said to him, with a solemn voice and countenance, 'Sir, there is something of consequence which I wish to impart to you: last night I had a dream; indeed I do not know whether I can properly call it one, in which methought my poor young master, disfigured by wounds, and stained with blood, came to me, and told me I should, when I least expected it, have the pleasure of discovering his murderer, and bringing him to condign punishment.'—Peter paused, and looked steadily at his master, who betrayed the greatest agitation.

"Was any thing else said to you?' demanded he, in a faltering voice.

'Yes (replied Peter), I asked him by what means I should discover his murderer, and he told me he would betray himself.

'You will (said he) mention my murder before him, and his guilty conscience will make him, if not by words, at least by agitation, declare his crime. Besides, my troubled spirit will be near you at the time, and accelerate the discovery.'

"Peter's master now declared he was taken very ill, and must go directly to his chamber. Scarcely had he spoken, when the dreadful creaking of an iron door was heard, and a faint light flashed upon him, from the spiral stair-case of an old tower, that had for centuries been uninhabited, from an idea of its being haunted.

'Lord, defend me! (cried Peter); I have the key of the iron door at the top of the tower in my possession, and no human hand could have opened it; the light, too, from the stair-case is quite a blue flame.'

"Hark (cried Floretta at this moment, with an affrighted countenance), what noise is that?"

"Noise!" (repeated Agatha, with an emotion of fear.)

"Oh! 'tis only the wind (continued she, listening a minute); it often comes in this way against the doors, as if it would burst them open; but bless me, Mam'selle (looking at Madeline), how deadly pale you are; I fear sitting up does not agree with you."

The spirits of Madeline, weakened by grief, were indeed affected, in spite of her reason, with a kind of superstitious awe, by the stories of her companions.

"Let us mull some wine (cried Agatha); it will do us all good."

"Ay, do (said Floretta), and I will make some toast."

Madeline now said she would step into the Countess's chamber, and try whether she still slept. She accordingly stole into it, and bending over her pillow, had the satisfaction of finding she continued in a tranquil sleep. This somewhat cheered her; and after taking a glass of the mulled wine, she felt the gloom of her spirits pretty well depressed. Agatha then resumed her story.

"Scarcely (said she) had Peter uttered the last word, when his master dropped senseless at his feet. Peter raised, and with difficulty recovered him. The moment he opened his eyes, he dropped upon his knees, implored the mercy of Heaven, and confessed he was the murderer of his cousin.

"Plunged into difficulties, he said, by his extravagance, which he was ashamed to avow, as soon as ever he heard of his cousin's expected return from the Holy Land, he laid the plan for destroying him, which succeeded but too well, and in which he was assisted by a servant, whom he afterwards murdered, for fear of his betraying him.

"Peter told him, if he would immediately resign the estate to the lawful heir, he would not give him up to the punishment he merited. This he readily consented to do; and every thing necessary being done, he retired to a monastery, where he soon after died of a broken heart. After his death, this story was divulged by the servant, whose assistance Peter had obtained for carrying into execution the scheme he had contrived for knowing whether or not his master had murdered his cousin."

The tale concluded, on which Floretta made many comments, a general silence ensued; it was now about the middle of the night, or rather the beginning of the morning, and the storm still raged with unabated violence. Madeline went to a window, and opened a shutter, to see whether the scene without was as dreary as fancy within had represented it to be, and found it, if possible, more so. The faint dawn o'er the western hills was overcast by heavy clouds, and the trees of the wood tumultuously agitated by the blast, which seemed threatening to tear them from the earth.

"How dreadful, how appalling is this hurricane (cried Madeline, as she leaned against the window). If it strikes such terror into a heart conscious of no crime, what fears, what horrors must it excite in one burdened with guilt. To such an one the war of the elements must indeed be dreadful, as seeming to declare the anger of an offended God."—Like the Poet, Madeline thought that such a heart would think

— — —The tempest blew his wrath,

The thunder was his voice, and the red flash

His speedy sword of justice.

Chilled by the melancholy prospect, she closed the shutter, and returned to the fire, before which her companions were now slumbering. In deep and pensive meditation, she sat a considerable time with her eyes fixed upon the crackling blaze, when the heavy crash of something falling in the lower part of the Castle, startled not only her, but her companions.

"Holy virgin! (exclaimed Agatha, turning pale), defend us—'tis the armour that has fallen."

"You had better try," (said Madeline, in a faint voice).

"Try (repeated Agatha); Lord, not for the world."

"Nor I, I am sure (said Floretta) if you could, or would give me a principality for doing so."

"I will then (cried Madeline, ashamed to propose what she would shrink from herself), I will go and endeavour to discover the occasion of the noise."

She went softly into the Countess's chamber, to try if she was disturbed by it, and finding her still asleep, she took up a light, and descended (though with trembling limbs, and a palpitating heart) to the great hall, from whence the noise had sounded. The light she held but partially dispersed its awful gloom, and her tremor and palpitation increased, as she proceeded to the extreme end, at which hung the ominous armour. She found this in its usual situation, and she was hastily moving from it, too much depressed and agitated to think of searching elsewhere for the cause of the noise, when a door opposite to her (which led to a suit of rooms that had been appropriated solely to the use of the Count, and since his death, shut up), slowly opened, and a tall figure, clad in black, came forth.

Madeline started behind a pillar; the conversation of her companions had raised the very spirit of superstition in her breast, and, with eyes almost bursting from their sockets, she now stood immovable, gazing upon the terrifying object that presented itself to her view; but when she saw it approaching her, which it did, with a slow, but steady step, her faculties returned, and dropping the light, she fled to the stair-case; but ere she had ascended many steps, she fell, through her extreme haste; and the surrounding darkness, and the exquisite pain she suffered, in consequence of bending her foot under her at the instant, prevented her from making an immediate effort for rising. She lay for about two minutes in this situation, when a faint light gleaming behind her, made her turn her head with quickness, and she beheld the object of her terror within a step of her. A cold dew instantly burst from her pores, her heart almost died within her, and she covered her face with her hands.

CHAP. VIII.

And art thou—of that sacred band?

Alas! for us too soon, tho' rais'd above

The reach of human pain, above the flight

Of human joy.

The well-known accents of Father Bertrand recalled the fainting spirits of Madeline; never were sounds before so delightful to her ear. She uncovered her face, started up, and exclaimed, "Gracious Heaven! is it possible! do I really behold Father Bertrand!"

"My dear young lady (said the good old man, with his usual mildness), what is the matter;—is our beloved benefactress worse?"

"No, I trust and believe not (replied Madeline); her sleep has been long and tranquil."

"If she is not worse then—if you did not come to call me to her, what could have brought you to the hall?"

Madeline, as briefly as possible, informed him; and in doing so, notwithstanding she wished to conceal it, in order to avoid the imputation of folly, betrayed the fright he had given her.

The good father was too well acquainted with human nature not to know, that the present hour was an improper one for reasoning with her against the weakness which exposed her to it. He determined, however, from a wish of promoting the happiness of a young creature, which he knew nothing would so materially injure as superstition, to take another opportunity of admonishing her against it.

He informed her, that his continuing the night in the Castle was owing to the express desire of the Countess; "but instead of going to bed (proceeded he), I procured the key of the library, well knowing, from the violence of the storm, that I could not sleep." He sighed as he spoke, and his eyes were involuntarily raised to Heaven.

Madeline looked at him with pity and reverence.

"Poor Caroline (said she to herself) is now present to his thoughts; Oh! what must have been his excruciating anguish at the time of her death, when even now, though so many years have passed since that event, his regret is so poignant."

"Never (cried she, addressing him), never again may I hear a storm so tremendous! I fear we shall have melancholy accounts tomorrow of the mischief it has done."

"I hope not (replied the Father); he, whose mighty spirit walks upon the careering winds, will, I humbly trust, prevent their fury from being destructive."

Madeline now enquired whether he heard the noise which had so much alarmed her and her companions. He replied in the affirmative, but said it had come from the gallery instead of the hall, and that he would now go up, and try to discover the cause of it, accompanied by Madeline. He accordingly ascended, and they soon discovered that it had been occasioned by the fall of the Countess's picture.

"Do you now, my child (said the Father), retire, and try to take some repose; for your spirits have been much agitated. I rejoice to hear that the rest of our noble friend has been so good; 'tis a favourable symptom; may the morning light witness the realization of the hopes it has inspired!"

"Heaven grant it may!" fervently rejoined Madeline. She then bade the good man farewell, and begged he would, on descending to the hall, try whether the light she had dropped was extinguished.

The moment she re-entered the dressing-room, Agatha and Floretta eagerly enquired if they were right in their conjectures. She assured them they were not, and then informed them of the cause of their alarm.—This excited little less consternation than if she had told them the armour was fallen;—so prone is superstition to dress up every circumstance in the garb of terror.

The dawn was now peeping through the shutters; the lights were therefore put out, and Agatha and Floretta then again began to slumber before the fire. They were soon, however, disturbed by a sudden gust of wind, which came with such violence against the doors, as almost to burst them open.

"Heaven defend us! (said Agatha), the storm grows worse, instead of better."

"Hark (cried Madeline, with a wild expression in her countenance, and laying her hand upon the arm of Agatha)—Hark!—there surely was a groan mingled in that blast."

"No, Mam'selle (said Agatha), 'tis only the howling of the wind."

"Again! (exclaimed Madeline);—Oh Heavens! (starting from her chair) 'tis the voice of the Countess!"

She rushed into the chamber, followed by her companions. The curtains of the bed were hastily drawn back, and the Countess was discovered in a fit: a scream of mingled terror and anguish burst from Madeline, and sinking on her knees, she clasped the nerveless hands of her friend between her's.

Agatha and Floretta used every effort to recover their lady, and at length succeeded. On opening her eyes, she turned them round with a wild stare, as if forgetting where she was, or by whom surrounded. Her recollection, however, appeared soon to return; her eyes suddenly lost their wildness, and were raised for some minutes to Heaven.—She then looked at Madeline, and spoke, but what she said was unintelligible: she seemed sensible of this herself, by mournfully shaking her head. Gently disengaging one hand from Madeline, she pointed it towards the door, looking earnestly in her face as she did so, as if to say, she wished her to bring some person to her.

"Father Bertrand!" cried Madeline, starting up.

A faint smile from the Countess was an affirmative; and she was flying from the chamber, when she was suddenly stopped by a deep groan.

"Has she relapsed?" cried she with a trembling voice, and a despairing look, again advancing to the bed.

"Never to recover, I fear," said Agatha, bursting into tears.

"'Tis too true! (cried Floretta), she is gone for ever."

Madeline grew sick; she could not weep; she could not speak; she could scarcely breathe; her sight grew dim; her head grew giddy; and the objects that she could discern seemed swimming before her. The grief and consternation of her companions prevented them from noticing her, till they saw her catching at a bed-post for support.—They then directly hastened to her assistance, and supporting her to a chair, opened a window. The keenness of the morning air, together with the water they sprinkled on her face, somewhat revived her, and a shower of tears came to her relief.

Agatha, whom her death-like coldness, and ghastly paleness greatly alarmed, would have led her from the room, but she resisted the effort, and tottering to the bed, threw herself upon it, and bedewed the pale face of her dear, her invaluable benefactress with tears of unutterable, of heart-felt anguish. Agatha now desired Floretta to ring a large bell, which hung in the gallery. This in a few minutes collected all the servants, and they came crowding into the room, preceded by Father Bertrand, and apprised by the sudden alarm of the melancholy event which had happened.

Few scenes could have been more distressing than that now exhibited by the old domestics, as they wept round the bed of their beloved lady, under whose protection they had passed the prime, and trusted to have closed the evening, of their days.

"Oh my friends and fellow-servants! (cried Agatha, whom grief made eloquent), our happiness in this world is gone for ever;—but 'tis a comfort to think, that, from the common course of nature, none of us can expect much longer to continue in it."

"My friends (said Father Bertrand, collecting all his spirits to his aid, and wiping away the tear which had bedewed his pale cheek), my friends (looking round him with the most benign compassion), moderate those transports of grief, by patiently acquiescing in the will of the Almighty; endeavour to deserve a continuance of some of his blessings.

"Peace (continued he, advancing to the foot of the bed, and kneeling before it, while his arms folded upon his breast, and his head gently reclined, seemed to denote that submission to the divine will which he preached to others), peace to the soul of the departed; and may we all, like her, be prepared for our latter end!"

"Let all (cried Agatha, as he rose from his knees) whose services are not required, now retire from the room."

Father Bertrand approached Madeline, who still lay, with her face covered, upon the bed; he took her hand, and entreated her to rise, but she had neither power to refuse nor to obey.

Perceiving her situation, he ordered her to be taken up, and carried into the next room; he was shocked beyond expression at the alteration which grief had effected in her appearance; her cheek and lips had lost all tinge of colour, and her eyes appeared too dim for her to distinguish any object.

Restoratives were administered to her, and by degrees the tears, which extreme agony had suspended, again began flowing, and somewhat relieved her.

Father Bertrand sat by her in silence; he knew the tribute of affection and sorrow must be paid, nor did he attempt to check it, till the first transports of the latter, by indulgence, were a little abated. He then addressed her in the mildest accents of consolation:—

"Oh! my daughter (he said), let the assurance of the felicity to which the spirit of your friend has departed, comfort you for her loss; life at best is but a state of pilgrimage. God, no doubt, to prevent our too great attachment to a state which we must resign, has chequered it with good and evil, so that few, after any long continuance in it, can, if possessed of reason and religion, regret a summons from it. To the Countess it was a happy release; her virtues had prepared her to meet it with fortitude, and her sorrows with pleasure; she knew she was about appearing before a merciful Being, who would reward the patience with which she bore those sorrows—sorrows that corroded the springs of life: so far am I permitted to say, in order to try and reconcile you to her loss, but the source of them I am bound to conceal. Endeavour (he proceeded) to compose yourself; Madame D'Alembert may soon be expected, and it will be some little comfort to the poor mourner to receive your soothing attentions. I am now compelled to retire to the convent, but at the close of day I shall return with some of my brother monks to say mass for the soul of the departed. farewell! (rising as he spoke) may the blessing of heaven rest upon you, and peace soon revisit your heart!"

He had scarcely left the room ere Agatha entered it. "Had you not better lay down Mam'selle (said she, in a voice broken by sobs); for my part I can hold up no longer; as soon as I have given orders about what is to be done I shall go to bed, and I little care if I never rise from it." The melancholy accent in which these words were pronounced, redoubled the tears of Madeline.

"We have lost indeed (cried she) the kindest, the best of friends; never can we expect again to meet with one like her."

The door now softly opened, and Floretta made her appearance; she came with a message of condolence from the physician, who had just arrived, to Madeline, and a request to know whether he could in any manner be serviceable to her.

"No (replied Madeline, mournfully) he cannot."

"The Notary has accompanied him (resumed Floretta) and he desired me to tell you that had he imagined the Countess so near her end, he would, notwithstanding the weather, have come hither yesterday."

"Alack—(cried Agatha) I grieve he did not; my Lady's kind intentions towards you will never now be fulfilled."

The idea of their being frustrated could not, in the present state of Madeline's mind, excite one sigh. Pale, faint, exhausted, she at last complied with the request of Agatha, and retiring to her chamber, threw herself upon the bed; but not even for an instant did sleep shed oblivion over her sorrows; she found the words of the Poet true, that

He, like the world, his ready visit pays

Where fortune smiles, the wretched he forsakes,

Swift on his downy pinions flies from woe,

And lights on lids unsully'd by a tear.

Rather fatigued than refreshed by laying down, she arose in about an hour, and opening a window, seated herself by it; for there was a faintness over her which she thought the air might remove. The heaviness of the sky was now dispersed; the sun looked out with refulgent glory, and the winds, whose fury had scattered the lawn with shattered boughs of trees and fragments from the chateau, were hushed into a calm; the trees, still surcharged with rain, displayed a brighter green, "and glittering as they trembled, cheered the day;" while the birds that sprung from amidst them, poured forth the softest notes of melody; but not that melody, not the blessed beams of the sun which it seemed to hail, could touch the sad heart of Madeline with pleasure.

"Ah! (she cried) after such a night as the last, how soon on the morning would my dear benefactress, if she had been spared to us, have gone forth to enquire what mischief was done, and give orders for repairing it! Oh! ye children of poverty and distress—ye, like the unhappy Madeline, have lost a mother."

Madeline knew not the strength or tenderness of her attachment to the Countess till she was deprived of her; in losing her, she lost all hope of comfort; for to none, as to her, could she impart the fears, the wishes, the expectations, which had so long, and still at times, agitated her heart; and which, by being concealed, she knew would fatally corrode its peace. Yet not for the tenderness which had poured balm upon its sorrows, not for the counsel which had regulated its impulses, not for the wisdom which had guarded its inexperience, did she lament alone; exclusive of all consideration for herself she bitterly wept the death of her benefactress, and imagined, was she but alive again, her own tranquillity would in some degree be restored, though the next moment she should be transported to an immeasurable distance from her.

The circumstances which occasioned her death, heightened the grief of Madeline for it, and the flattering hopes she had conceived of her amendment, from her uninterrupted rest, also aggravated her feelings.

She continued alone a considerable time; at length Agatha entered with some coffee. "I see Mam'selle, (cried she) that like me you could not rest; I might indeed as well have staid up as gone to bed."

"No, (said Madeline, looking mournfully in her face) I could not rest."

"Pray Mam'selle, (cried Agatha, as she laid the coffee on a little table before her) pray Mam'selle, do not take on so badly; though you have lost a good friend, you have still a kind father to love and to protect you; not like me, who in losing my lady, have lost my only friend. Ah, Mam'selle! (dropping into a chair opposite Madeline) 'tis a grievous thing for a poor old soul like me, to be neglected and forlorn."

"You will never be deserted or forlorn, I trust, and believe (cried Madeline); the noble daughter of your dear departed lady will never, I am convinced, desert any one that she loved."

"She is a noble lady, indeed (said Agatha) but— —"

"But what?" eagerly interrogated Madeline, on her suddenly pausing.

"Nothing, Mam'selle, (replied Agatha, sighing; then as if to change the discourse) do pray, Mam'selle (she continued) try and eat some breakfast; indeed, if you do not take more care of yourself, than you at present seem inclined to do, you will probably bring on a fit of sickness; and what a grievous thing would it be for my poor young lady on arriving, to find, not only her mother dead, but you unable to give her any comfort."

"Alas! (said Madeline) whether well or ill, I fear I shall be equally unable to give her comfort."—Agatha again pressed her to take some breakfast, but grief had destroyed all inclination for doing so, and the housekeeper soon left her to her melancholy meditations.—At the usual dinner hour they were again interrupted by the re-entrance of Agatha, who came to entreat her to descend to the dinner parlour. "Do, pray do, dear Mam'selle (she said); if you eat nothing, it will even do you good to stir a little."

Madeline had felt so forlorn whilst by herself, that she did not refuse this entreaty, and accordingly went down stairs; but when she entered the parlour—that parlour where she had first been welcomed to the chateau—where she had been embraced as the adopted child of the Countess—where she had passed with her so many happy hours, the composure she tried to assume vanished; she involuntarily started back, and bursting into tears, would have returned to her chamber, had not Agatha prevented her; the pathetic entreaties of the faithful creature at length prevailed on Madeline to sit down to the table, where she also insisted on Agatha's seating herself; but she could not eat—she could only weep.

The sorrowful looks of the servants—the solemn stillness which reigned throughout the chateau, so different from its former cheerfulness, augmented her tears. Agatha judged of Madeline by herself, and thinking those tears would be a relief to her overcharged heart, she did not attempt to stop them. They sat together till the close of day, when Agatha entreated her to retire to her chamber, and try and take that rest which she had been so long deprived of, and so materially wanted.

Madeline was convinced she could not sleep; but she did not hesitate to return to her chamber, at the door of which Agatha left her. Scarcely had she entered it, ere she resolved on going to her benefactress's, and indulging her sorrow by weeping over her remains. She accordingly proceeded thither; but when she reached the door, she paused, and shuddered at the solemn scene before her.

The chamber was hung with black, and a black velvet pall was thrown across the bed, which formed a melancholy contrast to the rich crimson curtains. Before the bed several rows of large wax tapers burned, and cast a gleam upon the face of the Countess that increased its ghastliness. Awe-struck, Madeline wanted resolution to enter; and it might perhaps have been many minutes ere she could have summoned sufficient for that purpose, had she not beheld Agatha and Floretta sitting in a remote corner of the room. She then, with light and trembling steps, approached the bed. The moment she cast her eyes upon the inanimate features of her friend, the composure, which sudden awe had inspired, gave way to her affliction.

"Is she gone? (she cried, looking round her with an eye of wildness, as if forgetting the scene of the morning—as if doubting the reality of what she saw); Oh! too surely—too surely she is (she continued, wringing her hands together); and who, in this wide world, can supply her loss to Madeline? Oh, most excellent of women! (kneeling beside the bed, while tears streamed in torrents down her cheeks); Thou—friend to the friendless—'tis now I feel the full extremity of grief; the sorrow, which I so lately deemed excruciating, seems light, seems trivial, in comparison of that which I now feel. Had you died (she went on, after a momentary pause, and as if the dull cold ear of death could have heard her pathetic lamentations), had you died according to the common course of nature, though my loss would have been equally great, my grief, I think, would not have been so poignant. To die by such horrible means (she added, with a kind of scream in her voice, and starting up as if she saw that very moment the poignard of the assassin pointed at her own breast); to die by such horrible means, is what overpowers me. Oh why—why did I not follow you the fatal night you went to the chapel?"

"Dear Mam'selle (said Agatha, rising and approaching her), try to compose yourself; no grief, no lamentations can recall my blessed lady."

"Oh! Agatha (cried Madeline), 'tis not a common friend; 'tis a mother I lament;—she was the only person from whom I ever experienced the tenderness of one. Do you not wonder (she continued, grasping the arm of Agatha) how any one could be so wicked as to injure such a woman—a woman who never, I am confident, in the whole course of her life, injured a mortal; whose hand was as liberal as her heart, and whose pity relieved, even when her reason condemned the sufferer? Would you not have thought, Agatha (again bending o'er the bed, from which she had a little retreated) that the innocence of that countenance might have disarmed the rage of a savage? What a smile is there still upon it; it seems to declare the happiness which is enjoyed by the spirit that once animated it!"

"My dear young lady (said Agatha, in a low voice), recollect yourself;—remember the promise you gave my lady in the chapel, never to mention or allude, by any means whatsoever, to the transaction that happened there."

"I thank you, Agatha (cried Madeline), for awakening me to recollection; never should I have forgiven myself, had I broken my promise. I will in future endeavour to have more command over my feelings." She still, however, remained by the bed, holding the arm of Agatha.

"And to this cold, this ghastly, this inanimate state, must we all, one day come!" she cried.

"Yes (replied a hollow voice behind her, the voice of Father Bertrand, who, unperceived, had entered some minutes before, accompanied by some of his brother monks, for the purpose of saying mass for the soul of the departed); the crime of disobedience has doomed us to that state, and the paths of fame and fortune lead but to the coffin and the grave."

He now proceeded to inform Madeline of the purpose for which he had entered.

"If (cried he) you think you can, without interrupting, attend to our solemn rites, and join in our orisons, remain; if not, retire to your chamber."

"I do think I can (replied Madeline); I also think, that, by staying, my mind will be composed."

Some of the most ancient of the domestics now entered, and the sacred service was begun, and ere concluded, the turbulence of Madeline's grief was abated: when over, Father Bertrand, who was tenderly interested about her, insisted on her retiring to her chamber, and gave her his benediction as she withdrew.

Overcome by fatigue, both of body and mind, she repaired to bed; but the sleep into which she sunk was broken and disturbed by frightful visions, and she arose pale and unrefreshed, at the first dawn of day, to seek some of her fellow-partners in affliction. To describe her feelings this day would be but to recapitulate those of the preceding one. They were now, as they were then, alternately perturbed, alternately calm; and

Father Bertrand, whose sympathy and counsel alone caused that calm, was convinced time only could restore them to their wonted state. She this day performed the painful task of acquainting her father with the melancholy loss they had sustained, which she did as follows:—

To M. Clermont,

"WHERE shall I find words to soften the melancholy tidings I have to communicate. Oh! my father, vainly would I try for expressions to do so; no language, no preparation I could use would mitigate them to you; but what I find it impossible to do, your own reason and religion will, I trust, perform.

"Heaven has been pleased to recall our estimable friend, my dear and lamented benefactress, to itself. The dawn of yesterday saw the seal of death impressed upon those eyes which scarcely ever opened but to cheer her family, or witness some good deeds of her own performing. So short was her illness, so unexpected her dissolution, that I feel myself at times quite bewildered by the shock, and tempted to think, that what has lately happened is but the dream of my own disordered imagination.

"Is she dead? I repeatedly ask myself;—the Countess de Merville dead? she whom but a few days ago I beheld so apparently well and happy? Alas! the gloom of every surrounding object gives a fatal affirmative to those self-questions.

"I wander to her favourite apartments, as if to seek for her, who never more will re-enter them; and start back, chilled and affrighted by their neglect and desertion, as if it was unexpected. Oh, my father, what a change has a few days produced! The sound of social mirth no longer enlivens the Castle; a death-like stillness reigns throughout it, scarcely ever interrupted but by the wind sighing through its long galleries, as if in unison with the grief of its inhabitants.

"Things without appear almost as dreary as they do within. The fury of a late storm has scattered the lawn with broken boughs and fragments from the chateau, and thus given the place an appearance of desolation saddening in the extreme. The poor peasants, too, who are employed within the wood, appear (to me at least) quite altered. They seem to pursue their labours with reluctance, and, often suspending them, look towards the Castle with a melancholy air, as if to say the comforts that cheered their toils, and supported their strength, died with its honoured and lamented owner.

"Their loss, indeed, is unspeakable;—not content with relieving the objects chance threw in her way, she herself explored the recesses of poverty, and, like a ministering angel from heaven, dispensed charity and compassion wherever she went. She delighted too in contriving little pastimes which should give relaxation to labour, and smiled to see the rough brow of industry smoothed by pleasure, and the peasants sporting on the sod which they had cultivated.

"This morning, as I stood at an upper window, which overlooked the old trees that waved before it, and saw the distant fields already beginning to wear the yellow tinge of Autumn; I recollected the manner in which she had planned to celebrate the conclusion of the ensuing harvest: she was to have given a feast and a dance upon the lawn to all her tenants, and I was to have mixed in the latter with the peasant girls. Alas! little did I think, when she spoke to me about it, that, ere the period destined for it, she would be laid within the narrow house of clay.

"To quit this place directly, to return to you, my dear father, and mingle those tears with your's, which should embalm her memory, would be my wish, had she not requested, almost in her last moments, that I might continue here to receive Madame D'Alembert, who is shortly expected, and also to give her my company while she staid, or whenever she came to the chateau alone—a request which the gratitude of your heart will not, I am convinced, permit me to disobey;—yet, alas! little benefit can she derive from my society. How can I comfort—how try to reconcile her to a loss which I feel myself nothing earthly can supply to me? But, perhaps, she may derive a melancholy pleasure from the company of a person who is a real mourner; I feel myself, that those of the Countess's family who are the most afflicted, are those to whom I am the most attached.

"It will, I am sure, impart to you the same satisfaction it has done to me, to know that, to the last, my beloved, my estimable benefactress, bestowed upon me those proofs of affection and esteem, which long since excited a gratitude in my heart, death or the loss of reason only can remove. The very morning on which she died so unexpectedly, her generous intentions towards me were to have been put into execution; that they were unfulfilled will, I am confident, be to you, as to me, a small source of regret, compared to that which we feel for her death. I am not now worse with respect to fortune than when she took me under her protection: the luxuries I enjoyed with her have not vitiated my taste, or rendered me unable to support with contentment the humble situation I am destined to. No, my dear father, her lessons and my affection for you guarded me against such perversion of disposition; and as I will still strive to deserve the protection of heaven, so I trust I shall obtain it, and never feel the pressure of worldly want. Do not suffer any apprehensions about my health to disturb your mind; my body has not sympathized as much as you might have supposed with my mind; I am not ill, indeed, though a little fatigued; but there is nothing now (alas! I sigh as I say so) to prevent my taking repose.

"I now regret more than ever the departure of my good friends, Madame Chatteneuf and her daughter; had they continued at V— — —, I am sure, on the first intimation of the melancholy event which has happened, they would have flown to the castle; and their society, I think, would a little have alleviated my feelings. When I sat down, I did not imagine I could have written above a few lines; but now I find that in writing to, as well as in conversing with, a beloved friend, one is insensibly drawn on, and comforted by being so.

"I have now, however, written almost to the extent of my paper; and as I have nothing of sufficient consequence to say to make me begin a new sheet, I shall bid you, my dearest father, farewell. Write as soon as possible, I entreat you; if you say (which I know you will not, except it is the case) that you are well, and somewhat composed after our great loss, you will give ease to my heart.

"I shall receive pleasure from hearing that our faithful Jaqueline, and all our good neighbours, are well: to all who may be so kind as to inquire after me, present my best wishes. Once more farewell! and believe me

"Your truly dutiful and affectionate child,

"Madeline Clermont."

CHAP. IX.

It is the wretch's comfort still to have
Some small reserve of near and inward woe—
Some unsuspected hoard of darling grief,
Which they, unseen, may wail, and weep, and mourn.

Congreve

In her letter to her father, Madeline carefully guarded against dropping any hint of the event which had accelerated the Countess's death, well knowing that, if she gave the most distant intimation of it, she should prompt inquiries from him, which it would be difficult for her to evade. The news of the Countess's decease soon spread throughout the neighbourhood, and several of her acquaintance sent to the castle to learn the particulars of it; how Mademoiselle Clermont was, and whether Madame D'Alembert was expected?

The respect of the servants to the commands of their lady did not expire with her; and, in conformity to the last she had issued, they answered the inquiries concerning the cause of her death, by saying that it was owing to a severe cold.

A dead calm now reigned throughout the castle; the domestics had nothing to do but to lament, and Madeline passed her time in wandering about the castle, like a ghost round the scene of its former happiness, or in watching by the pale remains of her friend, alternately wishing, alternately fearing the arrival of Madame D'Alembert. Ere she came, Father Bertrand determined to have the body of the Countess secured within its coffin, trusting by this measure to conceal for ever the injury it had suffered; convinced, from the strong affection Madame D'Alembert bore her mother, that to let her know the real cause of her death, would be upon the "quarry of that murdered deer," to add the death of her.

Eight days elapsed without any tidings of Madame D'Alembert; and before their expiration, the remains of the Countess were consigned to the coffin, and hid for ever from every mortal eye. At the end of that period, a messenger came post one morning to the castle to announce the near approach of Madame D'Alembert, who came, he said, merely attended by a few domestics. Madeline was astonished to hear she was unaccompanied by Monsieur D'Alembert; but Agatha, to whom she expressed that astonishment, replied, that Monsieur was of a gay disposition, and did not, she supposed, choose to come to the castle till the grief of his lady had a little abated.

"But who (cried Madeline) so able to support her under the pressure of that grief as an affectionate husband."

Agatha shook her head, but did not answer; and Madeline descended to the hall (from the dressing-room of her departed friend, where she had been sitting) to receive Madame D'Alembert, whose carriage at that instant was heard. In the hall Madeline found Father Bertrand and most of the servants assembled, whom the good priest earnestly besought to command their feelings, in order, if possible, to prevent letting Madame D'Alembert know the melancholy event which had happened, until a little prepared for it.

In a few minutes Madame D'Alembert entered, leaning on her woman—a female figure so interesting Madeline had never before seen. To that dignity which excites involuntary respect, she united that light elegance, that harmony of form, which inspires the beholder with mingled pleasure and admiration; she seemed not yet to have attained the prime of her days, and though the rose upon her cheek was pale, and the lustre of her fine blue eyes was fled, her countenance still retained an expression so animated, that language was scarcely necessary to develop her feelings.

She advanced to the middle of the hall; then paused, as if involuntarily, and casting a look around at the old domestics who were ranged on each side, exclaimed, in a tremulous voice, "Am I come too late? Have I arrived in time to receive the last blessing of my mother?"—The servants, instead of answering, hung their heads in mournful silence. Madeline, who had hitherto stood at a distance, pale and trembling, now stepped forward, followed by Father Bertrand; but the moment she had reached Madame D'Alembert, the fortitude she had struggled to assume forsook her; and dropping on her knees, she clasped her arms about her, and burst into tears.

"I see (said Madame D'Alembert, in the hollow voice of despair, and raising her hands towards heaven) I see that all is over—she is gone, and it is a stroke too heavy for me to bear."

She tottered, and would have fallen, had not some of the attendants timely caught her; they conveyed her into an adjoining apartment, but it was many minutes ere she showed any signs of returning sense. When recovered, instead of heeding Father Bertrand, who hung over her, like the delegate of heaven, to administer compassion, instead of regarding Madeline, who knelt beside her, and whose tears evinced her sympathy in her distress, or the domestics who surrounded her with looks of love and pity: she wildly started up, and demanded whether they had yet interred her mother. When answered in the negative, she insisted on going to her chamber: any opposition Father Bertrand was convinced, would be not only fruitless, but an aggravation of her grief.

He knew the violence of sorrow must, like that of the mountain torrent, have way, ere it can subside. Followed by him and Madeline, she ascended to the chamber, but when she reached the door, she stopped, or rather shrunk back, from a sensation of horror at only beholding the coffin, before which rows of tapers burned, every ray of day-light being excluded. In speechless agonies she leaned a minute upon the shoulders of Madeline, then raising her head, she looked at Father Bertrand; "had you the cruelty (she cried) to intend I never more should behold my mother?—never! never, will I acquiesce in such an intention. I command! (advancing into the room) I insist! nay, I entreat! (she continued, and tears, the first she had shed, began to steal down her cheeks) that the coffin may be opened; cold and inanimate as is the form it contains, it will sooth my sad heart once more to behold it. Oh, suffer the eyes of a child again to gaze upon an idolized parent! Oh let her tears of unutterable sorrow be shed over the dear, the lamented cause of them!"

"Impossible! impossible! (said Father Bertrand); the remains of my honoured friend must not be disturbed."

Madame D'Alembert, with a distracted air, now flung back the pall which was thrown over the coffin, as if she hoped herself to effect what she wished; but when the ghastly head of death, curiously engraved upon the lid, with the name and age of her parent, met her eye, she shivered, groaned, and sinking upon it, fainted away. They seized this opportunity to convey her to her chamber, where she was undressed and put to bed, which the female attendants declared was the properest place for her, as she had never stopped to rest from the commencement of her journey.

Father Bertrand now determined that the funeral of the Countess should take place that night, well knowing that, while her remains continued in the house, the feelings of her daughter would not subside, and accordingly issued the necessary orders for that purpose. Madeline staid by the bedside of Madame D'Alembert till the hour fixed on for the removal of the body, though, like every other person, she was totally unnoticed by her: the weakness she had been seized with, rendering her as unable, as from affliction she was unwilling to converse with any one. An express was sent for the surgeon who had attended the Countess, and he quieted the apprehensions of the family about her, by saying, that he trusted attention and time would restore her to her usual state of health. Madeline continued by her, as I have already said, till the hour for the funeral drew nigh; she then resigned her seat to Madame D'Alembert's woman, and descended to the hall, which was again lit up with all its usual splendour; but alas! how melancholy a scene did that light now display! in the centre lay the coffin, surrounded by a numerous body of monks from the neighbouring monastery, and the weeping domestics.

Madeline leaned, weeping, against a distant pillar, nor had power to move till the procession began; she then took a long mourning veil from Agatha, which she, knowing her intention of following the remains of her lady to the grave, had brought for her as soon as she entered the hall, and wrapping it round her, followed with the housekeeper.

The solemn requiem chanted by the monks, as they preceded the body, the glimmering light of the torches, carried by the servants, which as it fell in partial directions upon the old trees that canopied the garden walk through which they past to the valley, produced a thousand quivering and grotesque shadows; the melancholy notes of the birds, who, deceived by the light, started from their nests, and the low murmurs of the wind amongst the branches, altogether produced an effect upon Madeline that wrought her feelings up to agony.

Yet was that agony, if possible, increased when she entered the valley;—horror then seized her soul; and she shuddered as she thought she might, at that very moment perhaps, be treading in the steps of the Countess's murderers. The chapel was lighted up, but the light which gleamed from its windows, by rendering the decay and desolation of the building more conspicuous, served rather to increase than diminish its horrors; from its shattered towers the owls now hooted, and the ravens croaked amidst the surrounding trees, as if singing their nightly song of death, o'er the mouldering bodies which lay beneath them.

Father Bertrand met the procession as it entered the chapel; calmness and resignation in his look, but a more than usual paleness upon his cheek, on which Madeline also thought she could discover the traces of a tear. After meeting, he turned, and preceded the body to the grave, which was directly before the altar, and near those of the Count and his two sons. Madeline's heart felt bursting, and it was with difficulty she could prevent herself from breaking into lamentations; but when the solemn service begun—when she saw the coffin raised—when she saw it, by degrees, lowering into its last receptacle, she could no longer command herself, and a deep groan burst from her.—Father Bertrand paused in the sentence he was uttering over the body, and looked steadily at her; she instantly recollected herself, drew her veil entirely over her face, and buried her sobs in her bosom. He would then have proceeded, but as he attempted to speak, his voice faltered, the muscles of his face began to work, and a tear dropped from him into the grave of his benefactress; the weakness, however, which had overcome him was but momentary, and he resumed and finished the service with his usual steadiness; a solemn mass was then again said, for the soul of the departed, after which Father Bertrand pronounced a short and pathetic eulogium on her:—"The loss, my friends (said he, as he concluded it) which you have sustained by the death of this truly good woman, is indeed great; but man is born to suffer, and continually liable to such deprivations as you have experienced; murmur not therefore at the common lot, but, by patient resignation to the will of the Almighty, strive to deserve a continuance of your remaining blessings: instead of quitting this place with a vain sorrow, quit it with a noble resolution to perform your allotted parts, and to pursue, as far as lies in your power, the example of your lamented benefactress. So may you hope, at the last day, to ascend with her to life immortal."

The lights in the chapel, and the torches were now extinguished, and the monks repaired immediately from it to their convent, and Madeline and the servants returned to the castle. Agatha cried bitterly all the way back; " 'twas a grievous thing (she said to Madeline) to see the death of one's best, one's only friend; little did I imagine (she said) that I should ever have beheld the funeral of my lady—I who, when she was a nice prattling little girl, have often and often carried her about in my arms."

The moment Madeline re-entered the castle, she retired to her chamber, to give vent to that grief, which by being so long suppressed, had almost swelled her heart to bursting. When somewhat relieved by the tears she shed, she knelt down and implored heaven to strengthen her fortitude, that she might be enabled, not only to submit with patience to its divine will, but to pay proper attentions to the daughter of her lamented friend. "Regard not! (she cried with fervour) Oh, regard not! thou, from whom misery and happiness alike proceed, with any degree of displeasure, the sorrow of a weak creature, impressed with the sad idea of the world's being unable to make her any recompense for what she has lost."

In a short time she was sufficiently composed to be able to repair to the chamber of Madame D'Alembert, where she determined to pass the night. During that night, Madame D'Alembert continued almost in a state of insensibility, but on the morrow she appeared better, and again spoke. She asked, whether the interment of her mother had taken place? Father Bertrand desired, if such a question was asked, that he should be sent for to answer it, and for that purpose remained in the house; he was now called, and without hesitation informed her of the truth. The violence of her grief seemed renewed at this, and she reproached him with cruelty in not deferring the funeral till she was able to have attended it. He bore her reproaches with patience, with composure, and seized the first interval of silence to reason with her.

"For what purpose (cried he) would the interment have been delayed; merely to feed your grief, and continue your family in an unsettled state. Prove your affection to your departed parent, by striving to adhere to the precepts she always gave, to the example she always set you; with a sensibility as exquisite as your's, recall to mind the fortitude with which she bore the death of an idolized husband and two lovely sons, the darlings of her heart, the expected supporters of her noble house: instead of sinking into the supineness of sorrow, instead of withdrawing her cares from life, because that life had lost its brightest charms, she exerted herself to fulfil its incumbent duties; let the remembrance of those exertions inspire you to make similar ones; let it raise you from the bed of languor, let it rouse you from the torpor of affliction, let it animate you to perform your proper part, by tracing her steps; by doing as she has done, you will more truly prove your love, your reverence for her, than by passing years in fruitless lamentations over her tomb. Like her then, I again repeat, exert yourself; let the smile of your countenance again gladden the hearts of your friends, and your ear be again open to the voice of cheerfulness."

"She set me a glorious example indeed, (said Madame D'Alembert, on whom the language of the venerable man appeared to have made a deep impression); and in future I will strive to follow it."

"Do, (cried Father Bertrand) if you wish to retain your present blessings."

"My blessings!" repeated she mournfully.

"Yes, (resumed he) the many blessings you still possess."— Madame D'Alembert sighed deeply at those words, and shook her head with an air that seemed to imply a doubt of what he asserted.

"Amongst the least of these blessings (continued he, glancing at Madeline who sat beside the bed) I shall not rank the friend who now sighs to be presented to you."

"You would be wrong, I am sure, if you did," said Madame D'Alembert, raising herself a little upon her pillow, and extending her white hand, as if to receive Madeline's. Father Bertrand took it, and instantly put it into her's.—"You have both (said he, in a softened voice) lost a mother; be ye therefore as sisters to each other, a mutual comfort and support."

"I have long (cried Madame D'Alembert, turning her soft blue eyes on Madeline, and pressing her hand between her's) been prepared to love and to admire you; and she who prepared me to do so, I hoped would have introduced us to each other; but that hope, like many others, was indulged but to be disappointed." Madeline knelt down, and pressed her hand to her lips; Madame D'Alembert gently disengaged it, and throwing her arm round her neck, clasped her to a heart, whose strong emotions, for a few moments, overpowered her utterance. "Believe me (she cried, as soon as she had recovered her voice) when I declare, that the chief pleasure I look forward to, is that which I shall receive from your society; she who was beloved by my mother, and who loved her, must on these accounts, even if not possessed of half your powers of pleasing, be dear and precious to me; with the truest gratitude I now thank you for all your kind attentions to her."

"Ah Madam! (said Madeline, melting into tears) you surely must be ignorant of my great obligations to her, or you never could speak to me in this manner; did you know them, you would certainly think as I do, that I never did, never could do any thing adequate to the gratitude they excited; she was the only person from whom I ever received the tenderness of a mother, and as daughters must, I imagine, love their mothers, I loved her."

By degrees Madame D'Alembert grew composed, and the conversation then turned upon her deep regret at not arriving in time to behold her mother;—from Madeline, who, she understood, had attended her in her last moments, she entreated to hear the particulars of the disorder which had terminated so fatally. Father Bertrand, who had seated himself at the foot of the bed, now interposed his authority; he knew it would scarcely be possible for Madeline, if she complied with this entreaty, to avoid giving a too faithful narrative, and he therefore declared, that except she and Madame D'Alembert promised to converse no longer on the melancholy subject, they should be separated. "Why (said he, to the latter) do you feed your own grief, and augment her's, by dwelling on it?"

"I promise what you desire, (cried Madame D'Alembert) but Oh! let me be indulged by hearing, whether in her last moments my mother remembered her unhappy Viola!"

"Remembered! (repeated Madeline emphatically) Oh, Madam! after heaven you were her first consideration." She then, as far as it concerned Madame D'Alembert, related the conversation which had passed between the Countess and her the evening preceding her death.

"You will be my friend, my consoler then! (exclaimed Madame D'Alembert, from whom the relation drew floods of tears, extending her hand to Madeline as she spoke); I open my heart to receive your consolations; my mother wished me to do so, and as I perform what she wished, so do I hope that the blessing she left me, may draw another down."—Madeline sighed, and laid her face upon the hand she held, to conceal the feelings, which, for a few minutes stopped her utterance; fervently, though silently, she prayed for the fortitude which she now wanted, to perform the task enjoined her by her lamented friend. Yet, alas! she said to herself, as she had done in her letter to her father, how can I give to others that consolation which I want myself? Her evident inability to do so, rendered her, perhaps, a more soothing companion to Madame D'Alembert, than if the case had been reversed; it proved her deep and poignant sorrow more than any words could have done; and nothing perhaps attaches the heart of a mourner so soon, so truly, as a keen participation in its griefs. Madame D'Alembert eagerly enquired, whether she would not continue with her while she herself remained at the chateau? and whether she would not always accompany her to it, whenever she visited it alone? Madeline said, she believed she might promise to do so, as she was pretty certain her father would never refuse a request made by his honoured and lamented friend, or her daughter.

"How long Madam, (asked Father Bertrand), do you propose staying at the chateau?"

"About two months, (replied Madame D'Alembert); I shall then be obliged to return to Paris, where Monsieur D'Alembert proposes spending the winter."

"And how soon do you expect him here?" still interrogated Bertrand.

"I do not expect him at all, (answered Madame D'Alembert); he told me, just before we parted, that he was convinced some particular business, which prevented his accompanying me at the present melancholy juncture, would not be finished in time to permit him to follow me."

In two months then, thought Madeline, I shall be restored to the arms of my father; ah! how many distressing scenes have I gone through since I left them!

Father Bertrand now withdrew, but Madeline continued the remainder of the day with her friend, who, though unable at times to converse with her, seemed to derive pleasure from even looking at her. The following day, the exertions which Father Bertrand had animated her to make, enabled her to rise; and in two days more, the gentleman who attended her took his leave, declaring that time was the only physician whose aid she now required; but though health returned, cheerfulness still continued absent, nor had it more completely forsaken her breast than it had that of Madeline's.

The death of her benefactress, together with the disappointment she had experienced prior to it, left an impression of sadness upon her mind which she could not conquer;—had her efforts for doing so been aided by any external circumstance, they might perhaps, in some degree, have been successful; but her present companion and abode were gloomy in the extreme, and of themselves sufficient to have lowered even animated spirits.

Madame D'Alembert declined seeing any company; she received no visits but from Father Bertrand; and in answer to the compliments of condolence which she received from the neighbouring families, and which they anxiously wished to pay in person, she declared her utter inability of seeing them at present.

No more the feast of mirth and hospitality was spread within the hall of the chateau—no more its lofty roof re-echoed sounds of melody—no more the peasants danced upon the lawn, while Benevolence sat by in the form of the Countess, and smiled upon their sports. Solitude encompassed, and silence reigned within it; and the old domestics, whose grief for their lady knew no diminution, scrupled not to say, that the glory, the happiness of her house had, with her, forsaken it for ever.

So congenial was its gloom to the present feelings of Madame D'Alembert, that she never talked of quitting it without the deepest regret; exclusive of the above consideration, she was also attached to it from its having been the favourite residence of her parents, the place where the blossoms of her youth had blown. Here she wished to pass the remainder of her days—here, where she could be free from that restraint—that state—those tiresome ceremonies, which in a public situation the etiquette of the world obliged her to observe. Like the poet, she might have said,

"This shadowing desert, unfrequented woods,

I better brook than flourishing peopl'd towns.

Here I can sit alone, unseen of any,

And to the nightingale's complaining notes

Tune my distresses, and record my woes."

From words which sometimes dropped from Madame D'Alembert, Madeline was more than once led to imagine, that besides the death of her mother, she had another cause for sorrow; but whenever she reflected on her situation, that idea vanished, and she wondered how she could for a moment have harboured it; knowing, as she did, that Madame D'Alembert possessed those blessings, which in general are supposed to render life estimable—the affections of the man of her choice (for such Madeline always understood M. D'Alembert to be), friends who adored her, and even a superabundance of riches.

Those attentions, which pity for the afflicted Viola, and reverence for the commands of her benefactress, first prompted her to pay, Madeline now continued from affection.

Madame D'Alembert was a woman, whose temper and disposition, upon an intimacy, captivated the heart, as much as her beauty and elegance, at first sight, charmed the eye: besides, she treated Madeline exactly as a tender sister would have done, ordered the same mourning for her as for herself, nor suffered the servants to make any distinction between them.

In the course of the conversation Madeline discovered that Madame D'Alembert knew nothing of her or her father prior to her introduction at the chateau; and she felt from this circumstance more firmly convinced than ever that the private history of her father must be dreadful, when the Countess would not impart it even to her daughter.

A month elapsed without Madame D'Alembert's solitude being in the least interrupted, during which she and Madeline paid many visits to the grave of the Countess, which the latter could never approach without shuddering.

At the expiration of that period, as they sat at breakfast one morning, a letter was brought to Madame D'Alembert by her woman; who, as she put it into her hands, said, "From my master, Madam."

Her Lady turned pale at those words, and desiring her to retire, broke the seal with a trembling hand.

END OF VOL. II.

CHAP. I.

Thoughts succeed thoughts, like restless troubled waves,

Dashing out one another.

After perusing her letter, Madame D'Alembert leaned her head upon her hand and continued silent many minutes as if absorbed in profound meditation; then raising it, "my love (she cried to Madeline, whose eyes, though she had retired to a window were fastened on her), my love, (motioning for her to take a seat by her), I am now going to put your friendship to the test."

"I trust, Madame, (said Madeline as she seated herself), you do not doubt its being able to bear any trial you can put it to."

"I have no reason indeed, (replied Madame, taking her hand) to doubt your affection or sincerity; but the request I am about making appears to me unreasonable, consequently I fear its appearing much more so to you." She paused a minute, and then, tho' with rather a hesitating voice, proceeded.

"Monsieur D'Alembert is coming to the chateau; the letter I have just received came by an express to announce his approach,—in the course of this day I expect him. Reasons of the most powerful nature, but reasons which I cannot, must not, dare not declare, make me wish to prevent his seeing you, at least while you are under my protection."

"Dearest Madam (then said Madeline with quickness), let me return immediately to my father; how could you imagine I should think your requesting me to do so unreasonable; I have long wished to see him, and my regret at quitting you will now be lessened by knowing Monsieur D'Alembert will be your companion."

"My dear girl (cried Madame) you totally mistake me; though I do not wish you to see Monsieur D'Alembert, I by no means wish you to return to your father; on the contrary, should you insist on doing so, you will pain me beyond expression."

"But how, Madame, (asked Madeline with much surprise) how will it be possible to avoid being seen by Monsieur if I do not quit the chateau."

"By consenting to seclude yourself from society (answered Madame) while he is in it; his stay he informs me will be but short—was it a long one I could not be so selfish as to attempt to keep you; tell me then, my Madeline—terminate my suspense—will you gratify, will you comply with my wishes?" She paused and looked earnestly at Madeline for a reply, but it was many minutes ere Madeline could give one.

Amazed by what she had heard, and learning that Madame D'Alembert had powerful reasons for concealing her from her husband, her whole soul was engrossed in trying to develop those reasons; but like the other mysteries which had tortured it, she vainly tried to do so.

"Ah! Madeline (said Madame D'Alembert, in a melancholy voice) I fear this silence bodes me no good."

"My dearest Madam, (cried Madeline) I would at once have answered you, could I at once have determined how to act; but I will acknowledge though my affection for you prompts me to comply with your request, my pride makes me revolt from the idea of becoming the unknown guest of any person; besides—besides (with some little hesitation) there is a kind of apprehension mingled with that pride. I recollect the particular, the impressive manner, in which my beloved benefactress bade me remember, that whenever Monsieur D'Alembert came to the chateau, she did not desire me to continue in it; and her words, together with those you have uttered, make me fear that Monsieur has some secret enmity against me, though for what cause I cannot possibly conceive, unacquainted as I am with him."

"What a wild idea, (exclaimed Madame), to suppose a person who is really ignorant of your existence, can have any enmity to you?"

"Good heaven! Madam, (cried Madeline) how you astonish me!"

"I repeat, (said her friend) that Monsieur D'Alembert, at this moment, knows not that such a being as Madeline Clermont exists: when he comes to the chateau he certainly must hear about you, but your real residence I shall take care to have concealed from him: Come, tell me, do you longer hesitate how to act?"

Madeline sighed deeply; she was unwilling to stay, and yet unwilling to go: unwilling from motives of affection, and a fear that if she did she should be deemed ungrateful; rightly considering that those who will not sometimes tax their feelings for a friend, are themselves unworthy of the appellation of one.

"No, Madam, (said she, after the silence of a few minutes) I no longer hesitate,—do with me as you please; I should ill requite your favors if I disobeyed your wishes."

"A thousand thanks, my Madeline, for your compliance; (cried her friend, tenderly embracing her) it has removed a heavy burden of uneasiness from me: and now, my dear girl, to inform you of the plan which I have concerted for your concealment; a plan which only to those immediately concerned in carrying it into execution I shall impart, in order to avoid any danger of a discovery, and to prevent idle curiosity: I shall immediately have it circulated through the family that you are going to pay a visit to a relation some leagues off, and order Lubin, (in whom, his old godmother, Agatha, and Floretta, I alone mean to confide) to prepare horses for the journey; as soon as you are out of sight of the chateau, he shall conduct you to the grotto by the lake, where as soon as it is dark, Floretta shall be sent to re-conduct you home, and by a private door bring you to the chamber of my mother, which I think better adapted than your own for concealing you, as her death is too recent to permit the servants to wish to enter it.

"I hope my love (seeing Madeline turn pale) you have no objection to it?"

Madeline was ashamed to acknowledge she had.—

"No, Madam, (answered she falteringly) I have not."

"Consider, my dear, (said her friend, who was not perfectly satisfied by this assurance) your seclusion in it will be but short; and while you continue in it, Agatha and Floretta shall pass as much time as possible with you; every opportunity too which occurs for visiting you, without danger of detection, I shall seize: retire now, my love to your chamber, and in order to give the appeaance we wish to my plan, put on a riding habit."

Madeline withdrew, but instead of changing her dress, she sat down to reconsider all that had passed, and the more she reflected on it, the more her heart recoiled from the idea of continuing in the chateau.

"If discovered (said she) I may be insulted as an intruder, and degraded not only in my own eyes, but those of the family; but can I retract the promise I have given to Madame D'Alembert? No, it is impossible to do so—I cannot appear fickle, I cannot disappoint her; sooner than do so I will run the risk even of indignity."

While thus engrossed in thought, Madame D'Alembert, followed by Agatha and Floretta, entered: Madeline started and attempted to apologize for not having put on the habit.

"You are an idle girl, (cried her friend) the horses are waiting, and no time is to be lost."

In a few minutes she was ready, and with Madame D'Alembert descended to the hall, where she found many of the old servants, (who loved her for the sake of their dear departed lady as well as for her own) assembled to bid her farewell; having received and returned that farewell, and also a parting embrace from her friend, she mounted her horse and set off at a smart pace with Lubin: they soon penetrated into the thickest of the wood, and after proceeding about a mile through it, they turned into a winding path leading to the lake; here they both alighted, and Madeline, being acquainted with the way, walked on, while Lubin slowly led the horses after her. This was the very path which de Sevignie had taken the last evening she beheld him, and the moment she entered it, the remembrance of that evening rushed upon her mind; she sighed heavily: "Ah! how different (she cried to herself) were my feelings then to what they are now!—then I imagined myself the beloved of de Sevignie's heart, then believed him entitled, not only from affection but worth, to the possession of mine; but now no idea of that kind remains, and to that which I once entertained I look back as to a delightful dream, from which I have only been awakened to misery and horror.

"Yet can de Sevignie (she continued, as she pursued her way), can de Sevignie, (as if only now she had conceived the doubt) be perfidious, be unworthy? Oh! impossible! (cried she, yielding to the suggestions of a tenderness, which, though opposed, had never been in the least degree conquered), Oh! impossible! Vice could never wear such a semblance of virtue as he wore; the alteration in his manner must have been owing to some circumstances which pride prevented his revealing, and I should, I ought at once to have believed so: surely I had done so, had I not obeyed, (let me whisper it to myself) the dictates of disappointed tenderness and offended pride."

On reaching the grotto she seated herself on the moss-covered stone before it; the very seat on which she had once been alarmed by de Sevignie; the very seat on which she had once, while the pale stars glimmered o'er her head, so impatiently waited his approach.

"Oh! what minutes were those, (she exclaimed) Oh! what the palpitation of that moment which brought him to my feet! —" Again she beheld him in idea, again saw his fine eyes beaming on her with mingled love, hope and sorrow; again felt the soft pressure of his cold trembling hand; again heard the sighs, with which he declared there was an unconquerable necessity for their separation.

"Oh! de Sevignie (she cried) to know you happier now than when that declaration was made, would relieve my heart of an almost intolerable weight of anguish: she wished she could learn whether he had yet left V— — —; but to enquire without betraying her motives for doing so was impossible, and from the idea of discovering them she shrunk with affright.

"What satisfaction (she asked herself) could I derive by knowing he was still there? No hope of seeing him could be derived by such a knowledge."

She continued engrossed by this idea till she felt the tears dropping upon her cheeks; these brought her to a sense of her weakness. "Is it by indulging such feelings as my present ones, —is it by dwelling on the remembrance of Sevignie, (said she) that I adhere to the resolution I formed not to think about him, that I obey the injunctions of my lamented benefactress, or what I know must be the wishes of my father: what folly! instead of trying to drive him from my heart, to try and establish him more firmly than ever within it, by still believing him amiable! Ah, had he been really so, never would he have formed plans which he did not mean to realize; never would he have condemned my opening my heart to such a friend as I was blessed with; and 'tis only a sudden impulse of weak and culpable tenderness which could make me again consider him in the light I once did, an impulse which I will endeavour never more to yield to: Yes, de Sevignie, more resolutely than ever I will try to expel you from my heart." She wiped away her tears, but felt at the moment how arduous was the task which she had imposed upon herself.—

How difficult it would be, in moments of security and quiet, to banish de Sevignie from her thoughts, when scenes of grief and terror, such as she had lately experienced, had not had power to do so.

"Heaven, however, (cried she) strengthens those who wish to do right; I wish to do so, and to do so I think I must forget de Sevignie."

Lubin, who had hitherto been engaged in securing the horses within a cavity of the mountain, now approached, and opening a small basket of nice provisions, which Agatha had given him, he spread a napkin on the grass before Madeline, and laid the contents of the basket on it.

"'Tis time for you to take something Mademoiselle (said he) I dare say 'tis now far beyond your usual dinner hour; do pray, Mademoiselle, do take something, you look faint indeed."

Madeline felt weak and tired, and did not resist his entreaty: after her little repast was over, he removed the things to a respectful distance, and sat down to refresh himself. The parents of Lubin had passed the principal part of their lives in the service of the Countess and her family, and at their death, which happened when he was very young, she had taken him entirely under her protection; his gratitude and fidelity amply repaid her kindness, and she had considered him as she did Agatha, infinitely above the rest of the servants.

With true French gaiety after he had finished his repast, he amused himself with singing the following

Song

Come, sweet Content, thou ever smiling maid,

Come, sit with me beneath this old tree's shade;

Or ramble with me round yon green-clad hill,

Adown whose side soft steals the silvery rill.

If thou'rt an inmate of my humble home,

I would not change it for a gilded dome;

If blessed with thee, my table shall be crown'd
With sweets, in riot's banquet never found;

Careless with thee I'd roam at early day,
And join the warblers on the waving spray;
Or gaily tend my fleecy bleating fold,
And kindly guard them from the wint'ry cold.

Oh! let me fold thee to this throbbing heart,
Which sighs for peace thou only canst impart;
And let me with thee ever humbly bend,
Before each trial heav'n may please to send.

Like some kind star that gives a cheering ray,
To lead benighted mortals on their way,
Do thou appear to check each anxious thought,
And give that blessedness so long I've sought.

"Is that your own composition, Lubin?" (asked Madeline) whose mind was amused by listening to him.

"Yes, Mademoiselle, (replied he) I pass many of the long winter nights in scribbling, and then I set my own words to my own music, and they answer my purpose as well as the best song in the world."

"The purpose of amusing you," said Madeline.

"Yes, Mademoiselle, and keeping care from my mind: life is so short that one should, according to the old saying, 'learn to live all the days of their life', which they never can do if they yield to fretting or vexation."

"True, (cried Madeline), those who think as you do, Lubin, are only truly happy."

Lubin now rambled away, and Madeline also arose and walked about.

The day was now far advanced,

"And in the western sky the downward sun

"Look'd out effulgent from amid the flush

"Of broken clouds, gay shifting to his beams."

Those beautiful clouds, and all his dazzling splendour were reflected in the clear bosom of the lake, along with its verdant banks; where the laurestine just beginning to blossom, and the arbutis already in bloom, reared high their beauteous heads, while its soft murmurs intermingled in the wild concert of woodland choristers: a thousand golden beams played upon the forest, heightening the richness of its autumnal shades, and as they illumined the distant mountains, discovering some of their most romantic recesses. The mind of Madeline was soothed by the charming scene, and she felt that while she retained her present taste for the works of nature, she could not be entirely insensible to pleasure. The wild flowers that grew about now emitted their choicest fragrance, and the evening gale bore to her ear the bleating of distant flocks, and the far off whistle of the peasant the welcome signal to his companions in industry, to retire from their labours.

At the appointed time Floretta came to her; in about an hour Lubin said he would follow them to the chateau.

"Well to be sure, Mademoiselle, (said Floretta, as they walked towards it) 'tis with fear and trembling I came for you to-night; Lord I hope this may be the last time I shall ever be sent to the grotto."

"Is Monsieur D'Alembert come?" asked Madeline.

"Come, yes, and in a way that was not expected; he has brought three coaches full of company along with him."

"Brought company along with him?" repeated Madeline, in a voice of astonishment.

Yes, an equal number of ladies and gentlemen, and all gay souls I can assure you."

"Your lady's feelings must be extremely hurt," said Madeline.

"Aye to be sure; but if Monsieur never hurts them more severely, she will be very well off."

"This bringing so much company to the chateau seems as if he intended to make a long stay at it."

"Oh, no, Mademoiselle, (replied Floretta with quickness) I took care to inquire particularly from Lewis his valet de chambre, about his intentions, and he told me his master and his friends were taking a tour of pleasure, and the chateau lying in their way, had merely called at it for the purpose of resting themselves a few days."

"Or perhaps to request Madame D'Alembert's company," (said Madeline.)

"Not they indeed, (cried Floretta) she is quite too grave for my master, or the friends he likes, and tis a pity indeed that she should be so: Lord, what is the use of fine cloaths, or youth, or beauty, or fortune, if one lives moping and retired, as she does, for all the world like a hermit."

"Consider, Floretta, (said Madeline) the affliction your lady is at present in."

"And what does solitude do but increase that affliction; when a thing is over what is the good of lamenting it? Ah! Mam'selle, I have often thought what a fine figure I'd make if I had my lady's fine clothes, and jewels, and carriage to roll about in.

"I assure you, Mademoiselle, (continued she with a conceited simper) I could scarcely come to you to-night; Monsieur Lewis, whom I knew very well, when in Paris with my lady, would hardly let me leave him; he is one of the politest creatures in the world, and pays such pretty compliments; he says I am vastly improved by the country air, and that my natural roses would shame all the artificial ones in Paris. He and the other servants which accompanied him, have quite enlivened us again, all but poor Agatha; she has moped about ever since they came, but she is old, Mademoiselle, (proceeded Floretta, with a significant look) she is old, and that is the reason she cannot be animated like us."

"Poor Agatha!" exclaimed Madeline, who felt more attached than ever to the faithful creature, from finding she had feelings so congenial to her own.

She had now reached the chateau, and her heart palpitated with a fear of being discovered either by Monsieur D'Alembert, or some of his servants; but of this Floretta assured her there was no danger.

Through a private door in the rear of the castle, she led her up a flight of narrow stairs, seldom used, to the gallery, which was now gaily illumined by the lights that blazed in the hall: fearful of being discovered, Madeline hastened to the chamber, in which Floretta informed her she would find Agatha waiting to receive her; but ere she reached it, a shout of noisy laughter, ascended from an apartment contiguous to the hall, and shocked her, by making her feel as if an insult had been offered to the memory of the countess.

"If my feelings are so poignant upon the occasion, (said she to herself), ah, what must the feelings of her daughter be!—Surely, surely M. D'Alembert cannot have that sensibility which the husband of Viola should possess, or he would not thus have broken in upon the sacredness of her grief."

Floretta knocked softly at the chamber door and it was immediately opened by Agatha; but the moment Madeline entered it she started back, shocked and surprised at beholding it in the same state as when the remains of the countess were taken from it. Agatha took her hand, and, drawing her in, locked the door. "Pray be composed, dear Mademoiselle, (said she) my lady, who feared the sight of the hangings might affect you, would have had them removed had it been possible for me and Floretta to have taken them down; but as that was not the case, she she feared desiring the men to do so, lest it should excite suspicion."

"I own (cried Madeline, in a faint voice, with a face as pale as death) I own I would rather have continued in my own room; but if you or Floretta will have the goodness to pass the night in this with me, I shall not feel quite so reluctant to it."

"As to my staying with you, Mademoiselle, (exclaimed Floretta, instantly going to the door) that is utterly impossible; I have a thousand things to do, which Agatha, if she pleases can tell you of."

So saying she hastily unlocked the door, and departed without ceremony.

"For my part, (said Agatha, as soon as she had again secured it) I would stay with you with all my heart, but that I fear if I did I should be missed (as some of the maids rooms open into mine) and if I was, your being in the castle must be discovered, which I know would distress my lady exceedingly."

"And why should it distress her?" demanded Madeline with quickness, no longer able to suppress her curiosity.

"Why, (repeated Agatha, looking earnestly at her) because— dear Mademoiselle, (cried she as if suddenly recollecting herself) I am sure I can't tell you."

"Don't be alarmed, Agatha, (said Madeline, with affected composure), I shall not inquire into secrets, which I see your respect for your lady makes you solicitous to conceal; in silence I shall submit to her wishes, her kindness gives her a right to expect this from me."

Supper was prepared for Madeline, as was also provisions for the ensuing day, as till the next night, she was informed she could not be visited by any one. Agatha pressed her to sit down to table; she had no inclination to eat, she however complied with her entreaty, and made her also take a chair, being anxious to detain her as long as possible.

"Monsieur D'Alembert makes no long stay at the chateau, I understand, (said she), from Floretta."

"No, thank heaven, he soon quits it," replied Agatha.

"It seems he merely stopped to rest himself, and his party at it," resumed Madeline.

"So he and his good for nothing servants say, (cried Agatha) but I have reason to think he had some other motive for coming to it."

"Have you?" said Madeline eagerly.

"Yes; I imagine he came to it for the purpose of seeing what part of the estate would be the best to dispose of."

"Dispose of? (repeated Madeline, in amazement) surely Monsieur D'Alembert could not think of disposing of any part of it? surely his situation does not require his doing so?"

"'Tis a sign you know little of it, or you would not say so, (cried Agatha) his extravagance has long rendered him in want of money."

"His extravagance! (again repeated Madeline) Monsieur D'Alembert extravagant! Gracious heaven how you astonish me! By what means was the countess de Merville prevailed on to let her daughter marry a man of dissipation?"

"He appeared both to the Countess and her daughter a very different man before, to what he did after his marriage," answered Agatha.

"And to the too late discovery of his real character the melancholy of the Countess was to be imputed," said Madeline.

Agatha looked at her but made no reply.

A dreadful idea started in the mind of Madeline:—the words of Floretta, the solemn manner in which she had been bound by the countess to conceal the black transaction in the chapel, seemed to declare it was a just one: she grasped the arm of Agatha, she fastened her eyes upon her as if they would pierce into the very recesses of her soul.

"The horrible mystery then (said she) is explained;—Monsieur D'Alembert—the chapel—"

"Ha! (cried Agatha, starting from her chair and shaking off the hand of Madeline) what do you say? Beware, beware, Mademoiselle of what you utter; beware (with a dark frown) even of what you think. I know what you would have said, I know what you have imagined, but—"

"But I am not mistaken," said Madeline, in a hollow voice, and sinking against the back of the chair.

"You are; (exclaimed Agatha) you have done injustice to Monsieur D'Alembert."

"Heaven be praised, (cried Madeline, clasping her hands together) heaven be praised; had I continued much longer to believe the idea I formed of him a just one, I think I could not have preserved my reason."

"Dear heart, I am sure I should not have wondered if you had lost it directly, (said Agatha) it must have been horrible indeed to suppose that the husband of the daughter could have murdered the mother."

"Oh, horrible, most horrible!" exclaimed Madeline.

"Though Monsieur D'Alembert is gay and extravagant, and not the kind of man he appeared to be before his marriage, he is not such a villain as you supposed him," cried Agatha.

"I was not then mistaken in supposing that Madame D'Alembert had another cause for grief besides the death of her mother?" said Madeline.

"No, you were not mistaken as to that, (replied Agatha) poor thing she frets a great deal about Monsieur, and I am sure if he sells any part of the domain belonging to the chateau, it will go nigh to break her heart, for she loves every inch of it; and if any thing could raise my poor dear lady out of her grave, I am certain his doing so would."

"I hope he will not be so disrespectful to her memory, (said Madeline) as to do what he knows would have been contrary to her inclination, nor so inhuman to her daughter as to disregard her wishes."

"I fear he will, Mademoiselle: (cried Agatha) when once he takes a thing into his head, 'tis a difficult matter to make him give it up: but I hope when you see Madame you will not tell her any thing I have been saying."

"You may be assured I shall not," said Madeline.

"She means (resumed Agatha) to pay you a visit to-morrow night, if she can possibly steal from her company: poor soul tis very different company to what she has been accustomed to: Ah! Mademoiselle, if my dear lady had been living, such people would never have been permitted to enter the chateau. Alas! its glory and happiness are departed, and I shall never again behold such days as once I saw within it.

"Farewell Mademoiselle, (continued she, rising) tis time for me to leave you, for I hear the servants retiring to rest, heaven bless you and protect you."

Madeline locked the door after her with a trembling hand, and involuntarily shuddered as she turned from it at finding herself alone in a chamber so gloomy, and so remote from every one as her present one was. Her spirits were too much agitated, in consequence of her conversation with Agatha, to permit her to sleep; and, even if inclined to do so, she could not think of reposing on a bed where she had so lately seen the corpse of her friend; whenever she glanced at it, it was with a kind of terror, as if she almost expected to have beheld again upon it the same ghastly figure.

Within the chamber was a closet which contained a small selection of books; determined on sitting up the night, Madeline took one from it, with a hope that it would divert her thoughts and prevent her attention from dwelling on what distressed her; but this hope was a vain one, and the night wore heavily away. About the dawn of day she leaned back in the arm chair on which she was sitting, and slept for a little time; the ensuing hours were as tedious and melancholy as those she had recently passed; she waited most impatiently for the promised visit from some of her friends, particularly after it grew too dark for her to read. At length in about two hours after she had been compelled to lay aside her book, she heard a soft tap at the chamber door, she immediately opened it, and Floretta entered with a light, and a small basket of provisions. Madeline followed her to the table on which she laid them, as soon as she had re-locked the door, and then to her infinite amazement and terror first perceived that Floretta was weeping violently.

CHAP. II.

"Ah, fear, ah, frantic fear,

"I see, I see thee near:

"I know thy hurried step, thy haggard eye,

"Like thee I start, like thee disordered fly."

"What is the matter, Floretta?" asked Madeline, in a voice of alarm.

"Ah! Mademoiselle, (exclaimed Floretta, dropping into a chair, and wringing her hands) poor Agatha!"

"What of her?" cried Madeline, with an eagerness that shook her frame.

"She is dead!" replied Floretta.

"Dead! (repeated Madeline, receding a few paces and wildly staring) dead!" she exclaimed, with mingled doubt and horror.

"Yes, (said Floretta) and her death is attended with such appearances!"

Madeline trembled universally, her respiration grew faint, she sat down by Floretta, she laid her cold hand upon her, but it was many minutes ere she could speak.

"Her death has been attended with suspicious circumstances then?" said she.

"It has," replied Floretta.

Madeline started up, and wildly demanded whether she could not see Madame D'Alembert directly.

Without giving herself time to reflect how very improbable it was that they could have gained access to the castle to perpetrate the crime she accused them of, the moment Madeline heard of Agatha's death being attended with suspicious circumstances, she conceived the dreadful idea of her having fallen a victim to the murderers of the countess, in order to prevent their being discovered; and to a similar apprehension she could not doubt she would be sacrificed herself, as they had seen her in the chapel with Agatha.

It was this fear therefore that made her wish to see Madame D'Alembert directly that she might entreat her permission to return to her father without any farther delay.

"See my lady, Mademoiselle," said Floretta, also rising.

"Yes, (cried Madeline, almost gasping for breath), this house is no longer safe for me to dwell in, and she must let me quit it directly."

"I will go and try whether she can come to you Mademoiselle, (said Floretta, who, alarmed by her agitation, feared to oppose her), but indeed I fear she cannot, without Monsieurs knowledge, as she is now engaged with him and his company: I know she intends to visit you to-night, as she and my master are to have separate chambers, though it will be at a late hour; if you could wait till then it would be better."

"Well, (cried Madeline, growing a little composed and re-seating herself) if you are sure she intends to come, I will, however contrary to my inclination, wait her own time, rather than expose her to the displeasure of Monsieur D'Alembert: and yet, Floretta, (continued she looking earnestly at her) I cannot conceive why he should be displeased to hear I was in the chateau."

"Displeased! (repeated Floretta), Lord I am sure he would be rejoiced!"

"Rejoiced!" exclaimed Madeline.

"Yes, I have not a doubt but what he would," said Floretta.

"Then why (asked Madeline) am I concealed?"

"Because," cried Floretta—

"What?" eagerly demanded Madeline.

"Why to tell you the truth, Mademoiselle (cried Floretta) but remember it must go no farther, I believe my lady thinks you are too pretty to be seen by Monsieur."

"Heavens! (exclaimed Madeline) what would you have me imagine that your lady could harbour a suspicion of me?"

"Lord, no, to be sure I would not, (said Floretta) 'tis the very last thing in the world I would have you imagine, because it would be the most unjust idea you could form; 'tis not of you, but Monsieur, she harbours a suspicion; she knows if he saw you—"

"Would to God I had not consented to stay in the house," interrupted Madeline.

The motive for Madame D'Alembert's concealing her was now explained; the motive which prompted her lamented benefactress so repeatedly to tell her not to continue in the chateau, if Monsieur D'Alembert came to it.

"Oh! my father, (she sighed to herself) would to heaven I was again within your arms."

"I hope Mademoiselle, (said Floretta) you will not leave us; Monsieur departs in a few days, and I hope you will not mind a short confinement."

Madeline made no reply, but desired to hear the particulars of Agatha's death.

"About the middle of the night, (said Floretta) I and a fellow servant who sleeps with me were awoke by dreadful groans from the chamber of Agatha, which opened into ours; we directly jumped out of bed, and running into it, asked what was the matter; but groans were all we could hear: we grew dreadfully frightened, and called up more of the servants. A light was then procured, and we discovered Agatha in fits: the noise we made alarmed my master and mistress, o'er whose apartment we were, and throwing their wrappers over them they came up to inquire what was the matter. My lady appeared greatly shocked by the situation of Agatha, and directly ordered a physician to be sent for, but Monsieur countermanded this order; he said he had a medical friend in the house, who could do as much for her as any other person in the same line. He was accordingly sent for, and on examining Agatha, he declared her fits were owing to her having eaten something that disagreed with her. Scarcely had he spoken when she came to herself, and opening her eyes, in a hollow voice exclaimed, 'Poison! I am poisoned!'

'Good heavens! (cried Madame D'Alembert starting) what does she say? does she not say she is poisoned?'

'You are not to mind what she says, (replied Monsieur, in rather an angry voice) the woman raves, and I insist on your quitting her room directly, you are already sufficiently shocked by her.'

"My lady durst not disobey him, and re"My lady durst not disobey him, and retired, though I saw most unwillingly, with her woman."

'Send for father Bertrand, (again spoke Agatha, after the pause of a minute) for I am dying.'

'Nonsense, (exclaimed Monsieur D'Alembert) friend she will be well enough by and by, and I am sure I shall not permit my neighbourhood to be disturbed to gratify her, said my master.—['Ah! Mademoiselle, I fear he is but a bad christian']—I insist, therefore, (continued he) that not a servant in this castle shall go for father Bertrand, except they choose immediately to be dismissed my service.' Like my poor lady, none of us durst disobey him, he took care indeed that we should not, by continuing to watch us: In a little time Agatha relapsed, and died in a few minutes. She had scarcely breathed her last, ere she turned quite black and swelled to a great size; and, notwithstanding what my master and my master's friend says, we are all, that is, I mean, all the servants are of opinion, that she was poisoned; though how, or by whom, we cannot possibly conceive, as we know of no stranger that lately entered the castle, neither of any mortal that she ever offended."

"Tis a horrible affair," (said Madeline) who was now firmly convinced that the murderers of the countess had destroyed her.

"My master has insisted, (cried Floretta) upon our making no comment, at least no public comments on it; he declares if we do, he will have us severely punished. Poor Agatha, poor soul, there is nobody regrets her more than I do, though we had many little tiffs together; she was so good-natured and used to make me such a number of pretty little presents in the course of the year; if ever I wanted any thing nice, nice sweetmeats, or nice cordials, I had nothing to do but to ask her for them. Mr. Lubin will be holding up his head now I suppose, I fancy she has left me a legacy, I shall buy mourning for her."

"Poor Agatha! (said Madeline) she little thought she would have followed her dear lady so soon."

"True, Mademoiselle, (cried Floretta) but you look faint, let me give you a glass of wine?"

"First tell me (said Madeline, on whose agitated mind the dreadful idea of poison dwelt) first tell me, (said she, starting up) where or from whom did you procure this wine?"

"Lord bless me, Mademoiselle, (cried Floretta) how you frighten me by your looks; why, I stole it from the butler."

"Well, since you got it from him, I will take some of it, (cried Madeline.) She felt her spirits somewhat revived by doing so, and she then expressed her hopes that Floretta would stay with her till Madame D'Alembert came.

"'Tis quite out of my power to stay till then, (said Floretta, instantly rising, as if the very idea of doing so had terrified her) I must go, in order to watch for an opportunity for my lady to come to you."

"Hasten her to me I conjure you, (cried Madeline) as she followed Floretta to the door to lock it after her.

"O that I was out of this house, (exclaimed Madeline, as she turned from the door), danger and death surround me on every side."

She feared that Madame D'Alembert would oppose her quitting it, she feared she could not entreat her permission to do so without betraying in some degree the motive which prompted that entreaty. Impressed with terror, she knelt before a large crucifix near the head of the bed, and fervently implored the protection of heaven. As she prayed she was suddenly startled by the creaking of the closet door: she turned her head with quickness towards it, and beheld it half open; and the horror of that moment can better be conceived than described; a man whose face was shaded by a large hat leaning from it, and earnestly regarding her.

That the murderers of Agatha had by some means or other discovered her concealment, and from the garden had entered, through the closet window, with an intention of destroying her, was the dreadful idea which instantly started to her mind: all power of voice and motion forsook her, and straining an eye of agony and horror on the terrifying stranger, she still continued kneeling: in this situation she remained for about two minutes, when a soft tap came to the chamber door, the stranger hastily retreated, and shut the closet door; Madeline with a scream of mingled joy and terror then started from the ground, and flying to the door opened it and beheld Madame D'Alembert and Floretta.

Madeline fell upon the neck of the former, but for many minutes could only give vent to her feelings by sobs and broken sentences.

"Oh! you are come at last: (she exclaimed as she pressed her friend to her palpitating heart) you are come, the blessed instrument of providence, to save me from destruction; let us quit this chamber, and secure the door till the family can be alarmed and the closet searched."

"Heaven defend us! (cried Floretta, instantly retreating towards the gallery) what did you see within the closet, Mademoiselle?"

"Nothing to alarm her, I am sure," said Madame D'Alembert.

"Nothing to alarm her!" repeated Madeline emphatically.

"No, (cried Madame D'Alembert) every avenue to that closet is secured; tis therefore impossible any one could have entered it without your knowledge; your imagination affected by the gloom of your apartment has deceived you."

"Good heaven! Madam, (exclaimed Madeline) would you try to make me disbelieve my senses?"

"To prove how certain I am they have been deceived, I will search the closet myself," said Madame D'Alembert, advancing as she spoke into the chamber.

"Oh! do not be so rash, (cried Madeline, grasping her arm) do not too late repent your temerity."

Madame D'Alembert made no reply, but disengaging herself, she directly went to the closet, and flinging open the door, exclaimed,

"Come, see whether or not I have been mistaken."

Madeline approached her with trembling steps, and to her infinite amazement beheld there was no creature or trace of any creature within the closet.

"I am astonished indeed, (said she) but mysterious as was the entrance or disappearance of any person, that I saw some person is beyond a doubt."

"What kind of person, Mademoiselle?" asked Floretta.

Madeline, as clearly as she could, described him; but was hurt to find Madame D'Alembert still appeared incredulous.

"You see, (said she) that the window, the only way by which any person could have entered the closet, is secured within side."

"I see it is, (cried Madeline) I must therefore only suppose that it was a being of the other world I saw."

"No, no, my dear Madeline, (said Madame D'Alembert) I am sure you have too much sense to be superstitious."

"Ah! Madame, (replied Madeline) I should not wonder if my reason was impaired by the shocks I have lately received.—Wonder not, (she continued) if I declare I can no longer remain in this apartment. Oh! dearest Madam, be not surprised if I entreat your permission to return to my father; he wishes to see me; and who can wonder if I sigh to see him?"

"Unkind Madeline, (said Madame D'Alembert, shedding tears) will you then leave me? Will you disappoint the hopes I entertained of enjoying your society whilst I continued at the chateau? Your father, you must remember, in his last letter, assured you he did not expect, nay, he did not desire you to return, till I was going to Paris; and from all disagreeable confinement you will be released in two days, as Monsieur D'Alembert then departs."

Distressed, confused, perplexed, Madeline stood silent, irresolute how to act. Her fears, her reason urged her to quit the chateau directly, but her dread of being thought ungrateful, unfeeling, by Madame D'Alembert, if she did do so, almost tempted her to stay.

"Ah! (cried she to herself) how distressing a situation is mine; the fears which make me tremble to stay in the chateau I am bound by a solemn vow to conceal; and except I can assign better reasons for wishing to leave it than I have already done, (and to do so is impossible) Madame D'Alembert will certainly be offended at my quitting it."

Hurt by her silence, by her too evident wish of departing, Madame D'Alembert suddenly wiped away her tears, and while a crimson glow mantled her cheek, exclaimed,

"Against your inclination I will not detain you: no, Madeline, to inclination, not necessity, I must be indebted for your company. I see your reluctance to continue with me, and you are at liberty to depart the moment you please: I own—" and her voice faltered. "I had hoped, I had imagined, but it is no matter, 'tis not the first time I have been disappointed,—disappointed by those on whom my heart placed its tenderest affections, and by those it believed would sincerely return them."

Had a dagger pierced the bosom of Madeline it could scarcely have given her more pain than did the words of her friend: eager to be reinstated in her good opinion, she forgot those apprehensions which but a moment before had agitated her soul, and determined no longer to persist in desiring to quit the castle.

"Oh! Madam, (cried she, while tears trickled down her cheeks) how you have wounded me by your language: Do you then deem me unworthy? Do you think me ungrateful, forgetful of your kindness? Do you suppose I desire to fly from you?"

"Your words have intimated such a desire," replied Madame D'Alembert.

"Ah! Madame, (said Madeline) when I uttered them my senses were almost overpowered by terror; and if you wish me to continue in the castle,—"

"Wish you, (interrupted her friend) Ah! Madeline, (clasping her arms around her) do you doubt my wishing you to do so? Yes, my love, 'tis my wish, my entreaty, my earnest request, that you stay in the castle till I quit it. You shall not continue in your present chamber, I came on purpose to remove you from it, for, to be brief, Monsieur D'Alembert suspects your being in the castle, and may perhaps take it into his head to search it; I am therefore going to conduct you to a place where he will never think of looking for you."

"Oh! Madame, (cried Madeline, and she paused, fearful of again exciting the displeasure of her friend, for she had been on the point of again entreating permission to return to her father) to what place, Madame, (asked she, suddenly recollecting herself) are you going to take me."

"Ask me no questions at present, my love, (said Madame D'Alembert) our security perhaps depends upon our silence; for I know not at this very moment but we may be watched; follow me, therefore, I entreat in silence."

She now led the way from the chamber, and, preceded by Floretta carrying a light, they stole with trembling steps along the gallery, from whence they descended by the private stairs; opposite to them was a low arched door, which they past through, and proceeded along a dark passage to another flight of steep stone stairs, which seemed to lead to the subterraneous parts of the castle. Here Madeline paused, and entreated to know whither they were taking her.

"Be not alarmed, my love, (said Madame D'Alembert) be assured it is to a place of security."

The stairs were terminated by an iron door fastened by an immense padlock. Floretta laid down the light, and taking down a large rusty key with difficulty unlocked it, slowly opening with a grating noise, that absolutely struck terror into the soul of Madeline; it discovered to her view a black and hideous vault, dripping with damp, and from which a cold vapour issued that nearly extinguished the light; at its entrance Madeline again paused.

"Oh! heavens, (cried she, shuddering and leaning against the wall) whither are we going?"

"Ah! Madeline, (said Madame D'Alembert in a supplicating voice) after going so far will you at last disappoint me? Be not alarmed I again repeat; if you wish to confirm my obligations to you do not hesitate now: your life, your safety, are more precious to me than my own, follow therefore without fear, without hesitation, wherever I may lead."

To do so, however, was scarcely in the power of Madeline, and Madame D'Alembert taking her hand, rather drew than led her through a succession of gloomy vaults till they came to a low arched door, fastened by a bolt: Floretta undrew it, and Madeline, to her infinite horror and amazement, found herself in the chapel, beside the grave of her benefactress, and near the spot where she had received her fatal wound.

"Is this (said she, looking round her with terror and dismay) the place of security you said you were bringing me to? 'Tis all but secure; death and destruction hover o'er it. Oh! Madam! (wildly flinging herself at the feet of Madame D'Alembert) I cannot, cannot stay within it, for the murderer here takes his solitary rounds, to plunge his dagger in the heart of innocence and virtue."

"My love, (cried her friend, raising her from the ground) what do you mean? you strike me with horror by your words, you shake my very soul."

The energy of Madame D'Alembert recalled the scattered senses of Madeline, and made her reflect on the imprudence she had been guilty of; she shuddered as she considered she had nearly broken her solemn vow, and been on the point of planting unutterable and unappeasable sorrows in the heart of Madame D'Alembert.—Exerting all her resolution,

"Dear Madame, (said she) I know not what I said; my imagination was disordered by the gloom of the place."

"Surely my love, (said her friend) you could not imagine I would be so cruel as to intend to keep you here: no—to-night, as soon as it is dark, either Floretta or I, accompanied by Lubin, will come to re-conduct you to the castle, where you shall be again put in possession of your own apartment: my reason for bringing you to pass the day here, was to prevent your being seen by Monsieur D'Alembert, who, I will acknowledge, threatened to search the castle; but except he puts that threat in execution to-day, I am confident he never will, as to-morrow he will busy paying visits in the neighbourhood previous to his departure."

This assurance calmed the agitation of Madeline, and she grew still more composed when Madame D'Alembert declared she would not leave her till the morning was farther advanced.

They now ascended to the dormitory, which, as I have already said, was in an habitable state, and soon discovered a cell for Madeline to sit in, containing the remains of a wooden bedstead. Here Floretta left a small basket of provisions, and she and her lady continued with Madeline till the gloomy shadows of night had nearly fled, they then bade her adieu, and repeated their assurance of coming for her as soon as it grew dark.

Left to herself, the flurry of Madeline's spirits subsided, and she was able calmly to reconsider what was past and to reflect on her present situation; as she did so she bitterly regretted not having insisted on returning immediately to her father; for her longer residence in the castle, exposed her, she was convinced, to dangers of the most dreadful nature; that Agatha had fallen by the hands of the countess's murderers she could not doubt, neither that they had entered the closet with an intention of destroying her; for their strange and mysterious disappearance from it she accounted by supposing that behind some one of the large presses it contained there was a secret door.

"I cannot suppose, (said she) that one disappointment will make them lay aside their horrible intentions; by remaining in the castle I expose myself to their continual attempts, attempts which may perhaps at last be too successful, I must fly it therefore, (continued she) however unpleasant, however agonizing to my feelings to excite the displeasure of Madame D'Alembert; I must, when next we meet, entreat, implore her to let me return to my father."

As soon as the day was advanced Madeline descended to the chapel, in order to try and divert her mind from the dreadful ideas which depressed it, by examining the curious monuments within the building; the terror of Madeline's soul now gave way to awe and melancholy,—she felt chilled, she felt oppressed beyond expression, as she viewed the records of mortality, and trod the silent solitary aisles, which awfully echoed her lightest step, and whose gloom the beams of the sun that darted through the painted casements could not dissipate.

She had often (to use the words of an author, not less affecting than sublime) "Walked beneath the impending promontory's craggy cliff, sometimes trod the vast spaces of the lonely desert, and penetrated the inmost recesses of the dreary cavern, but had never, never before beheld nature louring with so tremendous an aspect,—never before felt such impressions of awe striking cold upon her heart, as now beneath the black browed arches, amidst the mouldy walls of the Monastery, where melancholy, deepest melancholy spread her raven wings."

Ah! if the children of vanity, of dissipation, sometimes visited a scene like this, surely (thought she) their hearts would be amended; they would be convinced of the littleness of this world, of the folly of placing their entire affections upon it, when they beheld "nobility arrayed in a winding sheet, grandeur mouldering in an urn, and the high grass waving round the hero's tomb, while his dusty banner, the banner which he once unfurled to strike consternation on his foes, hung idly fluttering o'er it."

At the grave of her benefactress she paused.

"Here (said she) gratitude and affection must ever linger. Oh! my friend, my mother, never can thy kindness be obliterated from my heart, never can my heart be consoled for thy loss: alas! from thy deep sleep the sighs of thy Madeline cannot awake thee! Cold is that breast which was the repository of her sorrows, silent the tongue which poured sympathy upon them."

When it grew dark she ascended to the cell, for the gloom of the chapel then grew too awful for her to bear. After sitting a considerable time there in a state of painful impatience, she went to a large folding door, which terminated the gallery, and commanded an extensive view of the valley, to try if she could discover any sign of Madame D'Alembert or Floretta, who had said, as I should previously have mentioned, that they would come to her through the garden; but no step, no voice, could she hear, no glimpse of any object could she distinguish.

"They cannot have forgotten me, (said she) they cannot let me pass the night amidst the dead; and yet 'tis far beyond the hour I expected them."

Her heart almost died away as she viewed the opposite mountains, whose dark brows seemed rising above the clouds, and from whose black cavities the wind issued with hoarse murmurs, like the yells of midnight murderers.

"Ah! (cried she, shuddering) within those cavities perhaps the murderers of the countess—of Agatha—the intended murderers of Madeline, may be now concealed; before to-morrow perhaps I may be cold and inanimate, like those o'er whose sculptured urns I so recently bent."

At this instant she thought she heard the echo of a light step outside the building; her heart palpitated, she bent forward, and caught a glimpse of a female figure habited in black, gliding into the Monastery and followed by a man wrapped up in a large dark coat: That it was Madame D'Alembert and Lubin she beheld she could not doubt, and in a transport of joy she instantly flew to the stairs to meet them, but at the head of the stairs she paused, and trembled, for as the low sound of voices reached her from below, she fancied she heard the voices of total strangers: she held in her breath that she might be better enabled to ascertain whether or not her fears were justly founded, and was soon convinced that it was neither Madame D'Alembert nor Lubin she had seen enter.

Alive only to one dreadful idea, to one apprehension, she now believed her fate approaching, and looked round for some place to secrete herself; she looked in vain however; for mouldering cells and narrow passages, choked with rubbish only, met her view.

At length she recollected, that near the cell where she had been sitting there was a long and winding gallery, pretty free from rubbish, and which Madame D'Alembert had informed her led to the innermost recesses of the building; down this she determined to fly.

At the head of the staircase which faced the body of the chapel was a large dismantled window, through which the moon, now beginning to rise, shed a faint light, but still sufficient to render objects conspicuous. Madeline therefore feared she should be seen as she crossed the staircase, she knew however there was no alternative, and that she must either run the risque of being discovered now, or remain where in a few minutes later she was sure of being so.

Madeline accordingly stepped forward, but though her step was too light to be heard, her figure was perceived, and she instantly heard a shout from the chapel, and ascending steps. Fear lent her wings, she flew to the gallery, but, just as she was darting into it, a large iron hook entangled her clothes: with a strength which desperation only could have given her, she attempted to tear them from it, but 'ere her efforts had succeeded her arm was rudely seized; she immediately turned her head and beheld the inflamed countenance of a man glaring upon her; the moment he saw her face he started back with a look which seemed to intimate she was not the person he expected to have seen, but the faint pleasure which this idea gave was quickly destroyed by his drawing a small dagger from his breast with which he again approached Madeline. Her death she now believed inevitable, and staggering back a few paces, "Ah! heaven have mercy upon me!" she said, and dropped lifeless on the floor.

As she recovered her senses she felt some one chafing her hands.

"Ah! (she cried, in a faint voice) do you restore me to life but to have the pleasure of depriving me of it?"

"My Madeline, my love, (exclaimed the soft voice of Madame D'Alembert) what has thus disordered your senses?"

Madeline raised her head from the ground, she looked at Madame D'Alembert,—she looked from her, and beheld Lubin.

"Gracious heaven! (cried she) do I dream or have I been in a frightful dream from which you have just awakened me?"

"My dearest girl, (said Madame D'Alembert) what has alarmed you?"

"Alarmed me? (repeated Madeline, wildly staring at her) Oh, heavens! surely it is but an instant ago since I saw the poignard of the murderer raised against me?"

"You terrify me," exclaimed her friend.

"Terrify you, (repeated Madeline, starting from the ground) Oh, let us fly this dreadful place directly, for even now perhaps our lives may be in danger."

"Don't be frightened, Mademoiselle, (cried Lubin) I am not unarmed."

"You strike me with horror, (said Madame D'Alembert) and take from me the power of moving: tell me what danger it is we have to apprehend, for no trace of any being, of any thing to alarm you, did we discover, and the swoon in which we found you we imputed to illness instead of terror."

Madeline in a few hasty words informed her of the manner in which she had been terrified, and whilst she gratefully returned her thanks to heaven for her safety, she expressed her astonishment at being uninjured.

"Oh! my love, (cried her friend, clasping her arms round her as she concluded) never, never can I requite you for what you have suffered on my account; never can I forgive myself for having exposed you to such alarms."

"I wish with all my soul (said Lubin, grasping the rusty sword he had brought from the chateau) I wish with all my soul I had caught the villain, I'll warrant if I had I should soon have made him confess what brought him hither; his companion I suppose, was only a man in disguise."

"Who these mysterious strangers were I cannot possibly conceive, (cried Madame D'Alembert) but that they certainly did not mean to harm you, however appearances may make you believe to the contrary, I think; for had such been their intention they most assuredly could have accomplished that intention 'ere we came."

"They only designed to rob her I suppose, (said Lubin) and frighten her to silence; pray search your pockets, Mademoiselle, to try if you have lost any thing."

"There was nothing of any value in them, (replied Madeline) so I need not take that trouble."

"They must certainly (resumed Lubin) have retreated, on hearing us, down that gallery," pointing to the one Madeline had attempted to conceal herself in; "I would give all the money I am worth for somebody now to assist me in searching it."

"Oh, Madeline! (cried her friend) I can no longer attempt to detain you: I came to half determined to let you return immediately to your father, as Monsieur D'Alembert, contrary to his first intention, has resolved on passing a month in the chateau; but I am now, in consequence of what I have heard, resolved on doing so; to-night therefore we part, and heaven knows whether we shall ever meet again."

"To-night!" repeated Madeline amazed.

"Yes, (replied Madame D'Alembert, whose tears scarcely permitted her to speak) to-night—was your journey postponed till to-morrow, Monsieur D'Alembert must discover that you have hitherto been concealed in the chateau, and the consequences of such a discovery would be extremely disagreeable to me."

"Heaven forbid then (said Madeline) I should delay my journey; and yet"—she paused, she recollected herself—and since her friend was anxious for her immediate departure, resolved not to mention the fears she felt at the idea of travelling by night.

"I confide you to the care of Lubin, (cried Madame D'Alembert) I know he is faithful, I know he is brave, and will fulfil the trust I repose in him."

"I humbly thank your Ladyship for your good opinion of me, (said Lubin, taking off his hat and making a low bow) it shall be my study to deserve it: I am sure I should be an ungrateful varlet if I would not go through fire and water for you, or any one beloved by you; and Mademoiselle may be assured, while I have an arm to stretch out in her defence, I will protect her."

"At the extremity of the wood surrounding the chateau, is the cottage of my nurse, (said Madame D'Alembert, addressing Madeline) thither Lubin must now conduct you, and there he will procure horses for your journey; for I am afraid to have any taken from the stables here, least a discovery should be the consequence of doing so: do not delay longer than is absolutely necessary at the cottage, I have important reasons for wishing you to get to a distance from the chateau, as soon as possible, when you are about half way between it and your father's house you can stop to rest."

"Yes, (replied Lubin) there is a snug house just thereabouts, where we can put up. You may recollect, Mademoiselle, (turning to Madeline) that you and my poor lady dined there last spring in your way to the chateau?"

A deep sigh stole from the breast of Madeline at the recollection of that happy period; and Madame D'Alembert was for a few minutes unable to speak.

"In the course of a few days, Madeline, (said she, as soon as she had recovered her voice) you may expect a letter, containing a full explanation of every thing that appeared mysterious in my conduct towards you. After suffering so much on my account you surely are entitled to know every secret of my heart—Oh! Madeline, that heart can never forget the gratitude it owes you."

"Ah, Madam, (cried Madeline, while tears trickled down her cheeks), do not hurt me by speaking in this manner; all that I could do, could never never repay the numerous favours I have received from you, 'tis I only have a right to speak of gratitude."

"Perhaps (resumed her friend) we may meet again: I will indulge such a hope, it will sooth, it will console me in some degree for your loss. Oh! Madeline, 'tis with pain, 'tis with agony I consent to our separation, but without murmuring I must submit to that as well as to many other sorrows."

She now took the trembling hand of Madeline, and they descended to the valley, thro' which they silently and swiftly passed, nor stopped 'till they came within sight of the chateau; Madame D'Alembert then paused, to give a last farewell to Madeline: locked in each others arms they continued many minutes unable to speak, unable to separate; at length Madame D'Alembert summoning all her resolution to her aid, disengaged herself from Madeline. "farewell, (said she) may heaven for ever bless, protect you, and make you as happy as you deserve to be." She turned away as she spoke as if fearful her resolution would fail her if she continued another moment with Madeline, and hastened to the chateau.

Silent and immovable Madeline stood gazing after her till addressed by Lubin.

"Come, Mademoiselle, (said he) we had better not delay any longer, 'twill be a late hour even as it is, I can assure you, 'ere we reach the house where we are to rest, this way, Mademoiselle."

Almost instinctively Madeline followed him to a door which opened from the garden to the lawn, but here she again stopped; the variety of distressing and terrifying scenes she had lately gone through had almost bewildered her senses, and she now felt as if she scarcely knew where she was, or whither she was going.

"Have I really taken my last leave of Madame D'Alembert? Am I really quitting the chateau?" said she, earnestly looking at Lubin.

"Lord, yes, that you have indeed Mademoiselle," answered he, somewhat surprised and alarmed.

"Gracious heaven! (cried she, with folded hands) if any person two months ago had told me I should quit the chateau in the manner I am at present doing, what little credit should I have given to their words.—

"Oh life! (she sighed to herself) how rapid are thy revolutions!—But a short time ago and that very mansion which I now leave with secrecy and precipitation, I entered with every hope of finding a permanent and happy home within it; but a short time ago and it was a refuge for distress, an asylum for innocence and virtue; but now the mendicant may wander to it in vain for relief, innocence and virtue seek protection without receiving it.

"With its virtues its honours must decline; for he who has not a heart to cherish the former, must surely want a spirit to support the latter.

"No more then shall the arm of valour unfurl its banners to the call of glory; no more shall the records of fame be swelled by its achievements; no more shall noble emulation be inspired by them.

"With its late owner its greatness and happiness departed; they are set, but set not like that sun whose splendours so lately brightened this scene, to rise again with renovated glory."

CHAP. III.

"Forlorn and lost I tread,

"With fainting steps and slow,

"Where wilds, immeasurably spread,

"Seem length'ning as I go.

"Ihope, Mademoiselle, (said Lubin, on hearing her sigh as she turned from the chateau) you are not frightened at the idea of going through the wood?"

"No;" replied Madeline.

"So much the better, so much the better, (said Lubin) but indeed I should not wonder if you were."

"Why, (cried Madeline) is it dangerous?"

"Not over safe indeed, but don't be frightened, Mademoiselle, (on seeing her suddenly stop) I shall bring you the shortest path through it."

"And when we get to the road we shall be safe, (cried Madeline) as there are cottages scattered all along it?"

"Yes, (said Lubin) but if you were in danger and expected any assistance from their inhabitants, you would be sadly disappointed, for those kind of people are so fatigued after their day's labour, that when once they get to bed one might as well try to waken the dead, as waken them: but don't be frightened, Mademoiselle."

"Frightened! (repeated Madeline) it is scarcely possible to be otherwise from the manner in which you talk; you have really made me tremble so that I can scarcely move."

"If you would condescend to accept my arm, Mademoiselle, we could make infinitely more haste than we do at present."

Madeline accepted the offer of Lubin, nor did they again pause till they had reached the cottage they were bound to; they found it shut up for the night, and Lubin knocked loudly with his stick against the door, but without effect.

"You see, Mademoiselle, (said he, after the silence of a few minutes) I was right in saying it was next to impossible to waken these cottagers."

"Poor people, (cried Madeline) it is a pity to disturb them."

"Oh, not at all, (said Lubin) they can go to bed immediately again, you know, and I warrant they will not rest the worse for having had their slumbers interrupted."

He now repeated the knocks with a violence that shook the door: at last a window was opened, and an old man, putting out his head, asked who came there. "Why, a friend, (replied Lubin) and a devilish time he has been trying to gain admittance: Come, come, Mr. Colin, you may open the door without any grumbling, for by the time I have taken to waken you it is pretty evident you have had a good spell."

"Pray what brings you here at this time of night?" cried a shrill female voice.

"I am come by the command of my lady to borrow two horses, (answered Lubin) I must get them directly, and without being asked whither I am going with them; pray make haste, I have a lady waiting with me for them."

"A lady!" the old couple repeated, and both thrust their heads together out of the window, to see whether he spoke truth or not.

The door was now opened in a minute, and the nurse invited Madeline into the cottage, while her husband went forth with Lubin to a little shed adjoining it, to prepare the horses: she had seen Madeline before at the cottage, and almost immediately recollected her; she was all amazement at now beholding her, nor could forbear inquiring the reason of it. Madeline waved the discourse, and expressed her regret at her having been disturbed.

The horses were ready in a few minutes, and the good couple having received a strict caution against mentioning her to any one, she was assisted by Lubin to mount, and they set off at a smart pace.

"How very curious old Colin and his wife were! (said Lubin) I dare say they would have given half they were worth to know the cause of our travelling by night, and not getting horses at the chateau."

"I don't wonder at their being so," cried Madeline.

"No, nor I neither, Mademoiselle; 'tis a comical thing to be sure our rambling about at night; it puts me in mind of the Fairy Tales I have read; heaven be praised our journey is but a short one."

They did not slacken their pace till they reached the gloomy forest, in which the gothic castle of Montmorenci stood; the heart of Madeline sunk as she approached it, and she trembled as she entered amidst its awful shades, and heard the breeze sweeping over them with a hollow murmur: the courage of Lubin too seemed a little to fail him.

"I wish with all my soul Mademoiselle, (said he) that the house we are going to was at this side of the forest instead of the other."

"I wish it was, (cried Madeline) or that we could get shelter elsewhere."

"That is impossible, Mademoiselle, (replied he) so we must only make what haste we can to it; Lord how glad I shall be when I find myself there; so will you, I dare say, Mademoiselle."

"Undoubtedly, (replied Madeline) the recollection of past danger will heighten present pleasure."

"I wish all our dangers were over, and our pleasures come, (cried Lubin) but Lord, Mademoiselle, the very worst of our way is still before us; the middle of the forest, which we have not yet reached, is a grand rendezvous, they say, for a gang of banditti, that have long infested the country; there they meet as soon as it grows dark, and settle their plans for the night. Well, of all places in the world I should not like to be robbed in a forest, it would be such an easy matter afterwards to murder one."

"Pray, Lubin, (said Madeline) do not talk any more in this manner, for if you do you'll make me tremble so I shall not be able to keep my seat."

"I ask your pardon, Mademoiselle; I am sure the last thing in the world I meant to do was to frighten you: To be sure I wish I had brought a pocket pistol or two with me from the chateau, instead of this rusty sword, to defend you; though, after all, what would avail my single arm against a whole gang? Heaven help us if they meet us! poor Colin may then go whistle for his horses; though upon recollection my Lady would certainly recompense him for their loss."

"Drop this dreadful subject I entreat you," said Madeline, in a tremulous voice.

"Come cheer up, Mademoiselle (exclaimed Lubin, who was now thoroughly convinced he had alarmed Madeline) we will keep as near as possible to the extremity of the forest, and if we ride fast we shall soon reach the house."

As fast as the intricacies of the path would permit them to go, they went, and at last reached in safety their destined goal.

Here Madeline, who had hitherto with difficulty kept her seat, alighted; but how impossible to describe her disappointment, and the disappointment of her companion, when after repeatedly knocking at the door they were at length convinced that the house was uninhabited. They stood for some minutes looking at each other, in a consternation that deprived them of speech.

Lubin was the first who broke silence.

"What's to be done, Mademoiselle?" said he.

"I am sure I can't tell," answered Madeline in a faint voice, and leaning against the wall.

"Faith, (cried Lubin) I have a good mind to break open the door and obtain shelter for the night, though, to my sorrow, I can't get a good supper; I meant to have ordered a nice omelet, the moment I arrived."

"For heaven's sake do not attempt to break open the door, (exclaimed Madeline) the consequences of such an action might be dreadful."

"What's to be done then I again ask? (said Lubin) you would not wish, I suppose, to sit down here without any shelter for the remainder of the night; neither would you, I suppose, like to mount your horse and go ten miles farther in search of another habitation, and nearer you need not expect to find one that would receive you."

"I am not able to go in search of another, (replied Madeline) the shocks I received and the fatigue I have gone through this night have quite overpowered me."

"Lord (cried Lubin, starting) perhaps the Marquis of Montmorenci may be come to his castle, only you were afraid Mademoiselle of that part of the forest, we might have past it, and been able perhaps to have discovered."

"And even if we had (said Madeline) what benefit should we have derived from that circumstance?"

"Why we should certainly have obtained a lodging in his castle."

"I should be afraid to disturb the family at this late hour," cried Madeline hesitatingly.

"Lord I am sure (cried Lubin) it is better to disturb them than run the risque of being murdered here."

"But suppose they are not there?" said Madeline.

"Why then, Mademoiselle, (cried Lubin hastily) we will try to find some niche about the wall where we can shelter ourselves for the night, since you are so scrupulous about the door of this house."

"But, (said Madeline) though the family may not be come to the castle, there may be inhabitants in it."

"Oh! I understand you, Mademoiselle, (interrupted Lubin) you are afraid that some of the banditti I was telling you of may have taken up their quarters there; but of that I am sure there's no danger, the castle was too well secured for them to gain admittance; so that except we find the right inhabitants in it, I am confident we shall not find any: come, Mademoiselle, let's lose no time, will you accept my arm, or would you choose to mount again?"

"No, (replied she) I would rather walk."

"Go before me then, (said he) and I will lead the horses."

Madeline obeyed him though with difficulty, for she felt so agitated that she could scarcely drag her weary limbs along. As she approached the castle her eyes were anxiously fastened on it, in hopes of discovering a light or some other sign of inhabitation, but all was dark and dreary around.

"I am afraid, Lubin, (said she, stopping and mournfully shaking her head) I am afraid the family have not yet returned."

"I do not quite despair about that, Mademoiselle, (replied Lubin); at so very late an hour as this you know we could not expect to have found any of them up."

"How shall we make ourselves heard by them then?" asked Madeline.

"Why I suppose we shall find a great bell at the gate, which I shall ring."

"But if the Marquis's family (cried Madeline, shuddering at the very idea) should not be in the castle, may not the ringing of that bell expose us to destruction? Do you forget the banditti you told me infested this forest?"

"Lord (said Lubin) that's true, the bell would certainly alarm them—well Mademoiselle, I'll tell you what we can do: I recollect taking notice last spring as I passed this castle, of the very bad repair in which the court wall was, so we will search about it for some gap to clamber through."

He accordingly fastened the horses to the gate, and had not long searched about 'ere he found a place which Madeline easily got over.

Immediately opposite this spot was an arched gateway, which led through a wing of the building to another court; to this Lubin conducted Madeline, who trembled so she could scarcely stand, but the moment she entered it she shrunk back, affrighted at the desolation she beheld, and fancied in the hoarse murmurs of the wind that sighed thro' the shattered buildings surrounding it, she heard portentous sounds.

On each side of the gateway were several doors; Lubin perceived one of them open, and through this he led his trembling companion: they then found themselves in a spacious stone hall, light with one gothic window, through which the twilight now cast a dim religious light, and opposite to which was a folding door, of heavy workmanship: there was a damp smell in this hall, which proclaimed it long deserted, and struck cold to the very heart of Madeline.

"Shall I go now, Mademoiselle, (asked Lubin) and try whether there is any one within the castle?"

"Not yet, (replied Madeline, sitting down upon a little bench which ran round the hall) "not yet," said she in a faint voice, and involuntarily leaning her head against his arm for support.

Lubin was terrified, he almost believed her dying.

"Dear, dear, Mademoiselle, (said he) cheer up, I shall not be long absent; and whether there is or is not any one in the castle, we are secure for the night."

Madeline grew a little better, and no longer opposed his going. It was some time 'ere he could open the folding door; when he did it disclosed to his view a long dark passage, down which the anxious eyes of Madeline pursued him till slowly closing, the door hid him from her view.

Scarcely was she left to herself 'ere she regretted not having accompanied him, for as her eye timidly glanced around, she shuddered at the profound gloom in which she was involved; never had she felt more forlorn, scarcely ever more disconsolate: the manner in which her first journey had been taken recurred to her recollection, and the contrast she drew between her situation now and then, heightened all the horrors of the present: so true is it, that the remembrance of past joys aggravates our present miseries.

From her melancholy retrospection she was roused by the opening of the door, tho' expecting Lubin, her spirits were so weak she involuntarily started from her seat.

"Don't be frightened Mademoiselle, (cried Lubin, in a whispering voice, as he softly closed the door after him) 'tis only I."

"Well, Lubin, (said Madeline, almost gasping for breath through agitation) what intelligence—did you see any one?"

"I can't tell you now, Mademoiselle, (cried he) we must be gone."

"Oh, heavens! (said Madeline) is there any danger."

"This is no time to ask questions, (replied Lubin) no place I can assure you to answer them; I again repeat it—we must be gone!"

To move was scarcely in the power of Madeline, so much was she overpowered by the terror Lubin's words had given her, she gave him her hand however, and he led her from the hall: but scarcely had they proceeded a few yards down the gateway, 'ere he started, suddenly stopped, and in a low voice exclaimed,

"There are some of them!"

"Gracious heaven! (cried Madeline) what do you mean?"

To repeat her question was unnecessary, for at that instant she beheld two men crossing the court. Lubin now drew, or rather carried her back to the hall, for her tremor had increased to such a degree that she could not stand, and he was compelled to support her upon the seat on which she sunk.

In a voice of agony she now conjured him to tell her what they had to fear, declaring that no certainty almost of danger could be more dreadful than the suspense she at present endured.

"Since you must know, Mademoiselle, (said he) we have nothing more to fear than being robbed and murdered!"

"Good heaven! (exclaimed Madeline) do you think the men we just beheld are murderers?"

"Yes," replied Lubin, ruefully shaking his head.

"What reason have you for so horrible a suspicion?" asked Madeline.

"Why you must know, Mademoiselle, I had not proceeded far down the dark passage 'ere I heard a noise, which sounded to me like the clattering of arms. A sudden panic instantly seized me, and I had a great mind to return directly and lead you from the castle: this, however, was but the thought of a minute, for when I reflected there was no probability of getting a lodging elsewhere, and how dismal a thing it would be to pass the remainder of the night in the open air, I resolved on going forward and trying to discover whether there were friends within.

"I accordingly proceeded till I came to the foot of a narrow flight of stairs, down which a faint light glimmered; up these I softly ascended to a half open door, from which the light issued, and peeping in I beheld a large ill-furnished chamber, with half a dozen men in it, as ill looking dogs as ever I beheld, before a huge fire, cleaning some fire arms: but that was not all—in one corner of the chamber lay the body of a man dreadfully mangled. The dogs laughed as they pursued their work, and talked of the exploits they had achieved and still hoped to achieve with their arms; in short, it was soon evident to me, that the banditti I had mentioned to you had thought proper to make free with the castle in the Marquis's absence, so I made the best of my way back to you, in order to take you directly from it; an intention which the rogues have disappointed."

"The horses will betray us," said Madeline in an agony.

"Aye, so I fear, (cried Lubin) it was devilish unlucky my fastening them to the gate."

"Hark! (exclaimed Madeline) do you not hear a noise?"

Both were instantly silent, and then clearly heard a violent shouting in the outer court. The dreadful fears it excited were soon however a little appeased by its growing fainter, as if the persons it came from had moved to a greater distance.

"I think, (cried Lubin, after the silence of a few minutes, and gasping for the breath he had before suppressed) I think I will now have another peep to try whether or not the coast is clear."

Madeline rising declared she would accompany him, that if there was an opportunity for escaping, not a moment might be lost.

Again therefore they quitted the hall, but had scarcely done so 'ere they once more retreated to it with precipitation, on hearing the shouting in the court renewed with double violence.

"The horses have, I am sure, as you feared, betrayed us; (cried Lubin) and I make no doubt search is now making for us."

"Oh! Lubin, (said Madeline) is there no way of escaping the impending danger?"

"None that I know of, (answered he) but don't be so frightened Mademoiselle, I promise you (he continued, grasping his rusty sword) those that attempt to harm you shall pay dearly for doing so: the villains perhaps may not be such villains as you imagine, they may have some little mercy in their hearts."

As he spoke the gateway resounded with the shouting, and a light glimmered beneath the door opening from it.

Madeline turned her eyes with dreadful expectation towards it; the next minute it was flung open, and several men entered: Her first impulse was to fall at their feet, and supplicate their mercy, but as she attempted to rise her senses totally receded, and she fell fainting upon the out stretched arm of Lubin.

When her reason returned she found herself supported between two women, and surrounded by men, amongst whom Lubin stood talking with earnestness. She looked round her wildly, too much disordered to understand the words of Lubin, or observe whether the appearance of the men was calculated to remove or confirm her fears.

Her clear perception was however soon restored by Lubin, who almost as soon as he saw her senses restored, exclaimed

"Come, cheer up, Mademoiselle, after all our fright we are in no danger; the noble owner of the castle has returned to it, and the fine fellows I saw cleaning the fire-arms, and whom I took, humbly begging their pardons, for robbers, which to be sure was a great wonder, seeing what honest countenances they have, were some of his Lordship's servants."

Madeline raised her eyes in thankfulness to heaven, and Lubin proceeded to inform her that the body he had seen had been one of the banditti, who the night before had made an unsuccessful attempt upon the castle, and that the tumult in the court originated from the domestics suspecting, in consequence of finding the horses fastened to the gate, that they were again lurking about it.

"Now that you find yourself in no dishonorable hands, I hope, Madam, you will speedily recover your spirits," said an elderly man, whose looks and manner denoted a conscious superiority over the rest of his companions.

Madeline thanked him for the hope he had expressed, and was going to explain the cause of her coming to the castle, when Lubin hastily interrupted her by saying, he had already explained every circumstance.

"My Lord (cried the man who had before addressed her, respectfully bowing as he spoke) has been already apprised of your situation, and has commissioned me, Madam, to present his compliments to you, and to entreat you to have the goodness to excuse his not doing the honors of his house himself, which the weak state of his health and spirits prevents: he also desired me to request you would honor his servants by your commands, and not think of quitting the castle till perfectly recovered from your late fatigue and fright."

Madeline felt truly grateful for this politeness, and rather happy than otherwise at not being introduced to the Marquis de Montmorenci, as her exhausted strength and spirits left her little inclination or ability to converse with a stranger.

The housekeeper, who was one of the women that had supported her, now conducted her down the passage, Lubin had before explored, to a large apartment near its termination; where, in a few minutes, a table was covered with refreshments. Lubin was taken to the servants hall, and Madeline, somewhat cheered by the knowledge of her safety, partook of the things provided for her: she found her companion extremely loquacious, and so she talked, not much caring whether it was questions she asked or answered.

Madeline inquired how long the Marquis had been indisposed.

"Many, many years, (replied the housekeeper, with a melancholy shake of the head) after the heavy afflictions he has sustained, it would be a wonder indeed if he had retained either his health or spirits."

Madeline, who perfectly recollected the account she had already heard of him, now made no inquiry concerning the nature of those afflictions; but of her own accord the housekeeper gave her a narrative of them.

"The Count St. Julian, his son, (continued she) was certainly one of the finest youths I ever beheld; his death undoubtedly caused that of my Lady Marchioness: 'tis generally imagined he fell by the hands of banditti, but some people have their doubts about that, and I own I am one of them."

"Good heaven! (cried Madeline) who but banditti could be suspected of murdering him?"

The housekeeper shook her head—

"There were people, Mademoiselle, but"—as if suddenly recollecting herself, "it does not become me to tell family secrets."

The curiosity of Madeline was highly raised, but into secrets which indeed she thought properly withheld, she could not think of prying.

"Would not the sympathizing society of friends be of some service to your Lord?" asked Madeline, after the pause of a minute.

"I scarcely think it would, Madam, (answered the housekeeper) but at any rate he will not try whether it would have any effect upon him; he lives the most strange and solitary life imaginable, rambling about from one seat to another, and never admitting any one to his presence, except his attendants, and now and then a kinsman, who lives some leagues from this, and will be his heir. This castle, in the life time of my Lady, was one of the finest and gayest places perhaps you can conceive; and 'tis a grievous thing to any one who knew it in it's glory, to see it now going to rack and ruin for want of a little repair, its courts full of rubbish, and its fine old towers mouldering away; but my Lord seems pleased at beholding its decay."

"Does he never go about the domain?" asked Madeline.

"No: he generally confines himself to a great lonely apartment, where he scarcely suffers a ray of the blessed day-light to enter, and frequently passes whole nights within the chapel, where he has caused a magnificent monument to be erected to the memory of his lady and son."

The conversation into which she had entered cast an involuntary gloom over the mind of Madeline, and by again depressing her spirits made her soon betray symptoms of languor and weariness.

The housekeeper then offered to conduct her to her chamber, an offer which she gladly accepted, and was accordingly led up a flight of stairs, at the end of the passage, to a gallery immediately over it; here she found a comfortable room prepared for her.

Too much fatigued to converse any longer with pleasure, Madeline would have been pleased if her companion had now retired, but the good woman was so fond of talking that she declared she would not leave her till she had seen her to bed.

Madeline had scarcely begun to undress when she missed her father's picture. Struck with consternation and regret at its loss, she threw herself on a chair, with a countenance so full of concern, that the housekeeper hastily demanded what was the matter: On being informed, she begged Madeline not to be so much distressed, at least till convinced she could not find it, declaring there was every probability of its being dropped in the hall at the time they were trying to recover her.

Madeline instantly started up with an intention of going in quest of it, but was prevented by the housekeeper, who assured her, that she herself would make a diligent search after it. This assurance however was not sufficient to prevent Madeline from wishing to join in it, till told that if she went now to the hall, she would run the chance of encountering the Marquis, who always passed through it in his way to the chapel, which he frequently visited at this hour.

As the housekeeper spoke somebody tapped at the door; she demanded who it was, and a voice which Madeline immediately recollected to be that of the Marquis's valet, who had so politely addressed her in the hall, replied,

"'Tis Lafroy.—My Lord presents his compliments to the young lady, and begs she may have the goodness to come to him for a few minutes."

"Lord have mercy upon me! (exclaimed the housekeeper, with uplifted hands and eyes) what can be the meaning of this? —Why, Lafroy (eagerly opening the door) you have quite astonished me!"

The surprise of Madeline, if possible, surpassed her companions; besides, with her's was intermingled something like fear.

"Aye, (cried Lafroy, in reply to the housekeeper) I don't wonder, indeed, Mrs. Beatrice, at your being astonished, 'tis quite a marvel to have my Lord desire to see a stranger, when he won't permit his own friends to come to him."

"But, pray, Lafroy, did he give no reason for desiring to see the young lady?"

"Why as I was lighting him to the chapel which, according to his usual custom, whenever he finds himself in very bad spirits, he was going to, he found in the hall a little picture, which he directly concluded must belong to the young lady; so instead of repairing to the chapel, he immediately returned to his apartment, declaring he must himself restore it to her."

"Dear heart, (cried Mrs. Beatrice) well, I protest he is very complaisant."

'Twas a complaisance, however, which Madeline would gladly have excused, and which she wondered a mind so afflicted as his could ever have thought of.

"I never saw my Lord more disturbed than he was just after finding the picture, (said Lafroy) I thought when he returned to his apartment he would have fainted."

"Since so disordered 'tis a greater wonder than ever that he should desire to see a stranger," cried the housekeeper.

"Aye, so I think too," said Lafroy.

Madeline saw he was impatient to conduct her to his Lord, and, though with a reluctance she could scarcely conceal, she did not hesitate to accompany him immediately.

He led her through a circuitous gallery to a very magnificent one, as well as she could discern by the faint light which glimmered through it; at the extreme end of which was the apartment the Marquis sat in: the moment he introduced her to it he retired, closing the door after him.

The Marquis sat at the head of the room; he bowed without rising at her entrance, and motioned for her to take a chair on his right hand.

Tremblingly, Madeline approached him, and obeyed his motion. It was some minutes 'ere he spoke, and as his eyes were bent upon the ground the timid ones of Madeline surveyed a form which inspired her with mingled reverence and pity, and which, though bent by age and sorrow, still retained traces of majesty and captivating beauty.

"Young lady, (said he, at last, raising his eyes to hers) I hope you had the goodness to excuse my not doing the honors of my house myself; affliction, (added he, with a deep sigh) has long rendered me unable to perform the rites of hospitality, to fulfil the claims of society."

"The rites of hospitality were so amply fulfilled towards me, my Lord, (cried Madeline) that I should deem myself highly remiss if I neglected this opportunity of assuring your Lordship of my heartfelt gratitude."

"Does this picture, young lady, (said he, displaying her father's, which he had hitherto concealed within his hand, and looking earnestly at her) belong to you?"

"It does my Lord," replied Madeline.

"Will you be so obliging (said he, still retaining it) as to inform me how it came into your possession?"

The strangeness of this question, and the look which accompanied it, threw Madeline into an agitation that made her tremble, and took from her all power of replying.

"You are surprised at my question, (proceeded he) nor do I wonder at your being so, but I trust you will excuse it, when I inform you I have important reasons for it: tell me therefore, I entreat, I conjure you, (he continued, with a vehemence Madeline did not think him capable of) how this picture became your's?"

"My father gave it to me, my Lord," answered Madeline.

"Your father!– – –Gracious heaven!–(He paused, as if overcome by strong emotions, but almost immediately recovering his voice,) his name I entreat!"

"Clermont, my Lord," said Madeline, with increasing wonder.

"Clermont! (repeated he, with a look strongly expressive of disappointment; then after the silence of some minutes) do you know by what means he obtained it?"

"It is his own, my Lord," replied Madeline.

"His own! (repeated the Marquis, with a wild and eager look) his own!–All gracious powers!" he arose and walked with disordered steps about the room.

Madeline amazed at all she saw and heard, remained trembling on her chair.

The Marquis suddenly stopped before her, and looked at her with an earnestness that made her droop her head.

"Yes, (cried he) I see traces in that face of one—which no time can wear from my remembrance."

He resumed his seat.—

"In what manner does your father live?" asked he.

"He lives in obscurity, my Lord," replied Madeline.

"What is his family?"

"It consists but of me, my Lord."

"You are acquainted I suppose with his real name, and the misfortunes which drove him to obscurity?"

"No, my Lord, I am not; I never knew he had a right to any name but that of Clermont; never knew he had been in a situation different from his present one."

"Tenderness to you made him, I suppose, conceal his misfortunes, (said the Marquis.) I see, (he continued, gazing upon Madeline, whose pale countenance was expressive of terror as well as agitation) that I have disturbed you; a curiosity raised as to your's has been, yet ungratified, is sufficient indeed to give you uneasiness; be satisfied, however, by an assurance that the present mystery shall perhaps, when least expected, be explained."

The too evident uneasiness of Madeline however was not solely owing to the cause he imputed it to. Ignorant of her father's connexions in life, she knew not whether to consider the Marquis as a friend or foe, and her uncertainty threw her into agony.

"No, my Lord, (she cried, determined if possible to terminate her suspense) 'tis not the pain of ungratified curiosity that now distresses my mind; 'tis the fear—she paused, trembled, and bent her eyes to the ground,—'tis the fear—resumed she in a few minutes, and summoning all her courage to her aid—that my father perhaps may have reason to regret the discovery of his residence."

"Never! (said the Marquis warmly) never will he have reason to regret my discovering it; no, never will he have reason to regret your seeking shelter beneath the roof of Montmorenci Castle. Accept my hand, (continued he, offering it to her) accept it as a pledge of friendship to you and your father."

Madeline received the proffered pledge with transport, and the Marquis, after gently pressing her hand between his, restored her father's picture.

He now told he would no longer detain her from the rest she appeared so much to require, and expressed his hopes, that 'till perfectly recovered from the effects of her late fright and fatigue, she would not quit the castle.

Madeline thanked him for his kind consideration about her, but said she was pretty sure she should be able to re-commence her journey the ensuing day.

The Marquis rung for Lafroy to reconduct her to her chamber, and cautioned her against mentioning the conversation which had passed between them to any one but her father.

Lafroy appeared in a few minutes, and Madeline on returning to her chamber found the housekeeper still there, all amazement and curiosity.

"Well, Mademoiselle, upon my word, (she exclaimed, the moment Madeline entered) you have had a long conversation with my Lord."

"Yes," said Madeline, who scarcely knew what she uttered, so much was her mind engrossed by wonder.

"And pray, Mademoiselle, how do you like him?" asked the inquisitive Mrs. Beatrice.

"Very well," replied Madeline, beginning to undress in order to get rid of her troublesome companion.

"Aye, (said Mrs. Beatrice) he is even now sometimes to be liked; in his youth there could not be a finer gentleman; he was so complaisant, and one of the best dancers I ever beheld."

She continued to extol what his Lordship had been 'till Madeline was in bed, she then bade her good-night, and desired her, when she chose to rise, to ring for a servant.

But solitude could not calm the agitation of Madeline's mind; the more she reflected on the conversation that had passed between her and the Marquis, the more her perplexity increased; she at last, however, endeavoured to compose herself by reflecting on the promise she had received from him of having the mystery explained, and his assurance of friendship to her father.

"Should that friendship (she cried), be something more than bare profession; should it have power to mitigate the sorrows he too visibly labours under, for ever blessed shall I consider the hour in which I entered Montmorenci Castle."

Exhausted by mental as well as bodily fatigue, she at last sunk to repose, from which she did not awaken till the morning was far advanced: she was ready to leave her chamber 'ere she rung for a servant, a maid immediately obeyed her summons, and informed her breakfast was already prepared for her by the housekeeper.

Through a number of winding passages Madeline was conducted to the grand staircase, which she descended to the hall. Here she involuntarily paused to examine the ancient ornaments surrounding her, which spoke of the splendour and the taste of other days: but with the admiration they excited, was intermingled a degree of sadness at the neglect and even desolation so every where apparent; the shields and other war-like trophies which hung upon the stately pillars of the hall, were covered with dust and cobwebs, the fine historical pictures which stretched from the side of the staircase to the ceiling, were discoloured by damp and dropping from the walls; and a great folding door half open, discovered the inner court strewed with rubbish, and encompassed by decaying buildings, before which the high grass waved in rank luxuriance, unbent by any foot.

"How dreary, how desolate, (said Madeline to herself) is this scene; but to this state every work of man sooner or later comes: who then should vaunt of possessions, which, like the hand that raised them, are doomed to swift decay? Like the Poet she said,

"Why dost thou build the hall, son of the winged days? Thou lookest from thy towers to-day, yet a few years and the blast of the desert comes; it howls in the empty court, and whistles round thy half worn shield."

The voice of Lubin roused her from her melancholy meditation. He came to inquire whether she was able to continue her journey that day. She immediately assured him she was, and desired him to have the horses ready against she had breakfasted.

She was then shown into a parlour adjoining the hall, where she found the housekeeper waiting at the breakfast-table to receive her. Mrs. Beatrice apologized for her Lord's not appearing, but said, for many years past he had not risen till the day was far advanced.

Directly after breakfast Madeline bade an adieu to Montmorenci Castle; as she did so, she requested Mrs. Beatrice to present her sincere acknowledgments to the Marquis for the politeness and hospitality she had received beneath his roof.

Lubin would gladly have chatted as they travelled, but the mind of Madeline was too much agitated to permit her to converse, and he was forced to amuse himself by whistling and singing.

The nearer Madeline drew to the habitation of her father, the more her agitation increased; all the scenes she had gone thro' since her separation from him recurred to her memory, and she feared his inquiries concerning them would be too minute; she trembled lest she should discover, notwithstanding all her precaution, the real state of her heart, discover that its affections were abused, its pride mortified, its expectations disappointed; well she knew such a discovery would wound him to the soul.

"And, Oh! (she cried) to add sorrow to his sorrow, to increase his misery already too oppressive, would be indeed to aggravate my own."

At the entrance of the valley, in which the cottage of her father stood, she alighted and desired Lubin to lead the horses after her.

Had her mind been less disturbed than it now was, she would have been enraptured with the lovely prospect she beheld: it was the autumnal season, and the promise of the spring was amply fulfilled by the luxuriance of the harvest; the grapes she had left in embryo, were now ripened into purple clusters, and the toils of the vintage had already commenced; a profusion of gay flowers enameled the bright sword of the valley, and the yellow mantle of Ceres covered the little vales that intersected many of the hills, and o'er the waving woods that hung upon those hills soft and solemn tints were just beginning to steal.

Madeline reached the valley when the sun had attained its meridian, an hour when the cattle lay pensively ruminating, and

— — — — — — — — — — "The daw,

"The rook and magpie, to the grey-grown oaks

"That the calm village in their verdant arms

"Shelt'ring, embrace, direct their lazy flight;

"Where on the mingling boughs they sit embower'd

"All the hot noon, 'till cooler hours arise:

"Faint, underneath, the household fowls convene;

"And, in a corner of the buzzing shade,

"The house-dog, with the vacant grey-hound, lie

"Out-stretch'd and sleepy.

"The children of industry have had their hopes amply fulfilled, (cried Madeline, as she cast her eyes around) mine, she sighed, mine, when I left this place, were, though different, as flattering as their's."

To describe her feelings when she came in sight of her beloved cottage would be impossible; they were such as almost swelled her heart to bursting; pain and pleasure were so intermingled, that it would have been hard to determine which was predominant. Her pleasure at the idea of beholding her father was damped by reflecting in how very different a manner she expected to have returned to him. She stopped at the little gate which opened into the grove, and leaned upon it, in order to try and gain some composure 'ere she should appear before him: old Bijou, the house dog, who lay slumbering beside it, woke at her approach, and instantly set up a cry of joy, which denoted his perfect recollection of her; as she patted his head, she endeavoured to quiet him, but without effect: the noise he made disturbed Jaqueline at her work, and excited her curiosity.

"What is the matter, you noisy rogue? (said she, coming from the cottage) what possesses you, Bijou, to keep such a barking?"

She approached the gate, stopped, screamed, and retreated—then again advanced—again retreated: at last she exclaimed,

"If you do not wish to deprive me of my senses, you will at once tell me whether or not you are Mademoiselle Madeline?"

"Do you doubt your eyes," cried Madeline, stretching out her hand.

Jaqueline instantly pulled open the gate, but instead of taking the proffered hand of Madeline, she clasped her arms about her, and for some minutes by her caresses prevented her from speaking.

"Is my father well?" at last asked Madeline, disengaging herself from the enraptured Jaqueline.

"Yes, Mademoiselle, very well; but how did you travel?— Bless me, looking over the gate, and perceiving Lubin with the horses) surely you did not ride?"

"Is my father within?" asked Madeline, not attending to this question.

"No, he is in the vineyard; I will run and inform him of your arrival."

"Do not be too precipitate, (said Madeline) break it to him by degrees for he does not expect me."

To practise any caution, however, was totally out of the power of Jaqueline; she flew to the vineyard; and Madeline all the way heard her exclaiming,

"She is come, she is come—O, Monsieur, Mademoiselle Madeline is come."

Madeline entered the parlour, she sat down, and tried to compose herself against the approaching interview; but she tried in vain. In a few minutes she heard the voice of her father; her heart throbbed as if it would burst her bosom: she rose, but had not power to meet him. Pale, disordered he rushed into the room, and Madeline sunk almost fainting into his extended arms.

It was some time 'ere either of them could speak. Clermont at last raised his eyes,

"Do I again behold you, my child, my Madeline, (he exclaimed) welcome, thrice welcome to my arms."

He held her to a distance from him; he gazed upon her; the alteration in her looks seemed to strike him to the very heart: the rose that had bloomed upon her cheek when they parted,—the lustre that had brightened her eye was fled, and sadness had taken entire possession of her.

"Oh! my child, (said he, looking mournfully at her) I fear, I fear, you have too bitterly lamented the death of our inestimable friend."

Madeline burst into tears.

"Our loss (resumed Clermont) is great indeed, but our grief is selfish: death to her was a removal to unutterable felicity; stem therefore these strong emotions in pity to me, check them, remember you are my only earthly consolation, the only prop I have to rest on."

"Alas! (sighed Madeline) how frail a prop!" She took his hand, she pressed it to her lips. "My father (she said) be assured no effort on my part shall be wanting to fulfil your expectations, and heaven I doubt not will strengthen the feeble hands and calm the agitated mind of her who prays to it for fortitude and composure to be enabled to perform its incumbent duties."

"Yes, my child, (cried Clermont embracing her) heaven always assists the virtuous."

He now inquired to what circumstance he owed her unexpected return, as in her last letter she had given no intimation of it. Madeline, without entering into the particulars of her late situation at the chateau, briefly informed him, that as soon as D'Alembert came to it, Madame D'Alembert wished her to leave it, and had promised in a few days to assign her reason for that wish.

Clermont was all astonishment; but as he could not possibly fathom the mystery, he endeavoured to turn his thoughts from it. Madeline was still too much agitated to be able to inform him of her adventures at Montmorenci castle, but she determined to devote the first minutes of returning composure to that purpose, deeming it highly necessary for him to be acquainted with them as soon as possible.

Her mind was a little relieved from the uneasiness that oppressed it by finding him silent respecting de Sevignie; yet while she rejoiced she wondered at that silence till she reflected that the Countess had promised never to acquaint him with the renewed attentions of de Sevignie, except they were terminated in a manner that she knew must be pleasing to him.

But though the Countess had kept her promise, though Clermont was silent respecting de Sevignie, his mind was occupied in thinking of him; he could not believe that the deep dejection of his daughter was owing solely to the death of her friend, as his words, from regard to her delicacy had intimated: to the disappointment of her hopes relative to de Sevignie he was convinced it was principally owing, and with anguish intolerable he looked upon this drooping blossom, whose fair promise of maturity seemed now utterly at an end.

"But a few days ago, (he cried to himself) and, from the recollection of former calamities, I thought I could not be more wretched than I then was: but, alas! I now find I was mistaken—now, when I behold the sole solace of affliction, my only earthly hope, sinking beneath a grief which seems bending her gentle head to swift decay. Oh! gracious heaven, if my child is destined to an early grave, close these sad eyes 'ere that destiny be accomplished."

He wished to have the sorrows of her heart acknowledged to him; the acknowledgment would give him a right to offer his sympathy and counsel: and the sympathy, the counsel of a parent, might perhaps, he thought, be efficacious. But though he wished such a divulgement, he would not desire it, well knowing the delicacy of the female mind, and how unwillingly it must confess a hopeless passion.

CHAP. IV.

"Ah! happy grove, dark and secure retreat
"Of sacred silence, rest's eternal seat;
"How well your cool and unfrequented shade
"Suits with the chaste retirement of a maid:
"Oh if kind heaven had been so much my friend,
"To make my fate upon my choice depend;
"All my ambition I would here confine,
"And only this elysium should be mine."

Clermont went out to see that Lubin was taken care of, thank him for the attention he had paid to Madeline, and inquire whether he would not stop a day or two at the cottage to rest himself; but Lubin said there was a necessity for his immediate return to the chateau, and that after dinner he must depart: he accordingly set out at the time he had fixed, and as he quitted the cottage received the grateful acknowledgments of Madeline for his care of her, and an entreaty that he would remind his lady of the promise she had given of writing soon.

Madeline, now more composed, no longer delayed acquainting her father of her visit to Montmorenci Castle. The instant she mentioned it he started, and betrayed the greatest emotion, but when she proceeded, when she informed him of her being summoned to the presence of the Marquis, of the inquiries he had made concerning the picture, he suddenly exclaimed with uplifted hands and eyes,

"Oh! Providence, how mysterious are thy ways!"

"The Marquis (said Madeline, obeying the motion which her father made for her to proceed) the Marquis promised that when least expected perhaps the mystery should be explained. —"

She paused, for at this moment she heard the trampling of horses feet—she looked towards the window and saw a man alighting at the gate, whom she immediately recollected to have seen at Montmorenci Castle.

"'Tis a messenger from the Marquis," cried Madeline, sinking back in her chair. Her father started up, and rushed from the room; he met the man at the entrance of the cottage, and Madeline heard them talking together for a few minutes, they then repaired to the study, the door of which was directly bolted, and Madeline remained two hours by herself in a situation that can be better conceived than described—her father then returned to the parlour pale, trembling, disordered; —he entered it, he spoke not to Madeline—he seemed to have no power to speak—but he put an open letter into her hand. With an agitation that shook her whole frame she cast her eyes over it, and read as follows.

"The sigh of repentance has at length prevailed—heaven has given me an opportunity of making some atonement for the injustice I committed in my youth:—

"Come then, son of a much injured and unhappy love, come to your rightful home, to the arms of your father—

"The lamp of life but feebly lights his eyes; hasten then, while he has power to see—to bless you he would add—but that he is unworthy of bestowing a blessing.

"Hasten, that he may sink to his grave with some degree of peace, at beholding his rightful heir acknowledged; at beholding an heir better calculated than himself for supporting the honors of montmorenci."

The variety of emotions that assailed the heart of Madeline on perusing this letter prevented all utterance, and she stood gazing on her father, the very image of astonishment.

"Yes, (said Clermont, at last, in a solemn voice), I am the son of a much injured and unhappy woman, the rightful though long unacknowledged heir of Montmorenci; called to a situation I was always entitled to, when too late for that situation to afford me any pleasure. So much am I attached to my present retirement, so congenial is it to my feelings, that nothing but respect to the memory of my mother, regard to the interest of my child, could tempt me to forego it."

"Heaven can witness for me, (cried Madeline) how little I desire you to leave it on my account. Oh! my father, no wealth, however great, no rank however exalted, can now confer happiness upon me."

"My child (exclaimed Clermont, clasping his arms round her) do not torture my soul by expressions which intimate such despondence. Oh, try to alleviate my misery, a misery which no time, no circumstance can banish from my mind, by letting me think that you will be happy,—by letting me think that the approaching change of situation will at least promote your felicity."

"I will try, my father, (said Madeline) I will try to be all you wish me."

"I have no longer any reason to conceal my former situation, (said Clermont) to-morrow therefore in our way to the Castle of Montmorenci, I shall relate a long and affecting story to you."

"To-morrow! (cried Madeline, gasping for breath) to-morrow do we go to Montmorenci Castle?"

"Yes, (replied Clermont) the servant who brought me the letter from his Lord and has just departed, informed me that a carriage would be here early in the morning, to convey us thither; tomorrow therefore I bid adieu to this cottage, in which I imagined my last sigh would have been breathed; to those shadowy woods which screened me from an invidious world; to those lonely shades which heard the voice of my complaining."

Madeline was not less affected than her father at the idea of quitting their retirement; the gaiety, the hopes, that would once have rendered her delighted with the prospect that now opened to her view, were fled, never, never she believed, to be revived.

Her father told her he meant merely to inform Jaqueline that they were going on a visit to a friend, but as soon as they were settled in Montmorenci Castle he intended to write to her and put her in possession of the cottage as a reward for her long and faithful services.

The preparations for their journey were made before they retired to rest; Madeline, at the time she accompanied the Countess de Merville had fortunately left some clothes behind, and these were now packed up for her.

In the solitude of her little chamber she gave vent to those feelings which tenderness for her father made her suppress in his presence.

"Alas! (she cried) are my hopes always to be disappointed? —must I resign the tranquillity of this cottage?—must I again launch into a world where I experienced little else than distress and danger?—Oh! scenes dear and congenial to my soul! (she exclaimed, as from a window she viewed the valley, now illumined by a bright moon), Oh! scenes dear and congenial to my soul, had I never left you I had never known the reality of falsehood, never been truly unhappy.

"I am now (she continued) about entering into a situation, which from disappointed hope I am incapable of enjoying; a situation which will give the world claims upon me, that from the sadness of my mind I shall be if not unable, at least totally unwilling to fulfil; far better, far happier than for me to remain in an obscurity, where, without strictures from others, or censures from myself, I might act as inclination prompted.

"But what do I say? (cried she, after a pause) do I repine at a change which restores my father to the rank he has been so long unjustly deprived of; at a change which will give to me the means of dispensing happiness to others. Oh! let me chase from my breast a grief so selfish, let me not wrap myself in sorrow and despair, and because the blessing I desired is not mine reject every other. Let me not, like a froward child, dash the proffered cup of joy from my lips, because there is not in it every ingredient I could wish. Yes, (she proceeded, as if animated by a new spirit), I will try to dispel a grief that enervates, that sinks me into languor, that makes me shrink from the idea of fulfilling the claims of society; and I make no doubt my efforts will be successful, for heaven strengthens those who wish to do right, and I shall be again, if not happy, at least tranquil; the felicity I shall have the means of bestowing on others, will soothe my feelings; the tears I wipe from the cheek of misery will dissipate my own, and the sigh I suppress in the bosom of affliction will prevent mine from rising."

The entrance of Jaqueline now disturbed her, she came to make those inquiries which the presence of Clermont had hitherto prevented.

"Dear Mademoiselle, (said she, sitting down by the little toilette as Madeline began to undress) what in the name of wonder occasioned your coming home in the sudden manner you did?"

"Nothing that can afford you any pleasure to hear, (replied Madeline) I therefore request you may ask no more questions about it."

"Lord, Mademoiselle, 'tis very natural to inquire about what has surprised one so much. Well, if you had taken my advice, you would never have gone with the Countess—I knew very well how she would serve you; I knew there was no dependence to be placed upon the promises of the great, and you find I was not wrong in thinking or saying so: you see after promising you so fine a fortune, how she has popped off without leaving you so much as a sous."

"You hurt me extremely by talking in this way, (said Madeline) I beg you may never speak again in such a manner of a person who was my best friend, and whose sudden death alone prevented her fulfilling her generous intentions towards me."

"Ah! Mademoiselle, you are a good soul, and willing to excuse every one; but people will have their own thoughts let you say what you will. One looks so foolish now, (she continued) for my chief consolation during your absence was telling the neighbours of the fine situation you had got into for life. 'She has been taken (says I) to one of the finest castles in Dauphine, and from thence she is to be carried to Paris, where, no doubt, she will get a grand match as the lady, her friend, intends to give her a very large fortune; and as soon as she is settled in a house of her own. I am to be sent for, either to be her own woman, or housekeeper, 'twill be at my own option which."

"And pray, Jaqueline, how came you to say such things, when you foresaw, as you yourself acknowledge that I should be disappointed by the Countess?"

Jaqueline looked confused—

"Why, Mademoiselle, (said she, after the hesitation of a minute) I was sometimes inclined to think that she might be as good as her word."

"Well, Jaqueline, let this be a caution to you never again to mention expectations which you are not pretty sure of having fulfilled."

"Aye, Mademoiselle, we all grow wiser every day."

She now expressed her regret at the intended departure of Clermont and Madeline, and endeavoured to discover whither they were going; but Madeline evaded her questions, and when nearly undressed dismissed her, highly mortified at not having had her curiosity gratified.

Madeline's mind was too much agitated to permit her to rest, and though she went to bed, she passed a restless night; towards the dawn of day she sunk into a slumber, from which however she was soon disturbed by Jaqueline, who came to tell her the carriage waited. She started up and hastily began to dress.

"Do pray, dear Mademoiselle, (said Jaqueline) do pray come to the window and look at the carriage, I dare say you never saw so fine a one; 'tis so beautifully ornamented, and drawn by six horses, and there are four out-riders and three postilions: dear me, it must be a charming thing to ride in it! I dare say it belongs to a very great man, I should certainly have inquired from the servants, but that my master told me he would be very angry if I asked them any questions."

"Tell my father, (said Madeline) I shall be with him very soon."

"Yes, Mademoiselle, (replied Jaqueline) and by the time you come down the coffee will be made."

Madeline was soon dressed and descended the stairs; but instead of going directly to the parlour, she stole into the garden, to take a last leave of

"The native bowers of innocence and ease,

Seats of her youth when ev'ry charm could please."

Scarcely a spot within the garden but what recalled some happy, some delightful hour to her mind; such hours as she never more expected to experience.

O'er the trees beneath whose shelter she had so often sported in childish gaiety, so often enjoyed a delightful retreat from the meridian sun; o'er the flowers which she had planted, and with her pencil so often amused herself by copying, she could now with difficulty prevent herself from weeping, and like the poet she exclaimed,

"Farewell, ye flow'rs, whose buds, with early care,
"I watch'd, and to the cheerful sun did rear;
"Who now shall bind your stems, or, when you fall,
"With fountain streams your fainting souls recall."
"No more, my goats, shall I behold you climb,
"The steepy cliffs, or crop the flowery thyme;
"No more extended in the grot below,
"Shall see you browsing on the mountain's brow;
"The prickly shrubs, and after on the bare,
"Lean down the deep abyss and hang in air."

A deep sigh from a little bower near her startled Madeline: she looked towards it, and beheld her father: he came out and taking her hand, led her into the house.

Breakfast was ready, they took some coffee and then rose to depart; Jaqueline cried bitterly, but Clermont comforted her by an assurance of writing soon, and informing her where he was; he also desired her to choose some neighbour for a companion: with a trembling hand he assisted his daughter into the coach, which set off the moment he had entered it. The deepest melancholy appeared to have taken possession of both, and both for a considerable time observed a profound silence."

CHAP. V.

"A parent's soft sorrows to mine led the way."

Clermont at last addressed Madeline.

"I shall now, my love, (said he) fulfil my promise, and relate those events which tenderness made me hitherto conceal from you.

"In the chateau, where you enjoyed the society of one of the most amiable of women, the early and the most happy part of my life was passed under the protection of Count de Valdore, father to your lamented Benefactress; I understood that I was the orphan son of a very particular friend of his, who, though of a respectable family, was unable to leave me any provision, and had in his last moments recommended me to the protection of the Count. Had I been in reality the son of the Count, he could not have paid me greater attention than he did; neither he nor the Countess made any distinction between me and their only child Elvira, with whom, her age being nearly the same of mine, I was educated; the most eminent masters in every branch of literature, and every elegant accomplishment, attending us constantly at the chateau.

"Naturally of a gay disposition, and surrounded by everything which could add to that gaiety, I basked in the sunshine, nor thought of any clouds that might hereafter obscure its brightness: indeed I had nothing to apprehend, for the Count had always promised me an ample provision. Alas! the happiness I then enjoyed but rendered the misery I afterwards experienced more acute; for recollected joys always sharpen the arrows of affliction.

"The first interruption my happiness received was by the death of the Countess, which happened when I was about eighteen; the grief I felt for her loss was such as an affectionate son must have felt for a tender mother, but, though poignant, it was faint to that experienced by the Count; nobly, however, he tried to check his own feelings, in order to appease those of his daughter and mine: his efforts in time succeeded; but, alas! scarcely were we beginning to regain some degree of tranquillity ere he was taken from us to that blessedness his whole life proved him deserving of. Smothered grief undermined his constitution, and in three months after the death of his lady he was re-united to her in those regions where they could never more be separated.

"When he felt his last moments approaching, he dismissed every one but me and Elvira from his room; we knelt on each side of the bed, and, in the most affecting language, he conjured us to submit, without repining, to the divine will; after he had bestowed a solemn and tender benediction upon his daughter, such as her filial piety deserved, he turned to me and took my hand:

'My dear Lausane, (said he, for so I was called) I should have died unhappy if I had not had an opportunity of thanking you for the respect, the attention you ever paid to me and mine.'

"I would have spoken, I would have told him how inadequate that respect, that attention was to the care, the affection I had experienced from him and his family, but the fullness of my heart prevented utterance.

"Had heaven spared my life (continued he) a little longer, I should have disclosed to you a most important secret; it was decreed however that from me you should never hear it; but in a small India box, in my cabinet, you will find a packet addressed to you, and containing all the particulars I would have informed you of: when you read them, you will find that without knowing misfortune you have been most unfortunate; that without feeling injury you have been most injured; but as you hope for prosperity in this world, endless happiness in that to come, I entreat you never rashly to resent those misfortunes, or endeavour to revenge those injuries. Should the author of both still withhold that justice you are entitled to, you will not find yourself under any necessity of accepting his bounty, which in such a case would be degrading to you, as in my will, which will be opened as soon as M. Valdore, my daughter's guardian arrives at the chateau, I have made such provision for you as will enable you to hold the same place in society you have hitherto done.'

"I cannot describe the feelings excited by the words of the Count: astonishment overwhelmed my senses, and I would not long have delayed to seek an explanation of them, had he not died almost immediately after he had ceased speaking.

"The confusion of the family, the grief of his daughter, who would only listen to consolation from me, and my own affliction then deadened my curiosity, and his interment had taken place ere I thought of visiting the cabinet; nor perhaps should I have done so as soon as I did, had I not found myself, the very evening after his funeral, seated with Elvira in the room where it stood. We were alone; for her guardian, who lived in a remote part of the kingdom, was not yet arrived. The moment I beheld the cabinet my curiosity was revived, and I eagerly wished to take from it the important papers; the eyes of Elvira followed mine, and the words of her father instantly recurred to her recollection.

'My dear Lausane, (said she) I am confident you must have suffered much from the suspension of your curiosity; delay no longer to gratify it—it may be requisite for you to be immediately acquainted with the secret my father spoke of; I will retire to give you a proper opportunity of perusing the packet.'

"No, Elvira, (I replied, taking her hand as she rose to withdraw), you have hitherto honored me with the appellation of brother, and heaven can witness for me I bear you the affection of one; a brother should have no secrets from an affectionate sister; since you therefore permit me to consider you as one, condescend to hear the mysterious words of your father explained; they have prepared me for a tale of distress, and if any thing can alleviate the sorrow it may perhaps excite, it can only be the gentle sympathy of such a friend as you are.'

"She re-seated herself, and tremblingly I approached and unlocked the cabinet: the first thing I beheld within it was the India box. I took it out, I drew back the lid, and beheld a large sealed packet, directed in the hand-writing of the Count to me. I felt my whole frame agitated, and could scarcely reach the sofa on which Elvira sat.

"Many minutes elapsed ere I could summon sufficient resolution to break the seal. I felt as if about to raise a veil which had hitherto concealed terrific images from my view, and shuddered at the idea of the horrors they might excite; at length I ventured to do so, and found several sheets of small paper within the envelope, all closely written, and in a hand entirely new to me. Elvira leaned over my shoulder, and together we began to peruse the following story."

Here Clermont paused; and, taking a manuscript from his pocket, he put it into the hand of his daughter, and desired her to read it to herself,

"When you have finished it, (said he) I will go on with my narrative."

Madeline bowed, and read as follows:

"Ere those pages meet your eye, the hand that wrote them will be crumbled into dust. Oh! my son, offspring of an unhappy and ill-requited love, long before you peruse them, every trace, every memorial of your unfortunate mother will be obliterated from your mind, nor will all your efforts be able to recall to recollection the period in which her bitter tears bedewed your innocent cheek, in which with happy playfulness you hid your head in her distracted bosom: — but I run into complaints ere I assign the sad occasion of them — I will, if possible, be brief.

"Ere I was born, love, unhappy love, I may say, laid in some degree the foundation of my misery. My mother, the daughter of Count St. Paul, whose family is well known for its antiquity and pride in the Province of Normandy; untinctured either by the ambition or avarice of her parents, selected for herself at an early age a partner whose only portion was merit, and thus disappointed the expectations which her birth, beauty, and accomplishments had raised in her family; in consequence of doing so she was utterly discarded by every member of it, her youngest brother excepted, who had then however nothing to bestow but — assurances of friendship.

"St. Foix, the descendant of a noble but reduced family, to whom she had united herself, was in the army, and with him she launched into the world, whose storms and distresses she had hitherto known only by report; too soon, alas! she had a sad experience of them.

"But with a noble fortitude she sustained them, not only from tenderness to her husband, but from a consciousness of having drawn them upon herself. St. Foix, however, the delirium of passion over, and the pressure of distress experienced, bitterly regretted having yielded to an affection which heightened his cares, by involving the woman he adored in sorrow, and in little more than two years after his marriage, and a few months after my birth, he fell a victim to his feelings. The grief of my mother may be imagined, but cannot be described, and in all probability she would soon have sunk beneath it, had not her brother flown to her relief: an union just then completed with an heiress of considerable fortune, gave him the power of serving her as he wished, and he endeavoured to calm her sorrows by assurances of being a never-failing friend to her, and of supplying to me, to the utmost of his power, the place of the parent I was so early deprived of. He immediately took a small cottage, in a sequestered and romantic part of Dauphine, for her, and settled upon her a yearly stipend, amply sufficient to procure her all that she could want or desire in retirement.

"Time and religion softened her anguish, and as I grew up, her heart again began to be sensible of pleasure; a pleasure, however, frequently embittered by a conviction of the unhappiness her brother experienced in consequence of serving her; for his wife, selfish and illiberal in her disposition, could not with any degree of patience bear the idea of his regarding any one out of his own immediate family, or of his expending on them any part of that fortune she so frequently boasted of having given to him.

"Long he withstood her solicitations to withdraw his bounty, long opposed her inclination; but at length, tired of domestic strife, of continual upbraidings for the intention he avowed of providing for his niece in a manner suitable to her birth, he hinted a wish to my mother for my retiring into a convent.

"This was an unexpected blow, and one which overwhelmed my mother, by destroying those hopes that, with the natural vanity and partiality of a parent, almost from my birth she had indulged, of seeing me at some period or other happily settled, and of enjoying beneath my roof that tranquillity which sorrow and dependence had hitherto prevented her from experiencing.

"With tears, with agonies which shook her frame, she conjured him not to deprive her of her only earthly comfort, not to entomb her child alive, or in one short minute undo all he had hitherto done.

"Ah! my mother, well had it been for your Madeline, if your lips had never uttered such a supplication; well had it been for her, if in the first bloom of life, ere her heart was sufficiently expanded to feel that tenderness which constitutes our greatest happiness or misery, the walls of a convent had immured her from a world, where her peace, her fame, were destined to be wrecked.

"My uncle was too generous to repeat a wish which gave such pain; he regretted ever having mentioned it, and strove to make amends for having done so, by reiterating the most solemn assurances of fulfilling the intentions he had before avowed towards me.

"Thus was the storm which threatened the peace of my mother, overblown; but, alas! the calm that succeeded it was to me of short duration. I had scarcely attained my sixteenth year when I was deprived of this inestimable parent. In the language of despair I wrote to my uncle, then at Paris, to inform him of this event; and at the same time enclosed a letter, written by my mother in her last hours, and, which I afterwards found contained a supplication not to permit me to enter a convent without I wished myself to do so, and an entreaty for his protection to be continued to me.

"He directly hastened to me, and used every method in his power to sooth my sorrows; he repeated his assurances of continued kindness, and declared from that period I should reside with him till I had a proper habitation of my own to go to.

"I accordingly accompanied him to Paris; and here, in all probability, the sadness of my heart might soon have been diverted by the novelty of every thing I saw, had I met with any of that tenderness I had always been accustomed to; but the most chilling coldness, or else the most contemptuous disdain, was the treatment I received from my aunt and her family. My uncle, in order to try and prevent my mind from dwelling on it, insisted on my being taken to all the places they frequented; but this, instead of alleviating, rather aggravated my misery, for my aunt soon took it into her head that I was a rival to her daughters. A year I dragged on in a state of wretchedness, which no language could justly express: at the expiration of that period, worn out with ill treatment, and agonized by beholding my benevolent protector in continual disquietude on my account, I determined, with a kind of desperate resolution, to terminate that disquietude and my indignities, by retiring to a cloister: but how impossible is it to express the pangs with which I formed and announced this resolution: yet what, you will say, could have occasioned those pangs? surely not the idea of renouncing a world which contained no tender friend to supply the place of the one I had lost?—

"Alas! it then contained a being dearer to me than life itself: —St. Julian, the Marquis of Montmorenci's son, visited at my uncle's, and had not long been known ere he was beloved! Those who knew him could not have wondered at my sudden attachment; every virtue, every grace which ennobles and adorns humanity he appeared to possess. Oh! St. Julian, Heaven surely endowed you with every virtue; for candour and benevolence sat upon your countenance, and it was only an improper education, or pernicious company that rendered you deceitful, and led you to betray the unsuspicious heart, which reposed upon you for happiness.

"Secretly I indulged my passion, yet without the smallest hope of having it returned; for though a soft beam from the eye of St. Julian sometimes tempted me to think I was not utterly indifferent to him, I never had reason to imagine he thought seriously about me; but, notwithstanding my hopelessness respecting him, so great, so exquisite was the pleasure I derived from seeing, from listening to him, that the idea of foregoing it was infinitely more painful to me than that of death.

"My uncle heard my determination of retiring to a cloister with a satisfaction which he could not disguise, though he attempted it; and my aunt and her children with evident delight: generous to the last, my uncle left me free to choose a convent—I accordingly fixed on one, with which I was well acquainted, near the habitation where alone I had been happy.

"Immediate preparations were made for my removal, and in a few days after I had avowed my intention of quitting it, I was hurried from my uncle's house.

"Accompanied by an old female domestic, I commenced my journey; what I suffered on doing so I shall not attempt to describe. I felt like a wretch going into a gloomy exile, where the features, the voice he loved, would never more charm his eye, or sooth his ear.

"At a late hour we stopped for the night. As soon as my companion had retired to her chamber, I locked myself up in mine, and gave way to the agonies of my soul. In the midst of my lamentations I was startled by a tap at the chamber-door; I listened attentively, and heard it repeated, and at the same time my name pronounced in a low voice. Still more surprised, I hastily unlocked the door, door, and beheld—ah! gracious Heaven! what were the feelings of that moment, St. Julian!—I involuntarily receded, and sunk half fainting upon a chair. The words, the tenderness of St. Julian soon revived me, and brought me to a perfect sense of my happiness; he implored my pardon for the agitation he had caused me.

"He had loved me, he declared, almost from the first moment he beheld me, and would at once have divulged his passion, had he not feared its being then discovered to my aunt, whose malice he knew would betray him to his father; he had therefore determined, if he beheld no chance of losing me, to conceal it till the expectations he entertained of a splendid independence at the death of a very old relative were realized, and he consequently secured from suffering any pecuniary distress through the displeasure of his father, which he could not deny his thinking would follow the disclosure of our union.

"My sudden resolution, (he proceeded to say) had been concealed from him till I had quitted my uncle's; with difficulty on hearing it he could hide his emotions, and almost instantly pursued me, trembling lest I should be lost to him for ever.

"He now implored me to consent to a private union, and put myself immediately under his protection, solemnly assuring me, that the moment he could acknowledge me as his wife, without involving me in distress, with equal pride and pleasure he would do so.

"You may well believe I did not, could not resist his supplications: — a carriage and confidential servants were in waiting, and we directly set out for Paris, which we reached at the dawn of the day, and, stopping at the first church we came to, were united.

"St. Julian then took lodgings for me in a retired part of the town, under a feigned name, passing himself for a secretary to a man of consequence, and unable, from his situation, to be always with me.

"I had now no drawback on my felicity but that which proceeded from sorrow at my mother's not being alive to witness it, and uneasiness at the disquiet, which I learned from St. Julian, who still continued to visit at his house, my uncle felt on my account, not being able to form the slightest conjecture of what had become of me: Perfect happiness, however, I knew was unattainable in this world, and as the best proof of my gratitude to Heaven for that portion which I enjoyed, I sedulously endeavoured to repel the sigh of regret that sometimes involuntarily heaved my bosom.

"Before the expiration of a year you were born. Oh! with what rapture did I receive you to my arms! with what delight did I present you to your father! and, with mingled emotions of tenderness and pleasure, beheld the tear which stole down his cheek, as I endeavoured in your infant features to discover a resemblance to his.

"I had now attained my summit of felicity; and my sun was soon to set in misery and despair.

"Soon after your birth, the visits of your father became less frequent; he did not assign any reason for their being so, nor did I inquire; for suspicion was a stranger to my breast; my faith was unbounded, great, and firm as my love; and while I wept his absence, I ever hailed his presence with a smile.

"At length a long space ensued in which I did not behold him; my spirits involuntarily drooped, and with them my health declined; yet, notwithstanding my sufferings, the moment I again saw him, I thought myself amply rewarded for them.

"The pleasure, however, which filled my heart on his entering my chamber, was quickly damped by the coldness of his manner: he scarcely returned my caresses, or noticed you.

'Well, Madeline, (said he, seating himself at a distance from me), I trust you have been well and happy since I last saw you.'

"As well and happy (I replied, looking at him with that tenderness which my heart experienced) as I could be without the society which constitutes my chief felicity."

'Ah! Madeline, (cried he) I trust when you mix more in the world, you will be able to enjoy felicity without that society.'

'Could the world (said I) produce any change in my present sentiments, I should wish for ever to be secluded from it.'

"He arose and approached me.

'I came, Madeline, (said he) with a hope of receiving proofs of your good sense instead of your tenderness; do not interrupt me, (continued he, seeing me about to speak) listen attentively to what I am about saying:

'All hopes of an independence are terminated by my uncle, who died some days ago, bequeathing the whole of his property to a religious house; I am therefore entirely at the mercy of my father; consequently to disclose our marriage would be to involve me in certain ruin, as I am convinced no supplications, no entreaties would ever prevail upon him to pardon so imprudent a step; 'tis absolutely necessary therefore that we should conceal it for ever.'

"'For ever! (repeated I) gracious Heaven! would it not be better to avow it, than to be teased with continual importunities (which must be the case) to form another connexion.'

"'I will not deny, Madeline, (said he) that it is not my intention to be deaf to such importunities: as our marriage is a profound secret, I mean it never shall be known; that from henceforth we shall be strangers to each other, and each again enter the world free to make another choice.'

"Good heavens! what words were those for a wife, for a mother to hear! – The blood run cold through my veins, and for some time the faculties of speech were suspended.

"Have I lived, (I at length exclaimed) have I lived to hear the husband I adore declare his intention of disowning me? Have I lived to hear St. Julian avow his design of branding his child with infamy?"

'Do not, Madeline, (said he) with the weakness peculiar to your sex, run into complaints at once unjust and unavailing; when you mix more in the world, and have opportunities of comparing my conduct with that of others, you will then be convinced that it is not quite so base or cruel as you now imagine; you will then see numbers of your sex, perhaps as amiable as yourself, cruelly forsaken after the first ardour of passion is extinguished, instead of which you will find yourself, if your obstinacy does not counteract my intentions, in possession of an ample provision, with which you can retire to some other part of France, where you are not known, and there, passing yourself as a widow, bring up your son, and, perhaps, make another choice more calculated than your present one to render you happy.'

"My heart felt bursting; but I strove to repress the grief, the indignation with which it laboured.

"No, St. Julian, (said I, in a solemn voice), never will I enter the road of infamy you have marked out for me to take; I am your wife, nor shall any power but that, whose mandate we must all obey, make me give up my claims. What! did you snatch me from the altar of my God, from the dwelling of piety and peace, but to plunge me into guilt and misery?"

'Madeline, (cried he) be wise, nor mar my good intentions towards you by useless endeavours to support claims, which I am determined to deny; 'tis impossible, you know, for you to prove your marriage; there were, you may recollect, no witnesses to it, and with the name of the priest who performed the ceremony you are unacquainted.'

"Alas! those were truths which could not be controverted, and destitute as I was of any friend to interfere in my behalf, my uncle having paid the last sad debt of nature some weeks before, I saw no means of escaping the fate he doomed me to. I wept, I upbraided, I supplicated, but all without effect; and I was soon convinced that every spark of his former affection was extinguished, and that some dangerous rival had taken entire possession of his heart.

"Agonized by this conviction, I might perhaps have silently submitted to his wishes, assured that his name, without his regard, could give me no happiness, had I not considered that with his unhappy mother the son of St. Julian must also sink; maternal tenderness urged me therefore to make some effort to counteract his cruel and unjust intentions.

"I accordingly formed the resolution of flying to Dauphine, to throw myself at the feet of his father, and implore his protection for the deserted wife and offspring of his son. Alas! it was a resolution which despair and ignorance of the world only could have prompted; for a heart occupied by avarice and ambition, as was the Marquis's, is ever dead to the nobler softer claims of justice and humanity.

"As St. Julian departed, he told me he would give me a day or two to consider of what he had said; if at the expiration of that time he found me inclined to accede to his wishes, he would at once secure to me the provision he had promised; but if, on the contrary, he found me still inclined to dispute them, he would, without farther hesitation abandon me to a world which would laugh at all the allegations I could make against him.

"I saw no time was to be lost; the moment therefore he had left me I stole from the house, and hired a carriage, which I ordered to meet me at an early hour, the next morning, at the end of the street. Faint, trembling, oppressed with a thousand horrors, I commenced my journey with you in my arms.

"Fearful of being pursued, I made the driver, as night approached, turn into an obscure village, some leagues from the road. Here a violent illness, brought on by the dreadful agitation I suffered, detained me two days, and when I recommenced my journey, I was more dead than alive.

"Oh! how impossible to describe the emotions which shook my frame as I approached the mansion of Montmorenci; as I stopped before those gates which I once hoped I should have entered as the acknowledged wife of St. Julian! for many minutes my feelings prevented my declaring to the astonished domestics the purport of my visit; at length I summoned sufficient resolution to desire to be shown into the presence of their Lord. I drew near his apartment more like an unhappy criminal about deprecating vengeance, than an injured sufferer going to implore justice: the moment I beheld his countenance, where pride and sternness only were visible, the faint hope of obtaining his protection, which had hitherto cheered my heart, died away; like the drowning wretch, however, grasping at every straw, I determined to essay every thing which had a chance of procuring me relief—I therefore cast myself at his feet, and poured forth my sorrows; but scarcely had I concluded my sad tale, scarcely had I raised my tearful eyes to his to try if I could perceive one gleam of pity in them, ere a door burst open, and St. Julian entered. He entered with a countenance inflamed by rage and every direful passion. Oh! had a dagger pierced my breast I could not have suffered greater agonies than I experienced when I beheld those eyes which had once beamed unutterable tenderness, now darting the keenest glances of resentment on me.

'You see, my Lord, (said he, addressing his father) that I was not mistaken with regard to this unhappy woman. I was well convinced of the lengths her artifice and ambition would carry her.'

'Such artifice in one so young is really astonishing, (replied the Marquis) and renders it absolutely necessary that we should prevent her having another opportunity of trying to deceive.'

"I attempted to speak, but was interrupted by St. Julian, who directly called in two servants, and ordered them to bear me to a remote apartment. Thither, shrieking with despair, and with you in my arms, I was carried and locked in. A kind of madness seized me—I could not weep—I could not speak—by cries, by groans I could alone express my misery.

"Night approached ere any one came near me; a young female then appeared—I merely cast a glance at her, and then averted my eyes, as a trembling wretch would have done from his executioner; for every heart in the mansion of Montmorenci I fancied steeled against me. She came to me and entreated me to take some refreshment.

"Surprised by the entreaty, and by the gentleness with which it was delivered, I looked at her, and beheld a tear stealing down her cheek; it was a sacred tear, which pity had engendered, and operated more powerfully in calming the violence of my feeling than any arguments could have done. Oh! how sweet, how soothing, when we believe ourselves utterly abandoned, utterly friendless, to be surprised by finding a heart that compassionates us!—

"My tears immediately began to flow, the fever in my brain abated, and I stretched out my hand to press her's to my bosom.

'Alas! unhappy lady, (she exclaimed) I pity you from my soul, and wish it was in my power to save you from the fate that awaits you.'

"What fate? (cried I, gazing on her) have they planned my death? Ah! no—they would not be so merciful as to terminate the anguish they have inflicted."

'About the middle of to-night (said she) they mean to put you into a carriage, and send you to a house of penitents near Paris, where you will for ever be confined from the world, and separated from your son.'

—"Horror for some time took from me the power of speech.

"Oh! St. Julian, (I at length exclaimed) is this the fate you have decreed for Madeline?—Is this the destiny you have doomed her to, whom but a few short months ago you wooed to your arms with vows of never-changing love?—Oh, never let my sex again confide in man!—Oh, never more let them gaze with pleasure upon the beam of tenderness, nor listen with delight to the language of love!'—

"On my knees I implored my informer to assist me to escape.

"Not on my own account (cried I) do I plead; stripes, dungeons, or perpetual imprisonment, could give little pain to her who has experienced the so much greater pain of being deserted by the man she loves; but on the account of him, who, if deprived of me, would surely be deprived of his only earthly friend; for those who exercised such unprecedented cruelty upon his mother, would no doubt but ill protect his helpless youth: By the God, then, which you worship; by that heaven which you hope to attain, assist me to fly with my son to some solitary gloom, where I may rear his youth with tenderness, or see him, while unconscious of calamity, laid within his grave."

"She raised me, and told me, if I would be calm, and thought I could brave the horrors of travelling through lonely woods at such an hour as the present, she would try to assist me in escaping. I gave her every assurance she desired, and she lost no time in conducting me down a flight of back stairs terminated by a door that opened into the forest. I gave her, at parting, almost all I had to bestow, my thanks, and put a little fancy ring upon her finger to bring me sometimes to her mind, and make her now and then offer up a prayer for me and my babe.

"My mind was too much disturbed to suffer me to arrange any plan for my future destiny: all I could think of was to seek some lonely cottage, where I might sequester myself till the heat of that pursuit, which I supposed would be made after me, should be over.

"Without knowing whither I went, or how far I had wandered, I found myself, as if instinct had guided me thither, about the middle of the night as well as I could conjecture, the hour which was to have borne me to endless confinement, near the habitation where I had resided with my mother, and which, since her death, had been unoccupied. Gently the moon dispensed her silvery light, and gave a perfect view of all the dear and lovely scenes of early youth: Oh! how agonizing were my feelings as I contrasted my present misery with the happiness I had enjoyed amongst them a happiness of which, like a bright vision, no trace remained but in my memory:—Oh! how excruciating my pangs as I gazed upon the cottage where I had experienced the care, the tenderness of a parent, and reflected that I was now a wretch forlorn, without one friend to protect me, without any covering for my head but the canopy of heaven, without any pillow to repose it on but the cold sod; nothing but religion, which had been early and strongly implanted in my mind, could have prevented my raising the hand of despair against a life, which from being no longer valuable to others, was hateful to myself.

"But I will not (said I) I will not, by any act of rashness forfeit that heaven, where only I can be recompensed for my sorrows."

"Exhausted by my sufferings, I threw myself upon the ground, and as I lulled you upon my bosom, sleep insensibly stole upon me.

"The horror of my waking thoughts tinctured my sleeping ones, and I suddenly awoke in terror: as I started from the ground I beheld a lady and gentleman standing by me, for the morning was far advanced; I gazed upon them wildly, and in the features of the female at length recognized those of the Countess de Valdore, who had married a few months previous to my mother's death, and with whom, from having resided both before and after her union near our cottage, I was well acquainted; she expressed the utmost astonishment at the situation in which she had discovered me, and with a degree of pity that quite overcame me: for as a profusion of viands will overpower the famished wretch, so will unexpected compassion the sad heart that has deemed itself utterly abandoned.

"A total weakness seized me, and I could only answer her inquiries with my tears. She seated herself on the ground, and supported my head on her lap, while the Count hastened to the chateau for a carriage to convey me thither. There I lay a week before I had power to disclose my unhappy story; when I concluded I had the comfort of finding I had secured two friends for my child, who would never desert him; and this comfort was surely requisite to save me from distraction, for I now learned that St. Julian had been married four months to the rich and beautiful heiress of Charette.

'To attempt now, therefore, to redress your wrongs, would be unavailing, (said the Count); whilst St. Julian is intoxicated with love and the attainment of his wishes, any effort to do so would in all probability expose you to his vengeance, and perhaps occasion your final separation from your son: we must therefore leave him to the workings of conscience; though sometimes slow, it is always sure in its operations, and will yet raise its scorpion stings within his breast.'

"With his amiable Countess the Count united in assurances of friendship and protection; the Countess told me of the high esteem and regard she had always felt for me, and that at the death of my mother both she and the Count would gladly have offered me an asylum in their house, had they not naturally supposed I preferred my uncle's; from the period of my quitting Dauphine, she had never heard concerning me.

'Had I sooner known your fate, (she said) I should sooner have tried to alleviate it.'

"Certain that St. Julian would make diligent search after me, in order to try and get me into his power, which if he once discovered me, it would be impossible to prevent his doing, from his having represented me as an artful woman, who had seduced his youth and endeavoured to ruin his character; it was deemed expedient that I should in future be secluded from the world: for such a purpose no place appeared so eligible as the deserted monastery in the valley; thither I was accordingly conveyed without the knowledge of any of the family but a confidential servant of the Countess. A few months after my retirement, I resigned you to the arms of my friend, for the purpose of having you conveyed to her house, as the orphan of an esteemed acquaintance of her Lords.

"Two years have elapsed since that period, during which I have heard of St. Julian's attaining his paternal title, of his having a son, born to his wishes, and of his leading a life of unbounded gaiety and pleasure—-Ah! how different from the one he has doomed me to!

"The attentions of the Count and Countess have been unremitted; could kindness, could compassion have healed the wounds of my heart, they would long since have been closed.

"In their visits to me you are often brought:—Ah! how does my breast heave with mingled pain and pleasure as I clasp you to it, and hear your lisping accents. Fair is the promise of your infancy, but never, my son, will your unfortunate mother see it fulfilled; affliction has undermined my health, I daily, hourly grow weaker; I fade like an early flower, o'er which the desolating blast has past, ere half its beauties are expanded; and long, long before the blossoms of your youth are blown, I shall be laid within my cold grave.

"From that grave, as you peruse this narrative, Oh! think the spirit of your mother speaks, and charges you to attend to the advice which it contains—charges you never, in resentment for her wrongs, to forget the respect due to your father; she wishes you to plead for your rights, to vindicate her character, and prove to the world, that the descendant of St. Paul, the daughter of St. Foix, never disgraced the noble families from which she sprung, but she wishes you to plead with calmness, and, if unsuccessful, to be resigned.

"She also charges you, if only acknowledged as the son of an illicit love, to fly from any overtures of kindness which may be made you.

"The Count and Countess de Valdore have promised never to withdraw their protection. Generous pair! may Heaven recompense their kindness to me and mine.

"They have also promised, ere they put this narrative into your hands, to prepare you in some degree for my unfortunate story: Sad and painful has been my task in writing it—Oh! agonizing in the extreme to divulge to my son the crimes of his father.

"Oh! St. Julian, beloved, though perjured from every mortal eye, I would have concealed those crimes, had not justice to your child compelled me to disclose them.

"Farewell, my boy—my child, farewell! I leave you all I have to bestow, my blessing—may your conduct ever entitle you to that of Heaven, may your mind be fair as your person, may your heart ever glow with fervour in the cause of virtue, and your hand never lie idle by your side when misery or innocence call for assistance!

"In happy ignorance and childish gaiety often perhaps will your light steps bound o'er the sod which covers my remains; but the period I trust will arrive when tenderness and sensibility shall guide you to it, to drop a tear to the memory of her whose last prayer will be breathed for your felicity, to bedew with the sacred drops of filial affection the grave of your mother.

"MADELINE ST. JULIAN."

The tears of Madeline fell as she perused the narrative of her unfortunate grandmother, which (too much affected by it to speak), she returned in silence to her father.

"You can better conceive than I can describe (said he) the feelings I experienced on perusing this story. I wept for my mother, I blushed for my father, and my heart was divided between affliction and resentment.

"With the natural impetuosity of youth, I determined not to let another day elapse without pleading for those rights which I had been so long and so unjustly deprived of; but convinced that my agitation would not permit me to plead for them in person, as I could wish, I resolved on sending a letter by a special messenger to the castle of Montmorenci, where I knew my father resided, declaring the late discovery of my birth, and the manner in which I had been protected from the distresses his desertion had exposed me to.

"I accordingly withdrew from Elvira as soon as I was sufficiently composed to pen my letter, which I did in the most respectful yet energetic manner, and enclosed within it a small miniature of myself, drawn by the Countess de Valdore's desire a few months previous to her death, along with her daughter's, for the purpose of ornamenting a cabinet, whence I now received it from Elvira: I sent it with a hope that it might perhaps, by recalling to his memory some feature of the woman he had injured, and once tenderly loved, soften his mind in my favour, and incline him to do me justice.

"My sufferings till the return of my messenger mock description. At his first appearance I flew with breathless haste to meet him. The Marquis of Montmorenci (he said) was too ill to answer my letter, but he desired me without delay to repair to his castle.

"Oh! gracious Heaven, how rapturous were the feelings of that moment!—I could not doubt but that he desired to see me for the purpose of blessing, of acknowledging me as his son, of vindicating the fame of my injured mother.

"Elvira thought as I did; and while a tear of regret for my intended departure strayed down her cheek, congratulated me in the most fervent manner on the prospect there appeared of having my wishes realized.

"I set out unattended for the mansion of my father, which I entered, though with hope, with emotions that shook my frame; the domestics were prepared to receive me, and immediately conducted me to the apartment where their Lord lay, apparently much indisposed, and exhibiting but the ruin of those graces which had captivated the too susceptible heart of my mother.

"Trembling I approached, and knelt before him, supplicating by my looks his blessing.

'With pleasure (said he, extending his hand) I acknowledge you as my son; to disown you never was my intention.'

"I pressed his hand to my lips, but could not speak; the reception I met with, the idea of being able to vindicate the fame of my mother, quite overpowered me. Alas! short was the duration of my joy.

'Rise, (continued my father) I have much to say; but ere I proceed, let me (looking as he spoke towards a young man who sat at some distance from the couch, and whom my agitation had hitherto prevented me from noticing) let me present you to the Count St. Julian, who has kindly promised to consider you as a brother.'

"Surprise, intermingled with indignation pervaded my heart, on hearing the Marquis address another person by the title to which alone I had a right. I suppressed those feelings however from a hope that an explanation would ensue, which should appease them.

'Chance (proceeded my father) made him acquainted with your story: During a late illness, from which I am now but barely recovered, I ordered every letter or message which came to me to be delivered to him—consequently your's fell into his hands; I therefore deemed it requisite that he should be present at our interview, deemed it an absolute duty to him, his mother, and myself, that he should, whilst he heard me acknowledge you as my son, solemnly disacknowledge you as the heir of Montmorenci; no ties but those of love ever existed between your mother and me, and if you have been credulous enough to give implicit credit to the artful tale she fabricated, all my schemes in your favour must be defeated:—Be wise, study your own interest, declare your total renunciation of your chimerical claims, and ensure my kindness and protection.'

"Never, my Lord, (cried I); if your kindness and protection can only be acquired by stigmatizing the character of my mother, and degrading myself, the son of Madeline St. Foix will never consent to be called the child of infamy; my opinion of her veracity is unalterable, and though I may not be able to support, I never will renounce my claims."

'Then you must for ever be an alien to me, (said the Marquis). Go, (he continued, with an agitated voice and a countenance inflamed by resentment), go, lest you should tempt me to curse the hour in which you were born.'

"With difficulty I suppressed the feelings which swelled my heart almost to bursting, but I determined not to forget that the author of my injuries was also the author of my being.

"I directly left the castle, and set out for the mansion which had fostered my helpless infancy. Ah! how different was the situation of my mind now from what it had been when I journeyed from it!—On entering it a servant informed me that M. de Valdore was arrived. I was too much disturbed to think of then paying my compliments to him, but I desired to be shown directly to Lady Elvira. Her tenderness, said I to myself, will soften the bitterness of disappointment; her gentleness will sooth the perturbations of my soul.

"I found her alone and in the deepest dejection. She started with astonishment at my unexpected appearance, and her eyes instantly brightened with pleasure; a brightness, however, which quickly vanished on surveying my countenance.

'My dear Lausane, (said she, extending her hand) what mean those looks?'

"Ah! my Elvira, (cried I) do they not render language unnecessary?—do they not tell you that my hopes were too sanguine?—that I have returned without finding the father I expected?'

'Good Heaven! (said she, bursting into tears) you overwhelm me with misery.—Oh! Lausane, what will become of you?'

"Do not, my dear Elvira, (cried I) aggravate my feelings, by giving way to your's. My situation is not desperate!—Reflect that the bounty of your noble parents secured me from experiencing any pecuniary distress through the desertion of my father."

'Oh! Lausane (exclaimed she in an agony) you are mistaken. M. de Valdore, who reached the chateau soon after you had left it, immediately opened the will of my father, in which your name was no where visible: this, I am convinced, unintentional omission, would give me little concern, could I immediately do what I know my father meant to have done for you; but M. de Valdore, without whose consent I cannot act, appears too selfish and illiberal to let me hope he will permit me to follow my wishes. Surely, surely my father was deceived with respect to the disposition of his relative, or he never would have chosen such a guardian for his Elvira; already he has told me, that if you returned to the castle, he would not suffer you to continue in it; views respecting me and his son, have, I am confident, inspired this resolution; he wishes an alliance to take place between us, and thinks that if you remained here, you might perhaps defeat those wishes: but I will kneel, I will supplicate him to drop the determination he has avowed; should he, however, have the cruelty to persevere in it, I can give you jewels of sufficient value to support you in the stile of life you have hitherto been accustomed to, till I am of age, when the doors of Elvira's mansion shall be again opened with delight to the adopted son of her parents, the friend of her youth, the brother of her heart.'

"Sad, silent, overwhelmed with misery, I listened to Elvira; her words gave the final stroke to my happiness; all the horrors of dependence stared me in the face, and ere she had ceased to speak, I had determined on ending the life upon which they seemed entailed.

"Formed for domestic comforts, (said I within myself) such comforts as my situation precludes my enjoying, life without them would be a burden. I will not, therefore, toil to support an existence valueless to me; I will not enter a world where I have no relative to guide, no friend to sooth me; where I might meet such men as the Marquis of Montmorenci and M. de Valdore; I will go to the mansion from which I am exiled, and gratify its master by destroying, perhaps in his presence, the being he detests.

"A kind of gloomy composure took possession of me from the moment I had conceived my fatal resolution. I made no comments to Elvira upon the conduct of her guardian; I attempted not to dissuade her from pleading to him in my favour, but pretending fatigue, I said I would retire for a little while to my chamber.

"As soon as I entered it, fearful of myself, fearful that my resolution would be shaken if I allowed myself a moment's thought, I put into my bosom a dagger, the gift of my late departed benefactor, and stealing out, bid, as I then thought, a last adieu to my hitherto happy home. I flew rather than walked, and about sun-set found myself in the gloomiest part of the forest of Montmorenci, and within view of the castle. Exhausted by fatigue and agitation, I threw myself upon the ground: it was a fine summer evening, and the beauty and serenity of nature formed a melancholy contrast to the horror and agony of my mind; the hour recalled a thousand tender images to my memory, a thousand happy scenes in which I had been engaged with the beloved protectors of my youth.

"Oh! joys departed! (I exclaimed) how bitter is your recollection!—but, for the last time, it now wrings my heart; to-morrow I shall be insensible of pain or pleasure.—Oh! sun, (I cried, raising my eyes to that resplendent orb, which in majestic glory was retiring from the world) never more will thy bright beams give me joy or vigour; ere they again visit the earth, I shall be cold and inanimate as the sod on which I now rest. Father of mercies! (I proceeded, raising myself on my knees) to thee I fly. I am forlorn, I am an outcast, where then but in thy bosom can I expect comfort or protection? Forgive me then, forgive me, for appearing in thy presence unsummoned; and,

Oh! should the eye of a father behold my remains, behold them with compunction, let, I implore thee, that compunction extenuate his errors, nor suffer the blood I shed to rest upon his head."

"I attempted to raise the dagger to my heart, but felt at the instant my arm seized. Astonished, I looked round, and beheld him who was unjustly titled St. Julian.

"I rose, and tried but in vain, to disengage myself from him—rage took immediate possession of my soul.

"Release me (cried I) directly, lest passion should endue me with double strength, and tempt me to raise that hand against your breast which now I only wish to turn against my own."

'Your threats are in vain, (said he); I will not release you till you assure me you have dropped your present dreadful intentions—till you assure me that you will have mercy upon your own soul.—Oh! kneel and deprecate the vengeance of heaven, for having thought of disobeying its most sacred injunctions, for having doubted its promises of protection, and despairingly determined on destroying what, as it gave, so only it should take.'

"The acknowledged heir of Montmorenci, the son of tenderness and prosperity, (cried I) may preach against a crime which he beholds no prospect of ever being tempted to commit; but were our situations reversed, was he, like me, an outcast, an exile from the house that should have sheltered and protected him, he would, like me, perhaps gladly resign a being valueless to himself from being so to others."

'To more strength of mind, more firmness than other men, (said he) I do not pretend; but still I humbly trust that in the very depth of misery the sacred sentiments of religion I have imbibed would guard me against an act which would for ever close the doors of happiness against me. You shall not (he continued) throw me from you; I will save, I will serve you—we are brothers, suffer us to be friends. My heart conceived a partiality for you the first moment I beheld you, and I should then have declared it, had I thought its disclosure would have been pleasing to you.'

"I will not, my love, (proceeded Clermont, after a short pause) dwell longer upon a scene which I perceive has already inspired you with horror; suffice it to say I was not able to resist his kindnesses, which, from being unexpected, had a double effect; his gentleness allayed the stormy passions of my soul, his arguments convinced me of the enormity of the crime I had been about committing, and I dropped the instrument of intended destruction to clasp his hand to a breast which heaved with strong emotion, forgetting in that moment that he was the usurper of my rights.

"Ah! had he been convinced he was the usurper of them, I am confident he would, without hesitation, have withdrawn from the place I should have filled; but the artful tale of the Marquis of Montmorenci completely deceived him: and while his generous heart acknowledged me as his brother, he considered me as the illegitimate son of his father.

"From the hour our friendship commenced I determined never more to mention the painful subject of my mother's wrongs and mine. But ere I would accept his offers of assistance, I made him assure me that his own feelings alone prompted him to serve me, solemnly vowing within my mind never through any hands, or by any means, to receive any mark of kindness from my father, except acknowledged by him in the light I wished.

"St. Julian (for so I now called him, though my heart swelled as I did so), informed me that in a few days he was going to Italy, and asked me to accompany him thither. This I gladly consented to do, and, in the interim he said he would bring me to the house of a cottager, where I might be secretly lodged: 'And ere we return to France, (continued he) we may think of some plan for your future establishment in life.'

"Ere I commenced my journey, I wrote to Elvira, acquainting her of the friend I had gained, and imploring her forgiveness for quitting her house in the abrupt manner I had done, carefully concealing, however, the motive which had prompted me to do so.

"St. Julian informed me, that his present excursion was merely for pleasure, as he had already made the tour of Europe.

"I shall pass over the admiration, the enthusiastic delight, which pervaded my mind as I ascended the Alps, and viewed nature in some of her most sublime forms.

"On the evening of the first day's journey St. Julian told me he meant to pass the night at the habitation of a very particular friend of his.

'Some months ago, (said he) as I was returning from Italy to France, I was severely hurt near his house by the overturning of my carriage, and from him, to whom I was then a total stranger, received every attention which politeness or humanity could dictate. I should therefore deem myself highly ungrateful if I could think of passing his door without paying him my respects.

'He is a foreigner, far advanced in life; a man of distinction, but unfortunate. Of the troubles which some years back agitated England, and its sister kingdom, I dare say you have heard. Lord Dunlere (so my friend is stiled) was one of the most faithful and zealous supporters of James the Second, and in consequence of his attachment to that unhappy Prince, became an exile from his native country, Ireland, and lost a considerable property in it:—with all he could preserve, a small pittance, he retired to the obscurity of these mountains, where, with two daughters, and a few affectionate followers, he lives a life of peaceful retirement, looking back on the world he has left without regret, and forward to the one to come with every hope of felicity.

' 'Tis impossible to give you any adequate idea of the benevolence of his disposition, the urbanity, the cheerfulness of his temper: he continually brings to mind the stories we have heard of the patriarchs; his simplicity, his hospitality, exactly accords with the account we have received of them.

'Of his daughters I must not speak, because I could not do them justice. I must, however, timely caution you against the charms of the elder, who is engaged to a gentleman, to whom she is prevented by particular circumstances from being immediately united; but the heart as well as the hand of the younger are at liberty I understand, and to wish them my brother's would be to wish him the greatest blessing man could possess.'

"Soon after this conversation we stopped at Lord Dunlere's. St. Julian went in first to prepare him for my reception, and in a few minutes returned with his venerable friend, whose looks were calculated to excite an immediate prepossession in his favour.

"He welcomed me with the utmost kindness, and conducted me to the apartment where his daughters sat. I cannot give you any idea of the surprise, the admiration which seized me on beholding them:—I saw indeed that my brother was right in not attempting to describe charms which no description could have done justice to. My eyes wandered for some time from one to the other, scarcely knowing which to give the preference of beauty to, but at last settled on the lovely face of Geraldine, the younger.

"Instead of staying but one night, we remained a week under the roof of Lord Dunlere—a week of such happiness as I had never before experienced—a week in which new feelings, new sentiments took possession of my soul, and taught me that I had hitherto been a stranger to the greatest pleasure, the greatest pain man can feel. I wished, I determined, however, if possible, to conceal my feelings—I regarded my passion as hopeless, and pride actuated me to hide it; but in vain I strove to do so; my melancholy, my total abstraction, amidst the new and lovely scenes through which I travelled, and the conversations into which I insensibly entered, betrayed me to St. Julian. He laughed, yet pitied, but neither desired me to hope nor despair.

'Lausane (said he, one morning, after we had been two or three weeks in Italy), would it be vastly disagreeable to you if, instead of passing two months here as we at first proposed, we returned to Lord Dunlere's, and spent them there?'

"Ah! St. Julian, (cried I) you know my heart too well to render it necessary for me to answer you."

"In short, without longer delay we returned to that mansion on which my thoughts continually dwelt. Here, in the presence of her whom my soul adored, I forgot my resolution of trying to conquer—to conceal my passion:—ah! how indeed could I do so, when in the soft glances of her eyes I sometimes fancied I saw an assurance of its being returned. At length the period for quitting her arrived—for quitting without the smallest hope of again beholding her: the most excruciating anguish filled my heart the moment it was announced, and with difficulty I concealed it.

"Unable to converse the evening preceding the day fixed for my departure, I left Lord Dunlere and St. Julian together, and withdrew to an alcove in a lonely and romantic part of the garden, where some of my happiest hours had been passed with Geraldine, indulging a melancholy kind of pleasure at the idea of there giving vent to my feelings.

"You may imagine what my emotions were, when, on entering it, the first object I beheld was Geraldine!—She was alone, and dejectedly leaning on a little table. Reason bid me fly, but passion overpowered, and at her feet I poured forth my sorrows. Ah! how amply did I think myself recompensed for those sorrows when I beheld the tear of pity stealing down her cheek, when I heard her soft and faltering accents declare I was not indifferent to her: — but the rapture that declaration gave was transient: I reflected on my situation, and my soul immediately upbraided me with cruelty to her, and treachery to Lord Dunlere, in avowing my passion, and pleading for a return to it, when no hope existed of our ever being united.

"Pity me, Geraldine, (said I, wildly starting from her feet), but no longer love me; yield not to sentiments which will, if indulged, entail anguish upon your gentle soul, such anguish as now pervades mine — the anguish of a hopeless passion: — we must part, part without an idea of again meeting; — I cannot, dare not ask you to become mine; cannot ask you to bestow your hand on him who is but a dependant. No, Geraldine, were it offered I would reject it, from a conviction that by accepting it I should plunge you in distress! — Oh! mild as your virtues may your destiny be, — different, ah! far different from that of the unhappy Lausane's!"

"A sudden rustling amongst the trees behind me made me turn round, and I beheld Lord Dunlere. I was a little startled, but the consciousness of not having attempted to take any advantage of the tenderness of his daughter, prevented my feeling that confusion I should otherwise have experienced at being thus surprised. I bowed, and was retiring from the alcove, when he stopped me —

'Lausane (said he), do not let me frighten you away: let me try (added he, with a benignant smile) whether I cannot obtain your pardon for my intrusion.'

"He seated himself by the almost fainting Geraldine, and motioned me to sit beside him.

'You will not, Lausane, (said he, after a pause) be surprised I think, when I inform you that I have overheard your conversation, nor will you, I hope, regret my having done so; it was one which reflected the highest honour on your heart. He who can soar above selfish considerations, who can resist the pleadings of passion for fear of inconveniencing the woman he loves, evinces a generosity, a sensibility, that does credit to human nature.

'I have long suspected your attachment; you will believe I did not disapprove it, when I confess I felt happy to think it was returned.

'To men of virtue, not to men of greatness, I always wished to give my daughters; they only, of all the numerous connexions which once blessed me, remain; consequently my felicity solely depends upon their's: I therefore determined never to control their inclinations, if such as reason could approve.'

"Oh! my Lord, (I exclaimed) I cannot give utterance to my feelings; but, ah! will you indeed persevere in your generous intentions when you hear my sad story, when you hear that I have been not only deprived of fortune, but the name I have a right to?"

'I am already acquainted with your story, (he replied); Count St. Julian related it a few days after your introduction to me. Your now mentioning it reminds me of a preliminary which must be settled ere I positively consent to give you my daughter, namely, that you solemnly promise never to enter again upon the subject of former grievances.'

"This was a promise which, even without having such an inducement as he now held out for making, I would not have hesitated to give, having long before determined to be silent about wrongs which I could not gain redress for.

'If then (resumed he) you think you can be happy in the retirement in which we live, for my fortune will not permit me to give you the power of entering the gay world, receive the hand of my daughter.'

"On my knees I expressed my gratitude, on my knees with truth assured him, that a desert with her would be a paradise. From his arms I received the most lovely and beloved of women. Oh! moment of ecstasy, in which I folded my Geraldine to my heart as my destined wife—in which I kissed away the tear that hung upon her glowing cheek, like the sweet dew of the morning on the silken leaves of the rose!

"St. Julian, who appeared almost overpowered with delight at my happiness, put off his journey in order to be present at my marriage, and gave me the most solemn assurances of dividing with me his paternal fortune whenever he came into possession of it.

"He left me the most blessed of men. Oh! days of delight, rapid in your course, and succeeded by years of misery and horror!

"I had been married about three months when I received a letter from my brother, informing me that he was ill, and anxiously desirous of seeing me. I sighed at the idea of even a transient separation from my love, but I could not resist the call of friendship, and accordingly set out for a cottage near the castle of Montmorenci, where St. Julian had once before lodged, and now appointed to see me.

"The heaviness of heart with which I commenced my journey was surely a presentiment of the ills that were approaching. Oh! venerable Dunlere, thy happiness and mine was then about setting!

"The chateau de Valdore lay in my way to the castle of Montmorenci; I could not think of passing it without inquiring after the friend of my youth, from whom I had heard but once since my departure from her house; our correspondence, as she then informed me, having been prohibited by her guardian. I went through a private path to the chateau, which conducted me directly to the hall occupied by the servants: here, amidst many strangers I soon discovered some of the old domestics, and from them learned that M. de Valdore and his family resided at the chateau, and that Lady Elvira's situation was unaltered. I sent to request an interview, and was almost immediately summoned to her: she received me with the most rapturous delight, and tears involuntarily fell from me as I recollected the kindness of her parents, and witnessed her pleasure at beholding me.

"When we grew a little composed, I answered her eager enquiries concerning all that had befallen me since our separation, and my present situation: but, Oh! what were my emotions when, as I mentioned that situation, I saw the blood forsake her cheeks, and discovered that it was more than friendship which she felt for me!

'Married!' she repeated in a faint voice—she paused—she seemed trying to recollect herself, and attempted to wish me joy; but her tongue could not utter what she wished to say, and her head sunk upon my shoulder. Oh! Geraldine, surely I did not wrong thy love by the tears, the tears of unutterable tenderness which I shed upon her pale cheek—by the sighs which heaved my bosom on hearing her's.

"She soon however recovered:—her mind was the seat of every virtue, and shrunk from the idea of betraying feelings contrary to propriety—

'Lausane, (said she) be assured I rejoice at your present happiness; the period I trust will arrive when I shall have an opportunity of beholding it; prepare your lady against that period to love and esteem me; tell her you have a friend, a sister, to introduce to her.'

"Already (cried I) she is acquainted with the virtues of Elvira; already taught to love and esteem her.'

"In pity to her feelings, which I saw she could ill suppress, I determined to shorten my visit: when she saw me rising to depart, she desired me to stop another moment—

'I have a present (said she) to send your lady: you know I often amused myself by copying pictures?—amongst the rest (continued she, with a blush) I copied your's, and now request you will take it to your lady.'

"She retired without permitting me to speak, and returned in a few minutes with it: it was the same which you now have, and which by being an exact copy of the one I sent my father, led to the late discovery.

"From that period particular circumstances, not necessary to explain, prevented my seeing or hearing any thing of the destiny of Elvira, till chance conducted her to our cottage. She then informed me, that soon after she was of age, she had united herself to the Count de Merville, whose virtues and tenderness rendered her, during his life time, one of the happiest of women, and thus rewarded her for the resolution with which she set about conquering her first attachment from the moment she knew it was improper to be indulged.

"From the chateau de Valdore I repaired to the cottage where my brother had desired to see me. He received me with the utmost affection, and I found he had not deceived me by saying he was ill; it was an illness however which seemed occasioned more by agitation than any bodily complaint; and I afterwards discovered I was not wrong in this opinion.

"Oh! had he confided in me; Oh! had he then opened his heart, divulged its cares, its anxieties, what misery, what horror would he have saved us both from experiencing!

"I had not been above a week with him when I was overwhelmed with sorrow by a letter from my wife, containing the melancholy intelligence of her lovely sister Eleanora's death.

"I could not hesitate a moment about returning to her directly; yet at the instant I determined on doing so, my heart was almost divided between her and my brother, who was seized with a violent fever the very day on which I heard from her.

"I will not pain your gentle soul, my Madeline, by describing the situation in which I found your mother, or relating the numerous train of calamities that followed the death of her sister; it is sufficient for me to say that within a few months after her decease I lost my brother and my wife.

"Ah, heavens! even at this distant period I shudder at the recollection of the excruciating anguish I endured on being deprived of friends so beloved. The world seemed a blank, and nothing but religion and tenderness for you could have prevented my quitting it; nor has time done more than appease the violence of that anguish.—Oh! never, never can the barb of sorrow be extracted from my heart; and respect for the memory of my mother, affection for you, could only have tempted me to quit a retirement, where unrestrained and unobserved I could have indulged my feelings.

"Lord Dunlere soon followed his children to their grave; the wreck of his fortune was placed in the hands of a banker at Paris, who failed about the time of his death. Thus, from necessity as well as choice, I sought the obscurity in which you were brought up.

"Disgusted with the world, I changed my name, in order to conceal myself from every one who had known me before, and thus prevent my retirement from being interrupted.

"I carefully concealed my story from you, well knowing from your sensibility the pain you would feel if acquainted with my injuries.

"Alas! too late is the hand of my father extended to do me justice; neither wealth nor titles can now confer pleasure upon me, and the coronet he is about placing upon my brow, I should reject, was it not to have the power of transmitting it to the child of my lamented love."

CHAP. VI.

"Thus conscience does make cowards of us all."

Here ceased Clermont, or, as we shall hereafter call him, St. Julian; but he ceased without gratifying the curiosity of Madeline: much of his story, she was convinced, remained untold, and she shuddered as she thought it was concealed merely because it was too dreadful to be known.

"Oh, surely, (she said, within herself) some mysterious circumstances must have attended the fate of my mother, or ere this my father would have mentioned her to me—ere this would have afforded me the melancholy pleasure of knowing I was descended from so amiable a woman, and taught me to reverence her memory; but what he wishes to hide I will not try to discover, confident as I am that if a full explanation of past events could have given me pleasure, I should have received it from him."

When St. Julian came within sight of his father's residence, the strong emotions which the idea of his approaching interview with that father inspired, took from him all further power of utterance.

The day was declining, and the deep gloom of the forest heightened the melancholy which the recital of past events had infused into the hearts of the travellers.

As soon as the carriage entered the court, the doors of the hall were thrown open, and a number of servants appeared, with eager impatience in their looks, to see and receive the newly declared heir of Montmorenci.

St. Julian now strove to regain his composure, that he might appear to bear the unexpected reverse in his situation with that calm dignity befitting a cultivated mind, and one which built not its happiness on the adventitious gifts of fortune; but vainly did he strive to do so. He trembled as he entered the ancient mansion of his forefathers, from which he had been so long unjustly exiled, trembled with violent emotion as he surveyed their warlike trophies, to which the spirit in his bosom told him he might have added, had not the hand of injustice plunged him in obscurity.

The resentment this idea excited was as transient however as involuntary, and though involuntary he repented it.

He was now called, he considered, to the presence of his father to receive from his hands, as far as in his power to make it, atonement for every wrong.

"And if such atonement satisfies heaven, (cried he) as we are assured it does, should it not amply satisfy weak and erring man?"

Agitation caused him to pause in the hall, and the domestics seemed pleased with the opportunity he thus afforded them of gratifying their curiosity; one of them bowing low at length spoke—

"The Marquis impatiently expects your arrival, my Lord, (said he); shall I have the honour of conducting you to him?"

St. Julian assented by an inclination of his head, and was immediately ushered up stairs to the apartment where his father sat.

On reaching the door he took the hand of Madeline, who with trembling steps had followed him to it.

The Marquis attempted to rise at their entrance, but neither his strength nor spirits seconded the effort, and faint and almost breathless he sunk back upon his chair.

St. Julian and Madeline knelt before him.

"Let the blessing of a father, (said St. Julian in a solemn voice) at length rejoice my heart."

The Marquis raised his venerable head—

"I am too unworthy to dare to give it (he exclaimed); but may heaven bless you, may all that can render life desirable be your's, long, long after I am laid within that grave where I now wish to shroud my sorrows and my shame!"

"Oh, my father (cried St. Julian, penetrated by his language), speak not so again; wish not again to deprive your son of an inexpressible comfort—the comfort of trying to mitigate your sorrows."

The Marquis embraced him, but was unable for some minutes to speak; then suddenly raising his head—

"Treat me not with tenderness, (he said, while a frown overspread his countenance) reproach, revile, neglect me, and you will show me mercy; for you will then save my heart from the intolerable pangs which kindness and attention so unmerited from you must give it. Oh! my son, my son, (he continued, clasping his hands together, and all the austerity of his countenance vanishing), you are now amply avenged, and I am amply punished. Had virtue been the guide of my actions, exclusive of that happiness which ever attends a quiet conscience, I should have had the happiness of being able to enjoy the society of my son; but now, what then would have been my blessing, almost becomes my curse; for not a word of tenderness that passes your lips, not a beam of love from your eye, but will come like daggers to my heart."

"Far better had it been then said (St. Julian) that I had remained in my obscurity, if I am only taken from it to aggravate the woes of a father: permit me, my Lord, (cried he, with increasing emotion), again to retire to it; permit me to withdraw from your presence a being so injurious to your tranquillity."

"No, (exclaimed the Marquis eagerly) never, never shall you, except you really wish to do so, withdraw yourself from me. Excuse what I have said, make some allowances for the agitation of such a meeting as our's; my composure will soon, I trust, return, and I shall then, I make no doubt, be able to enjoy your society.

"Rise now, my children, (extending a hand to St. Julian and Madeline) 'tis I should have knelt to you; but since you knelt for a blessing, though unworthy of giving, receive it: may happiness and honour, both in their fullest extent, ever be your's; may thy weakness (turning to Madeline, and kissing her soft cheek), ever find a tender guardian in thy father; and may his sufferings and filial piety to me be amply recompensed by thy affection and duty!"

He seated them on each side of himself, and the violence of his feelings having a little abated, began, notwithstanding the avowed wishes of St. Julian to the contrary, the history of his repentance.

"The dreadful fate of my son made me recollect my past conduct; all its enormities stared me in the face, and I wondered that the punishment of heaven had been so long delayed. Oh! wretch, (I cried, in the excruciating anguish of my soul) thy crimes have at length justly provoked the vengeance of Heaven, and drawn down destruction upon the head of thy son!— —

"The idea, that the sins of the father had been the occasion of the death of the son, almost shook Reason from her throne; horrors, beyond language to express, took possession of me:—to try to appease them, appease agonies which often urged me to complete the measure of my guilt, by raising the hand of suicide against my life.

"I sent for a Monk from a neighbouring Convent, to pour out my soul in confession to him; an holy act which I had long omitted, from a consciousness that till now it would have been a mockery of heaven, as till now the real sigh of repentance had never heaved my breast."

'My son, (cried the good man) you judge rightly in thinking that your conduct has caused your present afflictions; a merciful Being has sent them, in order to awaken you to repentance, and by suffering here, save your precious soul from suffering hereafter. Without further murmurs, therefore, submit to your deprivations as to a righteous punishment, and strive by every atonement in your power to expiate your crimes; so may you hope for a gleam of returning peace, so hope for support in the hour of death, when all the terrors of another world are opening to your view.'

"In consequence of his words, and the pleadings of my own conscience, I directly ordered the most diligent search to be made after you, but without effect. I then drew up a paper, acknowledging my marriage with your mother, and, consequently, you as my heir; which I lodged in the convent where my Confessor lived, that if by any chance either he or any of his holy brothers should hereafter hear of you, or any offspring of your's, they might be able to authenticate your title to the Castle of Montmorenci.

"Gratefully I return thanks to Heaven for permitting me to do that justice to you which I gave to others the power of performing; the pleasure derived from that idea will, I make no doubt, in a few days alleviate my feelings. But, Oh! my son, if your attentions have not always power to mitigate my sadness—if, whilst receiving them, the sigh of regret, the tear of tender recollection, should obtrude, be not offended, whilst I rejoice for the son I have recovered, I cannot help mourning for the one I have lost: he was all that the fondest father could desire! The proudest of the sons of men might have gloried in being called his parent. Ignorant as well as innocent of my great offences, his praises cannot displease you; but if they should, let the reflection of his being now in his cold and dreary tomb, where he can no longer interpose between you and your rights, remove your resentment."

"Oh! my father, (cried St. Julian, his tearful eye evincing the truth of his words) little do you know my heart if you think it can feel displeasure at the praises of my brother."

"I believe you, my son, (said the Marquis) and the belief gives me pleasure; for to think you will sometimes permit me to talk of him to you, sooths my feelings."

The appearance of a domestic now interrupted the conversation, and the Marquis led Madeline down stairs. The supper was laid out in one of the state apartments which had been long disused; and though every thing was magnificent, every thing was gloomy.

Fatigued by her journey, or rather by the emotions of her mind, Madeline soon after supper entreated permission to retire to her chamber; an attendant was accordingly summoned to conduct her to it, and on leaving the parlour she found the housekeeper waiting in the hall for that purpose.

"Well, I am happy, (cried she, simpering and courtesying), that I have an opportunity at last of wishing your La'ship joy. Dear me, I have been so surprised at what has lately happened! Who could ever have thought that the night I had the honour of seeing your La'ship here, I should have had the so much greater honour of calling you Mistress."

Madeline received her compliment with a faint smile, for her heart was too heavy to permit her to answer it as at another time she might have done; nor was her melancholy decreased on entering her spacious chamber, whose faded tapestry and tarnished furniture spoke of its long desertion and neglect.

"I hope your La'ship does not dislike this apartment, (said the housekeeper, on perceiving Madeline pause at the entrance, and look round her with a kind of dread); it is one of the most magnificent in the castle I can assure you, and was occupied by my late Lady, the Marchioness, since whose death it has neither been used or altered."

"No, (replied Madeline, advancing, and endeavouring to shake off the impression which its gloom had made upon her mind), I do not dislike it."

"That door (cried the housekeeper) opens into the dressing-room; there my lady used to pass many of her hours: it was fitted up entirely under her direction, and ornamented with portraits of several of her most particular friends; amongst the pictures is one of herself, and another of Lord Philippe, her son, drawn about a year before his death; the room still remains just in the same state as when she died."

An irresistible impulse prompted Madeline immediately to take a view of these pictures; and she directly entered the dressing-room still attended by the housekeeper.

The first she examined was the Marchioness: it represented a woman in all the bloom of youth and of the most exquisite beauty; she turned from it, after expressing her admiration, to Lord Philippe's. But, Oh! what were her feelings at that moment, when the exact resemblance of de Sevignie met her eyes.

With all the wildness of astonishment she gazed upon it: "Are you sure (cried she, glancing for an instant at the housekeeper, and speaking in almost breathless agitation) are you sure this picture was drawn for Lord Philippe?"

"Sure! (repeated the housekeeper) Lord, yes, that I am indeed. Why I saw him, myself sitting for it."

"Good heaven! (said Madeline to herself) what a likeness! Ah! how vain, (she continued) my resolves to forget de Sevignie while his image will be thus almost continually before me."

As if riveted by some spell to the spot, she still continued to stand before it: the more she gazed upon it, the more if possible the likeness grew upon her.

"Do you think it a handsome picture?" asked the housekeeper, elevating the light as she spoke as if to give Madeline a better opportunity of examining it.

"Handsome! (repeated Madeline emphatically and with a deep sigh), yes very handsome indeed."

"Aye, and so do I; (cried the housekeeper), what a sweet smile there is about the mouth!"

Yes, (thought Madeline) the fascinating smile of de Sevignie.

"And the eyes! (continued the housekeeper) how piercing, yet how mild!"

Madeline, who had turned to the housekeeper, again fastened her's upon them, and again fancied she beheld the dark eyes of de Sevignie beaming with unutterable tenderness upon her.

She sighed more deeply than before; and fearful that if she remained much longer in her present situation, she should not be able to conceal the feelings which now almost swelled her heart to bursting, she instantly left the dressing-room.

"Your La'ship looks disturbed, (said the housekeeper); I am afraid the picture of Lord Philippe has affected you, by bringing his melancholy fate to your mind: Poor youth, it was a sad thing indeed; but your La'ship must consider, that if he had not been taken off, your father would never have been restored to his rights; and heaven knows, he was kept long enough out of them."

"I must for ever regret (said Madeline) that his restoration to them was occasioned by the death of his brother."

"Why to be sure, (replied the housekeeper) it would have been better if they could have been regained by any other means; but that that would ever have been the case there was very little probability of; and, between ourselves, (proceeded she, lowering her voice) since your La'ship has hinted at the affair to me, I think even if it was openly proved, instead of being merely suspected, as it is at present, that the Count, your father, when his injuries were considered, would not be condemned; I, for my part, am one of those who would forgive him for what he did."

"For what he did! (repeated Madeline, starting), why what has he done to require forgiveness? What is the affair you say I have hinted at? Speak,—you have agitated my very soul."

The housekeeper receded a few steps in evident terror.

"Why, nothing, I assure your La'ship, (exclaimed she in faltering accents) I only meant that—that—"

Here she paused in the utmost confusion.

"Speak! (cried Madeline, in a voice that betrayed the most dreadful agitation—an agitation caused by recollecting at that instant the conversation which had passed between her and the housekeeper relative to the murder of Lord Philippe on the night she had sought for shelter in the castle); speak, I adjure you, (she repeated, with a distracted air) and relieve me from the horrors you have inspired."

"I am very sorry, I am sure, (said Mrs. Beatrice) that I have so distressed your La'ship; like an old woman, I must always be prating; I only meant, my Lady, I can assure you, to say, that if it was known that the Count, your father, rejoiced at, instead of regretted, the death of his brother, no one could wonder at it, considering the reason he had to hate him as the usurper of his rights."

"And was this all you really meant?" asked Madeline.

"Oh, all, I do assure your La'ship, upon the word of a true Christian; if you do not believe me, I will call all the Saints in Heaven to witness for me."

Madeline could not help smiling:

"As it is a call, perhaps, (said she) they might not obey; I will take your word."

She now endeavoured to compose herself; but not easily could she regain composure, nor dismiss remorse from her mind, for having yielded, but for a minute, to the horrid suggestions which had lately pervaded it.

"Oh! was my father acquainted with them, (cried she to herself), never, never would he forgive me. Ah! how can I forgive myself—Ah! how support, without betraying it, the pain I must ever feel, for having thought unjustly of him."

"You seem well acquainted with the affairs of this family?" said she, sitting down, and making an effort to appear composed.

"Yes, very well acquainted with them indeed, (replied the housekeeper, significantly shaking her head); I have lived in it almost ever since I was born; for my parents dying when I was very young, my aunt, who was housekeeper, took me immediately under her protection."

It now occurred to Madeline, that the domestic who had liberated her unhappy grandmother might still be living; and anxious, if she was, to pay her the tribute of respect she merited, she inquired; and heard, with pleasure, that her present attendant was the person who had performed that generous act.

"Yes, my lady, it was I, (cried the housekeeper, bridling up), who freed the poor unfortunate lady: I was then a fine lively young girl, as your La'ship indeed may well suppose, from the number of years which have passed since that event; and the most tender-hearted creature, though I say it myself, that perhaps ever lived. Dear me, I shall never forget how I cried, when I went with some food to her, and found her sitting on the ground, so pale, yet so beautiful, with her hair, the finest hair I ever saw, about one shade darker than your's, my lady, hanging about her shoulders, and her little baby lying on her lap, on whom her tears were falling so fast, while a cold wind whistled through the broken windows; for she was confined in an upper room, in one of the uninhabited towers."

"Could I see that room?" asked Madeline.

"Why, the stairs which lead to it are now very bad; but if you wish very much to go to it, I think you may venture some day or other. Poor soul!—it has not been opened I believe since she left it. I never shall forget the manner in which she thanked me as I led her from it; or the tears she shed as she put this little ring upon my finger."

Madeline started up and examined the ring; then, after a moment fastening her fine eyes swimming in tears upon the housekeeper,

"Blessed, for ever blessed, (she exclaimed) be the hand which aided the unhappy!"

"There was such a fuss, (resumed Mrs. Beatrice), when it was known that she had escaped, I was very near being dismissed from the castle; nothing but my youth could have obtained my forgiveness: so in it I continued, and on the death of my aunt obtained her place."

"And what was the general opinion about the unhappy Marchioness?" demanded Madeline.

"It was the opinion of the domestics, and such simple folks, (replied the housekeeper) that she was an unfortunate lady, who had been cruelly injured; but all the great people believed, or said they did at least, that she was an artful creature, who had drawn in the Count to have an amour with her."

After conversing a few minutes longer with the housekeeper, Madeline told her, she no longer required her attendance. The night was now indeed waning fast, and most of the inhabitants of the castle had retired to repose, ere she dismissed her; however so much was her imagination affected by the gloom of her apartment, that she could not avoid asking, whether there was an inhabited one near it?

"Not very near it," answered the housekeeper; "the one adjoining it," she said, "had belonged to Lord Philippe, but since his death had been shut up, with all the rest of the chambers in that gallery, except a few near the staircase, one of which had been now prepared for the Count St. Julian."

Left to herself, instead of retiring to rest, Madeline reseated herself by the toilette, and leaning her head pensively upon her hand, began to ruminate over past events. The picture of Lord Philippe, by recalling de Sevignie to her mind, had awakened a thousand tender recollections, which wrung her heart with agony; the idea of de Sevignie's falsehood had failed to conquer her tenderness; she still loved him, still doubted his duplicity, and felt more convinced than ever that all the splendour of her present situation could never restore the cheerfulness her disappointment relative to him had injured: again she regretted that situation, again regretted that situation, again regretted her elevation to a height which would render more conspicuous the melancholy she wished to conceal from every eye.

"The sadness that marks my brow will make me appear ungrateful to heaven, (cried she) for the wonderful change it has effected in my father's favour; and what ill-natured speculations may not be excited by seeing one so young so hopeless!"

Severely, however, did her heart reproach her for regretting that change—a change which removed from the memory of her grandmother the obloquy that had been so long attached to it.

From the sufferings of her grandmother her thoughts naturally reverted to those of her father, and the more she reflected on his narrative, the more firmly convinced she was that much of his life remained untold;—the recollected words of her departed friend confirmed this opinion.

"She told me, (cried Madeline) and her lips knew not falsehood, that the calamities of his life were unprecedented;

that its characters were marked by horror, and stained with blood;—but in the view he gave me of it, no such calamities, no such characters met my eye; 'tis therefore too evident, that much of it remained concealed.—Oh! may that concealment now continue, (she proceeded); Oh! may no hand more daring than mine withdraw the veil I have been so cautiously against raising; may no untoward circumstance reveal a mystery, whose elucidation I have now a presentiment would fill me with horror!"

She suddenly paused, for at this instant she thought she heard a groan from the adjoining chamber; which, it may be remembered, has already been mentioned as once belonging to Lord Philippe.

Her heart beat quick, and she turned her eyes towards the partition, as if they could have penetrated it, and discovered the cause of the sound that had alarmed her; but all again was profoundly still, and she at last began to think it was either the wind growling through the casements, she had heard, or some of those unaccountable noises, so common in old houses; such, she recollected, as had often startled her at the chateau of the Countess de Merville.

Thus trying to tranquillize her mind, she was beginning to undress, when the powers of motion were suddenly suspended by a repetition of the sound which had so recently alarmed her—a sound she could no longer ascribe to the causes she had already done.

Deep and dreadful groans now pierced her ear—groans which seemed bursting from the bosom of misery and despair, and which by degrees rose to a yell, intermingled with sighs and sobs.

That Madeline was not an entire stranger to superstition, must have been already perceived; that it was now awakened in her breast, cannot be denied, nor indeed scarcely wondered at, when her situation is considered; in a gloomy chamber, remote from every inhabited one, and assailed by noises from the long unoccupied apartment of a murdered relative.

For some minutes she was unable to move: at length her eyes timidly glanced round her chamber, dreading yet wishing to ascertain whether any terrific object was within it. They encountered a bell near the head of the bed, and which the housekeeper had previously informed her communicated with the gallery where the servants slept; to this she instantly darted, and rung it with violence;—almost immediately she heard a bustle over her head, and then descending steps.

She flew to the light, and taking it up, directly opened the door. Several of the male and female domestics approached, accompanied by her father.

"What is the matter, my love? (cried he), I have been called from my bed by the sound of passing steps."

"Listen!" exclaimed Madeline, with a countenance of horror, and glancing at the chamber.

The yell became, if possible, more savage; and the domestics began to cross themselves. Madeline looked at her father, with an intention of asking his opinion of the noise; but was prevented by observing the disorder and death-like paleness of his countenance.

"How long (demanded he) is it since this chamber was opened?"

"Two months at least, my Lord, (replied the housekeeper), and then it was only opened for a few hours, of a fine sunny day, merely to air it."

"Where is the key?" asked he.

"It hangs beside the door, my Lord;" answered Mrs. Beatrice.

"I will examine it then," cried he.

"Examine it! (repeated the housekeeper) Jesu Maria!—Why, surely my Lord, you could not think of such a thing; surely, surely you, of all men in the world, could not have courage to enter it?"

St. Julian started, and turned quick upon her; and a frown, such as Madeline had never before seen upon it, darkened his brow—his eyes, his piercing eyes, were fastened on her, as if wishing to discover the innermost recesses of her soul, and in an agitated voice he demanded what she meant.

"Meant, my Lord? (said the affrighted Beatrice) meant—why, nothing—nothing that could give your Lordship offence."

St. Julian looked doubtfully at her; then turning, he took down the key, and unlocked the chamber; the moment he opened the door, the women retreated from it, and shame alone, it was visible, prevented the men from following their example: —attended by them and Madeline he entered it, and the noise directly ceased.

The room, like Madeline's, was hung with tapestry; this was now raised, and the walls minutely examined, but no opening could be discovered, nor any means of entrance but by the door in the gallery.

"Were you ever before disturbed by any noise in this chamber?" asked St. Julian.

"No, (the servants replied) never before the present night."

"'Tis strange!" cried he, after pausing for a minute.

They then quitted the chamber, which he relocked.

"I shall keep the key myself, (said he, as he turned from it) it must undergo another examination; though destruction, certain destruction should overwhelm me for doing so, I will try to develop the mystery."

He now took the hand of Madeline, and led her to her room; he tried to tranquillize her, but the trembling of his frame, and disorder of his looks, mocked the efforts he made to do so.

"You look alarmed, my love?" cried he.

Madeline sighed, and might have said,

"And trust me, in mine eye, so do you."

"You have no reason for terror, (said he with a deep sigh), your conduct has made no enemies either in this world or the next."

"I trust not; (cried Madeline), but conscious innocence is not always able to guard the heart against the attacks of fear; and I own I am shocked beyond expression by the noise I have heard."

"I fear you are superstitious," exclaimed her father.

"Could you wonder if I was? (cried she); What we cannot account for, we can scarcely help ascribing to supernatural causes."

"Am I to infer, (said St. Julian, regarding her with earnestness) from what you say, that it is your opinion the groans proceeded from the spirit of the murdered Philippe?"

"With the Supreme nothing is impossible, (said Madeline), and I have been told that the spirits of the injured are sometimes permitted to revisit this world, for the purpose of obtaining retribution; and if 'tis true what the housekeeper once hinted to me,— — —"

St. Julian started,—"What did she hint?" asked he with eagerness.

Madeline paused for a minute; then with a faltering voice, and timidly raising her eyes to her father's face,

"She told me (said she) that Lord Philippe fell not by the hands of banditti, but—"

"By whom?" demanded St. Julian, in almost convulsive agitation.

"Some relative," replied Madeline.

"And did she acquaint you with the name of that relative?"

"No, and perhaps, after all, it was only an idle surmise of her own."

St. Julian left his seat, and traversed the apartment.

Madeline viewed him with consternation; her thoughts began to grow wild; and fears of the most frightful nature again assailed her heart.

"Oh, God! (she cried to herself, while every nerve was strained with agony at the idea) should the suspicions that now rack my breast be just!—-This torture of suspense is more than I can bear (continued she); I will throw myself at the feet of my father, I will disclose to him my suspicions; if false, he will pardon them, when he reflects on the combination of circumstances which exited them; if true, he will not surely shrink from reposing confidence in his child."

She rose, but almost instantly sunk upon her seat, recoiling from the dreadful idea of a child declaring to a parent her suspicion of his having committed one of the most horrible crimes which human nature can be capable of:—she shuddered, she wondered at her temerity, in having ever thought of doing so; and, as she wondered, the recollection of her father's precepts, his gentleness, his uniform piety, returning, she again began to believe, that in thinking he had ever deviated from integrity, she had done him the greatest injustice.

St. Julian, whose emotions prevented his noticing those of Madeline, soon resumed his seat; his countenance had lost its wildness, and a faint glow again mantled his cheek.

"I trust, my love, (cried he) you will not again listen to the idle surmises of the servants: even on the slightest foundation they are apt to raise improbabilities and horrors, which, in spite of reason, make too often a dangerous impression on the mind, and overturn its quiet, by engendering superstition:—Heaven knows, (he proceeded) the evils of life are sufficiently great without adding to them those of the imagination."

Madeline assured him she would never more encourage any conversation from the domestics, on family affairs.

"You look fatigued, (said he) and I will now (rising as he spoke) leave you to repose; retire to it, my love, without fear or trembling; blessed with conscious innocence, you can dread no evil, no angry spirit demanding retribution:—Oh! never may your bosom lose that peace which must ever belong to virtue!—Oh! never may reflection break your slumbers, or an offended conscience present terrific images to your view. farewell, my child, (tenderly embracing her) would to God thy father could sink to forgetfulness with a mind like thine!"

Heart-struck by the last words of her father, Madeline remained many minutes riveted to the spot on which he had left her, deeply ruminating on them; then starting, as if from a deep reverie,

"I must not think, (said she) since thought is so dreadful."

She felt fatigued, but it was more a mental than a bodily fatigue—that fatigue which repels, instead of inviting rest; besides a secret dread clung to her soul, which rendered her unwilling to go to bed; she therefore threw herself before a large crucifix that was placed near it, and continued to pray for her father, for herself, and for repose to the spirit of the murdered

Philippe, till day began to dawn through the shutters. With night her terror decreased, and undressing herself, she then retired to bed; but the sleep into which she soon fell was broken by horrid visions, and she arose in the morning, pale, and unrefreshed.

The sun beamed bright through the casements, and on the stately trees that waved before them, unnumbered birds poured forth their matin lay, intermingled with the simple carol of the woodman: but neither the bright beams of the sun, the melodious notes of soaring birds, nor the wild song of the peasant, could now, as heretofore, delight the mind of Madeline. Saddened beyond expression by obtrusive ideas, she strove to banish that sadness by banishing thought—but, ah! how vain the effort! the "vital spark of heavenly flame" within us must be extinguished, ere we can cease to think.

END OF VOL. III.

CHAP. I.

– – – – – – – – – – –Something still there lies

In Heaven's dark volume which I read through mists.

Dryden

On descending to the breakfast parlour, she found her father already there; he stood with his back to the door, and so deeply engaged in contemplating a large picture, that he did not hear her enter. Madeline approached him softly, and could not help being struck with horror on perceiving the picture was a representation of the murder of Abel. It was fancy, no doubt, which at that moment made her imagine, in the features of the agonized and affrighted Cain, there was a resemblance to her father's. A slight noise she made roused him; and, starting, he turned with evident confusion to her. He had scarcely recovered from it, when the Marquis entered the room. Contrary to his usual custom, he had forsaken his bed at an early hour, anxious, by every attention in his power, to make amends to his son for his long neglect.

After the usual salutations were over, – "I was sorry to hear (said he, as they seated themselves at the table), that your rest was disturbed last night; Lafroy informed me of the noise which alarmed you; I can no otherways account for it, than by supposing some ill-minded person resides in my family who wishes to overthrow its tranquillity by exciting superstitious fears. I have heard more than once of such tricks being played in other houses, by people who imagined they should reap advantage from the general confusion that was the consequence of them. If one is practised here, I will if possible detect it: this very morning I am determined to examine the chamber, to try if there is any other entrance to it than by the gallery; though that examination will be attended with the utmost pain, as I have never visited it since the death of my Philippe."

Lord St. Julian informed him he had secured the key for that purpose. As soon as breakfast was over, they accordingly repaired to it, accompanied by Madeline. The door was closed immediately on their entrance; and while the Marquis, overcome by afflicting recollections, sat almost motionless on the bed, the tapestry was raised, and the wall critically inspected, but without discovering any other crevices in it than those which time had made.

"'Tis strange (cried the Marquis, after the fruitless examination was over), I cannot now possibly conjecture from whence the noise could have proceeded:—what did it sound like?"

"Like the groans, or rather yells, of excruciating distress (replied St. Julian); never before did sounds so horrible pierce my ear."

"I shall place some of the servants I can depend on in the gallery as a watch upon this door to-night; and if any villainy is practised, I think (said the Marquis), by that means it will be detected. Though this room (continued he) affects, it also pleases me; it seems to me a place peculiarly consecrated to my Philippe, as since his death it never has been inhabited, nor never shall whilst I live. Will you indulge me by remaining a little longer in it with me?"

St. Julian and Madeline instantly seated themselves.

After some further conversation, the Marquis requested to hear the particulars of his son's life.

St. Julian seemed somewhat embarrassed: after a little hesitation, however, he gave the desired recital. But how great was the astonishment of Madeline to find it differ essentially from the one he had given her; every circumstance relative to his brother was now suppressed.

On finding his expectations of fortune blasted, he had set out for Italy, he said, with an intention of cultivating a taste for painting; trusting, from that source, he should be enabled at least to derive a support. "I had not proceeded far on my journey (continued he), ere an accident introduced me to the hospitable Lord Dunlere": he then gave the same account of that nobleman to the Marquis that he had already done to Madeline; and concluded by saying, he had lost his wife, and her father, in consequence of their grief for the premature death of his lovely sister-in-law: after which he had forsaken their habitations, unable to bear the scene of his former joys, and retired, changing his name, to a lonely cottage, amidst some of the most wild and romantic mountains of Dauphine.

The Marquis was affected by the sufferings of his son; but at the same time pleased to hear he had been united to a woman of rank and virtue: it gratified his pride to find the heiress of his fortunes could boast on every side of illustrious connexions.

But how different were the feelings of Madeline from his, on hearing this second narrative from her father: she was shocked to find so great a difference between the one he had given her, and the one he had given the Marquis. "Ah, why (cried she to herself) conceal the generosity of his noble brother!—Yet, perhaps (continued she, after some some minutes' reflection), he only forbore mentioning him, from a fear of awaking painful emotions in the Marquis's breast."

Soothed by this idea, the composure of her mind was returning, when again it was disturbed by the Marquis's suddenly enquiring on what part of the Alps the habitation in which Lord Dunlere had lived was situated, and by the agitation her father betrayed at the question: in faltering accents he answered it, and the Marquis instantly exclaimed—

"Oh, God! it was there my Philippe fell!—You resided with Lord Dunlere at that time (continued he, after the pause of a moment), and you heard perhaps of the murder?"

"A rumour of it (replied St. Julian), but without knowing the sufferer's name."

"You knew not then, till lately, that the vengeance of Heaven had overtaken me: the offended Majesty of Heaven could not indeed have inflicted any punishment upon me half so severe as that of depriving me of my son. Oh, Philippe! lovely and beloved! days, years have elapsed since your death,—but without witnessing any diminution of my grief!—Had I received your last sigh—had I paid the last sad duties to your remains, its poignancy I think would have been abated: but far from your kindred you fell!—and never will the tomb of your forefathers receive you."

"You have heard, perhaps (continued the Marquis), from your vicinity to the spot, where he fell—that the body could never be found. At the time he received his death wound, he was on his way to Italy, and had stopped for the night at a little obscure inn; from whence, tempted by the sublimity of the scene, he had wandered to an adjoining mountain, to pass an hour or two, attended by a favourite servant: both were unarmed; and the moment he was attacked, the servant fled for assistance; but, alas! ere he returned with it, the murdered and the murderer were gone. No doubt the body was dragged into some recess, a prey for the ravenous wolves which infest that part of the country; and even now, perhaps, his bones, unburied, lie bleaching in the mountain blast. Oh! never may my eyes be closed till they have seen vengeance fall upon the head of his murderer! accursed may he be! may his days be without comfort—his nights without repose!—and may his pangs, if possible, be more intolerable than those he has inflicted on my soul!"

"Perhaps (cried Madeline, in a faint voice), he does not live."

"Suggest not such an idea again (exclaimed the Marquis, with a kind of savage fury in his countenance); the hope of yet bringing him to punishment has hitherto, more than any other circumstance, supported me amidst my sufferings; to relinquish that hope, would be to relinquish almost all that could console me.—Still then will I retain it; still then will I trust, O God! that some heaven-directed hand shall point out the murderer of my son."

The Marquis and the Count sat on the same side, and Madeline directly opposite to them. As her grandfather uttered the last words, she withdrew her eyes from his for the purpose of stealing a glance at her father; but as she was turning to him, they were suddenly arrested by a sight which struck her with horror.

She beheld a hand thrust through the tapestry behind him, extended and pointing to him. Shrieking aloud, she started from her seat, and, with a desperate resolution, was flying to the wall in order to examine it, when her strength and senses suddenly receded, and she fell fainting on the floor.

Alarmed by her too evident terror and illness, St. Julian flew to her assistance; whilst the Marquis, scarcely less affected than her father, rung the bell with violence. Some of the servants immediately hastened to the room; and restoratives being procured, Madeline soon revived. The moment she opened her eyes, she raised her languid head from the shoulder of her father, and turned them to the spot from whence she had seen the dreadful hand extended. But it was gone; and she then begged to be carried to her chamber.

St. Julian would not permit any one to continue in it with her but himself. He had some secret reasons for wishing no one at present to listen to their conversation. He tried to sooth, he tried to tranquillize her, but without effect; and he besought her to acquaint him with the cause of her illness.

Unwilling to tell a falsehood, yet unable to declare the truth—"Oh! my father (cried she, bathing his hands with tears as she pressed them between her's), ask me no farther questions on the subject; place the same confidence in me now you have hitherto done, and believe that your Madeline will never have any concealments from which you can disapprove: you seem ill yourself," observing his pale and haggard looks.

"At my being disordered (cried he), you cannot wonder after what has passed."

"Passed!" repeated Madeline, recoiling with horror at the idea of his having seen the hand.

"Yes (replied St. Julian), after what has passed,—after being cursed by my father."

"Cursed!" cried Madeline aghast.

"Did you not hear him curse me?"

"No, surely not (answered Madeline); I heard him curse, but— — —she paused—she hesitated.

"But whom?" demanded St. Julian impatiently.

"The murderer of his son," replied Madeline in a faint voice, and turning her eyes from her father.

St. Julian groaned; he clasped his hands upon his breast and traversed the apartment.

"True (cried he, suddenly stopping, and flinging himself upon a chair); true, it was not me he cursed. I believe my reason is disordered by the sudden change in my situation. Ah! would to heaven (said he in a half-stifled voice), since so long delayed, that change had never taken place!"

"Would to heaven it never had!" said Madeline.

"Oh! my child (resumed St. Julian, rising and embracing her), you have no reason to join in that wish; the Castle of Montmorenci can lead you to no dreadful retrospections, can awaken no torturing recollections in your breast."

"Alas! my father (replied Madeline), if it has that effect upon your mind, mine must necessarily be disturbed: she whom you nurtured with tenderness, the child of your bosom, cannot, without the most agonizing sorrow, behold your distress."

At this moment a servant rapped at the door to announce dinner. Madeline declared herself unable either to go down or take any refreshment at present. But she promised her father she would exert herself to be able to attend him and the Marquis in the evening, and reluctantly he left her.

But how vain were the efforts she made to fulfil the promise she had given to her father; as well might she have attempted to still the wild waves of the ocean as the agitations of her breast, proceeding as they did from her newly-revived suspicions concerning him.

She hesitated whether she should disclose them or not. "Shall I throw myself at his feet (cried she, traversing her chamber with hasty steps), and entreat him to confirm my horrors, or dissipate my fears? Ah! what rapture to think he could do the latter!—but, alas! his unguarded expressions, the mysterious circumstances that have happened since our arrival at the castle, leave me little reason to imagine he can."

Absorbed by the dreadful ideas which had taken possession of her mind, Madeline heeded not the passing minutes, and was surprised by her father in a situation that made him start as he entered her apartment.

Never indeed was anguish more strongly depictured than by her; her hair, dishevelled, fell partly on a bosom whose tumultuous throbs indicated the disorder of her heart; and the wildness of her eyes declared the agitation that had mantled her cheeks with a feverish glow.

"Madeline (said her father as he approached her), is it thus you have kept your promise with me?"

She sighed.

"Your countenance (resumed he in a solemn voice, and taking her hand), renders concealment with you impossible; I shall not therefore ask what has disordered you, for your looks have informed me."

Madeline involuntarily averted her head.

"Yes (continued he), I know your present ideas. But, Oh,

Madeline! reflect on the tenor of my conduct, on the precepts I instilled into your mind, and then think whether you have done me justice or injustice in harbouring them?"

Madeline withdrew her hands, and covered her face.

"I forgive you, however (proceeded St. Julian), from my soul I forgive you. I know a strange combination of circumstances excited your suspicions—circumstance which I may yet perhaps satisfactorily account for: at any rate, be assured, at some period, perhaps not far distant, I will elucidate all the mysteries of my life, explain my reasons for sinking to the Marquis, and not to you, my intimacy with my brother."

"Oh! my father (cried Madeline, throwing herself at his feet), how can I ever sufficiently evince my gratitude for your forgiveness—a forgiveness which cannot be followed by my own. True, a strange combination of circumstances led me into error; but nothing can now justify me in my own opinion for it. Ah! never can I reflect without horror, that there were moments in which I doubted your integrity,—ah! never can I think myself punished enough for doing so; though my feelings, in consequence of such doubts, were such as almost to annihilate existence. You say you forgive me; but ah! my father, can I hope that you will ever look upon me again without internal resentment?"

"Without a trace of it shall I regard you (cried he, raising her from the ground): had our situations been reversed, I make no doubt I should just have thought as you did: let us now endeavour to banish all that is disagreeable from our recollections."

"With ecstasy (said Madeline). Oh! never, my father, shall my faith in your virtues be again shaken. Ah! happy should I now be, could I be reconciled to myself. Your words have removed a mountain from my breast; and all the horrors of doubt and suspicion are over."

"My happiness depends on your's (said St. Julian); the best proof, therefore, you can give me of your regard, is by endeavouring to recover your spirits."

"Every effort then shall be made (replied Madeline); and efforts in a right cause are generally successful."

Her father then led her to the apartment where the Marquis sat, who expressed much pleasure at seeing her better.

CHAP. II.

How would Philosophy enjoy this hour,
Did not grief's arrow in her bleeding side
Deep, deep infix'd, at every painful step
Pierce to the heart, and poison all her bliss.
Ev'n this calm solitude, this still serene,
Tranquillity, that to internal views
Recalls our scatter'd thoughts, and from the brow
Of ruffl'd passion steals its gloomy frown,
Is now my gentle foe; provokes the tear
From the pale eye of sorrow, and reminds
Despairing Friendship of its loss.— — —

West.

As they were drinking their coffee, Madeline was agreeably surprised by hearing there was a connexion between her family and that of her departed benefactress:—the father of Viola's husband was a near relation of the Marquis and next heir to his titles if he died without issue.

"As soon as I discovered I had a son in existence (said the Marquis), I wrote to Monsieur D'Alembert, whose chateau is about four leagues from this, acquainting him with the joyful event, and requesting his immediate presence, well convinced, from the generosity of his disposition, that he would rather rejoice than grieve at the discovery, though the means of destroying his prospect of my title and fortunes. I received a letter from him, breathing the warmest congratulations; and assuring me he would instantly have obeyed my summons, had not domestic calamity interposed to prevent his doing so. A dispatch had just arrived from his son, he continued, informing him of the illness of Madame D'Alembert."

"Her illness!" cried Madeline, turning pale.

"Yes (resumed the Marquis), an illness which threatened to end in a decline, and for which she was ordered directly to Bareges, whither Monsieur D'Alembert determined on accompanying her and his son."

Madeline, though inexpressibly shocked, was not surprised to hear this account of Madame D'Alembert, whose health she had long beheld declining. Almost confident, from the character of young D'Alembert, that he would not pay those attentions her situation required, Madeline could not forbear giving vent to her feelings, and exclaimed with energy—"Would to God I was now with her! would to God I was now permitted to pay to the daughter the debt of gratitude I owed the parent!"

"Impossible (cried the Marquis); Madame D'Alembert, accompanied as she is, cannot require additional attendance: besides, your presence in the castle is absolutely requisite, as an entertainment is already planned, and will be given in a few days, in honour of you and your father, at which you must preside. Of the travellers we shall receive the earliest intelligence, as Monsieur D'Alembert promised to write immediately on their arriving at Bareges: let this promise therefore contribute to quiet your mind."

Madeline bowed, and endeavoured to appear composed; but her heart swelled with sorrow at the idea of being separated from her friend, at a time when her attentions would have been so acceptable, perhaps necessary; and with difficulty she suppressed her tears.

When coffee was over, the Marquis and St. Julian sat down to chess, and Madeline withdrew to the court, from whence she was soon tempted to wander into the forest.

It was now the still, the dewy hour of eve, an hour in which she particularly loved to walk; and she proceeded, thinking of the happy period in which she had wandered, devoid of care, through the wild-wood walks surrounding her native valley; and sighing at the idea, that felicity such as she then experienced would never, never more return.

Unheeding whither or how far she went, she rambled on till her progress was unexpectedly stopped by the monumental pillar of Lord Philippe.

A kind of awful fear now took possession of her; a fear, which the idea of the distance she had wandered from the chateau, the lateness of the present hour, and the deep gloom surrounding her, inspired; a

— — —long cathedral aisle of shade

led to the pillar, around which clustered

cypress and bay,

Funereal, pensive birch, its languid arms

That droops, with waving willows, deem'd to weep,

And shiv'ring aspins— — —

The yellow radiance, diffused over the tall trees and the antique turrets of the castle, at her first setting out, was now entirely withdrawn, and scarcely a star-light ray penetrated to the spot on which she stood; whilst a breeze swept through the forest with a hollow murmur, that to her ear sounded like the lamentings of a troubled spirit.

The dreadful fate of him to whom the pillar was dedicated, rushed upon her recollection; and, shuddering, she was moving from it, when a deep groan arrested her steps. She paused,—she trembled; the surrounding trees faintly rustled; a figure slowly emerged from them, and gliding by her, gave as it passed a look at once tender and mournful—a look which presented to her view the exact features of de Sevignie.

"Oh, God! (cried she, recollecting the likeness between him and the picture of Lord Philippe), is it de Sevignie I saw, or the spirit of the murdered Philippe?"

The pale and hollow cheek presented to her view, the melancholy eye that beamed upon her, inclined her to believe the latter; and while a cold perspiration burst from every pore at the idea of having seen a supernatural being, she fled trembling up the long avenue that led from the pillar: at its termination she paused, uncertain which way to go, for the paths were here wild and entangled; but as she despairingly struck her breast from a fear of not finding her way, she beheld a light suddenly glimmering through the trees: from the castle she knew this must proceed; darting forward therefore, and still keeping it in view, she soon found herself at home.

She stopped for a few minutes in the hall in order to regain her breath and some degree of composure; she then repaired to the parlour where she found the gentlemen just rising from chess. In answer to their enquiries as to where she had been, she briefly replied, rambling about, but did not inform them how far or whither. Her paleness struck both the Marquis and St. Julian; both however imputed it to her grief for the illness of Madame D'Alembert.

On retiring to her chamber, Madeline was not sorry to find some of the servants stationed outside the chamber next to her's, for the purpose of apprising the Marquis and his son if there was any return of the noise that had alarmed the family the preceding night. Her spirits weakened by the idea of having seen a being of the other world she could ill have borne total solitude. Unable to sleep, she stood a considerable time at the window, contemplating that part of the forest where she had been terrified; yet without shuddering she could not look upon those trees, beneath whose covert she imagined the troubled spirit of Lord Philippe wandered.

CHAP. III.

Why I can smile, and murder while I smile,

And cry content to that which grieves my heart;

And wet my cheeks with artificial tears,

And frame my face to all occasions.

No noise this night disturbed the tranquillity of the castle; and the terror which had marked the countenances of the domestics began to vanish.

The Marquis had mentioned to Madeline his intention of giving an entertainment in honour of her and his Son; and preparations were now making for it—preparations which were unexpectedly interrupted by a letter from Monsieur D'Alembert, containing the melancholy intelligence of the death of his daughter-in-law on her way to Bareges.

Though this event was communicated in the most cautious manner to Madeline by her father, the shock it gave her nearly deprived her of her senses. Unwilling to distress him by the sight of her grief, yet unable at present to stem it, she requested permission to retire to her chamber; a request which he instantly complied with, from a hope that the unrestrained indulgence of her sorrow would abate its violence, and contribute to the restoration of her tranquillity.

In the solitude of her chamber she gave free vent to it. "But is not this a selfish sorrow? (she exclaimed, whilst tears trickled down her pale cheeks); do I not weep alone for the loss which the death of my friend will prove to me? for am I not convinced that death to her was a passport to unutterable felicity,—to that glorious world, where the cares, the disappointments that embitter this, can never obtrude—where all is happiness,—and where the kindred spirit of a Parent welcomed her pure and disembodied soul to that happiness.

These ideas, however, had not power to mitigate her feelings. Besides the tears she shed for the loss, the irreparable loss she sustained by the death of her friend, she wept from a fear, which the account she had received of the disposition of

D'Alembert inspired, namely, that his wife had not in her dying moments received those attentions that sooth the last struggles of nature; she feared that no

Soft complaint, no kind domestic tear

Pleas'd her pale ghost, or grac'd her mournful bier.

"Would to heaven! (she said) I had continued a little longer with her; it would have comforted me to have known that the kindnesses, the attentions, the nameless little offices of love, which soften the pangs of sickness and of death, had been paid to her."

From her melancholy meditations she was roused by a knock at the chamber-door. She started; hastily rose, and opening it, beheld her father.

"I hope, my dear Madeline (cried he, taking her hand) that the long and free indulgence of your grief has lightened your heart, and enabled you to make exertions against a sorrow, not only useless, but injurious. I hope (continued he, observing her trickling tears), that in the grave of your friend you have not buried all consideration for your father's peace—a father, who can know no happiness but what is derived from witnessing your's."

"Oh, my father (exclaimed Madeline, unspeakably affected by his words), every exertion you desire I will make."

Ever taught to consider her promise as sacred, she no longer gave way to her grief, and soon recovered, though not her cheerfulness, her composure.

The death of Madame D'Alembert caused the doors of the castle to be again barred against company, and an almost uninterrupted stillness once more reigned within it. Madeline rather rejoiced at than regretted the total solitude in which she lived; the spirits, the hopes, the expectations which would once have inclined her to gaiety, were fled, and she no longer wished to see or to be seen.

Nor did her father appear less pleased with his seclusion from the world; a deeper gloom than Madeline had ever before observed upon it, now almost continually clouded his brow. His wanderings from the castle became frequent; and were often prolonged till the curiosity of his father, and the fears of his daughter, were excited.

Tortured by beholding his increasing melancholy, Madeline was often tempted to implore him to reveal its source, from a hope that she might then be able to offer some consolation; but whenever she felt herself on the point of doing so, the solemn promise she had given her departed friend of never attempting to raise the veil which concealed the former events of his life, recurred to her recollection, and made her shrink back appalled from the idea.

"But has he not promised (she would then cry, endeavouring to strengthen her resolution), has he not promised, since his arrival at the castle, that he would himself raise that veil, and elucidate every mystery; Oh! let me then terminate my incertitude, my my suspense, by now imploring him to fulfil his promise."

Still however, whenever her lips opened for that purpose, a secret dread would again close them; and she was soon convinced that she could not summon resolution to urge the disclosure she so ardently desired.

About a fortnight after they had received the intelligence of Madame D'Alembert's death, a letter arrived from the elder D'Alembert, acquainting the Marquis with his intention of being at the castle that day. He arrived a short time before dinner, and paid his compliments to his newly-discovered relatives with the utmost warmth and affection. The prejudice Madeline had conceived against the son extended to the father; and, notwithstanding the warmth of his manner, she saw, or fancied she saw (which had just the same effect upon her mind), in his countenance a dissatisfaction that denoted his not feeling what he professed; his eye, she thought, often fastened upon her father with a malignant expression, as if the soul that animated it inwardly cursed the man who had stepped between him and the fortunes of Montmorenci.

After the first compliments were over, taking the hand of Madeline, he assured her that nothing but business of the most perplexing nature could have prevented his son from accompanying him to the chateau. "He is impatient (continued he) to be introduced to his amiable relations; above all, he is impatient for an opportunity of expressing to you his heartfelt gratitude for the attentions you paid to his wife."

The heart of Madeline was too full to permit her to speak: she bowed, and hastily averted her head to wipe away the tears which fell to the memory of the unhappy Viola.

Her father, perceiving her emotions, led her to a seat, and changed the discourse.

D'Alembert now informed them that his daughter (of whom Madeline had before heard the Marquis slightly speak) was at the Chateau de Merville with her brother. "In about a month I hope and expect (continued he), they will join me here."

"I hope so too (said the Marquis); for I think it is the want of society that lowers the spirits, and hurts the bloom of Madeline."

"Ah! (thought Madeline) 'tis not the society I am now debarred from, but the society I have lost, which deadens my cheerfulness, and fades my cheek."

"I shall insist (resumed the Marquis) on her father's taking her in the course of the winter to Paris; 'tis time for her to be introduced to the circles her rank entitles her to associate with."

D'Alembert by a bow silently assented to what the Marquis said.

From this period Madeline had but few opportunities of indulging her love for solitude; D'Alembert either was, or pretended to be, so delighted with her society, that he could not for any length of time endure her absence. Complaisance compelled her to humour a relation advanced in life, and also the guest of her grandfather; but the interruption he gave to her favourite inclinations, together with the extravagant eulogiums he bestowed upon her person and all she said or did, heightened, if possible, the dislike she had conceived against him from their first interview—a dislike, however, which she did not reveal; yet not without uneasiness could she hear her father declare he thought him a man worthy of esteem.

With the utmost pain she thought of the approaching visit from his son and daughter. "Ah! never (said she to herself), ah! never, without shuddering, without horror, shall I be able to look upon the man whose ill conduct I have reason to think occasioned the death of my beloved friend."

Within a week of the time she expected him, as she was walking one morning in that part of the forest which immediately surrounded the castle she beheld her father and D'Alembert at a little distance from her, apparently engaged in a deep and interesting discourse. Their eyes encountered her's almost at the moment she saw them; they instantly stopped;

and, after conversing together for about another minute, D'Alembert entered the court, and her father advanced to her: the gloom on his brow was somewhat lessened, and a languid smile faintly illumined his features.

"Madeline (said he, taking her hand, and walking on with her), D'Alembert and I have been talking of you."

"Of me!" cried Madeline.

"Yes, we have been sketching out a plan of felicity for you."

Madeline sighed, and looked earnestly at her father.

"A plan (resumed he) which I trust will meet your approbation."

"Explain yourself, my dearest father (cried Madeline), I am all impatience."

"To be explicit then (said St. Julian), D'Alembert has proposed an union between you and his son."

"Between me and his son! (repeated Madeline, involuntarily drawing her hand from her father's, and starting back a few paces)—between me and his son!—and you approved of the proposal!—Oh! my father, is this the felicity you planned for me?—sooner, ten thousand times sooner, would I immure myself for ever within the walls of a cloister, than become the wife of D'Alembert."

"Compose yourself (said St. Julian), you have no cause for the violent emotions you betray. You have always, I hope, found me, in every sense of the word, a parent: you should therefore have restrained your apprehensions, by being convinced I never would urge you to an act directly contrary to your inclinations. But whilst I give this assurance, I also declare that I will not, by rejecting every overture which may be made for your hand, sanction your attachment to an object who ought long since to have been forgotten."

"I solemnly declare (cried Madeline, clasping her hands together), that my repugnance to the union you have proposed, proceeds not entirely from the attachment you allude to."

"From what other cause (demanded St. Julian), can it proceed? you cannot have conceived a dislike against a man you never saw."

"'Tis true (replied Madeline), I know not the person of D'Alembert, but, I am acquainted with his character." She then briefly related all she had heard concerning him from Floretta and Agatha, the favourite and confidential servants of the Countess de Merville.

"I am shocked, I am astonished (cried St. Julian), at what you tell me; and with you I can readily believe, that the knowledge of his depravity accelerated the death of the mother, and occasioned that of the daughter."

"But had I never been informed of that depravity (resumed Madeline), I should have conceived an unconquerable dislike against him for his indelicacy in proposing for me so soon after his wife's death, and without being in the least degree acquainted with me."

"I own that part of his conduct appeared reprehensible to me (said St. Julian), and I gave my opinion of it to his father. He attempted to justify it by saying, that it was natural so young a man, and one of so domestic a turn as his son, should soon make another choice."

"But why let that choice devolve upon an object he had never beheld?" asked Madeline.

"Because a prepossession had been excited in her favour by the eulogiums of his wife; and he entreated his father to hasten to the castle, in order to pave the way for his addresses," St. Julian replied.

"Oh, my father (cried Madeline), I trust you will not delay declaring my utter repugnance to those addresses."

"Depend on me, my love (he said), for taking the earliest opportunity of informing D'Alembert they never can be successful: your grandfather, I hope, will be equally inclined to let you reject them."

"My grandfather! (repeated Madeline); was he then consulted on the subject?"

"So I understand from D'Alembert, and that he highly approved of the projected alliance: he wishes to have the fortunes of the family united."

"The fortunes of the family! (Madeline repeated); and are such the considerations that sway the great world?—Ah! no wonder, if the union of fortunes, not of hearts, is alone considered, that misery, vice, and dissipation from such connexions should ensue."

"I am almost convinced (resumed St. Julian), that the Marquis will not attempt to control your inclinations. But, my dear Madeline, though all idea of a connexion between you and D'Alembert shall on my part be relinquished, from a conviction that it never could promote your happiness, do not flatter yourself that, if a proposal came from an unexceptionable character, I would sanction a second rejection: 'tis not, be assured, from a vain pride of desiring an illustrious name to be continued to posterity, that I wish you to be married—no, 'tis from a wish of ensuring you protection when I shall be no longer able to extend it. I long to lodge my treasure in safe and honourable hands, ere I visit that country, from whose bourn I never shall return."

The words of her father opened a new source of disquietude to Madeline, who had flattered herself that her attachment to a single life would never be opposed: and still she tried to sooth her uneasiness by thinking, notwithstanding what he said, her father would never exert an arbitrary power over her.

They continued to walk till dinner time. At table Madeline turned with disgust from D'Alembert, whose looks expressed the utmost exultation. She withdrew almost immediately after dinner, and repaired to the garden, where she continued a considerable time uninterrupted, and deeply meditating on the conversation of the morning. At length she beheld D'Alembert approaching; and the alteration of his countenance convinced her that her father had communicated her sentiments to him.

She would have passed him in silence, but he prevented her by catching her hand.

"I came hither, Madam (said he in a sullen voice), on purpose to converse with you; I cannot therefore let you depart abruptly."

"Well, Sir (cried Madeline), I am ready to hear whatever you wish to say."

"But will you promise not to hear without regarding it?" demanded he in a gentler tone than he had before used.

"I never make promises I am not certain of fulfilling," replied Madeline.

"'Tis impossible (said he) to express the mortification, the disappointment, I feel in consequence of your rejection of the proposals which I made this morning; proposals approved by your father, and also sanctioned by the Marquis. Surely (he continued), you should not have rejected them, without being assured that their acceptance never could have contributed to your happiness; an assurance it is impossible you can have from your total ignorance of my son."

"Hopes which cannot be realized, cannot be too soon suppressed," exclaimed Madeline.

"And why, without knowing him, can you be so determined on destroying his hopes? (asked D'Alembert). Only see him—only hear him,—and then reject, if then you can disapprove."

"Was your son (said Madeline) all that the most romantic imagination can conceive of perfection, I would reject him."

"You would!" exclaimed D'Alembert, dropping her hand.

"I would," repeated Madeline.

"Did you ever hear aught against him?" demanded he, again catching her hand, and looking steadily upon her.

"Even supposing any thing could be alleged against him (replied Madeline, wishing to evade this question), in the family of his wife and mother-in-law, was it likely, do you think I should hear any thing to his prejudice?"

"'Tis evident (said D'Alembert, after musing a few minutes), that your heart is pre-engaged; nothing else could account for your absolute rejection of a man you never saw."

"Nothing else," repeated Madeline involuntarily, and looking in his face.

"No! confess, therefore that what I say, is true."

"Well (cried Madeline), if I do confess that my heart is devoted to another, will you drop all solicitation for your son?"

"No, never," exclaimed he in a furious voice, and with an inflamed countenance.

Madeline now attempted to free her hand. "I insist, Sir (said she), upon your releasing me immediately."

"I will, if you first promise to let my son plead his own cause on coming to the castle."

"Never," cried Madeline with vehemence, and struggling to disengage herself. "Are you then indeed inflexible? does that soft bosom really hide an obdurate heart? can no pity influence you to compassionate the pangs my son will feel when he hears of your rejection?"

"I never can feel pity for the pangs of disappointed avarice and ambition (replied Madeline); and avarice and ambition, I am convinced, alone influence your son's addresses to me; for how can he love or admire an object whose virtues he never knew, whose form he never saw? Your persecution, Sir, has forced me to be explicit: drop it, if you wish me to conceal my opinion."

"Insolent girl!" cried D'Alembert, flinging away her hand, and stamping on the ground.

A kind of terror pervaded the breast of Madeline at his violence; and she was hurrying to the castle when he overtook, and again stopped her.

"Insolent girl! (he repeated, grasping her hand, and looking at her with a fiend-like countenance); but such is the effect which unexpected elevation ever has upon little minds, raised from a cottage to a palace. Your head grows giddy, and you think you may with impunity look down upon the rest of mankind with contempt; you imagine there's nothing to fear;—but beware of indulging such an idea, lest too late you should find it erroneous. The pinnacle of greatness upon which you stand, already totters: beware lest by your conduct you provoke the breath which can in a moment overthrow it."

So saying, he once more flung her hand from him; and, turning into another path, left her abruptly, so much thunderstruck by his words, that for a few minutes she had not power to move. At length recovering her faculties, she condemned herself for weakness in permitting his expressions to affect her; expressions which she could only impute to malice and resentment for her rejection of his son. "He wished (said she), by alarming me, to be revenged in some degree, or else he imagined me weak, and hoped, by raising bugbears to my view, to terrify me to his purpose."

Her contempt and dislike were both increased by these ideas; and she resolved never more, if possible, to avoid it, to listen to his particular conversation.

She hastened to the castle, and in the gallery adjoining her chamber, met her father. "Well (asked he), has D'Alembert declared his disappointment to you? he sought you I know for the purpose of doing so."

"He has (replied Madeline); and I sincerely hope for the last time." She then enquired how her grandfather bore the rejection of his relative.

"As I expected (answered St. Julian); he declared his readiness to relinquish any alliance that accorded not with your inclination."

Madeline, without repeating all D'Alembert had said, now acknowledged that she felt herself too much agitated, in consequence of his conversation, to be able to mingle in society again that evening. Her father accordingly promised to apologize for her absence below stairs; and the remainder of the evening she passed alone.

CHAP. IV.

'Twas as at an hour when busy Nature lay

Dissolv'd in slumbers from the noisy day;

When gloomy shades and dusky atoms spread

A darkness o'er the universal bed,

And all the gaudy beams of light were fled.

The ensuing day Madeline was again teased with the importunities of D'Alembert: in vain she assured him her resolution was unalterable, in vain declared, that if his son came to the castle but for the purpose of addressing her, as he intimated, she would confine herself to her chamber. He still continued to persecute her. Finding her own arguments ineffectual, she spoke to her father to try his influence. He accordingly remonstrated with D'Alembert; and requested him, in rather a peremptory manner, to drop a subject so unpleasing.

In consequence of this request, she was unmolested with any solicitation the next day; but whenever her eyes encountered D'Alembert, an involuntary terror pervaded her heart at beholding the dark and malignant glances with which he regarded her: she strove, but in vain, to reason herself out of it; and felt, without knowing why, as if she was in his power.

When the hour for rest arrived, she dismissed her attendant; but she, instead of repairing to bed, took up a book, with a hope of being enabled, through its means, to amuse and compose her thoughts. They were too much disturbed, however, to permit this hope to be realised, and she soon threw it aside.

"Unconscious of any crime, unacquainted with D'Alembert almost till the present day, what (she asked herself, trying to reason away her terror), have I to fear from him? nothing on my own account.—(She paused; she mused for a few minutes). But my father—(she trembled, and started)—I know not the mysteries of his life! D'Alembert may not be equally ignorant, and through his heart perhaps intends to aim at mine." The recollected threat of D'Alembert rendered this idea but too probable; and agonies which no tongue could express directly seized her soul.

For some minutes the powers of articulation were suspended. At length, with a deep sigh and uplifted hands, she implored the protection of Heaven. "Trusting in that protection (cried she), which can defeat the malice of the most vile, Oh! let me again endeavour to regain some composure; let me also endeavour not to be too ready in anticipating evil."

She felt still disinclined to sleep, yet gladly would she have closed her eyes upon the gloom of her chamber—a gloom, rendered more awful by the profound stillness of the castle, and which was calculated to inspire ideas not easily to be resisted in the present state of her mind.

In short, imaginary horrors soon began to succeed the real ones that had lately agitated her; yet scarcely was she infected by them ere she blushed from a conviction of weakness, and resolved on going to bed. She began to undress, though with a trembling hand; nor could refrain from starting as the low murmurs of the wind (which now, in the decline of autumn, frequently growled through the forest, and shook the old battlements of the castle) sounded through her chamber.

She had not proceeded far in undressing, when she was suddenly alarmed by the shaking of the tapestry which hung behind the table at which she stood. Appalled, she started back; yet at the next instant was returning, under the idea of its having only been agitated by the wind, when again she saw it raised, and could then perfectly distinguish a human form behind it: with a wild and piercing shriek she instantly fled to the door; but ere her trembling hand could withdraw the rusty bolt, she was rudely seized.

Hopeless of mercy, she attempted not to supplicate it, but closed her eyes, unwilling to behold her executioner; for that a ruffian had secreted himself in her apartment, for the purpose of robbery and murder, she could not doubt.

From agonies, which only those who have been in a situation of equal danger can imagine or describe, she was soon however relieved by the voice of D'Alembert.

"Madeline (he cried, as he supported her upon his breast), revive; I come not to injure, but to entreat."

"Oh, heavens! (said she, opening her eyes, and wildly gazing on him), do I hear, do I behold aright?"

"Be composed (exclaimed he), I again entreat you; you have nothing to fear."

"Nothing to fear! (repeated Madeline as she disengaged herself from him), if I have nothing to fear, I have at least much to be offended at. Whence this intrusion, Sir?—Is it right, is it honourable, to steal like a midnight assassin to my chamber?"

"You yourself have compelled me to this conduct (he replied); you refused to hear me, and consequently forced me to devise a scheme to make you listen———"

"To make me listen! (repeated Madeline with haughtiness); no, Sir,—no scheme, no stratagem shall effect that purpose. Begone! (cried she, laying her hand upon the door) if you wish to avoid the punishment your temerity deserves."

"Suppress this haughtiness (said he, seizing her hands, and dragging her from the door ere she had power to open it); believe me, like your threats, it is unavailing. Hear me you must—hear me you shall: nay, more, you shall comply with what I desire."

"Never!" exclaimed Madeline in a resolute voice, and struggling to free herself.

"Then you shall tremble for the safety of a father," cried D'Alembert.

Madeline trembled; her heart grew cold; she ceased her struggles, and looked with mingled terror and melancholy upon him.

"Yes; I repeat (said he), you shall tremble for the safety of a father: I am the minister of fate to him; and only your acceptance of the proposals of my son can save him from that which now hangs over him."

"What fate that is not happy can he have provoked?" asked Madeline in a faint voice.

"I will not shock your ear (he replied), by divulging to you the one he merits; be satisfied, however, that all I know concerning him, and with the most important events of his life I am acquainted, shall be carefully concealed, if you swear solemnly, swear this minute to accept the hand of my son."

"No, (cried Madeline, after a moment's consideration, during which an idea struck her, that his insinuations against her father might be false, invented merely for the purpose of terrifying her into a promise which could not afterwards be cancelled), I will not swear; I will not take an oath my soul revolts against fulfilling."

"You are determined then," said D'Alembert with a forced calmness, while an ashy paleness stole upon his cheek.

"Unalterably determined," replied Madeline.

"But your resolution could be shaken, if you believed my allegations against your father."

"I trust I never shall have reason to believe them," said Madeline.

"Unhappy girl! dearly will you pay for your want of faith in me."

As he spoke, he put his hand into his bosom, and drew forth a small dagger.

Madeline recoiled a few paces, and involuntarily dropped upon her knees. "Oh, D'Alembert! (cried she with a quivering lip), have mercy upon your own soul, and spare me!"

"Be not alarmed (said he), I mean not to harm you; the blood of innocence shall not again, at least by my means, pollute this dagger: receive it (continued he), as a present for your father; when he looks upon it, you will be convinced I spoke but truth this night."

"Oh! in pity tell me (said Madeline with clasped hands), what you know concerning him, and terminate the horrors of suspense."

"No; the events of his life will come better from himself; events, which his knowing this dagger comes from me, will convince him I am acquainted with; events, which shall be buried in oblivion, if you remain no longer inflexible. To-morrow I shall again enquire your determination; if unpropitious, the long-suspended sword of justice shall at length strike. farewell! your own obstinacy has provoked your present pain."

So saying, he abruptly quitted the chamber, notwithstanding the entreaties of Madeline to remain a few minutes longer, and explain his terrifying and mysterious language.

Left to the dreadful solitude of her chamber, she continued a considerable time longer upon her knees, with her eyes fixed upon the dagger, which lay at a little distance from her. At length, slowly rising, she advanced to it, and taking it up, brought it to the light to examine it; the hilt was curiously studded with precious stones, but the blade was almost entirely covered with rust.

"He said (cried Madeline in a hollow voice), that the blood of innocence polluted it. Oh, God! (continued she, letting it drop with horror from her), in whose hand was it clenched at that fearful moment!"

The suspicions, which had agitated her on her first entrance into the castle, again rushed upon her mind; but when nearly sinking beneath them, the assurance her father had given her of being utterly unconcerned in the fate of Lord Philippe recurred to her recollection, and cheered her fainting heart. "He said he was innocent (exclaimed she), and to doubt his truth were impious; what then have I to fear from the threats of D'Alembert?"

But the calm produced by this idea was of short duration. Though assured of his innocence relative to Lord Philippe, she recollected she had never received an assurance of his being equally guiltless with regard to every other being: she recollected also the words of her departed friend, that the characters of his life were marked by horror, and stained with blood; and she shuddered at the too probable supposition of his having been involved in some deed as dreadful as that which she at first suspected—a deed with which it was evident D'Alembert was too well acquainted.

"Oh, let me then no longer hesitate how to act (exclaimed she),—let me no longer delay devoting myself to save my father! and yet (continued she, after the reflection of a minute), how am I convinced that my father is in the power of D'Alembert? may he not have said so merely for the purpose of frightening me into compliance with his wishes? should I not therefore be rash in the extreme if I doomed myself to misery without a conviction that my father's preservation depended on my doing so? But how can I doubt his veracity (proceeded she, wildly starting from the chair on which she had flung herself), how imagine he would ever make allegations he could not support? and yet, perhaps, he made them under the idea that I would never enquire into their truth: but shocked, appalled at the first intimation of danger to my father, promise at once to become the wife of his son: I will not then make that promise, till assured there is a necessity for doing so."

But how was she to receive this assurance? how—without enquiring from her father concerning the former events of his life? and, in making those enquiries, what painful recollections might not be awakened? what horrible fears might not be suggested?

"Oh, God! (cried she, kneeling upon the ground, half distracted with her incertitude how to act), teach me what I ought to do! Oh, let me not, in trying to avoid misery myself, draw misery upon him for whom I would willingly lay down my life."

The night passed away in a state of wretchedness which cannot be described, and the morning surprised her still undetermined. The bustle of the rising domestics at length made her recall her scattered thoughts, and recollect the necessity there was for appearing composed. She accordingly adjusted her hair, put on a morning-dress, and seated herself at a window with a book. Never was dissimulation so painful; agonized by conflicting terrors, scarcely could she prevent herself from traversing her room with a distracted step.

At the usual hour, a servant came to inform her breakfast was ready. Madeline desired her to bring up a cup of coffee as she was rather indisposed; but charged her, at the same time, not to alarm the Marquis or her father. As soon as she was gone, Madeline took up the dagger, which the skirt of her robe had concealed, and went into her dressing-room, with an intention of locking it up in a cabinet; resolving, in the course of the morning, to have another conversation with D'Alembert, and determine by that how she should act.

She had just unlocked the cabinet, when she felt her arm suddenly grasped. She started; and, turning with quickness, beheld her father. The dagger instantly dropped from her trembling hand; and, recoiling a few paces, she stood motionless, gazing alternately at it and St. Julian.

With the quickness of lightning he snatched it from the ground: but scarcely had his eye glanced on it, ere he let it fall; and, turning with a death-like countenance to her, demanded, in a faltering voice—from whence, or from whom she had got it?

"From D'Alembert," replied the almost fainting Madeline.

"From him! (repeated St. Julian, striking his breast, and starting); Oh, heavens! by what means did it come into his possession?"

"I know not," said Madeline.

"But you know the fearful story with which it is connected."

"Oh, my father! (cried Madeline), do not question me."

"This instant (exclaimed he in a frantic manner, advancing to her, and grasping her hands), declare what D'Alembert said; without hesitation, without equivocation, let me know all he told you."

"Oh, my father! (said Madeline sinking on her knees), do not be thus agitated."

"Once more (cried he), I command you to tell me all that passed between you and D'Alembert; if you longer delay, you will work me up to frenzy."

Thus urged, Madeline, in scarcely intelligible accents, and still kneeling, revealed the dreadful conversation. After she had concluded, St. Julian continued some minutes silent, immovable, and in an attitude of horror which almost froze her heart. He then knelt beside her; and, wrapping his arms round her, strained her in convulsive agitation to his breast, and leaned his head upon her shoulder.

At length, raising it, he looked up to heaven—"Almighty God! (he cried) I bend before thy will; thy chastisement is just, though dreadful; and vain are the arts by which we would elude it. The hour of retribution, though sometimes delayed, is never forgotten. Oh, my child! dear pledge of a tender, though disastrous love! sweet image of the most lovely and injured of women! conscious that I merited the vengeance of Heaven, not on my own account, but thine, did I wish to ward off the blow of justice; I wished to save thy gentle nature from the bitter pangs of seeing thy father dragged to torture, and the yet bitterer pangs of knowing he deserved it. But that wish is frustrated at the very time when its frustration was least expected; no doubt for the wisest purposes, to prove to mankind that guilt can never hope for lasting concealment.

How my unfortunate story became known to D'Alembert, I cannot conceive; but that it is, that fatal instrument of death too plainly proves. Yes, he spoke truth when he said the blood of innocence had polluted it; it did, and now cries aloud for mine."

"Oh, horror!" groaned Madeline.

"In mercy, in pity to me (exclaimed St. Julian, again straining her to his bosom), try to compose your feelings! Oh, let me not have the excruciating misery of thinking I destroyed my child: exert your resolution, my Madeline, and live to reconcile mankind, by your virtues, to the memory of your father."

"But though D'Alembert (cried Madeline, whose recollection sudden horror had for a few minutes suspended), is acquainted with your story, there is a method (she continued, rising from the floor), to prevail on him to conceal it."

"A method which I will never suffer you to adopt (exclaimed St. Julian); Oh, never shall my child be sacrificed to save my life."

"Ah, little do you know the soul of your child, if you suppose she will leave untried any expedient that may save you. Hear her solemnly swear (cried she, again kneeling), by that Being she worships—by the spirit of her mother—by all that is holy in his sight, to become the wife of young D'Alembert, if by doing so she can bind his father to inviolable secrecy."

"My inestimable child! (said St. Julian, raising and embracing her); alas! what a wretch am I to think I have doomed you to misery!"

"No (cried Madeline), you have not; my fate cannot be miserable if I know it has mitigated your's."

"I will no longer delay revealing my sad story to you (said St. Julian); perhaps after hearing it, some other expedient than a marriage with D'Alembert may strike you for preserving me.

"You expect, no doubt (resumed he after he had secured the doors, and seated himself by her), a tale of horrors; alas! that expectation will be but too dreadfully fulfilled!"

CHAP. V.

Prepare, to hear

A story that shall turn thee into stone.

Could there be hewn a monstrous gap in Nature,

A flaw made through the centre by some god,

Thro' which the groans of ghosts might strike thine ear,

They would not wound thee as this story will.

"Do not be too much shocked, my love (cried St. Julian) on finding that I deviated from truth, which in the course of this narrative you must discover; that deviation was occasioned by tenderness for you; for I was well convinced of the misery you would feel if I confessed the involuntary suspicions you entertained of me on our first coming to the castle were well founded;—alas! they were too just!"

He stopped for a minute as if overcome by agony; then again addressing her—"you recollect, I suppose (said he) all the particulars I informed you of in our journey hither?"

"I do," said Madeline.

"I told you (resumed he) of the letter I received from my brother, requesting me to leave my elizium on the Alps, and of my meeting him in the pursuance of it in the forest of Montmorenci. He was so much altered, that had I met him elsewhere by chance, I should scarcely have known him. He told me he had been long indisposed, and that it was in consequence of his indisposition and the languid state of his spirits, that he had requested to see me, certain that my presence would operate like a rich cordial upon him.

"In the cottage where he had lodged me on the commencement of our acquaintance, he again procured a chamber for me; it stood at the extremity of the forest, and belonged to a brother of Lafroy's, who was then valet to Lord Philippe; and by him I was introduced at it as an unfortunate young man taken under the patronage of his Lord.

"Every morning I met my brother, but met him without having the pleasure of seeing his health in the least amended. My regret at the continuance of his illness, joined to my uneasiness at being absent from home, rendered me extremely unhappy. I had been about a fortnight at the cottage, when one morning as I was preparing to walk out as usual to meet Lord Philippe, a letter arrived by a strange servant from the castle, informing me that he was so extremely ill he could not leave his room; and therefore requested, as the length of his confinement was uncertain, I would no longer delay returning home on his account.

"Notwithstanding this request, notwithstanding my strong anxiety, my ardent wishes to be again in that dear home, which contained a being more precious to me than existence, I could not bear the idea of departing, till assured he was at least out of danger."

"I wrote to this purpose, and entreated to hear from him as soon as possible. The day wore away, however, without any other tidings from the castle. As I sat, at its close, in a melancholy manner in my little chamber, ruminating over past scenes, and sometimes trying to cheer my heart by anticipating the happiness I should experience in again folding my Geraldine to it, I was suddenly startled by a loud knock at the cottage-door. Full of the idea of receiving a letter from the castle, I was rushing all impatience from the room, when the sound of a strange voice arrested my steps, and I was soon convinced that the man whom my host admitted had no business with me.

"I therefore returned to my seat, and was again sinking into a reverie, when a few words from the next room, which was only divided from mine by a thin partition, completely roused me, and made me, I may say, become all ear.

'Well, Claude (asked my host in a familiar voice), what journey have you been taking this time?'

'The old one (replied Claude); I have been to see my godfather who lives upon the Alps; he always makes me a handsome present when I visit him.'

'So he should, I am sure (said his companion); visiting him must be plaguey troublesome, considering the long and dangerous way you have to go.'

'Who do you think I met travelling that way this morning?' cried Claude.

'I am sure 'tis impossible for me to guess,' replied Josephe, the name of my host.

'No other than our young Lord the Marquis of Montmorenci's son,' said Claude, 'posting away as if the devil was at his heels.'

'Our young Lord! (repeated Josephe in a tone of astonishment), no, I'll be sworn you did not meet him; why, man, he is at this very moment confined to his room by a violent illness.'

'Well or ill, I say I met him (vociferated Claude, as if angry at being doubted), and your brother Lafroy along with him.'

'Your eyes certainly deceived you (said Josephe); what in the name of wonder should induce him to report he was ill except he really was so, or bring him the way you said you met him.'

'I certainly cannot assign a reason for his pretending illness (replied Claude); but I can give a very sufficient one for his journey to the Alps; has Lafroy never informed you?'

'No, never.'

'Ah, he is a close dog, he could have told you a great deal if he had had a mind, for he is quite in the confidence of his master. But to my story; you must know near the cottage of my godfather there stands a fine old castle, now inhabited by an Irishman of distinction, who was driven from his own country by some troubles in the state. On the two daughters of this nobleman the daughter of my godfather attends. About five months ago I was at his cottage. One evening, as the sun was setting, I attended him to collect his flocks which fed upon the heights surrounding the castle, and pen them for the night. While thus employed, from the court of the castle the most enchanting music stole upon mine ear: delighted with the sounds, I instantly paused, and turned to the place from whence they proceeded.'

'Tis the two young ladies you hear (said my companion); they both sing, and play upon the lute divinely; it often does my old heart good to hear them.'

'Lord (cried I), I wish I could have a peep at them.'

'You may easily gratify that wish (replied he), the wall about the court is broke in many places.'

'I instantly flew to it, and beheld two of the most lovely creatures imagination can conceive. After feasting my eyes some minutes, I carelessly cast them upon two gentlemen who sat beside them; guess the astonishment of that moment when I discovered one of those gentlemen who sat beside them; guess the astonishment of that moment when I discovered one of those gentlemen to be the Count St. Julian.

'I directly hastened to my godfather; informed him of the discovery I had made; and enquired from him whether he knew what had brought the Count to the castle.

'He smiled, and shook his head significantly. 'Chance (said he), first brought him to it, and inclination made him afterwards repeat the visit; he is a great friend to the family; he has lately provided a husband for the younger daughter.'

'He was secure of the eldest himself then I suppose (said I); for faith I think no man of any feeling could give up one handsome girl till sure of another to supply her place.'

'My godfather smiled; and some expressions dropped from him which excited my curiosity: but I questioned him in vain; like your brother Lafroy, he was a close codger, and refused to gratify me. I then determined to apply to his daughter: she came generally every morning to pay her duty to him. If a real woman (said I to myself), she will be glad of an opportunity to communicate a secret. I accordingly watched for her the next day: she came as I expected; but, instead of letting her enter the cottage, I prevailed on her to take a walk with me. I soon introduced the subject I wished to converse about.

'Your father, my dear (said I), informs me that my Lord is a great friend to the family you live with.'

'Ah, Mr. Claude (cried she), those who imagine he is a friend to the family are sadly mistaken; it would have been a happy thing he had never entered it.'

'Why, my soul (asked I), has he stole away the heart of one of the young ladies?'

She shook her head;—"'It does not become me to tell family secrets.'

'No, to be sure (said I), not to strangers; but to a person you know so well as you do me, there is not the least harm in the world in telling them.'

'Ah, if you could but make me believe that, I could tell you something would astonish you.'

'When a woman once begins to waver, we are sure of our point: I soon prevailed on my little companion to open her whole budget.

'Tis now some months (said she), since the Count St. Julian first entered Lord Dunlere's castle. Returning from Italy, he met with an accident near it which induced my Lord to offer him a lodging till able to continue his journey. The moment he and my lady Geraldine beheld each other, they were mutually smitten; and, in consequence of this attachment, they both devised a thousand excuses for his staying in the castle long after he was expected to leave it. At length he departed. Never shall I forget the wailing and weeping his going occasioned; my Lady Geraldine became but the shadow of herself, and wandered about like a ghost.

'One morning she called me into her chamber; and, after locking her door, 'My dear Blanche (said she with a flood of tears), I am now going to place the greatest confidence in you; a confidence which must convince you I think you a prudent, sensible, clever girl, one quite above the lower class.'

'I was quite confused by her praises, and could only courtesy, and say I hoped she never would have reason to repent any confidence she reposed in me.

'She then proceeded to say that the Count St. Julian had not only engaged her affections, but injured her honour; and that she was now in a situation that must soon expose her to open disgrace.

'I dare not tell my father or my sister (cried she); counsel me therefore, my dearest girl, how to act; though, alas! I have little hope that any advice will benefit me, as the silence of the Count since his departure inclines me to believe he will never fulfil his promises of marriage.'

'You must try him, Ma'am (said I as soon as I had recovered from my astonishment, and collected my wits together); write him one of the most cutting letters you can think of; and tell him you expect, as a man and a gentleman, he will make you immediate reparation for his injuries, by giving you his hand in marriage.'

'She accordingly wrote a letter to this purpose; and, at the expected time, an answer arrived, in which he informed her he still loved her to distraction; but that as to marriage, it was quite out of the question on account of his father, who would, he knew, if he so united himself, deprive him of all provision. He bid her, however, keep up her spirits, adding he would soon be at the castle; and had devised a scheme for preserving her from the indignation of her father, should her situation be discovered to him.

'Well, you may be convinced, we waited most impatiently for his arrival. He came soon after the receipt of his letter, accompanied by a very fine young man, the same you saw with him in the court last night; and my young lady was all anxiety till the scheme he had hinted at was disclosed to her. A villainous scheme, you will say,—no other than to have a marriage made up between my young lady and Monsieur Lausane, his companion.

'He is a natural son of my father's (said he to my lady; for I was in a closet adjoining the chamber in which they sat, and consequently heard all their conversation); and I mean, as soon as I come into possession of my paternal fortune, to make a handsome provision for him; this I shall mention to the Earl as a means of inducing him to consent to your union with him—an union, by which you will be guarded against your father's indignation should he ever discover our connexion, as he must then know the dreadful consequences that would attend its exposure;—an union also, which will give me a pretext, from our relationship, of visiting you much oftener than I could otherwise do.

'It was long, however, ere he could prevail on my poor lady to agree to his proposal; and nothing at last could have extorted her consent to it, but the hope of being shielded by her marriage from the rage of her father. Her consent once obtained, every thing was soon settled according to the Count's wishes. It was with difficulty (continued Blanche) I could prevail on myself to keep what I knew a secret from Monsieur Lausane; it grieved my very heart and soul to think so fine a young man should be so imposed upon.

'But, Blanche (said I), did you not say that Lady Geraldine was in a certain situation, and will not a premature birth open the eyes of her husband to the deceit that has been practised on him?'

'Oh, we have guarded against all that (replied she); about the time she expects to be confined, the Count St. Julian is to feign illness at the castle of Montmorenci, and write to his brother to pay him a visit. He is then to keep him there till my lady is recovered, and the child sent out of the way, whom he has promised to provide for.'

"How shall I describe the feelings that rose in my soul (proceeded St. Julian), as I listened to this horrible narrative? Not a doubt could I entertain of its authenticity; every recollected circumstance—the sudden friendship of my brother, notwithstanding the prejudices instilled into his mind against me by his father—the ready compliance of Lady Geraldine with my wishes, notwithstanding the short time we had been acquainted, and her knowing that I was an outcast from the house which should have sheltered me,—altogether proved that I was a dupe to the most perfidious art.

"Yes (I exclaimed within myself), my credulous nature has been imposed upon; and those whom I most loved, most trusted, have undone me. In the language of a poet of a sister country I might have said—

Two, two such,

(Oh! there's no further name), two such to me,

To me, who lock'd my soul within your breast,

Had no desire, no joy, no life, but you.

——————————————I had no use,

No fruit of all, but you;—a friend and mistress

Was all the world could give. Oh!—

————how could you betray

This tender heart, which, with an instant fondness,

Lay lull'd between your bosom, and there slept

Secure of injur'd faith. I can forgive

A foe, but not a mistress and a friend;

Treason is there in its most horrid shape

Where trust is greatest, and the soul resign'd

Is stabb'd by her own guards.

"I could only restrain myself till the narrative was concluded. The tempest in my bosom then broke forth, and, rushing into the next room, with the gripe, the fury of a lion, I seized the narrator, and bid him, as he valued his existence, instantly prove or disprove the truth of his assertions."

'By what right (cried he), do you desire this?'

"By the right of Lausane,' vociferated I, in a voice of thunder.

'Lausane! (repeated he, looking steadily upon me); ah! 'tis but too true; I now recollect your features. Well, it can't be help'd; the mischief is out, and there's an end of it. If it will give you any satisfaction, master, I will solemnly swear, that what I have told my friend Josephe here, I heard from Blanche, and she, I am sure, would not utter a falsehood; people seldom commit a sin without intending to derive some benefit from it; and what could accrue to her by defaming her mistress? I will also swear, that I met your brother this morning ascending the Alps; and that, while I was at the cottage of my godfather, Blanche told me that you had left home, and that her lady had lain in two days after your departure of a fine boy, who had been removed by her to a neighbouring cottage.'

"Ere I go in quest of vengeance (I cried, relinquishing my hold), I will ascertain whether the Count has left the castle.'

"I muffled myself up in a large cloak, and directly hastened to it. I thought my heart would have burst my bosom while waiting to have my enquiry answered.

'My young Lord, (said the porter) departed this morning, attended but by one servant; where he is gone, or when he will return is not known.'

"Never will he return to these walls,' exclaimed I inwardly as I turned from them.

"I re-entered the cottage merely to procure a horse from Josephe, in order to expedite my journey to the foot of the Alps; he tried to make me delay it, and endeavoured to allay my fury; I cursed him for the effort.

'You only aggravate the poor gentleman's feelings (said Claude to him); Lord! who can wonder at his being enraged at the vile imposition practised upon him? for my part, I think him so injured, that I am determined he shall have my services, if he will accept them, to the last drop of my blood; I would assist him in punishing his perfidious brother.'

"I extended my hand. I accept your proffered services (cried I); not to punish my deceiver, but to trace out for me every minute particular of his guilt, ere my vengeance falls upon him.

"He accordingly accompanied me to the Alps. We travelled with almost incredible expedition, and the second evening I found myself near that spot which but the day before I had thought of as a paradise. Unable to support the sight of it, I stopped, and, seating myself in the cavity of a rock, desired Claude to proceed, and gather what particulars he could from Blanche concerning the visit of the Count; charging him, at the same time, carefully to conceal my return from her, also my knowledge of the base deceit which had been practised on me, lest her regard for her mistress should make her inform her of the whole, and thus, in all probability, by putting her and my betrayer upon their guard, baffle the revenge I meant to take—a revenge which to hear of will make you tremble! I resolved on murdering my brother! after which it was my determination to hasten to the castle, acquaint the Earl with the baseness of his daughter, and terminate my existence in her sight.

"To his own ingenuity I left Claude to account for his unexpected return to the Alps; the minutes seemed hours till he came back to me.

"At length he appeared, and with a face full of importance—'Well, master (said he), I have seen Blanche. I shall not tire you by mentioning the excuses I made to her for my sudden appearance; suffice it to say, they were received in the manner I wished.'

"The Count," cried I impatiently.

'Arrived a few hours ago (said he), and is now in the chamber of Lady Geraldine, to which he was privately conducted by Blanche, who, in consequence of her lady's letter, was on the watch for him.

'She assigned a reason for what appeared so strange to us, namely, his having requested you to return home. He told Lady Geraldine he did so, fearful that, if you longer continued in the vicinity of Montmorenci Castle, you would discover his absence from it, and well knowing that here he could be concealed from you. He is now about leaving her for the night.'

"And whither does he go?' cried I, starting from my seat.

'He is to lodge in the cottage where his child is, (replied Claude); it stands upon yonder acclivity, and this is the way to it.'

"Enough (said I), retire.'

"He began to entreat permission to remain with me, but I hastily interrupted him. "I must not be opposed (cried I); my conversation with my brother will not admit of witnesses. farewell! retire to repose, and accept of my thanks and purse for your services."

'Neither, master (replied he); what I did was not from interested motives, but a pure wish of having perfidy punished.'

"I flung away the purse he had rejected, and motioned him to depart.

"The moment he was out of sight, I drew forth a dagger with which I always travelled, the one which the father of Elvira had given me, and the same with which I had attempted my life in the forest of Montmorenci; and, stationing myself behind a projecting fragment of rock, impatiently watched for my destined victim. The place in which I stood, seemed particularly adapted for a scene of horror: it was a little gloomy vale, sunk between stupendous mountains, bleak and bare of vegetation, crowned with snow, and full of frightful cavities, through which the wind grumbled with a dreadful violence. At last Lord Philippe appeared. Notwithstanding the detestation with which I then regarded him, never had he appeared so interesting to me; his pace was mournful and slow; and ever and anon he paused, and looked back, as if, inspired by some prophetic spirit, he was bidding what he knew would be a last adieu to the mansion he had quitted. As he drew near, I saw his cheek was pale, and the traces of tears upon it:—tears, said I, which he has shed over his Geraldine, at the relation of the dangers she has passed.

"When he was within a yard of my concealment, I sprung out. He started back astonished, and surveyed me for a minute with that kind of expression which seemed to say he could scarcely credit the evidence of his eyes; then approaching me with extended arms, he exclaimed, 'Ah, my brother! what—'

"I interrupted him; 'I disclaim the title (cried I, stepping up to him, and rudely seizing his arm); villain! I am well acquainted with thy perfidy; and this to thy heart to reward thee for it!'"

Madeline at those words instinctively caught hold of her father. She panted for breath, and her changing colour showed her strong emotions.

"My fears were but too just (said St. Julian); I was almost convinced my tale of horror would overcome your gentle nature."

'No, no (cried Madeline, after the pause of a few minutes), my fortitude will not again droop, for I have now surely heard the worst; go on therefore, my dearest father.'

"The unhappy Philippe instantly fell, (resumed St. Julian); he writhed for a moment in agony, and then expired with a deep groan.

"There is something dreadful in the sight of human blood to a heart not entirely callous. As his flowed at my feet, a faintness stole over me, and I leaned for support against the projecting fragment which had before concealed me. The scene in the forest of Montmorenci rushed upon my recollection. 'He could not bear to behold my blood (said I), and yet I spilled his without mercy!—Mercy! (repeated I starting), what mercy should I have extended to him who preserved my life but to entail dishonour upon it? I have taken but a just revenge (continued I)'; and my spirits were reanimated by the idea.

"Casting a look of savage triumph upon the body, I darted across it, and fled almost with the velocity of lightning towards the castle. As I was entering the court, I met a holy man, who lived in a neighbouring monastery, the confessor of the Earl and his family, coming out; I would have pushed by him, but he caught my arm.

'Alas, my son! (said he, in an accent of pity) your disordered looks too plainly prove your knowledge of the sad event which has happened in the castle during your absence. How unfortunate that you could not be found yesterday when your brother wrote to inform you of it, and request your company hither; your presence might have mitigated his transports.'

"A convulsive laugh broke from me at the idea of deception having also been practised upon the old man; yet, at the next instant, it struck me as something strange that he should know of my brother's visit to the castle.

"You speak enigmatically, holy father (said I); I know nothing of any letter my brother wrote, nor of any sad event that— — —.'

"I suddenly paused;—the dying groan of Philippe again, me—thought, sounded in my ear, and stopped my utterance.

'If the meaning of my words is incomprehensible (said the monk, regarding me with mingled horror and surprise), so is also the meaning of your looks: explain what has disordered you.'

"First say (cried I), what you know about my brother's visit to the castle; explain the reason of it."

'Concealment is no longer necessary (said he); the Count came to the castle to receive the last sigh of his wife.'

"His wife!" repeated I, starting and staring wildly.

'Yes, the lovely Elenora.'

"Elenora the wife of Philippe! no, 'tis not to be believed (exclaimed I); I see (endeavouring to shake him from me) you are but a sanctified villain, and in league with the rest to deceive me!"

'I know not what you mean (said he); I know nothing of any deceit that has been practised on you. Elenora was, by the holy cross I swear, (and he touched that which hung beside him the wife of your brother.)'

"I could no longer doubt his truth; a confused idea of treachery, of a snare having been spread to involve my unhappy brother and self in destruction, darted into my mind; all hell seemed opening to my view; I grew giddy, and would have fallen, but for the supporting arm of the monk.

'You are ill (said he); let me call for assistance.'

"No (replied I, exerting myself), I am now better. Tell me, ere I enter the castle, what has happened since my departure from it; and why the marriage of the Count with Elenora was concealed from me."

'It never was the wish of your brother to have it concealed from you,' said the monk, sitting down on the pavement, where I had seated myself unable to stand.

"'Tis now near a twelvemonth (continued he), since it took place; the ceremony was performed by me. The accident which introduced your brother to the castle you already know: almost from the first moment he and Lady Elenora beheld each other, they became mutually enamoured; the watchful eyes of a parent easily discovered their attachment; and the Earl soon demanded an explanation of your brother's intentions.

'It was his most ardent wish, the Count said, to be united to Lady Elenora; but it was a wish, he candidly confessed, which he durst not reveal to his father, whose avarice and ambition he knew, notwithstanding his extravagant partiality for him, would forbid his union with any one who could not increase the consequence, and add to the opulence of his house.

'Upon hearing this, the Earl, though gently, blamed him for having encouraged a tenderness for his daughter, and explicitly desired him to leave the castle. The Count, instead of promising to do so, fell at his feet, and besought him not to banish him from the woman he adored. 'Suffer me to marry her (cried he), and whilst my father lives to conceal my marriage.'

'The pride and rectitude of the Earl for a long time resisted this entreaty; but the repeated solicitations of the half-distracted St. Julian, and the tears of his daughter, at length extorted a consent to their union.

'On St. Julian's return to the habitation of his father, he met with you. Soon after that meeting, he planned a scheme for again visiting his lovely bride; you were the companion of his journey. Ere your appearance at the castle, the family were apprised of your intended visit and connexion with him.

'In his letter to the Earl, acquainting him with those particulars, he also said—'Against the loveliness of your Elenora I have guarded my Lausane, by informing him she was already engaged; but to the beauties of Geraldine I hope he will be as susceptible, as I wish her to be to his merits.'

'You came; and his wishes were accomplished by the attachment that grew between you.

'The Count mentioned to Lord Dunlere his intention of revealing his marriage to you; but the Earl opposed it. A long intercourse with the world had rendered him suspicious; and he feared your knowing of the affair, lest you should betray it to the Marquis, from a hope of benefiting by the resentment you would excite against your brother: 'and little pleasure (added he), should I derive from having one daughter enriched at the expense of the other.'

'Though the Count would not act in opposition to him, he resented the suspicion he harboured of you. 'In doubting the honour of Lausane (said he), you are guilty of the greatest injustice; no nature can be more noble, more pure than his; and I am confident he would sooner lose his life than harm me.'

"Oh, Philippe!" I groaned aloud.

"The monk looked earnestly at me. 'You are ill my son,' said he.

"Dear father (cried I), do not mind me; I am all impatience for you to go on."

'About the time you were married to Lady Geraldine, the Count beheld a prospect of an increase to his felicity; Elenora was with child. In pursuance of the Earl's advice, it was settled that when the period for her confinement arrived, your brother, pretending illness, should invite you to see him, and keep you away till she was recovered. It was also settled, that the child should be nursed at a neighbouring cottage, and when weaned, be brought back to the castle as the deserted orphan of some poor peasant.

'About ten days ago, almost immediately after your departure, Elenora lay in of a lovely boy. She continued as well as could be expected for a few days; a violent fever then seized her, and in a short time her life was despaired of. She retained her senses, and, sensible of her danger, begged her husband might be sent for, that she might have the pleasure of presenting her child to him, and breathing her last sigh in his arms.

'An express was accordingly dispatched; Geraldine and I met him upon his arrival: on not seeing you, as she expected, with him, she wildly demanded where you were. He replied, that the moment he had finished perusing the Earl's letter, he had sent it to you with a few lines, imploring your pardon for having had any concealment from you, and requesting your immediate attendance; but, to his great mortification, you were absent from the cottage; nor did the owner of it expect you back for a considerable time, as you had told him, he said, that you were going out upon a long ramble; to wait for your return was therefore, in his situation, impossible.

'He was conducted to the chamber of his Elenora; the agonies of death had already seized her; and he arrived but in time to receive the last sigh of her fleeting spirit. She has been dead some hours, but it is only a few minutes ago since he could be torn from her remains; nor could he have then been forced from them, but by the mention of his child; he is gone to weep over the poor babe, and I am now about following him.'

"You will wonder, no doubt, my dearest Madeline, how I could listen with calmness to this recital; you will wonder that I did not start into instant madness, and with a desperate hand, terminate my wretched existence; but horror had frozen up my blood, and suspended every faculty; my silence astonished the monk, and he looked steadily at me. At length I spoke—'Father (said I, in a hollow voice), do you not believe that evil spirits are sometimes let loose upon this world, to plague the sons of men, and tempt them to destruction?'

'Heaven forbid I should think so (he replied); the Almighty has declared his creatures never shall be tempted beyond their strength; 'tis not the ministers of darkness, but their own impetuous passions which hurry them to destruction.'

"I started up; 'farewell! (I cried); remember me in your prayers, and bid Geraldine not forget me in her orisons.'

'Whither are you going?' said he.

"To join my brother," replied I.

"No doubt I looked wild. He seized my arm—

'Your brother!' repeated he.

"Yes, to accompany his soul in its flight from this world.—His soul! (I repeated, starting and shrieking aloud with agony) Oh, no! heaven opens to receive his spirit, but the deepest abyss in hell now yawns for mine!"

'Some dreadful mystery lurks beneath those words (cried he); tell me, my son, what has distressed you?'

To tell you my distress is useless, since you cannot relieve it.'

'Though not able to remove, I might at least be able to mitigate it,' said he.

"No; except you could re-animate the dead;—except you could raise Philippe from the bloody turf, and bid him live again!"

"I tried to disengage myself, but he held me fast: in the conflict my strength and senses failed, and I fell fainting to the earth.

"When I recovered, I found myself in the hall of the castle, supported by my wife and the monk, and surrounded by the domestics, amidst whom the Earl stood. The minute I regained my senses, the monk dismissed the servants, and none remained with me but Geraldine, her father, and himself.

"He then besought me to reveal the cause of my distress. Geraldine and the Earl joined in his supplication. I raised my head from his shoulder, and withdrew myself from the arms of my wife. I knelt down; the fury of my soul had subsided.—

"Oh! my friends (I cried, while tears gushed from me), I am unworthy of your tenderness—I am unworthy of the light of heaven—I am the destroyer of your peace—the murderer of my brother!"

'Impossible!' cried Geraldine, whilst the deadly paleness of her cheek proved that her heart felt not the doubt her tongue implied.

'He raves,' said the Earl.

'Alas! (exclaimed the monk) I fear he utters a fatal truth. Be explicit (continued he, laying his hand upon my head), and sport not with the feelings of your friends.'

"He raised me to a seat. He again urged me to speak; and in faltering accents I began my tale of horror. As I ended it, Geraldine dropped, to all appearance lifeless, at my feet. I threw myself beside her. Oh, Philippe! (I cried) is the life of my wife required as an expiation of my crime?'

"Her wretched father hung over her.—'She dies! (said he); childless and forlorn I am doomed to descend to the grave!'

"The monk was alone collected; he raised her from the ground, and chafed her hands and temples; in a few minutes she showed signs of returning life. At length she opened her eyes: I was the first object they fell upon. 'Unhappy man! (she sighed) how could you doubt me?'

"Thus humbly kneeling, let me implore forgiveness for doing so (said I). Oh! amply, amply shall you be avenged; I fly this instant to throw myself into the arms of offended justice; and, by an ignominious death, atone for my wrongs to you and Philippe."

'And destroy your wife and her unborn infant,' cried she.

"This was the first time I had heard there was a prospect of my becoming a father; an idea of the felicity which but a few days before I should have received from such an intimation rushed upon my mind; and I sunk groaning to the earth at the contrast I now drew between it and my present feelings.

'Do not, by yielding to this wretchedness (said the monk), aggravate the misery of your wife and her father; 'tis the guilty heart, not the guilty hand, my son (proceeded he, trying to compose my mind), which merits the vengeance of heaven; your hand, not your heart, is guilty: the vilest arts could alone have turned it against your brother; and upon the contriver of such diabolical schemes, his blood must certainly rest; compose yourself, therefore, and you may again experience some degree of happiness.'

"I started up; 'repeat that word no more (cried I with fierceness); happiness and I must henceforth be as distant from each other as heaven and hell.'

'Promise (said Geraldine kneeling before me, and laying her cold and trembling hands upon me), promise that you will be guided by the holy father, and try to save a life upon which mine depends.'

"I snatched her to my breast. And can you wish to have the being saved (I asked), who doubted your purity?—Ah! surely the severest punishment is not more than he merits for having done so: yet, as you desire, he will act; here my friends (I continued, relinquishing her), I stand, the veriest wretch upon earth; death would be a release from torture; but do with me as you please; as you wish, I will either try to live, or prepare to die.'

'My son (said the monk), you must retire immediately to your chamber: night draws on apace; as soon as it is dark, I will repair to you, and inform you of the plan I have conceived for your avoiding the treachery by which I fear you are surrounded.'

'May I not accompany him?' said Geraldine, catching my hand as he was leading me from the room.

'No; I wish for your presence in order to consult with you as to the best mode of securing his safety.' This reason for preventing her attendance conquered all opposition.

"I shall not dwell upon the minutes I passed alone. The monk came according to his promise as soon as it was dark; he opened the door softly, and held a glimmering lamp in his hand. 'Follow me, my son,' said he.

"I implicitly obeyed, and pursued his cautious steps through winding passages, and down innumerable descents of steps. At length we stopped, and I found myself in a spacious and gloomy vault.

"Have you changed your mind (demanded I, after looking round me for a minute); have you at last thought me deserving of punishment, and brought me hither as to a prison."

'You wrong me by the supposition (said he); I have brought you to this vault but to secure you from danger; your destruction I have no doubt was intended as well as your brother's; the motive for such an intention I cannot conceive, nor perhaps may never be able to discover. Blanche has disappeared: I have every reason to believe she has joined that villain Claude. The moment I returned from your chamber, I sent for her, determined on trying to extort from her a confession of her guilt, but she was just gone out. On hearing this, I directly repaired to her father, a simple shepherd, long known to me, and one whom I have ever found conscientiously just in all his dealings. I enquired for his daughter; he had not seen her the whole day he said. I then in a careless manner asked him if he knew a person of the name of Claude?—No, he instantly replied.

'From his cottage I hastened to the valley where you said your brother had fallen; but the body was gone. Struck by a circumstance so strange, I stood as it were transfixed to the spot for a few minutes; at last I was turning away, when deep groans pierced my ear, and made me again pause.'

"As the monk uttered those words, I shrieked aloud—'Oh, God! (I cried), is it possible?—could I be mistaken?—does Philippe live?'

"The monk shook his head; 'would to heaven he did! (said he). But to proceed; the shades of night fell thick around me, and prevented my seeing to any distance; the groans still continued;—in the name of God (cried I), I conjure you, whoever you are, from whom those groans proceed, to speak, and direct me to your assistance.'

'Ah! father (said a voice, which I instantly recollected to be that of Lafroy, your brother's valet) heaven surely sent you hither.'

'Directed by his voice, I went up to him and found him sitting behind a low mound at a little distance from the spot on which I had first heard him. I enquired into the cause of his present situation; he burst into tears—'Ah! father (said he), do you not know what has happened? do you not know of the horrid murder that has been committed?—Ah! who could have thought that the hand of a brother could have perpetrated so cruel a deed!'

'I was wounded to the heart (said the monk) at hearing he was acquainted with the dreadful affair. I asked him what he knew concerning it.'

'I left the castle (answered he), a considerable time before my Lord, in order to apprise the nurse of his intended visit to the child. Tired at last of waiting for him, or rather apprehensive, from his long stay, that he was taken ill, and could not come, I was returning to the castle to terminate my suspense, when, in this very spot, I was suddenly stopped by surprise at seeing Monsieur Lausane a few yards before me, with a dagger in his hand, and an expression of the most violent rage in his face. I will not deny that I was panic-struck and unable to move even when I saw my Lord approaching. Oh! never shall I cease to regret my want of courage; though, alas! nothing but the greatest, the quickest exertion of it could have saved his life; for scarcely had his brother cast his eyes upon him, ere he stabbed him to the heart! Horror overcame me at that instant, and I fainted away, nor recovered my senses till a few minutes ago: when I recovered, I had not however power, or rather resolution to move; I feared beholding or stumbling over the body of my dear and murdered Lord.'

'I dreaded Lafroy's testimony against you (continued the monk); I therefore endeavoured to extenuate your conduct, and excite his pity by relating the artifices which had been practised on you. What I said had the desired effect; he no longer, he declared, considered you guilty, and, of his own accord, took a solemn oath never to give information against you.

'I asked him whether he had any knowledge of Claude, and also whether he did not think his brother in league with him? He had no personal knowledge of the villain, he replied; all he knew concerning him was that he was a vine-dresser, who lived a little way from his brother's cottage. As to his brother, in the most impassioned manner he protested a heart more noble, more humane than his never lodged within a breast; consequently it could not be supposed he had entered into so horrible a plot.

'I enquired whether he could form any conjecture about the first contrivers of it? None, he replied in a solemn manner. I then told him of my not being able to find the body: this renewed his grief, and by the first dawn of day, he said he would endeavour to discover it. As to Claude, he agreed with me there was little probability of any search after him being successful.

'I bid him return to the cottage, nor come to the castle unless sent for. I think his fidelity may be depended on; but I shall not put it to the test by entrusting him with your situation.

'The domestics are at present ignorant of the cause of your disorder, as well as of the death of your brother; there is no doubt but what they will soon be acquainted with the latter—they may then perhaps suspect the former; there is no knowing how they would act. I shall therefore, as soon as I leave you, inform them that you have been compelled to quit the castle, in order to attend a most particular friend to Italy; this will change the search, should one be made after you.'

"But think you not (cried I), that death would be preferable to a confinement here, which will deprive me of the society of all I love?'

'Your confinement here will not subject you to such a loss (he replied); a constant intercourse can easily be kept up between you and your Geraldine; and every thing that can possibly be brought hither for the purpose of adding to your comfort, shall be conveyed by me; the castle-vaults communicate with those belonging to the monastery—I shall therefore have free access at all times to you.'

"I shall no longer dwell upon the conversation that passed between us, neither upon the agonies I fell into on being left alone; pity for Geraldine only prevented me from dashing my desperate brains out.

"The next day the monk came to me sooner than I expected. 'Alas! (exclaimed he as he advanced), the unhappy father of your wife has not yet drained the cup of misery!' I thought of no sorrow but that which the death of Geraldine could occasion. Starting, therefore, I wrung my hands, and cried—'She is dead! my wife is dead, and I have murdered her!'

'No (replied he), 'tis not his Geraldine, but the babe of his departed Elenora he has lost.

'On coming to the castle this morning, I was surprised to see Lafroy just entering the hall before me. I accosted him in rather an angry tone, and asked what had brought him to it without my permission? He soon assigned a sufficient reason for his unexpected appearance. On returning to the cottage, he said he had thrown himself across a bed, where, overcome by grief and fatigue, towards morning he had fallen asleep. 'From my repose (he continued), I was soon roused by piercing shrieks; I instantly jumped up, and darted into the outside room, from whence they proceeded. Here I found the woman of the house alone, and almost in a state of distraction. It was some time ere she could speak and explain the cause of her disorder: at length she said the infant she had received from the castle was stolen whilst she was out milking her goats. That Claude was the author of this new misfortune I could not doubt; and I deemed it my duty to lose no time in informing the Earl of what had happened.'

'Alas! (resumed the monk) it was a heavy stroke to him; through the child he hoped to have received some little consolation for the death of the mother. This very day it was his intention to have written to the Marquis of Montmorenci to acquaint him with the marriage of his son, and implore his protection for the offspring of it; an intention he has now laid aside as unnecessary, except the child is found, to search for whom I have dispatched some agents I can depend upon. The death of your brother is now known throughout the castle; I invented a plausible story for Lafroy to repeat, which he did with little hesitation; and it is believed that your brother fell by the hand of a ruffian belonging to one of the numerous gangs of banditti which infest these mountains. Lafroy sets out this day for the castle of Montmorenci; and has solemnly promised to adhere to my instructions in announcing the death of his lamented master.'

"I asked the monk whether the body of the unfortunate Philippe had been discovered?—he replied in the negative.

"What he told me, if possible, increased my anguish. I then enquired when I should behold my Geraldine?—'At night,' he replied. I counted the tedious moments till she appeared. Ah! how pale, how languid, how different from the Geraldine I had left! She wept bitterly in my arms. 'Oh! my love, (I exclaimed), your tears distract me: yet I cannot wonder at your shedding them; you have reason indeed to weep the hard fate which united you to a murderer!'

'Ah! never, Lausane (said she), shall I lament the fate which bound me to you. Exclusive of your misfortunes, have I not reason to weep for the loss of my Elenora—the sister of my love—the sweet play-fellow of my infancy—the dear, the inestimable friend of my youth? Oh! Lausane, the most exalted prosperity with you could not have silenced my grief on her account.'

"A month passed away without any incident occurring to alarm my friends, and without any determination being formed relative to my future destiny. At the expiration of that time, the monk came to me one night at a very late hour; his countenance was disordered, and for a few minutes he could not speak.

'My son (said he at length), 'tis well that we took the precautions we did.'

"What has happened?" demanded I eagerly.

'To-night (resumed he), as I was returning to the monastery, I heard, from behind a low rock which lies at a little distance from the castle, a low murmur of voices. I paused and listened, for I thought I distinguished your name: I was not mistaken; in about a minute after I stopped, it was repeated. I then crept to the spot determined to run every risk rather than not try to discover any plot that might be forming against you. As I approached, I beheld two men, from whom a projection of the rock concealed me.

'To Italy (said one of them), you say he is gone.—'Tis so reported,' replied the other. 'Well, it shall be my business (again spoke the first), to discover what foundation there is for that report;—earth shall be searched for Lausane; for, whilst he lives, my wishes can never be accomplished.'

'They then walked away (continued the monk), and I hastened back to the castle to consult with your wife and her father about you. We soon agreed that a report of your death could alone, in all probability, save your life. I shall therefore send a young man, whom I can depend upon, to-morrow to the castle, for the purpose of declaring that you are no more. He shall say that in a small town in Italy, from whence he is just returned, he met you; that shortly after that meeting, you were taken ill; and, knowing whither he was bound, in your last moments had requested him to call upon your family, and inform them of your fate.

'This report will put a stop to all enquiries; and, as soon as your Geraldine has lain in, I will assist you in escaping with her to a part of the world where there can be no fear of your ever being discovered. To prevent any suspicion, Geraldine is to declare a resolution of renouncing the world as soon as her child is born; and, under the pretext of entering a cloister, she is to quit the castle: when settled in the manner you wish, the Earl and the infant are to follow.'

"I attempted not to oppose the scheme of the monk; any scheme, indeed, which flattered me with a hope of again enjoying the company of my Geraldine without interruption, was to me acceptable. 'Tis unnecessary to say the anxiety with which she longed for my release from confinement—a confinement which she endeavoured to soften by the most unremitting attentions. Oh! with what agony have I gazed upon this matchless woman in my dreary dungeon! pale, weeping, emaciated, sinking with horror, yet trying to conceal it! Oh! surely the wretch extended upon the rack could not have felt greater tortures than I at those moments experienced.

"The period now arrived for making me a father: my Geraldine did not come near me one entire day, and my heart throbbed with tumultuous fears on her account. The monk came at night; with an eagerness which shook my frame, I enquired for her. 'She is well (said he), but the Earl is indisposed; and, without exciting suspicion in the servants, she could not leave him:'—this excuse pacified me. Another day arrived without bringing her; two more followed, and still I saw her not. I then again began to be alarmed: 'I have been deceived I fear (said I); if Geraldine was well, she would surely have contrived some method for seeing me: to-night, though I rush into the arms of destruction by doing so, I will terminate my suspense.'

"Accordingly as soon as the monk came, I told him my determination of seeing her; he looked shocked, and endeavoured to oppose it; I hastily interrupted him—'No (cried I), I am resolved this night to know whether or not I have been deceived.' As I spoke, I rushed by him; and, with a velocity which mocked pursuit, fled through the intricate passages of the castle, nor stopped till I reached the chamber of Geraldine, which I gained without meeting with a being. I flung open the door—Ah, heavens what a sight presented itself! on the bed lay the lifeless body of Geraldine, already prepared for the grave, and bending over it the almost equally lifeless form of her father! For a minute I stood motionless; then shivering, shrieking with despair, I sprung to the bed, and fell fainting upon the clay-cold bosom of my love!—Short was the privation of my misery. When I revived, I found myself supported by the monk. I shall not attempt to describe the extravagancy of my grief, nor repeat the frantic reproaches I uttered at the deception practised on me. 'Oh! cruel, cruel (I cried), to deny me a last embrace! had the last beam of her eye fallen upon me—had her last sigh been breathed in my arms, I should not have been so wretched!'

'Mistaken idea! (said the monk); your wretchedness must have been augmented by witnessing the agonies of a creature so beloved. It was by her command alone any deception was practised on you. She knew her danger from the moment she lay in; and she knew, if acquainted with it, you would have insisted on seeing her. She charged me, therefore, not to acquaint you with her fate till her interment had taken place. And she charged me also to tell you, that if the love you professed for her was sincere, you would endeavour to combat your affliction, in order to support her father, and supply to her infant the loss she would sustain by her death.'

"Does my child then live?" said I.

'Yes (replied the monk); Providence is kind, and still reserves some blessings for you; forfeit them not by murmuring at its decrees. Look at that miserable old man (continued he, pointing to the Earl), and learn from him a lesson of submission to the will of the Almighty. Think you the anguish which wrings the heart of a husband can exceed that which rends the bosom of a parent? no—believe me it cannot: and yet, notwithstanding his deprivation, no loud complaint, no impious murmur, breaks from him; he bends before the stroke without repining, confident that it proceeds from a hand which cannot err.'

"The language of the venerable man allayed the tempest of my soul: I suffered him to lead me to the Earl, at whose feet I sunk. He turned from the bed, and attempted to speak, but his voice was inarticulate, and tears burst from him. I almost envied him the tears he shed; they relieved his oppression; but mine I could not lighten in that manner; mine was that deep, that silent grief which whispers the o'er-fraught heart, and bids it break.

'They are gone! (said he at length, and extending his trembling hand, he laid it on my shoulder); the pillars of my age are gone! No more shall the soft accents of my children attune my soul to peace! no more shall their bright eyes be opened to inspire me with gladness! the shroud already covers both, and on the cold bed of Elenora my Geraldine will soon be laid!'

"I groaned—grasped his hands convulsively in mine, and, in frantic exclamations, expressed my grief. The monk endeavoured to moderate my transports, and the Earl made a feeble effort to aid him.

'Oh! my son (said he), in pity to me, in pity to your child, exert yourself; let me not descend forlorn to my grave, neither let her be cast without a friend upon the world!'

"I started from the ground, and demanded to see my babe. You were laid in a distant chamber, and the monk instantly proceeded thither to dismiss the attendants, after which he cautiously conducted me to it. Oh, my child! how utterly impossible to describe the feelings which pervaded my breast as I gently raised the mantle that covered your sleeping face, and first cast my eyes upon you! I longed to strain you to my breast; yet I feared to breathe upon you lest I should injure you. I kneeled down, and gazed upon you till my sight grew dim! With difficulty the monk could tear me away. When he did, he would have reconducted me to my dungeon, but I pushed him aside, and again rushed to the chamber of death. For a long time I resisted his entreaties to leave it; nor should I at last, I believe, have been prevailed on to do so, had not the Earl at length bent his knee to me: I could not refuse the kneeling father of my Geraldine; and half-dragged, half-supported by the monk, I descended to my prison. Oh! what a night was that which followed the knowledge of my Geraldine's death: on the damp ground I lay stretched, and the gloomy echoes of the vaults were awakened by my moans!

"But I will not, by any longer dwelling on my feelings, lengthen out my story. It was determined that I should remain in my present situation during the life of the Earl, and, after his decease, seek another asylum with my child. Contrary to all expectation, the Earl survived the loss of his Geraldine two years; during which period no occurrence happened to disturb the melancholy quiet of the castle. As the infirmities of Lord Dunlere prevented his coming to me, I was frequently conducted to him by the monk, who, whilst I continued with him, always remained near the chamber to prevent our being surprised.

"Never shall I forget the last hours I passed with the father of my love at the decline of a lovely summer's day; I was brought to him to pay my then almost daily visit; I found him seated near an open window inhaling the sweet breeze which played around, whilst the setting sun beaming through it, cast a kind of luminous glory on the portraits of his daughters, before which, exhausted by play, you had fallen asleep.

'Ah! (said he, motioning for me to sit near him) how much should I have enjoyed the calmness of this delightful evening, had the blessings I once possessed been still mine! but let me not murmur at the decrees of the Almighty; something whispers to my soul I shall soon be re-united to those I regret. Oh! my son (he continued, observing a tear starting from me), do not too bitterly mourn my death; rather rejoice at what to me will be a release from misery as incurable as unspeakable: sink not beneath affliction at the very period your exertions will be most requisite. Oh! rouse your fortitude for the sake of Geraldine's child, and live to preserve one relic of the noble house of Dunlere! Yes, I repeat, noble was the house of Dunlere: and should any chance ever lead you to the isle in which it stands, you will find I have not been a vain boaster in calling it so. True, its honours are departed, its possessions are divided; but though its glory has set, it has set like yon bright orb, leaving a long tract of radiance behind it: 'tis on the flowery banks of the Shannon you would hear of the fame of my ancestors; 'tis there you would hear that they were ever foremost in the ranks of virtue and of valour; that their arms were never stretched against the feeble, nor their swords stained with the blood of innocence.' His eyes sparkled as he spoke, and the vigour of his soul seemed revived; but, alas! his was but the emanation of a departing spirit.

"Early the ensuing morning, contrary to his usual custom, the monk came to me. His unexpected visit, and agitated countenance, instantly alarmed me; and, in faltering accents, I pronounced your name.

'Your child is well (said he); the Earl too is well—he sleeps in peace; his soul has this day been called to heaven."

"I could not refrain my tears on hearing of this event; in losing the Earl, I lost the friend who soothed my sorrows by talking to me of my Geraldine. 'All then that now remains to me (cried I), of the friends I adored, (the wife I must eternally regret) is a poor helpless infant!'

'For her sake (said the monk), you must now exert yourself. Oh! rouse yourself (he continued, seeing me despondently shake my head), to guard her tender years from the cruelties and snares of the world! Ah, let not the sweet blossom, which gives so early a promise of perfection, fade untimely for want of a paternal shelter!'

"By degrees his language re-animated me to exertion, and we began to arrange plans for the future. He enquired to what part of the globe I was inclined to bend my steps? My broken spirits, I told him, rendered me, not only unwilling, but unable, to acquire new habits. I had, therefore, an unconquerable aversion to any strange country; and thought, from being so little known in my own, that I might, particularly as the story of my death was credited, remain in it with safety. The monk expressed his regret at my disinclination to quit France, but did not attempt to oppose it. After some consideration he mentioned the place he had come from, as a situation well calculated for retirement. I was enamoured of it from his description; and he assured me he would dispatch a confidential person that very day to procure a residence in it for me. He had already, he said, prepared the servants for dismission; and, before others came to supply their place, from the real owner of the castle, who had only lent it to the Earl as a temporary asylum, "my messenger (said he), will be returned, and every thing prepared for your departure. I have (continued he), prevented all enquiries as to the destination of your child, by declaring her solely committed to my charge: and when the hour for your quitting the castle approaches, I shall send the woman who now takes care of her after the other domestics.'

"Every thing succeeded according to our wishes. At the expected time the messenger arrived, after having taken the cottage for me in which you were brought up, and I set out for it a few days after the interment of the Earl. At the moment I was bidding a last adieu to the castle, the monk put you into my arms in order to revive my resolution, which he saw drooping. 'Tis said that our first parents lingered as they were quitting paradise; so I lingered as I was leaving what to me had been a paradise—so I paused and cast my tearful eyes upon it. With difficulty the monk could prevail on me to proceed; he insisted on accompanying me to the place, about half a league from the castle, where a guide and mules were stationed for me. As we proceeded thither, he exhorted me to patience and submission to the Divine will. Our farewell was solemn and affecting; I strained him to my breast, and attempted to express my gratitude for all his kindness. 'Oh! my son (cried the holy man, while tears bedewed his venerable face), I do not merit such thanks; I but performed my duty in the services I rendered you and the family of the Earl; for am I not the servant of a God, who pities the frailties of his creatures, and pours balm upon the wounds which his justice sees proper to inflict?' He promised to keep up a constant correspondence with me. 'When I cease to write (said he), you may be convinced that either my faculties have failed me, or—I am no more.'

"Our journey commenced at night; the ensuing day we lay by in an obscure cottage, and the following night reached our habitation. My domestic arrangements were soon made. I changed my name; and, from the retirement of my house, and its being entirely out of the beaten track, had not a fear of being discovered. Here had my bosom been free from the pangs of conscience, I might again have experienced some small degree of peace; but horror and remorse had taken possession of me, and the spirit of the murdered Philippe continually haunted my steps; life was so great a burden, that often should I have been tempted to raise a desperate hand against it but for your sake.

"To hide from you an anguish which I could not at times suppress, have I frequently wandered away to the wildest and most forlorn spots in our neighbourhood. No weather, no circumstance, could at these periods prevent those rambles; the dews of summer, the rains of winter, the closing hour of day, the midnight one of darkness were alike disregarded by me. Oh! how often have I stretched myself upon the damp earth, whilst the bleak winds of winter have whistled round me, to deprecate the wrath of Philippe's angry spirit: 'I plead not on my own account (I have cried), Oh! my brother, 'tis for the sake of my child I plead; in pity to her let not the thunders of vengeance burst upon my head! in pity to her, let me sink without infamy to my grave, that, as she bends over it, she may sooth the sorrows of her heart by saying, My father was virtuous, and his memory shall live for ever.'

"When I told you I would at some period or other elucidate the mysteries of my life, I said so but for the purpose of allaying your suspicions, hoping that, in consequence of such a promise, you would no longer imagine I had any dreadful secrets to disclose.

"Exclusive of the misery I felt from conscious guilt, I felt a considerable portion also from reflecting on the distresses to which, in all probability, you would be exposed after my death, as I could not hope that the farm would then, under the superintendence of a less interested person, yield such profits as it had before done; and I knew the small remainder of your grandfather's wealth, which the monk had deposited in my hands, and which I had most carefully husbanded, would be quite inadequate to your support.

"From this uneasiness I was relieved by our blessed friend the Countess de Merville. I should previously have told you of her seeing your mother; the visit I paid her on my way to Montmorenci Castle, was discovered by her guardian, and awakened his apprehensions. He wished to unite her to his son; and, ignorant of my situation, he imagined I had come back to the neighbourhood for the purpose of disappointing that wish, and profiting by the ascendancy he knew I had over her: he therefore, in order to baffle what he supposed were my designs, immediately determined on taking her to Italy. As he did not assign his real motive for this sudden journey, of course he received no explanation from her relative to me. They stopped for refreshment near the castle, and she contrived to escape to it to pay a visit to my wife; a visit, however, little attended to by Geraldine, who was then nearly distracted by the danger of her sister.

"In Italy the Countess first saw the Count de Merville, a French nobleman of amiable manners and illustrious descent; reason had conquered her hopeless passion, and in his arms she gladly sought a shelter from the tyranny of her guardian. They remained abroad some years after their marriage; and when, on their return to France, they stopped at the castle for the purpose of enquiring after me and mine, they could only receive a confused account of the sorrows and death of the family from an old woman who then took care of the mansion.

"To the Countess, on our unexpected meeting, I imparted all the particulars which I have related to you. She heard them with horror, grief, and astonishment; and, her emotions a little abating, bitterly regretted my not having applied to her friendship for protection; the reproaches she uttered for my not having done so, I at length stopped by reminding her of the danger which would have attended an application.

"She told me of the marriage of her daughter, and her connexion in consequence of it, with the House of Montmorenci. 'But though allied now in some degree to the Marquis (cried she), I never could prevail on myself to see him, so abhorrent to my soul has his cruelty to you and your mother made him: yet did I imagine that I could, by personally imploring his protection for you and your child, obtain it, I would instantly conquer my repugnance to an interview; but I am well convinced, that all supplications for justice would be unavailing, as I am confidently assured by those I cannot doubt, that he execrates the memory of those whom he has injured.'

'How much was she deceived when she believed that assurance! (exclaimed Madeline); my grandfather's acknowledging you as his rightful heir almost the moment he discovered your residence, proves he spoke truth when he assured us that his penitence for the injuries he had committed was extreme, and that his soul rejoiced at an opportunity of doing justice. The unworthy husband and father-in-law of her daughter were, I fear, the wretches who imposed upon her. But I interrupt your narrative.'

"The Countess (resumed St. Julian), assured me that, since her child was to be enriched by my birthright, she would take care to guard my daughter against the ills of poverty. How this generous intention was frustrated you best know.

"You may imagine I was not a little confounded when, on arriving at the castle, the first object almost I beheld was Lafroy: the alarm of my soul, which my countenance I believe too faithfully depicted, he however tried to dissipate by a secret look, and a slight pressure of his hand upon his heart, as if to assure me of his fidelity.

"At night, when I was undressing, he entered my apartment—'Pardon my intrusion, my Lord (said he), but I could not refrain from coming to express my joy at seeing you, as I may say, risen from the grave; for the monk assured me you were dead. He might have confided in me; I pledged a solemn oath never to betray you; and, though but a servant, I have ever been taught to consider a promise as sacred.'

"Excuse the caution of old age, Lafroy, (replied I); 'twas not by my desire the monk deceived you.'

'Certainly, my Lord (said he); I allow too much caution could not be practised then, nor is there less occasion for it now; as I am convinced, if the Marquis knew you were but accessary to the death of Lord Philippe, he would punish you with the most implacable vengeance. For my part, I think you more to be pitied than condemned; and that those who instigated you to the destruction of your brother, alone merit punishment.'

"Did you ever (asked I), discover any clue to unravel the horrid mysteries which involved me in guilt?"

'I once (cried Lafroy), had an opportunity of doing so, but, alas! I lost it.'

"Lost it! (repeated I); explain yourself."

'About seven years ago (resumed he), as I was attending the Marquis to a seat of his near Paris, at a post-house, to which I rode before the carriage for the purpose of securing horses, my eyes encountered that villain Claude: I instantly seized him by the arm, and, dragging him into a room, bolted the door—'Accursed wretch! (cried I), the long delayed punishment of heaven has at length overtaken you; the Marquis of Montmorenci approaches, and into his hands I shall consign you, as the immediate cause of his son's death.'

'Oh! have mercy (he exclaimed, and dropped upon his knees); I am not quite so guilty as you imagine: my poverty exposed me to temptation, and a base enemy of Lord Philippe's, by lavish promises, seduced me to evil. I have already made a full confession of every circumstance to a relation of the Marquis's; and I am ready to repeat the same to you, if you but promise not to give me into his power.'

'Well (said I, after some minutes of consideration), on this condition I give the promise you desire.' I accordingly raised him from the ground, and with an impatience which made me tremble, seated myself near him to hear his narrative. He had just opened his lips for the purpose of beginning it, when a violent knock came to the door, and the post-master bid me come out directly, for the Marquis of Montmorenci was dying. All horror and consternation, I obeyed him, and found a fellow-servant in the hall, who told me his Lord was in violent fits.'

'Secure the man in the parlour (cried I to the post-master as I sprung upon my horse to ride off to the carriage, which the servants had stopped for fear of rendering their Lord worse by the motion. It was long ere he regained his senses). We then slowly proceeded to the post-house; but think of my rage, my regret, when, upon enquiring for him, I learned that, during the bustle in the passage, Claude had slipped from the parlour, and escaped from the house by a back way, fearing, no doubt, that I would not keep my promise to him. 'Tis a true saying, my Lord, that a man generally judges of the disposition of others by his own, so Claude, being himself a deceiver, feared deception from me.'

"Lafroy then proceeded to inform me, that he had, ever since the death of my brother, been immediately about the person of the Marquis, and ended his conversation with assurances of being ever faithful to me and mine."

"It must have been to D'Alembert that Claude confessed his guilt," said Madeline.

"So I think (cried her father); I know of no other way by which he could have attained a knowledge of my life."

"Ah! what a base advantage does he take of the secret reposed in him!" said Madeline.

"A base one indeed (repeated St. Julian). Oh! my child, never can I consent to bribe him to silence by sacrificing you. What, to save a life upon which misery is entailed—a life already in its decline—shall I devote my heart's best treasure to wretchedness?—no, Madeline, no; sooner will I brave the threats, will I meet the vengeance of D'Alembert, than consent to such a measure."

"And do you think (cried Madeline), in an union with D'Alembert's son I could feel half the wretchedness I must experience if, by persevering in your present intentions, you provoke his resentment, and become its victim? no—believe me I could not. But I have sworn (continued she, wildly starting from her seat), I have sworn to become the wife of D'Alembert, if by no other means I can prevail upon his father to keep secret the fatal events of your life; the oath is recorded in heaven—what mortal then shall be daring enough to bid me break it?"

"My Madeline! my love! (cried her father, terrified by her strong emotions, and catching her hand), a thought has just struck me, which may perhaps extricate us from our present trouble; 'tis evident that neither D'Alembert nor his son would desire an union with you, but for the sake of the fortune you are to possess."

"Evident indeed," repeated Madeline.

"I think then (resumed St. Julian), that if we were to promise to resign that fortune to them, they would cease all further solicitations for your hand."

"A merciful God has surely inspired you with the idea (said Madeline, while tears of joy fell from her). Oh, I have no doubt but our persecution would immediately cease, if their avarice was once satisfied."

"Send then for D'Alembert (cried St. Julian), and tell him, if he vows inviolable secrecy with regard to me, and promises to relinquish all ideas of an union between you and his son, both you and your father will, without delay, sign any paper he may please to draw up, resigning to him and his heirs for ever all right and title to the fortunes of Montmorenci."

"I will send for him directly," exclaimed Madeline.

"Ah! my child (said St. Julian, still detaining and looking mournfully at her), must I then bid you sign away your birth-right? Must my crimes doom you to obscurity?—for me must you forfeit that wealth, that rank, you are entitled to?—"

"Talk not to me of wealth or rank (said Madeline); what happiness have I experienced from the possession of either?—Oh! my father, never did I know real peace since I left the dear cottage where I was brought up; to be again its humble inmate is the summit of my wishes."

"Gladly indeed shall I resign all pretensions to rank and splendour (cried St. Julian); gladly shall I quit this mansion, where the spirit of a murdered brother takes its nightly rounds to fill my soul with horror. Yes, Madeline, in the dead of the night, when all but misery and despair are sunk in repose, my ears are often pierced by dreadful groans and melancholy cries, such as disturbed the tranquillity of the family the first night we entered within these walls."

"Oh! would to heaven (exclaimed Madeline, shuddering and appalled), that our departure from the castle immediately followed our renunciation of the fortune appertaining to it."

"Would to heaven it did! (said St. Julian) but to quit it during the life-time of the Marquis is impossible."

"Let me no longer delay sending for D'Alembert," cried she. As she spoke, she disengaged her hand, and, flying to the bell rung it with violence. A servant almost instantly obeyed the summons, by whom she dispatched a message to D'Alembert, requesting to see him directly. Unwilling to meet him in the present agitated state of his mind, her father tenderly embraced her, and then left the room.

CHAP. VI.

Misfortunes on misfortunes press upon me,
Swell o'er my head like waves, and dash me down!
Sorrow and shame have torn my soul,
And blast the spring and promise of my year;
They hang like winter on my youthful hopes.
So flow'rs are gathered to adorn a grave,
To lose their freshness among bones and rottenness,
And have their odours stifled in the dust.

St. Julian had scarcely quitted the apartment ere D'Alembert entered it—"I am come, Madam (said he, bowing), to receive your commands."

"Rather say, Sir (cried Madeline, with a haughtiness she could not repress), you are come to pronounce my doom. I cannot (continued she, rising and closing the door), deny that you have my father, consequently me, completely in your power; I shall therefore no longer attempt to refuse—I shall only attempt to entreat."

"You already know my resolution (said D'Alembert, losing all the gentleness with which he had entered the apartment); urge, therefore, no entreaty which I must refuse."

"I trust I shall not (said Madeline); my entreaty is, that, instead of my hand, you would accept of a title to the fortunes I may possess for your son."

"I do not understand you," cried D'Alembert, looking steadily at her.

"I think my meaning is obvious (said Madeline); I offer to your son the charm which attracts him to me. Yes, D'Alembert, I am convinced that had I still been Madeline Clermont, the humble inmate of a lonely cottage, he never would have desired an alliance with me. Gladly, therefore, will I resign all that can now render him solicitous for that alliance; and am authorized by my father to tell you, that provided you promise, solemnly promise never to divulge the events of his unhappy life—events which, if properly stated, you must more compassionate than condemn him for, and withdraw the addresses of your son, he will, jointly with me, sign any paper you may please to draw up, resigning for ever to you and your heirs the fortunes of Montmorenci."

"Both you and your father are certainly entitled to the thanks of me and my son for your generous intentions (cried D'Alembert, bowing, and scornfully smiling). I will not pretend to say that either he or I are insensible of the value of riches, but we are not quite so interested as you imagine. The fortunes of Montmorenci would, to him, lose half their estimation, if the lovely Madeline was not attached to them. His therefore she must be, if she wishes to preserve the existence of her father, for on her compliance my secrecy depends."

Madeline dropped on her knees—"Kneel by me then (she exclaimed), and swear, if I promise to sacrifice myself, that that secrecy will never be violated."

"I swear (said D'Alembert, bending his knee to the ground), that if you become the wife of my son, all that I know concerning your father shall be buried within my breast."

"Dispose of me then (cried Madeline), as you please. Yet, Oh! D'Alembert (she continued, in a voice of agony, and raising her eyes to his face), if you value the happiness of your son, give not to his arms a reluctant wife—cold and joyless must be such a gift! In pity to him therefore, as well as me, give up all idea of our union."

"Never, (said D'Alembert, as he raised her from the floor); though you may marry with indifference, the tenderness of my son will soon, I am confident, convert that indifference into love."

"Love!" repeated Madeline. She involuntarily cast her eyes upon the portrait, which bore so strong a resemblance to de Sevignie. It was her disordered fancy, no doubt, which made her at that moment imagine the eyes regarded her with an expression of the deepest melancholy; every tender scene she had experienced with him rushed to her recollection. She felt she could never cease to adore him; she felt that, in the arms of another, she must still sigh for him: and, shuddering, almost shrieking, at the idea of the dreadful destiny which would soon render such sighs a crime, she fell in convulsive agitation upon the bosom of D'Alembert. He supported her to a window, and in a few minutes she began a little to revive. She then disengaged herself from his arms.

"You are still ill (said he); permit me therefore to support you."

"No (replied she, withholding the hand he attempted to take); upon the bosom which cannot pity me, I will not lean."

"You are now prejudiced against me (said D'Alembert); my professions, therefore, you would disregard; but I trust the period will shortly arrive in which you will believe me sincere when I say, that the esteem, the tenderness, your virtues merit, I feel for you. Will you now permit me (cried he, after a pause), to go and acquaint the Marquis with the happiness which awaits my son?"

Anxious to be relieved from his presence, Madeline desired him to do as he pleased, and he directly left her. The agonies of her soul then burst forth, and in tears and broken exclamations she vented her feelings. In this situation her father surprised her:—Pale, trembling, the very picture of melancholy and despair, he approached her.

"D'Alembert was then inflexible (said he). He has just announced to the Marquis and me your acceptance of his son. Oh! my child, can you pardon the father who has doomed you to wretchedness?"

Madeline flung herself into his arms. She would have spoken—she would have assured him, that the wretchedness of her destiny could not be as great as he imagined, from knowing that it had mitigated his; but sighs and sobs impeded her utterance. At length, raising her head—"Oh! my father (she said), do not torture me by such language; strengthen, instead of weakening me; aid me—advise me; enable me to perform the duties of the station I am about entering into. That God (cried she, lifting her streaming eyes to heaven), that God whom we both worship and adore, delights not in the miseries of his creatures: when, therefore, acting right, we may surely hope that he will mitigate our sorrows."

A summons to dinner prevented all further conversation. Madeline declared her utter inability of obeying it, and entreated her father to apologize for her absence.

Reluctantly he left her. Nothing could have prevailed upon him to do so, but a fear of distressing the Marquis if he absented himself from the table; and he promised to return as soon as he possibly could to her.

During his absence, Madeline determined to exert herself in order to regain some degree of composure. "But little shall I serve him (cried she), by the sacrifice of myself, if I let him know the anguish excited by that sacrifice."

He had been gone about half an hour when she heard a gentle knock at the dressing-room door. She started, but instantly recollecting herself, and supposing it to come from some one of the servants, she desired the door to be opened. She was obeyed directly, and a man, whom she had never seen before, made his appearance.

Madeline rose from her chair, and surveyed him with astonishment. He approached her with evident diffidence and agitation, and offered her a letter. "From whom does it come?" said Madeline without taking it.

"From a friend to virtue (he replied). Delay not to read it (continued he, dropping it at her feet, for surprise rendered her unable to extend her hand): observe its advice, and avoid destruction." So saying, he rushed from the room, and closed the door after him.

Madeline remained many minutes without motion. She then repeated his words—"And will this letter (cried she, taking it up) point out a way by which I can avoid destruction?" She broke the seal with a trembling hand, and read as follows:—

"Lady,

"The unhappy wife of young D'Alembert still exists; the story of her death was invented for the vilest purposes—purposes which, under Providence, I trust I shall be the humble instrument of defeating. Too long have I been the slave of vice—too long an accessary in all the horrid schemes of an iniquitous father and son! but heaven has at length awakened me to remorse; and, if the sincerest penitence for past enormities, and most strenuous endeavours to undo all the mischief I have done, can expiate error, I hope to be forgiven. I am now hastening to the place where the most lovely and most injured of her sex groans in captivity! but, till her liberation is effected, as you value her life (my worthless one I will not mention), keep secret the contents of this letter; were they prematurely known, there is no doubt but her death would be the immediate consequence. Oh! Lady, pray for her; pray that the efforts of a sorrowing and repentant wretch may be successful in rescuing virtue, and preserving innocence: and may that heaven, which must ever regard purity like thine, ever render abortive all schemes that wickedness may plan against thee!"

No language could do justice to the feelings of Madeline on perusing this letter; but the astonishment, the ecstasy, with which the knowledge of her friend's existence inspired her, soon gave way to apprehensions for her father. She trembled to think of the horrors which D'Alembert might entail upon him in revenge for the disappointment of his hopes. "It will gladden his cruel and malicious soul (cried she) to plunge my father into the gulf of destruction—that gulf, into which the discovery of his own crimes must precipitate himself."

Her heart throbbing with impatience, she anxiously listened for her father. The moment he appeared, she flew to him, and put the letter into his hand. Her looks prepared him for something wonderful, and he eagerly cast his eye over it.

"Oh, villains! (exclaimed he, ere he had half perused it), what punishment can be adequate to your crimes! My child (resumed he, after finishing the letter, tenderly embracing her as he spoke), thou art indeed, as the good must ever be, the peculiar care of Providence. Oh! with the most heartfelt gratitude do I acknowledge its goodness in preserving you from the snare which was set for you:—this instant would I expose the execrable contrivers of it to the fate they merit; this instant, notwithstanding the power which treachery has given them over me, brand them with infamy, did I not fear, in consequence of some part of this letter, taking any step of the kind till after the liberation of the unhappy Madame D'Alembert is effected. It would be an ill requital for the kindness of my dear lamented friend if, to gratify myself by punishing immediately an injury meditated against my child, I occasioned the destruction of her's."

"Oh! my father (cried Madeline, whose heart was now solely occupied by fears on his account), think not of punishing the monsters—think only how you may avoid their malice."

"Avoid it! (exclaimed St. Julian, looking sternly at her); no, I will brave it, I will brave their threats—I will brave the horrors they may draw upon me, to have the satisfaction of punishing myself their meditated injury against you."

This was what Madeline had dreaded; his indignation at their designs against her would, she feared, transport him beyond all consideration for himself.

She threw herself at his feet, and with tears besought him to sacrifice his resentment to his safety. "You have ever told me, ever taught me to believe (she exclaimed), that you tenderly regarded your Madeline; Oh! now, my father, prove that regard by endeavouring to preserve a life with which her's is entwined."

Her entreaties had at length the desired effect; passion gave way to pity; and, raising her from the ground, while he pressed her to his heart, St. Julian told her that the value she set upon his life made him in some degree value it himself. "I will therefore go (said he), to Lafroy—he is faithful and clever, and consult with him how I may best brave the coming storm: for, like you, I am convinced that, when once the villainy of D'Alembert is discovered, and consequently his hopes relative to you overthrown, he will reveal all he knows concerning me."

"Oh, go—go (cried Madeline, disengaging herself from his arms); go directly to Lafroy, and be quick, I entreat you, my father, in your return."

She followed him to the gallery, determined to wait there till he came back. A considerable time elapsed without bringing him; and the fears of Madeline were at length so excited by his long absence, that she was just going in quest of him, when she saw him and Lafroy approaching.

"I fear you have been uneasy at my not returning sooner (said he); but it required time to deliberate on what was to be done."

"What have you determined on?" said Madeline as they entered the dressing-room, and closed the door.

"On parting," replied he, in an accent of the deepest sorrow.

"On parting!" repeated Madeline, stepping back, and looking wildly at him.

"Yes; to remain in the castle, would be to await quietly the fate to which D'Alembert will expose me."

"It would indeed (said Lafroy); I have no doubt but that the moment his baseness is discovered, Monsieur D'Alembert will reveal every particular he knows concerning you: and I am sorry to say, from my knowledge of the Marquis's disposition, I am sure he will admit of no circumstance as a palliation of the murder of Lord Philippe."

Madeline shuddered at the word murder, and involuntarily averted her head from Lafroy.

"Murder sounds harshly in my daughter's ears," cried St. Julian in rather a resentful tone.

"I beg your pardon, my Lord (said Lafroy), for having spoken unguardedly; nothing, I can assure your Lordship, would distress me so much as to offend or give pain to either you or Lady Madeline; 'tis my most ardent wish to serve you both."

"And whither (cried Madeline, turning to her father), Oh! whither, if you quit this castle, can you betake yourself?"

"With the most wild and romantic solitudes of the Alps I am well acquainted (said he), and amongst them I mean to seek a shelter."

"The holy man, who was so kind to my mother and her unfortunate family, may then again befriend you," cried she.

"Alas! (exclaimed St. Julian) he is gone long since to receive the blessed reward his virtues merited: about eight years ago I was assured of his death by the termination of our correspondence."

"Oh! my father (cried Madeline, grasping his arm), may I not accompany you?"

"Lord! my Lady (exclaimed Lafroy), surely you could not think of such a thing; surely you could not think of abandoning all prospect of rank and independence?"

"Yes, (replied Madeline); to have the power of mitigating a father's distresses, I would abandon every prospect this world could present."

"But by accompanying him you would rather increase than mitigate his distresses. Situations which, on his own account, he would not mind, he would then tremble at on your's. Besides, you would retard the expedition it is necessary for him to make, and prevent his exploring the places best calculated for affording him an asylum."

"What reason can be assigned, what excuse offered to the Marquis for his quitting the castle, clandestinely quitting it," demanded Madeline.

"He must write a letter to the Marquis (resumed Lafroy), to be delivered the day after his departure, informing him that the misfortunes of his early life had given him such a distaste to society, that he had formed the resolution of renouncing the world; a resolution which, for fear of opposition, he would not acquaint him with till he had put it into execution."

"But when he finds, as no doubt from D'Alembert he will, that this was not his real motive for quitting the castle, how—how (cried Madeline), shall I be able to support his reproaches?"

"You must summon all your resolution to your aid (said Lafroy), and brave the storm from a certainty of having it soon over. The Marquis is old; he cannot punish you for an action committed by your father; and, after his death, if the Count is still compelled to seclude himself from a fear of the connexions of Lord Philippe, you may visit him without control."

"Well (said Madeline), I will exert myself; and, confiding my father to the mercy of a God whom he never wilfully offended, look forward to happier days. When must we part?" cried she, turning to St. Julian, who had thrown himself upon a sofa.

"To-night," replied he in a melancholy voice.

"To-night!" repeated Madeline.

"He must go while the coast is clear (said Lafroy); you know Monsieur D'Alembert's son is now shortly expected; and were he and his numerous retinue of servants once arrived, it would be impossible for my Lord the Count to escape without observation."

"Was it from a servant of young D'Alembert's I received the letter?"

"Yes, from an old confidential servant, well acquainted, no doubt, as he himself has said, with the villainy of his master."

"How does my father travel? (asked Madeline), or how, or by whose means am I to hear from him? for except I do hear, I shall be distracted."

"It shall be my care to settle every thing to his satisfaction and your's (said Lafroy): as soon as it is dark, I will conduct him to the house of a friend I can rely upon, a little beyond the forest, from whence he can procure a conveyance to the Alps, and to which his letters can be directed; by the same channel too you can forward your's, and also remit any supply of money he may want."

"Your ingenuity has obviated all our difficulties (said St. Julian, rising from the sofa). I trust I may yet have power to reward you, my good friend, for your zeal and fidelity; but if not, my beloved child will, I am convinced, readily pay off any debt of gratitude I may incur."

Every plan relative to him being now arranged, and the day declining, St. Julian sat down to pen his letter to his father, whilst his agonized Madeline hung over him, and Lafroy retired to pack up a few necessaries for him.

The letter concluded, he devoted the little time he had to remain in the castle to the purpose of consoling his Madeline, and exhorting her to fortitude. She promised to exert herself, but it was a promise given in such a manner, with such tears and sobs, as gave her father little hope she would ever be able to fulfil it.

With streaming eyes she watched the last lingering beams of day, and fancied that darkness had never before been so quick in its approach. At length Lafroy appeared; he carried a glimmering light, which he laid upon a table, and told the Count, in a whispering voice, that it was time to depart. He instantly arose—"farewell! my child, (said he, straining his Madeline to his heart), soul of my soul, life of my life—farewell! —Oh! for the sake of thy wandering and exiled father—Oh! to be enabled to give him future comfort, such comfort as shall repay him for past troubles, exert thyself!"

"I will, I will (cried Madeline); when the bitterness of this moment is over, I shall be better."

"Do not longer delay, my Lord (said Lafroy); I fear if you do, some interruption from the servants, who will soon be busy preparing for supper."

St. Julian gently withdrew his arms from his daughter. She did not attempt to detain him; and yet her very soul seemed fleeting after him as he turned from her. "Lafroy (cried she, following them to the gallery), the moment you return to the castle, you must come up to me."

"You may depend on my doing so," said he.

"And you, my father, (she resumed), must write to me without delay, if you wish to save me from distraction."

"The very minute I arrive at a place of safety, I will write to you," he replied, again embracing her.

Once more Lafroy conjured St. Julian to hasten with him; and, sighing out another adieu, the unhappy father turned from his weeping child. When she could no longer hear his steps from the gallery, she flew to her chamber, and, flinging up the sash, bent from the window to try if she could hear them in the forest; but a cold wind whistled through it, which prevented any other sound than that of its own murmurs from being distinguished; yet, though she could neither see nor hear him, she continued at the window till a sudden light flashing behind her, made her start from it; and, turning round, she beheld one of the female servants.

"I hope I have not frightened your Ladyship (said the girl, courtesying); I have brought you some refreshments from Mrs. Beatrice; and she desired me to say that she would have sent something before, only she heard you were engaged with my Lord the Count, and also that she would have come herself only she was unwell."

"I am sorry to hear she is ill," cried Madeline, sinking into a chair.

"She is indeed; but bless me, your Ladyship looks very ill too; had you not better take something, for you seem quite faint?"

Madeline was quite overpowered by weakness, and gladly took a little bread and wine to try and support her sinking frame.

"The cold wind which comes through this window, is enough to pierce your Ladyship," said the maid.

"It does (cried Madeline to herself, and sighing heavily), it does indeed pierce me to the heart, because I know my father is exposed to it. Good night, my good girl, (said she, addressing her attendant), good night; say nothing of my indisposition; I am sure I shall be better to-morrow."

"Your Ladyship will not then come down to-night."

"No;—who is with the Marquis?"

"Monsieur D'Alembert; my Lord the Count I understand is out. 'Tis very bold to be sure of me to speak on the subject, but I cannot help saying I wonder how he can like to ramble through the forest after it is dark."

Madeline rose in much agitation—"I suppose the Marquis (said she, wishing to change the conversation), will soon go to supper."

"Oh yes, Ma'am; you know, since my Lord the Count's custom of rambling has been known, the Marquis never waits for him after a certain hour."

"True," cried Madeline. She then repeated her good night, and the maid retired.

Alternately traversing her chamber, alternately looking from the window, Madeline passed two tedious hours ere Lafroy appeared. He then knocked gently at the door, which she eagerly opened, and as eagerly enquired about her father.

"He has begun his journey (said Lafroy); I readily procured the assistance of my friend, who will be his companion some part of the way."

"And can your friend really be depended on?" asked Madeline.

"I can as safely answer for his fidelity as my own (replied Lafroy); and mine I hope you do not doubt."

"No (cried Madeline), if I did, I should be completely wretched. Oh! Lafroy (she continued), how I dread to-morrow; I tremble to think of the interrogations of the Marquis; as long as it is possible to do so, postpone the delivery of the letter."

"You may be assured I shall not deliver it till there is an absolute necessity for doing so (he replied), and then I shall pretend I found it in the chamber of the Count."

"I shall keep out of the Marquis's way till he has read the letter," said Madeline.

"I think you will be right in doing so (cried Lafroy); you can plead indisposition, and confine yourself to your chamber entirely to-morrow; and depend on my ingenuity for devising some scheme to prevent your being disturbed either by the Marquis or the servants, even after the discovery of the Count's departure has taken place."

"Alas! (said Madeline), how trifling will be all I shall perhaps endure after this discovery, to what, in all probability, I shall suffer when the real cause of his departure is known!"

"You must only (cried Lafroy), as I said before, brave the storm, from a hope of having it soon over. The Marquis no doubt will be violent, and endeavour to wrest from you the secret of your father's residence; you must therefore deny your knowledge of it."

"No (exclaimed Madeline), I disdain a falsehood; to deny it would be to doubt my own resolution of keeping it. After all (continued she), upon reflection I do not think the Marquis can be so violent as you imagine; he must be convinced, and that conviction must surely mollify his resentment, that, had interested motives caused the death of Lord Philippe, my father, instead of retiring to obscurity, would have made some effort to obtain his favour."

"But to refute that idea, may it not be said (cried Lafroy), that he remained in obscurity so many years but to avoid suspicion, which he feared might be excited if he sooner threw himself in the way of his father?"

"He never threw himself in the way of the Marquis," interrupted Madeline.

"No, but he threw you, which was just the same thing; that is, I mean it may be said he did; it may be said that design, not chance, brought you to the castle; D'Alembert is equal to any falsehood."

"Heaven defend us from his machinations!" cried Madeline.

"I will now leave you to repose (said Lafroy); I am sure you need it, for the events of this day must certainly have agitated you not a little."

Madeline conjured him to come to her as soon as he possibly could after the delivery of the letter, which he promised to do, and then retired.

Kneeling down, Madeline then implored the protection of Heaven for her father, and its support for herself through the numerous trials she feared she had to encounter; after which, faint and exhausted by the agitations she had experienced, she went to bed. Her mind was too much disturbed to permit her slumbers to be tranquil; and she arose unrefreshed at the dawn of day. At the usual hour, a servant (the same who had attended her the preceding night) appeared to inform her breakfast was ready. Madeline said she was too unwell to go down, and desired her's to be brought to her dressing-room. She was accordingly obeyed; and, as the maid was laying the table—"The Count has gone out to ramble again this morning, Madam (said she); Lafroy went to call him to breakfast, and found his chamber-door locked on the outside."

The conversation her attendant was inclined to enter into was truly distressing to Madeline, and she soon dismissed her. In a state of perturbation which rendered her unable to read or work, or do any thing to try and amuse her thoughts, the heavy hours wore away without any creature coming near her till dinner time; Nannette then again appeared, and desired to know whether she would come down. Madeline replied in the negative, and dinner was brought to her.

"'Tis very extraordinary, Madam (cried Nannette as she stood behind the chair), very extraordinary indeed that the Count has not yet returned; don't you think so?"

"You may take away the things (said Madeline); and, Nannette, you need not come again till I ring for you."

"Very well, Madam. But dear heart! my Lady, you really have eaten no dinner; I am afraid you are fretting about the Count."

Madeline made no reply, but took up a book to signify her wish of being alone, and Nannette left her.

The moment she had retired, Madeline threw aside the book, and walked about the room in an agitation which shook her frame. "The hour approaches for the delivery of the letter (cried she); Oh! heaven forbid the Marquis should come to me after perusing it! this evening I could not summon sufficient spirits to support an interview."

She now every instant expected Lafroy; but two hours passed away without bringing him, during which she frequently stole to the gallery to try if she could hear him approaching. Tired at length of listening for him, she threw herself on a chair by the window, and gave way in tears to the oppression of her heart. Never had she before experienced such a degree of wretchedness; she felt neglected, abandoned by all! the gloom of closing day, the cold wind which rustled through the forest, bringing the leaves in showers from the trees, and bearing to her ear the dismal tolling of a distant convent bell, heightened if possible her melancholy.

"Oh! my father (she cried), to what misery have you left your Madeline!" The door creaked upon its rusty hinges; she started, and beheld Lafroy.

"Ah! (she exclaimed, rising to meet him), I thought you had forgotten me."

"Forgotten you!" he repeated as he cautiously closed the door.

"Has the Marquis received the letter?" eagerly interrupted Madeline.

"Yes."

"Well, and what (cried she, gasping for breath), does he say?"

"Ah! my dear young lady, I have bad news for you," exclaimed Lafroy.

"Bad news! what—does the Marquis suspect the truth? Has he sent to pursue my father?"

"He has not yet sent any one to pursue him (replied Lafroy), but he soon will; for—D'Alembert has discovered all."

The shock which those words gave to Madeline, was almost more than she could support, and she sunk, nearly fainting, against the shoulder of Lafroy.

"Do you think (cried she, raising her head in a few minutes from it), do you think that my father can baffle the pursuit?"

"I trust he may have a safe retreat secured ere it commences. But you must not turn your thoughts entirely upon him; you must not turn your thoughts entirely upon him; you must now think of yourself—think of escaping from the castle."

"Of escaping!" repeated Madeline.

"Yes, if you wish to avoid cruelty and oppression."

"Explain yourself," said Madeline.

"I will if you promise to compose yourself—if you promise not to interrupt me—briefly and explicitly inform you of the sufferings which await you if you continue in the castle."

"I promise," cried Madeline.

"To begin then (said Lafroy). After I had delivered the Count's letter to the Marquis, I stepped into an adjoining room to listen to the conversation which would ensue between him and D'Alembert in consequence of it. Long I had not remained in my concealment, ere my ears were shocked by hearing D'Alembert deride the assertion contained in the letter, and begin a horrid narrative of all he knew concerning your father. I will not pain you by repeating what the Marquis said; suffice it to say, he vowed the most implacable vengeance against the Count, and swore the world should be searched to discover him.

'His daughter to be sure (cried D'Alembert), who 'tis obvious wishes to have you, as well as your father, put out of the way in order to gain, without division, the fortunes of Montmorenci, is acquainted with the secret of his retreat.'

'No doubt (replied the Marquis), and I will obtain it from her.'

'I have little hope of your being able to do so,' cried D'Alembert.

'If gentle means will not prevail on her to reveal it (cried the Marquis), other methods shall be tried; every torture, every suffering, which can be devised, shall be practised upon her in this castle to wring it from her.'

"On hearing this (continued Lafroy), I hastened to you to apprise you of your danger, and assist you in escaping it."

"This instant let me go (cried Madeline), this instant let me fly from those hated walls—let me pursue the steps of my father."

"To do so would be madness (replied Lafroy); to follow his steps, would be to give a clue to his pursuers to discover him."

"Then guide me to a convent," cried Madeline.

"No; for a convent would be the worst asylum you could enter. The Marquis's power is great; on missing you, he will naturally conclude you have taken shelter in one, and will, I am confident, immediately get himself authorized to search throughout the religious houses for you, in order to get you again into his hands."

"Whither then (said Madeline in an agony), Oh! whither shall I go?"

"I have a female relation in Paris (cried Lafroy), who I am sure would be happy to afford you an asylum. She is far advanced in life; a woman of an amiable disposition, and housekeeper to a gentleman of large fortune, who, on the death of his wife, which happened some years ago, betook himself to travel, and left his house, a very fine one, to the entire care of my aunt; to her I can get my friend (the same who assisted your father in escaping) to convey you, and also a letter to her, imploring her protection for you."

"What reason will you assign for my requiring that protection?" demanded Madeline.

"I shall say (I trust you will excuse me for it, cried Lafroy), that your father is a particular friend of mine, who, from embarrassed circumstances, has been compelled to quit his residence near the castle of Montmorenci, for the purpose of seeking one elsewhere, and that, till he procures it, he has consigned you to my care."

Madeline felt truly grateful to Lafroy for the readiness with which he offered his services, yet at the same time most unwilling to accept them; and again she expressed a wish to retire to a convent—a wish, which was again opposed with vehemence by Lafroy, who assured her he was confident, if she went to one, that in a few days she would be dragged from it by the Marquis.—"By this (he continued), I dare say every plan relative to you and your father is settled; no time, therefore, is to be lost, for if the Marquis and D'Alembert once seize you, to escape will be beyond your power."

"I am ready (cried Madeline), I am ready this moment to fly."

A scarf hung upon the back of a chair, which Lafroy took up and wrapped about her; he then drew her trembling hand under his arm, and with light steps they stole down a flight of back stairs, and through a back court entered the forest.

They proceeded a considerable way through the forest before Lafroy would permit Madeline to slacken her pace for the purpose of asking whither they were now going.

When at length she had power to make the enquiry, "we are going (said he in reply to it) to the cottage of my friend, where every thing relative to your journey can be adjusted, and where it never will occur to the Marquis or D'Alembert to search for you."

CHAP. VII.

Wild hurrying thoughts

Start ev'ry way from my distracted soul

To find out hope, and only meet despair.

The habitation of Lafroy's friend stood about half a league from the forest;—it was a lonely and sequestered cottage, built by the side of a river, and shaded by fine old trees, above which a range of lofty mountains raised their proud heads. On reaching it, Lafroy seated Madeline on a little bench before it, and desired her to continue there till he had settled every thing relative to her journey with his friend: he then unlatched the door, and entered the cottage; in less than half an hour he returned to her, accompanied by an elderly man.

"Well, Mademoiselle, (said he, as he approached her) I have settled every thing, I hope, to your satisfaction. My friend has kindly promised to attend you to Paris, and is now going to L— — —, which is about two leagues off, to procure a proper conveyance for you."

"You must thank your friend for me (said Madeline, rising) for I have not language to express the gratitude I feel for his promised protection."

"My friend Oliver is a good soul (cried Lafroy), and does not require thanks."

"No! (exclaimed Oliver), I do not, indeed!"

"I think you had better now retire to a chamber, and try to take some repose, ere you commence your journey," said Lafroy.

"Do, Mademoiselle (cried Oliver), my daughter will be happy to attend you."

"I have taken care (said Lafroy, in a whispering voice to her), to guard you against all impertinent curiosity. I told a plausible story about you, and expressly desired that no one but Oliver's daughter should attend you;—she is a good girl, and has promised to make up a bundle of her clothes for you to take to Paris; when once there, you can easily procure others.—Excuse me if I ask, whether you do not want your purse replenished?"

"No, (replied Madeline), I do not; I have money enough, I am sure, to defray the expenses of my journey, and the sale of some valuable trinkets I have about me will, I hope, enable me, without inconvenience, to rejoin my father."

"As to the expenses of your present journey, they are already defrayed (said Lafroy); do not, my dear young lady, speak upon the subject; the money I acquired in your family can never be better expended than in the service of any one belonging to it."

"I cannot express my feelings (cried Madeline, melting into tears); 'tis only Heaven, Lafroy, that can properly reward your humanity."

"I must now bid you farewell, my dear lady (said Lafroy); if I stay much longer from the Castle I fear being missed, and my absence at this juncture would, I make no doubt, excite suspicion.—farewell! May Heaven and all its holy angels for ever watch over you!"

"Stop for one instant (cried Madeline, catching his arm). Oh! Lafroy! I entreat—I conjure you—the moment a letter arrives from my father, to forward it to me. I shall be all impatience—all agony—all distraction—till I hear of his safety, and know where or when I may rejoin him!"

"Rest assured (said Lafroy), that I shall do every thing you can wish. Once more, my dear young lady, farewell! Oliver has a letter to deliver to my aunt, which I wrote in the cottage; I am confident she will do every thing in her power to make you happy."

Madeline mournfully shook her head.—"Alas! (she cried to herself) any effort to make me happy will now, I fear, be unavailing."

"Come, Mademoiselle (said Oliver, as Lafroy turned from her), you had better step into the house."

"I will (replied Madeline, as with streaming eyes she still pursued the steps of Lafroy); but first tell me how long you think it will be ere you return with a carriage."

"About three hours, I think, (said Oliver); I shall ride to L—, and will, you may assure yourself, make as much haste as possible."

He now led her into the house, and conducted her to a chamber, at the door of which he left her, telling her, as he retired, that he should send his daughter Theresa to her with a light and supper. Left to herself, Madeline, instead of indulging tears and lamentations, tried to suppress both, and regain some little degree of composure.—"I am embarked upon a stormy sea (said she), and I must resolutely brave its dangers if I hope to gain a port of safety."

She every instant expected Theresa, but the minutes passed away without bringing her; this was a circumstance Madeline did not by any means regret, as solitude and silence best suited her present feelings. She continued a considerable time deeply ruminating over past events, when she was suddenly awakened from her reverie by strains of soft music from without the house; they were strains at once tender and solemn, and while they delighted, affected her to tears.—She went to a window, but just as she had gently opened it, for the purpose of more distinctly hearing them, they entirely ceased. The beautiful prospect, however, which the window commanded of the opposite mountains and the river, prevented her withdrawing immediately from it. It was a prospect to which the beams of a rising moon, and the stillness of the night gave additional charms—a stillness which (to borrow a description from a much-admired work) rendered the voice of the mountain waterfalls tremendous, as they all, in their variety of sounds, were re-echoed from every cavern, whilst the summits of the rocks began to receive the rays of the rising moon, and appeared as if crowned with turrets of silver, from which the stars departed for their nightly round.

"Ah! (cried Madeline, to whose recollection the present scene brought those she had been accustomed to), perhaps at this very moment my father gazes upon a landscape as sublime and beautiful as the one I now behold, with sadness, at the uncertainty of his Madeline ever again enjoying with him the works of nature."

She ceased, for again she heard the soft breathing of the oboe, though at a considerable distance from the house.

Thro' glades and glooms the mingl'd measure stole,

Or o'er some haunted streams with fond delay,

Round an holy calm diffusing,

Love of peace, and lonely musing,

In hollow murmurs died away.

The pensive pleasure which communicated itself to the feelings of Madeline, as with deep attention she listened to the enchanting strains, was soon interrupted by the now unwelcome appearance of her long expected visitor.

"Dear Mademoiselle! (cried she, as Madeline turned from the window to receive her), dear Mademoiselle! (as she laid down a little tray with refreshments) I hope you will have the goodness to excuse my not coming to you before, but I would not come to you till I brought you something to eat; do pray sit down and try this omelet! I flatter myself you will find it good."

"I am afraid (said Madeline), I have been the cause of a vast deal of trouble to you."

"Of pleasure, instead of trouble (replied the little voluble Theresa); but, Lord! Mademoiselle (continued she, going to it, and putting it down), how could you bear the window up so cold a night?"

"I opened it (said Madeline, as she seated herself at the table), for the purpose of listening to the most enchanting music I ever heard. Pray who plays so divinely on the oboe?"

"My brother," replied Theresa.

"Your brother! (repeated Madeline, somewhat surprised), why he seems a perfect master of music."

"Yes, that he is (said Theresa), and of many other accomplishments too. Lord! if I had but the key of that cabinet; for you must know, Mademoiselle, we are now in his room; it being the best in the house, my father procured it for you, I could show you such drawings of his as would I dare say astonish you: there is one hangs just over your head, a view of some fine place he saw, for he has been a great traveller."

Madeline stood up to examine it; but, Oh! what was her surprise, what the feelings of that moment, on beholding the landscape which de Sevignie had sketched of her native valley.

"Are you sure (cried Madeline, looking wildly at Theresa), are you sure your brother drew this landscape—are you sure it is not a copy instead of an original?"

"Very sure indeed (replied Theresa); he told me himself he had drawn it, and I know he would not utter a falsehood."

"Yes (cried Madeline to herself), 'tis evident de Sevignie is the son of a cottager, and every thing which before appeared strange and mysterious in his conduct, is now explained. Oh! de Sevignie, had no false pride restrained you—had you candidly, explicitly confessed your situation, what happiness might now have been our's! for well am I convinced that neither my father nor my friend would have objected to our union when once thoroughly assured of your worth."

"What is your brother's name?" asked Madeline, wishing to remove every doubt, as to what she suspected, from her mind.

"Henri de Sevignie Melicour. Melicour is the name of his family, and he was called Henri de Sevignie after a great gentleman who stood godfather to him, and by whose desire he received so different an education from the rest of his family."

"And did he do nothing more than desire him to be well educated?" said Madeline.

"Why—yes—he made him handsome presents at times, and enabled him to travel and keep fine company; and I believe that lately he would have made a certain provision for him, but that they have disagreed."

"Disagreed!" repeated Madeline, in an agitated voice.

"Yes—Henri's patron wants him to marry some great young lady, who has fallen desperately in love with him, and he has positively refused to do so.

"Who is the lady?" asked Madeline, in a voice scarcely intelligible.

"I really don't know, Ma'am; if I did, I would tell you; but my father never entrusts me with a secret, lest I should blab it; though I am sure I should never think of doing so; and so 'tis only by listening here, and listening there, I ever come to the knowledge of any thing. Poor Henri! my father has also quarrelled with him, because he has rejected this great offer: 'tis a cruel thing to do so; for, to be sure, it is but natural to suppose he would accept it, if he could; but when a person is already in love, what can one do?"

"In love! (repeated Madeline), do you think your brother is in love?"

"Yes, I am sure he is."

"But how sure: did he ever tell you he was?"

"No—but one can easily guess he is, by the alteration in his looks and manner.—Lord, he is grown so pale, and so melancholy, he mopes about the whole day by himself; and at night he wanders away to the bleak mountains, where he passes whole hours playing that melancholy music, which almost breaks one's heart to hear."

"It does indeed," said Madeline with a deep sigh.

"Bless me, Mademoiselle, how pale you look; let me give you a glass of wine."

Madeline felt almost fainting, and took one in silence; after which, recovering a little, she begged Theresa to leave her—"I will lay down upon the bed (cried she), and try to rest myself till your father returns."

"Well, Mam'selle (said Theresa), since you desire it, I will bid you good night; but had I not better draw the window-curtains, and leave you a light?"

"No, (replied Madeline), I prefer the shadowy light of the moon to any other; good night, as soon as your father comes back, let me be called."

Theresa promised she should, and retired.

"Oh! de Sevignie, dear, unhappy de Sevignie! (exclaimed Madeline the moment she was left to herself), what an aggravation of my misery is the knowledge of your wretchedness—is the conviction of its being experienced on my account?—Yes, I well recollect your telling me, that it was on my account your youth was wasted, your hopes o'erthrown, your prospects blasted!—Yet, notwithstanding your sufferings, I could cruelly, unjustly condemn you, and expose you to the censure of others; falsely and rashly I judged your conduct, and for ever shall I regret my doing so.

"It was him no doubt (she continued), whom I beheld near the monumental pillar of Lord Philippe; from his vicinity to the castle, he must have heard of the occurrences which took place there, and he wandered to the forest perhaps from a hope of seeing me.

"What would he feel if now acquainted with the reverse in my situation? what will he not feel when he hears it—when he hears that his Madeline was sheltered beneath the roof of his father? But perhaps the latter circumstance he may never learn; —if it would add to his misery, Oh! may he never hear it!—Oh! may sorrow and unavailing regret be removed from his heart;— may his hopes be revived, his prospects rebrightened, and may———!" She paused—she could not bring herself to wish him united to another—could not bring herself to wish that he should take another to his heart, and expunge her for ever from it. "And yet am I not selfish (cried she), in still desiring to retain his regard? our union is now impossible; for was he even to see me again (which 'tis very improbable he ever will), and offer me his hand, I would reject it;—reject it, because I could not now in dowry with my heart, bring any thing but simple wishes for his happiness. My destiny is fixed; the lonely solitude of my father shall be my home: and should he descend before me to the grave, the remainder of my days I'll pass within a cloister."

Exhausted by fatigue and agitation, she threw herself upon the bed, but sleep was a stranger to her eye-lids: she wept bitterly—wept o'er her misfortunes—yet wept with a kind of pleasure at the idea of her tears falling upon the pillow on which, perhaps, de Sevignie had often sighed forth her name.

The day was just dawning, when she heard the rumbling of a distant carriage. She directly started from the bed, and the next instant Theresa entered the chamber.

"My father is come, Mademoiselle (said she), and impatient for you to be gone; I have brought you a hat, and given him a bundle of things for you."

Madeline, as she tied on the hat, thanked her for her kindness and attention; and then with a fervent, though silent prayer for the happiness of de Sevignie, whom she never more expected to hear of, or behold, she quitted the chamber.

Oliver was waiting for her in the hall; he told her he had left the chaise at the opposite side of the river, but that they had only to cross the bridge, which was but a little way above the cottage, to reach it. He offered her his arm, which, weak and trembling, she accepted, and in a few minutes found herself within the carriage.

From their quitting the cottage to their arrival in Paris, nothing happened worth relating; they were three days travelling to it, and entered it when it was almost dark. The dejection of Madeline was not in the least abated; nor could the busy hum of voices, the bustle in the streets, or the rattling of the carriages, for a moment divert her attention from her sorrows.

After going through a considerable part of the town, the chaise stopped, and Oliver exclaimed, "We have at length reached the habitation of Madame Fleury." Madeline directly looked from the window, but could only distinguish a black wall. Oliver desired the postilion to alight, and knock at a small door he pointed to:—the postilion accordingly obeyed, and in a few minutes the door was opened by a female; but what kind of female it was too dark for Madeline to perceive.

"Is Madame Fleury at home?" asked Oliver.

"Lord, that she is (said the woman); it is many a good day since my mistress has been out at so late an hour as this."

"I'll step in before you (cried Oliver to Madeline), and present Lafroy's letter; as soon as she has read it, I will come back for you."

He accordingly left the carriage. In about fifteen minutes he returned to it—"Madame Fleury (said he, as he opened the chaise door), is impatient to see you."

He handed Madeline across a spacious court; and they entered a hall so long and badly lighted by one small lamp, that Madeline could not perceive its termination. Here Madame Fleury waited to receive her. She took her hand, and as she led her into an old fashioned parlour, scarcely less gloomy than the hall, welcomed her to the house. "I shall be happy, my dear (said she), to render you every kindness in my power, not only on my nephew's account, but your own; for your countenance is itself a letter of recommendation."

Madeline attempted to express her thanks, but an agony of tears and sobs—an agony excited by the idea of the forlorn situation which had thus cast her upon the kindness of strangers, suppressed her utterance; and, sinking upon a chair, she covered her face with her hands.

"Come, come (said Madame Fleury, tapping her upon the shoulder), you must not give way to low spirits. Come, come (continued she, going to the side-board and bringing her a glass of wine), you must take this, and I'll answer for it you'll be better."

It was many minutes, however, ere her emotions were in the least abated. As soon as Oliver saw her a little composed, he declared he must be gone. Madame Fleury asked him if he could not stay the night? he replied in the negative, saying he had some relations in Paris whom he wished to visit; and as he meant to leave it the ensuing morning, no time was to be lost.

Madeline conjured him to remind Lafroy of his promise, which he solemnly assured her he would; and she saw him depart, though the father of de Sevignie, without the least regret; for neither in his looks or manner was there the least resemblance to his son, or any thing which could conciliate esteem.

As her composure returned, she was able to make observations upon her companion—observations by no means to her advantage; and she felt, that if she had been at liberty to choose a protector, Madame Fleury would have been the last person in the world the choice would have devolved upon. Like Oliver, neither her looks or manner were in the smallest degree prepossessing; the first were coarse and assured, the latter bold and vulgar.

Almost immediately after the departure of Oliver, she ordered supper; and as they sat at table, attended by an elderly female servant, dirty and mean in her appearance, Madame Fleury tried to force consolation as well as food upon Madeline.

"You must not, my dear (cried she), as I have said before, give way to low spirits; there is nothing hurts a young person so much as melancholy—it destroys all vivacity; and what is a young person without vivacity? why a mere log. You must reflect, that when things are at the worst, they always mend; and that a stormy night is often succeeded by a fine day. Come, take a glass of wine (continued she, filling out a bumper for herself, and another for Madeline), it will cheer your heart. Nothing does one so much good when one's melancholy as a little wine: I speak from experience; I have led a dismal life, one that has hurt my spirits very much for some years past. My nephew, I suppose, told you about the gentleman to whom this house belongs."

Madeline bowed.

"Well, upon his quitting it, for the purpose of travelling, all the servants were discharged; and ever since, that poor woman and I (pointing to the servant), have led the most solitary life imaginable, just like two poor lonely hermits." (Madeline could not forbear smiling at those words; very like hermits indeed, thought she, as she cast her eyes over the table, which was covered with delicacies.)—"Just like two poor lonely hermits, fasting and praying," said Madame Fleury, with a deep sigh.

It may easily be supposed that Madeline soon grew tired of conversation of this kind; her timid heart shrunk from the attentions of Madame Fleury, instead of expanding to receive them; yet she condemned the strong prejudice which she had conceived against her.—"I will try to conquer it (said she to herself), because it is unjust—unjust to dislike a person merely because they have been cast in one of the rough moulds of Nature, and their manners, in consequence of the difference of education, are unlike mine."

Madame Fleury seemed inclined to sit up to a late hour, which Madeline perceiving, she pleaded fatigue, and begged permission to retire to her chamber. Madame Fleury instantly rising, took up a light, and said she would conduct her to it. Madeline followed her down the hall, at the bottom of which was a folding door, that on being opened, discovered a spacious stair-case.—"This appears to be a very large house," said Madeline, as ascending the stairs, she beheld numerous passages and doors.

"Oh, quite a wilderness of a house (replied Madame Fleury); I am sometimes a year without seeing half the apartments."

"I wonder you are not afraid to live in it (said Madeline), without more servants."

"Why all the valuable things were removed from it on the desertion of its master, so that prevents my having many fears; besides, I take good care to see all the doors secured before I go to bed."

The room allotted for Madeline was spacious, but dirty and ill furnished; nor was there aught within it that gave evidence of better days, except a few faded portraits, large as the life, which still hung against the brown and dusty wainscot.

"Is your chamber near this?" asked Madeline, as she cast her eye around.

"Oh, yes, I shall be your neighbour; so don't be uneasy," replied Madame Fleury. Madeline assured her she would not; and then, anxious to be alone, begged she might no longer detain her.—"Good night then, my dear (said Madame Fleury); I shall call you when it is time to breakfast."

Madeline looked behind the window-curtain ere she locked the door; she then recommended herself to the protection of Heaven; and, worn out both by bodily and mental fatigue, repaired to bed, where she slept till her usual hour of rising.

When dressed, she drew up the window curtain; but how different the prospect she beheld from the prospects she had been accustomed to; instead of sublime mountains towering to the clouds, or rich meadows, scattered over with flocks and herds, she now beheld high and dirty walls, which completely enclosed a small spot of ground planted with a few stunted trees. She sighed, and a tear stole from her to think she might never more enjoy the sweets of Nature, or mark

——————how spring the tended plants,

How blows the citron grove, what drops the myrrh,

And what the balmy reed—how Nature paints

Her colours—how the bee sits on the bloom

Extracting liquid sweets.

Her melancholy reflections were soon interrupted by the voice of Madame Fleury; she immediately opened the door, and, after the usual salutations of the morning were over, accompanied her to breakfast, which was laid out in the room where they had supped the preceding night, and which, like the chamber of Madeline, looked into what Madame Fleury called the garden.

After breakfast she rose, and told Madeline she must leave her—"I go every morning to church (cried she); while I am absent, you can amuse yourself with reading; you'll find some books in that closet," pointing to one at the end of the room.

Madeline thought it odd her not being asked to accompany her to church; and she was just on the point of requesting permission to do so, when she recollected, that perhaps

Madame Fleury might have some places after the service was over to call at, which she did not wish to bring her to; she therefore timely checked herself, and said she would either walk in the garden, or read.

As soon as she was alone, she examined the books, but she found none that pleased her; and even if she had, her mind was too much disturbed to permit her to derive amusement from them; she therefore went into the garden, where, deeply ruminating o'er past events, she heeded not the lapse of time, and was astonished when the maid came out to inform her that her mistress had been returned some time, and dinner waited. Madeline hastily followed her into the house, but on reaching the parlour, she involuntarily started back on perceiving a young man with Madame Fleury.

"Bless my soul (said Madame Fleury, laughing immoderately), bless my soul (cried she, taking the hand of Madeline), you look terrified. Well, you are the first girl I ever saw frightened at the sight of a young man; let me introduce my nephew to you, and you'll find you have no reason to be afraid of him;—Dupont, this is Mademoiselle Jernac," the assumed name Lafroy had chosen for Madeline."

Dupont saluted Madeline with much politeness, and expressed his regret at having caused her any disagreeable surprise: she bowed, and endeavoured to recollect herself, in order to avoid the coarse raillery which her confusion excited in Madame Fleury, and permitted him to lead her to the table.

When they were seated at it, Madame Fleury began to sound the praises of her nephew;—"I can assure you, Mademoiselle (cried she) when you know him better, you will like him much; he is a good soul, I cannot help saying so, though to his face: he is secretary to a nobleman of high rank and consequence; and, though from his situation he might be conceited and dissipated, he is neither the one nor the other, nor disdains to come now and then, and take a snug dinner with his old aunt." While she was speaking, Madeline could not help attentively regarding Dupont, whose face appeared familiar to her; but where or when she had seen the person whom he resembled, she could not possibly recollect.

Dupont was young, handsome, and rather elegant; yet almost the moment Madeline beheld him, she conceived a prejudice against him;—his gentleness seemed assumed, and there was a fierceness, a boldness in his eyes, which at once alarmed and confused her.

When dinner was over, Madame Fleury proposed cards. Madeline immediately rose, and, declaring she never played, desired leave to retire to her chamber.

"No, (cried Dupont, also rising and taking her hand, whilst he gazed upon her with the most impassioned tenderness), we cannot let you go; we'll give up cards; we'll not think, not act, but as you like."

"I should be sorry, Sir (cried Madeline coldly, and withdrawing her hand), that the inclination of any person was sacrificed to mine; at present I am much better calculated for solitude than society, and must therefore again entreat Madame Fleury's permission to retire to my room."

"Then you will entreat in vain I assure you (cried she); I have no notion of letting you go to mope about by yourself."

"If you thus restrain me, Madam (said Madeline, who every moment grew more anxious to quit Dupont), you will prevent me from having the pleasure of thinking myself at home."

"True (cried Dupont), where there is restraint, there can be no pleasure; permit Mademoiselle Jernac, therefore, Madame (addressing his aunt) to leave us, since she is so cruel as to desire to do so; perhaps our ready compliance with her wishes will at some other time incline her to be more propitious to our's."

"Well, you may go, child (said Madame Fleury); but indeed 'tis only to oblige my nephew that I let you."

Dupont led Madeline to the door, where, in spite of all her efforts to prevent him, he imprinted a kiss upon her hand.

Her heart throbbing tumultuously, she hastily ascended the stairs; she saw, or fancied she saw, looks exchanged between the aunt and nephew which terrified her: stories of designing men and deceitful women rushed to her recollection; and she trembled at the idea of her forlorn situation—at the idea of being solely in the power of strangers, without a being near her to protect her, if protection should be necessary. She wished to know whether she was in an inhabited part of the town, which the darkness of the hour she had arrived at Madame Fleury's prevented her ascertaining, that in case there was a necessity for quitting her present residence, she might have a chance of easily procuring another; and accordingly determined to avail herself of the present opportunity, and explore her way, if possible to the front of the house. The gallery in which her chamber stood, was terminated by a door, which she softly opened, and discovered a winding passage: without hesitation she entered it, and proceeded till stopped by another door; this she opened with difficulty, for the key was rusty, and for a long time resisted all her efforts to turn it: when at length she had succeeded, she found herself in a chamber as spacious as her own, but stripped of all the furniture except a bare bedstead. She stepped lightly to a window, and to her great mortification, found herself still at the back of the house; she directly turned away, and was hastening from the room, when, carelessly glancing her eye over it, a stain of blood upon the floor filled her with horror, and riveted her to the spot. "Oh! God, (she cried, while her arms dropped nerveless by the side), what dreadful evidence of guilt do I behold!" A heavy hand fell upon her shoulder; she shrieked—and, starting, beheld Madame Fleury—"What, in the name of wonder, brought you hither?" demanded she in rather an angry voice.

"I did not conceive there was the least impropriety in examining the apartments," said Madeline.

"Impropriety, why no; but then you might have told me you were curious. Come, let us quit this chamber; I hate it."

"Have you reason to hate it?" asked Madeline, her eyes still fastened upon the blood-stained floor. She felt the hand of Madame Fleury tremble.—"Why to tell you the truth, (said she, going to the bedstead and sitting down), my nephew, Dupont, (speaking in an agitated voice), once met with an ugly accident in it; he fell and hurt himself so much, we thought he never would have recovered; the stains of his blood are still upon the floor; nothing would take them out."

"Blood sinks deep!" said Madeline in a hollow voice, and raising her eyes, she fixed them upon Madame Fleury.

"Pray let us leave this chamber," cried her companion, rising in visible confusion. She seized the arm of Madeline, and drawing her from it, locked the door, and put the key into her pocket. "I came up (said she, as they proceeded to the chamber of Madeline), to ask you whether you would not choose a book, and if I should not send you some coffee."

"No (replied Madeline), neither a book nor coffee; all I desire is to be left without interruption to myself to-night."

"I am afraid you are a fanciful girl," said Madame Fleury.

"Would to Heaven I was only affected by fancies!" exclaimed Madeline with fervour.

"Well, since you wish to be alone, I will leave you (cried Madame Fleury), nor shall you again be interrupted."

"In doubting Madame Fleury (said Madeline, when left to herself), do I not doubt Lafroy, of whose fidelity I have received such proofs, that to harbour a suspicion of him, makes me feel guilty of ingratitude. Oh! surely (she continued, and her mind grew composed by the idea), he never would have confided me to the care of his relation, had he not been convinced she was worthy of the trust; and, in giving way to my present fears, I torment myself without a cause. Every thing may be as Madame Fleury has stated; her nephew may have been hurt in the chamber; and his attentions to me may be dictated by what he imagines politeness. I will then exert myself (she cried); I will combat my fears, nor to the pressure of real evils add those of imaginary ones."

To reason herself out of her fears was not, however, as easy as she imagined; they still clung to her heart, and she wished, fervently wished, that she had never entered the residence of Madame Fleury. She determined the next morning to ask to accompany her to church—"I shall then (said she), know what kind of neighbourhood I am in, and whether there is any convent near the house, to which I could fly in case any thing disagreeable again occurred in it."

As soon as it grew dark, the maid brought her a light, which she kept burning all the night. She was scarcely dressed in the morning, when Madame Fleury tapped at the door to inform her breakfast was ready. Madeline immediately opened the door, and attended her to the parlour, where, to her great vexation, she found Dupont.

"So, so (said his aunt, as if a little surprised by seeing him), you are here! what, I suppose you could not rest till you had paid your devoirs to Mademoiselle?"

"I should be sorry (said Madeline, with some degree of haughtiness), to place to my own account a visit which I neither expected nor desired."

"And yet you would be right in doing so," cried Dupont.

Madeline made no reply, but addressed herself on some indifferent subject to Madame Fleury.

After breakfast, which was rendered extremely disagreeable to Madeline by the looks and attentions of Dupont, Madame Fleury rose, and said it was time to go to church. "I hope, Madam (cried Madeline, also rising), you will permit me to accompany you this morning."

"No, indeed I shall not (exclaimed she); you can be much better employed at home, for my nephew will stay with you."

There was something in those words which shocked Madeline so much, that for a moment she had not the power of utterance.—"I can assure you, Madam, then (said she), that if you do not let me go, I will confine myself to my chamber until your return."

"That is, if my nephew is such a fool as to permit you."

Madeline could no longer restrain herself. "If this is the manner in which you mean to treat me, Madam (she exclaimed), you cannot be surprised if my continuance with you is of short duration. 'Tis not (she continued, with increasing warmth), the mere shelter of a roof that I require—'tis kindness, 'tis protection, 'tis the attentions which sooth the sorrows of the heart, and lighten the pangs of dependence;—except assured of my receiving these, your nephew, Lafroy, I am confident would never have entrusted me to your care; and candidly and explicitly I now tell you, I shall withdraw myself from it, if longer subjected to freedoms I abhor."

Madame Fleury only replied to this speech by a contemptuous smile; then turning on her heel, she darted out of the room, and shut the door after her. Madeline attempted to follow her, but was prevented by Dupont, who, seizing her hand, dragged her back to a seat. She grew terrified, but tried to conceal her terrors. "I insist on your releasing me immediately, Sir," said she.

"I cannot (cried he), I cannot be so much my own enemy."

"Though Madame Fleury has forgot what is due to her sex, I hope (resumed Madeline), you will not forget what is due to your's; to insult an unhappy woman, is surely a degradation to the character of a man."

"I do not mean to insult you (replied Dupont); my honourable addresses cannot surely insult you?"

"Your honourable addresses!" repeated Madeline, surveying

him with mingled surprise and contempt.

"Yes—I love, I adore you; and now entreat you to accept my hand and heart."

"I shall not say I reject them (replied Madeline), because I do not think you serious in offering them; I cannot believe that any man in his senses can offer himself to a woman he scarcely knows."

"I am serious, by all that is sacred!" cried he with vehemence.

"Then believe me equally serious (said Madeline), when I assure you, that could you with your hand and heart offer me the wealth of the universe, I would reject them. You are, no doubt, acquainted with my unhappy story—Oh! do not, therefore (she continued), do not render unpleasant the asylum your aunt has afforded me, by persevering in attentions which never can have the desired effect."

"Perseverance does much (said Dupont); I will try it."

"To my torment then, and your own disappointment you will try it," cried Madeline.

"How can you be so inflexible?" said he, looking on her with the most passionate tenderness.

Madeline grew more alarmed than ever by his manner. "If you have generosity, if you have compassion (exclaimed she), you will now let me retire."

"Well (said he), to show my readiness to oblige you, however I may mortify myself by doing so, I will now let you leave me; but ere you go, suffer me to say I never will drop my suit."

Anxious to leave him, Madeline made no reply. Her first impulse on quitting the parlour, was to fly directly from a house in which she was exposed to insult and persecution; but a moment's reflection convinced her of the impracticability of such a measure at present, when in all probability Dupont was upon the watch: she therefore determined not to attempt escaping till a more favourable opportunity for that purpose offered. Still anxious, before that opportunity occurred, to discover in what kind of neighbourhood she was, instead of repairing to her chamber, she hastily turned into a long passage off of the great stair-case, in which several doors appeared.

CHAP. VIII.

Oh! take me in a fellow-mourner with thee;
I'll number groan for groan, and tear for tear!
And when the fountains of thy eyes are dry,
Mine shall supply the stream, and weep for both.

Madeline tried many doors, but found them fastened. She resolved, however, not to return without attempting all, and was just laying her hand upon another lock, when a dreadful groan from the bottom of the passage pierced her ear, and penetrated to her heart. She hesitated whether she should advance or retreat; but at length humanity triumphed over fear, and she determined to go on, and try if she could be of any service to the person from whom the groan proceeded. At the bottom of the passage she perceived, what the darkness it was involved in had before concealed from her, a narrow stair-case in the side of the wall: this she eagerly ascended, and came to a small door half open; here she paused, and looking in, beheld, with equal horror and astonishment, an old woman wretchedly clad, and worn to a skeleton, kneeling in the corner of an ill-furnished room, before a wooden crucifix.

"Oh! heavenly father (the miserable object exclaimed, almost the moment Madeline had reached the door), may I, dare I, hope for thy forgiveness!—Oh! no, 'tis impossible thou canst ever grant it;—thou never canst forgive the wretch who caused the anguish of the most amiable of women—the misery and death of the most noble of men! Yet, if suffering could entitle me to mercy, I might hope for it.—Oh! if my blood can atone for that I caused to be shed, thou, thou shalt have it!"

So saying, she seized a knotted cord that lay beside her, and struck herself with it: Madeline instantly sprung forward—"Have mercy upon yourself (she exclaimed, as she caught her emaciated hand); God only requires real contrition as an atonement for error." The miserable wretch looked wildly at her for a moment; then uttering a piercing shriek, she convulsively wrested her hand from her and fell fainting on the floor.

The situation of Madeline was distressing in the extreme; she feared calling for assistance, lest the knowledge of her having discovered the miserable object before her should be productive of unpleasant consequences; and yet she feared her own efforts would never recover her. She knelt down and chafed her temples; but it was many minutes ere she showed any signs of returning life. At length opening her eyes, she again fastened them upon Madeline with the wildest expression of fear, and in a feeble voice exclaimed, "You are come then, come from the realms of bliss, for the purpose of summoning my soul to that tribunal where it must answer for all its crimes?"

"I know not what you mean (said Madeline, endeavouring to raise her head, and support it upon her breast); the voice of distress drew me to this apartment, not from idle curiosity, but from a hope of being serviceable to the person from whom it proceeded; and my motive will I trust excuse any intrusion I may appear guilty of."

"From whence, or from whom do you come?" demanded the unhappy woman.

"Alas! (replied Madeline), I have neither strength nor spirits now to enable me to relate my sad story; all I can tell you is, that I am an unfortunate girl, without any friend, I fear, to afford me the protection I require."

"Perhaps I may be able to serve you (said the stranger); that voice—that look—Ah! how powerfully do they plead in your behalf! What part of the house do you inhabit?"

"I am so little acquainted with the house (cried Madeline), that perhaps I may confound one place with another; my chamber is at the end of a great gallery."

"What kind of a chamber is it?"

"'Tis wainscoted, and ornamented with faded portraits."

"Amongst which is there not a remarkable one of a lady in mourning with a drawn dagger?"

"Yes."

"Well, since I know your chamber, I will, if there is a possibility of getting to it, pay you a visit, and tell you of a plan I have thought of for your escape."

Madeline, in an ecstasy of gratitude and hope, caught her hand, and was raising it to her lips, when a sudden, though distant, noise made her drop it.

"Oh! heavens (cried the stranger), if we are discovered, we are lost!—Fly—regain your chamber, if possible, without delay; and as you value your safety, as you value your life and mine, keep secret our interview."

Madeline started from the ground—"Oh! tell me ere I go (she cried), when I may expect you."

"Away, away (said the stranger), a moment's delay may be fatal!"

Madeline could no longer hesitate about departing, and swiftly and lightly she descended the stairs; at the bottom she paused to listen and look down the passage, but she neither heard any noise, nor beheld any object: she was therefore proceeding with quickness when suddenly she heard an approaching step.

From the words of the stranger, she believed destruction inevitable if discovered in her present situation; she therefore determined to try and gain admittance into one of the adjacent chambers, and secrete herself within it till all danger of detection was over. She accordingly tried the nearest door, and, to her inexpressible transport, the lock yielded to her first effort. The instant she entered the room, she bolted the door, against which she then leaned to try if she could hear the approach of the step that had so much alarmed her; but all again was profoundly still. Somewhat composed by this, she ventured to turn, and to her infinite amazement, beheld herself in a most magnificent chamber. "What new mystery (said she), is this? Madame Fleury assured me her chamber was near mine; and yet who but Madame Fleury can occupy this room?"

This was a mystery soon explained; for as she was stealing from the door to the window, she beheld the clothes which Dupont had on the preceding day lying upon a chair.—"Ah! heavens (exclaimed Madeline, recoiling with horror, as if it was Dupont himself she saw); Dupont then is the inhabitant of this chamber! Oh! for what vile purpose is his residence here concealed? Oh! Lafroy, you were either deceived yourself, or basely deceived me when you sent me to this house; new horrors every moment open to my view, and my senses are scarcely equal to the conflicts I endure!"

She was returning to the door for the purpose of endeavouring to quit the room, when some letters scattered upon a dressing-table caught her attention: she darted to them; but how impossible to describe the horror she experienced, when upon all the hated name of D'Alembert met her eye. She snatched up one, and while the blood ran cold to her heart, read as follows: —

"The lovely Madeline will soon be in your power; Lafroy has completely secured her for you: may you profit by his stratagems! Adieu! — Believe me ever your affectionate father,

"G. D'ALEMBERT."

Not when she trembled beneath the poignard of a supposed assassin — when she shuddered at the idea of having seen a being of the other world — when she groaned from a conviction of her father's being a murderer — did Madeline receive such a shock, did she experience such horrors as she now felt on discovering Lafroy to be a villain! She dropped upon her knees, and raised her eyes and trembling hands to heaven, though unable to articulate a prayer.

She had not been in this situation above two minutes, when a loud knock came to the door. Madeline started wildly from the floor, and looked round to see if there was any place which could afford her concealment; but no such place presented itself to her view. The knock was repeated with increased violence; and scarcely could she prevent the wild shriek of despair from bursting from her lips. Her silence, however, availed her but little; for the knock was repeated, and the moment after, the door burst open by Dupont; the room rung with the shriek which she uttered at that instant.

"Well (exclaimed he), by coming to my chamber, you have saved me the trouble of going to your's."

As he spoke, he attempted to catch her in his arms, but she eluded his grasp, and springing past him, fled towards her chamber; he pursued her, and, overtaking her just as she had reached the door, rushed into the room along with her.

She now threw herself upon her knees — "I am in your power (said she, in almost breathless agitation); be generous, and use it nobly."

"And do you deserve any thing like generosity from me? (cried he); do you not merit the severest punishment for having clandestinely entered my chamber, and treacherously examined my letters."

The fear of Madeline gave way to indignation; her eyes flashed fire; she rose, and looked upon him with scorn.

"And what punishment does the villain merit who forced me to such actions? (she exclaimed). What punishment does he merit who assumes a name but for the purpose of deceiving, who spreads his snares for the friendless and unhappy?"

"You compelled me to assume another name (said he), because you objected to me for bearing that of D'Alembert."

Madeline turned from him with contempt; he followed her.

"Madeline (cried he), let all trifling cease between us: you are, as you have yourself observed, completely in my power; be politic therefore, and no longer reject my overtures."

"Monster! (exclaimed Madeline), do you insult me by still pleading for my hand, knowing, as you must, that I am acquainted with the existence of your wife?"

"I do not plead for your hand (replied he with the most deliberate coolness), 'tis for your heart: consent to be mine; consent to accept the only proposals I can now make you; and, in return, I will not only secure you an independence and a delightful asylum, where you can fear nothing, but solemnly promise, if ever I have power to do so, to make you my wife."

"I will not attempt (said Madeline), to express my indignation and contempt—I shall content myself with merely saying, that, were you even dear to my heart, I would reject offers which could entail infamy upon me: think, therefore, whether there is a probability of my accepting them, when I tell you, that, united to my horror at your baseness, is an aversion to you too strong for any language to describe."

The most violent rage took possession of D'Alembert at those words; but the terror which his rage inspired, was trifling to the shock which Madeline received, when in his inflamed countenance she traced the dreadful countenance of him beneath whose poignard she had trembled at midnight in the ruined monastery of Valdore.

"Oh! God (she cried, starting back), do I behold the murderer of the Countess?"

The crimson of D'Alembert's cheek faded at those words; his eyes lost their fury, and he trembled, but in a minute almost he recovered from his confusion. "Insolent girl! (cried he, stepping fiercely to Madeline), of what new crime will you next accuse me? Beware how you provoke me; do not go too far, lest you tempt me to retaliate—retaliate in a manner most dreadful to you—on your father."

"He is beyond your power (exclaimed Madeline, with a wild scream, and clasping her hands together); he is safe, he is secure."

"As I could wish," cried D'Alembert, with a malicious smile.

An idea of treachery having been practised upon her father as well as upon herself now started in the mind of Madeline, and her heart almost died away. "My father is safe!" she repeated, with a quivering lip, and a faltering voice.

"Yes—beneath this roof."

"Oh, God!" cried Madeline as she sunk upon the floor.

D'Alembert raised her, and used every method in his power to revive her: it was many minutes, however, ere she was able to stand or speak. At length, sinking from his arms—"Forgive me (she exclaimed, as she knelt at his feet), Oh! forgive me if I have said aught to offend you; make allowances for my wounded feelings, for my distress, my irritation at finding myself deceived where I most confided, and drop all resentment; be noble, and give up every intention hostile to my father's peace and mine; restore me to his arms, and suffer us to depart together to some distant spot, where, in security and solitude, we may pass our days;—do this, and receive from me the most solemn assurances of our never disturbing your tranquillity, or uttering an expression which can be unpleasing to you."

D'Alembert raised and pressed her to his heart; she trembled—she resented. "But I am in the grasp of the lion (said she to herself), and I must try by gentleness to disengage myself from it."

"You plead in vain, Madeline (cried he); I have run every risk to secure you, and never will give you up. But while I say this, let me quiet your apprehensions by assuring you, that though solely in my power, I never will make an ungenerous use of that power by using any violence; I will not force you to return my love; but if you continue much longer to disdain it, I shall not hesitate to surrender your father to the fate he merits."

"He is not, he is not in your power (exclaimed Madeline); you have said so but for the purpose of awaking my fears, from a hope of being able to take a base advantage of them."

"Well, though you doubt my words, I suppose you will not doubt the evidence of your own eyes."

Madeline trembled; the faint hope which had just darted into her mind, of his assertion relative to her father being merely for the purpose of terrifying her, now utterly died away.

"I will this instant, if you please (said D'Alembert), conduct you to the chamber of your father; but ere I take you to it, I must prepare you for the situation in which you will find him."

"The situation!" repeated Madeline, starting.

"Yes; I had an idea I should be compelled to bring you to him, in order to convince you he was in my power; and therefore ordered an opiate to be given to him this morning, which has thrown him into a state of insensibility, and thus precluded all possibility of his either hearing or uttering complaints."

"The ear of the Almighty will be open to his complaints and mine (said Madeline); they will reach the throne of Heaven, before which you must one day answer for your crimes."

"Do you choose to see him?" asked D'Alembert.

Madeline made no reply; but, breaking from his arms, she moved towards the door; he followed her, and, taking her trembling hand, led her in silence to the end of the gallery, from whence they turned into a long passage, terminated by another door. D'Alembert took a key from his pocket, and unlocked it—"We are now (said he), in the chamber of your father."

The curtains of the bed were closed; Madeline snatched her hand from D'Alembert, and pulling them back, beheld her father extended on it—thin, ghastly, to all appearance dead. She shrieked aloud—"He is dead! (cried she), he is dead!—Oh! monster, you have murdered my father!"

"No, (said D'Alembert); you frighten yourself without a cause; the ghastly look of his countenance is occasioned by the opiate."

Madeline laid her hand upon his heart; she felt it faintly flutter; and a scream of joy burst from her lips. "Yet have I reason to rejoice at his existence (she cried), when I reflect upon his situation?"

"'Tis in your power (said D'Alembert), to change that situation—to restore him to liberty, to free him from danger, to ensure him protection."

"In my power!" repeated Madeline.

"Yes; accept my offers, and all that the most duteous, the most tender son could do for a father, I will do for your's."

"And think you (said Madeline), my father would thank me for freedom and security, if purchased by dishonour? no, believe me he would not; I know his soul too well—know that death, in its most frightful form, would not be half so dreadful to him as the knowledge of his daughter's infamy:—never then will that daughter deviate from the path he early in life marked out for her to take:—never then, though surrounded by dangers and difficulties,—the dangers, the difficulties of him who is dearer, infinitely dearer to her than existence, will she act contrary to the principles he implanted in her mind, or forego her hopes of Heaven's protection, by striving to attain safety at the expense of virtue."

"Your resolution is then fixed," said D'Alembert.

"It is," replied Madeline in a firm voice.

"Mine is also fixed," cried D'Alembert. As he spoke, he approached her—"You continue no longer in this chamber," said he.

Madeline retreated. "You cannot, you will not surely (she cried), be so inhuman as to force me from it? Oh! let me watch by my father!—Oh! suffer me to remain with him I entreat, I conjure you!"

"In vain," said D'Alembert; and he again advanced to seize her. Madeline screamed; and, throwing herself upon the bed, she clasped her arms around her father—"Awake, awake (she cried), my father, awake, and hear, Oh! hear the agonizing shrieks of your child!"

"It will be many hours ere he awakes (exclaimed D'Alembert, as unlocking the hands of Madeline, he raised her from the bed); and when he does, it will be in an apartment very different from his present one, except you relent."

She forcibly disengaged herself from him, and sunk at his feet—"Have mercy (she exclaimed, with streaming eyes and uplifted hands), have mercy upon my father and me, and entitle yourself to that of Heaven! Oh! let those tears, those agonies, plead for us! let them express the feelings which language cannot utter!"

"I have already told you (said D'Alembert, with savage fury in his countenance), that my resolution is fixed; I now swear it—swear to give up your father to the offended laws of his country, except you consent to return my love."

He caught her in his arms, from which she vainly tried to disengage herself, and bore her shrieking and struggling to her chamber.

"Now, Madeline (cried he), speak—but ere you speak, deliberate; for on your words depends the fate of your father."

"Wretch! (exclaimed the agonized Madeline), you already know my determination."

"Farewell! then (said he), I go for the officers of justice."

"Oh! D'Alembert (cried Madeline, wildly catching his arm as he was about quitting the room), you cannot be so inhuman; you cannot surely think of giving up to death a man, who has been basely betrayed into your power—a man, infinitely more unfortunate than guilty!—Again I kneel before you to supplicate your pity for him. Oh! could you look into my heart, could you ascertain the dreadful feelings which now pervade it, I am convinced you would be softened to compassion."

"My compassion can easily be obtained (said D'Alembert)—your love."

"Villain! (exclaimed Madeline, rising from the floor), begone! never more will I address you: to God alone will I look, up to him, whose power can in a moment defeat your purposes; he has promised to protect the innocent; I will think of that promise, and support my fainting heart."

"Again then (said D'Alembert), I bid you farewell! you have yourself provoked your father's fate."

With feelings which can better be conceived than described, Madeline saw him quit the chamber. "He is gone then (said she, as she heard him close the door), he is gone for the ministers of justice!" The dreadful and approaching sufferings of her father rushed to her mind; she saw the torturing rack—she beheld his mangled form upon it—she heard his deep groans, expressive of excruciating agony, and the loud shouts of the rabble mocking his pangs, and applauding the hand which inflicted punishment upon the fratricide.

She shrieked aloud; she flew to the door, but it was fastened on the outside: she called upon D'Alembert; she conjured him to return—to return to assure her he would have mercy upon her father; but she called in vain. She then attempted to force the door, but her strength was unequal to the effort. The agony and disappointment she experienced were too much for her; her brain maddened; and wild as the waves which destroy the hopes of the mariners, she raved about the room, till, utterly exhausted by the violence of her emotions, she dropped upon the floor, where her shrieks sunk into groans, which by degrees died away in hollow murmurs, and a total insensibility came over her.

In this situation she must have continued many hours; for when she recovered, she found the gloom of closing day had already pervaded the chamber. Her ideas at first felt confused; but by degrees a perfect recollection of all that had passed returned, and clasping her cold and trembling hands together, she called upon her father.

As she called upon him, she heard a faint noise outside the door; she started, but had not power to rise; and almost immediately it was opened, and the miserable woman she had seen in the morning entered.

"Rise (exclaimed she in a whispering voice), and follow me."

"Whither?" said Madeline, without obeying her.

"To your father; he waits to conduct you from this detestable house. I released him from his chamber, in the door of which D'Alembert left the key when he dragged you from it. But ask me no farther questions; D'Alembert but deferred going for the officers of justice till it grew dark; a moment's delay may therefore be fatal, and cut off all opportunity of escaping."

"Oh! let us fly, let us fly then," said Madeline, starting from the ground.

Softly and silently they descended to the hall, and turned down a long passage, terminated by a flight of steep stone stairs; these they also descended, and Madeline then found herself in a subterraneous room; a faint light glimmered from a recess at the extremity of it, which startled her, and she caught the arm of her companion.

"Her terror, however, was but of short duration; almost instantly the voice of her father reached her ear, and she saw him approaching with extended arms; she sprung forward, and flung herself into them. "Oh! my child (he exclaimed, as he clasped her to his heart), in what a situation do I behold you!"

"My father, my dearest father (cried Madeline), do not let us complain of our situation; Oh! rather let us express our gratitude to that Being who has alleviated it, by giving us a friend who will extricate us from this abode of terror and of death;—but the moments are precious; we should lose no time."

"They are precious indeed (said the old woman); that door (pointing to one in the recess), opens upon a flight of steps which ascend to the court; here is the key of it," continued she, presenting it to St. Julian.

"But how shall we escape from the court?" demanded Madeline.

"Your father will be able with ease to unbar the door; and as Madame Fleury always sits at the back of the house, there is no danger of your being discovered."

"Oh! let us be quick," exclaimed Madeline.

St. Julian advanced to the door; but scarcely had he attempted to open it, when a violent tumult was heard without the court, and immediately after the steps of many people entering it. He paused—listened—and looked at his daughter. Horror almost froze her blood—"They are come (cried she), the ministers of death are come."

"I fear so (said the old woman). Hark! they have entered the house, and are now ranging through the apartments!"

"Is there no hope—is there no way of escaping?" asked Madeline distractedly.

"None (replied the old woman mournfully), but through the court."

"Is there no place of concealment?"

"No."

"Nor any fastening to this door?" advancing to the one through which they had entered.

"None, except a weak bolt that could be burst in a moment."

"Then all hope is over (cried Madeline, turning to her father). Oh! God (she continued, looking up to heaven), take me, take me from this scene of horror! let me die within the arms of my father!"—Almost fainting, she sunk upon his breast.

The tumult within and without became every instant more violent; and it was evident that one party surrounded the house for the purpose of guarding every passage, whilst another searched throughout it.

Madeline suddenly started from the arms of her father, and extinguished the light. "Let us go within the recess (cried she); if they do come down, they may not perhaps do more than merely look into the room." They accordingly crept into it, and placed themselves as close as they possibly could against the wall.

They had not been in this situation above two minutes, when they heard descending steps. "They are coming," cried Madeline, with a panting heart, whilst a cold dew burst from every pore.

She had scarcely spoken, when a light glimmered through the room, and a party of men rushed in it. "He is not here," vociferated one.—"Let us search elsewhere then," exclaimed another.—(Heaven hears our prayers, thought Madeline).—"We will first examine this room (said a third); these subterraneous chambers are generally surrounded with places for concealment."

The heart of Madeline died away at those words; and with a faint cry she sunk to the earth.

"Have pity upon my child (exclaimed the wretched St. Julian, bending over her, whilst the shouts of the men pierced his ears, and re-echoed through the chamber); have pity upon her, and aid me in recovering her ere you tear me from her!"

"Tear you from her! (repeated a voice which made him start from his daughter—the tender, the well-remembered voice of de Sevignie)—Oh! never (cried he, darting from amidst his companions, and snatching the still senseless Madeline from the ground), Oh! never shall Madeline be torn from the arms of her father!"

Something like a ray of hope gleamed upon the mind of St. Julian—"I am all amazement!" exclaimed he.

"You are free—you are safe (said de Sevignie); 'tis friends, not foes, that you behold; but I can give no explanation till this suffering angel is revived."

His promised explanation we shall anticipate in the following Chapter.

CHAP. IX.

Endure and conquer: Jove will soon dispose
To future good your past and present woes.
Resume your courage, and dismiss your care;
An hour will come, with pleasure to relate
Your sorrows past; as benefits of fate
Endure the hardships of your present state;
Live, and reserve yourselves for better fate.

The elder D'Alembert was son to the Marquis of Montmorenci's sister, and heir to his titles and fortunes if he died without children. He was brought up with a taste for pleasure and extravagance—a taste which, on becoming his own master, a circumstance that took place at a very early period in life, he indulged to the utter derangement of his paternal income. From the distresses which he was consequently involved in, and which his assumed character of steadiness and propriety prevented his disclosing to his uncle, he extricated himself by an union with an opulent heiress, whom the elegance and insinuation of his manners captivated, and was thus enabled again to set forward in the career of dissipation which his embarrassments had a little interrupted. Lafroy, the son of his nurse, his companion from the cradle, and attendant from the time he required an attendant, was the confident of all his profligate pursuits, and assisted him in the expenditure of such sums as materially injured his income, and again plunged him in distress.

To reveal that distress, he was now more unwilling than ever to do, from a conviction, that now more than ever he should be condemned for the dissipation which had involved him in it: he therefore set his wits to work to contrive ways and means for supplying his emergencies, and concealing it.

Knowing as he did, that if the Marquis of Montmorenci was without a son, he should, as his heir, gain what credit he required, he could not look upon the young Philippe but with eyes of envy and malignancy—as upon a person who prevented his being extricated from his difficulties. Philippe, however, was of a delicate constitution; and he indulged a hope, that if he once entered the world without the watchful eye of a parent over him, he might be led into such courses as would eventually destroy his health, and terminate his existence: it was a hope derived from a self-experience of the dangerous situation in which a young man of rank and fashion stands when unacquainted with the world, and unguarded by any friend. As a means of poisoning his mind, he had often wished to get Lafroy into his service; he knew of no person better calculated for sowing the seeds of vice, and leading the unwary into the flowery paths of dissipation. Accordingly, on a continental tour being settled for Philippe, he offered Lafroy to the Marquis for his son: having already made that tour himself, he said he knew the necessity there was for a young man being accompanied in it by some person on whom he could depend; he therefore recommended Lafroy as such a person, as one whose principles no temptation could warp, and whose integrity would be a guard for him against the designs of the artful.

The Marquis, who believed the offer of D'Alembert (as he himself indeed declared it) to be suggested by the purest friendship, accepted it with the most heartfelt gratitude, and Lafroy was taken into the suite of his son.

From Italy Lafroy wrote an account of all his operations to D'Alembert; and with the utmost chagrin, one declared, and the other heard, that the mind of Philippe was too well fortified by virtue and reflection to be led astray.

Notwithstanding the ill success of his plan, and the inconveniences he was often subjected to from the loss of Lafroy, D'Alembert would not recall him, still trusting that time and perseverance would sap the foundation which had hitherto resisted all the attacks that were made upon it.

So silent, so imperceptible were those attacks, that Philippe never was alarmed by them; they were like the sting of the asp,

That best of thieves, who with an easy key

Dost open life, and unperceiv'd by us,

Ev'n steal us from ourselves, discharging so

Death's dreadful office better than himself;

Touching our limbs so gently into slumber,

That Death stands by, deceived by his own image,

And thinks himself but sleep.

Lord Philippe returned to France without the smallest alteration in his principles; and the hopes of D'Alembert died away—hopes, however, which revived on Philippe's declaring his resolution of going back to Italy, when he had been but a few months returned from it. Something more than a mere inclination to travel he was convinced attracted him so immediately from home; and he gave the necessary instructions to Lafroy to watch him narrowly.

Lafroy suspected an attachment between him and Lady Elenora Dunlere; and his suspicions were confirmed by Lord Philippe's passing that time at the castle of her father, which, on quitting his own home, he had declared he would spend in Italy. To know the nature of the attachment, what kind of connexion it had formed, or was likely to form, between them, he laid himself out to gain the confidence of Blanche, with whose perfect knowledge of all that passed in the family he was acquainted. Ignorant, innocent, the very child of simplicity, Blanche was not long proof to his artifices—artifices which were aided by every blandishment that had power to touch a susceptible heart, and her virtue and promised secrecy to her ladies were soon sacrificed to him. From being taken into the family of the Earl when quite a child, and brought up in a great degree with his daughters, Blanche was treated more as an humble friend than servant, and entrusted with the most important secrets. Her protectors doubted not the principles which they had implanted, nor the sincerity of the attachment which their tenderness deserved, and she professed. With the marriage of both her ladies, with the relationship between their husbands, and the concealment of Lord Philippe's marriage from his brother, she was acquainted, and all those particulars she communicated to Lafroy, who transmitted them to his employer.

Scarcely were they known to D'Alembert ere they suggested a most horrid and complicated scheme of baseness and cruelty to him; a scheme of which there appeared every probability of success. That Lausane, the injured son of the Marquis, could easily be worked up to the destruction of a brother, who deprived him of his right, he could not doubt; and if Philippe fell, it would surely, he thought, be an easy matter to get rid of Lausane. On Lafroy's return to the Castle of Montmorenci, he finally adjusted and arranged his plans. The manner in which they were executed and accomplished is already known.

Josephe, at whose cottage Lausane lodged, was, as has been already mentioned, the brother of Lafroy, and Claude was a companion and particular friend, whom D'Alembert, on parting with him, took at his recommendation to supply his place.

D'Alembert charged Lafroy to secure Blanche, lest any after-repentance should tempt her to betray them: he accordingly inveigled her from the castle, by representing the delights she would experience if she went to Paris; and immediately after the fatal rencounter between the brothers, he put her into the hands of Claude, who conveyed her thither to the house of Madame Fleury. D'Alembert also charged him to destroy the son of Philippe, whose existence interfered as much with his prospects, as that of the father's had done. Lafroy promised obedience to all his commands; but the last was one he never meant to fulfil. He was so great a villain himself, he could place no confidence in others; and therefore believed, that if he had no tie upon D'Alembert, he never should receive the rewards he had been promised, and thought his services entitled to. He therefore determined to preserve the infant: nor was he stimulated to his preservation by a mere distrust of D'Alembert; another motive equally powerful influenced him, namely the aggrandizement of his own family through his means. Proud, ambitious, and disdainful of his dependant situation, he resolved on bringing up the son of Lord Philippe as his own nephew, the child of his brother Josephe; and at a proper age, insisting on an union taking place between him and the daughter of D'Alembert; "when supposed to be allied to the proud House of Montmorenci (said he), I shall no longer be permitted to be a dependant in it; the family will then enrich, will then ennoble me and mine."

As soon as he had securely lodged the child in the hands of Josephe, who, immediately after the departure of Lausane from his cottage, repaired to the Alps for the purpose of receiving it, and easily prevailed on his wife to acknowledge it as her's; he disclosed his scheme to D'Alembert, solemnly declaring at the moment he did so, that if he did not acquiesce in it, he would betray him to the Marquis. This threat—a threat which, from the disposition of Lafroy, D'Alembert doubted not his putting into execution if incensed, conquered all opposition to it; and he agreed, at a proper age, to give his daughter to the supposed son of Josephe.

But he was still more in the power of Lafroy than he imagined: Lafroy and Claude had watched the meeting between the brothers; and on Lausane's flying from the bleeding body of Philippe, they hastened to it. As they bent over it with a kind of savage triumph at the success of the execrable scheme they had been concerned in, they suddenly beheld it tremble. Lafroy was startled, and laid his hand upon the breast; he felt the heart faintly flutter; "Lausane (he exclaimed), has but ill-performed the work we gave him."

"I'll try if I cannot do it better," said Claude, and he snatched up the dagger, with which Lausane had stabbed Lord Philippe, and which lay beside him.

"Hold! (cried Lafroy, catching his arm as he raised it for the purpose of striking Lord Philippe to the heart), a thought strikes me—we had better endeavour to preserve than destroy his existence;—the life of his son is precarious; if our schemes relative to him are accomplished, we can easily destroy the father; if they are disappointed, our declaring his existence will at all times compel D'Alembert to comply with our demands, be they ever so extravagant."

"True (cried Claude); but how will you conceal him, or manage about his wounds?"

"There is an extensive cave (replied Lafroy), contiguous to the vaults of the castle, known but to few, and which Blanche showed to me; the former inhabitants of the castle used it as a place for depositing treasure in, and accordingly fortified it with iron doors. Thither, with your assistance, I can now convey him; and, as I have a knowledge of surgery, I shall dress his wound, and from the castle bring whatever I deem necessary for him:—for the purpose of attending him, I shall continue here till Josephe has left the child with his wife; he shall then return to supply my place; and as his affinity affinity to me is not known, his appearance can excite no suspicion."

"But inhabited as the castle is (said Claude), you cannot, without danger of detection, secrete him long within the cave."

"No (replied Lafroy), I cannot; as soon, therefore, as he regains sufficient strength to enable him to bear the fatigue of the journey, I shall return hither, and with your assistance and Josephe's convey him elsewhere."

This cruel scheme, which doomed the unfortunate Philippe to worse than death, to lingering misery, was put into practice without farther hesitation; and Claude was then dispatched for Blanche, who waited impatiently to commence her journey with him to Paris.

No sooner was D'Alembert informed of the death of Philippe, than he devised a scheme for the destruction of Lausane. This, it may be supposed, he meant easily to effect accusing him of murder, and consequently drawing upon him the vengeance of an enraged and afflicted father. But this was not by any means his intention;—an open accusation would, he knew, occasion a public trial, at which there could be no doubt but Lausane would declare the artifices which had instigated him to the destruction of his brother—a declaration that might, that would indeed, in all probability, D'Alembert feared, raise suspicions against himself. To prevent, therefore, all danger of such suspicions, he determined to have him privately destroyed; for which purpose, he meant to dispatch some of his well-tried emissaries to the habitation of Lord Dunlere, habited as officers of justice, to demand Lausane as a murderer; whom, on getting into their hands, they were to convey to a proper place for such a deed of horror, and put to death, but in such a manner, that his death should seem the effect of some sudden disorder. To aid in this diabolical plan, he himself travelled in disguise to the Alps, with his emissaries; and he was the person who alarmed the good monk so much by declaring his intention of searching every where for Lausane. The story invented in consequence of that declaration, completely frustrated his designs; and he returned not a little delighted to his home, at the idea of Death's having proved such a friend to him, by freeing him both from the trouble and danger of putting Lausane out of the way himself. With him died away all apprehension of detection, and all fears of disappointment relative to the estates of Montmorenci; and his dissipation, in consequence of the certainty of his expectations being realized, was unbounded.

Lafroy still remained in the service of the Marquis, who felt strongly attached to him from an idea of his having been a faithful and affectionate servant to his son. That unfortunate son recovered from his wound; and, as soon as he was able to bear a removal, was conveyed in the dead of the night by Josephe, Lafroy, and their partner in iniquity, Claude, to a lonely cottage at some distance from the castle, and well calculated, from its frightful solitude, for the purpose for which it was taken. Here, under the care of Josephe, he remained till after the death of Lord Dunlere; he was then re-conveyed to the castle, which Lafroy had art enough to prevail on D'Alembert to purchase, by pretending he should like it for a future habitation. In reality, he knew no place so well calculated for concealing the unhappy Philippe, no place in which he could so easily make away with him, when he should find his existence no longer necessary. As it was not possible to keep Josephe longer from his home without exciting suspicions and enquiries, he dispatched him to it, and placed in the castle a sister of their's and her husband, whose dispositions too much resembled his own to make him fear any thing from them.

Every thing now went smoothly on with D'Alembert: his wife, whom he had never loved, died shortly after the supposed death of the two brothers, and every one considered, and treated him with additional respect in consequence of that consideration, as the heir of Montmorenci. The unhappy Marquis, tortured with remorse, and anxious to expiate his crimes by atoning to those he had injured, made the most diligent enquiries after his eldest son—enquiries in which D'Alembert, with the warmest zeal appeared to join, but which in reality he baffled, wishing, for obvious reasons, to conceal from the Marquis every thing relative to him. The only drawback he had upon his happiness, was the idea of the degradation he should suffer by the union of his daughter with the supposed son of Josephe, a peasant upon the Montmorenci estate. But as he knew this was a measure which could not be avoided without the exposure of his iniquities, he tried to reconcile himself to it by a hope, that his rank and fortune would stifle at least the open censures of the world. The consequence which he knew he should lose by his daughter's connexion, he determined to try and re-acquire by the marriage of his son; and for this purpose, looked out amongst the most illustrious for a partner for him. His choice soon devolved upon the young and lovely heiress of the Count de Merville, who was then just presented at the French Court by her mother, and was the most admired object at it. Her heart was not gained without difficulty; but when gained, her hand soon followed it. The prize attained, the tendernesses and attentions by which it was won, were soon discontinued; and the mask of gentleness and sensibility cast aside, discovered to the unhappy mother and daughter features of the utmost deformity and horror. To reform, instead of reproach, was however the ardent wish of both—a wish which they were soon convinced was not to be accomplished; and with unutterable anguish, the Countess beheld her amiable and beloved child united to a hardened libertine. To try and alleviate her bitter destiny, she remained with her a considerable time after her marriage, till driven from her residence by the insulting treatment of D'Alembert, whose expenses far exceeded both the fortune of his wife, and the income allowed by his father, made him demand supplies from her, which she refusing, provoked him to language and conduct not more wounding to her as a woman to receive, than degrading to him as a man to use. She refused those supplies, not only because she thought it a sin to furnish vice with the means of gratifying itself, but because she wished to reserve something like an independence for her daughter, in case she was ever plunged into pecuniary distresses (of which she beheld every probability) by the thoughtless and unbounded extravagance of her husband.

During her own life this independence could only be acquired, for at her death her fortune, which, in right of her father she enjoyed, was entailed upon her daughter; and would, she was convinced, on devolving to her, be swept, like all her other possessions, into the vortex of dissipation.

To avoid the insults of D'Alembert, and to diminish her expenses, she was hastening to her chateau at the time she met with the accident which introduced her to the cottage of Clermont. No sooner was she acquainted with his situation, than she formed the resolution of taking his daughter under her protection, and dividing with her whatever she could save, and meant to have appropriated solely to Madame D'Alembert's use.

Her departure from the habitation of D'Alembert did not exempt her from his solicitations, or reproaches on finding those solicitations still unsuccessful. A letter from him, couched in a more insulting stile than any she had before received from him, was the occasion of the illness and dejection which shocked and alarmed Madeline so much on her return from Madame Chatteneuf's—an illness and dejection, for which the Countess would never assign the real cause. To conceal domestic troubles—troubles which could not be remedied, she always conceived to be the wisest plan; rightly considering, that the world always took a divided part; and, though convinced one side was culpable, never exempted the other entirely from blame.

Enraged, disappointed, and distressed by her continued refusals, D'Alembert formed the horrible resolution of assassinating her—a resolution which he scrupled not to avow to his father, who had ever been his abettor in all his villainous schemes and profligate pursuits. His father did more than sanction it by silence; he commended it as a proof of real spirit, which would not quietly submit to ill-treatment; and recommended Claude, who still continued in his service, as a proper person for assisting in such a scheme: of this young D'Alembert was already convinced, having before tried his abilities in one scarcely less iniquitous than the present. Disguised, they both travelled to the chateau, and in the ruined monastery acted the dreadful scene which has been already described. Notwithstanding her injuries, the just resentment she must have felt for them, the Countess determined never to reveal their author; the consequence of doing so would, she was convinced, be either death or distraction to her daughter. She died, imploring heaven to forgive him as she had done, and for ever conceal from his wife her having fallen by the hand of her husband.

Her solemn injunction to Madeline upon her death bed, not to continue in the house if he came to it, was occasioned by her perfect knowledge of his libertine disposition. Beauty like her's could not fail, she was sure, of exciting his regards: she was equally sure that he would not hesitate going any length to gratify his passions. She therefore, though without informing Madeline of the danger she dreaded on her account, earnestly conjured her to avoid it. Of his baseness and profligacy she had had a fatal proof during her residence beneath his roof.

Soon after his marriage, ere they were thoroughly acquainted with his disposition, she and Madame D'Alembert took under their protection a young and lovely girl, the orphan of a noble but reduced family, with whom they had been well acquainted. They took her with an intention of amply providing for her, and still keeping her amongst the circles she had been accustomed to. Long she had not been under their care, ere her charms attracted the admiration of D'Alembert; and, in defiance of the laws of hospitality, honour, and humanity, he insulted her with the basest proposals, and threatened revenge when he found them treated with the contempt they merited. Tenderness for her patronesses made her long conceal his conduct: at length she grew alarmed, and revealed it. In consequence of this disclosure, they determined to send her to a convent in Dauphine, and lodge her there till they could hear of a respectable family who would receive her as a boarder, and under whose protection she could with safety and propriety again enjoy some of the pleasures of life. Under the care of proper attendants she commenced her journey; but how great was the horror, the consternation of the Countess and Madame D'Alembert, when those attendants returned to inform them, that from the inn where they had stopped for the night, she had eloped.

The idea of her having eloped was not for an instant conceived either by the Countess or Madame D'Alembert; they knew the innocence of the unhappy girl—they knew her total ignorance of all with whom they were not acquainted, and suspicion immediately glanced at D'Alembert: they hesitated not to inform him of that suspicion; they did more—they declared their positive conviction of his having had her carried off by means of some of his agents: he denied the justice of the charge—he resented it; and, in reply to their threats (for supplications they soon found unavailing), said he was ready to deny before any tribunal they might cite him to, the crime they accused him of. His declarations of innocence gained no credit with them; they were convinced of his guilt, but could not prove it; and the unfortunate Adelaide, who had no friends out of their family interested about her, was never after heard of by them, notwithstanding their diligent and unceasing enquiries, and promises of liberally rewarding any one who could give the smallest intelligence concerning her.

As fearful as her mother of having Madeline seen by her husband, yet unwilling to relinquish her society, Madame D'Alembert determined, instead of sending her from it, to secrete her in the chateau when Monsieur D'Alembert so unexpectedly announced his intention of coming to it, for the purpose, as Agatha suspected, of seeing what part of the estate would be the best to dispose of. Amongst the domestics who attended Madame D'Alembert to the chateau, was a young female, whose principles her master had entirely perverted. His improper influence over her was, however, carefully concealed from her mistress, over whom he placed her as a kind of spy, an office she too faithfully executed. She overheard the conversation between Madame D'Alembert and Madeline, and communicated it to D'Alembert almost immediately after his arrival at the chateau. Eager to behold beauty so extolled, he rested not till he had gained access to the chamber in which Madeline was concealed, and which he effected by means of a sliding-door in the closet, with which she was unacquainted.

The moment he beheld her, he was captivated by her, and determined to leave no means untried of securing charms which he had never seen equalled. For the purpose of concerting a plan for the accomplishment of his wishes, he appointed an interview in the ruined monastery with his female confidant. The shock which Madeline received in consequence of that interview, is already known. As she lay senseless at his feet, instead of being moved to pity by her situation, he conceived the horrid idea of availing himself of it; and determined to send to the chateau for some of his emissaries to carry her off, when the unexpected approach of his wife and Lubin frustrated this intention. Not knowing who were approaching, he and his companion fled at the first sound of their steps, and thus lost the conversation which took place between Madeline and her friend.

He returned the next morning to the monastery, and explored every part of it for her; the chateau next underwent a search. When convinced she was gone, his rage knew no bounds; he openly accused his wife of perfidy, of meanness; insisted she had infringed her duty in having had any concealment from him; and peremptorily commanded her to tell him (if she hoped for his forgiveness), whither she had sent her lovely charge; this she as peremptorily refused doing. Words, in consequence of that refusal, grew high between them; and the party which had accompanied him to the chateau, were dismissed abruptly from it by him. As a justification of his conduct, and an excuse for it, he assured them that his wife's temper would not permit him to have them with pleasure to themselves any longer under his roof.

When freed from their observation, and the little restraint which they had imposed upon him, he treated the unhappy Madame D'Alembert with the utmost brutality. To avoid his inhumanity, she never stirred from her chamber, except compelled to do so by his commands; and now endeavoured to beguile her wretchedness by beginning her promised narrative to Madeline—a narrative, however, which she doubted ever having the power of sending to her, as D'Alembert solemnly swore she never should be permitted to leave the chateau, or hold converse of any kind with any person out of it, till she had communicated to him all he desired to know concerning her lovely friend.

His temper, it may be supposed, was not improved when his father arrived at the chateau to inform him of the existence of Clermont, and his being acknowledged as the son and rightful heir of the Marquis of Montmorenci. This was a blow not more unexpected than dreadful—a blow which completely demolished all his hopes of independence, all his hopes of being extricated from his difficulties. He raved, and imprecated curses upon the memory of those who had deceived his father relative to Clermont. His rage and regret at not having secured Madeline, were augmented when he understood that she was the daughter of Clermont; and reflected, that had she been carried off by him, the discovery relative to her father would never, in all probability, have taken place.

"How unfortunate (exclaimed old D'Alembert, in reply to what he had said concerning her), how unfortunate that you are not at liberty to offer your hand, and thus gratify your love and your ambition. Were you free, I am convinced I could soon effect a marriage between you and St. Julian's daughter."

His son started; a flush of savage joy overspread his countenance—"I can easily regain my liberty (said he); I have long sighed for it; a noble soul will ever try to break chains which are oppressive. My wife is but a mortal; the hand which gave a quietus to the mother, can easily give the same to the daughter. We can manage the affair between us so secretly, that no soul shall know of it, no eye behold it."

His father sighed heavily, and shook his head. Remorse had lately begun to visit his breast; and he trembled to think there was an eye over all their actions—an eye which could not be deceived. "I like not the shedding of blood," said he.

"You were not always averse to it," cried his son with a malignant sneer.

"True, because my designs could be by no other means accomplished; where mercy can be shown, I wish to be merciful; you can get rid of your wife without destroying her: the report of her death will as effectually serve your purposes as if she had really died; and in the castle on the Alps she can be too securely lodged ever to have an opportunity of proving the fallacy of that report."

D'Alembert detested his wife; and could not, without the utmost reluctance, think of sparing her life; when his father at length prevailed upon him to promise to do so. They soon concerted their schemes relative to her. It was determined that he should apologize to her for his unkindness; and, as an atonement for it, insist upon her accompanying him to Bareges, in order to try and recover her health, which to herself alone he should acknowledge his fears of having injured. Their plans arranged, they immediately separated. Old D'Alembert was in haste to return to his house from whence he had privately departed for the purpose of consulting his son on the sudden change in their prospects; Claude alone knew of his departure, and was ordered to detain the Marquis's messenger, and invent a plausible excuse for the letter he brought not being answered directly.

The purport of the letter which D'Alembert wrote in reply to it has been already mentioned. After writing it, he had a private interview with Lafroy, to whom he imparted the new scene of cruelty and baseness he and his son were about acting; and gave such instructions as he deemed necessary. These instructions were merely to do every thing which could gain the favour and confidence of St. Julian, and render him unsuspicious of the designs upon his daughter. To forward which designs, it was determined that all the horrors of superstition should be awakened in his breast; when once infected, once enervated by them, he might easily, D'Alembert believed, be made the dupe of art and villainy. For the purpose of exciting those horrors, Lafroy secreted himself in the chamber of Lord Philippe, to which he gained access by a way not known to many of the family, and forgotten by those who did know it, from its being long disused. Immediately behind the bedstead was a small door which opened into a dark closet, communicating with a flight of back stairs; those stairs, and this closet, previous to his residence at the castle, had been shut up, and chance first discovered them to him. A valuable ring of his Lord's was mislaid one day, and, in searching for it, he pushed aside the bedstead, and perceived the door; curiosity made him eagerly unbar it, and explore the places beyond it. Of those long deserted places he determined to avail himself when the plan of alarming St. Julian was first suggested, and his was the hand which, extended through the tapestry, had so greatly shocked and terrified Madeline.

The rage of D'Alembert at her obstinate refusal of his son, was even greater than he expressed; he soon found that solicitations were vain, and that stratagem alone could effect his purposes. The stratagem he called in to his aid is already known: but whilst exulting at the idea of the success with which there was every appearance of its being crowned, he was suddenly plunged into despair by the intelligence of his daughter-in-law's existence being discovered to Madeline and her father—a despair, however, from which the ready genius of Lafroy soon relieved him.

The letter which Madeline received relative to her friend, was written and delivered by Claude. A fit of illness, which endangered his life, effected a thorough reformation in his principles; and he rose from the bed of sickness resolved to make every atonement in his power for his former enormities. To openly declare the existence of Madame D'Alembert and the unfortunate Philippe, would be, he was convinced, to occasion their immediate destruction; for so well was he acquainted with the hardened wickedness of D'Alembert, his son, and Lafroy, that he doubted not their declaring such an assertion the assertion of a madman, and instantly dispatching some of the well-tried and diabolical agents, by which they were surrounded, to destroy Philippe and Viola ere any person from the Marquis could be deputed to search for them. He knew the necessity therefore there was for going secretly to work, and, having once gained access to the castle, to warn Madeline of her danger, determined to set out alone for the Alps. He learned from a domestic of D'Alembert's who was sent home, that Madeline confined herself to her chamber; and, acquainted as he was with every avenue in the castle, he found it no difficult matter to steal to her unperceived by any of the family.

His letter, which St. Julian, in the full conviction of his fidelity, imparted to Lafroy, was immediately shown by him to D'Alembert. For leaving him so abruptly, Lafroy apologized to St. Julian by saying he wished to be alone in his chamber, in order to consider what was to be done.

D'Alembert, on reading the letter, struck his forehead in a frenzy, and exclaimed that all was lost. Lafroy, however, soon convinced him to the contrary. The conversation which passed between him and Madeline, and which has already been related, sufficiently explains his plot.

St. Julian, instead of meeting a friendly guide at the extremity of the forest, as he had been taught to expect, was met by two ruffians, who rudely seized him, and forced him into a chaise, in which he was conveyed to Madame Fleury's, where too late he discovered, that by the person in whom he had most confided, he had been most deceived.

Josephe, Lafroy's brother, was the person who accompanied Madeline to Paris, under the assumed name of Oliver. An express from the Castle of Montmorenci informed young D'Alembert of all the transactions at it, and of St. Julian and his daughter being consigned to the care of Madame Fleury till he had determined their fate. He immediately conceived the idea of passing himself as the nephew of Madame Fleury, and under that assumed character, offering his hand to Madeline, falsely imagining her friendless situation would make her readily embrace any offer which gave her a promise of protection. When tired of her, which he doubted not being soon the case, he resolved on destroying her, as a sure method of preventing another disappointment relative to the fortune of Montmorenci: her father's death he would not have delayed an hour, but that he was withheld from it, by considering, if artifice failed with Madeline, fears for her father might accomplish his designs. In the house of Madame Fleury, he knew any scene of iniquity might be acted with impunity. She was a woman of the most infamous description, and avowedly kept a house for the encouragement of vice. Beneath her roof the innocent and lovely Adelaide lost her life; bribed to the horrid deed by D'Alembert, the owner of the inn at which she slept put her into his power, and, on finding no other way of escaping his violence, she stabbed herself to the heart with a knife which she concealed about her; her body was thrown into a vault beneath the house; and it was the traces of her blood which had so much alarmed Madeline. Blanche, the once faithful servant of her mother's, was the unhappy penitent she discovered before the crucifix: the seeds of virtue which had been early implanted in her mind, the artifices of Lafroy had not been able entirely to destroy; and ere she was many months with Madame Fleury, Blanche bitterly regretted her misconduct, and wished to leave her. This was a wish, however, which Madame Fleury was peremptorily commanded by D'Alembert not to gratify, lest her releasement should occasion the discovery of his crimes.

The resemblance which Madeline bore to Lady Geraldine immediately struck her; the effect it had upon her has been already described. On Madeline's quitting her, she followed her to the head of the gallery, and heard the scene which passed between her and D'Alembert. Whilst he was pursuing Madeline, she stepped into his chamber, and read his letters, which clearly explained the real name of Madeline, and the situation of her and her father—a situation which, on discovering who they really were, Blanche was determined to run every risk to rescue them from. She was acquainted with all the passages in the house, and knew she never was suspected of leaving her chamber; she therefore flattered herself she could easily effect their delivery. As soon as it grew dark, she unlocked the door of St. Julian's prison, who had by that time entirely recovered from the effects of the opiate, and briefly informed him of her wishes and intention to serve him. He heard her with grateful transport; and was conducted by her to the vault communicating with the court, from whence she ascended to bring his daughter to him.

During this transaction D'Alembert was seated quietly with Madame Fleury, exulting at the probability there was of his schemes being now successful in consequence of the terror into which he had thrown Madeline, whom he meant shortly to visit, and inform that the officers of justice were coming to the house to seize her father. But great as was his exultation, it was trifling compared to that which his father experienced, who, on the removal of St. Julian and Madeline from the Castle of Montmorenci, had not a fear remaining of any future disappointment. Till Madeline was secured, he deemed it unsafe to say any thing about her father to the Marquis; he therefore made him believe, till she had departed, that his unfortunate son, oppressed with the deepest melancholy, wandered about the forest to indulge it the whole day, and only returned at night to take some trifling refreshment, and go to bed.

As soon as Madeline was consigned to the care of Josephe, a letter was presented to the Marquis, which exactly imitated the writing of his son, and was signed with his name. This letter contained a full confession of the murder of his brother, and went on as follows:—"It was a murder to which I was stimulated by revenge at the usurpation of my rights, and a hope, that if he was once out of the way, you would not be averse to doing me justice. That hope has been realized, but without yielding me happiness. Since my arrival at the castle, remorse has been awakened by means not more awful than mysterious, in my breast; and, in consequence of that remorse, I have determined to resign all claim to the fortunes of Montmorenci, and seclude myself for ever from the world. Nor shall my daughter enjoy them; they would entail misery instead of happiness upon her: a convent is her doom; to her God I shall devote her; the offering I trust will be acceptable, and cause him to look with an eye of compassion and forgiveness upon my miseries and crimes."

The feelings of the Marquis on perusing this letter were too dreadful to be described; he accused himself as the cause of death to one son, and guilt to the other; and all idea of vengeance for the murder of Philippe was lost in the reflection of his having occasioned that murder himself. His life, in all probability, would have been terminated in a few days by the anguish he suffered, had not that Being, who accepts our penitence as an atonement for our errors, unexpectedly relieved him from the horrors of despair.

D'Alembert dispatched two emissaries after Claude for the purpose of destroying him. Fatigued by his exertions, he had stepped aside to rest himself in a little grotesque hollow at some distance from the road they took, and thus escaped falling into their merciless hands. From his concealment he had a perfect view of them, and the moment he beheld them, he conjectured their horrible designs. All hope of succouring Madame D'Alembert now died away; all hope of escaping the vengeance of her husband and his father; for whether he advanced or retreated, he was confident equal danger awaited him. Overwhelmed with fear and anguish, he flung himself despairingly on the ground, determined rather to die there, than by stirring from the spot, expose himself to the hand of an assassin. In this situation he heard a party of travellers approaching; he was in that desperate state which tempts a man to adventure every thing. He accordingly started up, and resolved on applying to them for protection for himself, and assistance for Madame D'Alembert. The instant they drew near, he threw himself before them, and in a supplicating voice, besought them to stop and listen to a story calculated to awaken all the feelings of compassion, and to interest every generous heart. His words and manner claimed immediate attention, and he began his strange narrative. Scarcely had he concluded it, when a sudden exclamation of mingled grief and indignation burst from some of the party, which convinced him he had applied to the friends of Madame D'Alembert in her behalf. To her most tender, most affectionate friends he had indeed applied—to Madame Chatteneuf and her daughter, who were returning from Italy to France, accompanied by an Italian Nobleman, (to whom a few days before the commencement of her journey, Olivia had given her hand), his friend, and a numerous retinue of servants. To the dreary castle they immediately bent their course, and rescued the unhappy Viola from worse than death—from lingering misery!

Her safety ensured, Claude mentioned the imprisonment of Philippe. His reason for not declaring it to Madeline was owing to his doubts of the existence of the unhappy captive at the time he set out for the Alps, having heard a few days before that he was in so weak a state, his life was despaired of: he therefore feared raising expectations in the breast of Madeline which might be disappointed, being well convinced, that if Philippe died ere he reached the castle, the assertion of his having lived to that period, would be considered as the mere fabrication of his brain. To the gloomy tower in which he was confined, he led the way, and found him, as he had been taught to expect, on the very brink of the grave—that grave to which he had long wished himself consigned; for, torn as he was from all that could render life desirable, life was a burden which he ardently wished to resign! But with the change in his prospects, an immediate change took place in his sentiments, and the soothing attentions of compassion—attentions to which he had been long a stranger; the joy of unexpected deliverance, and rapturous idea of beholding his son, soon effected such an alteration in his appearance, as not more delighted than astonished his friends, gave them every hope of his speedy recovery, and enabled them, even sooner than they had expected, to proceed to the castle of Montmorenci. Within a little way of it, all the carriages but Madame Chatteneuf's, stopped and, accompanied by her son-in-law, she proceeded to it, and demanded a private interview with the Marquis. After the first ceremonies of meeting were over, she told him she had something to relate to him not more affecting than interesting; but declared she could not commence her relation till he had given orders for Monsieur D'Alembert and Lafroy being secured.

Strange as was this desire, the impressive manner in which it was delivered, would not permit the Marquis to hesitate about obeying it. He accordingly summoned some of the domestics he most confided in, and gave them a strict charge to have an eye over D'Alembert and Lafroy, and inform him if they attempted to quit the castle.

Madame Chatteneuf then began her promised narrative;—nothing but the knowledge which the Marquis had of her character, could have prevented him from interrupting her in the midst of it, and declaring his doubts of its truth. When she had concluded the recital of the injustice which had been done to Madame D'Alembert, and her sufferings in consequence of it, she paused—paused from the emotions she experienced at the idea of those which the fond father would feel when informed the long-lamented darling of his heart was about being restored to his arms. She approached him with eyes swimming in tears, and taking his hand, pressed it between her's. "A yet greater, a yet more affecting surprise than that received by hearing of Madame D'Alembert's existence, awaits you (cried she); Oh! endeavour to bear it with composure—endeavour to hear with moderation—that he, whom long you have mourned, still lives—lives to demand a father's blessing, and recompense the bitter sorrow he has occasioned."

Great joy and great sorrow are often alike in their effects. Madame Chatteneuf had scarcely uttered the last word, ere the Marquis fainted in her arms. She directly desired a servant to be dispatched for the rest of her party; and the first object the Marquis beheld on recovering, was his long-lost Philippe. The scene which followed can better be conceived than described; it was such as drew tears from every spectator. Yet amidst the Marquis's raptures, the keenest pangs of anguish seized his heart at beholding the devastation which suffering had made upon his son, no more he beheld eyes darting fire, cheeks painted with the liveliest bloom of health, and a form graceful and elastic. "But happiness (he exclaimed), happiness never is perfect in this life!"

When Philippe grew a little more composed, he mentioned his son, and besought him to be sent for. This was a new surprise, a new source of delight to the Marquis; and an express was directly dispatched to the cottage of Josephe for him. Orders were also given for the confinement of D'Alembert and Lafroy.

Ignorant of the late transactions at the castle, de Sevignie, whilst he obeyed the summons to it, could not otherwise account for that summons, than by supposing his residence near Madeline had been discovered by her father, and awakened his apprehensions of their attachment being renewed in consequence of their vicinity to each other; to prevent which, he had sent for him to request he would go elsewhere. "If he makes such a request, I will obey it (cried de Sevignie, as in a melancholy manner he followed the messenger); go where I will, I shall still retain the idea of Madeline; and, though my situation cannot gain the approbation, my conduct shall merit the esteem, of her father."

Oh! how impossible to describe the feelings of Philippe when he presented himself to his view? How equally impossible to do justice to those of the Marquis, when, in the youthful Henri, he beheld the exact resemblance of his beloved son—his resemblance, when all the graces, all the charms of elegance and youth were his. Surprised by the reception he met with, by the emotions with which he was alternately clasped to the bosom of Lord Philippe and the Marquis, de Sevignie looked the very picture of astonishment. He was not permitted to remain long in ignorance of his real situation; and with a delight not inferior to that experienced by his new-found relatives, he knelt to receive their blessing. But short was the duration of his joy when informed of Madeline and her father having been spirited away from the castle; informed of the too probable dangers which surrounded them, the most dreadful anguish pervaded his soul; and striking his hand distractedly against his forehead, he exclaimed, that happiness was lost for ever!

D'Alembert and Lafroy had been brought into the apartment, taxed with their guilt, and strictly interrogated concerning St. Julian and his daughter; to which interrogations both had hitherto observed a profound silence—a silence the former determined to persevere in, from a fiend-like wish of rendering others as miserable as himself; but which the latter resolved on breaking if he could, by doing so, escape the punishment he merited. In reply, therefore, to what de Sevignie had said, he declared there was still a chance of happiness being restored to him.

"If (cried he), the Marquis will promise to pardon me, and not cast me without provision upon the world, I will, without delay, reveal the place to which the Count and his daughter have been taken."

"Oh! promise him all he asks (exclaimed de Sevignie, grasping the arm of the Marquis); promise him pardon—promise him wealth, protection, if he but declares the situation of Madeline and her father."

"Solemnly I promise to grant him all he desires," said the Marquis.

"May his information come too late! (cried D'Alembert, who, finding his baseness could not even be palliated, determined no longer to conceal the deformity of his soul); may his information come too late! ere this, I trust, the fate of the father and daughter is decided—the dreadful fate to which they both were doomed."

"Infernal monster! (exclaimed de Sevignie, catching him by the breast, then suddenly flinging him from him); you are a defenceless man (he exclaimed), that consideration alone saves you from my fury. Villain as you are, I will not strike where there can be no resistance. Oh! tell me (he continued, turning to Lafroy), Oh! tell me whither I can fly to rescue Madeline and her father."

Lafroy, having made his conditions, informed him without hesitation, and the Count Manfredonia, the husband of Olivia, and his friend Count Durasso, both declared their resolution of accompanying him directly to Paris.

Whilst the carriages were preparing, the Marquis wrote a hasty letter to a nobleman of high rank and power there, requesting him to give whatever authority was necessary to de Sevignie for searching the house of Madame Fleury. De Sevignie never stopped till he reached Paris, except when compelled to do so for the purpose of changing horses.

The moment the nobleman to whom the Marquis's letter was addressed, had perused it, he procured proper officers to accompany de Sevignie to Madame Fleury's. She and D'Alembert were immediately secured, and the house searched for Madeline and her father. But when de Sevignie found it searched in vain, no language could describe what he felt; he flew to the prisoners, and implored them to reveal the place to which they had conveyed the unfortunate St. Julian and his daughter. They heard his supplications unmoved: what he asked they could not indeed have granted; yet, in order to torture him, they pretended that they could. Though unable to account for the escape of St. Julian and Madeline, they yet believed they had effected it, and rejoiced at the idea, not only on the account of the anguish which they perceived the uncertainty of their fate gave to de Sevignie, but from a hope that they might be able to extricate themselves from his power, and regain the fugitives.

De Sevignie was sinking beneath the horrors of despair, when the subterraneous chambers were mentioned by the officers; thither he directly fled, and there discovered the objects of his search; from thence he bore the senseless Madeline to the parlour, which was cleared for her reception. Oh! how utterly impossible to describe her feelings when, on recovering, she perceived de Sevignie—when, as he pressed her to his throbbing heart, from his lips she received an assurance of her safety and her father's: but great as was the rapture of those feelings, it was faint compared to that which she experienced on being informed of the existence of Philippe. At first she doubted the reality of what she heard, and accused de Sevignie of an intention of deceiving her; then besought him, if he wished to be credited, to give a solemn assurance of the truth of his assertion. This solemn assurance was instantly given, and received by Madeline with a wild scream of joy: then, flying to her father, who, on the first mention of his brother, had sunk motionless upon a chair, she flung herself into his arms; her caresses restored him to sensibility. He disengaged himself from her, and knelt down—"Oh! God (he cried, his uplifted hands folded together), accept my thanks—accept my thanks for preventing me from being in reality a murderer, a fratricide. In adversity I besought thee to give me fortitude to bear it; in prosperity I now beseech thee to give me moderation to sustain it; Oh! teach, teach me to support with composure this sudden reverse of situation!"

"Oh! ecstasy (cried Madeline, kneeling beside him), to know your guiltless brother lives; to know you have nothing more to fear, repays me amply for all my sufferings."

When they grew a little composed, de Sevignie continued his narration.

"The web of deceit is at length unravelled (said St. Julian, as soon as he had concluded it), and the ways of Providence are justified to man. We now perceive, that however successful the schemes of wickedness may be at first, they are, in the end, completely defeated and overthrown. We now perceive, that God wounds but to heal, strikes but to save, punishes us in this life, but to correct our passions, and render us deserving of happiness in that which is to come."

Blanche, who had followed them to the parlour, shared their transports, and now made herself known; for time and sorrow had so altered her, that St. Julian had not the smallest recollection of her. He freely granted the pardon she asked for the part she had had in his sufferings, and he promised to send her to the place of her nativity, where she earnestly wished to end her days.

Anxious to terminate the anxiety of his friends, it was determined that the journey to the Castle of Montmorenci should be commenced at the dawn of day. Accordingly at the settled time they left the detested mansion of Madame Fleury, leaving her and D'Alembert in it under the care of the officers of justice, till it should be known whether the charges against them would occasion their being confined elsewhere. They travelled with the utmost expedition, nor slackened their speed, till within a short distance of the castle, in order to send forward a servant to inform the Marquis of their approach, lest their appearance, if unexpected, should affect him too much; but, notwithstanding this precaution, the emotions he felt on beholding them—on beholding the long separated brothers folded in the arms of each other, were such as nearly overcame him, and "shook his frame almost to dissolution."

In the most affecting language St. Julian implored Lord Philippe's pardon, which he, in terms not less affecting, granted.

"My sons (said a reverend Monk from a neighbouring convent, the same to whom the Marquis had given such particular directions about his eldest son before he was discovered), take my advice, and let a veil be drawn over past transactions, never to be raised except it is for the purpose of instructing youth, by displaying to them the fearful scenes which uncontrolled passions may occasion—uncontrolled passions I repeat, for to such were all your miseries owing. The Marquis, by gratifying his love at the expense of honour and humanity, entailed remorse upon himself, and all the horrors which must ever attend our conviction of being under the immediate displeasure of heaven: and you (addressing St. Julian), by madly following the bent of resentment, plunged yourself, to all appearance, into an abyss of guilt, from whence you scarcely dared to raise your eyes to heaven to implore its protection against the designs of the cruel, and the punishment you thought you had merited; whilst your brother, by gratifying the impulse of inclination, without obtaining, or trying to obtain, the sanction of a parent, left himself exposed to the most base designs, and, by practising deceit himself, taught others to practise it upon him. In the course of your sufferings, I dare say you have often accused fate of being the occasion of them; when, in reality, had you properly reflected, you would have found they entirely originated with yourselves: that they are terminated can scarcely excite more pleasure in your hearts than in mine: may your happiness never again know diminution, and your past sorrows, if mentioned, only be mentioned for the purpose of keeping alive a fervent gratitude to that Being who so wonderfully dispersed them!

"From your strange and eventful story, the virtuous may be convinced that they should never despair—the guilty, that they should never exult, as the hour of deliverance to one, and retribution to the other, often arrives when least expected: both should also learn by it, that a merciful God makes allowances for human frailty, and accepts sincere repentance as an atonement for error." In the words of the poet the holy man might have concluded,

Heaven has but

Our sorrows for our sins, and then delights

To pardon erring man. Sweet mercy seems

Its darling attribute, which limits justice,

As if there were degrees in Infinite,

And Infinite would rather want perfection,

Than punish to extent.

"The affection subsisting between my sons (said the Marquis), prevents my feeling that uneasiness I should otherwise experience at the idea of leaving one almost wholly depending upon the other."

"We will know no difference of fortune (exclaimed St. Julian); all that I could do for my brother, all that I could bestow upon him, could never be a sufficient recompense for the sufferings I occasioned him."

"Most amply can you recompense them," said Philippe.

"In what manner?" cried St. Julian with eagerness.

"Need I explain my meaning? (said Philippe, and he glanced alternately at Madeline and de Sevignie, whose attachment he had been previously informed of); need I say that it is by giving your daughter to my son, you can make me amends for all my sorrows."

"That I shall readily make such amends, you will believe (cried St. Julian), when I tell you, that by so doing, I shall ensure my own happiness; in seeing the precious offspring of Elenora and Geraldine united, the most ardent wishes of my heart will be accomplished: in giving her to de Sevignie, I give her to a man, in whose favour I felt a predilection, excited not only by his manner, but his strong resemblance to you. Take her (he continued, presenting her hand to de Sevignie), take her with the fond blessing of her father; and may the felicity you both deserve, be ever your's!"

The feelings of de Sevignie and Madeline were such as language could not have done justice to; but their eyes, more eloquently than any words could have done, expressed them.

Sorrow now seemed removed from every heart but that of Madame D'Alembert's; with the deepest melancholy she ruminated over her sad prospects, and resolved to retire from the castle of Montmorenci to a convent, as soon as some settlement had taken place relative to her husband and his iniquitous father. On her account (well knowing, notwithstanding her abhorrence to them she would sensibly feel their exposure to public disgrace), the Marquis determined not to give them up to the punishment they merited, provided they solemnly promised, ere he liberated them, never more to molest her, or attempt injuring the property she inherited in right of her mother. He had already spoken on the subject to D'Alembert, but could not extort a reply from him; he therefore resolved on sending an express to the son, to inform him of the conditions on which he would restore him to liberty.

On the evening of this happy day which restored them to the Castle of Montmorenci, de Sevignie and Madeline wandered into the forest, and there he informed her of all he had suffered on her account. "In a manner very different from the family to which I was supposed to belong (said he), I was brought up, by the desire, it was said, of Monsieur D'Alembert, my godfather. Not qualified from my education to partake of the amusements, or join in the pursuits of my family, I found home unpleasant, and early conceived a passion for wandering about; which passion the presents I received from D'Alembert, and the indulgence of my father, permitted me to gratify. In the course of my wanderings, I beheld and became acquainted with you: the feelings you inspired, what followed that acquaintance must have already explained. Though formed to adorn the highest station, I yet flattered myself the unambitious disposition of your father would incline him to bestow you on me, provided I could prove myself possessed of a competency, and worthy, from my past conduct, of his approbation. To do the latter would, I knew, be easy; and to do the former, would, I trusted, be scarcely more difficult, for D'Alembert had always promised to secure me a handsome establishment, and I now hoped he might be prevailed on to fulfil his promises. I wrote to my father, opened my whole heart to him, and besought him to apply to D'Alembert in my behalf. I received an immediate answer to this letter, in which my father charged me, except I wished to incur his severest malediction, never to think more about you, declaring that my sole prosperity in life depended on my union with D'Alembert's daughter, who, in my visits to the chateau, he said, had conceived a partiality for me, which her father, rather than destroy her peace, had determined to gratify. My resolution, on perusing this letter, was instantly formed: I resolved never to marry a woman I disliked, nor unite myself to one I loved, except assured I could add to, instead of injure, her happiness. Notwithstanding my determination, I lingered in your house till the altered looks of your father plainly convinced me he wished for my departure: the pangs which rend soul and body, could not, I am sure, have been greater than those I endured on tearing myself from you.

"I returned to my father's house; he treated me ill, and I resumed my wanderings, with a hope that change of scene might alleviate my anguish; but this hope was disappointed; no change of scene could change the feelings of my soul; no company could amuse, no prospect delight; upon the loveliest productions of Nature I often gazed with a vacant eye—prospects which, in the early days of youth, when expectation sat smiling at my heart, I had often contemplated with a degree of rapturous enthusiasm which seemed to raise me from earth to heaven, and inspiring me with a sublime devotion, made me look up through Nature's works to Nature's God.

"Not all the attention, the hospitality I received at V———, to which chance alone conducted me, could dissipate the thoughts that corroded my peace; but, as if I had a presentiment of your coming to it, I could not bring myself to leave it. Strange and inconsistent you found me: that strangeness, that inconsistency, was owing to a passion which I wished to conquer, yet could not forbear nourishing—which I wished, yet dreaded, to have returned, conscious as I was that that return would plunge the object of my love in sorrow.

"But how weak is the mind of man, how frail his best resolves! When I found I had an interest in that tender heart, every idea but of felicity fled from me; and I was tempted to ask you to unite your destiny to mine: a sudden interruption to our conversation alone prevented my doing so. Scarcely however, had I left your presence, ere Reason resumed her empire, and represented the baseness of what I had intended. Shall I then persevere in such an intention? (I cried); shall I take advantage of her tenderness?—shall I requite it by plunging her into difficulties—by transplanting her from the genial soil in which she has flourished, to one of penury?—shall I sink, instead of exalting, my love?—shall I requite the humanity of the father, by blasting the hopes he entertains about his child?—Oh! no, (I exclaimed, maddening at the idea), I will not be such a villain; I will not, Madeline, merit your after-reproaches and my own by such conduct; every hope relative to you—hopes which but now raised my soul to heaven, I will relinquish. How I acted in consequence of this determination you know; but you know not, nor can I give you any adequate idea of the anguish which I endured in consequence of it—the anguish which I felt at observing the resentment that glowed upon your cheek, and sparkled in your eye at the idea of my being either deceitful or capricious; scarcely on witnessing it, could I withhold myself from kneeling at your feet, and fully explaining the motives of my conduct. You may wonder, perhaps, at my not revealing myself on hearing of the Countess de Merville's kind intentions towards me; I was prevented doing so, by an idea of her being, notwithstanding all her worth, too proud, like the rest of the French noblesse, to think of bestowing her Madeline—she, whose graces, whose loveliness fitted her for the most exalted station, upon the son of a peasant, when once she had discovered his origin: to disclose my situation I therefore deemed unnecessary. After our parting I lingered some time longer at V———, and might not perhaps have left it so soon as I did, had I not received a positive command from my father to return home:—on doing so, he renewed his importunities for a marriage with D'Alembert's daughter; I told him my positive determination relative to her, and he behaved with outrage. I should immediately have quitted home, had he not assured me, if I did so, his curses would pursue me. Though I considered his conduct unjustifiable, I shrunk from his malediction, and accordingly obeyed him. Chance first produced the discovery of my vicinity to her who engrossed all my thoughts. Ah! little did I think, when I first heard of the newly-acknowledged son of the Marquis of Montmorenci, that Clermont was that son: Ah! little did I think, when I heard of the beauty, the goodness of his daughter, that it was to the praises of Madeline I was listening.

"I saw you one day in the forest; surprise riveted me to the spot, nor had I power to move till you disappeared. A domestic belonging to the castle was passing me at the moment; I enquired from him about you, and heard your real situation. From that period I haunted the forest in hopes of catching a glimpse of you; and you may recollect seeing me one evening near the monumental pillar.

"Great have been my sufferings, but amply are they recompensed; my present felicity is such as, in the most sanguine moments of expectation, I never could have thought of experiencing. To find myself allied to beings congenial to my heart—to find myself on the point of being united to the woman I adore, is a happiness which requires the utmost efforts of reason to bear with any moderation."

As he spoke, they heard an approaching step, and the next instant St. Julian appeared before them:—he looked agitated; and Madeline, in a voice of alarm, enquired the cause of that agitation;—he briefly informed her.

An express, he said, had just arrived from Paris to announce the death of young D'Alembert. Maddened at finding his schemes discovered, and his hopes defeated, in a paroxysm of fury he had stabbed himself; but scarcely had he committed the rash act ere he repented it, and implored immediate assistance; this assistance was procured but to confirm his apprehensions of the wound being mortal. After suffering excruciating pangs of body and mind, he endeavoured to ease the latter by a full avowal of all his enormities. He accordingly confessed his having occasioned the death of a young girl, called Adelaide St. Pierre; his having assassinated the Countess de Merville, and poisoned her house-keeper, Agatha, for fear of her betraying him; after which confession he shortly expired.

Madeline was so shocked by hearing of his crimes, that it was many minutes ere she had power to move. At length the fond caresses of her father and attentions of de Sevignie, restored her in some degree to herself.

Her father then informed her he had sought her for the purpose of bringing her to the castle, in order to assist him in breaking the affair to Madame D'Alembert. "Though all affection for her husband must long since (cried he), have been destroyed by his unworthy conduct, I am yet convinced, from her feelings, she will be shocked to hear of his dying by his own hand. His confession I mean carefully to conceal from her; for to know her mother was murdered—murdered by her husband, would, I am confident, entail horror and wretchedness upon her days."

Madeline now hastened to the castle, and D'Alembert's death was communicated with the utmost caution to Madame D'Alembert;—it filled her with horror; but, as St. Julian had said, all affection for him having long before ceased, every hope was entertained of the melancholy impression which it made upon her mind being soon erased. On his father it had the most dreadful effect, the moment he heard it; the proud disdainful silence which he had observed from the first discovery of his baseness, vanished, and he vented his misery in groans and exclamations, accusing himself of being the cause of his son's destruction. Every attention which humanity could dictate was paid him, but paid in vain. Attentions from those he had injured, rather aggravated than soothed his feelings; and in about two days after his son's death, he declared his resolution of renouncing the world. He accordingly withdrew from the castle of Montmorenci to La Trappe, the most rigid of all the religious houses in France, where he soon ended a miserable existence. Immediately after his departure Lafroy was dismissed, having first, according to the promise that was made him, received a handsome provision, which, by giving him the power of gratifying his inordinate passions, soon occasioned his death. Josephe, his iniquitous brother, was compelled to retire from the vicinity of the castle; but though he deserved punishment and misery, the Marquis was too generous to permit him to feel any inconvenience in consequence of this measure. Claude and Blanche, alike penitent, were, by their own desire, sent to the places from whence they originally came, amply secured from the ills of poverty. Thus did the Marquis and his sons fulfil every promise they had made, and by the mercy they extended to others, proved their gratitude to heaven for that which they had themselves experienced.

As soon as tranquillity was restored to the inhabitants of the castle, the nuptials of de Sevignie and Madeline were solemnized; after which they accompanied Madame D'Alembert, (who with her friend Madame Chatteneuf and her party, had only waited to see them united,) to the Chateau de Valdore. Without mingled emotions of pain and pleasure Madeline could not re-enter it, nor could de Sevignie, without experiencing similar ones, behold the walks where he had often wandered to watch for Madeline, and despairingly sigh forth her name. A constant intercourse was kept up between the families of Madame D'Alembert and Madame Chatteneuf, in the course of which Count Durasso, who from the first interview had been captivated by her graces, made the impression he wished upon the heart of Viola. To the softness of the Italian he united the vivacity of the French, and was in every respect worthy of her. Till the happy period which united them, de Sevignie and Madeline divided their time alternately between the Castle of Montmorenci and the Chateau de Valdore.

With Durasso, Viola enjoyed a long course of uninterrupted happiness—happiness which could only be equalled by that which her beloved friends de Sevignie and Madeline experienced.

Having now, to use the words of Adam, brought "my story to the sum of earthly bliss," I shall conclude with an humble hope, that however unworthy of public favour it may be deemed, its not aspiring to fame will guard it from severity.

FINIS

Northanger Abbey

By Jane Austin

ADVERTISEMENT BY THE AUTHORESS, TO NORTHANGER ABBEY

This little work was finished in the year 1803, and intended for immediate publication. It was disposed of to a bookseller, it was even advertised, and why the business proceeded no farther, the author has never been able to learn. That any bookseller should think it worth-while to purchase what he did not think it worth-while to publish seems extraordinary. But with this, neither the author nor the public have any other concern than as some observation is necessary upon those parts of the work which thirteen years have made comparatively obsolete. The public are entreated to bear in mind that thirteen years have passed since it was finished, many more since it was begun, and that during that period, places, manners, books, and opinions have undergone considerable changes.

CHAPTER 1

No one who had ever seen Catherine Morland in her infancy would have supposed her born to be an heroine. Her situation in life, the character of her father and mother, her own person and disposition, were all equally against her. Her father was a clergyman, without being neglected, or poor, and a very respectable man, though his name was Richard—and he had never been handsome. He had a considerable independence besides two good livings—and he was not in the least addicted to locking up his daughters. Her mother was a woman of useful plain sense, with a good temper, and, what is more remarkable, with a good constitution. She had three sons before Catherine was born; and instead of dying in bringing the latter into the world, as anybody might expect, she still lived on—lived to have six children more—to see them growing up around her, and to enjoy excellent health herself. A family of ten children will be always called a fine family, where there are heads and arms and legs enough for the number; but the Morlands had little other right to the word, for they were in general very plain, and Catherine, for many years of her life, as plain as any. She had a thin awkward figure, a sallow skin without colour, dark lank hair, and strong features—so much for her person; and not less unpropitious for heroism seemed her mind. She was fond of all boys' plays, and greatly preferred cricket not merely to dolls, but to the more heroic enjoyments of infancy, nursing a dormouse, feeding a canary-bird, or watering a rose-bush. Indeed she had no taste for a garden; and if she gathered flowers at all, it was chiefly for the pleasure of mischief—at least so it was conjectured from her always preferring those which she was forbidden to take. Such were her propensities—her abilities were quite as extraordinary. She never could learn or understand anything before she was taught; and sometimes not even then, for she was often inattentive, and occasionally stupid. Her mother was three months in teaching her only to repeat the "Beggar's Petition"; and after all, her next sister, Sally, could say it better than she did. Not that Catherine was always stupid—by no means; she learnt the fable of "The Hare and Many Friends" as quickly as any girl in England. Her mother wished her to learn music; and Catherine was sure she should like it, for she was very fond of tinkling the keys of the old forlorn spinnet; so, at eight years old she began. She learnt a year, and could not bear it; and Mrs. Morland, who did not insist on her daughters being accomplished in spite of incapacity or distaste, allowed her to leave off. The day which dismissed the music-master was one of the happiest of Catherine's life. Her taste for drawing was not superior; though whenever she could obtain the outside of a letter from her mother or seize upon any other odd piece of paper, she did what she could in that way, by drawing houses and trees, hens and chickens, all very much like one another. Writing and accounts she was taught by her father; French by her mother: her proficiency in either was not remarkable, and she shirked her lessons in both whenever she could. What a strange, unaccountable character!—for with all these symptoms of profligacy at ten years old, she had neither a bad heart nor a bad temper, was seldom stubborn, scarcely ever quarrelsome, and very kind to the little ones, with few interruptions of tyranny; she was moreover noisy and wild, hated confinement and cleanliness, and loved nothing so well in the world as rolling down the green slope at the back of the house.

Such was Catherine Morland at ten. At fifteen, appearances were mending; she began to curl her hair and long for balls; her complexion improved, her features were softened by plumpness and colour, her eyes gained more animation, and her figure more consequence. Her love of dirt gave way to an inclination for finery, and she grew clean as she grew smart; she had now the pleasure of sometimes hearing her father and mother remark on her personal improvement. "Catherine grows quite a good-looking girl—she is almost pretty to-day," were words which caught her ears now and then; and how welcome were the sounds! To look almost pretty is an acquisition of higher delight to a girl who has been looking plain the first fifteen years of her life than a beauty from her cradle can ever receive.

Mrs. Morland was a very good woman, and wished to see her children everything they ought to be; but her time was so much occupied in lying-in and teaching the little ones, that her elder daughters were inevitably left to shift for themselves; and it was not very wonderful that Catherine, who had by nature nothing heroic about her, should prefer cricket, baseball, riding on horseback, and running about the country at the age of fourteen, to books—or at least books of information—for, provided that nothing like useful knowledge could be gained from them, provided they were all story and no reflection, she had never any objection to books at all. But from fifteen to seventeen she was in training for a heroine; she read all such works as heroines must read to supply their memories with those quotations which are so serviceable and so soothing in the vicissitudes of their eventful lives.

From Pope, she learnt to censure those who

"bear about the mockery of woe."

From Gray, that

"Many a flower is born to blush unseen,

"And waste its fragrance on the desert air."

From Thomson, that—

"It is a delightful task

"To teach the young idea how to shoot."

And from Shakespeare she gained a great store of information—amongst the rest, that—

"Trifles light as air,

"Are, to the jealous, confirmation strong,

"As proofs of Holy Writ."

That

"The poor beetle, which we tread upon,

"In corporal sufferance feels a pang as great

"As when a giant dies."

And that a young woman in love always looks—

"like Patience on a monument

"Smiling at Grief."

So far her improvement was sufficient—and in many other points she came on exceedingly well; for though she could not write sonnets, she brought herself to read them; and though there seemed no chance of her throwing a whole party into raptures by a prelude on the pianoforte, of her own composition, she could listen to other people's performance with very little fatigue. Her greatest deficiency was in the pencil—she had no notion of drawing—not enough even to attempt a sketch of her lover's profile, that she might be detected in the design. There she fell miserably short of the true heroic height. At present she did not know her own poverty, for she had no lover to portray. She had reached the age of seventeen, without having seen one amiable youth who could call forth her sensibility, without having inspired one real passion, and without having excited even any admiration but what was very moderate and very transient. This was strange indeed! But strange things may be generally accounted for if their cause be fairly searched out. There was not one lord in the neighbourhood; no—not even a baronet. There was not one family among their acquaintance who had reared and supported a boy accidentally found at their door—not one young man whose origin was unknown. Her father had no ward, and the squire of the parish no children.

But when a young lady is to be a heroine, the perverseness of forty surrounding families cannot prevent her. Something must and will happen to throw a hero in her way.

Mr. Allen, who owned the chief of the property about Fullerton, the village in Wiltshire where the Morlands lived, was ordered to Bath for the benefit of a gouty constitution—and his lady, a good-humoured woman, fond of Miss Morland, and probably aware that if adventures will not befall a young lady in her own village, she must seek them abroad, invited her to go with them. Mr. and Mrs. Morland were all compliance, and Catherine all happiness.

CHAPTER 2

In addition to what has been already said of Catherine Morland's personal and mental endowments, when about to be launched into all the difficulties and dangers of a six weeks' residence in Bath, it may be stated, for the reader's more certain information, lest the following pages should otherwise fail of giving any idea of what her character is meant to be, that her heart was affectionate; her disposition cheerful and open, without conceit or affectation of any kind—her manners just removed from the awkwardness and shyness of a girl; her person pleasing, and, when in good looks, pretty—and her mind about as ignorant and uninformed as the female mind at seventeen usually is.

When the hour of departure drew near, the maternal anxiety of Mrs. Morland will be naturally supposed to be most severe. A thousand alarming presentiments of evil to her beloved Catherine from this terrific separation must oppress her heart with sadness, and drown her in tears for the last day or two of their being together; and advice of the most important and applicable nature must of course flow from her wise lips in their parting conference in her closet. Cautions against the violence of such noblemen and baronets as delight in forcing young ladies away to some remote farm-house, must, at such a moment, relieve the fulness of her heart. Who would not think so? But Mrs. Morland knew so little of lords and baronets, that she entertained no notion of their general mischievousness, and was wholly unsuspicious of danger to her daughter from their machinations. Her cautions were confined to the following points. "I beg, Catherine, you will always wrap yourself up very warm about the throat, when you come from the Rooms at night; and I wish you would try to keep some account of the money you spend; I will give you this little book on purpose."

Sally, or rather Sarah (for what young lady of common gentility will reach the age of sixteen without altering her name as far as she can?), must from situation be at this time the intimate friend and confidante of her sister. It is remarkable, however, that she neither insisted on Catherine's writing by every post, nor exacted her promise of transmitting the character of every new acquaintance, nor a detail of every interesting conversation that Bath might produce. Everything indeed relative to this important journey was done, on the part of the Morlands, with a degree of moderation and composure, which seemed rather consistent with the common feelings of common life, than with the refined susceptibilities, the tender emotions which the first separation of a heroine from her family ought always to excite. Her father, instead of giving her an unlimited order on his banker, or even putting an hundred pounds bank-bill into her hands, gave her only ten guineas, and promised her more when she wanted it.

Under these unpromising auspices, the parting took place, and the journey began. It was performed with suitable quietness and uneventful safety. Neither robbers nor tempests befriended them, nor one lucky overturn to introduce them to the hero. Nothing more alarming occurred than a fear, on Mrs. Allen's side, of having once left her clogs behind her at an inn, and that fortunately proved to be groundless.

They arrived at Bath. Catherine was all eager delight—her eyes were here, there, everywhere, as they approached its fine and striking environs, and afterwards drove through those streets which conducted them to the hotel. She was come to be happy, and she felt happy already.

They were soon settled in comfortable lodgings in Pulteney Street.

It is now expedient to give some description of Mrs. Allen, that the reader may be able to judge in what manner her actions will hereafter tend to promote the general distress of the work, and how she will, probably, contribute to reduce poor Catherine to all the desperate wretchedness of which a last volume is capable—whether by her imprudence, vulgarity, or jealousy—whether by intercepting her letters, ruining her character, or turning her out of doors.

Mrs. Allen was one of that numerous class of females, whose society can raise no other emotion than surprise at there being any men in the world who could like them well enough to marry them. She had neither beauty, genius, accomplishment, nor manner. The air of a gentlewoman, a great deal of quiet, inactive good temper, and a trifling turn of mind were all that could account for her being the choice of a sensible, intelligent man like Mr. Allen. In one respect she was admirably fitted to introduce a young lady into public, being as fond of going everywhere and seeing everything herself as any young lady could be. Dress was her passion. She had a most harmless delight in being fine; and our heroine's entree into life could not take place till after three or four days had been spent in learning what was mostly worn, and her chaperon was provided with a dress of the newest fashion. Catherine too made some purchases herself, and when all these matters were arranged, the important evening came which was to usher her into the Upper

Rooms. Her hair was cut and dressed by the best hand, her clothes put on with care, and both Mrs. Allen and her maid declared she looked quite as she should do. With such encouragement, Catherine hoped at least to pass uncensured through the crowd. As for admiration, it was always very welcome when it came, but she did not depend on it.

Mrs. Allen was so long in dressing that they did not enter the ballroom till late. The season was full, the room crowded, and the two ladies squeezed in as well as they could. As for Mr. Allen, he repaired directly to the card-room, and left them to enjoy a mob by themselves. With more care for the safety of her new gown than for the comfort of her protégée, Mrs. Allen made her way through the throng of men by the door, as swiftly as the necessary caution would allow; Catherine, however, kept close at her side, and linked her arm too firmly within her friend's to be torn asunder by any common effort of a struggling assembly. But to her utter amazement she found that to proceed along the room was by no means the way to disengage themselves from the crowd; it seemed rather to increase as they went on, whereas she had imagined that when once fairly within the door, they should easily find seats and be able to watch the dances with perfect convenience. But this was far from being the case, and though by unwearied diligence they gained even the top of the room, their situation was just the same; they saw nothing of the dancers but the high feathers of some of the ladies. Still they moved on—something better was yet in view; and by a continued exertion of strength and ingenuity they found themselves at last in the passage behind the highest bench. Here there was something less of crowd than below; and hence Miss Morland had a comprehensive view of all the company beneath her, and of all the dangers of her late passage through them. It was a splendid sight, and she began, for the first time that evening, to feel herself at a ball: she longed to dance, but she had not an acquaintance in the room. Mrs. Allen did all that she could do in such a case by saying very placidly, every now and then, "I wish you could dance, my dear—I wish you could get a partner." For some time her young friend felt obliged to her for these wishes; but they were repeated so often, and proved so totally ineffectual, that Catherine grew tired at last, and would thank her no more.

They were not long able, however, to enjoy the repose of the eminence they had so laboriously gained. Everybody was shortly in motion for tea, and they must squeeze out like the rest. Catherine began to feel something of disappointment—she was tired of being continually pressed against by people, the generality of whose faces possessed nothing to interest, and with all of whom she was so wholly unacquainted that she could not relieve the irksomeness of imprisonment by the exchange of a syllable with any of her fellow captives; and when at last arrived in the tea-room, she felt yet more the awkwardness of having no party to join, no acquaintance to claim, no gentleman to assist them. They saw nothing of Mr. Allen; and after looking about them in vain for a more eligible situation, were obliged to sit down at the end of a table, at which a large party were already placed, without having anything to do there, or anybody to speak to, except each other.

Mrs. Allen congratulated herself, as soon as they were seated, on having preserved her gown from injury. "It would have been very shocking to have it torn," said she, "would not it? It is such a delicate muslin. For my part I have not seen anything I like so well in the whole room, I assure you."

"How uncomfortable it is," whispered Catherine, "not to have a single acquaintance here!"

"Yes, my dear," replied Mrs. Allen, with perfect serenity, "it is very uncomfortable indeed."

"What shall we do? The gentlemen and ladies at this table look as if they wondered why we came here—we seem forcing ourselves into their party."

"Aye, so we do. That is very disagreeable. I wish we had a large acquaintance here."

"I wish we had any;—it would be somebody to go to."

"Very true, my dear; and if we knew anybody we would join them directly. The Skinners were here last year—I wish they were here now."

"Had not we better go away as it is? Here are no tea-things for us, you see."

"No more there are, indeed. How very provoking! But I think we had better sit still, for one gets so tumbled in such a crowd! How is my head, my dear? Somebody gave me a push that has hurt it, I am afraid."

"No, indeed, it looks very nice. But, dear Mrs. Allen, are you sure there is nobody you know in all this multitude of people? I think you must know somebody."

"I don't, upon my word—I wish I did. I wish I had a large acquaintance here with all my heart, and then I should get you a partner. I should be so glad to have you dance. There goes a strange-looking woman! What an odd gown she has got on! How old-fashioned it is! Look at the back."

After some time they received an offer of tea from one of their neighbours; it was thankfully accepted, and this introduced a light conversation with the gentleman who offered it, which was the only time that anybody spoke to them during the evening, till they were discovered and joined by Mr. Allen when the dance was over.

"Well, Miss Morland," said he, directly, "I hope you have had an agreeable ball."

"Very agreeable indeed," she replied, vainly endeavouring to hide a great yawn.

"I wish she had been able to dance," said his wife; "I wish we could have got a partner for her. I have been saying how glad I should be if the Skinners were here this winter instead of last; or if the Parrys had come, as they talked of once, she might have danced with George Parry. I am so sorry she has not had a partner!"

"We shall do better another evening I hope," was Mr. Allen's consolation.

The company began to disperse when the dancing was over—enough to leave space for the remainder to walk about in some comfort; and now was the time for a heroine, who had not yet played a very distinguished part in the events of the evening, to be noticed and admired. Every five minutes, by removing some of the crowd, gave greater openings for her charms. She was now seen by many young men who had not been near her before. Not one, however, started with rapturous wonder on beholding her, no whisper of eager inquiry ran round the room, nor was she once called a divinity by anybody. Yet Catherine was in very good looks, and had the company only seen her three years before, they would now have thought her exceedingly handsome.

She was looked at, however, and with some admiration; for, in her own hearing, two gentlemen pronounced her to be a pretty girl. Such words had their due effect; she immediately thought the evening pleasanter than she had found it before—her humble vanity was contented—she felt more obliged to the two young men for this simple praise than a true quality heroine would have been for fifteen sonnets in celebration of her charms, and went to her chair in good humour with everybody, and perfectly satisfied with her share of public attention.

CHAPTER 3

Every morning now brought its regular duties—shops were to be visited; some new part of the town to be looked at; and the Pump-room to be attended, where they paraded up and down for an hour, looking at everybody and speaking to no one. The wish of a numerous acquaintance in Bath was still uppermost with Mrs. Allen, and she repeated it after every fresh proof, which every morning brought, of her knowing nobody at all.

They made their appearance in the Lower Rooms; and here fortune was more favourable to our heroine. The master of the ceremonies introduced to her a very gentleman-like young man as a partner; his name was Tilney. He seemed to be about four or five and twenty, was rather tall, had a pleasing countenance, a very intelligent and lively eye, and, if not quite handsome, was very near it. His address was good, and Catherine felt herself in high luck. There was little leisure for speaking while they danced; but when they were seated at tea, she found him as agreeable as she had already given him credit for being. He talked with fluency and spirit—and there was an archness and pleasantry in his manner which interested, though it was hardly understood by her. After chatting some time on such matters as naturally arose from the objects around them, he suddenly addressed her with—"I have hitherto been very remiss, madam, in the proper attentions of a partner here; I have not yet asked you how long you have been in Bath; whether you were ever here before; whether you have been at the Upper Rooms, the theatre, and the concert; and how you like the place altogether. I have been very negligent—but are you now at leisure to satisfy me in these particulars? If you are I will begin directly."

"You need not give yourself that trouble, sir."

"No trouble, I assure you, madam." Then forming his features into a set smile, and affectedly softening his voice, he added, with a simpering air, "Have you been long in Bath, madam?"

"About a week, sir," replied Catherine, trying not to laugh.

"Really!" with affected astonishment.

"Why should you be surprised, sir?"

"Why, indeed!" said he, in his natural tone. "But some emotion must appear to be raised by your reply, and surprise is more easily assumed, and not less reasonable than any other.

Now let us go on. Were you never here before, madam?"

"Never, sir."

"Indeed! Have you yet honoured the Upper Rooms?"

"Yes, sir, I was there last Monday."

"Have you been to the theatre?"

"Yes, sir, I was at the play on Tuesday."

"To the concert?"

"Yes, sir, on Wednesday."

"And are you altogether pleased with Bath?"

"Yes—I like it very well."

"Now I must give one smirk, and then we may be rational again." Catherine turned away her head, not knowing whether she might venture to laugh.

"I see what you think of me," said he gravely—"I shall make but a poor figure in your journal to-morrow."

"My journal!"

"Yes, I know exactly what you will say: Friday, went to the Lower Rooms; wore my sprigged muslin robe with blue trimmings—plain black shoes—appeared to much advantage; but was strangely harassed by a queer, half-witted man, who would make me dance with him, and distressed me by his nonsense."

"Indeed I shall say no such thing."

"Shall I tell you what you ought to say?"

"If you please."

"I danced with a very agreeable young man, introduced by Mr. King; had a great deal of conversation with him—seems a most extraordinary genius—hope I may know more of him. That, madam, is what I wish you to say."

"But, perhaps, I keep no journal."

"Perhaps you are not sitting in this room, and I am not sitting by you. These are points in which a doubt is equally possible. Not keep a journal! How are your absent cousins to understand the tenor of your life in Bath without one? How are the civilities and compliments of every day to be related as they ought to be, unless noted down every evening in a journal? How are your various dresses to be remembered, and the particular state of your complexion, and curl of your hair to be described in all their diversities, without having constant recourse to a journal? My dear madam, I am not so ignorant of young ladies' ways as you wish to believe me; it is this delightful habit of journaling which largely contributes to form the easy style of writing for which ladies are so generally celebrated. Everybody allows that the talent of writing agreeable letters is peculiarly female. Nature may have done something, but I am sure it must be essentially assisted by the practice of keeping a journal."

"I have sometimes thought," said Catherine, doubtingly, "whether ladies do write so much better letters than gentlemen! That is—I should not think the superiority was always on our side."

"As far as I have had opportunity of judging, it appears to me that the usual style of letter-writing among women is faultless, except in three particulars."

"And what are they?"

"A general deficiency of subject, a total inattention to stops, and a very frequent ignorance of grammar."

"Upon my word! I need not have been afraid of disclaiming the compliment. You do not think too highly of us in that way."

"I should no more lay it down as a general rule that women write better letters than men, than that they sing better duets, or draw better landscapes. In every power, of which taste is the foundation, excellence is pretty fairly divided between the sexes."

They were interrupted by Mrs. Allen: "My dear Catherine," said she, "do take this pin out of my sleeve; I am afraid it has torn a hole already; I shall be quite sorry if it has, for this is a favourite gown, though it cost but nine shillings a yard."

"That is exactly what I should have guessed it, madam," said Mr. Tilney, looking at the muslin.

"Do you understand muslins, sir?"

"Particularly well; I always buy my own cravats, and am allowed to be an excellent judge; and my sister has often trusted me in the choice of a gown. I bought one for her the other day, and it was pronounced to be a prodigious bargain by every lady who saw it. I gave but five shillings a yard for it, and a true Indian muslin."

Mrs. Allen was quite struck by his genius. "Men commonly take so little notice of those things," said she; "I can never get Mr. Allen to know one of my gowns from another. You must be a great comfort to your sister, sir."

"I hope I am, madam."

"And pray, sir, what do you think of Miss Morland's gown?"

"It is very pretty, madam," said he, gravely examining it; "but I do not think it will wash well; I am afraid it will fray."

"How can you," said Catherine, laughing, "be so—" She had almost said "strange."

"I am quite of your opinion, sir," replied Mrs. Allen; "and so I told Miss Morland when she bought it."

"But then you know, madam, muslin always turns to some account or other; Miss Morland will get enough out of it for a handkerchief, or a cap, or a cloak. Muslin can never be said to be wasted. I have heard my sister say so forty times, when she has been extravagant in buying more than she wanted, or careless in cutting it to pieces."

"Bath is a charming place, sir; there are so many good shops here. We are sadly off in the country; not but what we have very good shops in Salisbury, but it is so far to go—eight miles is a long way; Mr. Allen says it is nine, measured nine; but I am sure it cannot be more than eight; and it is such a fag—I come back tired to death. Now, here one can step out of doors and get a thing in five minutes."

Mr. Tilney was polite enough to seem interested in what she said; and she kept him on the subject of muslins till the dancing recommenced. Catherine feared, as she listened to their discourse, that he indulged himself a little too much with the foibles of others. "What are you thinking of so earnestly?" said he, as they walked back to the ballroom; "not of your partner, I hope, for, by that shake of the head, your meditations are not satisfactory."

Catherine coloured, and said, "I was not thinking of anything."

"That is artful and deep, to be sure; but I had rather be told at once that you will not tell me."

"Well then, I will not."

"Thank you; for now we shall soon be acquainted, as I am authorized to tease you on this subject whenever we meet, and nothing in the world advances intimacy so much."

They danced again; and, when the assembly closed, parted, on the lady's side at least, with a strong inclination for continuing the acquaintance. Whether she thought of him so much, while she drank her warm wine and water, and prepared herself for bed, as to dream of him when there, cannot be ascertained; but I hope it was no more than in a slight slumber, or a morning doze at most; for if it be true, as a celebrated writer has maintained, that no young lady can be justified in falling in love before the gentleman's love is declared,[1] it must be very improper that a young lady should dream of a gentleman before the gentleman is first known to have dreamt of her. How proper Mr. Tilney might be as a dreamer or a lover had not yet perhaps entered Mr. Allen's head, but that he was not objectionable as a common acquaintance for his young charge he was on inquiry satisfied; for he had early in the evening taken pains to know who her partner was, and had been assured of Mr. Tilney's being a clergyman, and of a very respectable family in Gloucestershire.

[1] Vide a letter from Mr. Richardson, No. 97, Vol. ii, Rambler.

CHAPTER 4

With more than usual eagerness did Catherine hasten to the pump-room the next day, secure within herself of seeing Mr. Tilney there before the morning were over, and ready to meet him with a smile; but no smile was demanded—Mr. Tilney did not appear. Every creature in Bath, except himself, was to be seen in the room at different periods of the fashionable hours; crowds of people were every moment passing in and out, up the steps and down; people whom nobody cared about, and nobody wanted to see; and he only was absent. "What a delightful place Bath is," said Mrs. Allen as they sat down near the great clock, after parading the room till they were tired; "and how pleasant it would be if we had any acquaintance here."

This sentiment had been uttered so often in vain that Mrs. Allen had no particular reason to hope it would be followed with more advantage now; but we are told to "despair of nothing we would attain," as "unwearied diligence our point would gain"; and the unwearied diligence with which she had every day wished for the same thing was at length to have its just reward, for hardly had she been seated ten minutes before a lady of about her own age, who was sitting by her, and had been looking at her attentively for several minutes, addressed her with great complaisance in these words: "I think, madam, I cannot be mistaken; it is a long time since I had the pleasure of seeing you, but is not your name Allen?" This question answered, as it readily was, the stranger pronounced hers to be Thorpe; and Mrs. Allen immediately recognized the features of a former schoolfellow and intimate, whom she had seen only once since their respective marriages, and that many years ago. Their joy on this meeting was very great, as well it might, since they had been contented to know nothing of each other for the last fifteen years. Compliments on good looks now passed; and, after observing how time had slipped away since they were last together, how little they had thought of meeting in Bath, and what a pleasure it was to see an old friend, they proceeded to make inquiries and give intelligence as to their families, sisters, and cousins, talking both together, far more ready to give than to receive information, and each hearing very little of what the other said. Mrs. Thorpe, however, had one great advantage as a talker, over Mrs. Allen, in a family of children; and when she expatiated on the talents of her sons, and the beauty of her daughters, when she related their different situations and views—that John was at Oxford, Edward at Merchant Taylors', and William at sea—and all of them more beloved and respected in their different station than any other three beings ever were, Mrs. Allen had no similar information to give, no similar triumphs to press on the unwilling and unbelieving ear of her friend, and was forced to sit and appear to listen to all these maternal effusions, consoling herself, however, with the discovery, which her keen eyes soon made, that the lace on Mrs. Thorpe's pelisse was not half so handsome as that on her own.

"Here come my dear girls," cried Mrs. Thorpe, pointing at three smart-looking females who, arm in arm, were then moving towards her. "My dear Mrs. Allen, I long to introduce them; they will be so delighted to see you: the tallest is Isabella, my eldest; is not she a fine young woman? The others are very much admired too, but I believe Isabella is the handsomest."

The Miss Thorpes were introduced; and Miss Morland, who had been for a short time forgotten, was introduced likewise. The name seemed to strike them all; and, after speaking to her with great civility, the eldest young lady observed aloud to the rest, "How excessively like her brother Miss Morland is!"

"The very picture of him indeed!" cried the mother—and "I should have known her anywhere for his sister!" was repeated by them all, two or three times over. For a moment Catherine was surprised; but Mrs. Thorpe and her daughters had scarcely begun the history of their acquaintance with Mr. James Morland, before she remembered that her eldest brother had lately formed an intimacy with a young man of his own college, of the name of Thorpe; and that he had spent the last week of the Christmas vacation with his family, near London.

The whole being explained, many obliging things were said by the Miss Thorpes of their wish of being better acquainted with her; of being considered as already friends, through the friendship of their brothers, etc., which Catherine heard with pleasure, and answered with all the pretty expressions she could command; and, as the first proof of amity, she was soon invited to accept an arm of the eldest Miss Thorpe, and take a turn with her about the room. Catherine was delighted with this extension of her Bath acquaintance, and almost forgot Mr. Tilney while she talked to Miss Thorpe. Friendship is certainly the finest balm for the pangs of disappointed love.

Their conversation turned upon those subjects, of which the free discussion has generally much to do in perfecting a sudden intimacy between two young ladies: such as dress, balls, flirtations, and quizzes. Miss Thorpe, however, being four years older than Miss Morland, and at least four years better informed, had a very decided advantage in discussing such points; she could compare the balls of Bath with those of Tunbridge, its fashions with the fashions of London; could rectify the opinions of her new friend in many articles of tasteful attire; could discover a flirtation between any gentleman and lady who only smiled on each other; and point out a quiz through the thickness of a crowd. These powers received due admiration from Catherine, to whom they were entirely new; and the respect which they naturally inspired might have been too great for familiarity, had not the easy gaiety of Miss Thorpe's manners, and her frequent expressions of delight on this acquaintance with her, softened down every feeling of awe, and left nothing but tender affection. Their increasing attachment was not to be satisfied with half a dozen turns in the pump-room, but required, when they all quitted it together, that Miss Thorpe should accompany Miss Morland to the very door of Mr. Allen's house; and that they should there part with a most affectionate and lengthened shake of hands, after learning, to their mutual relief, that they should see each other across the theatre at night, and say their prayers in the same chapel the next morning. Catherine then ran directly upstairs, and watched Miss Thorpe's progress down the street from the drawing-room window; admired the graceful spirit of her walk, the fashionable air of her figure and dress; and felt grateful, as well she might, for the chance which had procured her such a friend.

Mrs. Thorpe was a widow, and not a very rich one; she was a good-humoured, well-meaning woman, and a very indulgent mother. Her eldest daughter had great personal beauty, and the younger ones, by pretending to be as handsome as their sister, imitating her air, and dressing in the same style, did very well.

This brief account of the family is intended to supersede the necessity of a long and minute detail from Mrs. Thorpe herself, of her past adventures and sufferings, which might otherwise be expected to occupy the three or four following chapters; in which the worthlessness of lords and attorneys might be set forth, and conversations, which had passed twenty years before, be minutely repeated.

CHAPTER 5

Catherine was not so much engaged at the theatre that evening, in returning the nods and smiles of Miss Thorpe, though they certainly claimed much of her leisure, as to forget to look with an inquiring eye for Mr. Tilney in every box which her eye could reach; but she looked in vain. Mr. Tilney was no fonder of the play than the pump-room. She hoped to be more fortunate the next day; and when her wishes for fine weather were answered by seeing a beautiful morning, she hardly felt a doubt of it; for a fine Sunday in Bath empties every house of its inhabitants, and all the world appears on such an occasion to walk about and tell their acquaintance what a charming day it is.

As soon as divine service was over, the Thorpes and Allens eagerly joined each other; and after staying long enough in the pump-room to discover that the crowd was insupportable, and that there was not a genteel face to be seen, which everybody discovers every Sunday throughout the season, they hastened away to the Crescent, to breathe the fresh air of better company. Here Catherine and Isabella, arm in arm, again tasted the sweets of friendship in an unreserved conversation; they talked much, and with much enjoyment; but again was Catherine disappointed in her hope of reseeing her partner. He was nowhere to be met with; every search for him was equally unsuccessful, in morning lounges or evening assemblies; neither at the Upper nor Lower Rooms, at dressed or undressed balls, was he perceivable; nor among the walkers, the horsemen, or the curricle-drivers of the morning. His name was not in the pump-room book, and curiosity could do no more. He must be gone from Bath. Yet he had not mentioned that his stay would be so short! This sort of mysteriousness, which is always so becoming in a hero, threw a fresh grace in Catherine's imagination around his person and manners, and increased her anxiety to know more of him. From the Thorpes she could learn nothing, for they had been only two days in Bath before they met with Mrs. Allen. It was a subject, however, in which she often indulged with her fair friend, from whom she received every possible encouragement to continue to think of him; and his impression on her fancy was not suffered therefore to weaken. Isabella was very sure that he must be a charming young man, and was equally sure that he must have been delighted with her dear Catherine, and would therefore shortly return. She liked him the better for being a clergyman, "for she must confess herself very partial to the profession"; and something like a sigh escaped her as she said it. Perhaps Catherine was wrong in not demanding the cause of that gentle emotion—but she was not experienced enough in the finesse of love, or the duties of friendship, to know when delicate raillery was properly called for, or when a confidence should be forced.

Mrs. Allen was now quite happy—quite satisfied with Bath. She had found some acquaintance, had been so lucky too as to find in them the family of a most worthy old friend; and, as the completion of good fortune, had found these friends by no means so expensively dressed as herself. Her daily expressions were no longer, "I wish we had some acquaintance in Bath!" They were changed into, "How glad I am we have met with Mrs. Thorpe!" and she was as eager in promoting the intercourse of the two families, as her young charge and Isabella themselves could be; never satisfied with the day unless she spent the chief of it by the side of Mrs. Thorpe, in what they called conversation, but in which there was scarcely ever any exchange of opinion, and not often any resemblance of subject, for Mrs. Thorpe talked chiefly of her children, and Mrs. Allen of her gowns.

The progress of the friendship between Catherine and Isabella was quick as its beginning had been warm, and they passed so rapidly through every gradation of increasing tenderness that there was shortly no fresh proof of it to be given to their friends or themselves. They called each other by their Christian name, were always arm in arm when they walked, pinned up each other's train for the dance, and were not to be divided in the set; and if a rainy morning deprived them of other enjoyments, they were still resolute in meeting in defiance of wet and dirt, and shut themselves up, to read novels together. Yes, novels; for I will not adopt that ungenerous and impolitic custom so common with novel-writers, of degrading by their contemptuous censure the very performances, to the number of which they are themselves adding—joining with their greatest enemies in bestowing the harshest epithets on such works, and scarcely ever permitting them to be read by their own heroine, who, if she accidentally take up a novel, is sure to turn over its insipid pages with disgust. Alas! If the heroine of one novel be not patronized by the heroine of another, from whom can she expect protection and regard? I cannot approve of it. Let us leave it to the reviewers to abuse such effusions of fancy at their leisure, and over every new novel to talk in threadbare strains of the trash with which the press now groans. Let us not desert one another; we are an injured body. Although our productions have afforded more extensive and unaffected pleasure than those of any other literary corporation in the world, no species of composition has been so much decried. From pride, ignorance, or fashion, our foes are almost as many as our readers. And while the abilities of the nine-hundredth abridger of the History of England, or of the man who collects and publishes in a volume some dozen lines of Milton, Pope, and Prior, with a paper from the Spectator, and a chapter from Sterne, are eulogized by a thousand pens—there seems almost a general wish of decrying the capacity and undervaluing the labour of the novelist, and of slighting the performances which have only genius, wit, and taste to recommend them. "I am no novel-reader—I seldom look into novels—Do not imagine that I often read novels—It is really very well for a novel." Such is the common cant. "And what are you reading, Miss— —?" "Oh! It is only a novel!" replies the young lady, while she lays down her book with affected indifference, or momentary shame. "It is only Cecilia, or Camilla, or Belinda"; or, in short, only some work in which the greatest powers of the mind are displayed, in which the most thorough knowledge of human nature, the happiest delineation of its varieties, the liveliest effusions of wit and humour, are conveyed to the world in the best-chosen language. Now, had the same young lady been engaged with a volume of the Spectator, instead of such a work, how proudly would she have produced the book, and told its name; though the chances must be against her being occupied by any part of that voluminous publication, of which either the matter or manner would not disgust a young person of taste: the substance of its papers so often consisting in the statement of improbable circumstances, unnatural characters, and topics of conversation which no longer concern anyone living; and their language, too, frequently so coarse as to give no very favourable idea of the age that could endure it.

CHAPTER 6

The following conversation, which took place between the two friends in the pump-room one morning, after an acquaintance of eight or nine days, is given as a specimen of their very warm attachment, and of the delicacy, discretion, originality of thought, and literary taste which marked the reasonableness of that attachment.

They met by appointment; and as Isabella had arrived nearly five minutes before her friend, her first address naturally was, "My dearest creature, what can have made you so late? I have been waiting for you at least this age!"

"Have you, indeed! I am very sorry for it; but really I thought I was in very good time. It is but just one. I hope you have not been here long?"

"Oh! These ten ages at least. I am sure I have been here this half hour. But now, let us go and sit down at the other end of the room, and enjoy ourselves. I have an hundred things to say to you. In the first place, I was so afraid it would rain this morning, just as I wanted to set off; it looked very showery, and that would have thrown me into agonies! Do you know, I saw the prettiest hat you can imagine, in a shop window in Milsom Street just now—very like yours, only with coquelicot ribbons instead of green; I quite longed for it. But, my dearest Catherine, what have you been doing with yourself all this morning? Have you gone on with Udolpho?"

"Yes, I have been reading it ever since I woke; and I am got to the black veil."

"Are you, indeed? How delightful! Oh! I would not tell you what is behind the black veil for the world! Are not you wild to know?"

"Oh! Yes, quite; what can it be? But do not tell me—I would not be told upon any account. I know it must be a skeleton, I am sure it is Laurentina's skeleton. Oh! I am delighted with the book! I should like to spend my whole life in reading it. I assure you, if it had not been to meet you, I would not have come away from it for all the world."

"Dear creature! How much I am obliged to you; and when you have finished Udolpho, we will read the Italian together; and I have made out a list of ten or twelve more of the same kind for you."

"Have you, indeed! How glad I am! What are they all?"

"I will read you their names directly; here they are, in my pocketbook. Castle of Wolfenbach, Clermont, Mysterious Warnings, Necromancer of the Black Forest, Midnight Bell, Orphan of the Rhine, and Horrid Mysteries. Those will last us some time."

"Yes, pretty well; but are they all horrid, are you sure they are all horrid?"

"Yes, quite sure; for a particular friend of mine, a Miss Andrews, a sweet girl, one of the sweetest creatures in the world, has read every one of them. I wish you knew Miss Andrews, you would be delighted with her. She is netting herself the sweetest cloak you can conceive. I think her as beautiful as an angel, and I am so vexed with the men for not admiring her! I scold them all amazingly about it."

"Scold them! Do you scold them for not admiring her?"

"Yes, that I do. There is nothing I would not do for those who are really my friends. I have no notion of loving people by halves; it is not my nature. My attachments are always excessively strong. I told Captain Hunt at one of our assemblies this winter that if he was to tease me all night, I would not dance with him, unless he would allow Miss Andrews to be as beautiful as an angel. The men think us incapable of real friendship, you know, and I am determined to show them the difference. Now, if I were to hear anybody speak slightingly of you, I should fire up in a moment: but that is not at all likely, for you are just the kind of girl to be a great favourite with the men."

"Oh, dear!" cried Catherine, colouring. "How can you say so?"

"I know you very well; you have so much animation, which is exactly what Miss Andrews wants, for I must confess there is something amazingly insipid about her. Oh! I must tell you, that just after we parted yesterday, I saw a young man looking at you so earnestly—I am sure he is in love with you." Catherine coloured, and disclaimed again. Isabella laughed. "It is very true, upon my honour, but I see how it is; you are indifferent to everybody's admiration, except that of one gentleman, who shall be nameless. Nay, I cannot blame you"—speaking more seriously—"your feelings are easily understood. Where the heart is really attached, I know very well how little one can be pleased with the attention of anybody else. Everything is so insipid, so uninteresting, that does not relate to the beloved object! I can perfectly comprehend your feelings."

"But you should not persuade me that I think so very much about Mr. Tilney, for perhaps I may never see him again."

"Not see him again! My dearest creature, do not talk of it. I am sure you would be miserable if you thought so!"

"No, indeed, I should not. I do not pretend to say that I was not very much pleased with him; but while I have Udolpho to read, I feel as if nobody could make me miserable. Oh! The dreadful black veil! My dear Isabella, I am sure there must be Laurentina's skeleton behind it."

"It is so odd to me, that you should never have read Udolpho before; but I suppose Mrs. Morland objects to novels."

"No, she does not. She very often reads Sir Charles Grandison herself; but new books do not fall in our way."

"Sir Charles Grandison! That is an amazing horrid book, is it not? I remember Miss Andrews could not get through the first volume."

"It is not like Udolpho at all; but yet I think it is very entertaining."

"Do you indeed! You surprise me; I thought it had not been readable. But, my dearest Catherine, have you settled what to wear on your head to-night? I am determined at all events to be dressed exactly like you. The men take notice of that sometimes, you know."

"But it does not signify if they do," said Catherine, very innocently.

"Signify! Oh, heavens! I make it a rule never to mind what they say. They are very often amazingly impertinent if you do not treat them with spirit, and make them keep their distance."

"Are they? Well, I never observed that. They always behave very well to me."

"Oh! They give themselves such airs. They are the most conceited creatures in the world, and think themselves of so much importance! By the by, though I have thought of it a hundred times, I have always forgot to ask you what is your favourite complexion in a man. Do you like them best dark or fair?"

"I hardly know. I never much thought about it. Something between both, I think. Brown—not fair, and—and not very dark."

"Very well, Catherine. That is exactly he. I have not forgot your description of Mr. Tilney—'a brown skin, with dark eyes, and rather dark hair.' Well, my taste is different. I prefer light eyes, and as to complexion—do you know—I like a sallow better than any other. You must not betray me, if you should ever meet with one of your acquaintance answering that description."

"Betray you! What do you mean?"

"Nay, do not distress me. I believe I have said too much. Let us drop the subject."

Catherine, in some amazement, complied, and after remaining a few moments silent, was on the point of reverting to what interested her at that time rather more than anything else in the world, Laurentina's skeleton, when her friend prevented her, by saying, "For heaven's sake! Let us move away from this end of the room. Do you know, there are two odious young men who have been staring at me this half hour. They really put me quite out of countenance. Let us go and look at the arrivals. They will hardly follow us there."

Away they walked to the book; and while Isabella examined the names, it was Catherine's employment to watch the proceedings of these alarming young men.

"They are not coming this way, are they? I hope they are not so impertinent as to follow us. Pray let me know if they are coming. I am determined I will not look up."

In a few moments Catherine, with unaffected pleasure, assured her that she need not be longer uneasy, as the gentlemen had just left the pump-room.

"And which way are they gone?" said Isabella, turning hastily round. "One was a very good-looking young man."

"They went towards the church-yard."

"Well, I am amazingly glad I have got rid of them! And now, what say you to going to Edgar's Buildings with me, and looking at my new hat? You said you should like to see it."

Catherine readily agreed. "Only," she added, "perhaps we may overtake the two young men."

"Oh! Never mind that. If we make haste, we shall pass by them presently, and I am dying to show you my hat."

"But if we only wait a few minutes, there will be no danger of our seeing them at all."

"I shall not pay them any such compliment, I assure you. I have no notion of treating men with such respect. That is the way to spoil them."

Catherine had nothing to oppose against such reasoning; and therefore, to show the independence of Miss Thorpe, and her resolution of humbling the sex, they set off immediately as fast as they could walk, in pursuit of the two young men.

CHAPTER 7

Half a minute conducted them through the pump-yard to the archway, opposite Union Passage; but here they were stopped. Everybody acquainted with Bath may remember the difficulties of crossing Cheap Street at this point; it is indeed a street of so impertinent a nature, so unfortunately connected with the great London and Oxford roads, and the principal inn of the city, that a day never passes in which parties of ladies, however important their business, whether in quest of pastry, millinery, or even (as in the present case) of young men, are not detained on one side or other by carriages, horsemen, or carts. This evil had been felt and lamented, at least three times a day, by Isabella since her residence in Bath; and she was now fated to feel and lament it once more, for at the very moment of coming opposite to Union Passage, and within view of the two gentlemen who were proceeding through the crowds, and threading the gutters of that interesting alley, they were prevented crossing by the approach of a gig, driven along on bad pavement by a most knowing-looking coachman with all the vehemence that could most fitly endanger the lives of himself, his companion, and his horse.

"Oh, these odious gigs!" said Isabella, looking up. "How I detest them." But this detestation, though so just, was of short duration, for she looked again and exclaimed, "Delightful! Mr. Morland and my brother!"

"Good heaven! 'Tis James!" was uttered at the same moment by Catherine; and, on catching the young men's eyes, the horse was immediately checked with a violence which almost threw him on his haunches, and the servant having now scampered up, the gentlemen jumped out, and the equipage was delivered to his care.

Catherine, by whom this meeting was wholly unexpected, received her brother with the liveliest pleasure; and he, being of a very amiable disposition, and sincerely attached to her, gave every proof on his side of equal satisfaction, which he could have leisure to do, while the bright eyes of Miss Thorpe were incessantly challenging his notice; and to her his devoirs were speedily paid, with a mixture of joy and embarrassment which might have informed Catherine, had she been more expert in the development of other people's feelings, and less simply engrossed by her own, that her brother thought her friend quite as pretty as she could do herself.

John Thorpe, who in the meantime had been giving orders about the horses, soon joined them, and from him she directly received the amends which were her due; for while he slightly and carelessly touched the hand of Isabella, on her he bestowed a whole scrape and half a short bow. He was a stout young man of middling height, who, with a plain face and ungraceful form, seemed fearful of being too handsome unless he wore the dress of a groom, and too much like a gentleman unless he were easy where he ought to be civil, and impudent where he might be allowed to be easy. He took out his watch: "How long do you think we have been running it from Tetbury, Miss Morland?"

"I do not know the distance." Her brother told her that it was twenty-three miles.

"Three-and-twenty!" cried Thorpe, "five-and-twenty if it is an inch." Morland remonstrated, pleaded the authority of road-books, innkeepers, and milestones; but his friend disregarded them all; he had a surer test of distance. "I know it must be five-and-twenty," said he, "by the time we have been doing it. It is now half after one; we drove out of the inn-yard at Tetbury as the town clock struck eleven; and I defy any man in England to make my horse go less than ten miles an hour in harness; that makes it exactly twenty-five."

"You have lost an hour," said Morland; "it was only ten o'clock when we came from Tetbury."

"Ten o'clock! It was eleven, upon my soul! I counted every stroke. This brother of yours would persuade me out of my senses, Miss Morland; do but look at my horse; did you ever see an animal so made for speed in your life?" (The servant had just mounted the carriage and was driving off.) "Such true blood! Three hours and and a half indeed coming only three and twenty miles! Look at that creature, and suppose it possible if you can."

"He does look very hot, to be sure."

"Hot! He had not turned a hair till we came to Walcot Church; but look at his forehand; look at his loins; only see how he moves; that horse cannot go less than ten miles an hour: tie his legs and he will get on. What do you think of my gig, Miss Morland? A neat one, is not it? Well hung; town-built; I have not had it a month. It was built for a Christchurch man, a friend of mine, a very good sort of fellow; he ran it a few weeks, till, I believe, it was convenient to have done with it. I happened just then to be looking out for some light thing of the kind, though I had pretty well determined on a curricle too; but I chanced to meet him on Magdalen Bridge, as he was driving into Oxford, last term: 'Ah! Thorpe,' said he, 'do you happen to want such a little thing as this? It is a capital one of the kind, but I am cursed tired of it.' 'Oh! D—,' said I; 'I am your man; what do you ask?' And how much do you think he did, Miss Morland?"

"I am sure I cannot guess at all."

"Curricle-hung, you see; seat, trunk, sword-case, splashing-board, lamps, silver moulding, all you see complete; the iron-work as good as new, or better. He asked fifty guineas; I closed with him directly, threw down the money, and the carriage was mine."

"And I am sure," said Catherine, "I know so little of such things that I cannot judge whether it was cheap or dear."

"Neither one nor t'other; I might have got it for less, I dare say; but I hate haggling, and poor Freeman wanted cash."

"That was very good-natured of you," said Catherine, quite pleased.

"Oh! D— — it, when one has the means of doing a kind thing by a friend, I hate to be pitiful."

An inquiry now took place into the intended movements of the young ladies; and, on finding whither they were going, it was decided that the gentlemen should accompany them to Edgar's Buildings, and pay their respects to Mrs. Thorpe. James and Isabella led the way; and so well satisfied was the latter with her lot, so contentedly was she endeavouring to ensure a pleasant walk to him who brought the double recommendation of being her brother's friend, and her friend's brother, so pure and uncoquettish were her feelings, that, though they overtook and passed the two offending young men in Milsom Street, she was so far from seeking to attract their notice, that she looked back at them only three times.

John Thorpe kept of course with Catherine, and, after a few minutes' silence, renewed the conversation about his gig. "You will find, however, Miss Morland, it would be reckoned a cheap thing by some people, for I might have sold it for ten guineas more the next day; Jackson, of Oriel, bid me sixty at once; Morland was with me at the time."

"Yes," said Morland, who overheard this; "but you forget that your horse was included."

"My horse! Oh, d— — it! I would not sell my horse for a hundred. Are you fond of an open carriage, Miss Morland?"

"Yes, very; I have hardly ever an opportunity of being in one; but I am particularly fond of it."

"I am glad of it; I will drive you out in mine every day."

"Thank you," said Catherine, in some distress, from a doubt of the propriety of accepting such an offer.

"I will drive you up Lansdown Hill to-morrow."

"Thank you; but will not your horse want rest?"

"Rest! He has only come three and twenty miles to-day; all nonsense; nothing ruins horses so much as rest; nothing knocks them up so soon. No, no; I shall exercise mine at the average of four hours every day while I am here."

"Shall you indeed!" said Catherine very seriously. "That will be forty miles a day."

"Forty! Aye, fifty, for what I care. Well, I will drive you up Lansdown to-morrow; mind, I am engaged."

"How delightful that will be!" cried Isabella, turning round. "My dearest Catherine, I quite envy you; but I am afraid, brother, you will not have room for a third."

"A third indeed! No, no; I did not come to Bath to drive my sisters about; that would be a good joke, faith! Morland must take care of you."

This brought on a dialogue of civilities between the other two; but Catherine heard neither the particulars nor the result. Her companion's discourse now sunk from its hitherto animated pitch to nothing more than a short decisive sentence of praise or condemnation on the face of every woman they met; and Catherine, after listening and agreeing as long as she could, with all the civility and deference of the youthful female mind, fearful of hazarding an opinion of its own in opposition to that of a self-assured man, especially where the beauty of her own sex is concerned, ventured at length to vary the subject by a question which had been long uppermost in her thoughts; it was, "Have you ever read Udolpho, Mr. Thorpe?"

"Udolpho! Oh, Lord! Not I; I never read novels; I have something else to do."

Catherine, humbled and ashamed, was going to apologize for her question, but he prevented her by saying, "Novels are all so full of nonsense and stuff; there has not been a tolerably decent one come out since Tom Jones, except The Monk; I read that t'other day; but as for all the others, they are the stupidest things in creation."

"I think you must like Udolpho, if you were to read it; it is so very interesting."

"Not I, faith! No, if I read any, it shall be Mrs. Radcliffe's; her novels are amusing enough; they are worth reading; some fun and nature in them."

"Udolpho was written by Mrs. Radcliffe," said Catherine, with some hesitation, from the fear of mortifying him.

"No, sure; was it? Aye, I remember, so it was; I was thinking of that other stupid book, written by that woman they make such a fuss about, she who married the French emigrant."

"I suppose you mean Camilla?"

"Yes, that's the book; such unnatural stuff! An old man playing at see-saw, I took up the first volume once and looked it over, but I soon found it would not do; indeed I guessed what sort of stuff it must be before I saw it: as soon as I heard she had married an emigrant, I was sure I should never be able to get through it."

"I have never read it."

"You had no loss, I assure you; it is the horridest nonsense you can imagine; there is nothing in the world in it but an old man's playing at see-saw and learning Latin; upon my soul there is not."

This critique, the justness of which was unfortunately lost on poor Catherine, brought them to the door of Mrs. Thorpe's lodgings, and the feelings of the discerning and unprejudiced reader of Camilla gave way to the feelings of the dutiful and affectionate son, as they met Mrs. Thorpe, who had descried them from above, in the passage. "Ah, Mother! How do you do?" said he, giving her a hearty shake of the hand. "Where did you get that quiz of a hat? It makes you look like an old witch. Here is Morland and I come to stay a few days with you, so you must look out for a couple of good beds somewhere near." And this address seemed to satisfy all the fondest wishes of the mother's heart, for she received him with the most delighted and exulting affection. On his two younger sisters he then bestowed an equal portion of his fraternal tenderness, for he asked each of them how they did, and observed that they both looked very ugly.

These manners did not please Catherine; but he was James's friend and Isabella's brother; and her judgment was further bought off by Isabella's assuring her, when they withdrew to see the new hat, that John thought her the most charming girl in the world, and by John's engaging her before they parted to dance with him that evening. Had she been older or vainer, such attacks might have done little; but, where youth and diffidence are united, it requires uncommon steadiness of reason to resist the attraction of being called the most charming girl in the world, and of being so very early engaged as a partner; and the consequence was that, when the two Morlands, after sitting an hour with the Thorpes, set off to walk together to Mr. Allen's, and James, as the door was closed on them, said, "Well, Catherine, how do you like my friend Thorpe?" instead of answering, as she probably would have done, had there been no friendship and no flattery in the case, "I do not like him at all," she directly replied, "I like him very much; he seems very agreeable."

"He is as good-natured a fellow as ever lived; a little of a rattle; but that will recommend him to your sex, I believe: and how do you like the rest of the family?"

"Very, very much indeed: Isabella particularly."

"I am very glad to hear you say so; she is just the kind of young woman I could wish to see you attached to; she has so much good sense, and is so thoroughly unaffected and amiable; I always wanted you to know her; and she seems very fond of you. She said the highest things in your praise that could possibly be; and the praise of such a girl as Miss Thorpe even you, Catherine," taking her hand with affection, "may be proud of."

"Indeed I am," she replied; "I love her exceedingly, and am delighted to find that you like her too. You hardly mentioned anything of her when you wrote to me after your visit there."

"Because I thought I should soon see you myself. I hope you will be a great deal together while you are in Bath. She is a most amiable girl; such a superior understanding! How fond all the family are of her; she is evidently the general favourite; and how much she must be admired in such a place as this—is not she?"

"Yes, very much indeed, I fancy; Mr. Allen thinks her the prettiest girl in Bath."

"I dare say he does; and I do not know any man who is a better judge of beauty than Mr. Allen. I need not ask you whether you are happy here, my dear Catherine; with such a companion and friend as Isabella Thorpe, it would be impossible for you to be otherwise; and the Allens, I am sure, are very kind to you?"

"Yes, very kind; I never was so happy before; and now you are come it will be more delightful than ever; how good it is of you to come so far on purpose to see me."

James accepted this tribute of gratitude, and qualified his conscience for accepting it too, by saying with perfect sincerity, "Indeed, Catherine, I love you dearly."

Inquiries and communications concerning brothers and sisters, the situation of some, the growth of the rest, and other family matters now passed between them, and continued, with only one small digression on James's part, in praise of Miss Thorpe, till they reached Pulteney Street, where he was welcomed with great kindness by Mr. and Mrs. Allen, invited by the former to dine with them, and summoned by the latter to guess the price and weigh the merits of a new muff and tippet. A pre-engagement in Edgar's Buildings prevented his accepting the invitation of one friend, and obliged him to hurry away as soon as he had satisfied the demands of the other. The time of the two parties uniting in the Octagon Room being correctly adjusted, Catherine was then left to the luxury of a raised, restless, and frightened imagination over the pages of Udolpho, lost from all worldly concerns of dressing and dinner, incapable of soothing Mrs. Allen's fears on the delay of an expected dressmaker, and having only one minute in sixty to bestow even on the reflection of her own felicity, in being already engaged for the evening.

CHAPTER 8

In spite of Udolpho and the dressmaker, however, the party from Pulteney Street reached the Upper Rooms in very good time. The Thorpes and James Morland were there only two minutes before them; and Isabella having gone through the usual ceremonial of meeting her friend with the most smiling and affectionate haste, of admiring the set of her gown, and envying the curl of her hair, they followed their chaperons, arm in arm, into the ballroom, whispering to each other whenever a thought occurred, and supplying the place of many ideas by a squeeze of the hand or a smile of affection.

The dancing began within a few minutes after they were seated; and James, who had been engaged quite as long as his sister, was very importunate with Isabella to stand up; but John was gone into the card-room to speak to a friend, and nothing, she declared, should induce her to join the set before her dear Catherine could join it too. "I assure you," said she, "I would not stand up without your dear sister for all the world; for if I did we should certainly be separated the whole evening." Catherine accepted this kindness with gratitude, and they continued as they were for three minutes longer, when Isabella, who had been talking to James on the other side of her, turned again to his sister and whispered, "My dear creature, I am afraid I must leave you, your brother is so amazingly impatient to begin; I know you will not mind my going away, and I dare say John will be back in a moment, and then you may easily find me out." Catherine, though a little disappointed, had too much good nature to make any opposition, and the others rising up, Isabella had only time to press her friend's hand and say, "Good-bye, my dear love," before they hurried off. The younger Miss Thorpes being also dancing, Catherine was left to the mercy of Mrs. Thorpe and Mrs. Allen, between whom she now remained. She could not help being vexed at the non-appearance of Mr. Thorpe, for she not only longed to be dancing, but was likewise aware that, as the real dignity of her situation could not be known, she was sharing with the scores of other young ladies still sitting down all the discredit of wanting a partner. To be disgraced in the eye of the world, to wear the appearance of infamy while her heart is all purity, her actions all innocence, and the misconduct of another the true source of her debasement, is one of those circumstances which peculiarly belong to the heroine's life, and her fortitude under it what particularly dignifies her character. Catherine had fortitude too; she suffered, but no murmur passed her lips.

From this state of humiliation, she was roused, at the end of ten minutes, to a pleasanter feeling, by seeing, not Mr. Thorpe, but Mr. Tilney, within three yards of the place where they sat; he seemed to be moving that way, but he did not see her, and therefore the smile and the blush, which his sudden reappearance raised in Catherine, passed away without sullying her heroic importance. He looked as handsome and as lively as ever, and was talking with interest to a fashionable and pleasing-looking young woman, who leant on his arm, and whom Catherine immediately guessed to be his sister; thus unthinkingly throwing away a fair opportunity of considering him lost to her forever, by being married already. But guided only by what was simple and probable, it had never entered her head that Mr. Tilney could be married; he had not behaved, he had not talked, like the married men to whom she had been used; he had never mentioned a wife, and he had acknowledged a sister. From these circumstances sprang the instant conclusion of his sister's now being by his side; and therefore, instead of turning of a deathlike paleness and falling in a fit on Mrs. Allen's bosom, Catherine sat erect, in the perfect use of her senses, and with cheeks only a little redder than usual.

Mr. Tilney and his companion, who continued, though slowly, to approach, were immediately preceded by a lady, an acquaintance of Mrs. Thorpe; and this lady stopping to speak to her, they, as belonging to her, stopped likewise, and Catherine, catching Mr. Tilney's eye, instantly received from him the smiling tribute of recognition. She returned it with pleasure, and then advancing still nearer, he spoke both to her and Mrs. Allen, by whom he was very civilly acknowledged. "I am very happy to see you again, sir, indeed; I was afraid you had left Bath." He thanked her for her fears, and said that he had quitted it for a week, on the very morning after his having had the pleasure of seeing her.

"Well, sir, and I dare say you are not sorry to be back again, for it is just the place for young people—and indeed for everybody else too. I tell Mr. Allen, when he talks of being sick of it, that I am sure he should not complain, for it is so very agreeable a place, that it is much better to be here than at home at this dull time of year. I tell him he is quite in luck to be sent here for his health."

"And I hope, madam, that Mr. Allen will be obliged to like the place, from finding it of service to him."

"Thank you, sir. I have no doubt that he will. A neighbour of ours, Dr. Skinner, was here for his health last winter, and came away quite stout."

"That circumstance must give great encouragement."

"Yes, sir—and Dr. Skinner and his family were here three months; so I tell Mr. Allen he must not be in a hurry to get away."

Here they were interrupted by a request from Mrs. Thorpe to Mrs. Allen, that she would move a little to accommodate Mrs. Hughes and Miss Tilney with seats, as they had agreed to join their party. This was accordingly done, Mr. Tilney still continuing standing before them; and after a few minutes' consideration, he asked Catherine to dance with him. This compliment, delightful as it was, produced severe mortification to the lady; and in giving her denial, she expressed her sorrow on the occasion so very much as if she really felt it, that had Thorpe, who joined her just afterwards, been half a minute earlier, he might have thought her sufferings rather too acute. The very easy manner in which he then told her that he had kept her waiting did not by any means reconcile her more to her lot; nor did the particulars which he entered into while they were standing up, of the horses and dogs of the friend whom he had just left, and of a proposed exchange of terriers between them, interest her so much as to prevent her looking very often towards that part of the room where she had left Mr. Tilney. Of her dear Isabella, to whom she particularly longed to point out that gentleman, she could see nothing. They were in different sets. She was separated from all her party, and away from all her acquaintance; one mortification succeeded another, and from the whole she deduced this useful lesson, that to go previously engaged to a ball does not necessarily increase either the dignity or enjoyment of a young lady. From such a moralizing strain as this, she was suddenly roused by a touch on the shoulder, and turning round, perceived Mrs. Hughes directly behind her, attended by Miss Tilney and a gentleman. "I beg your pardon, Miss Morland," said she, "for this liberty—but I cannot anyhow get to Miss Thorpe, and Mrs. Thorpe said she was sure you would not have the least objection to letting in this young lady by you." Mrs. Hughes could not have applied to any creature in the room more happy to oblige her than Catherine. The young ladies were introduced to each other, Miss Tilney expressing a proper sense of such goodness, Miss Morland with the real delicacy of a generous mind making light of the obligation; and Mrs. Hughes, satisfied with having so respectably settled her young charge, returned to her party.

Miss Tilney had a good figure, a pretty face, and a very agreeable countenance; and her air, though it had not all the decided pretension, the resolute stylishness of Miss Thorpe's, had more real elegance. Her manners showed good sense and good breeding; they were neither shy nor affectedly open; and she seemed capable of being young, attractive, and at a ball without wanting to fix the attention of every man near her, and without exaggerated feelings of ecstatic delight or inconceivable vexation on every little trifling occurrence. Catherine, interested at once by her appearance and her relationship to Mr. Tilney, was desirous of being acquainted with her, and readily talked therefore whenever she could think of anything to say, and had courage and leisure for saying it. But the hindrance thrown in the way of a very speedy intimacy, by the frequent want of one or more of these requisites, prevented their doing more than going through the first rudiments of an acquaintance, by informing themselves how well the other liked Bath, how much she admired its buildings and surrounding country, whether she drew, or played, or sang, and whether she was fond of riding on horseback.

The two dances were scarcely concluded before Catherine found her arm gently seized by her faithful Isabella, who in great spirits exclaimed, "At last I have got you. My dearest creature, I have been looking for you this hour. What could induce you to come into this set, when you knew I was in the other? I have been quite wretched without you."

"My dear Isabella, how was it possible for me to get at you? I could not even see where you were."

"So I told your brother all the time—but he would not believe me. Do go and see for her, Mr. Morland, said I—but all in vain—he would not stir an inch. Was not it so, Mr. Morland? But you men are all so immoderately lazy! I have been scolding him to such a degree, my dear Catherine, you would be quite amazed. You know I never stand upon ceremony with such people."

"Look at that young lady with the white beads round her head," whispered Catherine, detaching her friend from James. "It is Mr. Tilney's sister."

"Oh! Heavens! You don't say so! Let me look at her this moment. What a delightful girl! I never saw anything half so beautiful! But where is her all-conquering brother? Is he in the room? Point him out to me this instant, if he is. I die to see him. Mr. Morland, you are not to listen. We are not talking about you."

"But what is all this whispering about? What is going on?"

"There now, I knew how it would be. You men have such restless curiosity! Talk of the curiosity of women, indeed! 'Tis nothing. But be satisfied, for you are not to know anything at all of the matter."

"And is that likely to satisfy me, do you think?"

"Well, I declare I never knew anything like you. What can it signify to you, what we are talking of. Perhaps we are talking about you; therefore I would advise you not to listen, or you may happen to hear something not very agreeable."

In this commonplace chatter, which lasted some time, the original subject seemed entirely forgotten; and though Catherine was very well pleased to have it dropped for a while, she could not avoid a little suspicion at the total suspension of all Isabella's impatient desire to see Mr. Tilney. When the orchestra struck up a fresh dance, James would have led his fair partner away, but she resisted. "I tell you, Mr. Morland," she cried, "I would not do such a thing for all the world. How can you be so teasing; only conceive, my dear Catherine, what your brother wants me to do. He wants me to dance with him again, though I tell him that it is a most improper thing, and entirely against the rules. It would make us the talk of the place, if we were not to change partners."

"Upon my honour," said James, "in these public assemblies, it is as often done as not."

"Nonsense, how can you say so? But when you men have a point to carry, you never stick at anything. My sweet Catherine, do support me; persuade your brother how impossible it is. Tell him that it would quite shock you to see me do such a thing; now would not it?"

"No, not at all; but if you think it wrong, you had much better change."

"There," cried Isabella, "you hear what your sister says, and yet you will not mind her. Well, remember that it is not my fault, if we set all the old ladies in Bath in a bustle. Come along, my dearest Catherine, for heaven's sake, and stand by me." And off they went, to regain their former place. John Thorpe, in the meanwhile, had walked away; and Catherine, ever willing to give Mr. Tilney an opportunity of repeating the agreeable request which had already flattered her once, made her way to Mrs. Allen and Mrs. Thorpe as fast as she could, in the hope of finding him still with them—a hope which, when it proved to be fruitless, she felt to have been highly unreasonable. "Well, my dear," said Mrs. Thorpe, impatient for praise of her son, "I hope you have had an agreeable partner."

"Very agreeable, madam."

"I am glad of it. John has charming spirits, has not he?"

"Did you meet Mr. Tilney, my dear?" said Mrs. Allen.

"No, where is he?"

"He was with us just now, and said he was so tired of lounging about, that he was resolved to go and dance; so I thought perhaps he would ask you, if he met with you."

"Where can he be?" said Catherine, looking round; but she had not looked round long before she saw him leading a young lady to the dance.

"Ah! He has got a partner; I wish he had asked you," said Mrs. Allen; and after a short silence, she added, "he is a very agreeable young man."

"Indeed he is, Mrs. Allen," said Mrs. Thorpe, smiling complacently; "I must say it, though I am his mother, that there is not a more agreeable young man in the world."

This inapplicable answer might have been too much for the comprehension of many; but it did not puzzle Mrs. Allen, for after only a moment's consideration, she said, in a whisper to Catherine, "I dare say she thought I was speaking of her son."

Catherine was disappointed and vexed. She seemed to have missed by so little the very object she had had in view; and this persuasion did not incline her to a very gracious reply, when John Thorpe came up to her soon afterwards and said, "Well, Miss Morland, I suppose you and I are to stand up and jig it together again."

"Oh, no; I am much obliged to you, our two dances are over; and, besides, I am tired, and do not mean to dance any more."

"Do not you? Then let us walk about and quiz people. Come along with me, and I will show you the four greatest quizzers in the room; my two younger sisters and their partners. I have been laughing at them this half hour."

Again Catherine excused herself; and at last he walked off to quiz his sisters by himself. The rest of the evening she found very dull; Mr. Tilney was drawn away from their party at tea, to attend that of his partner; Miss Tilney, though belonging to it, did not sit near her, and James and Isabella were so much engaged in conversing together that the latter had no leisure to bestow more on her friend than one smile, one squeeze, and one "dearest Catherine."

CHAPTER 9

The progress of Catherine's unhappiness from the events of the evening was as follows. It appeared first in a general dissatisfaction with everybody about her, while she remained in the rooms, which speedily brought on considerable weariness and a violent desire to go home. This, on arriving in Pulteney Street, took the direction of extraordinary hunger, and when that was appeased, changed into an earnest longing to be in bed; such was the extreme point of her distress; for when there she immediately fell into a sound sleep which lasted nine hours, and from which she awoke perfectly revived, in excellent spirits, with fresh hopes and fresh schemes. The first wish of her heart was to improve her acquaintance with Miss Tilney, and almost her first resolution, to seek her for that purpose, in the pump-room at noon. In the pump-room, one so newly arrived in Bath must be met with, and that building she had already found so favourable for the discovery of female excellence, and the completion of female intimacy, so admirably adapted for secret discourses and unlimited confidence, that she was most reasonably encouraged to expect another friend from within its walls. Her plan for the morning thus settled, she sat quietly down to her book after breakfast, resolving to remain in the same place and the same employment till the clock struck one; and from habitude very little incommoded by the remarks and ejaculations of Mrs. Allen, whose vacancy of mind and incapacity for thinking were such, that as she never talked a great deal, so she could never be entirely silent; and, therefore, while she sat at her work, if she lost her needle or broke her thread, if she heard a carriage in the street, or saw a speck upon her gown, she must observe it aloud, whether there were anyone at leisure to answer her or not. At about half past twelve, a remarkably loud rap drew her in haste to the window, and scarcely had she time to inform Catherine of there being two open carriages at the door, in the first only a servant, her brother driving Miss Thorpe in the second, before John Thorpe came running upstairs, calling out, "Well, Miss Morland, here I am. Have you been waiting long? We could not come before; the old devil of a coachmaker was such an eternity finding out a thing fit to be got into, and now it is ten thousand to one but they break down before we are out of the street. How do you do, Mrs. Allen? A famous ball last night, was not it? Come, Miss Morland, be quick, for the others are in a confounded hurry to be off. They want to get their tumble over."

"What do you mean?" said Catherine. "Where are you all going to?"

"Going to? Why, you have not forgot our engagement! Did not we agree together to take a drive this morning? What a head you have! We are going up Claverton Down."

"Something was said about it, I remember," said Catherine, looking at Mrs. Allen for her opinion; "but really I did not expect you."

"Not expect me! That's a good one! And what a dust you would have made, if I had not come."

Catherine's silent appeal to her friend, meanwhile, was entirely thrown away, for Mrs. Allen, not being at all in the habit of conveying any expression herself by a look, was not aware of its being ever intended by anybody else; and Catherine, whose desire of seeing Miss Tilney again could at that moment bear a short delay in favour of a drive, and who thought there could be no impropriety in her going with Mr. Thorpe, as Isabella was going at the same time with James, was therefore obliged to speak plainer. "Well, ma'am, what do you say to it? Can you spare me for an hour or two? Shall I go?"

"Do just as you please, my dear," replied Mrs. Allen, with the most placid indifference. Catherine took the advice, and ran off to get ready. In a very few minutes she reappeared, having scarcely allowed the two others time enough to get through a few short sentences in her praise, after Thorpe had procured Mrs. Allen's admiration of his gig; and then receiving her friend's parting good wishes, they both hurried downstairs. "My dearest creature," cried Isabella, to whom the duty of friendship immediately called her before she could get into the carriage, "you have been at least three hours getting ready. I was afraid you were ill. What a delightful ball we had last night. I have a thousand things to say to you; but make haste and get in, for I long to be off."

Catherine followed her orders and turned away, but not too soon to hear her friend exclaim aloud to James, "What a sweet girl she is! I quite dote on her."

"You will not be frightened, Miss Morland," said Thorpe, as he handed her in, "if my horse should dance about a little at first setting off. He will, most likely, give a plunge or two, and perhaps take the rest for a minute; but he will soon know his master. He is full of spirits, playful as can be, but there is no vice in him."

Catherine did not think the portrait a very inviting one, but it was too late to retreat, and she was too young to own herself frightened; so, resigning herself to her fate, and trusting to the animal's boasted knowledge of its owner, she sat peaceably down, and saw Thorpe sit down by her. Everything being then arranged, the servant who stood at the horse's head was bid in an important voice "to let him go," and off they went in the quietest manner imaginable, without a plunge or a caper, or anything like one. Catherine, delighted at so happy an escape, spoke her pleasure aloud with grateful surprise; and her companion immediately made the matter perfectly simple by assuring her that it was entirely owing to the peculiarly judicious manner in which he had then held the reins, and the singular discernment and dexterity with which he had directed his whip. Catherine, though she could not help wondering that with such perfect command of his horse, he should think it necessary to alarm her with a relation of its tricks, congratulated herself sincerely on being under the care of so excellent a coachman; and perceiving that the animal continued to go on in the same quiet manner, without showing the smallest propensity towards any unpleasant vivacity, and (considering its inevitable pace was ten miles an hour) by no means alarmingly fast, gave herself up to all the enjoyment of air and exercise of the most invigorating kind, in a fine mild day of February, with the consciousness of safety. A silence of several minutes succeeded their first short dialogue; it was broken by Thorpe's saying very abruptly, "Old Allen is as rich as a Jew—is not he?" Catherine did not understand him—and he repeated his question, adding in explanation, "Old Allen, the man you are with."

"Oh! Mr. Allen, you mean. Yes, I believe, he is very rich."

"And no children at all?"

"No—not any."

"A famous thing for his next heirs. He is your godfather, is not he?"

"My godfather! No."

"But you are always very much with them."

"Yes, very much."

"Aye, that is what I meant. He seems a good kind of old fellow enough, and has lived very well in his time, I dare say; he is not gouty for nothing. Does he drink his bottle a day now?"

"His bottle a day! No. Why should you think of such a thing? He is a very temperate man, and you could not fancy him in liquor last night?"

"Lord help you! You women are always thinking of men's being in liquor. Why, you do not suppose a man is overset by a bottle? I am sure of this—that if everybody was to drink their bottle a day, there would not be half the disorders in the world there are now. It would be a famous good thing for us all."

"I cannot believe it."

"Oh! Lord, it would be the saving of thousands. There is not the hundredth part of the wine consumed in this kingdom that there ought to be. Our foggy climate wants help."

"And yet I have heard that there is a great deal of wine drunk in Oxford."

"Oxford! There is no drinking at Oxford now, I assure you. Nobody drinks there. You would hardly meet with a man who goes beyond his four pints at the utmost. Now, for instance, it was reckoned a remarkable thing, at the last party in my rooms, that upon an average we cleared about five pints a head. It was looked upon as something out of the common way. Mine is famous good stuff, to be sure. You would not often meet with anything like it in Oxford—and that may account for it. But this will just give you a notion of the general rate of drinking there."

"Yes, it does give a notion," said Catherine warmly, "and that is, that you all drink a great deal more wine than I thought you did. However, I am sure James does not drink so much."

This declaration brought on a loud and overpowering reply, of which no part was very distinct, except the frequent exclamations, amounting almost to oaths, which adorned it, and Catherine was left, when it ended, with rather a strengthened belief of there being a great deal of wine drunk in Oxford, and the same happy conviction of her brother's comparative sobriety.

Thorpe's ideas then all reverted to the merits of his own equipage, and she was called on to admire the spirit and freedom with which his horse moved along, and the ease which his paces, as well as the excellence of the springs, gave the motion of the carriage. She followed him in all his admiration as well as she could. To go before or beyond him was impossible. His knowledge and her ignorance of the subject, his rapidity of expression, and her diffidence of herself put that out of her power; she could strike out nothing new in commendation, but she readily echoed whatever he chose to assert, and it was finally settled between them without any difficulty that his equipage was altogether the most complete of its kind in England, his carriage the neatest, his horse the best goer, and himself the best coachman. "You do not really think, Mr. Thorpe," said Catherine, venturing after some time to consider the matter as entirely decided, and to offer some little variation on the subject, "that James's gig will break down?"

"Break down! Oh, lord! Did you ever see such a little tittuppy thing in your life? There is not a sound piece of iron about it. The wheels have been fairly worn out these ten years at least—and as for the body! Upon my soul, you might shake it to pieces yourself with a touch. It is the most devilish little rickety business I ever beheld! Thank God! we have got a better. I would not be bound to go two miles in it for fifty thousand pounds."

"Good heavens!" cried Catherine, quite frightened. "Then pray let us turn back; they will certainly meet with an accident if we go on. Do let us turn back, Mr. Thorpe; stop and speak to my brother, and tell him how very unsafe it is."

"Unsafe! Oh, lord! What is there in that? They will only get a roll if it does break down; and there is plenty of dirt; it will be excellent falling. Oh, curse it! The carriage is safe enough, if a man knows how to drive it; a thing of that sort in good hands will last above twenty years after it is fairly worn out. Lord bless you! I would undertake for five pounds to drive it to York and back again, without losing a nail."

Catherine listened with astonishment; she knew not how to reconcile two such very different accounts of the same thing; for she had not been brought up to understand the propensities of a rattle, nor to know to how many idle assertions and impudent falsehoods the excess of vanity will lead. Her own family were plain, matter-of-fact people who seldom aimed at wit of any kind; her father, at the utmost, being contented with a pun, and her mother with a proverb; they were not in the habit therefore of telling lies to increase their importance, or of asserting at one moment what they would contradict the next. She reflected on the affair for some time in much perplexity, and was more than once on the point of requesting from Mr. Thorpe a clearer insight into his real opinion on the subject; but she checked herself, because it appeared to her that he did not excel in giving those clearer insights, in making those things plain which he had before made ambiguous; and, joining to this, the consideration that he would not really suffer his sister and his friend to be exposed to a danger from which he might easily preserve them, she concluded at last that he must know the carriage to be in fact perfectly safe, and therefore would alarm herself no longer. By him the whole matter seemed entirely forgotten; and all the rest of his conversation, or rather talk, began and ended with himself and his own concerns. He told her of horses which he had bought for a trifle and sold for incredible sums; of racing matches, in which his judgment had infallibly foretold the winner; of shooting parties, in which he had killed more birds (though without having one good shot) than all his companions together; and described to her some famous day's sport, with the fox-hounds, in which his foresight and skill in directing the dogs had repaired the mistakes of the most experienced huntsman, and in which the boldness of his riding, though it had never endangered his own life for a moment, had been constantly leading others into difficulties, which he calmly concluded had broken the necks of many.

Little as Catherine was in the habit of judging for herself, and unfixed as were her general notions of what men ought to be, she could not entirely repress a doubt, while she bore with the effusions of his endless conceit, of his being altogether completely agreeable. It was a bold surmise, for he was Isabella's brother; and she had been assured by James that his manners would recommend him to all her sex; but in spite of this, the extreme weariness of his company, which crept over her before they had been out an hour, and which continued unceasingly to increase till they stopped in Pulteney Street again, induced her, in some small degree, to resist such high authority, and to distrust his powers of giving universal pleasure.

When they arrived at Mrs. Allen's door, the astonishment of Isabella was hardly to be expressed, on finding that it was too late in the day for them to attend her friend into the house: "Past three o'clock!" It was inconceivable, incredible, impossible! And she would neither believe her own watch, nor her brother's, nor the servant's; she would believe no assurance of it founded on reason or reality, till Morland produced his watch, and ascertained the fact; to have doubted a moment longer then, would have been equally inconceivable, incredible, and impossible; and she could only protest, over and over again, that no two hours and a half had ever gone off so swiftly before, as Catherine was called on to confirm; Catherine could not tell a falsehood even to please Isabella; but the latter was spared the misery of her friend's dissenting voice, by not waiting for her answer. Her own feelings entirely engrossed her; her wretchedness was most acute on finding herself obliged to go directly home. It was ages since she had had a moment's conversation with her dearest Catherine; and, though she had such thousands of things to say to her, it appeared as if they were never to be together again; so, with smiles of most exquisite misery, and the laughing eye of utter despondency, she bade her friend adieu and went on.

Catherine found Mrs. Allen just returned from all the busy idleness of the morning, and was immediately greeted with, "Well, my dear, here you are," a truth which she had no greater inclination than power to dispute; "and I hope you have had a pleasant airing?"

"Yes, ma'am, I thank you; we could not have had a nicer day."

"So Mrs. Thorpe said; she was vastly pleased at your all going."

"You have seen Mrs. Thorpe, then?"

"Yes, I went to the pump-room as soon as you were gone, and there I met her, and we had a great deal of talk together. She says there was hardly any veal to be got at market this morning, it is so uncommonly scarce."

"Did you see anybody else of our acquaintance?"

"Yes; we agreed to take a turn in the Crescent, and there we met Mrs. Hughes, and Mr. and Miss Tilney walking with her."

"Did you indeed? And did they speak to you?"

"Yes, we walked along the Crescent together for half an hour. They seem very agreeable people. Miss Tilney was in a very pretty spotted muslin, and I fancy, by what I can learn, that she always dresses very handsomely. Mrs. Hughes talked to me a great deal about the family."

"And what did she tell you of them?"

"Oh! A vast deal indeed; she hardly talked of anything else."

"Did she tell you what part of Gloucestershire they come

from?"

"Yes, she did; but I cannot recollect now. But they are very good kind of people, and very rich. Mrs. Tilney was a Miss Drummond, and she and Mrs. Hughes were schoolfellows; and Miss Drummond had a very large fortune; and, when she married, her father gave her twenty thousand pounds, and five hundred to buy wedding-clothes. Mrs. Hughes saw all the clothes after they came from the warehouse."

"And are Mr. and Mrs. Tilney in Bath?"

"Yes, I fancy they are, but I am not quite certain. Upon recollection, however, I have a notion they are both dead; at least the mother is; yes, I am sure Mrs. Tilney is dead, because Mrs. Hughes told me there was a very beautiful set of pearls that Mr. Drummond gave his daughter on her wedding-day and that Miss Tilney has got now, for they were put by for her when her mother died."

"And is Mr. Tilney, my partner, the only son?"

"I cannot be quite positive about that, my dear; I have some idea he is; but, however, he is a very fine young man, Mrs. Hughes says, and likely to do very well."

Catherine inquired no further; she had heard enough to feel that Mrs. Allen had no real intelligence to give, and that she was most particularly unfortunate herself in having missed such a meeting with both brother and sister. Could she have foreseen such a circumstance, nothing should have persuaded her to go out with the others; and, as it was, she could only lament her ill luck, and think over what she had lost, till it was clear to her that the drive had by no means been very pleasant and that John Thorpe himself was quite disagreeable.

CHAPTER 10

The Allens, Thorpes, and Morlands all met in the evening at the theatre; and, as Catherine and Isabella sat together, there was then an opportunity for the latter to utter some few of the many thousand things which had been collecting within her for communication in the immeasurable length of time which had divided them. "Oh, heavens! My beloved Catherine, have I got you at last?" was her address on Catherine's entering the box and sitting by her. "Now, Mr. Morland," for he was close to her on the other side, "I shall not speak another word to you all the rest of the evening; so I charge you not to expect it. My sweetest Catherine, how have you been this long age? But I need not ask you, for you look delightfully. You really have done your hair in a more heavenly style than ever; you mischievous creature, do you want to attract everybody? I assure you, my brother is quite in love with you already; and as for Mr. Tilney—but that is a settled thing—even your modesty cannot doubt his attachment now; his coming back to Bath makes it too plain. Oh! What would not I give to see him! I really am quite wild with impatience. My mother says he is the most delightful young man in the world; she saw him this morning, you know; you must introduce him to me. Is he in the house now? Look about, for heaven's sake! I assure you, I can hardly exist till I see him."

"No," said Catherine, "he is not here; I cannot see him anywhere."

"Oh, horrid! Am I never to be acquainted with him? How do you like my gown? I think it does not look amiss; the sleeves were entirely my own thought. Do you know, I get so immoderately sick of Bath; your brother and I were agreeing this morning that, though it is vastly well to be here for a few weeks, we would not live here for millions. We soon found out that our tastes were exactly alike in preferring the country to every other place; really, our opinions were so exactly the same, it was quite ridiculous! There was not a single point in which we differed; I would not have had you by for the world; you are such a sly thing, I am sure you would have made some droll remark or other about it."

"No, indeed I should not."

"Oh, yes you would indeed; I know you better than you know yourself. You would have told us that we seemed born for each other, or some nonsense of that kind, which would have distressed me beyond conception; my cheeks would have been as red as your roses; I would not have had you by for the world."

"Indeed you do me injustice; I would not have made so improper a remark upon any account; and besides, I am sure it would never have entered my head."

Isabella smiled incredulously and talked the rest of the evening to James.

Catherine's resolution of endeavouring to meet Miss Tilney again continued in full force the next morning; and till the usual moment of going to the pump-room, she felt some alarm from the dread of a second prevention. But nothing of that kind occurred, no visitors appeared to delay them, and they all three set off in good time for the pump-room, where the ordinary course of events and conversation took place; Mr. Allen, after drinking his glass of water, joined some gentlemen to talk over the politics of the day and compare the accounts of their newspapers; and the ladies walked about together, noticing every new face, and almost every new bonnet in the room. The female part of the Thorpe family, attended by James Morland, appeared among the crowd in less than a quarter of an hour, and Catherine immediately took her usual place by the side of her friend. James, who was now in constant attendance, maintained a similar position, and separating themselves from the rest of their party, they walked in that manner for some time, till Catherine began to doubt the happiness of a situation which, confining her entirely to her friend and brother, gave her very little share in the notice of either. They were always engaged in some sentimental discussion or lively dispute, but their sentiment was conveyed in such whispering voices, and their vivacity attended with so much laughter, that though Catherine's supporting opinion was not unfrequently called for by one or the other, she was never able to give any, from not having heard a word of the subject. At length however she was empowered to disengage herself from her friend, by the avowed necessity of speaking to Miss Tilney, whom she most joyfully saw just entering the room with Mrs. Hughes, and whom she instantly joined, with a firmer determination to be acquainted, than she might have had courage to command, had she not been urged by the disappointment of the day before. Miss Tilney met her with great civility, returned her advances with equal goodwill, and they continued talking together as long as both parties remained in the room; and though in all probability not an observation was made, nor an expression used by either which had not been made and used some thousands of times before, under that roof, in every Bath season, yet the merit of their being spoken with simplicity and truth, and without personal conceit, might be something uncommon.

"How well your brother dances!" was an artless exclamation of Catherine's towards the close of their conversation, which at once surprised and amused her companion.

"Henry!" she replied with a smile. "Yes, he does dance very well."

"He must have thought it very odd to hear me say I was engaged the other evening, when he saw me sitting down. But I really had been engaged the whole day to Mr. Thorpe." Miss Tilney could only bow. "You cannot think," added Catherine after a moment's silence, "how surprised I was to see him again. I felt so sure of his being quite gone away."

"When Henry had the pleasure of seeing you before, he was in Bath but for a couple of days. He came only to engage lodgings for us."

"That never occurred to me; and of course, not seeing him anywhere, I thought he must be gone. Was not the young lady he danced with on Monday a Miss Smith?"

"Yes, an acquaintance of Mrs. Hughes."

"I dare say she was very glad to dance. Do you think her pretty?"

"Not very."

"He never comes to the pump-room, I suppose?"

"Yes, sometimes; but he has rid out this morning with my father."

Mrs. Hughes now joined them, and asked Miss Tilney if she was ready to go. "I hope I shall have the pleasure of seeing you again soon," said Catherine. "Shall you be at the cotillion ball to-morrow?"

"Perhaps we—Yes, I think we certainly shall."

"I am glad of it, for we shall all be there." This civility was duly returned; and they parted—on Miss Tilney's side with some knowledge of her new acquaintance's feelings, and on Catherine's, without the smallest consciousness of having explained them.

She went home very happy. The morning had answered all her hopes, and the evening of the following day was now the object of expectation, the future good. What gown and what head-dress she should wear on the occasion became her chief concern. She cannot be justified in it. Dress is at all times a frivolous distinction, and excessive solicitude about it often destroys its own aim. Catherine knew all this very well; her great aunt had read her a lecture on the subject only the Christmas before; and yet she lay awake ten minutes on Wednesday night debating between her spotted and her tamboured muslin, and nothing but the shortness of the time prevented her buying a new one for the evening. This would have been an error in judgment, great though not uncommon, from which one of the other sex rather than her own, a brother rather than a great aunt, might have warned her, for man only can be aware of the insensibility of man towards a new gown. It would be mortifying to the feelings of many ladies, could they be made to understand how little the heart of man is affected by what is costly or new in their attire; how little it is biased by the texture of their muslin, and how unsusceptible of peculiar tenderness towards the spotted, the sprigged, the mull, or the jackonet. Woman is fine for her own satisfaction alone. No man will admire her the more, no woman will like her the better for it. Neatness and fashion are enough for the former, and a something of shabbiness or impropriety will be most endearing to the latter. But not one of these grave reflections troubled the tranquillity of Catherine.

She entered the rooms on Thursday evening with feelings very different from what had attended her thither the Monday before. She had then been exulting in her engagement to Thorpe, and was now chiefly anxious to avoid his sight, lest he should engage her again; for though she could not, dared not expect that Mr. Tilney should ask her a third time to dance, her wishes, hopes, and plans all centred in nothing less. Every young lady may feel for my heroine in this critical moment, for every young lady has at some time or other known the same agitation. All have been, or at least all have believed themselves to be, in danger from the pursuit of someone whom they wished to avoid; and all have been anxious for the attentions of someone whom they wished to please. As soon as they were joined by the Thorpes, Catherine's agony began; she fidgeted about if John Thorpe came towards her, hid herself as much as possible from his view, and when he spoke to her pretended not to hear him. The cotillions were over, the country-dancing beginning, and she saw nothing of the Tilneys.

"Do not be frightened, my dear Catherine," whispered Isabella, "but I am really going to dance with your brother again. I declare positively it is quite shocking. I tell him he ought to be ashamed of himself, but you and John must keep us in countenance. Make haste, my dear creature, and come to us. John is just walked off, but he will be back in a moment."

Catherine had neither time nor inclination to answer. The others walked away, John Thorpe was still in view, and she gave herself up for lost. That she might not appear, however, to observe or expect him, she kept her eyes intently fixed on her fan; and a self-condemnation for her folly, in supposing that among such a crowd they should even meet with the Tilneys in any reasonable time, had just passed through her mind, when she suddenly found herself addressed and again solicited to dance, by Mr. Tilney himself. With what sparkling eyes and ready motion she granted his request, and with how pleasing a flutter of heart she went with him to the set, may be easily imagined. To escape, and, as she believed, so narrowly escape John Thorpe, and to be asked, so immediately on his joining her, asked by Mr. Tilney, as if he had sought her on purpose!—it did not appear to her that life could supply any greater felicity.

Scarcely had they worked themselves into the quiet possession of a place, however, when her attention was claimed by John Thorpe, who stood behind her. "Heyday, Miss Morland!" said he. "What is the meaning of this? I thought you and I were to dance together."

"I wonder you should think so, for you never asked me."

"That is a good one, by Jove! I asked you as soon as I came into the room, and I was just going to ask you again, but when I turned round, you were gone! This is a cursed shabby trick! I only came for the sake of dancing with you, and I firmly believe you were engaged to me ever since Monday. Yes; I remember, I asked you while you were waiting in the lobby for your cloak. And here have I been telling all my acquaintance that I was going to dance with the prettiest girl in the room; and when they see you standing up with somebody else, they will quiz me famously."

"Oh, no; they will never think of me, after such a description as that."

"By heavens, if they do not, I will kick them out of the room for blockheads. What chap have you there?" Catherine satisfied his curiosity. "Tilney," he repeated. "Hum—I do not know him.

A good figure of a man; well put together. Does he want a horse? Here is a friend of mine, Sam Fletcher, has got one to sell that would suit anybody. A famous clever animal for the road—only forty guineas. I had fifty minds to buy it myself, for it is one of my maxims always to buy a good horse when I meet with one; but it would not answer my purpose, it would not do for the field. I would give any money for a real good hunter. I have three now, the best that ever were backed. I would not take eight hundred guineas for them. Fletcher and I mean to get a house in Leicestershire, against the next season. It is so d— — uncomfortable, living at an inn."

This was the last sentence by which he could weary Catherine's attention, for he was just then borne off by the resistless pressure of a long string of passing ladies. Her partner now drew near, and said, "That gentleman would have put me out of patience, had he stayed with you half a minute longer. He has no business to withdraw the attention of my partner from me. We have entered into a contract of mutual agreeableness for the space of an evening, and all our agreeableness belongs solely to each other for that time. Nobody can fasten themselves on the notice of one, without injuring the rights of the other. I consider a country-dance as an emblem of marriage. Fidelity and complaisance are the principal duties of both; and those men who do not choose to dance or marry themselves, have no business with the partners or wives of their neighbours."

"But they are such very different things!"

"—That you think they cannot be compared together."

"To be sure not. People that marry can never part, but must go and keep house together. People that dance only stand opposite each other in a long room for half an hour."

"And such is your definition of matrimony and dancing. Taken in that light certainly, their resemblance is not striking; but I think I could place them in such a view. You will allow, that in both, man has the advantage of choice, woman only the power of refusal; that in both, it is an engagement between man and woman, formed for the advantage of each; and that when once entered into, they belong exclusively to each other till the moment of its dissolution; that it is their duty, each to endeavour to give the other no cause for wishing that he or she had bestowed themselves elsewhere, and their best interest to keep their own imaginations from wandering towards the perfections of their neighbours, or fancying that they should have been better off with anyone else. You will allow all this?"

"Yes, to be sure, as you state it, all this sounds very well; but still they are so very different. I cannot look upon them at all in the same light, nor think the same duties belong to them."

"In one respect, there certainly is a difference. In marriage, the man is supposed to provide for the support of the woman, the woman to make the home agreeable to the man; he is to purvey, and she is to smile. But in dancing, their duties are exactly changed; the agreeableness, the compliance are expected from him, while she furnishes the fan and the lavender water. That, I suppose, was the difference of duties which struck you, as rendering the conditions incapable of comparison."

"No, indeed, I never thought of that."

"Then I am quite at a loss. One thing, however, I must observe. This disposition on your side is rather alarming. You totally disallow any similarity in the obligations; and may I not thence infer that your notions of the duties of the dancing state are not so strict as your partner might wish? Have I not reason to fear that if the gentleman who spoke to you just now were to return, or if any other gentleman were to address you, there would be nothing to restrain you from conversing with him as long as you chose?"

"Mr. Thorpe is such a very particular friend of my brother's, that if he talks to me, I must talk to him again; but there are hardly three young men in the room besides him that I have any acquaintance with."

"And is that to be my only security? Alas, alas!"

"Nay, I am sure you cannot have a better; for if I do not know anybody, it is impossible for me to talk to them; and, besides, I do not want to talk to anybody."

"Now you have given me a security worth having; and I shall proceed with courage. Do you find Bath as agreeable as when I had the honour of making the inquiry before?"

"Yes, quite—more so, indeed."

"More so! Take care, or you will forget to be tired of it at the proper time. You ought to be tired at the end of six weeks."

"I do not think I should be tired, if I were to stay here six months."

"Bath, compared with London, has little variety, and so everybody finds out every year. 'For six weeks, I allow Bath is pleasant enough; but beyond that, it is the most tiresome place in the world.' You would be told so by people of all descriptions, who come regularly every winter, lengthen their six weeks into ten or twelve, and go away at last because they can afford to stay no longer."

"Well, other people must judge for themselves, and those who go to London may think nothing of Bath. But I, who live in a small retired village in the country, can never find greater sameness in such a place as this than in my own home; for here are a variety of amusements, a variety of things to be seen and done all day long, which I can know nothing of there."

"You are not fond of the country."

"Yes, I am. I have always lived there, and always been very happy. But certainly there is much more sameness in a country life than in a Bath life. One day in the country is exactly like another."

"But then you spend your time so much more rationally in the country."

"Do I?"

"Do you not?"

"I do not believe there is much difference."

"Here you are in pursuit only of amusement all day long."

"And so I am at home—only I do not find so much of it. I walk about here, and so I do there; but here I see a variety of people in every street, and there I can only go and call on Mrs. Allen."

Mr. Tilney was very much amused.

"Only go and call on Mrs. Allen!" he repeated. "What a picture of intellectual poverty! However, when you sink into this abyss again, you will have more to say. You will be able to talk of Bath, and of all that you did here."

"Oh! Yes. I shall never be in want of something to talk of again to Mrs. Allen, or anybody else. I really believe I shall always be talking of Bath, when I am at home again—I do like it so very much. If I could but have Papa and Mamma, and the rest of them here, I suppose I should be too happy! James's coming (my eldest brother) is quite delightful—and especially as it turns out that the very family we are just got so intimate with are his intimate friends already. Oh! Who can ever be tired of Bath?"

"Not those who bring such fresh feelings of every sort to it as you do. But papas and mammas, and brothers, and intimate friends are a good deal gone by, to most of the frequenters of Bath—and the honest relish of balls and plays, and everyday sights, is past with them."

Here their conversation closed, the demands of the dance becoming now too importunate for a divided attention.

Soon after their reaching the bottom of the set, Catherine perceived herself to be earnestly regarded by a gentleman who stood among the lookers-on, immediately behind her partner. He was a very handsome man, of a commanding aspect, past the bloom, but not past the vigour of life; and with his eye still directed towards her, she saw him presently address Mr. Tilney in a familiar whisper. Confused by his notice, and blushing from the fear of its being excited by something wrong in her appearance, she turned away her head. But while she did so, the gentleman retreated, and her partner, coming nearer, said, "I see that you guess what I have just been asked. That gentleman knows your name, and you have a right to know his. It is General Tilney, my father."

Catherine's answer was only "Oh!"—but it was an "Oh!" expressing everything needful: attention to his words, and perfect reliance on their truth. With real interest and strong admiration did her eye now follow the general, as he moved through the crowd, and "How handsome a family they are!" was her secret remark.

In chatting with Miss Tilney before the evening concluded, a new source of felicity arose to her. She had never taken a country walk since her arrival in Bath. Miss Tilney, to whom all the commonly frequented environs were familiar, spoke of them in terms which made her all eagerness to know them too; and on her openly fearing that she might find nobody to go with her, it was proposed by the brother and sister that they should join in a walk, some morning or other. "I shall like it," she cried, "beyond anything in the world; and do not let us put it off—let us go to-morrow." This was readily agreed to, with only a proviso of Miss Tilney's, that it did not rain, which

Catherine was sure it would not. At twelve o'clock, they were to call for her in Pulteney Street; and "Remember—twelve o'clock," was her parting speech to her new friend. Of her other, her older, her more established friend, Isabella, of whose fidelity and worth she had enjoyed a fortnight's experience, she scarcely saw anything during the evening. Yet, though longing to make her acquainted with her happiness, she cheerfully submitted to the wish of Mr. Allen, which took them rather early away, and her spirits danced within her, as she danced in her chair all the way home.

CHAPTER 11

The morrow brought a very sober-looking morning, the sun making only a few efforts to appear, and Catherine augured from it everything most favourable to her wishes. A bright morning so early in the year, she allowed, would generally turn to rain, but a cloudy one foretold improvement as the day advanced. She applied to Mr. Allen for confirmation of her hopes, but Mr. Allen, not having his own skies and barometer about him, declined giving any absolute promise of sunshine. She applied to Mrs. Allen, and Mrs. Allen's opinion was more positive. "She had no doubt in the world of its being a very fine day, if the clouds would only go off, and the sun keep out."

At about eleven o'clock, however, a few specks of small rain upon the windows caught Catherine's watchful eye, and "Oh! dear, I do believe it will be wet," broke from her in a most desponding tone.

"I thought how it would be," said Mrs. Allen.

"No walk for me to-day," sighed Catherine; "but perhaps it may come to nothing, or it may hold up before twelve."

"Perhaps it may, but then, my dear, it will be so dirty."

"Oh! That will not signify; I never mind dirt."

"No," replied her friend very placidly, "I know you never mind dirt."

After a short pause, "It comes on faster and faster!" said Catherine, as she stood watching at a window.

"So it does indeed. If it keeps raining, the streets will be very wet."

"There are four umbrellas up already. How I hate the sight of an umbrella!"

"They are disagreeable things to carry. I would much rather take a chair at any time."

"It was such a nice-looking morning! I felt so convinced it would be dry!"

"Anybody would have thought so indeed. There will be very few people in the pump-room, if it rains all the morning. I hope Mr. Allen will put on his greatcoat when he goes, but I dare say he will not, for he had rather do anything in the world than walk out in a greatcoat; I wonder he should dislike it, it must be so comfortable."

The rain continued—fast, though not heavy. Catherine went every five minutes to the clock, threatening on each return that, if it still kept on raining another five minutes, she would give up the matter as hopeless. The clock struck twelve, and it still rained. "You will not be able to go, my dear."

"I do not quite despair yet. I shall not give it up till a quarter after twelve. This is just the time of day for it to clear up, and I do think it looks a little lighter. There, it is twenty minutes after twelve, and now I shall give it up entirely. Oh! That we had such weather here as they had at Udolpho, or at least in Tuscany and the south of France!—the night that poor St. Aubin died!—such beautiful weather!"

At half past twelve, when Catherine's anxious attention to the weather was over and she could no longer claim any merit from its amendment, the sky began voluntarily to clear. A gleam of sunshine took her quite by surprise; she looked round; the clouds were parting, and she instantly returned to the window to watch over and encourage the happy appearance. Ten minutes more made it certain that a bright afternoon would succeed, and justified the opinion of Mrs. Allen, who had "always thought it would clear up." But whether Catherine might still expect her friends, whether there had not been too much rain for Miss Tilney to venture, must yet be a question.

It was too dirty for Mrs. Allen to accompany her husband to the pump-room; he accordingly set off by himself, and Catherine had barely watched him down the street when her notice was claimed by the approach of the same two open carriages, containing the same three people that had surprised her so much a few mornings back.

"Isabella, my brother, and Mr. Thorpe, I declare! They are coming for me perhaps—but I shall not go—I cannot go indeed, for you know Miss Tilney may still call." Mrs. Allen agreed to it. John Thorpe was soon with them, and his voice was with them yet sooner, for on the stairs he was calling out to Miss Morland to be quick. "Make haste! Make haste!" as he threw open the door. "Put on your hat this moment—there is no time to be lost—we are going to Bristol. How d'ye do, Mrs. Allen?"

"To Bristol! Is not that a great way off? But, however, I cannot go with you to-day, because I am engaged; I expect some friends every moment." This was of course vehemently talked down as no reason at all; Mrs. Allen was called on to second him, and the two others walked in, to give their assistance. "My sweetest Catherine, is not this delightful? We shall have a most heavenly drive. You are to thank your brother and me for the scheme; it darted into our heads at breakfast-time, I verily believe at the same instant; and we should have been off two hours ago if it had not been for this detestable rain. But it does not signify, the nights are moonlight, and we shall do delightfully. Oh! I am in such ecstasies at the thoughts of a little country air and quiet! So much better than going to the Lower Rooms. We shall drive directly to Clifton and dine there; and, as soon as dinner is over, if there is time for it, go on to Kingsweston."

"I doubt our being able to do so much," said Morland.

"You croaking fellow!" cried Thorpe. "We shall be able to do ten times more. Kingsweston! Aye, and Blaize Castle too, and anything else we can hear of; but here is your sister says she will not go."

"Blaize Castle!" cried Catherine. "What is that?"

"The finest place in England—worth going fifty miles at any time to see."

"What, is it really a castle, an old castle?"

"The oldest in the kingdom."

"But is it like what one reads of?"

"Exactly—the very same."

"But now really—are there towers and long galleries?"

"By dozens."

"Then I should like to see it; but I cannot—I cannot go."

"Not go! My beloved creature, what do you mean?"

"I cannot go, because"—looking down as she spoke, fearful of Isabella's smile—"I expect Miss Tilney and her brother to call on me to take a country walk. They promised to come at twelve, only it rained; but now, as it is so fine, I dare say they will be here soon."

"Not they indeed," cried Thorpe; "for, as we turned into Broad Street, I saw them—does he not drive a phaeton with bright chestnuts?"

"I do not know indeed."

"Yes, I know he does; I saw him. You are talking of the man you danced with last night, are not you?"

"Yes."

"Well, I saw him at that moment turn up the Lansdown Road, driving a smart-looking girl."

"Did you indeed?"

"Did upon my soul; knew him again directly, and he seemed to have got some very pretty cattle too."

"It is very odd! But I suppose they thought it would be too dirty for a walk."

"And well they might, for I never saw so much dirt in my life. Walk! You could no more walk than you could fly! It has not been so dirty the whole winter; it is ankle-deep everywhere."

Isabella corroborated it: "My dearest Catherine, you cannot form an idea of the dirt; come, you must go; you cannot refuse going now."

"I should like to see the castle; but may we go all over it? May we go up every staircase, and into every suite of rooms?"

"Yes, yes, every hole and corner."

"But then, if they should only be gone out for an hour till it is dryer, and call by and by?"

"Make yourself easy, there is no danger of that, for I heard Tilney hallooing to a man who was just passing by on horseback, that they were going as far as Wick Rocks."

"Then I will. Shall I go, Mrs. Allen?"

"Just as you please, my dear."

"Mrs. Allen, you must persuade her to go," was the general cry. Mrs. Allen was not inattentive to it: "Well, my dear," said she, "suppose you go." And in two minutes they were off.

Catherine's feelings, as she got into the carriage, were in a very unsettled state; divided between regret for the loss of one great pleasure, and the hope of soon enjoying another, almost its equal in degree, however unlike in kind. She could not think the Tilneys had acted quite well by her, in so readily giving up their engagement, without sending her any message of excuse. It was now but an hour later than the time fixed on for the beginning of their walk; and, in spite of what she had heard of the prodigious accumulation of dirt in the course of that hour, she could not from her own observation help thinking that they might have gone with very little inconvenience. To feel herself slighted by them was very painful. On the other hand, the delight of exploring an edifice like Udolpho, as her fancy represented Blaize Castle to be, was such a counterpoise of good as might console her for almost anything.

They passed briskly down Pulteney Street, and through Laura Place, without the exchange of many words. Thorpe talked to his horse, and she meditated, by turns, on broken promises and broken arches, phaetons and false hangings, Tilneys and trap-doors. As they entered Argyle Buildings, however, she was roused by this address from her companion, "Who is that girl who looked at you so hard as she went by?"

"Who? Where?"

"On the right-hand pavement—she must be almost out of sight now." Catherine looked round and saw Miss Tilney leaning on her brother's arm, walking slowly down the street. She saw them both looking back at her. "Stop, stop, Mr. Thorpe," she impatiently cried; "it is Miss Tilney; it is indeed. How could you tell me they were gone? Stop, stop, I will get out this moment and go to them." But to what purpose did she speak? Thorpe only lashed his horse into a brisker trot; the Tilneys, who had soon ceased to look after her, were in a moment out of sight round the corner of Laura Place, and in another moment she was herself whisked into the marketplace. Still, however, and during the length of another street, she entreated him to stop. "Pray, pray stop, Mr. Thorpe. I cannot go on. I will not go on. I must go back to Miss Tilney." But Mr. Thorpe only laughed, smacked his whip, encouraged his horse, made odd noises, and drove on; and Catherine, angry and vexed as she was, having no power of getting away, was obliged to give up the point and submit. Her reproaches, however, were not spared. "How could you deceive me so, Mr. Thorpe? How could you say that you saw them driving up the Lansdown Road? I would not have had it happen so for the world. They must think it so strange, so rude of me! To go by them, too, without saying a word! You do not know how vexed I am; I shall have no pleasure at Clifton, nor in anything else. I had rather, ten thousand times rather, get out now, and walk back to them. How could you say you saw them driving out in a phaeton?" Thorpe defended himself very stoutly, declared he had never seen two men so much alike in his life, and would hardly give up the point of its having been Tilney himself.

Their drive, even when this subject was over, was not likely to be very agreeable. Catherine's complaisance was no longer what it had been in their former airing. She listened reluctantly, and her replies were short. Blaize Castle remained her only comfort; towards that, she still looked at intervals with pleasure; though rather than be disappointed of the promised walk, and especially rather than be thought ill of by the Tilneys, she would willingly have given up all the happiness which its walls could supply – the happiness of a progress through a long suite of lofty rooms, exhibiting the remains of magnificent furniture, though now for many years deserted – the happiness of being stopped in their way along narrow, winding vaults, by a low, grated door; or even of having their lamp, their only lamp, extinguished by a sudden gust of wind, and of being left in total darkness. In the meanwhile, they proceeded on their journey without any mischance, and were within view of the town of Keynsham, when a halloo from Morland, who was behind them, made his friend pull up, to know what was the matter. The others then came close enough for conversation, and Morland said, "We had better go back, Thorpe; it is too late to go on to-day; your sister thinks so as well as I. We have been exactly an hour coming from Pulteney Street, very little more than seven miles; and, I suppose, we have at least eight more to go. It will never do. We set out a great deal too late. We had much better put it off till another day, and turn round."

"It is all one to me," replied Thorpe rather angrily; and instantly turning his horse, they were on their way back to Bath.

"If your brother had not got such a d— — beast to drive," said he soon afterwards, "we might have done it very well. My horse would have trotted to Clifton within the hour, if left to himself, and I have almost broke my arm with pulling him in to that cursed broken-winded jade's pace. Morland is a fool for not keeping a horse and gig of his own."

"No, he is not," said Catherine warmly, "for I am sure he could not afford it."

"And why cannot he afford it?"

"Because he has not money enough."

"And whose fault is that?"

"Nobody's, that I know of." Thorpe then said something in the loud, incoherent way to which he had often recourse, about its being a d— — thing to be miserly; and that if people who rolled in money could not afford things, he did not know who could, which Catherine did not even endeavour to understand. Disappointed of what was to have been the consolation for her first disappointment, she was less and less disposed either to be agreeable herself or to find her companion so; and they returned to Pulteney Street without her speaking twenty words.

As she entered the house, the footman told her that a gentleman and lady had called and inquired for her a few minutes after her setting off; that, when he told them she was gone out with Mr. Thorpe, the lady had asked whether any message had been left for her; and on his saying no, had felt for a card, but said she had none about her, and went away. Pondering over these heart-rending tidings, Catherine walked slowly upstairs. At the head of them she was met by Mr. Allen, who, on hearing the reason of their speedy return, said, "I am glad your brother had so much sense; I am glad you are come back. It was a strange, wild scheme."

They all spent the evening together at Thorpe's. Catherine was disturbed and out of spirits; but Isabella seemed to find a pool of commerce, in the fate of which she shared, by private partnership with Morland, a very good equivalent for the quiet and country air of an inn at Clifton. Her satisfaction, too, in not being at the Lower Rooms was spoken more than once. "How I pity the poor creatures that are going there! How glad I am that I am not amongst them! I wonder whether it will be a full ball or not! They have not begun dancing yet. I would not be there for all the world. It is so delightful to have an evening now and then to oneself. I dare say it will not be a very good ball. I know the Mitchells will not be there. I am sure I pity everybody that is. But I dare say, Mr. Morland, you long to be at it, do not you? I am sure you do. Well, pray do not let anybody here be a restraint on you. I dare say we could do very well without you;

but you men think yourselves of such consequence."

Catherine could almost have accused Isabella of being wanting in tenderness towards herself and her sorrows, so very little did they appear to dwell on her mind, and so very inadequate was the comfort she offered. "Do not be so dull, my dearest creature," she whispered. "You will quite break my heart. It was amazingly shocking, to be sure; but the Tilneys were entirely to blame. Why were not they more punctual? It was dirty, indeed, but what did that signify? I am sure John and I should not have minded it. I never mind going through anything, where a friend is concerned; that is my disposition, and John is just the same; he has amazing strong feelings. Good heavens! What a delightful hand you have got! Kings, I vow! I never was so happy in my life! I would fifty times rather you should have them than myself."

And now I may dismiss my heroine to the sleepless couch, which is the true heroine's portion; to a pillow strewed with thorns and wet with tears. And lucky may she think herself, if she get another good night's rest in the course of the next three months.

CHAPTER 12

"Mrs. Allen," said Catherine the next morning, "will there be any harm in my calling on Miss Tilney to-day? I shall not be easy till I have explained everything."

"Go, by all means, my dear; only put on a white gown; Miss Tilney always wears white."

Catherine cheerfully complied, and being properly equipped, was more impatient than ever to be at the pump-room, that she might inform herself of General Tilney's lodgings, for though she believed they were in Milsom Street, she was not certain of the house, and Mrs. Allen's wavering convictions only made it more doubtful. To Milsom Street she was directed, and having made herself perfect in the number, hastened away with eager steps and a beating heart to pay her visit, explain her conduct, and be forgiven; tripping lightly through the church-yard, and resolutely turning away her eyes, that she might not be obliged to see her beloved Isabella and her dear family, who, she had reason to believe, were in a shop hard by. She reached the house without any impediment, looked at the number, knocked at the door, and inquired for Miss Tilney. The man believed Miss Tilney to be at home, but was not quite certain. Would she be pleased to send up her name? She gave her card. In a few minutes the servant returned, and with a look which did not quite confirm his words, said he had been mistaken, for that Miss Tilney was walked out. Catherine, with a blush of mortification, left the house. She felt almost persuaded that Miss Tilney was at home, and too much offended to admit her; and as she retired down the street, could not withhold one glance at the drawing-room windows, in expectation of seeing her there, but no one appeared at them. At the bottom of the street, however, she looked back again, and then, not at a window, but issuing from the door, she saw Miss Tilney herself. She was followed by a gentleman, whom Catherine believed to be her father, and they turned up towards Edgar's Buildings. Catherine, in deep mortification, proceeded on her way. She could almost be angry herself at such angry incivility; but she checked the resentful sensation; she remembered her own ignorance. She knew not how such an offence as hers might be classed by the laws of worldly politeness, to what a degree of unforgivingness it might with propriety lead, nor to what rigours of rudeness in return it might justly make her amenable.

Dejected and humbled, she had even some thoughts of not going with the others to the theatre that night; but it must be confessed that they were not of long continuance, for she soon recollected, in the first place, that she was without any excuse for staying at home; and, in the second, that it was a play she wanted very much to see. To the theatre accordingly they all went; no Tilneys appeared to plague or please her; she feared that, amongst the many perfections of the family, a fondness for plays was not to be ranked; but perhaps it was because they were habituated to the finer performances of the London stage, which she knew, on Isabella's authority, rendered everything else of the kind "quite horrid." She was not deceived in her own expectation of pleasure; the comedy so well suspended her care that no one, observing her during the first four acts, would have supposed she had any wretchedness about her. On the beginning of the fifth, however, the sudden view of Mr. Henry Tilney and his father, joining a party in the opposite box, recalled her to anxiety and distress. The stage could no longer excite genuine merriment—no longer keep her whole attention. Every other look upon an average was directed towards the opposite box; and, for the space of two entire scenes, did she thus watch Henry Tilney, without being once able to catch his eye. No longer could he be suspected of indifference for a play; his notice was never withdrawn from the stage during two whole scenes. At length, however, he did look towards her, and he bowed—but such a bow! No smile, no continued observance attended it; his eyes were immediately returned to their former direction. Catherine was restlessly miserable; she could almost have run round to the box in which he sat and forced him to hear her explanation. Feelings rather natural than heroic possessed her; instead of considering her own dignity injured by this ready condemnation—instead of proudly resolving, in conscious innocence, to show her resentment towards him who could harbour a doubt of it, to leave to him all the trouble of seeking an explanation, and to enlighten him on the past only by avoiding his sight, or flirting with somebody else—she took to herself all the shame of misconduct, or at least of its appearance, and was only eager for an opportunity of explaining its cause.

The play concluded—the curtain fell—Henry Tilney was no longer to be seen where he had hitherto sat, but his father remained, and perhaps he might be now coming round to their box. She was right; in a few minutes he appeared, and, making his way through the then thinning rows, spoke with like calm politeness to Mrs. Allen and her friend. Not with such calmness was he answered by the latter: "Oh! Mr. Tilney, I have been quite wild to speak to you, and make my apologies. You must have thought me so rude; but indeed it was not my own fault, was it, Mrs. Allen? Did not they tell me that Mr. Tilney and his sister were gone out in a phaeton together? And then what could I do? But I had ten thousand times rather have been with you; now had not I, Mrs. Allen?"

"My dear, you tumble my gown," was Mrs. Allen's reply.

Her assurance, however, standing sole as it did, was not thrown away; it brought a more cordial, more natural smile into his countenance, and he replied in a tone which retained only a little affected reserve: "We were much obliged to you at any rate for wishing us a pleasant walk after our passing you in Argyle Street: you were so kind as to look back on purpose."

"But indeed I did not wish you a pleasant walk; I never thought of such a thing; but I begged Mr. Thorpe so earnestly to stop; I called out to him as soon as ever I saw you; now, Mrs. Allen, did not—Oh! You were not there; but indeed I did; and, if Mr. Thorpe would only have stopped, I would have jumped out and run after you."

Is there a Henry in the world who could be insensible to such a declaration? Henry Tilney at least was not. With a yet sweeter smile, he said everything that need be said of his sister's concern, regret, and dependence on Catherine's honour. "Oh, do not say Miss Tilney was not angry," cried Catherine, "because I know she was; for she would not see me this morning when I called; I saw her walk out of the house the next minute after my leaving it; I was hurt, but I was not affronted. Perhaps you did not know I had been there."

"I was not within at the time; but I heard of it from Eleanor, and she has been wishing ever since to see you, to explain the reason of such incivility; but perhaps I can do it as well. It was nothing more than that my father—they were just preparing to walk out, and he being hurried for time, and not caring to have it put off—made a point of her being denied. That was all, I do assure you. She was very much vexed, and meant to make her apology as soon as possible."

Catherine's mind was greatly eased by this information, yet a something of solicitude remained, from which sprang the following question, thoroughly artless in itself, though rather distressing to the gentleman: "But, Mr. Tilney, why were you less generous than your sister? If she felt such confidence in my good intentions, and could suppose it to be only a mistake, why should you be so ready to take offence?"

"Me! I take offence!"

"Nay, I am sure by your look, when you came into the box, you were angry."

"I angry! I could have no right."

"Well, nobody would have thought you had no right who saw your face." He replied by asking her to make room for him, and talking of the play.

He remained with them some time, and was only too agreeable for Catherine to be contented when he went away. Before they parted, however, it was agreed that the projected walk should be taken as soon as possible; and, setting aside the misery of his quitting their box, she was, upon the whole, left one of the happiest creatures in the world.

While talking to each other, she had observed with some surprise that John Thorpe, who was never in the same part of the house for ten minutes together, was engaged in conversation with General Tilney; and she felt something more than surprise when she thought she could perceive herself the object of their attention and discourse. What could they have to say of her? She feared General Tilney did not like her appearance: she found it was implied in his preventing her admittance to his daughter, rather than postpone his own walk a few minutes. "How came Mr. Thorpe to know your father?" was her anxious inquiry, as she pointed them out to her companion. He knew nothing about it; but his father, like every military man, had a very large acquaintance.

When the entertainment was over, Thorpe came to assist them in getting out. Catherine was the immediate object of his gallantry; and, while they waited in the lobby for a chair, he prevented the inquiry which had travelled from her heart almost to the tip of her tongue, by asking, in a consequential manner, whether she had seen him talking with General Tilney: "He is a fine old fellow, upon my soul! Stout, active—looks as young as his son. I have a great regard for him, I assure you: a gentleman-like, good sort of fellow as ever lived."

"But how came you to know him?"

"Know him! There are few people much about town that I do not know. I have met him forever at the Bedford; and I knew his face again to-day the moment he came into the billiard-room. One of the best players we have, by the by; and we had a little touch together, though I was almost afraid of him at first: the odds were five to four against me; and, if I had not made one of the cleanest strokes that perhaps ever was made in this world—I took his ball exactly—but I could not make you understand it without a table; however, I did beat him. A very fine fellow; as rich as a Jew. I should like to dine with him; I dare say he gives famous dinners. But what do you think we have been talking of? You. Yes, by heavens! And the general thinks you the finest girl in Bath."

"Oh! Nonsense! How can you say so?"

"And what do you think I said?"—lowering his voice—"well done, general, said I; I am quite of your mind."

Here Catherine, who was much less gratified by his admiration than by General Tilney's, was not sorry to be called away by Mr. Allen. Thorpe, however, would see her to her chair, and, till she entered it, continued the same kind of delicate flattery, in spite of her entreating him to have done.

That General Tilney, instead of disliking, should admire her, was very delightful; and she joyfully thought that there was not one of the family whom she need now fear to meet. The evening had done more, much more, for her than could have been expected.

CHAPTER 13

Monday, Tuesday, Wednesday, Thursday, Friday, and Saturday have now passed in review before the reader; the events of each day, its hopes and fears, mortifications and pleasures, have been separately stated, and the pangs of Sunday only now remain to be described, and close the week. The Clifton scheme had been deferred, not relinquished, and on the afternoon's Crescent of this day, it was brought forward again. In a private consultation between Isabella and James, the former of whom had particularly set her heart upon going, and the latter no less anxiously placed his upon pleasing her, it was agreed that, provided the weather were fair, the party should take place on the following morning; and they were to set off very early, in order to be at home in good time. The affair thus determined, and Thorpe's approbation secured, Catherine only remained to be apprised of it. She had left them for a few minutes to speak to Miss Tilney. In that interval the plan was completed, and as soon as she came again, her agreement was demanded; but instead of the gay acquiescence expected by Isabella, Catherine looked grave, was very sorry, but could not go. The engagement which ought to have kept her from joining in the former attempt would make it impossible for her to accompany them now. She had that moment settled with Miss Tilney to take their proposed walk to-morrow; it was quite determined, and she would not, upon any account, retract. But that she must and should retract, was instantly the eager cry of both the Thorpes; they must go to Clifton to-morrow, they would not go without her, it would be nothing to put off a mere walk for one day longer, and they would not hear of a refusal. Catherine was distressed, but not subdued. "Do not urge me, Isabella. I am engaged to Miss Tilney. I cannot go." This availed nothing. The same arguments assailed her again; she must go, she should go, and they would not hear of a refusal. "It would be so easy to tell Miss Tilney that you had just been reminded of a prior engagement, and must only beg to put off the walk till Tuesday."

"No, it would not be easy. I could not do it. There has been no prior engagement." But Isabella became only more and more urgent, calling on her in the most affectionate manner, addressing her by the most endearing names. She was sure her dearest, sweetest Catherine would not seriously refuse such a trifling request to a friend who loved her so dearly. She knew her beloved Catherine to have so feeling a heart, so sweet a temper, to be so easily persuaded by those she loved. But all in vain; Catherine felt herself to be in the right, and though pained by such tender, such flattering supplication, could not allow it to influence her. Isabella then tried another method. She reproached her with having more affection for Miss Tilney, though she had known her so little a while, than for her best and oldest friends, with being grown cold and indifferent, in short, towards herself. "I cannot help being jealous, Catherine, when I see myself slighted for strangers, I, who love you so excessively! When once my affections are placed, it is not in the power of anything to change them. But I believe my feelings are stronger than anybody's; I am sure they are too strong for my own peace; and to see myself supplanted in your friendship by strangers does cut me to the quick, I own. These Tilneys seem to swallow up everything else."

Catherine thought this reproach equally strange and unkind. Was it the part of a friend thus to expose her feelings to the notice of others? Isabella appeared to her ungenerous and selfish, regardless of everything but her own gratification. These painful ideas crossed her mind, though she said nothing. Isabella, in the meanwhile, had applied her handkerchief to her eyes; and Morland, miserable at such a sight, could not help saying, "Nay, Catherine. I think you cannot stand out any longer now. The sacrifice is not much; and to oblige such a friend—I shall think you quite unkind, if you still refuse."

This was the first time of her brother's openly siding against her, and anxious to avoid his displeasure, she proposed a compromise. If they would only put off their scheme till Tuesday, which they might easily do, as it depended only on themselves, she could go with them, and everybody might then be satisfied. But "No, no, no!" was the immediate answer; "that could not be, for Thorpe did not know that he might not go to town on Tuesday." Catherine was sorry, but could do no more; and a short silence ensued, which was broken by Isabella, who in a voice of cold resentment said, "Very well, then there is an end of the party. If Catherine does not go, I cannot. I cannot be the only woman. I would not, upon any account in the world, do so improper a thing."

"Catherine, you must go," said James.

"But why cannot Mr. Thorpe drive one of his other sisters? I dare say either of them would like to go."

"Thank ye," cried Thorpe, "but I did not come to Bath to drive my sisters about, and look like a fool. No, if you do not go, d— — me if I do. I only go for the sake of driving you."

"That is a compliment which gives me no pleasure." But her words were lost on Thorpe, who had turned abruptly away.

The three others still continued together, walking in a most uncomfortable manner to poor Catherine; sometimes not a word was said, sometimes she was again attacked with supplications or reproaches, and her arm was still linked within Isabella's, though their hearts were at war. At one moment she was softened, at another irritated; always distressed, but always steady.

"I did not think you had been so obstinate, Catherine," said James; "you were not used to be so hard to persuade; you once were the kindest, best-tempered of my sisters."

"I hope I am not less so now," she replied, very feelingly; "but indeed I cannot go. If I am wrong, I am doing what I believe to be right."

"I suspect," said Isabella, in a low voice, "there is no great struggle."

Catherine's heart swelled; she drew away her arm, and Isabella made no opposition. Thus passed a long ten minutes, till they were again joined by Thorpe, who, coming to them with a gayer look, said, "Well, I have settled the matter, and now we may all go to-morrow with a safe conscience. I have been to Miss Tilney, and made your excuses."

"You have not!" cried Catherine.

"I have, upon my soul. Left her this moment. Told her you had sent me to say that, having just recollected a prior engagement of going to Clifton with us to-morrow, you could not have the pleasure of walking with her till Tuesday. She said very well, Tuesday was just as convenient to her; so there is an end of all our difficulties. A pretty good thought of mine—hey?"

Isabella's countenance was once more all smiles and good humour, and James too looked happy again.

"A most heavenly thought indeed! Now, my sweet Catherine, all our distresses are over; you are honourably acquitted, and we shall have a most delightful party."

"This will not do," said Catherine; "I cannot submit to this. I must run after Miss Tilney directly and set her right."

Isabella, however, caught hold of one hand, Thorpe of the other, and remonstrances poured in from all three. Even James was quite angry. When everything was settled, when Miss Tilney herself said that Tuesday would suit her as well, it was quite ridiculous, quite absurd, to make any further objection.

"I do not care. Mr. Thorpe had no business to invent any such message. If I had thought it right to put it off, I could have spoken to Miss Tilney myself. This is only doing it in a ruder way; and how do I know that Mr. Thorpe has—He may be mistaken again perhaps; he led me into one act of rudeness by his mistake on Friday. Let me go, Mr. Thorpe; Isabella, do not hold me."

Thorpe told her it would be in vain to go after the Tilneys; they were turning the corner into Brock Street, when he had overtaken them, and were at home by this time.

"Then I will go after them," said Catherine; "wherever they are I will go after them. It does not signify talking. If I could not be persuaded into doing what I thought wrong, I never will be tricked into it." And with these words she broke away and hurried off. Thorpe would have darted after her, but Morland withheld him. "Let her go, let her go, if she will go."

"She is as obstinate as—"

Thorpe never finished the simile, for it could hardly have been a proper one.

Away walked Catherine in great agitation, as fast as the crowd would permit her, fearful of being pursued, yet determined to persevere. As she walked, she reflected on what had passed. It was painful to her to disappoint and displease them, particularly to displease her brother; but she could not repent her resistance. Setting her own inclination apart, to have failed a second time in her engagement to Miss Tilney, to have retracted a promise voluntarily made only five minutes before, and on a false pretence too, must have been wrong. She had not been withstanding them on selfish principles alone, she had not consulted merely her own gratification; that might have been ensured in some degree by the excursion itself, by seeing Blaize Castle; no, she had attended to what was due to others, and to her own character in their opinion. Her conviction of being right, however, was not enough to restore her composure; till she had spoken to Miss Tilney she could not be at ease; and quickening her pace when she got clear of the Crescent, she almost ran over the remaining ground till she gained the top of Milsom Street. So rapid had been her movements that in spite of the Tilneys' advantage in the outset, they were but just turning into their lodgings as she came within view of them; and the servant still remaining at the open door, she used only the ceremony of saying that she must speak with Miss Tilney that moment, and hurrying by him proceeded upstairs. Then, opening the first door before her, which happened to be the right, she immediately found herself in the drawing-room with General Tilney, his son, and daughter. Her explanation, defective only in being—from her irritation of nerves and shortness of breath—no explanation at all, was instantly given. "I am come in a great hurry—It was all a mistake—I never promised to go—I told them from the first I could not go.—I ran away in a great hurry to explain it.—I did not care what you thought of me.—I would not stay for the servant."

The business, however, though not perfectly elucidated by this speech, soon ceased to be a puzzle. Catherine found that John Thorpe had given the message; and Miss Tilney had no scruple in owning herself greatly surprised by it. But whether her brother had still exceeded her in resentment, Catherine, though she instinctively addressed herself as much to one as to the other in her vindication, had no means of knowing. Whatever might have been felt before her arrival, her eager declarations immediately made every look and sentence as friendly as she could desire.

The affair thus happily settled, she was introduced by Miss Tilney to her father, and received by him with such ready, such solicitous politeness as recalled Thorpe's information to her mind, and made her think with pleasure that he might be sometimes depended on. To such anxious attention was the General's civility carried, that not aware of her extraordinary swiftness in entering the house, he was quite angry with the servant whose neglect had reduced her to open the door of the apartment herself. "What did William mean by it? He should make a point of inquiring into the matter." And if Catherine had not most warmly asserted his innocence, it seemed likely that William would lose the favour of his master forever, if not his place, by her rapidity.

After sitting with them a quarter of an hour, she rose to take leave, and was then most agreeably surprised by General Tilney's asking her if she would do his daughter the honour of dining and spending the rest of the day with her. Miss Tilney added her own wishes. Catherine was greatly obliged; but it was quite out of her power. Mr. and Mrs. Allen would expect her back every moment. The general declared he could say no more; the claims of Mr. and Mrs. Allen were not to be superseded; but on some other day he trusted, when longer notice could be given, they would not refuse to spare her to her friend. "Oh, no; Catherine was sure they would not have the least objection, and she should have great pleasure in coming." The general attended her himself to the street-door, saying everything gallant as they went downstairs, admiring the elasticity of her walk, which corresponded exactly with the spirit of her dancing, and making her one of the most graceful bows she had ever beheld, when they parted.

Catherine, delighted by all that had passed, proceeded gaily to Pulteney Street, walking, as she concluded, with great elasticity, though she had never thought of it before. She reached home without seeing anything more of the offended party; and now that she had been triumphant throughout, had carried her point, and was secure of her walk, she began (as the flutter of her spirits subsided) to doubt whether she had been perfectly right. A sacrifice was always noble; and if she had given way to their entreaties, she should have been spared the distressing idea of a friend displeased, a brother angry, and a scheme of great happiness to both destroyed, perhaps through her means. To ease her mind, and ascertain by the opinion of an unprejudiced person what her own conduct had really been, she took occasion to mention before Mr. Allen the half-settled scheme of her brother and the Thorpes for the following day. Mr. Allen caught at it directly. "Well," said he, "and do you think of going too?"

"No; I had just engaged myself to walk with Miss Tilney before they told me of it; and therefore you know I could not go with them, could I?"

"No, certainly not; and I am glad you do not think of it. These schemes are not at all the thing. Young men and women driving about the country in open carriages! Now and then it is very well; but going to inns and public places together! It is not right; and I wonder Mrs. Thorpe should allow it. I am glad you do not think of going; I am sure Mrs. Morland would not be pleased. Mrs. Allen, are not you of my way of thinking? Do not you think these kind of projects objectionable?"

"Yes, very much so indeed. Open carriages are nasty things. A clean gown is not five minutes' wear in them. You are splashed getting in and getting out; and the wind takes your hair and your bonnet in every direction. I hate an open carriage myself."

"I know you do; but that is not the question. Do not you think it has an odd appearance, if young ladies are frequently driven about in them by young men, to whom they are not even related?"

"Yes, my dear, a very odd appearance indeed. I cannot bear to see it."

"Dear madam," cried Catherine, "then why did not you tell me so before? I am sure if I had known it to be improper, I would not have gone with Mr. Thorpe at all; but I always hoped you would tell me, if you thought I was doing wrong."

"And so I should, my dear, you may depend on it; for as I told Mrs. Morland at parting, I would always do the best for you in my power. But one must not be over particular. Young people will be young people, as your good mother says herself. You know I wanted you, when we first came, not to buy that sprigged muslin, but you would. Young people do not like to be always thwarted."

"But this was something of real consequence; and I do not think you would have found me hard to persuade."

"As far as it has gone hitherto, there is no harm done," said Mr. Allen; "and I would only advise you, my dear, not to go out with Mr. Thorpe any more."

"That is just what I was going to say," added his wife.

Catherine, relieved for herself, felt uneasy for Isabella, and after a moment's thought, asked Mr. Allen whether it would not be both proper and kind in her to write to Miss Thorpe, and explain the indecorum of which she must be as insensible as herself; for she considered that Isabella might otherwise perhaps be going to Clifton the next day, in spite of what had passed. Mr. Allen, however, discouraged her from doing any such thing. "You had better leave her alone, my dear; she is old enough to know what she is about, and if not, has a mother to advise her. Mrs. Thorpe is too indulgent beyond a doubt; but, however, you had better not interfere. She and your brother choose to go, and you will be only getting ill will."

Catherine submitted, and though sorry to think that Isabella should be doing wrong, felt greatly relieved by Mr. Allen's approbation of her own conduct, and truly rejoiced to be preserved by his advice from the danger of falling into such an error herself. Her escape from being one of the party to Clifton was now an escape indeed; for what would the Tilneys have thought of her, if she had broken her promise to them in order to do what was wrong in itself, if she had been guilty of one breach of propriety, only to enable her to be guilty of another?

CHAPTER 14

The next morning was fair, and Catherine almost expected another attack from the assembled party. With Mr. Allen to support her, she felt no dread of the event: but she would gladly be spared a contest, where victory itself was painful, and was heartily rejoiced therefore at neither seeing nor hearing anything of them. The Tilneys called for her at the appointed time; and no new difficulty arising, no sudden recollection, no unexpected summons, no impertinent intrusion to disconcert their measures, my heroine was most unnaturally able to fulfil her engagement, though it was made with the hero himself. They determined on walking round Beechen Cliff, that noble hill whose beautiful verdure and hanging coppice render it so striking an object from almost every opening in Bath.

"I never look at it," said Catherine, as they walked along the side of the river, "without thinking of the south of France."

"You have been abroad then?" said Henry, a little surprised.

"Oh! No, I only mean what I have read about. It always puts me in mind of the country that Emily and her father travelled through, in The Mysteries of Udolpho. But you never read novels, I dare say?"

"Why not?"

"Because they are not clever enough for you—gentlemen read better books."

"The person, be it gentleman or lady, who has not pleasure in a good novel, must be intolerably stupid. I have read all Mrs. Radcliffe's works, and most of them with great pleasure. The Mysteries of Udolpho, when I had once begun it, I could not lay down again; I remember finishing it in two days—my hair standing on end the whole time."

"Yes," added Miss Tilney, "and I remember that you undertook to read it aloud to me, and that when I was called away for only five minutes to answer a note, instead of waiting for me, you took the volume into the Hermitage Walk, and I was obliged to stay till you had finished it."

"Thank you, Eleanor—a most honourable testimony. You see, Miss Morland, the injustice of your suspicions. Here was I, in my eagerness to get on, refusing to wait only five minutes for my sister, breaking the promise I had made of reading it aloud, and keeping her in suspense at a most interesting part, by running away with the volume, which, you are to observe, was her own, particularly her own. I am proud when I reflect on it, and I think it must establish me in your good opinion."

"I am very glad to hear it indeed, and now I shall never be ashamed of liking Udolpho myself. But I really thought before, young men despised novels amazingly."

"It is amazingly; it may well suggest amazement if they do—for they read nearly as many as women. I myself have read hundreds and hundreds. Do not imagine that you can cope with me in a knowledge of Julias and Louisas. If we proceed to particulars, and engage in the never-ceasing inquiry of 'Have you read this?' and 'Have you read that?' I shall soon leave you as far behind me as—what shall I say?—I want an appropriate simile.—as far as your friend Emily herself left poor Valancourt when she went with her aunt into Italy. Consider how many years I have had the start of you. I had entered on my studies at Oxford, while you were a good little girl working your sampler at home!"

"Not very good, I am afraid. But now really, do not you think Udolpho the nicest book in the world?"

"The nicest—by which I suppose you mean the neatest. That must depend upon the binding."

"Henry," said Miss Tilney, "you are very impertinent. Miss Morland, he is treating you exactly as he does his sister. He is forever finding fault with me, for some incorrectness of language, and now he is taking the same liberty with you. The word 'nicest,' as you used it, did not suit him; and you had better change it as soon as you can, or we shall be overpowered with Johnson and Blair all the rest of the way."

"I am sure," cried Catherine, "I did not mean to say anything wrong; but it is a nice book, and why should not I call it so?"

"Very true," said Henry, "and this is a very nice day, and we are taking a very nice walk, and you are two very nice young ladies. Oh! It is a very nice word indeed! It does for everything. Originally perhaps it was applied only to express neatness, propriety, delicacy, or refinement—people were nice in their dress, in their sentiments, or their choice. But now every commendation on every subject is comprised in that one word."

"While, in fact," cried his sister, "it ought only to be applied to you, without any commendation at all. You are more nice than wise. Come, Miss Morland, let us leave him to meditate over our faults in the utmost propriety of diction, while we praise Udolpho in whatever terms we like best. It is a most interesting work. You are fond of that kind of reading?"

"To say the truth, I do not much like any other."

"Indeed!"

"That is, I can read poetry and plays, and things of that sort, and do not dislike travels. But history, real solemn history, I cannot be interested in. Can you?"

"Yes, I am fond of history."

"I wish I were too. I read it a little as a duty, but it tells me nothing that does not either vex or weary me. The quarrels of popes and kings, with wars or pestilences, in every page; the men all so good for nothing, and hardly any women at all—it is very tiresome: and yet I often think it odd that it should be so dull, for a great deal of it must be invention. The speeches that are put into the heroes' mouths, their thoughts and designs—the chief of all this must be invention, and invention is what delights me in other books."

"Historians, you think," said Miss Tilney, "are not happy in their flights of fancy. They display imagination without raising interest. I am fond of history—and am very well contented to take the false with the true. In the principal facts they have sources of intelligence in former histories and records, which may be as much depended on, I conclude, as anything that does not actually pass under one's own observation; and as for the little embellishments you speak of, they are embellishments, and I like them as such. If a speech be well drawn up, I read it with pleasure, by whomsoever it may be made—and probably with much greater, if the production of Mr. Hume or Mr. Robertson, than if the genuine words of Caractacus, Agricola, or Alfred the Great."

"You are fond of history! And so are Mr. Allen and my father; and I have two brothers who do not dislike it. So many instances within my small circle of friends is remarkable! At this rate, I shall not pity the writers of history any longer. If people like to read their books, it is all very well, but to be at so much trouble in filling great volumes, which, as I used to think, nobody would willingly ever look into, to be labouring only for the torment of little boys and girls, always struck me as a hard fate; and though I know it is all very right and necessary, I have often wondered at the person's courage that could sit down on purpose to do it."

"That little boys and girls should be tormented," said Henry, "is what no one at all acquainted with human nature in a civilized state can deny; but in behalf of our most distinguished historians, I must observe that they might well be offended at being supposed to have no higher aim, and that by their method and style, they are perfectly well qualified to torment readers of the most advanced reason and mature time of life. I use the verb 'to torment,' as I observed to be your own method, instead of 'to instruct,' supposing them to be now admitted as synonymous."

"You think me foolish to call instruction a torment, but if you had been as much used as myself to hear poor little children first learning their letters and then learning to spell, if you had ever seen how stupid they can be for a whole morning together, and how tired my poor mother is at the end of it, as I am in the habit of seeing almost every day of my life at home, you would allow that to torment and to instruct might sometimes be used as synonymous words."

"Very probably. But historians are not accountable for the difficulty of learning to read; and even you yourself, who do not altogether seem particularly friendly to very severe, very intense application, may perhaps be brought to acknowledge that it is very well worth-while to be tormented for two or three years of one's life, for the sake of being able to read all the rest of it. Consider—if reading had not been taught, Mrs. Radcliffe would have written in vain—or perhaps might not have written at all."

Catherine assented—and a very warm panegyric from her on that lady's merits closed the subject. The Tilneys were soon engaged in another on which she had nothing to say. They were viewing the country with the eyes of persons accustomed to drawing, and decided on its capability of being formed into pictures, with all the eagerness of real taste. Here Catherine was quite lost. She knew nothing of drawing—nothing of taste: and she listened to them with an attention which brought her little profit, for they talked in phrases which conveyed scarcely any idea to her. The little which she could understand, however, appeared to contradict the very few notions she had entertained on the matter before. It seemed as if a good view were no longer to be taken from the top of an high hill, and that a clear blue sky was no longer a proof of a fine day. She was heartily ashamed of her ignorance. A misplaced shame. Where people wish to attach, they should always be ignorant. To come with a well-informed mind is to come with an inability of administering to the vanity of others, which a sensible person would always wish to avoid. A woman especially, if she have the misfortune of knowing anything, should conceal it as well as she can.

The advantages of natural folly in a beautiful girl have been already set forth by the capital pen of a sister author; and to her treatment of the subject I will only add, in justice to men, that though to the larger and more trifling part of the sex, imbecility in females is a great enhancement of their personal charms, there is a portion of them too reasonable and too well informed themselves to desire anything more in woman than ignorance. But Catherine did not know her own advantages—did not know that a good-looking girl, with an affectionate heart and a very ignorant mind, cannot fail of attracting a clever young man, unless circumstances are particularly untoward. In the present instance, she confessed and lamented her want of knowledge, declared that she would give anything in the world to be able to draw; and a lecture on the picturesque immediately followed, in which his instructions were so clear that she soon began to see beauty in everything admired by him, and her attention was so earnest that he became perfectly satisfied of her having a great deal of natural taste. He talked of foregrounds, distances, and second distances—side-screens and perspectives—lights and shades; and Catherine was so hopeful a scholar that when they gained the top of Beechen Cliff, she voluntarily rejected the whole city of Bath as unworthy to make part of a landscape. Delighted with her progress, and fearful of wearying her with too much wisdom at once, Henry suffered the subject to decline, and by an easy transition from a piece of rocky fragment and the withered oak which he had placed near its summit, to oaks in general, to forests, the enclosure of them, waste lands, crown lands and government, he shortly found himself arrived at politics; and from politics, it was an easy step to silence. The general pause which succeeded his short disquisition on the state of the nation was put an end to by Catherine, who, in rather a solemn tone of voice, uttered these words, "I have heard that something very shocking indeed will soon come out in London."

Miss Tilney, to whom this was chiefly addressed, was startled, and hastily replied, "Indeed! And of what nature?"

"That I do not know, nor who is the author. I have only heard that it is to be more horrible than anything we have met with yet."

"Good heaven! Where could you hear of such a thing?"

"A particular friend of mine had an account of it in a letter from London yesterday. It is to be uncommonly dreadful. I shall expect murder and everything of the kind."

"You speak with astonishing composure! But I hope your friend's accounts have been exaggerated; and if such a design is known beforehand, proper measures will undoubtedly be taken by government to prevent its coming to effect."

"Government," said Henry, endeavouring not to smile, "neither desires nor dares to interfere in such matters. There must be murder; and government cares not how much."

The ladies stared. He laughed, and added, "Come, shall I make you understand each other, or leave you to puzzle out an explanation as you can? No—I will be noble. I will prove myself a man, no less by the generosity of my soul than the clearness of my head. I have no patience with such of my sex as disdain to let themselves sometimes down to the comprehension of yours. Perhaps the abilities of women are neither sound nor acute—neither vigorous nor keen. Perhaps they may want observation, discernment, judgment, fire, genius, and wit."

"Miss Morland, do not mind what he says; but have the goodness to satisfy me as to this dreadful riot."

"Riot! What riot?"

"My dear Eleanor, the riot is only in your own brain. The confusion there is scandalous. Miss Morland has been talking of nothing more dreadful than a new publication which is shortly to come out, in three duodecimo volumes, two hundred and seventy-six pages in each, with a frontispiece to the first, of two tombstones and a lantern—do you understand? And you, Miss Morland—my stupid sister has mistaken all your clearest expressions. You talked of expected horrors in London—and instead of instantly conceiving, as any rational creature would have done, that such words could relate only to a circulating library, she immediately pictured to herself a mob of three thousand men assembling in St. George's Fields, the Bank attacked, the Tower threatened, the streets of London flowing with blood, a detachment of the Twelfth Light Dragoons (the hopes of the nation) called up from Northampton to quell the insurgents, and the gallant Captain Frederick Tilney, in the moment of charging at the head of his troop, knocked off his horse by a brickbat from an upper window. Forgive her stupidity. The fears of the sister have added to the weakness of the woman; but she is by no means a simpleton in general."

Catherine looked grave. "And now, Henry," said Miss Tilney, "that you have made us understand each other, you may as well make Miss Morland understand yourself—unless you mean to have her think you intolerably rude to your sister, and a great brute in your opinion of women in general. Miss Morland is not used to your odd ways."

"I shall be most happy to make her better acquainted with them."

"No doubt; but that is no explanation of the present."

"What am I to do?"

"You know what you ought to do. Clear your character handsomely before her. Tell her that you think very highly of the understanding of women."

"Miss Morland, I think very highly of the understanding of all the women in the world—especially of those—whoever they may be—with whom I happen to be in company."

"That is not enough. Be more serious."

"Miss Morland, no one can think more highly of the understanding of women than I do. In my opinion, nature has given them so much that they never find it necessary to use more than half."

"We shall get nothing more serious from him now, Miss Morland. He is not in a sober mood. But I do assure you that he must be entirely misunderstood, if he can ever appear to say an unjust thing of any woman at all, or an unkind one of me."

It was no effort to Catherine to believe that Henry Tilney could never be wrong. His manner might sometimes surprise, but his meaning must always be just: and what she did not understand, she was almost as ready to admire, as what she did. The whole walk was delightful, and though it ended too soon, its conclusion was delightful too; her friends attended her into the house, and Miss Tilney, before they parted, addressing herself with respectful form, as much to Mrs. Allen as to Catherine, petitioned for the pleasure of her company to dinner on the day after the next. No difficulty was made on Mrs. Allen's side, and the only difficulty on Catherine's was in concealing the excess of her pleasure.

The morning had passed away so charmingly as to banish all her friendship and natural affection, for no thought of Isabella or James had crossed her during their walk. When the Tilneys were gone, she became amiable again, but she was amiable for some time to little effect; Mrs. Allen had no intelligence to give that could relieve her anxiety; she had heard nothing of any of them. Towards the end of the morning, however, Catherine, having occasion for some indispensable yard of ribbon which must be bought without a moment's delay, walked out into the town, and in Bond Street overtook the second Miss Thorpe as she was loitering towards Edgar's Buildings between two of the sweetest girls in the world, who had been her dear friends all the morning. From her, she soon learned that the party to Clifton had taken place. "They set off at eight this morning," said Miss Anne, "and I am sure I do not envy them their drive. I think you and I are very well off to be out of the scrape. It must be the dullest thing in the world, for there is not a soul at Clifton at this time of year. Belle went with your brother, and John drove Maria."

Catherine spoke the pleasure she really felt on hearing this part of the arrangement.

"Oh! yes," rejoined the other, "Maria is gone. She was quite wild to go. She thought it would be something very fine. I cannot say I admire her taste; and for my part, I was determined from the first not to go, if they pressed me ever so much."

Catherine, a little doubtful of this, could not help answering, "I wish you could have gone too. It is a pity you could not all go."

"Thank you; but it is quite a matter of indifference to me. Indeed, I would not have gone on any account. I was saying so to Emily and Sophia when you overtook us."

Catherine was still unconvinced; but glad that Anne should have the friendship of an Emily and a Sophia to console her, she bade her adieu without much uneasiness, and returned home, pleased that the party had not been prevented by her refusing to join it, and very heartily wishing that it might be too pleasant to allow either James or Isabella to resent her resistance any longer.

CHAPTER 15

Early the next day, a note from Isabella, speaking peace and tenderness in every line, and entreating the immediate presence of her friend on a matter of the utmost importance, hastened Catherine, in the happiest state of confidence and curiosity, to Edgar's Buildings. The two youngest Miss Thorpes were by themselves in the parlour; and, on Anne's quitting it to call her sister, Catherine took the opportunity of asking the other for some particulars of their yesterday's party. Maria desired no greater pleasure than to speak of it; and Catherine immediately learnt that it had been altogether the most delightful scheme in the world, that nobody could imagine how charming it had been, and that it had been more delightful than anybody could conceive. Such was the information of the first five minutes; the second unfolded thus much in detail—that they had driven directly to the York Hotel, ate some soup, and bespoke an early dinner, walked down to the pump-room, tasted the water, and laid out some shillings in purses and spars; thence adjourned to eat ice at a pastry-cook's, and hurrying back to the hotel, swallowed their dinner in haste, to prevent being in the dark; and then had a delightful drive back, only the moon was not up, and it rained a little, and Mr. Morland's horse was so tired he could hardly get it along.

Catherine listened with heartfelt satisfaction. It appeared that Blaize Castle had never been thought of; and, as for all the rest, there was nothing to regret for half an instant. Maria's intelligence concluded with a tender effusion of pity for her sister Anne, whom she represented as insupportably cross, from being excluded the party.

"She will never forgive me, I am sure; but, you know, how could I help it? John would have me go, for he vowed he would not drive her, because she had such thick ankles. I dare say she will not be in good humour again this month; but I am determined I will not be cross; it is not a little matter that puts me out of temper."

Isabella now entered the room with so eager a step, and a look of such happy importance, as engaged all her friend's notice. Maria was without ceremony sent away, and Isabella, embracing Catherine, thus began: "Yes, my dear Catherine, it is so indeed; your penetration has not deceived you. Oh, that arch eye of yours! It sees through everything."

Catherine replied only by a look of wondering ignorance.

"Nay, my beloved, sweetest friend," continued the other, "compose yourself. I am amazingly agitated, as you perceive. Let us sit down and talk in comfort. Well, and so you guessed it the moment you had my note? Sly creature! Oh! My dear Catherine, you alone, who know my heart, can judge of my present happiness. Your brother is the most charming of men. I only wish I were more worthy of him. But what will your excellent father and mother say? Oh! Heavens! When I think of them I am so agitated!"

Catherine's understanding began to awake: an idea of the truth suddenly darted into her mind; and, with the natural blush of so new an emotion, she cried out, "Good heaven! My dear Isabella, what do you mean? Can you—can you really be in love with James?"

This bold surmise, however, she soon learnt comprehended but half the fact. The anxious affection, which she was accused of having continually watched in Isabella's every look and action, had, in the course of their yesterday's party, received the delightful confession of an equal love. Her heart and faith were alike engaged to James. Never had Catherine listened to anything so full of interest, wonder, and joy. Her brother and her friend engaged! New to such circumstances, the importance of it appeared unspeakably great, and she contemplated it as one of those grand events, of which the ordinary course of life can hardly afford a return. The strength of her feelings she could not express; the nature of them, however, contented her friend. The happiness of having such a sister was their first effusion, and the fair ladies mingled in embraces and tears of joy.

Delighting, however, as Catherine sincerely did, in the prospect of the connection, it must be acknowledged that Isabella far surpassed her in tender anticipations. "You will be so infinitely dearer to me, my Catherine, than either Anne or Maria: I feel that I shall be so much more attached to my dear Morland's family than to my own."

This was a pitch of friendship beyond Catherine.

"You are so like your dear brother," continued Isabella, "that I quite doted on you the first moment I saw you. But so it always is with me; the first moment settles everything. The very first day that Morland came to us last Christmas—the very first moment I beheld him—my heart was irrecoverably gone. I remember I wore my yellow gown, with my hair done up in braids; and when I came into the drawing-room, and John introduced him, I thought I never saw anybody so handsome before."

Here Catherine secretly acknowledged the power of love; for, though exceedingly fond of her brother, and partial to all his endowments, she had never in her life thought him handsome.

"I remember too, Miss Andrews drank tea with us that evening, and wore her puce-coloured sarsenet; and she looked so heavenly that I thought your brother must certainly fall in love with her; I could not sleep a wink all night for thinking of it. Oh! Catherine, the many sleepless nights I have had on your brother's account! I would not have you suffer half what I have done! I am grown wretchedly thin, I know; but I will not pain you by describing my anxiety; you have seen enough of it. I feel that I have betrayed myself perpetually—so unguarded in speaking of my partiality for the church! But my secret I was always sure would be safe with you."

Catherine felt that nothing could have been safer; but ashamed of an ignorance little expected, she dared no longer contest the point, nor refuse to have been as full of arch penetration and affectionate sympathy as Isabella chose to consider her. Her brother, she found, was preparing to set off with all speed to Fullerton, to make known his situation and ask consent; and here was a source of some real agitation to the mind of Isabella. Catherine endeavoured to persuade her, as she was herself persuaded, that her father and mother would never oppose their son's wishes. "It is impossible," said she, "for parents to be more kind, or more desirous of their children's happiness; I have no doubt of their consenting immediately."

"Morland says exactly the same," replied Isabella; "and yet I dare not expect it; my fortune will be so small; they never can consent to it. Your brother, who might marry anybody!"

Here Catherine again discerned the force of love.

"Indeed, Isabella, you are too humble. The difference of fortune can be nothing to signify."

"Oh! My sweet Catherine, in your generous heart I know it would signify nothing; but we must not expect such disinterestedness in many. As for myself, I am sure I only wish our situations were reversed. Had I the command of millions, were I mistress of the whole world, your brother would be my only choice."

This charming sentiment, recommended as much by sense as novelty, gave Catherine a most pleasing remembrance of all the heroines of her acquaintance; and she thought her friend never looked more lovely than in uttering the grand idea. "I am sure they will consent," was her frequent declaration; "I am sure they will be delighted with you."

"For my own part," said Isabella, "my wishes are so moderate that the smallest income in nature would be enough for me. Where people are really attached, poverty itself is wealth; grandeur I detest: I would not settle in London for the universe. A cottage in some retired village would be ecstasy. There are some charming little villas about Richmond."

"Richmond!" cried Catherine. "You must settle near Fullerton. You must be near us."

"I am sure I shall be miserable if we do not. If I can but be near you, I shall be satisfied. But this is idle talking! I will not allow myself to think of such things, till we have your father's answer. Morland says that by sending it to-night to Salisbury, we may have it to-morrow. To-morrow? I know I shall never have courage to open the letter. I know it will be the death of me."

A reverie succeeded this conviction—and when Isabella spoke again, it was to resolve on the quality of her wedding-gown.

Their conference was put an end to by the anxious young lover himself, who came to breathe his parting sigh before he set off for Wiltshire. Catherine wished to congratulate him, but knew not what to say, and her eloquence was only in her eyes. From them, however, the eight parts of speech shone out most expressively, and James could combine them with ease. Impatient for the realization of all that he hoped at home, his adieus were not long; and they would have been yet shorter, had he not been frequently detained by the urgent entreaties of his fair one that he would go. Twice was he called almost from the door by her eagerness to have him gone. "Indeed, Morland, I must drive you away. Consider how far you have to ride. I cannot bear to see you linger so. For heaven's sake, waste no more time. There, go, go—I insist on it."

The two friends, with hearts now more united than ever, were inseparable for the day; and in schemes of sisterly happiness the hours flew along. Mrs. Thorpe and her son, who were acquainted with everything, and who seemed only to want Mr. Morland's consent, to consider Isabella's engagement as the most fortunate circumstance imaginable for their family, were allowed to join their counsels, and add their quota of significant looks and mysterious expressions to fill up the measure of curiosity to be raised in the unprivileged younger sisters. To Catherine's simple feelings, this odd sort of reserve seemed neither kindly meant, nor consistently supported; and its unkindness she would hardly have forborne pointing out, had its inconsistency been less their friend; but Anne and Maria soon set her heart at ease by the sagacity of their "I know what"; and the evening was spent in a sort of war of wit, a display of family ingenuity, on one side in the mystery of an affected secret, on the other of undefined discovery, all equally acute.

Catherine was with her friend again the next day, endeavouring to support her spirits and while away the many tedious hours before the delivery of the letters; a needful exertion, for as the time of reasonable expectation drew near, Isabella became more and more desponding, and before the letter arrived, had worked herself into a state of real distress. But when it did come, where could distress be found? "I have had no difficulty in gaining the consent of my kind parents, and am promised that everything in their power shall be done to forward my happiness," were the first three lines, and in one moment all was joyful security. The brightest glow was instantly spread over Isabella's features, all care and anxiety seemed removed, her spirits became almost too high for control, and she called herself without scruple the happiest of mortals.

Mrs. Thorpe, with tears of joy, embraced her daughter, her son, her visitor, and could have embraced half the inhabitants of Bath with satisfaction. Her heart was overflowing with tenderness. It was "dear John" and "dear Catherine" at every word; "dear Anne and dear Maria" must immediately be made sharers in their felicity; and two "dears" at once before the name of Isabella were not more than that beloved child had now well earned. John himself was no skulker in joy. He not only bestowed on Mr. Morland the high commendation of being one of the finest fellows in the world, but swore off many sentences in his praise.

The letter, whence sprang all this felicity, was short, containing little more than this assurance of success; and every particular was deferred till James could write again. But for particulars Isabella could well afford to wait. The needful was comprised in Mr. Morland's promise; his honour was pledged to make everything easy; and by what means their income was to be formed, whether landed property were to be resigned, or funded money made over, was a matter in which her disinterested spirit took no concern. She knew enough to feel secure of an honourable and speedy establishment, and her imagination took a rapid flight over its attendant felicities. She saw herself at the end of a few weeks, the gaze and admiration of every new acquaintance at Fullerton, the envy of every valued old friend in Putney, with a carriage at her command, a new name on her tickets, and a brilliant exhibition of hoop rings on her finger.

When the contents of the letter were ascertained, John Thorpe, who had only waited its arrival to begin his journey to London, prepared to set off. "Well, Miss Morland," said he, on finding her alone in the parlour, "I am come to bid you good-bye." Catherine wished him a good journey. Without appearing to hear her, he walked to the window, fidgeted about, hummed a tune, and seemed wholly self-occupied.

"Shall not you be late at Devizes?" said Catherine. He made no answer; but after a minute's silence burst out with, "A famous good thing this marrying scheme, upon my soul! A clever fancy of Morland's and Belle's. What do you think of it, Miss Morland? I say it is no bad notion."

"I am sure I think it a very good one."

"Do you? That's honest, by heavens! I am glad you are no enemy to matrimony, however. Did you ever hear the old song, 'Going to One Wedding Brings on Another?' I say, you will come to Belle's wedding, I hope."

"Yes; I have promised your sister to be with her, if possible."

"And then you know"—twisting himself about and forcing a foolish laugh—"I say, then you know, we may try the truth of this same old song."

"May we? But I never sing. Well, I wish you a good journey. I dine with Miss Tilney to-day, and must now be going home."

"Nay, but there is no such confounded hurry. Who knows when we may be together again? Not but that I shall be down again by the end of a fortnight, and a devilish long fortnight it will appear to me."

"Then why do you stay away so long?" replied Catherine—finding that he waited for an answer.

"That is kind of you, however—kind and good-natured. I shall not forget it in a hurry. But you have more good nature and all that, than anybody living, I believe. A monstrous deal of good nature, and it is not only good nature, but you have so much, so much of everything; and then you have such—upon my soul, I do not know anybody like you."

"Oh! dear, there are a great many people like me, I dare say, only a great deal better. Good morning to you."

"But I say, Miss Morland, I shall come and pay my respects at Fullerton before it is long, if not disagreeable."

"Pray do. My father and mother will be very glad to see you."

"And I hope—I hope, Miss Morland, you will not be sorry to see me."

"Oh! dear, not at all. There are very few people I am sorry to see. Company is always cheerful."

"That is just my way of thinking. Give me but a little cheerful company, let me only have the company of the people I love, let me only be where I like and with whom I like, and the devil take the rest, say I. And I am heartily glad to hear you say the same. But I have a notion, Miss Morland, you and I think pretty much alike upon most matters."

"Perhaps we may; but it is more than I ever thought of. And as to most matters, to say the truth, there are not many that I know my own mind about."

"By Jove, no more do I. It is not my way to bother my brains with what does not concern me. My notion of things is simple enough. Let me only have the girl I like, say I, with a comfortable house over my head, and what care I for all the rest? Fortune is nothing. I am sure of a good income of my own; and if she had not a penny, why, so much the better."

"Very true. I think like you there. If there is a good fortune on one side, there can be no occasion for any on the other. No matter which has it, so that there is enough. I hate the idea of one great fortune looking out for another. And to marry for money I think the wickedest thing in existence. Good day. We shall be very glad to see you at Fullerton, whenever it is convenient." And away she went. It was not in the power of all his gallantry to detain her longer. With such news to communicate, and such a visit to prepare for, her departure was not to be delayed by anything in his nature to urge; and she hurried away, leaving him to the undivided consciousness of his own happy address, and her explicit encouragement.

The agitation which she had herself experienced on first learning her brother's engagement made her expect to raise no inconsiderable emotion in Mr. and Mrs. Allen, by the communication of the wonderful event. How great was her disappointment! The important affair, which many words of preparation ushered in, had been foreseen by them both ever since her brother's arrival; and all that they felt on the occasion was comprehended in a wish for the young people's happiness, with a remark, on the gentleman's side, in favour of Isabella's beauty, and on the lady's, of her great good luck. It was to Catherine the most surprising insensibility. The disclosure, however, of the great secret of James's going to Fullerton the day before, did raise some emotion in Mrs. Allen. She could not listen to that with perfect calmness, but repeatedly regretted the necessity of its concealment, wished she could have known his intention, wished she could have seen him before he went, as she should certainly have troubled him with her best regards to his father and mother, and her kind compliments to all the Skinners.

CHAPTER 16

Catherine's expectations of pleasure from her visit in Milsom Street were so very high that disappointment was inevitable; and accordingly, though she was most politely received by General Tilney, and kindly welcomed by his daughter, though Henry was at home, and no one else of the party, she found, on her return, without spending many hours in the examination of her feelings, that she had gone to her appointment preparing for happiness which it had not afforded. Instead of finding herself improved in acquaintance with Miss Tilney, from the intercourse of the day, she seemed hardly so intimate with her as before; instead of seeing Henry Tilney to greater advantage than ever, in the ease of a family party, he had never said so little, nor been so little agreeable; and, in spite of their father's great civilities to her—in spite of his thanks, invitations, and compliments—it had been a release to get away from him. It puzzled her to account for all this. It could not be General Tilney's fault. That he was perfectly agreeable and good-natured, and altogether a very charming man, did not admit of a doubt, for he was tall and handsome, and Henry's father. He could not be accountable for his children's want of spirits, or for her want of enjoyment in his company. The former she hoped at last might have been accidental, and the latter she could only attribute to her own stupidity. Isabella, on hearing the particulars of the visit, gave a different explanation: "It was all pride, pride, insufferable haughtiness and pride! She had long suspected the family to be very high, and this made it certain. Such insolence of behaviour as Miss Tilney's she had never heard of in her life! Not to do the honours of her house with common good breeding! To behave to her guest with such superciliousness! Hardly even to speak to her!"

"But it was not so bad as that, Isabella; there was no superciliousness; she was very civil."

"Oh, don't defend her! And then the brother, he, who had appeared so attached to you! Good heavens! Well, some people's feelings are incomprehensible. And so he hardly looked once at you the whole day?"

"I do not say so; but he did not seem in good spirits."

"How contemptible! Of all things in the world inconstancy is my aversion. Let me entreat you never to think of him again, my dear Catherine; indeed he is unworthy of you."

"Unworthy! I do not suppose he ever thinks of me."

"That is exactly what I say; he never thinks of you. Such fickleness! Oh! How different to your brother and to mine! I really believe John has the most constant heart."

"But as for General Tilney, I assure you it would be impossible for anybody to behave to me with greater civility and attention; it seemed to be his only care to entertain and make me happy."

"Oh! I know no harm of him; I do not suspect him of pride. I believe he is a very gentleman-like man. John thinks very well of him, and John's judgment—"

"Well, I shall see how they behave to me this evening; we shall meet them at the rooms."

"And must I go?"

"Do not you intend it? I thought it was all settled."

"Nay, since you make such a point of it, I can refuse you nothing. But do not insist upon my being very agreeable, for my heart, you know, will be some forty miles off. And as for dancing, do not mention it, I beg; that is quite out of the question. Charles Hodges will plague me to death, I dare say; but I shall cut him very short. Ten to one but he guesses the reason, and that is exactly what I want to avoid, so I shall insist on his keeping his conjecture to himself."

Isabella's opinion of the Tilneys did not influence her friend; she was sure there had been no insolence in the manners either of brother or sister; and she did not credit there being any pride in their hearts. The evening rewarded her confidence; she was met by one with the same kindness, and by the other with the same attention, as heretofore: Miss Tilney took pains to be near her, and Henry asked her to dance.

Having heard the day before in Milsom Street that their elder brother, Captain Tilney, was expected almost every hour, she was at no loss for the name of a very fashionable-looking, handsome young man, whom she had never seen before, and who now evidently belonged to their party. She looked at him with great admiration, and even supposed it possible that some people might think him handsomer than his brother, though, in her eyes, his air was more assuming, and his countenance less prepossessing. His taste and manners were beyond a doubt decidedly inferior; for, within her hearing, he not only protested against every thought of dancing himself, but even laughed openly at Henry for finding it possible. From the latter circumstance it may be presumed that, whatever might be our heroine's opinion of him, his admiration of her was not of a very dangerous kind; not likely to produce animosities between the brothers, nor persecutions to the lady. He cannot be the instigator of the three villains in horsemen's greatcoats, by whom she will hereafter be forced into a traveling-chaise and four, which will drive off with incredible speed. Catherine, meanwhile, undisturbed by presentiments of such an evil, or of any evil at all, except that of having but a short set to dance down, enjoyed her usual happiness with Henry Tilney, listening with sparkling eyes to everything he said; and, in finding him irresistible, becoming so herself.

At the end of the first dance, Captain Tilney came towards them again, and, much to Catherine's dissatisfaction, pulled his brother away. They retired whispering together; and, though her delicate sensibility did not take immediate alarm, and lay it down as fact, that Captain Tilney must have heard some malevolent misrepresentation of her, which he now hastened to communicate to his brother, in the hope of separating them forever, she could not have her partner conveyed from her sight without very uneasy sensations. Her suspense was of full five minutes' duration; and she was beginning to think it a very long quarter of an hour, when they both returned, and an explanation was given, by Henry's requesting to know, if she thought her friend, Miss Thorpe, would have any objection to dancing, as his brother would be most happy to be introduced to her. Catherine, without hesitation, replied that she was very sure Miss Thorpe did not mean to dance at all. The cruel reply was passed on to the other, and he immediately walked away.

"Your brother will not mind it, I know," said she, "because I heard him say before that he hated dancing; but it was very good-natured in him to think of it. I suppose he saw Isabella sitting down, and fancied she might wish for a partner; but he is quite mistaken, for she would not dance upon any account in the world."

Henry smiled, and said, "How very little trouble it can give you to understand the motive of other people's actions."

"Why? What do you mean?"

"With you, it is not, How is such a one likely to be influenced, What is the inducement most likely to act upon such a person's feelings, age, situation, and probable habits of life considered—but, How should I be influenced, What would be my inducement in acting so and so?"

"I do not understand you."

"Then we are on very unequal terms, for I understand you perfectly well."

"Me? Yes; I cannot speak well enough to be unintelligible."

"Bravo! An excellent satire on modern language."

"But pray tell me what you mean."

"Shall I indeed? Do you really desire it? But you are not aware of the consequences; it will involve you in a very cruel embarrassment, and certainly bring on a disagreement between us."

"No, no; it shall not do either; I am not afraid."

"Well, then, I only meant that your attributing my brother's wish of dancing with Miss Thorpe to good nature alone convinced me of your being superior in good nature yourself to all the rest of the world."

Catherine blushed and disclaimed, and the gentleman's predictions were verified. There was a something, however, in his words which repaid her for the pain of confusion; and that something occupied her mind so much that she drew back for some time, forgetting to speak or to listen, and almost forgetting where she was; till, roused by the voice of Isabella, she looked up and saw her with Captain Tilney preparing to give them hands across.

Isabella shrugged her shoulders and smiled, the only explanation of this extraordinary change which could at that time be given; but as it was not quite enough for Catherine's comprehension, she spoke her astonishment in very plain terms to her partner.

"I cannot think how it could happen! Isabella was so determined not to dance."

"And did Isabella never change her mind before?"

"Oh! But, because—And your brother! After what you told him from me, how could he think of going to ask her?"

"I cannot take surprise to myself on that head. You bid me be surprised on your friend's account, and therefore I am; but as for my brother, his conduct in the business, I must own, has been no more than I believed him perfectly equal to. The fairness of your friend was an open attraction; her firmness, you know, could only be understood by yourself."

"You are laughing; but, I assure you, Isabella is very firm in general."

"It is as much as should be said of anyone. To be always firm must be to be often obstinate. When properly to relax is the trial of judgment; and, without reference to my brother, I really think Miss Thorpe has by no means chosen ill in fixing on the present hour."

The friends were not able to get together for any confidential discourse till all the dancing was over; but then, as they walked about the room arm in arm, Isabella thus explained herself: "I do not wonder at your surprise; and I am really fatigued to death. He is such a rattle! Amusing enough, if my mind had been disengaged; but I would have given the world to sit still."

"Then why did not you?"

"Oh! My dear! It would have looked so particular; and you know how I abhor doing that. I refused him as long as I possibly could, but he would take no denial. You have no idea how he pressed me. I begged him to excuse me, and get some other partner—but no, not he; after aspiring to my hand, there was nobody else in the room he could bear to think of; and it was not that he wanted merely to dance, he wanted to be with me. Oh! Such nonsense! I told him he had taken a very unlikely way to prevail upon me; for, of all things in the world, I hated fine speeches and compliments; and so—and so then I found there would be no peace if I did not stand up. Besides, I thought Mrs. Hughes, who introduced him, might take it ill if I did not: and your dear brother, I am sure he would have been miserable if I had sat down the whole evening. I am so glad it is over! My spirits are quite jaded with listening to his nonsense: and then, being such a smart young fellow, I saw every eye was upon us."

"He is very handsome indeed."

"Handsome! Yes, I suppose he may. I dare say people would admire him in general; but he is not at all in my style of beauty. I hate a florid complexion and dark eyes in a man. However, he is very well. Amazingly conceited, I am sure. I took him down several times, you know, in my way."

When the young ladies next met, they had a far more interesting subject to discuss. James Morland's second letter was then received, and the kind intentions of his father fully explained. A living, of which Mr. Morland was himself patron and incumbent, of about four hundred pounds yearly value, was to be resigned to his son as soon as he should be old enough to take it; no trifling deduction from the family income, no niggardly assignment to one of ten children. An estate of at least equal value, moreover, was assured as his future inheritance.

James expressed himself on the occasion with becoming gratitude; and the necessity of waiting between two and three years before they could marry, being, however unwelcome, no more than he had expected, was borne by him without discontent. Catherine, whose expectations had been as unfixed as her ideas of her father's income, and whose judgment was now entirely led by her brother, felt equally well satisfied, and heartily congratulated Isabella on having everything so pleasantly settled.

"It is very charming indeed," said Isabella, with a grave face. "Mr. Morland has behaved vastly handsome indeed," said the gentle Mrs. Thorpe, looking anxiously at her daughter. "I only wish I could do as much. One could not expect more from him, you know. If he finds he can do more by and by, I dare say he will, for I am sure he must be an excellent good-hearted man. Four hundred is but a small income to begin on indeed, but your wishes, my dear Isabella, are so moderate, you do not consider how little you ever want, my dear."

"It is not on my own account I wish for more; but I cannot bear to be the means of injuring my dear Morland, making him sit down upon an income hardly enough to find one in the common necessaries of life. For myself, it is nothing; I never think of myself."

"I know you never do, my dear; and you will always find your reward in the affection it makes everybody feel for you. There never was a young woman so beloved as you are by everybody that knows you; and I dare say when Mr. Morland sees you, my dear child—but do not let us distress our dear Catherine by talking of such things. Mr. Morland has behaved so very handsome, you know. I always heard he was a most excellent man; and you know, my dear, we are not to suppose but what, if you had had a suitable fortune, he would have come down with something more, for I am sure he must be a most liberal-minded man."

"Nobody can think better of Mr. Morland than I do, I am sure. But everybody has their failing, you know, and everybody has a right to do what they like with their own money."

Catherine was hurt by these insinuations. "I am very sure," said she, "that my father has promised to do as much as he can afford."

Isabella recollected herself. "As to that, my sweet Catherine, there cannot be a doubt, and you know me well enough to be sure that a much smaller income would satisfy me. It is not the want of more money that makes me just at present a little out of spirits; I hate money; and if our union could take place now upon only fifty pounds a year, I should not have a wish unsatisfied. Ah! my Catherine, you have found me out. There's the sting. The long, long, endless two years and a half that are to pass before your brother can hold the living."

"Yes, yes, my darling Isabella," said Mrs. Thorpe, "we perfectly see into your heart. You have no disguise. We perfectly understand the present vexation; and everybody must love you the better for such a noble honest affection."

Catherine's uncomfortable feelings began to lessen. She endeavoured to believe that the delay of the marriage was the only source of Isabella's regret; and when she saw her at their next interview as cheerful and amiable as ever, endeavoured to forget that she had for a minute thought otherwise. James soon followed his letter, and was received with the most gratifying kindness.

CHAPTER 17

The Allens had now entered on the sixth week of their stay in Bath; and whether it should be the last was for some time a question, to which Catherine listened with a beating heart. To have her acquaintance with the Tilneys end so soon was an evil which nothing could counterbalance. Her whole happiness seemed at stake, while the affair was in suspense, and everything secured when it was determined that the lodgings should be taken for another fortnight. What this additional fortnight was to produce to her beyond the pleasure of sometimes seeing Henry Tilney made but a small part of Catherine's speculation. Once or twice indeed, since James's engagement had taught her what could be done, she had got so far as to indulge in a secret "perhaps," but in general the felicity of being with him for the present bounded her views: the present was now comprised in another three weeks, and her happiness being certain for that period, the rest of her life was at such a distance as to excite but little interest. In the course of the morning which saw this business arranged, she visited Miss Tilney, and poured forth her joyful feelings. It was doomed to be a day of trial. No sooner had she expressed her delight in Mr. Allen's lengthened stay than Miss Tilney told her of her father's having just determined upon quitting Bath by the end of another week. Here was a blow! The past suspense of the morning had been ease and quiet to the present disappointment. Catherine's countenance fell, and in a voice of most sincere concern she echoed Miss Tilney's concluding words, "By the end of another week!"

"Yes, my father can seldom be prevailed on to give the waters what I think a fair trial. He has been disappointed of some friends' arrival whom he expected to meet here, and as he is now pretty well, is in a hurry to get home."

"I am very sorry for it," said Catherine dejectedly; "if I had known this before—"

"Perhaps," said Miss Tilney in an embarrassed manner, "you would be so good—it would make me very happy if—"

The entrance of her father put a stop to the civility, which Catherine was beginning to hope might introduce a desire of their corresponding. After addressing her with his usual politeness, he turned to his daughter and said, "Well, Eleanor, may I congratulate you on being successful in your application to your fair friend?"

"I was just beginning to make the request, sir, as you came in."

"Well, proceed by all means. I know how much your heart is in it. My daughter, Miss Morland," he continued, without leaving his daughter time to speak, "has been forming a very bold wish. We leave Bath, as she has perhaps told you, on Saturday se'nnight. A letter from my steward tells me that my presence is wanted at home; and being disappointed in my hope of seeing the Marquis of Longtown and General Courteney here, some of my very old friends, there is nothing to detain me longer in Bath. And could we carry our selfish point with you, we should leave it without a single regret. Can you, in short, be prevailed on to quit this scene of public triumph and oblige your friend Eleanor with your company in Gloucestershire? I am almost ashamed to make the request, though its presumption would certainly appear greater to every creature in Bath than yourself. Modesty such as yours—but not for the world would I pain it by open praise. If you can be induced to honour us with a visit, you will make us happy beyond expression. 'Tis true, we can offer you nothing like the gaieties of this lively place; we can tempt you neither by amusement nor splendour, for our mode of living, as you see, is plain and unpretending; yet no endeavours shall be wanting on our side to make Northanger Abbey not wholly disagreeable."

Northanger Abbey! These were thrilling words, and wound up Catherine's feelings to the highest point of ecstasy. Her grateful and gratified heart could hardly restrain its expressions within the language of tolerable calmness. To receive so flattering an invitation! To have her company so warmly solicited! Everything honourable and soothing, every present enjoyment, and every future hope was contained in it; and her acceptance, with only the saving clause of Papa and Mamma's approbation, was eagerly given. "I will write home directly," said she, "and if they do not object, as I dare say they will not—"

General Tilney was not less sanguine, having already waited on her excellent friends in Pulteney Street, and obtained their sanction of his wishes. "Since they can consent to part with you," said he, "we may expect philosophy from all the world."

Miss Tilney was earnest, though gentle, in her secondary civilities, and the affair became in a few minutes as nearly settled as this necessary reference to Fullerton would allow.

The circumstances of the morning had led Catherine's feelings through the varieties of suspense, security, and disappointment; but they were now safely lodged in perfect bliss; and with spirits elated to rapture, with Henry at her heart, and Northanger Abbey on her lips, she hurried home to write her letter. Mr. and Mrs. Morland, relying on the discretion of the friends to whom they had already entrusted their daughter, felt no doubt of the propriety of an acquaintance which had been formed under their eye, and sent therefore by return of post their ready consent to her visit in Gloucestershire. This indulgence, though not more than Catherine had hoped for, completed her conviction of being favoured beyond every other human creature, in friends and fortune, circumstance and chance. Everything seemed to cooperate for her advantage. By the kindness of her first friends, the Allens, she had been introduced into scenes where pleasures of every kind had met her. Her feelings, her preferences, had each known the happiness of a return. Wherever she felt attachment, she had been able to create it. The affection of Isabella was to be secured to her in a sister. The Tilneys, they, by whom, above all, she desired to be favourably thought of, outstripped even her wishes in the flattering measures by which their intimacy was to be continued. She was to be their chosen visitor, she was to be for weeks under the same roof with the person whose society she mostly prized—and, in addition to all the rest, this roof was to be the roof of an abbey! Her passion for ancient edifices was next in degree to her passion for Henry Tilney—and castles and abbeys made usually the charm of those reveries which his image did not fill. To see and explore either the ramparts and keep of the one, or the cloisters of the other, had been for many weeks a darling wish, though to be more than the visitor of an hour had seemed too nearly impossible for desire. And yet, this was to happen. With all the chances against her of house, hall, place, park, court, and cottage, Northanger turned up an abbey, and she was to be its inhabitant. Its long, damp passages, its narrow cells and ruined chapel, were to be within her daily reach, and she could not entirely subdue the hope of some traditional legends, some awful memorials of an injured and ill-fated nun.

It was wonderful that her friends should seem so little elated by the possession of such a home, that the consciousness of it should be so meekly borne. The power of early habit only could account for it. A distinction to which they had been born gave no pride. Their superiority of abode was no more to them than their superiority of person.

Many were the inquiries she was eager to make of Miss Tilney; but so active were her thoughts, that when these inquiries were answered, she was hardly more assured than before, of Northanger Abbey having been a richly endowed convent at the time of the Reformation, of its having fallen into the hands of an ancestor of the Tilneys on its dissolution, of a large portion of the ancient building still making a part of the present dwelling although the rest was decayed, or of its standing low in a valley, sheltered from the north and east by rising woods of oak.

CHAPTER 18

With a mind thus full of happiness, Catherine was hardly aware that two or three days had passed away, without her seeing Isabella for more than a few minutes together. She began first to be sensible of this, and to sigh for her conversation, as she walked along the pump-room one morning, by Mrs. Allen's side, without anything to say or to hear; and scarcely had she felt a five minutes' longing of friendship, before the object of it appeared, and inviting her to a secret conference, led the way to a seat. "This is my favourite place," said she as they sat down on a bench between the doors, which commanded a tolerable view of everybody entering at either; "it is so out of the way."

Catherine, observing that Isabella's eyes were continually bent towards one door or the other, as in eager expectation, and remembering how often she had been falsely accused of being arch, thought the present a fine opportunity for being really so; and therefore gaily said, "Do not be uneasy, Isabella, James will soon be here."

"Psha! My dear creature," she replied, "do not think me such a simpleton as to be always wanting to confine him to my elbow. It would be hideous to be always together; we should be the jest of the place. And so you are going to Northanger! I am amazingly glad of it. It is one of the finest old places in England, I understand. I shall depend upon a most particular description of it."

"You shall certainly have the best in my power to give. But who are you looking for? Are your sisters coming?"

"I am not looking for anybody. One's eyes must be somewhere, and you know what a foolish trick I have of fixing mine, when my thoughts are an hundred miles off. I am amazingly absent; I believe I am the most absent creature in the world. Tilney says it is always the case with minds of a certain stamp."

"But I thought, Isabella, you had something in particular to tell me?"

"Oh yes, and so I have. But here is a proof of what I was saying. My poor head, I had quite forgot it. Well, the thing is this: I have just had a letter from John; you can guess the contents."

"No, indeed, I cannot."

"My sweet love, do not be so abominably affected. What can he write about, but yourself? You know he is over head and ears in love with you."

"With me, dear Isabella!"

"Nay, my sweetest Catherine, this is being quite absurd! Modesty, and all that, is very well in its way, but really a little common honesty is sometimes quite as becoming. I have no idea of being so overstrained! It is fishing for compliments. His attentions were such as a child must have noticed. And it was but half an hour before he left Bath that you gave him the most positive encouragement. He says so in this letter, says that he as good as made you an offer, and that you received his advances in the kindest way; and now he wants me to urge his suit, and say all manner of pretty things to you. So it is in vain to affect ignorance."

Catherine, with all the earnestness of truth, expressed her astonishment at such a charge, protesting her innocence of every thought of Mr. Thorpe's being in love with her, and the consequent impossibility of her having ever intended to encourage him. "As to any attentions on his side, I do declare, upon my honour, I never was sensible of them for a moment—except just his asking me to dance the first day of his coming. And as to making me an offer, or anything like it, there must be some unaccountable mistake. I could not have misunderstood a thing of that kind, you know! And, as I ever wish to be believed, I solemnly protest that no syllable of such a nature ever passed between us. The last half hour before he went away! It must be all and completely a mistake—for I did not see him once that whole morning."

"But that you certainly did, for you spent the whole morning in Edgar's Buildings—it was the day your father's consent came—and I am pretty sure that you and John were alone in the parlour some time before you left the house."

"Are you? Well, if you say it, it was so, I dare say—but for the life of me, I cannot recollect it. I do remember now being with you, and seeing him as well as the rest—but that we were ever alone for five minutes— However, it is not worth arguing about, for whatever might pass on his side, you must be convinced, by my having no recollection of it, that I never thought, nor expected, nor wished for anything of the kind from him. I am excessively concerned that he should have any regard for me—but indeed it has been quite unintentional on my side; I never had the smallest idea of it. Pray undeceive him as soon as you can, and tell him I beg his pardon—that is—I do not know what I ought to say—but make him understand what I mean, in the properest way. I would not speak disrespectfully of a brother of yours, Isabella, I am sure; but you know very well that if I could think of one man more than another—he is not the person." Isabella was silent. "My dear friend, you must not be angry with me. I cannot suppose your brother cares so very much about me. And, you know, we shall still be sisters."

"Yes, yes" (with a blush), "there are more ways than one of our being sisters. But where am I wandering to? Well, my dear Catherine, the case seems to be that you are determined against poor John—is not it so?"

"I certainly cannot return his affection, and as certainly never meant to encourage it."

"Since that is the case, I am sure I shall not tease you any further. John desired me to speak to you on the subject, and therefore I have. But I confess, as soon as I read his letter, I thought it a very foolish, imprudent business, and not likely to promote the good of either; for what were you to live upon, supposing you came together? You have both of you something, to be sure, but it is not a trifle that will support a family nowadays; and after all that romancers may say, there is no doing without money. I only wonder John could think of it; he could not have received my last."

"You do acquit me, then, of anything wrong?—You are convinced that I never meant to deceive your brother, never suspected him of liking me till this moment?"

"Oh! As to that," answered Isabella laughingly, "I do not pretend to determine what your thoughts and designs in time past may have been. All that is best known to yourself. A little harmless flirtation or so will occur, and one is often drawn on to give more encouragement than one wishes to stand by. But you may be assured that I am the last person in the world to judge you severely. All those things should be allowed for in youth and high spirits. What one means one day, you know, one may not mean the next. Circumstances change, opinions alter."

"But my opinion of your brother never did alter; it was always the same. You are describing what never happened."

"My dearest Catherine," continued the other without at all listening to her, "I would not for all the world be the means of hurrying you into an engagement before you knew what you were about. I do not think anything would justify me in wishing you to sacrifice all your happiness merely to oblige my brother, because he is my brother, and who perhaps after all, you know, might be just as happy without you, for people seldom know what they would be at, young men especially, they are so amazingly changeable and inconstant. What I say is, why should a brother's happiness be dearer to me than a friend's? You know I carry my notions of friendship pretty high. But, above all things, my dear Catherine, do not be in a hurry. Take my word for it, that if you are in too great a hurry, you will certainly live to repent it. Tilney says there is nothing people are so often deceived in as the state of their own affections, and I believe he is very right. Ah! Here he comes; never mind, he will not see us, I am sure."

Catherine, looking up, perceived Captain Tilney; and Isabella, earnestly fixing her eye on him as she spoke, soon caught his notice. He approached immediately, and took the seat to which her movements invited him. His first address made Catherine start. Though spoken low, she could distinguish, "What! Always to be watched, in person or by proxy!"

"Psha, nonsense!" was Isabella's answer in the same half whisper. "Why do you put such things into my head? If I could believe it—my spirit, you know, is pretty independent."

"I wish your heart were independent. That would be enough for me."

"My heart, indeed! What can you have to do with hearts? You men have none of you any hearts."

"If we have not hearts, we have eyes; and they give us torment enough."

"Do they? I am sorry for it; I am sorry they find anything so disagreeable in me. I will look another way. I hope this pleases you" (turning her back on him); "I hope your eyes are not tormented now."

"Never more so; for the edge of a blooming cheek is still in view—at once too much and too little."

Catherine heard all this, and quite out of countenance, could listen no longer. Amazed that Isabella could endure it, and jealous for her brother, she rose up, and saying she should join Mrs. Allen, proposed their walking. But for this Isabella showed no inclination. She was so amazingly tired, and it was so odious to parade about the pump-room; and if she moved from her seat she should miss her sisters; she was expecting her sisters every moment; so that her dearest Catherine must excuse her, and must sit quietly down again. But Catherine could be stubborn too; and Mrs. Allen just then coming up to propose their returning home, she joined her and walked out of the pump-room, leaving Isabella still sitting with Captain Tilney. With much uneasiness did she thus leave them. It seemed to her that Captain Tilney was falling in love with Isabella, and Isabella unconsciously encouraging him; unconsciously it must be, for Isabella's attachment to James was as certain and well acknowledged as her engagement. To doubt her truth or good intentions was impossible; and yet, during the whole of their conversation her manner had been odd. She wished Isabella had talked more like her usual self, and not so much about money, and had not looked so well pleased at the sight of Captain Tilney. How strange that she should not perceive his admiration! Catherine longed to give her a hint of it, to put her on her guard, and prevent all the pain which her too lively behaviour might otherwise create both for him and her brother.

The compliment of John Thorpe's affection did not make amends for this thoughtlessness in his sister. She was almost as far from believing as from wishing it to be sincere; for she had not forgotten that he could mistake, and his assertion of the offer and of her encouragement convinced her that his mistakes could sometimes be very egregious. In vanity, therefore, she gained but little; her chief profit was in wonder. That he should think it worth his while to fancy himself in love with her was a matter of lively astonishment. Isabella talked of his attentions; she had never been sensible of any; but Isabella had said many things which she hoped had been spoken in haste, and would never be said again; and upon this she was glad to rest altogether for present ease and comfort.

CHAPTER 19

A few days passed away, and Catherine, though not allowing herself to suspect her friend, could not help watching her closely. The result of her observations was not agreeable. Isabella seemed an altered creature. When she saw her, indeed, surrounded only by their immediate friends in Edgar's Buildings or Pulteney Street, her change of manners was so trifling that, had it gone no farther, it might have passed unnoticed. A something of languid indifference, or of that boasted absence of mind which Catherine had never heard of before, would occasionally come across her; but had nothing worse appeared, that might only have spread a new grace and inspired a warmer interest. But when Catherine saw her in public, admitting Captain Tilney's attentions as readily as they were offered, and allowing him almost an equal share with James in her notice and smiles, the alteration became too positive to be passed over. What could be meant by such unsteady conduct, what her friend could be at, was beyond her comprehension. Isabella could not be aware of the pain she was inflicting; but it was a degree of wilful thoughtlessness which Catherine could not but resent. James was the sufferer. She saw him grave and uneasy; and however careless of his present comfort the woman might be who had given him her heart, to her it was always an object. For poor Captain Tilney too she was greatly concerned. Though his looks did not please her, his name was a passport to her goodwill, and she thought with sincere compassion of his approaching disappointment; for, in spite of what she had believed herself to overhear in the pump-room, his behaviour was so incompatible with a knowledge of Isabella's engagement that she could not, upon reflection, imagine him aware of it. He might be jealous of her brother as a rival, but if more had seemed implied, the fault must have been in her misapprehension. She wished, by a gentle remonstrance, to remind Isabella of her situation, and make her aware of this double unkindness; but for remonstrance, either opportunity or comprehension was always against her. If able to suggest a hint, Isabella could never understand it. In this distress, the intended departure of the Tilney family became her chief consolation; their journey into Gloucestershire was to take place within a few days, and Captain Tilney's removal would at least restore peace to every heart but his own. But Captain Tilney had at present no intention of removing; he was not to be of the party to Northanger; he was to continue at Bath. When Catherine knew this, her resolution was directly made. She spoke to Henry Tilney on the subject, regretting his brother's evident partiality for Miss Thorpe, and entreating him to make known her prior engagement.

"My brother does know it," was Henry's answer.

"Does he? Then why does he stay here?"

He made no reply, and was beginning to talk of something else; but she eagerly continued, "Why do not you persuade him to go away? The longer he stays, the worse it will be for him at last. Pray advise him for his own sake, and for everybody's sake, to leave Bath directly. Absence will in time make him comfortable again; but he can have no hope here, and it is only staying to be miserable."

Henry smiled and said, "I am sure my brother would not wish to do that."

"Then you will persuade him to go away?"

"Persuasion is not at command; but pardon me, if I cannot even endeavour to persuade him. I have myself told him that Miss Thorpe is engaged. He knows what he is about, and must be his own master."

"No, he does not know what he is about," cried Catherine; "he does not know the pain he is giving my brother. Not that James has ever told me so, but I am sure he is very uncomfortable."

"And are you sure it is my brother's doing?"

"Yes, very sure."

"Is it my brother's attentions to Miss Thorpe, or Miss Thorpe's admission of them, that gives the pain?"

"Is not it the same thing?"

"I think Mr. Morland would acknowledge a difference. No man is offended by another man's admiration of the woman he loves; it is the woman only who can make it a torment."

Catherine blushed for her friend, and said, "Isabella is wrong. But I am sure she cannot mean to torment, for she is very much attached to my brother. She has been in love with him ever since they first met, and while my father's consent was uncertain, she fretted herself almost into a fever. You know she must be attached to him."

"I understand: she is in love with James, and flirts with Frederick."

"Oh no, not flirts. A woman in love with one man cannot flirt with another."

"It is probable that she will neither love so well, nor flirt so well, as she might do either singly. The gentlemen must each give up a little."

After a short pause, Catherine resumed with, "Then you do not believe Isabella so very much attached to my brother?"

"I can have no opinion on that subject."

"But what can your brother mean? If he knows her engagement, what can he mean by his behaviour?"

"You are a very close questioner."

"Am I? I only ask what I want to be told."

"But do you only ask what I can be expected to tell?"

"Yes, I think so; for you must know your brother's heart."

"My brother's heart, as you term it, on the present occasion, I assure you I can only guess at."

"Well?"

"Well! Nay, if it is to be guesswork, let us all guess for ourselves. To be guided by second-hand conjecture is pitiful. The premises are before you. My brother is a lively and perhaps sometimes a thoughtless young man; he has had about a week's acquaintance with your friend, and he has known her engagement almost as long as he has known her."

"Well," said Catherine, after some moments' consideration, "you may be able to guess at your brother's intentions from all this; but I am sure I cannot. But is not your father uncomfortable about it? Does not he want Captain Tilney to go away? Sure, if your father were to speak to him, he would go."

"My dear Miss Morland," said Henry, "in this amiable solicitude for your brother's comfort, may you not be a little mistaken? Are you not carried a little too far? Would he thank you, either on his own account or Miss Thorpe's, for supposing that her affection, or at least her good behaviour, is only to be secured by her seeing nothing of Captain Tilney? Is he safe only in solitude? Or is her heart constant to him only when unsolicited by anyone else? He cannot think this—and you may be sure that he would not have you think it. I will not say, 'Do not be uneasy,' because I know that you are so, at this moment; but be as little uneasy as you can. You have no doubt of the mutual attachment of your brother and your friend; depend upon it, therefore, that real jealousy never can exist between them; depend upon it that no disagreement between them can be of any duration. Their hearts are open to each other, as neither heart can be to you; they know exactly what is required and what can be borne; and you may be certain that one will never tease the other beyond what is known to be pleasant."

Perceiving her still to look doubtful and grave, he added, "Though Frederick does not leave Bath with us, he will probably remain but a very short time, perhaps only a few days behind us. His leave of absence will soon expire, and he must return to his regiment. And what will then be their acquaintance? The mess-room will drink Isabella Thorpe for a fortnight, and she will laugh with your brother over poor Tilney's passion for a month."

Catherine would contend no longer against comfort. She had resisted its approaches during the whole length of a speech, but it now carried her captive. Henry Tilney must know best. She blamed herself for the extent of her fears, and resolved never to think so seriously on the subject again.

Her resolution was supported by Isabella's behaviour in their parting interview. The Thorpes spent the last evening of Catherine's stay in Pulteney Street, and nothing passed between the lovers to excite her uneasiness, or make her quit them in apprehension. James was in excellent spirits, and Isabella most engagingly placid. Her tenderness for her friend seemed rather the first feeling of her heart; but that at such a moment was allowable; and once she gave her lover a flat contradiction, and once she drew back her hand; but Catherine remembered Henry's instructions, and placed it all to judicious affection. The embraces, tears, and promises of the parting fair ones may be fancied.

CHAPTER 20

Mr. and Mrs. Allen were sorry to lose their young friend, whose good humour and cheerfulness had made her a valuable companion, and in the promotion of whose enjoyment their own had been gently increased. Her happiness in going with Miss Tilney, however, prevented their wishing it otherwise; and, as they were to remain only one more week in Bath themselves, her quitting them now would not long be felt. Mr. Allen attended her to Milsom Street, where she was to breakfast, and saw her seated with the kindest welcome among her new friends; but so great was her agitation in finding herself as one of the family, and so fearful was she of not doing exactly what was right, and of not being able to preserve their good opinion, that, in the embarrassment of the first five minutes, she could almost have wished to return with him to Pulteney Street.

Miss Tilney's manners and Henry's smile soon did away some of her unpleasant feelings; but still she was far from being at ease; nor could the incessant attentions of the general himself entirely reassure her. Nay, perverse as it seemed, she doubted whether she might not have felt less, had she been less attended to. His anxiety for her comfort—his continual solicitations that she would eat, and his often-expressed fears of her seeing nothing to her taste—though never in her life before had she beheld half such variety on a breakfast-table—made it impossible for her to forget for a moment that she was a visitor. She felt utterly unworthy of such respect, and knew not how to reply to it. Her tranquillity was not improved by the General's impatience for the appearance of his eldest son, nor by the displeasure he expressed at his laziness when Captain Tilney at last came down. She was quite pained by the severity of his father's reproof, which seemed disproportionate to the offence; and much was her concern increased when she found herself the principal cause of the lecture, and that his tardiness was chiefly resented from being disrespectful to her. This was placing her in a very uncomfortable situation, and she felt great compassion for Captain Tilney, without being able to hope for his goodwill.

He listened to his father in silence, and attempted not any defence, which confirmed her in fearing that the inquietude of his mind, on Isabella's account, might, by keeping him long sleepless, have been the real cause of his rising late. It was the first time of her being decidedly in his company, and she had hoped to be now able to form her opinion of him; but she scarcely heard his voice while his father remained in the room; and even afterwards, so much were his spirits affected, she could distinguish nothing but these words, in a whisper to Eleanor, "How glad I shall be when you are all off."

The bustle of going was not pleasant. The clock struck ten while the trunks were carrying down, and the general had fixed to be out of Milsom Street by that hour. His greatcoat, instead of being brought for him to put on directly, was spread out in the curricle in which he was to accompany his son. The middle seat of the chaise was not drawn out, though there were three people to go in it, and his daughter's maid had so crowded it with parcels that Miss Morland would not have room to sit; and, so much was he influenced by this apprehension when he handed her in, that she had some difficulty in saving her own new writing-desk from being thrown out into the street. At last, however, the door was closed upon the three females, and they set off at the sober pace in which the handsome, highly fed four horses of a gentleman usually perform a journey of thirty miles: such was the distance of Northanger from Bath, to be now divided into two equal stages. Catherine's spirits revived as they drove from the door; for with Miss Tilney she felt no restraint; and, with the interest of a road entirely new to her, of an abbey before, and a curricle behind, she caught the last view of Bath without any regret, and met with every milestone before she expected it. The tediousness of a two hours' wait at Petty France, in which there was nothing to be done but to eat without being hungry, and loiter about without anything to see, next followed—and her admiration of the style in which they travelled, of the fashionable chaise and four—postilions handsomely liveried, rising so regularly in their stirrups, and numerous outriders properly mounted, sunk a little under this consequent inconvenience. Had their party been perfectly agreeable, the delay would have been nothing; but General Tilney, though so charming a man, seemed always a check upon his children's spirits, and scarcely anything was said but by himself; the observation of which, with his discontent at whatever the inn afforded, and his angry impatience at the waiters, made Catherine grow every moment more in awe of him, and appeared to lengthen the two hours into four. At last, however, the order of release was given; and much was Catherine then surprised by the General's proposal of her taking his place in his son's curricle for the rest of the journey: "the day was fine, and he was anxious for her seeing as much of the country as possible."

The remembrance of Mr. Allen's opinion, respecting young men's open carriages, made her blush at the mention of such a plan, and her first thought was to decline it; but her second was of greater deference for General Tilney's judgment; he could not propose anything improper for her; and, in the course of a few minutes, she found herself with Henry in the curricle, as happy a being as ever existed. A very short trial convinced her that a curricle was the prettiest equipage in the world; the chaise and four wheeled off with some grandeur, to be sure, but it was a heavy and troublesome business, and she could not easily forget its having stopped two hours at Petty France. Half the time would have been enough for the curricle, and so nimbly were the light horses disposed to move, that, had not the general chosen to have his own carriage lead the way, they could have passed it with ease in half a minute. But the merit of the curricle did not all belong to the horses; Henry drove so well—so quietly—without making any disturbance, without parading to her, or swearing at them: so different from the only gentleman-coachman whom it was in her power to compare him with! And then his hat sat so well, and the innumerable capes of his greatcoat looked so becomingly important! To be driven by him, next to being dancing with him, was certainly the greatest happiness in the world. In addition to every other delight, she had now that of listening to her own praise; of being thanked at least, on his sister's account, for her kindness in thus becoming her visitor; of hearing it ranked as real friendship, and described as creating real gratitude. His sister, he said, was uncomfortably circumstanced—she had no female companion—and, in the frequent absence of her father, was sometimes without any companion at all.

"But how can that be?" said Catherine. "Are not you with her?"

"Northanger is not more than half my home; I have an establishment at my own house in Woodston, which is nearly twenty miles from my father's, and some of my time is necessarily spent there."

"How sorry you must be for that!"

"I am always sorry to leave Eleanor."

"Yes; but besides your affection for her, you must be so fond of the abbey! After being used to such a home as the abbey, an ordinary parsonage-house must be very disagreeable."

He smiled, and said, "You have formed a very favourable idea of the abbey."

"To be sure, I have. Is not it a fine old place, just like what one reads about?"

"And are you prepared to encounter all the horrors that a building such as 'what one reads about' may produce? Have you a stout heart? Nerves fit for sliding panels and tapestry?"

"Oh! yes—I do not think I should be easily frightened, because there would be so many people in the house—and besides, it has never been uninhabited and left deserted for years, and then the family come back to it unawares, without giving any notice, as generally happens."

"No, certainly. We shall not have to explore our way into a hall dimly lighted by the expiring embers of a wood fire—nor be obliged to spread our beds on the floor of a room without windows, doors, or furniture. But you must be aware that when a young lady is (by whatever means) introduced into a dwelling of this kind, she is always lodged apart from the rest of the family. While they snugly repair to their own end of the house, she is formally conducted by Dorothy, the ancient housekeeper, up a different staircase, and along many gloomy passages, into an apartment never used since some cousin or kin died in it about twenty years before. Can you stand such a ceremony as this? Will not your mind misgive you when you find yourself in this gloomy chamber—too lofty and extensive for you, with only the feeble rays of a single lamp to take in its size—its walls hung with tapestry exhibiting figures as large as life, and the bed, of dark green stuff or purple velvet, presenting even a funereal appearance? Will not your heart sink within you?"

"Oh! But this will not happen to me, I am sure."

"How fearfully will you examine the furniture of your apartment! And what will you discern? Not tables, toilettes, wardrobes, or drawers, but on one side perhaps the remains of a broken lute, on the other a ponderous chest which no efforts can open, and over the fireplace the portrait of some handsome warrior, whose features will so incomprehensibly strike you, that you will not be able to withdraw your eyes from it. Dorothy, meanwhile, no less struck by your appearance, gazes on you in great agitation, and drops a few unintelligible hints. To raise your spirits, moreover, she gives you reason to suppose that the part of the abbey you inhabit is undoubtedly haunted, and informs you that you will not have a single domestic within call. With this parting cordial she curtsies off—you listen to the sound of her receding footsteps as long as the last echo can reach you—and when, with fainting spirits, you attempt to fasten your door, you discover, with increased alarm, that it has no lock."

"Oh! Mr. Tilney, how frightful! This is just like a book! But it cannot really happen to me. I am sure your housekeeper is not really Dorothy. Well, what then?"

"Nothing further to alarm perhaps may occur the first night. After surmounting your unconquerable horror of the bed, you will retire to rest, and get a few hours' unquiet slumber. But on the second, or at farthest the third night after your arrival, you will probably have a violent storm. Peals of thunder so loud as to seem to shake the edifice to its foundation will roll round the neighbouring mountains—and during the frightful gusts of wind which accompany it, you will probably think you discern (for your lamp is not extinguished) one part of the hanging more violently agitated than the rest. Unable of course to repress your curiosity in so favourable a moment for indulging it, you will instantly arise, and throwing your dressing-gown around you, proceed to examine this mystery. After a very short search, you will discover a division in the tapestry so artfully constructed as to defy the minutest inspection, and on opening it, a door will immediately appear—which door, being only secured by massy bars and a padlock, you will, after a few efforts, succeed in opening—and, with your lamp in your hand, will pass through it into a small vaulted room."

"No, indeed; I should be too much frightened to do any such thing."

"What! Not when Dorothy has given you to understand that there is a secret subterraneous communication between your apartment and the chapel of St. Anthony, scarcely two miles off. Could you shrink from so simple an adventure? No, no, you will proceed into this small vaulted room, and through this into several others, without perceiving anything very remarkable in either. In one perhaps there may be a dagger, in another a few drops of blood, and in a third the remains of some instrument of torture; but there being nothing in all this out of the common way, and your lamp being nearly exhausted, you will return towards your own apartment. In repassing through the small vaulted room, however, your eyes will be attracted towards a large, old-fashioned cabinet of ebony and gold, which, though narrowly examining the furniture before, you had passed unnoticed. Impelled by an irresistible presentiment, you will eagerly advance to it, unlock its folding doors, and search into every drawer—but for some time without discovering anything of importance—perhaps nothing but a considerable hoard of diamonds. At last, however, by touching a secret spring, an inner compartment will open—a roll of paper appears—you seize it—it contains many sheets of manuscript—you hasten with the precious treasure into your own chamber, but scarcely have you been able to decipher 'Oh thou, whomsoever thou mayst be, into whose hands these memoirs of the wretched Matilda may fall'—when your lamp suddenly expires in the socket, and leaves you in total darkness."

"Oh, no, no; do not say so. Well, go on."

But Henry was too much amused by the interest he had raised to be able to carry it farther; he could no longer command solemnity either of subject or voice, and was obliged to entreat her to use her own fancy in the perusal of Matilda's woes. Catherine, recollecting herself, grew ashamed of her eagerness, and began earnestly to assure him that her attention had been fixed without the smallest apprehension of really meeting with what he related. "Miss Tilney, she was sure, would never put her into such a chamber as he had described! She was not at all afraid."

As they drew near the end of their journey, her impatience for a sight of the abbey—for some time suspended by his conversation on subjects very different—returned in full force, and every bend in the road was expected with solemn awe to afford a glimpse of its massy walls of grey stone, rising amidst a grove of ancient oaks, with the last beams of the sun playing in beautiful splendour on its high Gothic windows. But so low did the building stand, that she found herself passing through the great gates of the lodge into the very grounds of Northanger, without having discerned even an antique chimney.

She knew not that she had any right to be surprised, but there was a something in this mode of approach which she certainly had not expected. To pass between lodges of a modern appearance, to find herself with such ease in the very precincts of the abbey, and driven so rapidly along a smooth, level road of fine gravel, without obstacle, alarm, or solemnity of any kind, struck her as odd and inconsistent. She was not long at leisure, however, for such considerations. A sudden scud of rain, driving full in her face, made it impossible for her to observe anything further, and fixed all her thoughts on the welfare of her new straw bonnet; and she was actually under the abbey walls, was springing, with Henry's assistance, from the carriage, was beneath the shelter of the old porch, and had even passed on to the hall, where her friend and the general were waiting to welcome her, without feeling one awful foreboding of future misery to herself, or one moment's suspicion of any past scenes of horror being acted within the solemn edifice. The breeze had not seemed to waft the sighs of the murdered to her; it had wafted nothing worse than a thick mizzling rain; and having given a good shake to her habit, she was ready to be shown into the common drawing-room, and capable of considering where she was.

An abbey! Yes, it was delightful to be really in an abbey! But she doubted, as she looked round the room, whether anything within her observation would have given her the consciousness. The furniture was in all the profusion and elegance of modern taste. The fireplace, where she had expected the ample width and ponderous carving of former times, was contracted to a Rumford, with slabs of plain though handsome marble, and ornaments over it of the prettiest English china. The windows, to which she looked with peculiar dependence, from having heard the general talk of his preserving them in their Gothic form with reverential care, were yet less what her fancy had portrayed. To be sure, the pointed arch was preserved—the form of them was Gothic—they might be even casements—but every pane was so large, so clear, so light! To an imagination which had hoped for the smallest divisions, and the heaviest stone-work, for painted glass, dirt, and cobwebs, the difference was very distressing.

The general, perceiving how her eye was employed, began to talk of the smallness of the room and simplicity of the furniture, where everything, being for daily use, pretended only to comfort, etc.; flattering himself, however, that there were some apartments in the Abbey not unworthy her notice—and was proceeding to mention the costly gilding of one in particular, when, taking out his watch, he stopped short to pronounce it with surprise within twenty minutes of five! This seemed the word of separation, and Catherine found herself hurried away by Miss Tilney in such a manner as convinced her that the strictest punctuality to the family hours would be expected at Northanger.

Returning through the large and lofty hall, they ascended a broad staircase of shining oak, which, after many flights and many landing-places, brought them upon a long, wide gallery. On one side it had a range of doors, and it was lighted on the other by windows which Catherine had only time to discover looked into a quadrangle, before Miss Tilney led the way into a chamber, and scarcely staying to hope she would find it comfortable, left her with an anxious entreaty that she would make as little alteration as possible in her dress.

CHAPTER 21

A moment's glance was enough to satisfy Catherine that her apartment was very unlike the one which Henry had endeavoured to alarm her by the description of. It was by no means unreasonably large, and contained neither tapestry nor velvet. The walls were papered, the floor was carpeted; the windows were neither less perfect nor more dim than those of the drawing-room below; the furniture, though not of the latest fashion, was handsome and comfortable, and the air of the room altogether far from uncheerful. Her heart instantaneously at ease on this point, she resolved to lose no time in particular examination of anything, as she greatly dreaded disobliging the general by any delay. Her habit therefore was thrown off with all possible haste, and she was preparing to unpin the linen package, which the chaise-seat had conveyed for her immediate accommodation, when her eye suddenly fell on a large high chest, standing back in a deep recess on one side of the fireplace. The sight of it made her start; and, forgetting everything else, she stood gazing on it in motionless wonder, while these thoughts crossed her:

"This is strange indeed! I did not expect such a sight as this! An immense heavy chest! What can it hold? Why should it be placed here? Pushed back too, as if meant to be out of sight! I will look into it—cost me what it may, I will look into it—and directly too—by daylight. If I stay till evening my candle may go out." She advanced and examined it closely: it was of cedar, curiously inlaid with some darker wood, and raised, about a foot from the ground, on a carved stand of the same. The lock was silver, though tarnished from age; at each end were the imperfect remains of handles also of silver, broken perhaps prematurely by some strange violence; and, on the centre of the lid, was a mysterious cipher, in the same metal. Catherine bent over it intently, but without being able to distinguish anything with certainty. She could not, in whatever direction she took it, believe the last letter to be a T; and yet that it should be anything else in that house was a circumstance to raise no common degree of astonishment. If not originally theirs, by what strange events could it have fallen into the Tilney family?

Her fearful curiosity was every moment growing greater; and seizing, with trembling hands, the hasp of the lock, she resolved at all hazards to satisfy herself at least as to its contents. With difficulty, for something seemed to resist her efforts, she raised the lid a few inches; but at that moment a sudden knocking at the door of the room made her, starting, quit her hold, and the lid closed with alarming violence. This ill-timed intruder was Miss Tilney's maid, sent by her mistress to be of use to Miss Morland; and though Catherine immediately dismissed her, it recalled her to the sense of what she ought to be doing, and forced her, in spite of her anxious desire to penetrate this mystery, to proceed in her dressing without further delay. Her progress was not quick, for her thoughts and her eyes were still bent on the object so well calculated to interest and alarm; and though she dared not waste a moment upon a second attempt, she could not remain many paces from the chest. At length, however, having slipped one arm into her gown, her toilette seemed so nearly finished that the impatience of her curiosity might safely be indulged. One moment surely might be spared; and, so desperate should be the exertion of her strength, that, unless secured by supernatural means, the lid in one moment should be thrown back. With this spirit she sprang forward, and her confidence did not deceive her. Her resolute effort threw back the lid, and gave to her astonished eyes the view of a white cotton counterpane, properly folded, reposing at one end of the chest in undisputed possession!

She was gazing on it with the first blush of surprise when Miss Tilney, anxious for her friend's being ready, entered the room, and to the rising shame of having harboured for some minutes an absurd expectation, was then added the shame of being caught in so idle a search. "That is a curious old chest, is not it?" said Miss Tilney, as Catherine hastily closed it and turned away to the glass. "It is impossible to say how many generations it has been here. How it came to be first put in this room I know not, but I have not had it moved, because I thought it might sometimes be of use in holding hats and bonnets. The worst of it is that its weight makes it difficult to open. In that corner, however, it is at least out of the way."

Catherine had no leisure for speech, being at once blushing, tying her gown, and forming wise resolutions with the most violent dispatch. Miss Tilney gently hinted her fear of being late; and in half a minute they ran downstairs together, in an alarm not wholly unfounded, for General Tilney was pacing the drawing-room, his watch in his hand, and having, on the very instant of their entering, pulled the bell with violence, ordered "Dinner to be on table directly!"

Catherine trembled at the emphasis with which he spoke, and sat pale and breathless, in a most humble mood, concerned for his children, and detesting old chests; and the general, recovering his politeness as he looked at her, spent the rest of his time in scolding his daughter for so foolishly hurrying her fair friend, who was absolutely out of breath from haste, when there was not the least occasion for hurry in the world: but Catherine could not at all get over the double distress of having involved her friend in a lecture and been a great simpleton herself, till they were happily seated at the dinner-table, when the General's complacent smiles, and a good appetite of her own, restored her to peace. The dining-parlour was a noble room, suitable in its dimensions to a much larger drawing-room than the one in common use, and fitted up in a style of luxury and expense which was almost lost on the unpractised eye of Catherine, who saw little more than its spaciousness and the number of their attendants. Of the former, she spoke aloud her admiration; and the general, with a very gracious countenance, acknowledged that it was by no means an ill-sized room, and further confessed that, though as careless on such subjects as most people, he did look upon a tolerably large eating-room as one of the necessaries of life; he supposed, however, "that she must have been used to much better-sized apartments at Mr. Allen's?"

"No, indeed," was Catherine's honest assurance; "Mr. Allen's dining-parlour was not more than half as large," and she had never seen so large a room as this in her life. The General's good humour increased. Why, as he had such rooms, he thought it would be simple not to make use of them; but, upon his honour, he believed there might be more comfort in rooms of only half their size. Mr. Allen's house, he was sure, must be exactly of the true size for rational happiness.

The evening passed without any further disturbance, and, in the occasional absence of General Tilney, with much positive cheerfulness. It was only in his presence that Catherine felt the smallest fatigue from her journey; and even then, even in moments of languor or restraint, a sense of general happiness preponderated, and she could think of her friends in Bath without one wish of being with them.

The night was stormy; the wind had been rising at intervals the whole afternoon; and by the time the party broke up, it blew and rained violently. Catherine, as she crossed the hall, listened to the tempest with sensations of awe; and, when she heard it rage round a corner of the ancient building and close with sudden fury a distant door, felt for the first time that she was really in an abbey. Yes, these were characteristic sounds; they brought to her recollection a countless variety of dreadful situations and horrid scenes, which such buildings had witnessed, and such storms ushered in; and most heartily did she rejoice in the happier circumstances attending her entrance within walls so solemn! She had nothing to dread from midnight assassins or drunken gallants. Henry had certainly been only in jest in what he had told her that morning. In a house so furnished, and so guarded, she could have nothing to explore or to suffer, and might go to her bedroom as securely as if it had been her own chamber at Fullerton. Thus wisely fortifying her mind, as she proceeded upstairs, she was enabled, especially on perceiving that Miss Tilney slept only two doors from her, to enter her room with a tolerably stout heart; and her spirits were immediately assisted by the cheerful blaze of a wood fire. "How much better is this," said she, as she walked to the fender—"how much better to find a fire ready lit, than to have to wait shivering in the cold till all the family are in bed, as so many poor girls have been obliged to do, and then to have a faithful old servant frightening one by coming in with a faggot! How glad I am that Northanger is what it is! If it had been like some other places, I do not know that, in such a night as this, I could have answered for my courage: but now, to be sure, there is nothing to alarm one."

She looked round the room. The window curtains seemed in motion. It could be nothing but the violence of the wind penetrating through the divisions of the shutters; and she stepped boldly forward, carelessly humming a tune, to assure herself of its being so, peeped courageously behind each curtain, saw nothing on either low window seat to scare her, and on placing a hand against the shutter, felt the strongest conviction of the wind's force. A glance at the old chest, as she turned away from this examination, was not without its use; she scorned the causeless fears of an idle fancy, and began with a most happy indifference to prepare herself for bed. "She should take her time; she should not hurry herself; she did not care if she were the last person up in the house. But she would not make up her fire; that would seem cowardly, as if she wished for the protection of light after she were in bed." The fire therefore died away, and Catherine, having spent the best part of an hour in her arrangements, was beginning to think of stepping into bed, when, on giving a parting glance round the room, she was struck by the appearance of a high, old-fashioned black cabinet, which, though in a situation conspicuous enough, had never caught her notice before. Henry's words, his description of the ebony cabinet which was to escape her observation at first, immediately rushed across her; and though there could be nothing really in it, there was something whimsical, it was certainly a very remarkable coincidence! She took her candle and looked closely at the cabinet. It was not absolutely ebony and gold; but it was japan, black and yellow japan of the handsomest kind; and as she held her candle, the yellow had very much the effect of gold. The key was in the door, and she had a strange fancy to look into it; not, however, with the smallest expectation of finding anything, but it was so very odd, after what Henry had said. In short, she could not sleep till she had examined it. So, placing the candle with great caution on a chair, she seized the key with a very tremulous hand and tried to turn it; but it resisted her utmost strength. Alarmed, but not discouraged, she tried it another way; a bolt flew, and she believed herself successful; but how strangely mysterious! The door was still immovable. She paused a moment in breathless wonder. The wind roared down the chimney, the rain beat in torrents against the windows, and everything seemed to speak the awfulness of her situation. To retire to bed, however, unsatisfied on such a point, would be vain, since sleep must be impossible with the consciousness of a cabinet so mysteriously closed in her immediate vicinity. Again, therefore, she applied herself to the key, and after moving it in every possible way for some instants with the determined celerity of hope's last effort, the door suddenly yielded to her hand: her heart leaped with exultation at such a victory, and having thrown open each folding door, the second being secured only by bolts of less wonderful construction than the lock, though in that her eye could not discern anything unusual, a double range of small drawers appeared in view, with some larger drawers above and below them; and in the centre, a small door, closed also with a lock and key, secured in all probability a cavity of importance.

Catherine's heart beat quick, but her courage did not fail her. With a cheek flushed by hope, and an eye straining with curiosity, her fingers grasped the handle of a drawer and drew it forth. It was entirely empty. With less alarm and greater eagerness she seized a second, a third, a fourth; each was equally empty. Not one was left unsearched, and in not one was anything found. Well read in the art of concealing a treasure, the possibility of false linings to the drawers did not escape her, and she felt round each with anxious acuteness in vain. The place in the middle alone remained now unexplored; and though she had "never from the first had the smallest idea of finding anything in any part of the cabinet, and was not in the least disappointed at her ill success thus far, it would be foolish not to examine it thoroughly while she was about it." It was some time however before she could unfasten the door, the same difficulty occurring in the management of this inner lock as of the outer; but at length it did open; and not vain, as hitherto, was her search; her quick eyes directly fell on a roll of paper pushed back into the further part of the cavity, apparently for concealment, and her feelings at that moment were indescribable. Her heart fluttered, her knees trembled, and her cheeks grew pale. She seized, with an unsteady hand, the precious manuscript, for half a glance sufficed to ascertain written characters; and while she acknowledged with awful sensations this striking exemplification of what Henry had foretold, resolved instantly to peruse every line before she attempted to rest.

The dimness of the light her candle emitted made her turn to it with alarm; but there was no danger of its sudden extinction; it had yet some hours to burn; and that she might not have any greater difficulty in distinguishing the writing than what its ancient date might occasion, she hastily snuffed it. Alas! It was snuffed and extinguished in one. A lamp could not have expired with more awful effect. Catherine, for a few moments, was motionless with horror. It was done completely; not a remnant of light in the wick could give hope to the rekindling breath. Darkness impenetrable and immovable filled the room. A violent gust of wind, rising with sudden fury, added fresh horror to the moment. Catherine trembled from head to foot. In the pause which succeeded, a sound like receding footsteps and the closing of a distant door struck on her affrighted ear. Human nature could support no more. A cold sweat stood on her forehead, the manuscript fell from her hand, and groping her way to the bed, she jumped hastily in, and sought some suspension of agony by creeping far underneath the clothes. To close her eyes in sleep that night, she felt must be entirely out of the question. With a curiosity so justly awakened, and feelings in every way so agitated, repose must be absolutely impossible. The storm too abroad so dreadful! She had not been used to feel alarm from wind, but now every blast seemed fraught with awful intelligence. The manuscript so wonderfully found, so wonderfully accomplishing the morning's prediction, how was it to be accounted for? What could it contain? To whom could it relate? By what means could it have been so long concealed? And how singularly strange that it should fall to her lot to discover it! Till she had made herself mistress of its contents, however, she could have neither repose nor comfort; and with the sun's first rays she was determined to peruse it. But many were the tedious hours which must yet intervene. She shuddered, tossed about in her bed, and envied every quiet sleeper. The storm still raged, and various were the noises, more terrific even than the wind, which struck at intervals on her startled ear. The very curtains of her bed seemed at one moment in motion, and at another the lock of her door was agitated, as if by the attempt of somebody to enter. Hollow murmurs seemed to creep along the gallery, and more than once her blood was chilled by the sound of distant moans. Hour after hour passed away, and the wearied Catherine had heard three proclaimed by all the clocks in the house before the tempest subsided or she unknowingly fell fast asleep.

CHAPTER 22

The housemaid's folding back her window-shutters at eight o'clock the next day was the sound which first roused Catherine; and she opened her eyes, wondering that they could ever have been closed, on objects of cheerfulness; her fire was already burning, and a bright morning had succeeded the tempest of the night. Instantaneously, with the consciousness of existence, returned her recollection of the manuscript; and springing from the bed in the very moment of the maid's going away, she eagerly collected every scattered sheet which had burst from the roll on its falling to the ground, and flew back to enjoy the luxury of their perusal on her pillow. She now plainly saw that she must not expect a manuscript of equal length with the generality of what she had shuddered over in books, for the roll, seeming to consist entirely of small disjointed sheets, was altogether but of trifling size, and much less than she had supposed it to be at first.

Her greedy eye glanced rapidly over a page. She started at its import. Could it be possible, or did not her senses play her false? An inventory of linen, in coarse and modern characters, seemed all that was before her! If the evidence of sight might be trusted, she held a washing-bill in her hand. She seized another sheet, and saw the same articles with little variation; a third, a fourth, and a fifth presented nothing new. Shirts, stockings, cravats, and waistcoats faced her in each. Two others, penned by the same hand, marked an expenditure scarcely more interesting, in letters, hair-powder, shoe-string, and breeches-ball. And the larger sheet, which had enclosed the rest, seemed by its first cramp line, "To poultice chestnut mare"—a farrier's bill! Such was the collection of papers (left perhaps, as she could then suppose, by the negligence of a servant in the place whence she had taken them) which had filled her with expectation and alarm, and robbed her of half her night's rest! She felt humbled to the dust. Could not the adventure of the chest have taught her wisdom? A corner of it, catching her eye as she lay, seemed to rise up in judgment against her. Nothing could now be clearer than the absurdity of her recent fancies. To suppose that a manuscript of many generations back could have remained undiscovered in a room such as that, so modern, so habitable!—Or that she should be the first to possess the skill of unlocking a cabinet, the key of which was open to all!

How could she have so imposed on herself? Heaven forbid that Henry Tilney should ever know her folly! And it was in a great measure his own doing, for had not the cabinet appeared so exactly to agree with his description of her adventures, she should never have felt the smallest curiosity about it. This was the only comfort that occurred. Impatient to get rid of those hateful evidences of her folly, those detestable papers then scattered over the bed, she rose directly, and folding them up as nearly as possible in the same shape as before, returned them to the same spot within the cabinet, with a very hearty wish that no untoward accident might ever bring them forward again, to disgrace her even with herself.

Why the locks should have been so difficult to open, however, was still something remarkable, for she could now manage them with perfect ease. In this there was surely something mysterious, and she indulged in the flattering suggestion for half a minute, till the possibility of the door's having been at first unlocked, and of being herself its fastener, darted into her head, and cost her another blush.

She got away as soon as she could from a room in which her conduct produced such unpleasant reflections, and found her way with all speed to the breakfast-parlour, as it had been pointed out to her by Miss Tilney the evening before. Henry was alone in it; and his immediate hope of her having been undisturbed by the tempest, with an arch reference to the character of the building they inhabited, was rather distressing. For the world would she not have her weakness suspected, and yet, unequal to an absolute falsehood, was constrained to acknowledge that the wind had kept her awake a little. "But we have a charming morning after it," she added, desiring to get rid of the subject; "and storms and sleeplessness are nothing when they are over. What beautiful hyacinths! I have just learnt to love a hyacinth."

"And how might you learn? By accident or argument?"

"Your sister taught me; I cannot tell how. Mrs. Allen used to take pains, year after year, to make me like them; but I never could, till I saw them the other day in Milsom Street; I am naturally indifferent about flowers."

"But now you love a hyacinth. So much the better. You have gained a new source of enjoyment, and it is well to have as many holds upon happiness as possible. Besides, a taste for flowers is always desirable in your sex, as a means of getting you out of doors, and tempting you to more frequent exercise than you would otherwise take. And though the love of a hyacinth may be rather domestic, who can tell, the sentiment once raised, but you may in time come to love a rose?"

"But I do not want any such pursuit to get me out of doors. The pleasure of walking and breathing fresh air is enough for me, and in fine weather I am out more than half my time. Mamma says I am never within."

"At any rate, however, I am pleased that you have learnt to love a hyacinth. The mere habit of learning to love is the thing; and a teachableness of disposition in a young lady is a great blessing. Has my sister a pleasant mode of instruction?"

Catherine was saved the embarrassment of attempting an answer by the entrance of the general, whose smiling compliments announced a happy state of mind, but whose gentle hint of sympathetic early rising did not advance her composure.

The elegance of the breakfast set forced itself on Catherine's notice when they were seated at table; and, luckily, it had been the General's choice. He was enchanted by her approbation of his taste, confessed it to be neat and simple, thought it right to encourage the manufacture of his country; and for his part, to his uncritical palate, the tea was as well flavoured from the clay of Staffordshire, as from that of Dresden or Sêve. But this was quite an old set, purchased two years ago. The manufacture was much improved since that time; he had seen some beautiful specimens when last in town, and had he not been perfectly without vanity of that kind, might have been tempted to order a new set. He trusted, however, that an opportunity might ere long occur of selecting one—though not for himself. Catherine was probably the only one of the party who did not understand him.

Shortly after breakfast Henry left them for Woodston, where business required and would keep him two or three days. They all attended in the hall to see him mount his horse, and immediately on re-entering the breakfast-room, Catherine walked to a window in the hope of catching another glimpse of his figure. "This is a somewhat heavy call upon your brother's fortitude," observed the general to Eleanor. "Woodston will make but a sombre appearance to-day."

"Is it a pretty place?" asked Catherine.

"What say you, Eleanor? Speak your opinion, for ladies can best tell the taste of ladies in regard to places as well as men. I think it would be acknowledged by the most impartial eye to have many recommendations. The house stands among fine meadows facing the south-east, with an excellent kitchen-garden in the same aspect; the walls surrounding which I built and stocked myself about ten years ago, for the benefit of my son. It is a family living, Miss Morland; and the property in the place being chiefly my own, you may believe I take care that it shall not be a bad one. Did Henry's income depend solely on this living, he would not be ill-provided for. Perhaps it may seem odd, that with only two younger children, I should think any profession necessary for him; and certainly there are moments when we could all wish him disengaged from every tie of business. But though I may not exactly make converts of you young ladies, I am sure your father, Miss Morland, would agree with me in thinking it expedient to give every young man some employment. The money is nothing, it is not an object, but employment is the thing. Even Frederick, my eldest son, you see, who will perhaps inherit as considerable a landed property as any private man in the county, has his profession."

The imposing effect of this last argument was equal to his wishes. The silence of the lady proved it to be unanswerable.

Something had been said the evening before of her being shown over the house, and he now offered himself as her conductor; and though Catherine had hoped to explore it accompanied only by his daughter, it was a proposal of too much happiness in itself, under any circumstances, not to be gladly accepted; for she had been already eighteen hours in the abbey, and had seen only a few of its rooms. The netting-box, just leisurely drawn forth, was closed with joyful haste, and she was ready to attend him in a moment. "And when they had gone over the house, he promised himself moreover the pleasure of accompanying her into the shrubberies and garden." She curtsied her acquiescence. "But perhaps it might be more agreeable to her to make those her first object. The weather was at present favourable, and at this time of year the uncertainty was very great of its continuing so. Which would she prefer? He was equally at her service. Which did his daughter think would most accord with her fair friend's wishes? But he thought he could discern. Yes, he certainly read in Miss Morland's eyes a judicious desire of making use of the present smiling weather. But when did she judge amiss? The abbey would be always safe and dry. He yielded implicitly, and would fetch his hat and attend them in a moment." He left the room, and Catherine, with a disappointed, anxious face, began to speak of her unwillingness that he should be taking them out of doors against his own inclination, under a mistaken idea of pleasing her; but she was stopped by Miss Tilney's saying, with a little confusion, "I believe it will be wisest to take the morning while it is so fine; and do not be uneasy on my father's account; he always walks out at this time of day."

Catherine did not exactly know how this was to be understood. Why was Miss Tilney embarrassed? Could there be any unwillingness on the General's side to show her over the abbey? The proposal was his own. And was not it odd that he should always take his walk so early? Neither her father nor Mr. Allen did so. It was certainly very provoking. She was all impatience to see the house, and had scarcely any curiosity about the grounds. If Henry had been with them indeed! But now she should not know what was picturesque when she saw it. Such were her thoughts, but she kept them to herself, and put on her bonnet in patient discontent.

She was struck, however, beyond her expectation, by the grandeur of the abbey, as she saw it for the first time from the lawn. The whole building enclosed a large court; and two sides of the quadrangle, rich in Gothic ornaments, stood forward for admiration. The remainder was shut off by knolls of old trees, or luxuriant plantations, and the steep woody hills rising behind, to give it shelter, were beautiful even in the leafless month of March. Catherine had seen nothing to compare with it; and her feelings of delight were so strong, that without waiting for any better authority, she boldly burst forth in wonder and praise. The general listened with assenting gratitude; and it seemed as if his own estimation of Northanger had waited unfixed till that hour.

The kitchen-garden was to be next admired, and he led the way to it across a small portion of the park.

The number of acres contained in this garden was such as Catherine could not listen to without dismay, being more than double the extent of all Mr. Allen's, as well as her father's, including church-yard and orchard. The walls seemed countless in number, endless in length; a village of hot-houses seemed to arise among them, and a whole parish to be at work within the enclosure. The general was flattered by her looks of surprise, which told him almost as plainly, as he soon forced her to tell him in words, that she had never seen any gardens at all equal to them before; and he then modestly owned that, "without any ambition of that sort himself—without any solicitude about it—he did believe them to be unrivalled in the kingdom. If he had a hobby-horse, it was that. He loved a garden. Though careless enough in most matters of eating, he loved good fruit—or if he did not, his friends and children did. There were great vexations, however, attending such a garden as his. The utmost care could not always secure the most valuable fruits. The pinery had yielded only one hundred in the last year. Mr. Allen, he supposed, must feel these inconveniences as well as himself."

"No, not at all. Mr. Allen did not care about the garden, and never went into it."

With a triumphant smile of self-satisfaction, the general wished he could do the same, for he never entered his, without being vexed in some way or other, by its falling short of his plan.

"How were Mr. Allen's succession-houses worked?" describing the nature of his own as they entered them.

"Mr. Allen had only one small hot-house, which Mrs. Allen had the use of for her plants in winter, and there was a fire in it now and then."

"He is a happy man!" said the general, with a look of very happy contempt.

Having taken her into every division, and led her under every wall, till she was heartily weary of seeing and wondering, he suffered the girls at last to seize the advantage of an outer door, and then expressing his wish to examine the effect of some recent alterations about the tea-house, proposed it as no unpleasant extension of their walk, if Miss Morland were not tired. "But where are you going, Eleanor? Why do you choose that cold, damp path to it? Miss Morland will get wet. Our best way is across the park."

"This is so favourite a walk of mine," said Miss Tilney, "that I always think it the best and nearest way. But perhaps it may be damp."

It was a narrow winding path through a thick grove of old Scotch firs; and Catherine, struck by its gloomy aspect, and eager to enter it, could not, even by the General's disapprobation, be kept from stepping forward. He perceived her inclination, and having again urged the plea of health in vain, was too polite to make further opposition. He excused himself, however, from attending them: "The rays of the sun were not too cheerful for him, and he would meet them by another course." He turned away; and Catherine was shocked to find how much her spirits were relieved by the separation. The shock, however, being less real than the relief, offered it no injury; and she began to talk with easy gaiety of the delightful melancholy which such a grove inspired.

"I am particularly fond of this spot," said her companion, with a sigh. "It was my mother's favourite walk."

Catherine had never heard Mrs. Tilney mentioned in the family before, and the interest excited by this tender remembrance showed itself directly in her altered countenance, and in the attentive pause with which she waited for something more.

"I used to walk here so often with her!" added Eleanor; "though I never loved it then, as I have loved it since. At that time indeed I used to wonder at her choice. But her memory endears it now."

"And ought it not," reflected Catherine, "to endear it to her husband? Yet the general would not enter it." Miss Tilney continuing silent, she ventured to say, "Her death must have been a great affliction!"

"A great and increasing one," replied the other, in a low voice. "I was only thirteen when it happened; and though I felt my loss perhaps as strongly as one so young could feel it, I did not, I could not, then know what a loss it was." She stopped for a moment, and then added, with great firmness, "I have no sister, you know—and though Henry—though my brothers are very affectionate, and Henry is a great deal here, which I am most thankful for, it is impossible for me not to be often solitary."

"To be sure you must miss him very much."

"A mother would have been always present. A mother would have been a constant friend; her influence would have been beyond all other."

"Was she a very charming woman? Was she handsome? Was there any picture of her in the abbey? And why had she been so partial to that grove? Was it from dejection of spirits?"—were questions now eagerly poured forth; the first three received a ready affirmative, the two others were passed by; and Catherine's interest in the deceased Mrs. Tilney augmented with every question, whether answered or not. Of her unhappiness in marriage, she felt persuaded. The general certainly had been an unkind husband. He did not love her walk: could he therefore have loved her? And besides, handsome as he was, there was a something in the turn of his features which spoke his not having behaved well to her.

"Her picture, I suppose," blushing at the consummate art of her own question, "hangs in your father's room?"

"No; it was intended for the drawing-room; but my father was dissatisfied with the painting, and for some time it had no place. Soon after her death I obtained it for my own, and hung it in my bed-chamber—where I shall be happy to show it you; it is very like." Here was another proof. A portrait—very like—of a departed wife, not valued by the husband! He must have been dreadfully cruel to her!

Catherine attempted no longer to hide from herself the nature of the feelings which, in spite of all his attentions, he had previously excited; and what had been terror and dislike before, was now absolute aversion. Yes, aversion! His cruelty to such a charming woman made him odious to her. She had often read of such characters, characters which Mr. Allen had been used to call unnatural and overdrawn; but here was proof positive of the contrary.

She had just settled this point when the end of the path brought them directly upon the general; and in spite of all her virtuous indignation, she found herself again obliged to walk with him, listen to him, and even to smile when he smiled. Being no longer able, however, to receive pleasure from the surrounding objects, she soon began to walk with lassitude; the general perceived it, and with a concern for her health, which seemed to reproach her for her opinion of him, was most urgent for returning with his daughter to the house. He would follow them in a quarter of an hour. Again they parted—but Eleanor was called back in half a minute to receive a strict charge against taking her friend round the abbey till his return. This second instance of his anxiety to delay what she so much wished for struck Catherine as very remarkable.

CHAPTER 23

An hour passed away before the general came in, spent, on the part of his young guest, in no very favourable consideration of his character. "This lengthened absence, these solitary rambles, did not speak a mind at ease, or a conscience void of reproach." At length he appeared; and, whatever might have been the gloom of his meditations, he could still smile with them. Miss Tilney, understanding in part her friend's curiosity to see the house, soon revived the subject; and her father being, contrary to Catherine's expectations, unprovided with any pretence for further delay, beyond that of stopping five minutes to order refreshments to be in the room by their return, was at last ready to escort them.

They set forward; and, with a grandeur of air, a dignified step, which caught the eye, but could not shake the doubts of the well-read Catherine, he led the way across the hall, through the common drawing-room and one useless antechamber, into a room magnificent both in size and furniture—the real drawing-room, used only with company of consequence. It was very noble—very grand—very charming!—was all that Catherine had to say, for her indiscriminating eye scarcely discerned the colour of the satin; and all minuteness of praise, all praise that had much meaning, was supplied by the general: the costliness or elegance of any room's fitting-up could be nothing to her; she cared for no furniture of a more modern date than the fifteenth century. When the general had satisfied his own curiosity, in a close examination of every well-known ornament, they proceeded into the library, an apartment, in its way, of equal magnificence, exhibiting a collection of books, on which an humble man might have looked with pride. Catherine heard, admired, and wondered with more genuine feeling than before—gathered all that she could from this storehouse of knowledge, by running over the titles of half a shelf, and was ready to proceed. But suites of apartments did not spring up with her wishes. Large as was the building, she had already visited the greatest part; though, on being told that, with the addition of the kitchen, the six or seven rooms she had now seen surrounded three sides of the court, she could scarcely believe it, or overcome the suspicion of there being many chambers secreted. It was some relief, however, that they were to return to the rooms in common use, by passing through a few of less importance, looking into the court, which, with occasional passages, not wholly unintricate, connected the different sides; and she was further soothed in her progress by being told that she was treading what had once been a cloister, having traces of cells pointed out, and observing several doors that were neither opened nor explained to her—by finding herself successively in a billiard-room, and in the General's private apartment, without comprehending their connection, or being able to turn aright when she left them; and lastly, by passing through a dark little room, owning Henry's authority, and strewed with his litter of books, guns, and greatcoats.

From the dining-room, of which, though already seen, and always to be seen at five o'clock, the general could not forgo the pleasure of pacing out the length, for the more certain information of Miss Morland, as to what she neither doubted nor cared for, they proceeded by quick communication to the kitchen—the ancient kitchen of the convent, rich in the massy walls and smoke of former days, and in the stoves and hot closets of the present. The General's improving hand had not loitered here: every modern invention to facilitate the labour of the cooks had been adopted within this, their spacious theatre; and, when the genius of others had failed, his own had often produced the perfection wanted. His endowments of this spot alone might at any time have placed him high among the benefactors of the convent.

With the walls of the kitchen ended all the antiquity of the abbey; the fourth side of the quadrangle having, on account of its decaying state, been removed by the General's father, and the present erected in its place. All that was venerable ceased here. The new building was not only new, but declared itself to be so; intended only for offices, and enclosed behind by stable-yards, no uniformity of architecture had been thought necessary. Catherine could have raved at the hand which had swept away what must have been beyond the value of all the rest, for the purposes of mere domestic economy; and would willingly have been spared the mortification of a walk through scenes so fallen, had the general allowed it; but if he had a vanity, it was in the arrangement of his offices; and as he was convinced that, to a mind like Miss Morland's, a view of the accommodations and comforts by which the labours of her inferiors were softened, must always be gratifying, he should make no apology for leading her on. They took a slight survey of all; and Catherine was impressed, beyond her expectation, by their multiplicity and their convenience. The purposes for which a few shapeless pantries and a comfortless scullery were deemed sufficient at Fullerton, were here carried on in appropriate divisions, commodious and roomy. The number of servants continually appearing did not strike her less than the number of their offices. Wherever they went, some pattened girl stopped to curtsy, or some footman in dishabille sneaked off. Yet this was an abbey! How inexpressibly different in these domestic arrangements from such as she had read about—from abbeys and castles, in which, though certainly larger than Northanger, all the dirty work of the house was to be done by two pair of female hands at the utmost. How they could get through it all had often amazed Mrs. Allen; and, when Catherine saw what was necessary here, she began to be amazed herself.

They returned to the hall, that the chief staircase might be ascended, and the beauty of its wood, and ornaments of rich carving might be pointed out: having gained the top, they turned in an opposite direction from the gallery in which her room lay, and shortly entered one on the same plan, but superior in length and breadth. She was here shown successively into three large bed-chambers, with their dressing-rooms, most completely and handsomely fitted up; everything that money and taste could do, to give comfort and elegance to apartments, had been bestowed on these; and, being furnished within the last five years, they were perfect in all that would be generally pleasing, and wanting in all that could give pleasure to Catherine. As they were surveying the last, the general, after slightly naming a few of the distinguished characters by whom they had at times been honoured, turned with a smiling countenance to Catherine, and ventured to hope that henceforward some of their earliest tenants might be "our friends from Fullerton." She felt the unexpected compliment, and deeply regretted the impossibility of thinking well of a man so kindly disposed towards herself, and so full of civility to all her family.

The gallery was terminated by folding doors, which Miss Tilney, advancing, had thrown open, and passed through, and seemed on the point of doing the same by the first door to the left, in another long reach of gallery, when the general, coming forwards, called her hastily, and, as Catherine thought, rather angrily back, demanding whither she were going?—And what was there more to be seen?—Had not Miss Morland already seen all that could be worth her notice?—And did she not suppose her friend might be glad of some refreshment after so much exercise? Miss Tilney drew back directly, and the heavy doors were closed upon the mortified Catherine, who, having seen, in a momentary glance beyond them, a narrower passage, more numerous openings, and symptoms of a winding staircase, believed herself at last within the reach of something worth her notice; and felt, as she unwillingly paced back the gallery, that she would rather be allowed to examine that end of the house than see all the finery of all the rest. The General's evident desire of preventing such an examination was an additional stimulant. Something was certainly to be concealed; her fancy, though it had trespassed lately once or twice, could not mislead her here; and what that something was, a short sentence of Miss Tilney's, as they followed the general at some distance downstairs, seemed to point out: "I was going to take you into what was my mother's room—the room in which she died—" were all her words; but few as they were, they conveyed pages of intelligence to Catherine. It was no wonder that the general should shrink from the sight of such objects as that room must contain; a room in all probability never entered by him since the dreadful scene had passed, which released his suffering wife, and left him to the stings of conscience.

She ventured, when next alone with Eleanor, to express her wish of being permitted to see it, as well as all the rest of that side of the house; and Eleanor promised to attend her there, whenever they should have a convenient hour. Catherine understood her: the general must be watched from home, before that room could be entered. "It remains as it was, I suppose?" said she, in a tone of feeling.

"Yes, entirely."

"And how long ago may it be that your mother died?"

"She has been dead these nine years." And nine years, Catherine knew, was a trifle of time, compared with what generally elapsed after the death of an injured wife, before her room was put to rights.

"You were with her, I suppose, to the last?"

"No," said Miss Tilney, sighing; "I was unfortunately from home. Her illness was sudden and short; and, before I arrived it was all over."

Catherine's blood ran cold with the horrid suggestions which naturally sprang from these words. Could it be possible? Could Henry's father—? And yet how many were the examples to justify even the blackest suspicions! And, when she saw him in the evening, while she worked with her friend, slowly pacing the drawing-room for an hour together in silent thoughtfulness, with downcast eyes and contracted brow, she felt secure from all possibility of wronging him. It was the air and attitude of a Montoni! What could more plainly speak the gloomy workings of a mind not wholly dead to every sense of humanity, in its fearful review of past scenes of guilt? Unhappy man! And the anxiousness of her spirits directed her eyes towards his figure so repeatedly, as to catch Miss Tilney's notice. "My father," she whispered, "often walks about the room in this way; it is nothing unusual."

"So much the worse!" thought Catherine; such ill-timed exercise was of a piece with the strange unseasonableness of his morning walks, and boded nothing good.

After an evening, the little variety and seeming length of which made her peculiarly sensible of Henry's importance among them, she was heartily glad to be dismissed; though it was a look from the general not designed for her observation which sent his daughter to the bell. When the butler would have lit his master's candle, however, he was forbidden. The latter was not going to retire. "I have many pamphlets to finish," said he to Catherine, "before I can close my eyes, and perhaps may be poring over the affairs of the nation for hours after you are asleep. Can either of us be more meetly employed? My eyes will be blinding for the good of others, and yours preparing by rest for future mischief."

But neither the business alleged, nor the magnificent compliment, could win Catherine from thinking that some very different object must occasion so serious a delay of proper repose. To be kept up for hours, after the family were in bed, by stupid pamphlets was not very likely. There must be some deeper cause: something was to be done which could be done only while the household slept; and the probability that Mrs. Tilney yet lived, shut up for causes unknown, and receiving from the pitiless hands of her husband a nightly supply of coarse food, was the conclusion which necessarily followed. Shocking as was the idea, it was at least better than a death unfairly hastened, as, in the natural course of things, she must ere long be released. The suddenness of her reputed illness, the absence of her daughter, and probably of her other children, at the time—all favoured the supposition of her imprisonment. Its origin—jealousy perhaps, or wanton cruelty—was yet to be unravelled.

In revolving these matters, while she undressed, it suddenly struck her as not unlikely that she might that morning have passed near the very spot of this unfortunate woman's confinement—might have been within a few paces of the cell in which she languished out her days; for what part of the abbey could be more fitted for the purpose than that which yet bore the traces of monastic division? In the high-arched passage, paved with stone, which already she had trodden with peculiar awe, she well remembered the doors of which the general had given no account. To what might not those doors lead? In support of the plausibility of this conjecture, it further occurred to her that the forbidden gallery, in which lay the apartments of the unfortunate Mrs. Tilney, must be, as certainly as her memory could guide her, exactly over this suspected range of cells, and the staircase by the side of those apartments of which she had caught a transient glimpse, communicating by some secret means with those cells, might well have favoured the barbarous proceedings of her husband. Down that staircase she had perhaps been conveyed in a state of well-prepared insensibility!

Catherine sometimes started at the boldness of her own surmises, and sometimes hoped or feared that she had gone too far; but they were supported by such appearances as made their dismissal impossible.

The side of the quadrangle, in which she supposed the guilty scene to be acting, being, according to her belief, just opposite her own, it struck her that, if judiciously watched, some rays of light from the General's lamp might glimmer through the lower windows, as he passed to the prison of his wife; and, twice before she stepped into bed, she stole gently from her room to the corresponding window in the gallery, to see if it appeared; but all abroad was dark, and it must yet be too early. The various ascending noises convinced her that the servants must still be up. Till midnight, she supposed it would be in vain to watch; but then, when the clock had struck twelve, and all was quiet, she would, if not quite appalled by darkness, steal out and look once more. The clock struck twelve—and Catherine had been half an hour asleep.

CHAPTER 24

The next day afforded no opportunity for the proposed examination of the mysterious apartments. It was Sunday, and the whole time between morning and afternoon service was required by the general in exercise abroad or eating cold meat at home; and great as was Catherine's curiosity, her courage was not equal to a wish of exploring them after dinner, either by the fading light of the sky between six and seven o'clock, or by the yet more partial though stronger illumination of a treacherous lamp. The day was unmarked therefore by anything to interest her imagination beyond the sight of a very elegant monument to the memory of Mrs. Tilney, which immediately fronted the family pew. By that her eye was instantly caught and long retained; and the perusal of the highly strained epitaph, in which every virtue was ascribed to her by the inconsolable husband, who must have been in some way or other her destroyer, affected her even to tears.

That the general, having erected such a monument, should be able to face it, was not perhaps very strange, and yet that he could sit so boldly collected within its view, maintain so elevated an air, look so fearlessly around, nay, that he should even enter the church, seemed wonderful to Catherine. Not, however, that many instances of beings equally hardened in guilt might not be produced. She could remember dozens who had persevered in every possible vice, going on from crime to crime, murdering whomsoever they chose, without any feeling of humanity or remorse; till a violent death or a religious retirement closed their black career. The erection of the monument itself could not in the smallest degree affect her doubts of Mrs. Tilney's actual decease. Were she even to descend into the family vault where her ashes were supposed to slumber, were she to behold the coffin in which they were said to be enclosed—what could it avail in such a case? Catherine had read too much not to be perfectly aware of the ease with which a waxen figure might be introduced, and a supposititious funeral carried on.

The succeeding morning promised something better. The General's early walk, ill-timed as it was in every other view, was favourable here; and when she knew him to be out of the house, she directly proposed to Miss Tilney the accomplishment of her promise. Eleanor was ready to oblige her; and Catherine reminding her as they went of another promise, their first visit in consequence was to the portrait in her bed-chamber. It represented a very lovely woman, with a mild and pensive countenance, justifying, so far, the expectations of its new observer; but they were not in every respect answered, for Catherine had depended upon meeting with features, hair, complexion, that should be the very counterpart, the very image, if not of Henry's, of Eleanor's—the only portraits of which she had been in the habit of thinking, bearing always an equal resemblance of mother and child. A face once taken was taken for generations. But here she was obliged to look and consider and study for a likeness. She contemplated it, however, in spite of this drawback, with much emotion, and, but for a yet stronger interest, would have left it unwillingly.

Her agitation as they entered the great gallery was too much for any endeavour at discourse; she could only look at her companion. Eleanor's countenance was dejected, yet sedate; and its composure spoke her inured to all the gloomy objects to which they were advancing. Again she passed through the folding doors, again her hand was upon the important lock, and Catherine, hardly able to breathe, was turning to close the former with fearful caution, when the figure, the dreaded figure of the general himself at the further end of the gallery, stood before her! The name of "Eleanor" at the same moment, in his loudest tone, resounded through the building, giving to his daughter the first intimation of his presence, and to Catherine terror upon terror. An attempt at concealment had been her first instinctive movement on perceiving him, yet she could scarcely hope to have escaped his eye; and when her friend, who with an apologizing look darted hastily by her, had joined and disappeared with him, she ran for safety to her own room, and, locking herself in, believed that she should never have courage to go down again. She remained there at least an hour, in the greatest agitation, deeply commiserating the state of her poor friend, and expecting a summons herself from the angry general to attend him in his own apartment. No summons, however, arrived; and at last, on seeing a carriage drive up to the abbey, she was emboldened to descend and meet him under the protection of visitors. The breakfast-room was gay with company; and she was named to them by the general as the friend of his daughter, in a complimentary style, which so well concealed his resentful ire, as to make her feel secure at least of life for the present. And Eleanor, with a command of countenance which did honour to her concern for his character, taking an early occasion of saying to her, "My father only wanted me to answer a note," she began to hope that she had either been unseen by the general, or that from some consideration of policy she should be allowed to suppose herself so. Upon this trust she dared still to remain in his presence, after the company left them, and nothing occurred to disturb it.

In the course of this morning's reflections, she came to a resolution of making her next attempt on the forbidden door alone. It would be much better in every respect that Eleanor should know nothing of the matter. To involve her in the danger of a second detection, to court her into an apartment which must wring her heart, could not be the office of a friend. The General's utmost anger could not be to herself what it might be to a daughter; and, besides, she thought the examination itself would be more satisfactory if made without any companion. It would be impossible to explain to Eleanor the suspicions, from which the other had, in all likelihood, been hitherto happily exempt; nor could she therefore, in her presence, search for those proofs of the General's cruelty, which however they might yet have escaped discovery, she felt confident of somewhere drawing forth, in the shape of some fragmented journal, continued to the last gasp. Of the way to the apartment she was now perfectly mistress; and as she wished to get it over before Henry's return, who was expected on the morrow, there was no time to be lost. The day was bright, her courage high; at four o'clock, the sun was now two hours above the horizon, and it would be only her retiring to dress half an hour earlier than usual.

It was done; and Catherine found herself alone in the gallery before the clocks had ceased to strike. It was no time for thought; she hurried on, slipped with the least possible noise through the folding doors, and without stopping to look or breathe, rushed forward to the one in question. The lock yielded to her hand, and, luckily, with no sullen sound that could alarm a human being. On tiptoe she entered; the room was before her; but it was some minutes before she could advance another step. She beheld what fixed her to the spot and agitated every feature. She saw a large, well-proportioned apartment, an handsome dimity bed, arranged as unoccupied with an housemaid's care, a bright Bath stove, mahogany wardrobes, and neatly painted chairs, on which the warm beams of a western sun gaily poured through two sash windows! Catherine had expected to have her feelings worked, and worked they were. Astonishment and doubt first seized them; and a shortly succeeding ray of common sense added some bitter emotions of shame. She could not be mistaken as to the room; but how grossly mistaken in everything else!—in Miss Tilney's meaning, in her own calculation! This apartment, to which she had given a date so ancient, a position so awful, proved to be one end of what the General's father had built. There were two other doors in the chamber, leading probably into dressing-closets; but she had no inclination to open either. Would the veil in which Mrs. Tilney had last walked, or the volume in which she had last read, remain to tell what nothing else was allowed to whisper? No: whatever might have been the General's crimes, he had certainly too much wit to let them sue for detection. She was sick of exploring, and desired but to be safe in her own room, with her own heart only privy to its folly; and she was on the point of retreating as softly as she had entered, when the sound of footsteps, she could hardly tell where, made her pause and tremble. To be found there, even by a servant, would be unpleasant; but by the general (and he seemed always at hand when least wanted), much worse! She listened—the sound had ceased; and resolving not to lose a moment, she passed through and closed the door. At that instant a door underneath was hastily opened; someone seemed with swift steps to ascend the stairs, by the head of which she had yet to pass before she could gain the gallery. She had no power to move. With a feeling of terror not very definable, she fixed her eyes on the staircase, and in a few moments it gave Henry to her view. "Mr. Tilney!" she exclaimed in a voice of more than common astonishment. He looked astonished too. "Good God!" she continued, not attending to his address. "How came you here? How came you up that staircase?"

"How came I up that staircase!" he replied, greatly surprised. "Because it is my nearest way from the stable-yard to my own chamber; and why should I not come up it?"

Catherine recollected herself, blushed deeply, and could say no more. He seemed to be looking in her countenance for that explanation which her lips did not afford. She moved on towards the gallery. "And may I not, in my turn," said he, as he pushed back the folding doors, "ask how you came here? This passage is at least as extraordinary a road from the breakfast-parlour to your apartment, as that staircase can be from the stables to mine."

"I have been," said Catherine, looking down, "to see your mother's room."

"My mother's room! Is there anything extraordinary to be seen there?"

"No, nothing at all. I thought you did not mean to come back till to-morrow."

"I did not expect to be able to return sooner, when I went away; but three hours ago I had the pleasure of finding nothing to detain me. You look pale. I am afraid I alarmed you by running so fast up those stairs. Perhaps you did not know—you were not aware of their leading from the offices in common use?"

"No, I was not. You have had a very fine day for your ride."

"Very; and does Eleanor leave you to find your way into all the rooms in the house by yourself?"

"Oh no! she showed me over the greatest part on Saturday—and we were coming here to these rooms—but only," dropping her voice, "your father was with us."

"And that prevented you," said Henry, earnestly regarding her. "Have you looked into all the rooms in that passage?"

"No, I only wanted to see—Is not it very late? I must go and dress."

"It is only a quarter past four," showing his watch; "and you are not now in Bath. No theatre, no rooms to prepare for. Half an hour at Northanger must be enough."

She could not contradict it, and therefore suffered herself to be detained, though her dread of further questions made her, for the first time in their acquaintance, wish to leave him. They walked slowly up the gallery. "Have you had any letter from Bath since I saw you?"

"No, and I am very much surprised. Isabella promised so faithfully to write directly."

"Promised so faithfully! A faithful promise! That puzzles me. I have heard of a faithful performance. But a faithful promise—the fidelity of promising! It is a power little worth knowing, however, since it can deceive and pain you. My mother's room is very commodious, is it not? Large and cheerful-looking, and the dressing-closets so well disposed! It always strikes me as the most comfortable apartment in the house, and I rather wonder that Eleanor should not take it for her own. She sent you to look at it, I suppose?"

"No."

"It has been your own doing entirely?" Catherine said nothing. After a short silence, during which he had closely observed her, he added, "As there is nothing in the room in itself to raise curiosity, this must have proceeded from a sentiment of respect for my mother's character, as described by

Eleanor, which does honour to her memory. The world, I believe, never saw a better woman. But it is not often that virtue can boast an interest such as this. The domestic, unpretending merits of a person never known do not often create that kind of fervent, venerating tenderness which would prompt a visit like yours. Eleanor, I suppose, has talked of her a great deal?"

"Yes, a great deal. That is—no, not much, but what she did say was very interesting. Her dying so suddenly" (slowly, and with hesitation it was spoken), "and you—none of you being at home—and your father, I thought—perhaps had not been very fond of her."

"And from these circumstances," he replied (his quick eye fixed on hers), "you infer perhaps the probability of some negligence—some"—(involuntarily she shook her head)—"or it may be—of something still less pardonable." She raised her eyes towards him more fully than she had ever done before. "My mother's illness," he continued, "the seizure which ended in her death, was sudden. The malady itself, one from which she had often suffered, a bilious fever—its cause therefore constitutional. On the third day, in short, as soon as she could be prevailed on, a physician attended her, a very respectable man, and one in whom she had always placed great confidence. Upon his opinion of her danger, two others were called in the next day, and remained in almost constant attendance for four and twenty hours. On the fifth day she died. During the progress of her disorder, Frederick and I (we were both at home) saw her repeatedly; and from our own observation can bear witness to her having received every possible attention which could spring from the affection of those about her, or which her situation in life could command. Poor Eleanor was absent, and at such a distance as to return only to see her mother in her coffin."

"But your father," said Catherine, "was he afflicted?"

"For a time, greatly so. You have erred in supposing him not attached to her. He loved her, I am persuaded, as well as it was possible for him to—we have not all, you know, the same tenderness of disposition—and I will not pretend to say that while she lived, she might not often have had much to bear, but though his temper injured her, his judgment never did. His value of her was sincere; and, if not permanently, he was truly afflicted by her death."

"I am very glad of it," said Catherine; "it would have been very shocking!"

"If I understand you rightly, you had formed a surmise of such horror as I have hardly words to—Dear Miss Morland, consider the dreadful nature of the suspicions you have entertained. What have you been judging from? Remember the country and the age in which we live. Remember that we are English, that we are Christians. Consult your own understanding, your own sense of the probable, your own observation of what is passing around you. Does our education prepare us for such atrocities? Do our laws connive at them? Could they be perpetrated without being known, in a country like this, where social and literary intercourse is on such a footing, where every man is surrounded by a neighbourhood of voluntary spies, and where roads and newspapers lay everything open? Dearest Miss Morland, what ideas have you been admitting?"

They had reached the end of the gallery, and with tears of shame she ran off to her own room.

CHAPTER 25

The visions of romance were over. Catherine was completely awakened. Henry's address, short as it had been, had more thoroughly opened her eyes to the extravagance of her late fancies than all their several disappointments had done. Most grievously was she humbled. Most bitterly did she cry. It was not only with herself that she was sunk—but with Henry. Her folly, which now seemed even criminal, was all exposed to him, and he must despise her forever. The liberty which her imagination had dared to take with the character of his father—could he ever forgive it? The absurdity of her curiosity and her fears—could they ever be forgotten? She hated herself more than she could express. He had—she thought he had, once or twice before this fatal morning, shown something like affection for her. But now—in short, she made herself as miserable as possible for about half an hour, went down when the clock struck five, with a broken heart, and could scarcely give an intelligible answer to Eleanor's inquiry if she was well. The formidable Henry soon followed her into the room, and the only difference in his behaviour to her was that he paid her rather more attention than usual. Catherine had never wanted comfort more, and he looked as if he was aware of it.

The evening wore away with no abatement of this soothing politeness; and her spirits were gradually raised to a modest tranquillity. She did not learn either to forget or defend the past; but she learned to hope that it would never transpire farther, and that it might not cost her Henry's entire regard. Her thoughts being still chiefly fixed on what she had with such causeless terror felt and done, nothing could shortly be clearer than that it had been all a voluntary, self-created delusion, each trifling circumstance receiving importance from an imagination resolved on alarm, and everything forced to bend to one purpose by a mind which, before she entered the abbey, had been craving to be frightened. She remembered with what feelings she had prepared for a knowledge of Northanger. She saw that the infatuation had been created, the mischief settled, long before her quitting Bath, and it seemed as if the whole might be traced to the influence of that sort of reading which she had there indulged.

Charming as were all Mrs. Radcliffe's works, and charming even as were the works of all her imitators, it was not in them perhaps that human nature, at least in the Midland counties of England, was to be looked for. Of the Alps and Pyrenees, with their pine forests and their vices, they might give a faithful delineation; and Italy, Switzerland, and the south of France might be as fruitful in horrors as they were there represented. Catherine dared not doubt beyond her own country, and even of that, if hard pressed, would have yielded the northern and western extremities. But in the central part of England there was surely some security for the existence even of a wife not beloved, in the laws of the land, and the manners of the age. Murder was not tolerated, servants were not slaves, and neither poison nor sleeping potions to be procured, like rhubarb, from every druggist. Among the Alps and Pyrenees, perhaps, there were no mixed characters. There, such as were not as spotless as an angel might have the dispositions of a fiend. But in England it was not so; among the English, she believed, in their hearts and habits, there was a general though unequal mixture of good and bad. Upon this conviction, she would not be surprised if even in Henry and Eleanor Tilney, some slight imperfection might hereafter appear; and upon this conviction she need not fear to acknowledge some actual specks in the character of their father, who, though cleared from the grossly injurious suspicions which she must ever blush to have entertained, she did believe, upon serious consideration, to be not perfectly amiable.

Her mind made up on these several points, and her resolution formed, of always judging and acting in future with the greatest good sense, she had nothing to do but to forgive herself and be happier than ever; and the lenient hand of time did much for her by insensible gradations in the course of another day. Henry's astonishing generosity and nobleness of conduct, in never alluding in the slightest way to what had passed, was of the greatest assistance to her; and sooner than she could have supposed it possible in the beginning of her distress, her spirits became absolutely comfortable, and capable, as heretofore, of continual improvement by anything he said. There were still some subjects, indeed, under which she believed they must always tremble—the mention of a chest or a cabinet, for instance—and she did not love the sight of japan in any shape: but even she could allow that an occasional memento of past folly, however painful, might not be without use.

The anxieties of common life began soon to succeed to the alarms of romance. Her desire of hearing from Isabella grew every day greater. She was quite impatient to know how the Bath world went on, and how the rooms were attended; and especially was she anxious to be assured of Isabella's having matched some fine netting-cotton, on which she had left her intent; and of her continuing on the best terms with James. Her only dependence for information of any kind was on Isabella.

James had protested against writing to her till his return to Oxford; and Mrs. Allen had given her no hopes of a letter till she had got back to Fullerton. But Isabella had promised and promised again; and when she promised a thing, she was so scrupulous in performing it! This made it so particularly strange!

For nine successive mornings, Catherine wondered over the repetition of a disappointment, which each morning became more severe: but, on the tenth, when she entered the breakfast-room, her first object was a letter, held out by Henry's willing hand. She thanked him as heartily as if he had written it himself. "'Tis only from James, however," as she looked at the direction. She opened it; it was from Oxford; and to this purpose:

"Dear Catherine,

"Though, God knows, with little inclination for writing, I think it my duty to tell you that everything is at an end between Miss Thorpe and me. I left her and Bath yesterday, never to see either again. I shall not enter into particulars—they would only pain you more. You will soon hear enough from another quarter to know where lies the blame; and I hope will acquit your brother of everything but the folly of too easily thinking his affection returned. Thank God! I am undeceived in time! But it is a heavy blow! After my father's consent had been so kindly given—but no more of this. She has made me miserable forever! Let me soon hear from you, dear Catherine; you are my only friend; your love I do build upon. I wish your visit at Northanger may be over before Captain Tilney makes his engagement known, or you will be uncomfortably circumstanced. Poor Thorpe is in town: I dread the sight of him; his honest heart would feel so much. I have written to him and my father. Her duplicity hurts me more than all; till the very last, if I reasoned with her, she declared herself as much attached to me as ever, and laughed at my fears. I am ashamed to think how long I bore with it; but if ever man had reason to believe himself loved, I was that man. I cannot understand even now what she would be at, for there could be no need of my being played off to make her secure of Tilney. We parted at last by mutual consent—happy for me had we never met! I can never expect to know such another woman! Dearest Catherine, beware how you give your heart.

"Believe me," &c.

Catherine had not read three lines before her sudden change of countenance, and short exclamations of sorrowing wonder, declared her to be receiving unpleasant news; and Henry, earnestly watching her through the whole letter, saw plainly that it ended no better than it began. He was prevented, however, from even looking his surprise by his father's entrance. They went to breakfast directly; but Catherine could hardly eat anything. Tears filled her eyes, and even ran down her cheeks as she sat. The letter was one moment in her hand, then in her lap, and then in her pocket; and she looked as if she knew not what she did. The general, between his cocoa and his newspaper, had luckily no leisure for noticing her; but to the other two her distress was equally visible. As soon as she dared leave the table she hurried away to her own room; but the housemaids were busy in it, and she was obliged to come down again. She turned into the drawing-room for privacy, but Henry and Eleanor had likewise retreated thither, and were at that moment deep in consultation about her. She drew back, trying to beg their pardon, but was, with gentle violence, forced to return; and the others withdrew, after Eleanor had affectionately expressed a wish of being of use or comfort to her.

After half an hour's free indulgence of grief and reflection, Catherine felt equal to encountering her friends; but whether she should make her distress known to them was another consideration. Perhaps, if particularly questioned, she might just give an idea—just distantly hint at it—but not more. To expose a friend, such a friend as Isabella had been to her—and then their own brother so closely concerned in it! She believed she must waive the subject altogether. Henry and Eleanor were by themselves in the breakfast-room; and each, as she entered it, looked at her anxiously. Catherine took her place at the table, and, after a short silence, Eleanor said, "No bad news from Fullerton, I hope? Mr. and Mrs. Morland—your brothers and sisters—I hope they are none of them ill?"

"No, I thank you" (sighing as she spoke); "they are all very well. My letter was from my brother at Oxford."

Nothing further was said for a few minutes; and then speaking through her tears, she added, "I do not think I shall ever wish for a letter again!"

"I am sorry," said Henry, closing the book he had just opened; "if I had suspected the letter of containing anything unwelcome, I should have given it with very different feelings."

"It contained something worse than anybody could suppose! Poor James is so unhappy! You will soon know why."

"To have so kind-hearted, so affectionate a sister," replied Henry warmly, "must be a comfort to him under any distress."

"I have one favour to beg," said Catherine, shortly afterwards, in an agitated manner, "that, if your brother should be coming here, you will give me notice of it, that I may go away."

"Our brother! Frederick!"

"Yes; I am sure I should be very sorry to leave you so soon, but something has happened that would make it very dreadful for me to be in the same house with Captain Tilney."

Eleanor's work was suspended while she gazed with increasing astonishment; but Henry began to suspect the truth, and something, in which Miss Thorpe's name was included, passed his lips.

"How quick you are!" cried Catherine: "you have guessed it, I declare! And yet, when we talked about it in Bath, you little thought of its ending so. Isabella — no wonder now I have not heard from her — Isabella has deserted my brother, and is to marry yours! Could you have believed there had been such inconstancy and fickleness, and everything that is bad in the world?"

"I hope, so far as concerns my brother, you are misinformed. I hope he has not had any material share in bringing on Mr. Morland's disappointment. His marrying Miss Thorpe is not probable. I think you must be deceived so far. I am very sorry for Mr. Morland — sorry that anyone you love should be unhappy; but my surprise would be greater at Frederick's marrying her than at any other part of the story."

"It is very true, however; you shall read James's letter yourself. Stay — There is one part — " recollecting with a blush the last line.

"Will you take the trouble of reading to us the passages which concern my brother?"

"No, read it yourself," cried Catherine, whose second thoughts were clearer. "I do not know what I was thinking of" (blushing again that she had blushed before); "James only means to give me good advice."

He gladly received the letter, and, having read it through, with close attention, returned it saying, "Well, if it is to be so, I can only say that I am sorry for it. Frederick will not be the first man who has chosen a wife with less sense than his family expected. I do not envy his situation, either as a lover or a son."

Miss Tilney, at Catherine's invitation, now read the letter likewise, and, having expressed also her concern and surprise, began to inquire into Miss Thorpe's connections and fortune.

"Her mother is a very good sort of woman," was Catherine's answer.

"What was her father?"

"A lawyer, I believe. They live at Putney."

"Are they a wealthy family?"

"No, not very. I do not believe Isabella has any fortune at all: but that will not signify in your family. Your father is so very liberal! He told me the other day that he only valued money as it allowed him to promote the happiness of his children." The brother and sister looked at each other. "But," said Eleanor, after a short pause, "would it be to promote his happiness, to enable him to marry such a girl? She must be an unprincipled one, or she could not have used your brother so. And how strange an infatuation on Frederick's side! A girl who, before his eyes, is violating an engagement voluntarily entered into with another man! Is not it inconceivable, Henry? Frederick too, who always wore his heart so proudly! Who found no woman good enough to be loved!"

"That is the most unpromising circumstance, the strongest presumption against him. When I think of his past declarations, I give him up. Moreover, I have too good an opinion of Miss Thorpe's prudence to suppose that she would part with one gentleman before the other was secured. It is all over with Frederick indeed! He is a deceased man—defunct in understanding. Prepare for your sister-in-law, Eleanor, and such a sister-in-law as you must delight in! Open, candid, artless, guileless, with affections strong but simple, forming no pretensions, and knowing no disguise."

"Such a sister-in-law, Henry, I should delight in," said Eleanor with a smile.

"But perhaps," observed Catherine, "though she has behaved so ill by our family, she may behave better by yours. Now she has really got the man she likes, she may be constant."

"Indeed I am afraid she will," replied Henry; "I am afraid she will be very constant, unless a baronet should come in her way; that is Frederick's only chance. I will get the Bath paper, and look over the arrivals."

"You think it is all for ambition, then? And, upon my word, there are some things that seem very like it. I cannot forget that, when she first knew what my father would do for them, she seemed quite disappointed that it was not more. I never was so deceived in anyone's character in my life before."

"Among all the great variety that you have known and studied."

"My own disappointment and loss in her is very great; but, as for poor James, I suppose he will hardly ever recover it."

"Your brother is certainly very much to be pitied at present; but we must not, in our concern for his sufferings, undervalue yours. You feel, I suppose, that in losing Isabella, you lose half yourself: you feel a void in your heart which nothing else can occupy. Society is becoming irksome; and as for the amusements in which you were wont to share at Bath, the very idea of them without her is abhorrent. You would not, for instance, now go to a ball for the world. You feel that you have no longer any friend to whom you can speak with unreserve, on whose regard you can place dependence, or whose counsel, in any difficulty, you could rely on. You feel all this?"

"No," said Catherine, after a few moments' reflection, "I do not—ought I? To say the truth, though I am hurt and grieved, that I cannot still love her, that I am never to hear from her, perhaps never to see her again, I do not feel so very, very much afflicted as one would have thought."

"You feel, as you always do, what is most to the credit of human nature. Such feelings ought to be investigated, that they may know themselves."

Catherine, by some chance or other, found her spirits so very much relieved by this conversation that she could not regret her being led on, though so unaccountably, to mention the circumstance which had produced it.

CHAPTER 26

From this time, the subject was frequently canvassed by the three young people; and Catherine found, with some surprise, that her two young friends were perfectly agreed in considering Isabella's want of consequence and fortune as likely to throw great difficulties in the way of her marrying their brother. Their persuasion that the general would, upon this ground alone, independent of the objection that might be raised against her character, oppose the connection, turned her feelings moreover with some alarm towards herself. She was as insignificant, and perhaps as portionless, as Isabella; and if the heir of the Tilney property had not grandeur and wealth enough in himself, at what point of interest were the demands of his younger brother to rest? The very painful reflections to which this thought led could only be dispersed by a dependence on the effect of that particular partiality, which, as she was given to understand by his words as well as his actions, she had from the first been so fortunate as to excite in the general; and by a recollection of some most generous and disinterested sentiments on the subject of money, which she had more than once heard him utter, and which tempted her to think his disposition in such matters misunderstood by his children.

They were so fully convinced, however, that their brother would not have the courage to apply in person for his father's consent, and so repeatedly assured her that he had never in his life been less likely to come to Northanger than at the present time, that she suffered her mind to be at ease as to the necessity of any sudden removal of her own. But as it was not to be supposed that Captain Tilney, whenever he made his application, would give his father any just idea of Isabella's conduct, it occurred to her as highly expedient that Henry should lay the whole business before him as it really was, enabling the general by that means to form a cool and impartial opinion, and prepare his objections on a fairer ground than inequality of situations. She proposed it to him accordingly; but he did not catch at the measure so eagerly as she had expected. "No," said he, "my father's hands need not be strengthened, and Frederick's confession of folly need not be forestalled. He must tell his own story."

"But he will tell only half of it."

"A quarter would be enough."

A day or two passed away and brought no tidings of Captain Tilney. His brother and sister knew not what to think.

Sometimes it appeared to them as if his silence would be the natural result of the suspected engagement, and at others that it was wholly incompatible with it. The general, meanwhile, though offended every morning by Frederick's remissness in writing, was free from any real anxiety about him, and had no more pressing solicitude than that of making Miss Morland's time at Northanger pass pleasantly. He often expressed his uneasiness on this head, feared the sameness of every day's society and employments would disgust her with the place, wished the Lady Frasers had been in the country, talked every now and then of having a large party to dinner, and once or twice began even to calculate the number of young dancing people in the neighbourhood. But then it was such a dead time of year, no wild-fowl, no game, and the Lady Frasers were not in the country. And it all ended, at last, in his telling Henry one morning that when he next went to Woodston, they would take him by surprise there some day or other, and eat their mutton with him. Henry was greatly honoured and very happy, and Catherine was quite delighted with the scheme. "And when do you think, sir, I may look forward to this pleasure? I must be at Woodston on Monday to attend the parish meeting, and shall probably be obliged to stay two or three days."

"Well, well, we will take our chance some one of those days. There is no need to fix. You are not to put yourself at all out of your way. Whatever you may happen to have in the house will be enough. I think I can answer for the young ladies making allowance for a bachelor's table. Let me see; Monday will be a busy day with you, we will not come on Monday; and Tuesday will be a busy one with me. I expect my surveyor from Brockham with his report in the morning; and afterwards I cannot in decency fail attending the club. I really could not face my acquaintance if I stayed away now; for, as I am known to be in the country, it would be taken exceedingly amiss; and it is a rule with me, Miss Morland, never to give offence to any of my neighbours, if a small sacrifice of time and attention can prevent it. They are a set of very worthy men. They have half a buck from Northanger twice a year; and I dine with them whenever I can. Tuesday, therefore, we may say is out of the question. But on Wednesday, I think, Henry, you may expect us; and we shall be with you early, that we may have time to look about us. Two hours and three quarters will carry us to Woodston, I suppose; we shall be in the carriage by ten; so, about a quarter before one on Wednesday, you may look for us."

A ball itself could not have been more welcome to Catherine than this little excursion, so strong was her desire to be acquainted with Woodston; and her heart was still bounding with joy when Henry, about an hour afterwards, came booted and greatcoated into the room where she and Eleanor were sitting, and said, "I am come, young ladies, in a very moralizing strain, to observe that our pleasures in this world are always to be paid for, and that we often purchase them at a great disadvantage, giving ready-monied actual happiness for a draft on the future, that may not be honoured. Witness myself, at this present hour. Because I am to hope for the satisfaction of seeing you at Woodston on Wednesday, which bad weather, or twenty other causes, may prevent, I must go away directly, two days before I intended it."

"Go away!" said Catherine, with a very long face. "And why?"

"Why! How can you ask the question? Because no time is to be lost in frightening my old housekeeper out of her wits, because I must go and prepare a dinner for you, to be sure."

"Oh! Not seriously!"

"Aye, and sadly too—for I had much rather stay."

"But how can you think of such a thing, after what the general said? When he so particularly desired you not to give yourself any trouble, because anything would do."

Henry only smiled. "I am sure it is quite unnecessary upon your sister's account and mine. You must know it to be so; and the general made such a point of your providing nothing extraordinary: besides, if he had not said half so much as he did, he has always such an excellent dinner at home, that sitting down to a middling one for one day could not signify."

"I wish I could reason like you, for his sake and my own. Good-bye. As to-morrow is Sunday, Eleanor, I shall not return."

He went; and, it being at any time a much simpler operation to Catherine to doubt her own judgment than Henry's, she was very soon obliged to give him credit for being right, however disagreeable to her his going. But the inexplicability of the General's conduct dwelt much on her thoughts. That he was very particular in his eating, she had, by her own unassisted observation, already discovered; but why he should say one thing so positively, and mean another all the while, was most unaccountable! How were people, at that rate, to be understood? Who but Henry could have been aware of what his father was at?

From Saturday to Wednesday, however, they were now to be without Henry. This was the sad finale of every reflection: and Captain Tilney's letter would certainly come in his absence; and Wednesday she was very sure would be wet. The past, present, and future were all equally in gloom. Her brother so unhappy, and her loss in Isabella so great; and Eleanor's spirits always affected by Henry's absence! What was there to interest or amuse her? She was tired of the woods and the shrubberies—always so smooth and so dry; and the abbey in itself was no more to her now than any other house. The painful remembrance of the folly it had helped to nourish and perfect was the only emotion which could spring from a consideration of the building. What a revolution in her ideas! She, who had so longed to be in an abbey! Now, there was nothing so charming to her imagination as the unpretending comfort of a well-connected parsonage, something like Fullerton, but better: Fullerton had its faults, but Woodston probably had none. If Wednesday should ever come!

It did come, and exactly when it might be reasonably looked for. It came—it was fine—and Catherine trod on air. By ten o'clock, the chaise and four conveyed the trio from the abbey; and, after an agreeable drive of almost twenty miles, they entered Woodston, a large and populous village, in a situation not unpleasant. Catherine was ashamed to say how pretty she thought it, as the general seemed to think an apology necessary for the flatness of the country, and the size of the village; but in her heart she preferred it to any place she had ever been at, and looked with great admiration at every neat house above the rank of a cottage, and at all the little chandler's shops which they passed. At the further end of the village, and tolerably disengaged from the rest of it, stood the parsonage, a new-built substantial stone house, with its semicircular sweep and green gates; and, as they drove up to the door, Henry, with the friends of his solitude, a large Newfoundland puppy and two or three terriers, was ready to receive and make much of them.

Catherine's mind was too full, as she entered the house, for her either to observe or to say a great deal; and, till called on by the general for her opinion of it, she had very little idea of the room in which she was sitting. Upon looking round it then, she perceived in a moment that it was the most comfortable room in the world; but she was too guarded to say so, and the coldness of her praise disappointed him.

"We are not calling it a good house," said he. "We are not comparing it with Fullerton and Northanger—we are considering it as a mere parsonage, small and confined, we allow, but decent, perhaps, and habitable; and altogether not inferior to the generality; or, in other words, I believe there are few country parsonages in England half so good. It may admit of improvement, however. Far be it from me to say otherwise; and anything in reason—a bow thrown out, perhaps—though, between ourselves, if there is one thing more than another my aversion, it is a patched-on bow."

Catherine did not hear enough of this speech to understand or be pained by it; and other subjects being studiously brought forward and supported by Henry, at the same time that a tray full of refreshments was introduced by his servant, the general was shortly restored to his complacency, and Catherine to all her usual ease of spirits.

The room in question was of a commodious, well-proportioned size, and handsomely fitted up as a dining-parlour; and on their quitting it to walk round the grounds, she was shown, first into a smaller apartment, belonging peculiarly to the master of the house, and made unusually tidy on the occasion; and afterwards into what was to be the drawing-room, with the appearance of which, though unfurnished, Catherine was delighted enough even to satisfy the general. It was a prettily shaped room, the windows reaching to the ground, and the view from them pleasant, though only over green meadows; and she expressed her admiration at the moment with all the honest simplicity with which she felt it. "Oh! Why do not you fit up this room, Mr. Tilney? What a pity not to have it fitted up! It is the prettiest room I ever saw; it is the prettiest room in the world!"

"I trust," said the general, with a most satisfied smile, "that it will very speedily be furnished: it waits only for a lady's taste!"

"Well, if it was my house, I should never sit anywhere else. Oh! What a sweet little cottage there is among the trees—apple trees, too! It is the prettiest cottage!"

"You like it—you approve it as an object—it is enough. Henry, remember that Robinson is spoken to about it. The cottage remains."

Such a compliment recalled all Catherine's consciousness, and silenced her directly; and, though pointedly applied to by the general for her choice of the prevailing colour of the paper and hangings, nothing like an opinion on the subject could be drawn from her. The influence of fresh objects and fresh air, however, was of great use in dissipating these embarrassing associations; and, having reached the ornamental part of the premises, consisting of a walk round two sides of a meadow, on which Henry's genius had begun to act about half a year ago, she was sufficiently recovered to think it prettier than any pleasure-ground she had ever been in before, though there was not a shrub in it higher than the green bench in the corner.

A saunter into other meadows, and through part of the village, with a visit to the stables to examine some improvements, and a charming game of play with a litter of puppies just able to roll about, brought them to four o'clock, when Catherine scarcely thought it could be three. At four they were to dine, and at six to set off on their return. Never had any day passed so quickly!

She could not but observe that the abundance of the dinner did not seem to create the smallest astonishment in the general; nay, that he was even looking at the side-table for cold meat which was not there. His son and daughter's observations were of a different kind. They had seldom seen him eat so heartily at any table but his own, and never before known him so little disconcerted by the melted butter's being oiled.

At six o'clock, the general having taken his coffee, the carriage again received them; and so gratifying had been the tenor of his conduct throughout the whole visit, so well assured was her mind on the subject of his expectations, that, could she have felt equally confident of the wishes of his son, Catherine would have quitted Woodston with little anxiety as to the How or the When she might return to it.

CHAPTER 27

The next morning brought the following very unexpected letter from Isabella:

Bath, April

My dearest Catherine,

I received your two kind letters with the greatest delight, and have a thousand apologies to make for not answering them sooner. I really am quite ashamed of my idleness; but in this horrid place one can find time for nothing. I have had my pen in my hand to begin a letter to you almost every day since you left Bath, but have always been prevented by some silly trifler or other. Pray write to me soon, and direct to my own home. Thank God, we leave this vile place to-morrow. Since you went away, I have had no pleasure in it—the dust is beyond anything; and everybody one cares for is gone. I believe if I could see you I should not mind the rest, for you are dearer to me than anybody can conceive. I am quite uneasy about your dear brother, not having heard from him since he went to Oxford; and am fearful of some misunderstanding. Your kind offices will set all right: he is the only man I ever did or could love, and I trust you will convince him of it. The spring fashions are partly down; and the hats the most frightful you can imagine. I hope you spend your time pleasantly, but am afraid you never think of me. I will not say all that I could of the family you are with, because I would not be ungenerous, or set you against those you esteem; but it is very difficult to know whom to trust, and young men never know their minds two days together. I rejoice to say that the young man whom, of all others, I particularly abhor, has left Bath. You will know, from this description, I must mean Captain Tilney, who, as you may remember, was amazingly disposed to follow and tease me, before you went away. Afterwards he got worse, and became quite my shadow. Many girls might have been taken in, for never were such attentions; but I knew the fickle sex too well. He went away to his regiment two days ago, and I trust I shall never be plagued with him again. He is the greatest coxcomb I ever saw, and amazingly disagreeable. The last two days he was always by the side of Charlotte Davis: I pitied his taste, but took no notice of him. The last time we met was in Bath Street, and I turned directly into a shop that he might not speak to me; I would not even look at him. He went into the pump-room afterwards; but I would not have followed him for all the world. Such a contrast between him and your brother! Pray send me some news of the latter—I am quite unhappy about him; he seemed so uncomfortable when he went away, with a cold, or something that affected his spirits. I would write to him myself, but have mislaid his direction; and, as I hinted above, am afraid he took something in my conduct amiss. Pray explain everything to his satisfaction; or, if he still harbours any doubt, a line from himself to me, or a call at Putney when next in town, might set all to rights. I have not been to the Rooms this age, nor to the play, except going in last night with the Hodges, for a frolic, at half price: they teased me into it; and I was determined they should not say I shut myself up because Tilney was gone. We happened to sit by the Mitchells, and they pretended to be quite surprised to see me out. I knew their spite: at one time they could not be civil to me, but now they are all friendship; but I am not such a fool as to be taken in by them. You know I have a pretty good spirit of my own. Anne Mitchell had tried to put on a turban like mine, as I wore it the week before at the Concert, but made wretched work of it—it happened to become my odd face, I believe, at least Tilney told me so at the time, and said every eye was upon me; but he is the last man whose word I would take. I wear nothing but purple now: I know I look hideous in it, but no matter—it is your dear brother's favourite colour. Lose no time, my dearest, sweetest Catherine, in writing to him and to me,

Who ever am, etc.

Such a strain of shallow artifice could not impose even upon Catherine. Its inconsistencies, contradictions, and falsehood struck her from the very first. She was ashamed of Isabella, and ashamed of having ever loved her. Her professions of attachment were now as disgusting as her excuses were empty, and her demands impudent. "Write to James on her behalf! No, James should never hear Isabella's name mentioned by her again."

On Henry's arrival from Woodston, she made known to him and Eleanor their brother's safety, congratulating them with sincerity on it, and reading aloud the most material passages of her letter with strong indignation. When she had finished it—"So much for Isabella," she cried, "and for all our intimacy! She must think me an idiot, or she could not have written so; but perhaps this has served to make her character better known to me than mine is to her. I see what she has been about. She is a vain coquette, and her tricks have not answered. I do not believe she had ever any regard either for James or for me, and I wish I had never known her."

"It will soon be as if you never had," said Henry.

"There is but one thing that I cannot understand. I see that she has had designs on Captain Tilney, which have not succeeded; but I do not understand what Captain Tilney has been about all this time. Why should he pay her such attentions as to make her quarrel with my brother, and then fly off himself?"

"I have very little to say for Frederick's motives, such as I believe them to have been. He has his vanities as well as Miss Thorpe, and the chief difference is, that, having a stronger head, they have not yet injured himself. If the effect of his behaviour does not justify him with you, we had better not seek after the cause."

"Then you do not suppose he ever really cared about her?"

"I am persuaded that he never did."

"And only made believe to do so for mischief's sake?"

Henry bowed his assent.

"Well, then, I must say that I do not like him at all. Though it has turned out so well for us, I do not like him at all. As it happens, there is no great harm done, because I do not think Isabella has any heart to lose. But, suppose he had made her very much in love with him?"

"But we must first suppose Isabella to have had a heart to lose—consequently to have been a very different creature; and, in that case, she would have met with very different treatment."

"It is very right that you should stand by your brother."

"And if you would stand by yours, you would not be much distressed by the disappointment of Miss Thorpe. But your mind is warped by an innate principle of general integrity, and therefore not accessible to the cool reasonings of family partiality, or a desire of revenge."

Catherine was complimented out of further bitterness. Frederick could not be unpardonably guilty, while Henry made himself so agreeable. She resolved on not answering Isabella's letter, and tried to think no more of it.

CHAPTER 28

Soon after this, the general found himself obliged to go to London for a week; and he left Northanger earnestly regretting that any necessity should rob him even for an hour of Miss Morland's company, and anxiously recommending the study of her comfort and amusement to his children as their chief object in his absence. His departure gave Catherine the first experimental conviction that a loss may be sometimes a gain. The happiness with which their time now passed, every employment voluntary, every laugh indulged, every meal a scene of ease and good humour, walking where they liked and when they liked, their hours, pleasures, and fatigues at their own command, made her thoroughly sensible of the restraint which the General's presence had imposed, and most thankfully feel their present release from it. Such ease and such delights made her love the place and the people more and more every day; and had it not been for a dread of its soon becoming expedient to leave the one, and an apprehension of not being equally beloved by the other, she would at each moment of each day have been perfectly happy; but she was now in the fourth week of her visit; before the general came home, the fourth week would be turned, and perhaps it might seem an intrusion if she stayed much longer. This was a painful consideration whenever it occurred; and eager to get rid of such a weight on her mind, she very soon resolved to speak to Eleanor about it at once, propose going away, and be guided in her conduct by the manner in which her proposal might be taken.

Aware that if she gave herself much time, she might feel it difficult to bring forward so unpleasant a subject, she took the first opportunity of being suddenly alone with Eleanor, and of Eleanor's being in the middle of a speech about something very different, to start forth her obligation of going away very soon. Eleanor looked and declared herself much concerned. She had "hoped for the pleasure of her company for a much longer time—had been misled (perhaps by her wishes) to suppose that a much longer visit had been promised—and could not but think that if Mr. and Mrs. Morland were aware of the pleasure it was to her to have her there, they would be too generous to hasten her return." Catherine explained: "Oh! As to that, Papa and Mamma were in no hurry at all. As long as she was happy, they would always be satisfied."

"Then why, might she ask, in such a hurry herself to leave them?"

"Oh! Because she had been there so long."

"Nay, if you can use such a word, I can urge you no farther. If you think it long—"

"Oh! No, I do not indeed. For my own pleasure, I could stay with you as long again." And it was directly settled that, till she had, her leaving them was not even to be thought of. In having this cause of uneasiness so pleasantly removed, the force of the other was likewise weakened. The kindness, the earnestness of Eleanor's manner in pressing her to stay, and Henry's gratified look on being told that her stay was determined, were such sweet proofs of her importance with them, as left her only just so much solicitude as the human mind can never do comfortably without. She did—almost always—believe that Henry loved her, and quite always that his father and sister loved and even wished her to belong to them; and believing so far, her doubts and anxieties were merely sportive irritations.

Henry was not able to obey his father's injunction of remaining wholly at Northanger in attendance on the ladies, during his absence in London, the engagements of his curate at Woodston obliging him to leave them on Saturday for a couple of nights. His loss was not now what it had been while the general was at home; it lessened their gaiety, but did not ruin their comfort; and the two girls agreeing in occupation, and improving in intimacy, found themselves so well sufficient for the time to themselves, that it was eleven o'clock, rather a late hour at the abbey, before they quitted the supper-room on the day of Henry's departure. They had just reached the head of the stairs when it seemed, as far as the thickness of the walls would allow them to judge, that a carriage was driving up to the door, and the next moment confirmed the idea by the loud noise of the house-bell. After the first perturbation of surprise had passed away, in a "Good heaven! What can be the matter?" it was quickly decided by Eleanor to be her eldest brother, whose arrival was often as sudden, if not quite so unseasonable, and accordingly she hurried down to welcome him.

Catherine walked on to her chamber, making up her mind as well as she could, to a further acquaintance with Captain Tilney, and comforting herself under the unpleasant impression his conduct had given her, and the persuasion of his being by far too fine a gentleman to approve of her, that at least they should not meet under such circumstances as would make their meeting materially painful. She trusted he would never speak of Miss Thorpe; and indeed, as he must by this time be ashamed of the part he had acted, there could be no danger of it; and as long as all mention of Bath scenes were avoided, she thought she could behave to him very civilly. In such considerations time passed away, and it was certainly in his favour that Eleanor should be so glad to see him, and have so much to say, for half an hour was almost gone since his arrival, and Eleanor did not come up.

At that moment Catherine thought she heard her step in the gallery, and listened for its continuance; but all was silent. Scarcely, however, had she convicted her fancy of error, when the noise of something moving close to her door made her start; it seemed as if someone was touching the very doorway—and in another moment a slight motion of the lock proved that some hand must be on it. She trembled a little at the idea of anyone's approaching so cautiously; but resolving not to be again overcome by trivial appearances of alarm, or misled by a raised imagination, she stepped quietly forward, and opened the door. Eleanor, and only Eleanor, stood there. Catherine's spirits, however, were tranquillized but for an instant, for Eleanor's cheeks were pale, and her manner greatly agitated. Though evidently intending to come in, it seemed an effort to enter the room, and a still greater to speak when there. Catherine, supposing some uneasiness on Captain Tilney's account, could only express her concern by silent attention, obliged her to be seated, rubbed her temples with lavender water, and hung over her with affectionate solicitude. "My dear Catherine, you must not—you must not indeed—" were Eleanor's first connected words. "I am quite well. This kindness distracts me—I cannot bear it—I come to you on such an errand!"

"Errand! To me!"

"How shall I tell you! Oh! How shall I tell you!"

A new idea now darted into Catherine's mind, and turning as pale as her friend, she exclaimed, "'Tis a messenger from Woodston!"

"You are mistaken, indeed," returned Eleanor, looking at her most compassionately; "it is no one from Woodston. It is my father himself." Her voice faltered, and her eyes were turned to the ground as she mentioned his name. His unlooked-for return was enough in itself to make Catherine's heart sink, and for a few moments she hardly supposed there were anything worse to be told. She said nothing; and Eleanor, endeavouring to collect herself and speak with firmness, but with eyes still cast down, soon went on. "You are too good, I am sure, to think the worse of me for the part I am obliged to perform. I am indeed a most unwilling messenger. After what has so lately passed, so lately been settled between us—how joyfully, how thankfully on my side!—as to your continuing here as I hoped for many, many weeks longer, how can I tell you that your kindness is not to be accepted—and that the happiness your company has hitherto given us is to be repaid by—But I must not trust myself with words. My dear Catherine, we are to part. My father has recollected an engagement that takes our whole family away on Monday. We are going to Lord Longtown's, near Hereford, for a fortnight. Explanation and apology are equally impossible. I cannot attempt either."

"My dear Eleanor," cried Catherine, suppressing her feelings as well as she could, "do not be so distressed. A second engagement must give way to a first. I am very, very sorry we are to part—so soon, and so suddenly too; but I am not offended, indeed I am not. I can finish my visit here, you know, at any time; or I hope you will come to me. Can you, when you return from this lord's, come to Fullerton?"

"It will not be in my power, Catherine."

"Come when you can, then."

Eleanor made no answer; and Catherine's thoughts recurring to something more directly interesting, she added, thinking aloud, "Monday—so soon as Monday; and you all go. Well, I am certain of—I shall be able to take leave, however. I need not go till just before you do, you know. Do not be distressed, Eleanor, I can go on Monday very well. My father and mother's having no notice of it is of very little consequence. The general will send a servant with me, I dare say, half the way—and then I shall soon be at Salisbury, and then I am only nine miles from home."

"Ah, Catherine! Were it settled so, it would be somewhat less intolerable, though in such common attentions you would have received but half what you ought. But—how can I tell you?—to-morrow morning is fixed for your leaving us, and not even the hour is left to your choice; the very carriage is ordered, and will be here at seven o'clock, and no servant will be offered you."

Catherine sat down, breathless and speechless. "I could hardly believe my senses, when I heard it; and no displeasure, no resentment that you can feel at this moment, however justly great, can be more than I myself—but I must not talk of what I felt. Oh! That I could suggest anything in extenuation! Good

God! What will your father and mother say! After courting you from the protection of real friends to this—almost double distance from your home, to have you driven out of the house, without the considerations even of decent civility! Dear, dear Catherine, in being the bearer of such a message, I seem guilty myself of all its insult; yet, I trust you will acquit me, for you must have been long enough in this house to see that I am but a nominal mistress of it, that my real power is nothing."

"Have I offended the general?" said Catherine in a faltering voice.

"Alas! For my feelings as a daughter, all that I know, all that I answer for, is that you can have given him no just cause of offence. He certainly is greatly, very greatly discomposed; I have seldom seen him more so. His temper is not happy, and something has now occurred to ruffle it in an uncommon degree; some disappointment, some vexation, which just at this moment seems important, but which I can hardly suppose you to have any concern in, for how is it possible?"

It was with pain that Catherine could speak at all; and it was only for Eleanor's sake that she attempted it. "I am sure," said she, "I am very sorry if I have offended him. It was the last thing I would willingly have done. But do not be unhappy, Eleanor. An engagement, you know, must be kept. I am only sorry it was not recollected sooner, that I might have written home. But it is of very little consequence."

"I hope, I earnestly hope, that to your real safety it will be of none; but to everything else it is of the greatest consequence: to comfort, appearance, propriety, to your family, to the world. Were your friends, the Allens, still in Bath, you might go to them with comparative ease; a few hours would take you there; but a journey of seventy miles, to be taken post by you, at your age, alone, unattended!"

"Oh, the journey is nothing. Do not think about that. And if we are to part, a few hours sooner or later, you know, makes no difference. I can be ready by seven. Let me be called in time." Eleanor saw that she wished to be alone; and believing it better for each that they should avoid any further conversation, now left her with, "I shall see you in the morning."

Catherine's swelling heart needed relief. In Eleanor's presence friendship and pride had equally restrained her tears, but no sooner was she gone than they burst forth in torrents. Turned from the house, and in such a way! Without any reason that could justify, any apology that could atone for the abruptness, the rudeness, nay, the insolence of it. Henry at a distance—not able even to bid him farewell. Every hope, every expectation from him suspended, at least, and who could say how long? Who could say when they might meet again? And all this by such a man as General Tilney, so polite, so well bred, and heretofore so particularly fond of her! It was as incomprehensible as it was mortifying and grievous. From what it could arise, and where it would end, were considerations of equal perplexity and alarm. The manner in which it was done so grossly uncivil, hurrying her away without any reference to her own convenience, or allowing her even the appearance of choice as to the time or mode of her travelling; of two days, the earliest fixed on, and of that almost the earliest hour, as if resolved to have her gone before he was stirring in the morning, that he might not be obliged even to see her. What could all this mean but an intentional affront? By some means or other she must have had the misfortune to offend him. Eleanor had wished to spare her from so painful a notion, but Catherine could not believe it possible that any injury or any misfortune could provoke such ill will against a person not connected, or, at least, not supposed to be connected with it.

Heavily passed the night. Sleep, or repose that deserved the name of sleep, was out of the question. That room, in which her disturbed imagination had tormented her on her first arrival, was again the scene of agitated spirits and unquiet slumbers. Yet how different now the source of her inquietude from what it had been then—how mournfully superior in reality and substance! Her anxiety had foundation in fact, her fears in probability; and with a mind so occupied in the contemplation of actual and natural evil, the solitude of her situation, the darkness of her chamber, the antiquity of the building, were felt and considered without the smallest emotion; and though the wind was high, and often produced strange and sudden noises throughout the house, she heard it all as she lay awake, hour after hour, without curiosity or terror.

Soon after six Eleanor entered her room, eager to show attention or give assistance where it was possible; but very little remained to be done. Catherine had not loitered; she was almost dressed, and her packing almost finished. The possibility of some conciliatory message from the general occurred to her as his daughter appeared. What so natural, as that anger should pass away and repentance succeed it? And she only wanted to know how far, after what had passed, an apology might properly be received by her. But the knowledge would have been useless here; it was not called for; neither clemency nor dignity was put to the trial—Eleanor brought no message. Very little passed between them on meeting; each found her greatest safety in silence, and few and trivial were the sentences exchanged while they remained upstairs, Catherine in busy agitation completing her dress, and Eleanor with more goodwill than experience intent upon filling the trunk. When everything was done they left the room, Catherine lingering only half a minute behind her friend to throw a parting glance on every well-known, cherished object, and went down to the breakfast-parlour, where breakfast was prepared. She tried to eat, as well to save herself from the pain of being urged as to make her friend comfortable; but she had no appetite, and could not swallow many mouthfuls. The contrast between this and her last breakfast in that room gave her fresh misery, and strengthened her distaste for everything before her. It was not four and twenty hours ago since they had met there to the same repast, but in circumstances how different! With what cheerful ease, what happy, though false, security, had she then looked around her, enjoying everything present, and fearing little in future, beyond Henry's going to Woodston for a day! Happy, happy breakfast! For Henry had been there; Henry had sat by her and helped her. These reflections were long indulged undisturbed by any address from her companion, who sat as deep in thought as herself; and the appearance of the carriage was the first thing to startle and recall them to the present moment. Catherine's colour rose at the sight of it; and the indignity with which she was treated, striking at that instant on her mind with peculiar force, made her for a short time sensible only of resentment. Eleanor seemed now impelled into resolution and speech.

"You must write to me, Catherine," she cried; "you must let me hear from you as soon as possible. Till I know you to be safe at home, I shall not have an hour's comfort. For one letter, at all risks, all hazards, I must entreat. Let me have the satisfaction of knowing that you are safe at Fullerton, and have found your family well, and then, till I can ask for your correspondence as I ought to do, I will not expect more. Direct to me at Lord Longtown's, and, I must ask it, under cover to Alice."

"No, Eleanor, if you are not allowed to receive a letter from me, I am sure I had better not write. There can be no doubt of my getting home safe."

Eleanor only replied, "I cannot wonder at your feelings. I will not importune you. I will trust to your own kindness of heart when I am at a distance from you." But this, with the look of sorrow accompanying it, was enough to melt Catherine's pride in a moment, and she instantly said, "Oh, Eleanor, I will write to you indeed."

There was yet another point which Miss Tilney was anxious to settle, though somewhat embarrassed in speaking of. It had occurred to her that after so long an absence from home, Catherine might not be provided with money enough for the expenses of her journey, and, upon suggesting it to her with most affectionate offers of accommodation, it proved to be exactly the case. Catherine had never thought on the subject till that moment, but, upon examining her purse, was convinced that but for this kindness of her friend, she might have been turned from the house without even the means of getting home; and the distress in which she must have been thereby involved filling the minds of both, scarcely another word was said by either during the time of their remaining together. Short, however, was that time. The carriage was soon announced to be ready; and Catherine, instantly rising, a long and affectionate embrace supplied the place of language in bidding each other adieu; and, as they entered the hall, unable to leave the house without some mention of one whose name had not yet been spoken by either, she paused a moment, and with quivering lips just made it intelligible that she left "her kind remembrance for her absent friend." But with this approach to his name ended all possibility of restraining her feelings; and, hiding her face as well as she could with her handkerchief, she darted across the hall, jumped into the chaise, and in a moment was driven from the door.

CHAPTER 29

Catherine was too wretched to be fearful. The journey in itself had no terrors for her; and she began it without either dreading its length or feeling its solitariness. Leaning back in one corner of the carriage, in a violent burst of tears, she was conveyed some miles beyond the walls of the abbey before she raised her head; and the highest point of ground within the park was almost closed from her view before she was capable of turning her eyes towards it. Unfortunately, the road she now travelled was the same which only ten days ago she had so happily passed along in going to and from Woodston; and, for fourteen miles, every bitter feeling was rendered more severe by the review of objects on which she had first looked under impressions so different. Every mile, as it brought her nearer Woodston, added to her sufferings, and when within the distance of five, she passed the turning which led to it, and thought of Henry, so near, yet so unconscious, her grief and agitation were excessive.

The day which she had spent at that place had been one of the happiest of her life. It was there, it was on that day, that the general had made use of such expressions with regard to Henry and herself, had so spoken and so looked as to give her the most positive conviction of his actually wishing their marriage. Yes, only ten days ago had he elated her by his pointed regard—had he even confused her by his too significant reference! And now—what had she done, or what had she omitted to do, to merit such a change?

The only offence against him of which she could accuse herself had been such as was scarcely possible to reach his knowledge. Henry and her own heart only were privy to the shocking suspicions which she had so idly entertained; and equally safe did she believe her secret with each. Designedly, at least, Henry could not have betrayed her. If, indeed, by any strange mischance his father should have gained intelligence of what she had dared to think and look for, of her causeless fancies and injurious examinations, she could not wonder at any degree of his indignation. If aware of her having viewed him as a murderer, she could not wonder at his even turning her from his house. But a justification so full of torture to herself, she trusted, would not be in his power.

Anxious as were all her conjectures on this point, it was not, however, the one on which she dwelt most. There was a thought yet nearer, a more prevailing, more impetuous concern. How Henry would think, and feel, and look, when he returned on the morrow to Northanger and heard of her being gone, was a question of force and interest to rise over every other, to be never ceasing, alternately irritating and soothing; it sometimes suggested the dread of his calm acquiescence, and at others was answered by the sweetest confidence in his regret and resentment. To the general, of course, he would not dare to speak; but to Eleanor—what might he not say to Eleanor about her?

In this unceasing recurrence of doubts and inquiries, on any one article of which her mind was incapable of more than momentary repose, the hours passed away, and her journey advanced much faster than she looked for. The pressing anxieties of thought, which prevented her from noticing anything before her, when once beyond the neighbourhood of Woodston, saved her at the same time from watching her progress; and though no object on the road could engage a moment's attention, she found no stage of it tedious. From this, she was preserved too by another cause, by feeling no eagerness for her journey's conclusion; for to return in such a manner to Fullerton was almost to destroy the pleasure of a meeting with those she loved best, even after an absence such as hers—an eleven weeks' absence. What had she to say that would not humble herself and pain her family, that would not increase her own grief by the confession of it, extend an useless resentment, and perhaps involve the innocent with the guilty in undistinguishing ill will? She could never do justice to Henry and Eleanor's merit; she felt it too strongly for expression; and should a dislike be taken against them, should they be thought of unfavourably, on their father's account, it would cut her to the heart.

With these feelings, she rather dreaded than sought for the first view of that well-known spire which would announce her within twenty miles of home. Salisbury she had known to be her point on leaving Northanger; but after the first stage she had been indebted to the post-masters for the names of the places which were then to conduct her to it; so great had been her ignorance of her route. She met with nothing, however, to distress or frighten her. Her youth, civil manners, and liberal pay procured her all the attention that a traveller like herself could require; and stopping only to change horses, she travelled on for about eleven hours without accident or alarm, and between six and seven o'clock in the evening found herself entering Fullerton.

A heroine returning, at the close of her career, to her native village, in all the triumph of recovered reputation, and all the dignity of a countess, with a long train of noble relations in their several phaetons, and three waiting-maids in a travelling chaise and four, behind her, is an event on which the pen of the contriver may well delight to dwell; it gives credit to every conclusion, and the author must share in the glory she so liberally bestows. But my affair is widely different; I bring back my heroine to her home in solitude and disgrace; and no sweet elation of spirits can lead me into minuteness. A heroine in a hack post-chaise is such a blow upon sentiment, as no attempt at grandeur or pathos can withstand. Swiftly therefore shall her post-boy drive through the village, amid the gaze of Sunday groups, and speedy shall be her descent from it.

But, whatever might be the distress of Catherine's mind, as she thus advanced towards the parsonage, and whatever the humiliation of her biographer in relating it, she was preparing enjoyment of no everyday nature for those to whom she went; first, in the appearance of her carriage—and secondly, in herself. The chaise of a traveller being a rare sight in Fullerton, the whole family were immediately at the window; and to have it stop at the sweep-gate was a pleasure to brighten every eye and occupy every fancy—a pleasure quite unlooked for by all but the two youngest children, a boy and girl of six and four years old, who expected a brother or sister in every carriage. Happy the glance that first distinguished Catherine! Happy the voice that proclaimed the discovery! But whether such happiness were the lawful property of George or Harriet could never be exactly understood.

Her father, mother, Sarah, George, and Harriet, all assembled at the door to welcome her with affectionate eagerness, was a sight to awaken the best feelings of Catherine's heart; and in the embrace of each, as she stepped from the carriage, she found herself soothed beyond anything that she had believed possible. So surrounded, so caressed, she was even happy! In the joyfulness of family love everything for a short time was subdued, and the pleasure of seeing her, leaving them at first little leisure for calm curiosity, they were all seated round the tea-table, which Mrs. Morland had hurried for the comfort of the poor traveller, whose pale and jaded looks soon caught her notice, before any inquiry so direct as to demand a positive answer was addressed to her.

Reluctantly, and with much hesitation, did she then begin what might perhaps, at the end of half an hour, be termed, by the courtesy of her hearers, an explanation; but scarcely, within that time, could they at all discover the cause, or collect the particulars, of her sudden return. They were far from being an irritable race; far from any quickness in catching, or bitterness in resenting, affronts: but here, when the whole was unfolded, was an insult not to be overlooked, nor, for the first half hour, to be easily pardoned. Without suffering any romantic alarm, in the consideration of their daughter's long and lonely journey, Mr. and Mrs. Morland could not but feel that it might have been productive of much unpleasantness to her; that it was what they could never have voluntarily suffered; and that, in forcing her on such a measure, General Tilney had acted neither honourably nor feelingly—neither as a gentleman nor as a parent. Why he had done it, what could have provoked him to such a breach of hospitality, and so suddenly turned all his partial regard for their daughter into actual ill will, was a matter which they were at least as far from divining as Catherine herself; but it did not oppress them by any means so long; and, after a due course of useless conjecture, that "it was a strange business, and that he must be a very strange man," grew enough for all their indignation and wonder; though Sarah indeed still indulged in the sweets of incomprehensibility, exclaiming and conjecturing with youthful ardour. "My dear, you give yourself a great deal of needless trouble," said her mother at last; "depend upon it, it is something not at all worth understanding."

"I can allow for his wishing Catherine away, when he recollected this engagement," said Sarah, "but why not do it civilly?"

"I am sorry for the young people," returned Mrs. Morland; "they must have a sad time of it; but as for anything else, it is no matter now; Catherine is safe at home, and our comfort does not depend upon General Tilney." Catherine sighed. "Well," continued her philosophic mother, "I am glad I did not know of your journey at the time; but now it is all over, perhaps there is no great harm done. It is always good for young people to be put upon exerting themselves; and you know, my dear Catherine, you always were a sad little scatter-brained creature; but now you must have been forced to have your wits about you, with so much changing of chaises and so forth; and I hope it will appear that you have not left anything behind you in any of the pockets."

Catherine hoped so too, and tried to feel an interest in her own amendment, but her spirits were quite worn down; and, to be silent and alone becoming soon her only wish, she readily agreed to her mother's next counsel of going early to bed. Her parents, seeing nothing in her ill looks and agitation but the natural consequence of mortified feelings, and of the unusual exertion and fatigue of such a journey, parted from her without any doubt of their being soon slept away; and though, when they all met the next morning, her recovery was not equal to their hopes, they were still perfectly unsuspicious of there being any deeper evil. They never once thought of her heart, which, for the parents of a young lady of seventeen, just returned from her first excursion from home, was odd enough!

As soon as breakfast was over, she sat down to fulfil her promise to Miss Tilney, whose trust in the effect of time and distance on her friend's disposition was already justified, for already did Catherine reproach herself with having parted from Eleanor coldly, with having never enough valued her merits or kindness, and never enough commiserated her for what she had been yesterday left to endure. The strength of these feelings, however, was far from assisting her pen; and never had it been harder for her to write than in addressing Eleanor Tilney. To compose a letter which might at once do justice to her sentiments and her situation, convey gratitude without servile regret, be guarded without coldness, and honest without resentment—a letter which Eleanor might not be pained by the perusal of—and, above all, which she might not blush herself, if Henry should chance to see, was an undertaking to frighten away all her powers of performance; and, after long thought and much perplexity, to be very brief was all that she could determine on with any confidence of safety. The money therefore which Eleanor had advanced was enclosed with little more than grateful thanks, and the thousand good wishes of a most affectionate heart.

"This has been a strange acquaintance," observed Mrs. Morland, as the letter was finished; "soon made and soon ended. I am sorry it happens so, for Mrs. Allen thought them very pretty kind of young people; and you were sadly out of luck too in your Isabella. Ah! Poor James! Well, we must live and learn; and the next new friends you make I hope will be better worth keeping."

Catherine coloured as she warmly answered, "No friend can be better worth keeping than Eleanor."

"If so, my dear, I dare say you will meet again some time or other; do not be uneasy. It is ten to one but you are thrown together again in the course of a few years; and then what a pleasure it will be!"

Mrs. Morland was not happy in her attempt at consolation. The hope of meeting again in the course of a few years could only put into Catherine's head what might happen within that time to make a meeting dreadful to her. She could never forget Henry Tilney, or think of him with less tenderness than she did at that moment; but he might forget her; and in that case, to meet—! Her eyes filled with tears as she pictured her acquaintance so renewed; and her mother, perceiving her comfortable suggestions to have had no good effect, proposed, as another expedient for restoring her spirits, that they should call on Mrs. Allen.

The two houses were only a quarter of a mile apart; and, as they walked, Mrs. Morland quickly dispatched all that she felt on the score of James's disappointment. "We are sorry for him," said she; "but otherwise there is no harm done in the match going off; for it could not be a desirable thing to have him engaged to a girl whom we had not the smallest acquaintance with, and who was so entirely without fortune; and now, after such behaviour, we cannot think at all well of her. Just at present it comes hard to poor James; but that will not last forever; and I dare say he will be a discreeter man all his life, for the foolishness of his first choice."

This was just such a summary view of the affair as Catherine could listen to; another sentence might have endangered her complaisance, and made her reply less rational; for soon were all her thinking powers swallowed up in the reflection of her own change of feelings and spirits since last she had trodden that well-known road. It was not three months ago since, wild with joyful expectation, she had there run backwards and forwards some ten times a day, with an heart light, gay, and independent; looking forward to pleasures untasted and unalloyed, and free from the apprehension of evil as from the knowledge of it. Three months ago had seen her all this; and now, how altered a being did she return!

She was received by the Allens with all the kindness which her unlooked-for appearance, acting on a steady affection, would naturally call forth; and great was their surprise, and warm their displeasure, on hearing how she had been treated—though Mrs. Morland's account of it was no inflated representation, no studied appeal to their passions. "Catherine took us quite by surprise yesterday evening," said she. "She travelled all the way post by herself, and knew nothing of coming till Saturday night; for General Tilney, from some odd fancy or other, all of a sudden grew tired of having her there, and almost turned her out of the house. Very unfriendly, certainly; and he must be a very odd man; but we are so glad to have her amongst us again! And it is a great comfort to find that she is not a poor helpless creature, but can shift very well for herself."

Mr. Allen expressed himself on the occasion with the reasonable resentment of a sensible friend; and Mrs. Allen thought his expressions quite good enough to be immediately made use of again by herself. His wonder, his conjectures, and his explanations became in succession hers, with the addition of this single remark—"I really have not patience with the general"—to fill up every accidental pause. And, "I really have not patience with the general," was uttered twice after Mr. Allen left the room, without any relaxation of anger, or any material digression of thought. A more considerable degree of wandering attended the third repetition; and, after completing the fourth, she immediately added, "Only think, my dear, of my having got that frightful great rent in my best Mechlin so charmingly mended, before I left Bath, that one can hardly see where it was. I must show it you some day or other. Bath is a nice place, Catherine, after all. I assure you I did not above half like coming away. Mrs. Thorpe's being there was such a comfort to us, was not it? You know, you and I were quite forlorn at first."

"Yes, but that did not last long," said Catherine, her eyes brightening at the recollection of what had first given spirit to her existence there.

"Very true: we soon met with Mrs. Thorpe, and then we wanted for nothing. My dear, do not you think these silk gloves wear very well? I put them on new the first time of our going to the Lower Rooms, you know, and I have worn them a great deal since. Do you remember that evening?"

"Do I! Oh! Perfectly."

"It was very agreeable, was not it? Mr. Tilney drank tea with us, and I always thought him a great addition, he is so very agreeable. I have a notion you danced with him, but am not quite sure. I remember I had my favourite gown on."

Catherine could not answer; and, after a short trial of other subjects, Mrs. Allen again returned to—"I really have not patience with the general! Such an agreeable, worthy man as he seemed to be! I do not suppose, Mrs. Morland, you ever saw a better-bred man in your life. His lodgings were taken the very day after he left them, Catherine. But no wonder; Milsom Street, you know."

As they walked home again, Mrs. Morland endeavoured to impress on her daughter's mind the happiness of having such steady well-wishers as Mr. and Mrs. Allen, and the very little consideration which the neglect or unkindness of slight acquaintance like the Tilneys ought to have with her, while she could preserve the good opinion and affection of her earliest friends. There was a great deal of good sense in all this; but there are some situations of the human mind in which good sense has very little power; and Catherine's feelings contradicted almost every position her mother advanced. It was upon the behaviour of these very slight acquaintance that all her present happiness depended; and while Mrs. Morland was successfully confirming her own opinions by the justness of her own representations, Catherine was silently reflecting that now Henry must have arrived at Northanger; now he must have heard of her departure; and now, perhaps, they were all setting off for Hereford.

CHAPTER 30

Catherine's disposition was not naturally sedentary, nor had her habits been ever very industrious; but whatever might hitherto have been her defects of that sort, her mother could not but perceive them now to be greatly increased. She could neither sit still nor employ herself for ten minutes together, walking round the garden and orchard again and again, as if nothing but motion was voluntary; and it seemed as if she could even walk about the house rather than remain fixed for any time in the parlour. Her loss of spirits was a yet greater alteration. In her rambling and her idleness she might only be a caricature of herself; but in her silence and sadness she was the very reverse of all that she had been before.

For two days Mrs. Morland allowed it to pass even without a hint; but when a third night's rest had neither restored her cheerfulness, improved her in useful activity, nor given her a greater inclination for needlework, she could no longer refrain from the gentle reproof of, "My dear Catherine, I am afraid you are growing quite a fine lady. I do not know when poor Richard's cravats would be done, if he had no friend but you. Your head runs too much upon Bath; but there is a time for everything—a time for balls and plays, and a time for work. You have had a long run of amusement, and now you must try to be useful."

Catherine took up her work directly, saying, in a dejected voice, that "her head did not run upon Bath—much."

"Then you are fretting about General Tilney, and that is very simple of you; for ten to one whether you ever see him again. You should never fret about trifles." After a short silence—"I hope, my Catherine, you are not getting out of humour with home because it is not so grand as Northanger. That would be turning your visit into an evil indeed. Wherever you are you should always be contented, but especially at home, because there you must spend the most of your time. I did not quite like, at breakfast, to hear you talk so much about the French bread at Northanger."

"I am sure I do not care about the bread. It is all the same to me what I eat."

"There is a very clever essay in one of the books upstairs upon much such a subject, about young girls that have been spoilt for home by great acquaintance—The Mirror, I think. I will look it out for you some day or other, because I am sure it will do you good."

Catherine said no more, and, with an endeavour to do right, applied to her work; but, after a few minutes, sunk again, without knowing it herself, into languor and listlessness, moving herself in her chair, from the irritation of weariness, much oftener than she moved her needle. Mrs. Morland watched the progress of this relapse; and seeing, in her daughter's absent and dissatisfied look, the full proof of that repining spirit to which she had now begun to attribute her want of cheerfulness, hastily left the room to fetch the book in question, anxious to lose no time in attacking so dreadful a malady. It was some time before she could find what she looked for; and other family matters occurring to detain her, a quarter of an hour had elapsed ere she returned downstairs with the volume from which so much was hoped. Her avocations above having shut out all noise but what she created herself, she knew not that a visitor had arrived within the last few minutes, till, on entering the room, the first object she beheld was a young man whom she had never seen before. With a look of much respect, he immediately rose, and being introduced to her by her conscious daughter as "Mr. Henry Tilney," with the embarrassment of real sensibility began to apologize for his appearance there, acknowledging that after what had passed he had little right to expect a welcome at Fullerton, and stating his impatience to be assured of Miss Morland's having reached her home in safety, as the cause of his intrusion. He did not address himself to an uncandid judge or a resentful heart. Far from comprehending him or his sister in their father's misconduct, Mrs. Morland had been always kindly disposed towards each, and instantly, pleased by his appearance, received him with the simple professions of unaffected benevolence; thanking him for such an attention to her daughter, assuring him that the friends of her children were always welcome there, and entreating him to say not another word of the past.

He was not ill-inclined to obey this request, for, though his heart was greatly relieved by such unlooked-for mildness, it was not just at that moment in his power to say anything to the purpose. Returning in silence to his seat, therefore, he remained for some minutes most civilly answering all Mrs. Morland's common remarks about the weather and roads. Catherine meanwhile—the anxious, agitated, happy, feverish Catherine—said not a word; but her glowing cheek and brightened eye made her mother trust that this good-natured visit would at least set her heart at ease for a time, and gladly therefore did she lay aside the first volume of The Mirror for a future hour.

Desirous of Mr. Morland's assistance, as well in giving encouragement, as in finding conversation for her guest, whose embarrassment on his father's account she earnestly pitied, Mrs. Morland had very early dispatched one of the children to summon him; but Mr. Morland was from home—and being thus without any support, at the end of a quarter of an hour she had nothing to say. After a couple of minutes' unbroken silence, Henry, turning to Catherine for the first time since her mother's entrance, asked her, with sudden alacrity, if Mr. and Mrs. Allen were now at Fullerton? And on developing, from amidst all her perplexity of words in reply, the meaning, which one short syllable would have given, immediately expressed his intention of paying his respects to them, and, with a rising colour, asked her if she would have the goodness to show him the way. "You may see the house from this window, sir," was information on Sarah's side, which produced only a bow of acknowledgment from the gentleman, and a silencing nod from her mother; for Mrs. Morland, thinking it probable, as a secondary consideration in his wish of waiting on their worthy neighbours, that he might have some explanation to give of his father's behaviour, which it must be more pleasant for him to communicate only to Catherine, would not on any account prevent her accompanying him. They began their walk, and Mrs. Morland was not entirely mistaken in his object in wishing it. Some explanation on his father's account he had to give; but his first purpose was to explain himself, and before they reached Mr. Allen's grounds he had done it so well that Catherine did not think it could ever be repeated too often. She was assured of his affection; and that heart in return was solicited, which, perhaps, they pretty equally knew was already entirely his own; for, though Henry was now sincerely attached to her, though he felt and delighted in all the excellencies of her character and truly loved her society, I must confess that his affection originated in nothing better than gratitude, or, in other words, that a persuasion of her partiality for him had been the only cause of giving her a serious thought. It is a new circumstance in romance, I acknowledge, and dreadfully derogatory of an heroine's dignity; but if it be as new in common life, the credit of a wild imagination will at least be all my own.

A very short visit to Mrs. Allen, in which Henry talked at random, without sense or connection, and Catherine, wrapt in the contemplation of her own unutterable happiness, scarcely opened her lips, dismissed them to the ecstasies of another tête-à-tête; and before it was suffered to close, she was enabled to judge how far he was sanctioned by parental authority in his present application. On his return from Woodston, two days before, he had been met near the abbey by his impatient father, hastily informed in angry terms of Miss Morland's departure, and ordered to think of her no more.

Such was the permission upon which he had now offered her his hand. The affrighted Catherine, amidst all the terrors of expectation, as she listened to this account, could not but rejoice in the kind caution with which Henry had saved her from the necessity of a conscientious rejection, by engaging her faith before he mentioned the subject; and as he proceeded to give the particulars, and explain the motives of his father's conduct, her feelings soon hardened into even a triumphant delight. The general had had nothing to accuse her of, nothing to lay to her charge, but her being the involuntary, unconscious object of a deception which his pride could not pardon, and which a better pride would have been ashamed to own. She was guilty only of being less rich than he had supposed her to be. Under a mistaken persuasion of her possessions and claims, he had courted her acquaintance in Bath, solicited her company at Northanger, and designed her for his daughter-in-law. On discovering his error, to turn her from the house seemed the best, though to his feelings an inadequate proof of his resentment towards herself, and his contempt of her family.

John Thorpe had first misled him. The general, perceiving his son one night at the theatre to be paying considerable attention to Miss Morland, had accidentally inquired of Thorpe if he knew more of her than her name. Thorpe, most happy to be on speaking terms with a man of General Tilney's importance, had been joyfully and proudly communicative; and being at that time not only in daily expectation of Morland's engaging Isabella, but likewise pretty well resolved upon marrying Catherine himself, his vanity induced him to represent the family as yet more wealthy than his vanity and avarice had made him believe them. With whomsoever he was, or was likely to be connected, his own consequence always required that theirs should be great, and as his intimacy with any acquaintance grew, so regularly grew their fortune. The expectations of his friend Morland, therefore, from the first overrated, had ever since his introduction to Isabella been gradually increasing; and by merely adding twice as much for the grandeur of the moment, by doubling what he chose to think the amount of Mr. Morland's preferment, trebling his private fortune, bestowing a rich aunt, and sinking half the children, he was able to represent the whole family to the general in a most respectable light. For Catherine, however, the peculiar object of the General's curiosity, and his own speculations, he had yet something more in reserve, and the ten or fifteen thousand pounds which her father could give her would be a pretty addition to Mr. Allen's estate. Her intimacy there had made him seriously determine on her being handsomely legacied hereafter; and to speak of her therefore as the almost acknowledged future heiress of Fullerton naturally followed. Upon such intelligence the general had proceeded; for never had it occurred to him to doubt its authority. Thorpe's interest in the family, by his sister's approaching connection with one of its members, and his own views on another (circumstances of which he boasted with almost equal openness), seemed sufficient vouchers for his truth; and to these were added the absolute facts of the Allens being wealthy and childless, of Miss Morland's being under their care, and—as soon as his acquaintance allowed him to judge—of their treating her with parental kindness. His resolution was soon formed. Already had he discerned a liking towards Miss Morland in the countenance of his son; and thankful for Mr. Thorpe's communication, he almost instantly determined to spare no pains in weakening his boasted interest and ruining his dearest hopes. Catherine herself could not be more ignorant at the time of all this, than his own children. Henry and Eleanor, perceiving nothing in her situation likely to engage their father's particular respect, had seen with astonishment the suddenness, continuance, and extent of his attention; and though latterly, from some hints which had accompanied an almost positive command to his son of doing everything in his power to attach her, Henry was convinced of his father's believing it to be an advantageous connection, it was not till the late explanation at Northanger that they had the smallest idea of the false calculations which had hurried him on. That they were false, the general had learnt from the very person who had suggested them, from Thorpe himself, whom he had chanced to meet again in town, and who, under the influence of exactly opposite feelings, irritated by Catherine's refusal, and yet more by the failure of a very recent endeavour to accomplish a reconciliation between Morland and Isabella, convinced that they were separated forever, and spurning a friendship which could be no longer serviceable, hastened to contradict all that he had said before to the advantage of the Morlands—confessed himself to have been totally mistaken in his opinion of their circumstances and character, misled by the rhodomontade of his friend to believe his father a man of substance and credit, whereas the transactions of the two or three last weeks proved him to be neither; for after coming eagerly forward on the first overture of a marriage between the families, with the most liberal proposals, he had, on being brought to the point by the shrewdness of the relator, been constrained to acknowledge himself incapable of giving the young people even a decent support. They were, in fact, a necessitous family; numerous, too, almost beyond example; by no means respected in their own neighbourhood, as he had lately had particular opportunities of discovering; aiming at a style of life which their fortune could not warrant; seeking to better themselves by wealthy connections; a forward, bragging, scheming race.

The terrified general pronounced the name of Allen with an inquiring look; and here too Thorpe had learnt his error. The Allens, he believed, had lived near them too long, and he knew the young man on whom the Fullerton estate must devolve. The general needed no more. Enraged with almost everybody in the world but himself, he set out the next day for the abbey, where his performances have been seen.

I leave it to my reader's sagacity to determine how much of all this it was possible for Henry to communicate at this time to Catherine, how much of it he could have learnt from his father, in what points his own conjectures might assist him, and what portion must yet remain to be told in a letter from James. I have united for their ease what they must divide for mine. Catherine, at any rate, heard enough to feel that in suspecting General Tilney of either murdering or shutting up his wife, she had scarcely sinned against his character, or magnified his cruelty.

Henry, in having such things to relate of his father, was almost as pitiable as in their first avowal to himself. He blushed for the narrow-minded counsel which he was obliged to expose. The conversation between them at Northanger had been of the most unfriendly kind. Henry's indignation on hearing how Catherine had been treated, on comprehending his father's views, and being ordered to acquiesce in them, had been open and bold. The general, accustomed on every ordinary occasion to give the law in his family, prepared for no reluctance but of feeling, no opposing desire that should dare to clothe itself in words, could ill brook the opposition of his son, steady as the sanction of reason and the dictate of conscience could make it. But, in such a cause, his anger, though it must shock, could not intimidate Henry, who was sustained in his purpose by a conviction of its justice. He felt himself bound as much in honour as in affection to Miss Morland, and believing that heart to be his own which he had been directed to gain, no unworthy retraction of a tacit consent, no reversing decree of unjustifiable anger, could shake his fidelity, or influence the resolutions it prompted.

He steadily refused to accompany his father into Herefordshire, an engagement formed almost at the moment to promote the dismissal of Catherine, and as steadily declared his intention of offering her his hand. The general was furious in his anger, and they parted in dreadful disagreement. Henry, in an agitation of mind which many solitary hours were required to compose, had returned almost instantly to Woodston, and, on the afternoon of the following day, had begun his journey to Fullerton.

CHAPTER 31

Mr. and Mrs. Morland's surprise on being applied to by Mr. Tilney for their consent to his marrying their daughter was, for a few minutes, considerable, it having never entered their heads to suspect an attachment on either side; but as nothing, after all, could be more natural than Catherine's being beloved, they soon learnt to consider it with only the happy agitation of gratified pride, and, as far as they alone were concerned, had not a single objection to start. His pleasing manners and good sense were self-evident recommendations; and having never heard evil of him, it was not their way to suppose any evil could be told. Goodwill supplying the place of experience, his character needed no attestation. "Catherine would make a sad, heedless young housekeeper to be sure," was her mother's foreboding remark; but quick was the consolation of there being nothing like practice.

There was but one obstacle, in short, to be mentioned; but till that one was removed, it must be impossible for them to sanction the engagement. Their tempers were mild, but their principles were steady, and while his parent so expressly forbade the connection, they could not allow themselves to encourage it. That the general should come forward to solicit the alliance, or that he should even very heartily approve it, they were not refined enough to make any parading stipulation; but the decent appearance of consent must be yielded, and that once obtained—and their own hearts made them trust that it could not be very long denied—their willing approbation was instantly to follow. His consent was all that they wished for. They were no more inclined than entitled to demand his money. Of a very considerable fortune, his son was, by marriage settlements, eventually secure; his present income was an income of independence and comfort, and under every pecuniary view, it was a match beyond the claims of their daughter.

The young people could not be surprised at a decision like this. They felt and they deplored—but they could not resent it; and they parted, endeavouring to hope that such a change in the general, as each believed almost impossible, might speedily take place, to unite them again in the fulness of privileged affection. Henry returned to what was now his only home, to watch over his young plantations, and extend his improvements for her sake, to whose share in them he looked anxiously forward; and Catherine remained at Fullerton to cry. Whether the torments of absence were softened by a clandestine correspondence, let us not inquire. Mr. and Mrs. Morland never did—they had been too kind to exact any promise; and whenever Catherine received a letter, as, at that time, happened pretty often, they always looked another way.

The anxiety, which in this state of their attachment must be the portion of Henry and Catherine, and of all who loved either, as to its final event, can hardly extend, I fear, to the bosom of my readers, who will see in the tell-tale compression of the pages before them, that we are all hastening together to perfect felicity. The means by which their early marriage was effected can be the only doubt: what probable circumstance could work upon a temper like the General's? The circumstance which chiefly availed was the marriage of his daughter with a man of fortune and consequence, which took place in the course of the summer—an accession of dignity that threw him into a fit of good humour, from which he did not recover till after Eleanor had obtained his forgiveness of Henry, and his permission for him "to be a fool if he liked it!"

The marriage of Eleanor Tilney, her removal from all the evils of such a home as Northanger had been made by Henry's banishment, to the home of her choice and the man of her choice, is an event which I expect to give general satisfaction among all her acquaintance. My own joy on the occasion is very sincere. I know no one more entitled, by unpretending merit, or better prepared by habitual suffering, to receive and enjoy felicity. Her partiality for this gentleman was not of recent origin; and he had been long withheld only by inferiority of situation from addressing her. His unexpected accession to title and fortune had removed all his difficulties; and never had the general loved his daughter so well in all her hours of companionship, utility, and patient endurance as when he first hailed her "Your Ladyship!" Her husband was really deserving of her; independent of his peerage, his wealth, and his attachment, being to a precision the most charming young man in the world. Any further definition of his merits must be unnecessary; the most charming young man in the world is instantly before the imagination of us all. Concerning the one in question, therefore, I have only to add—aware that the rules of composition forbid the introduction of a character not connected with my fable—that this was the very gentleman whose negligent servant left behind him that collection of washing-bills, resulting from a long visit at Northanger, by which my heroine was involved in one of her most alarming adventures.

The influence of the Viscount and Viscountess in their brother's behalf was assisted by that right understanding of Mr. Morland's circumstances which, as soon as the general would allow himself to be informed, they were qualified to give. It taught him that he had been scarcely more misled by Thorpe's first boast of the family wealth than by his subsequent malicious overthrow of it; that in no sense of the word were they necessitous or poor, and that Catherine would have three thousand pounds. This was so material an amendment of his late expectations that it greatly contributed to smooth the descent of his pride; and by no means without its effect was the private intelligence, which he was at some pains to procure, that the Fullerton estate, being entirely at the disposal of its present proprietor, was consequently open to every greedy speculation.

On the strength of this, the general, soon after Eleanor's marriage, permitted his son to return to Northanger, and thence made him the bearer of his consent, very courteously worded in a page full of empty professions to Mr. Morland. The event which it authorized soon followed: Henry and Catherine were married, the bells rang, and everybody smiled; and, as this took place within a twelvemonth from the first day of their meeting, it will not appear, after all the dreadful delays occasioned by the General's cruelty, that they were essentially hurt by it. To begin perfect happiness at the respective ages of twenty-six and eighteen is to do pretty well; and professing myself moreover convinced that the General's unjust interference, so far from being really injurious to their felicity, was perhaps rather conducive to it, by improving their knowledge of each other, and adding strength to their attachment, I leave it to be settled, by whomsoever it may concern, whether the tendency of this work be altogether to recommend parental tyranny, or reward filial disobedience.

Milton Keynes UK
Ingram Content Group UK Ltd.
UKHW021938081024
449407UK00008B/153

9 781965 179086